The Island of Sea Women

Lisa See

SCRIBNER

LONDON NEW YORK SYDNEY TORONTO NEW DELHI

First published in the United States by Scribner, an imprint of
Simon & Schuster, Inc., 2019

First published in Great Britain by Scribner, an imprint of
Simon & Schuster UK Ltd, 2019
This paperback edition published by Scribner, an imprint of
Simon & Schuster UK Ltd, 2020

Copyright © Lisa See, 2019

SCRIBNER and design are registered trademarks of The Gale Group, Inc.,
used under licence by Simon & Schuster Inc.

The right of Lisa See to be identified as author of this work has been asserted
in accordance with the Copyright, Designs and Patents Act, 1988.

7 9 10 8 6

Simon & Schuster UK Ltd
1st Floor
222 Gray's Inn Road
London WC1X 8HB

Simon & Schuster Australia, Sydney
Simon & Schuster India, New Delhi

www.simonandschuster.co.uk
www.simonandschuster.com.au
www.simonandschuster.co.in

A CIP catalogue record for this book
is available from the British Library

Paperback ISBN: 978-1-4711-8383-6
eBook ISBN: 978-1-4711-8382-9
Audio ISBN: 978-1-4711-8472-7

This book is a work of fiction. Names, characters, places and incidents are either
a product of the author's imagination or are used fictitiously. Any resemblance
to actual people living or dead, events or locales is entirely coincidental.

Printed and bound by CPI Group (UK) Ltd, Croydon CR0 4YY

MIX
Paper from
responsible sources
FSC® C171272

Author's Note

Although parts of the story take place when the McCune-Reischauer system of romanization was standard, I have used Revised Romanization of Korean, which was formalized in 2000. All personal names are rendered in common spelling. Wherever possible, I have used Jeju words. On the mainland, *halmeoni* means "grandmother." On Jeju, in a fitting example of the respect in which women are held for their strength, independence, and persistence, *halmang* means both "grandmother" and "goddess." According to tradition, the title of *halmang* should follow the name, but to avoid confusion I have put it first: Seolmundae Halmang becomes Halmang Seolmundae or Grandmother Seolmundae.

Day 1: 2008

An old woman sits on the beach, a cushion strapped to her bottom, sorting algae that's washed ashore. She's used to spending time in the water, but even on land she's vigilant to the environment around her. Jeju is her home, an island known for Three Abundances: wind, stones, and women. Today the most capricious of these—the wind—is but a gentle breeze. Not a single cloud smudges the sky. The sun warms her head, neck, and back through her bonnet and other clothing. So soothing. Her house perches on the rocky shoreline overlooking the sea. It doesn't look like much—just two small structures made from native stone, but the location . . . Her children and grandchildren have suggested she allow them to convert the buildings into a restaurant and bar. "Oh, Granny, you'll be rich. You'll never have to work again." One of her neighbors did as the younger generation asked. Now that woman's home is a guesthouse and an Italian restaurant. On Young-sook's beach. In her village. She will never let that happen to her house. "There isn't enough money in all the pockets in all Korea to make me leave," Young-sook has said many times. How could she? Her house is the nest where she hides the joy, laughter, sorrows, and regrets of her life.

She is not alone in her work on the beach. Other women around her age—in their eighties and nineties—also pick through the algae that has come to rest on the sand, putting what's salable in small bags and leaving the rest. Up on the walkway that separates this cove from the road, young couples—honeymooners, probably—walk hand in hand, heads together, sometimes even kissing, in front of everyone, in broad daylight. She sees a tourist family, clearly from the mainland. The children and husband are so obvious in their matching polka-dot T-shirts and lime-green shorts. The wife wears the same polka-dot T-shirt, but otherwise every bit of her skin is protected from the sun by long pants, sleeve guards, gloves, hat, and a cloth mask. Children from the village climb over the rocks that spill across the sand and into the sea. Soon they're playing in the shallow depths, giggling, and challenging each other to be the first to reach the deepest rock, locate a piece of sea glass, or find a sea urchin, if they're lucky enough to spot one. She smiles to herself. How differently life will unfurl for these young ones . . .

She also observes other people—some not even trying to hide their curiosity—who stare at her before shifting their gazes to some of the other old women on the shore today. Which granny looks the nicest? The most accessible? What those people don't understand is that Young-sook and her friends are appraising them too. Are they scholars, journalists, or documentarians? Will they pay? Will they be knowledgeable about the haenyeo—sea women? They'll want to take her photo. They'll shove a microphone in her face and ask the same predictable questions: "Do you consider yourself a granny of the sea? Or do you think of yourself more like a mermaid?" "The government labels the haenyeo a cultural heritage treasure—something dying out that must be preserved, if only in memory. How does it feel to be the last of the last?" If they're academics, they'll want to talk about Jeju's matrifocal culture, explaining, "It's not a matriarchy. Rather, it's a society *focused* on women." Then they'll begin to probe: "Were you really in charge in your household? Did you give your husband an allowance?" Often she'll get a young woman who'll ask the question Young-sook's heard discussed her entire life. "Is it better to be a man or a woman?" No matter what the inquiry, she always answers the same way: "I was the best haenyeo!" She prefers to leave it at that. When a visitor persists, Young-sook will say gruffly, "If you want to know about me, go to the Haenyeo Museum. You can see my photo. You can watch the video about me!" If they *still* won't go . . . Well, then, she becomes even more direct. "Leave me alone! I have work to do!"

Her response usually depends on how her body feels. Today, the sun is bright, the water glistens, and she perceives in her bones—even though she's only sitting on the shore—the weightlessness of the sea, the surge that massages the aches in her muscles, the enveloping chill that cools the heat in her joints, so she allows herself to be photographed, even pushing back the brim of her bonnet so one young man can "see your face better." She watches as he edges toward the inevitable awkward subject, until he finally arrives at his query: "Did your family suffer during the April Third Incident?"

Aigo, of course she suffered. Of course. Of course. Of course. "Everyone on Jeju Island suffered," she answers. But that is all she will say about it. Ever. Better to tell him this is the happiest time of her life. And it is. She still works, but she's not too busy to visit friends and travel. Now she can look at her great-granddaughters and think, *That's a pretty one. That's the smartest one yet.* Or *That one better marry well.* Her grandchildren and great-grandchildren give her the greatest joy. Why couldn't she have thought like that when she was younger? But she couldn't have imagined how her life would turn out back then. She couldn't have imagined today even in a dream.

The young man wanders off. He tries to talk to another woman, Kang Gu-ja, who's working about ten meters to Young-sook's left. Gu-ja, always crotchety, won't even look up. He presses on to Gu-ja's younger sister, Gu-sun, who yells at him. "Go away!" Young-sook snorts appreciatively.

When her small bag is full, she shakily gets to her feet and shuffles to the collection of larger bags she's been filling. Once the small bag is emptied, she hobbles to an area of the beach untouched by the others. She settles back down, positioning her cushion beneath her. Her hands, though gnarled from work and deeply creased from years of exposure to the sun, are agile. The sound of the sea . . . The caress of warm air . . . The knowledge that she is protected by the thousands of goddesses who live on this island . . . Even Gu-sun's colorful epithets can't sour her mood.

Then in Young-sook's peripheral vision she glimpses another family group. They aren't dressed alike, and they don't look alike. The husband is white, the wife is Korean, and the children—a small boy and a teenage girl—are mixed. Young-sook can't help it, but seeing those half-and-half children makes her uncomfortable: the boy in shorts, a superhero T-shirt, and clunky tennis shoes, the girl in shorts that scarcely cover what they're supposed to cover, earbuds plugged into her ears, and wires trailing down over her barely-there breasts. Young-sook guesses they're Americans, and she watches warily as they approach.

"Are you Kim Young-sook?" the woman, pale and pretty, asks. When Young-sook gives a slight nod, the woman continues. "My name is Ji-young, but everyone calls me Janet."

Young-sook tries out the name on her tongue. "Janet."

"And this is my husband, Jim, and my children, Clara and Scott. We're wondering if you remember my grandmother?" Janet speaks . . . What does she speak exactly? It's not Korean, but it's not the Jeju dialect either. "Her name was Mi-ja. Her family name was Han—"

"I don't know that person."

The softest frown crinkles the space above the bridge of the woman's nose. "But didn't you both live in this village?"

"I live here, but I don't know who you're talking about." Young-sook's voice comes out even sharper and louder than Gu-sun's, causing both Kang sisters to look her way. *Are you all right?*

But the American woman is undeterred. "Let me show you her photograph."

She scrounges through her satchel, pulls out a manila envelope, and paws through it until she finds what she's been looking for. She stretches out her hand and shows Young-sook a black-and-white photograph of a girl dressed in the white bathing costume of the past. Her nipples are like a pair of octopus eyes peering out from the protection of a cave. Her hair is hidden under a matching white scarf. Her face is round, her slim arms show the definition of muscles, her legs are sturdy, and her smile is wide and unabashed.

"I'm sorry," Young-sook says. "I don't know her."

"I have more photos," the woman goes on.

As Janet once again peers into her envelope, rifling through what must be more photographs, Young-sook smiles up at the white man. "You have phone?" she asks in English, which she realizes must sound far worse than his wife's Korean, and then holds an imaginary phone to her ear. She's used this tactic many times to save herself from bothersome intruders. If it's a young woman, she might say, "Before I answer your questions, I need to talk to my grandson." If it's a man—of any age—she'll ask, "Are you married yet? My great-niece is lovely, and she's in college too. I'll have her come so the two of you can meet." It's amazing how many people fall for her tricks. Sure enough, the foreign man pats his pockets as he searches for his phone. He smiles. Bright white, very straight teeth, like a shark's. But the teenage girl gets her phone out first. It's one of those new iPhones, exactly like the ones Young-sook bought for her great-grandchildren for their birthdays this year.

Without bothering to remove her earbuds, Clara says, "Tell me the number." The sound of her voice further ruffles Young-sook. The girl has spoken in the Jeju dialect. It's not perfect, but it's passable, and her inflection causes goosebumps to rise along Young-sook's arms.

She recites the number, while Clara taps the buttons on the phone. Once she's done, she unplugs the phone and extends it to Young-sook, who feels strangely paralyzed. On impulse—it has to be impulse, right?—the girl leans over and puts the phone to Young-sook's ear. Her touch . . . Like lava . . . A small cross on a gold chain slips out from under the girl's T-shirt and swings in front of Young-sook's eyes. Now she notices that the mother, Janet, wears a cross too.

The four foreigners stare at her expectantly. They think she's going to help them. She speaks rapidly into the phone. Janet's brow furrows once again as she tries to understand the words, but Young-sook has spoken pure Jeju, which is as different from standard Korean as French is from Japanese, or so she's been told. Once the call is done, Clara tucks the phone in her back pocket and watches, embarrassed, as her mother starts pulling out more photographs.

"Here is my father when he was young," Janet says, thrusting a blurry image before Young-sook's eyes. "Do you remember him? Here's another photo of my grandmother. It was taken on her wedding day. I was told the girl beside her is you. Won't you please take a few minutes to talk to us?"

But Young-sook has gone back to sorting, only occasionally glancing at the photos to be polite but registering nothing on her face that would reveal the feelings of her heart.

A few minutes later, a motorcycle with a cart attached to the back comes bumping along the beach. When it reaches her, she struggles to stand. The foreign man takes her elbow to steady her. It's been a long time since she's been touched by someone so white, and she instinctively pulls away.

"He only wants to help," Clara says in her childish Jeju dialect.

Young-sook watches the strangers try to assist her grandson as he loads the bags of algae onto the flatbed. Once everything is secured, she climbs behind her grandson and wraps her arms around his waist. She nudges him with the back of her hand. "Go!" Once they've cleared the beach and have bounced up onto the road, she says in a softer tone, "Drive me around for a while. I don't want them to see where I live."

PART I

Friendship

1938

Swallowing Water Breath

April 1938

My first day of sea work started hours before sunrise when even the crows were still asleep. I dressed and made my way through the dark to our latrine. I climbed the ladder to the stone structure and positioned myself over the hole in the floor. Below, our pigs gathered, snuffling eagerly. A big stick leaned against the wall in the corner in case one of them became too enthusiastic and tried to leap up. Yesterday I'd had to hit one pretty hard. They must have remembered, because this morning they waited for my private business to drop to the ground to fight among themselves for it. I returned to the house, tied my baby brother to my back, and went outside to draw water from the village well. Three round trips, carrying earthenware jugs in my hands, were required to get enough water to satisfy our morning needs. Next, I gathered dung to burn for heating and cooking. This also had to be done early, because I had a lot of competition from other women and girls in the village. My chores done, my baby brother and I headed home.

Three generations of my family lived within the same fence—with Mother, Father, and us children in the big house and Grandmother in the little house across the courtyard. Both structures were built from stone and had thatch roofs weighed down with additional stones to keep the island wind from blowing them away. The big house had three rooms: a kitchen, the main room, and a special room for women to use on their wedding nights and after they'd given birth. In the main room, oil lamps flickered and sputtered. Our sleeping mats had already been folded and stacked against the wall.

Grandmother was awake, dressed, and drinking hot water.

11

Her hair was covered by a scarf. Her face and hands were bony and the color of chestnuts. My first and second brothers, twelve and ten years old, sat cross-legged on the floor, knees touching. Across from them, Third Brother squirmed as only a seven-year-old boy can. My little sister, six years younger than I was, helped our mother pack three baskets. Mother's face was set in concentration as she checked and double-checked that she had everything, while Little Sister tried to show she was already training to be a good haenyeo.

Father ladled the thin millet soup that he'd prepared into bowls. I loved him. He had Grandmother's narrow face. His long, tapered hands were soft. His eyes were deep and warm. His callused feet were almost always bare. He wore his favorite dog-fur hat pulled down over his ears and many layers of clothes, which helped to disguise how he sacrificed food, so his children could eat more. Mother, never wasting a moment, joined us on the floor and nursed my baby brother as she ate. As soon as she was done with her soup and the feeding, she handed the baby to my father. Like all haenyeo husbands, he would spend the rest of the day under the village tree in Hado's central square with other fathers. Together, they'd look after infants and young children. Satisfied that Fourth Brother was content in Father's arms, Mother motioned for me to hurry. Anxiety rattled through me. I so hoped to prove myself today.

The sky was just beginning to turn pink when Mother, Grandmother, and I stepped outside. Now that it was light, I could see my steamy breath billowing then dissipating in the cold air. Grandmother moved slowly, but Mother had efficiency in every step and gesture. Her legs and arms were strong. Her basket was on her back, and she helped me with mine, securing the straps. Here I was, going to work, helping to feed and care for my family, and becoming a part of the long tradition of haenyeo. Suddenly I felt like a woman.

Mother hoisted the third basket, holding it before her, and together we stepped through the opening in the stone wall that protected our small piece of property from prying eyes and the relentless wind. We wended our way through the olle—one of thousands of stone-walled pathways that ran between houses and also gave us routes to crisscross the island. We stayed alert for Japanese soldiers. Korea had now been a Japanese colony for twenty-eight years. We hated the Japanese, and they hated us. They were cruel. They stole food. Inland, they rustled livestock. They took and took and took. They'd killed Grandmother's parents, and she called them chokpari—cloven-footed ones. Mother always said that if I was ever alone and saw colonists, whether soldiers or civilians, I should run and hide, because they'd ruined many girls on Jeju.

We came around a corner and into a long straightaway. Ahead in the distance, my friend Mi-ja danced from foot to foot, to keep warm, from excitement. Her skin was perfect, and the morning light glowed on her cheeks. I'd grown up in the Gul-dong section of Hado, while Mi-ja lived in the Sut-dong section, and the two of us always met in this spot. Even before we reached her, she bowed deeply to show her gratitude and humility to my mother, who bent at her waist just enough to acknowledge Mi-ja's deference. Then Mother wordlessly strapped the third basket to Mi-ja's back.

"You girls learned to swim together," Mother said. "You've watched and learned as apprentices. You, Mi-ja, have worked especially hard."

I didn't mind that Mother singled out Mi-ja. She'd earned it.

"I can never thank you enough." Mi-ja's voice was as delicate as flower petals. "You have been a mother to me, and I will always be grateful."

"You are another daughter to me," Mother replied. "Today, Halmang Samseung's job is done. As the goddess who oversees pregnancy, childbirth, and raising a child to the age of fifteen, she is now fully released from her duties. Many girls have friends, but the two of you are closer than friends. You are like sisters, and I expect you to take care of each other today and every day as those tied by blood would do."

It was as much a blessing as a warning.

Mi-ja was the first to voice her fears. "I understand about swallowing water breath before going beneath the waves. I must hold as much air within me as possible. But what if I don't know when to come up? What if I can't make a good sumbisori?"

Swallowing water breath is the process all haenyeo use to gather enough air in their lungs to sustain them as they submerge. The sumbisori is the special sound—like a whistle or a dolphin's call—a haenyeo makes as she breaches the surface of the sea and releases the air she's held in her lungs, followed by a deep intake of breath.

"Sucking in air shouldn't be troublesome," Mother said. "You breathe in every day as you walk about the earth."

"But what if I run out of it in the watery depths?" Mi-ja asked.

"Breathing in, breathing out. Every beginning haenyeo worries about this," Grandmother blurted before my mother could answer. She could be impatient with Mi-ja.

"Your body will know what to do," Mother said reassuringly. "And even if it doesn't, I will be there with you. I'm responsible for every woman's safe return to shore. I listen for the sumbisori of all women in our collective. Together our sumbisori create a song of the air and wind on Jeju. Our sumbisori is the innermost sound of the world. It connects us to the future and the past. Our sumbisori allows us first to serve our parents and then our children."

I found this comforting, but I also became aware of Mi-ja staring at me expectantly. Yesterday we'd agreed to tell my mother of our worries. Mi-ja had volunteered hers, but I was hesitant about revealing mine. There were many ways to die in the sea, and I was scared. My mother may have said that Mi-ja was like a daughter— and I loved her for loving my friend—but I was an actual daughter, and I didn't want her to see me as less than Mi-ja.

I was saved from having to say anything when Mother started walking. Mi-ja and I trailed after her, with Grandmother following us. We passed house after house—all made of stone with thatch roofs. The main square was deserted except for women, who were being pulled to the sea by the scent of salt air and the sound of waves. Just before reaching the beach, we stopped to pick a handful of leaves from a bank of wild mugwort, which we tucked into our baskets. We turned another corner and reached the shore. We stepped over sharp rocks, making our way to the bulteok—the fire space. It was a round, roofless structure made of stacked lava rocks. Instead of a door, two curved walls overlapped to prevent those outside from seeing in. A similar structure sat in the shallows. This was where people bathed and washed their clothes.

THE ISLAND OF SEA WOMEN

And just offshore, where the water reached no higher than our knees, was an area walled with stone. Here, anchovies washed in at high tide, were trapped at low tide, and then we waded through with nets to catch them.

We had seven bulteoks in Hado—one for each neighborhood's diving collective. Our group had thirty members. Logic would say that the entrance should face the sea, since haenyeo go back and forth from it all day, but having the entrance at the back gave an added barrier against the constant winds blowing in from the water. Above the crash of waves, we could hear women's voices— teasing, laughing, and shouting well-worn gibes back and forth. As we entered, the gathered women turned to see who'd arrived. They all wore padded jackets and trousers.

Mi-ja set down her basket and hurried to the fire.

"No need for you to worry about tending the fire now," Yang Do-saeng called out good-naturedly. She had high cheekbones and sharp elbows. She was the only person I knew who kept her hair in braids at all times. She was a little older than my mother, and they were diving partners and best friends. Do-saeng's husband had given her one son and one daughter, and that was the end. A sadness, to be sure. Nevertheless, our two families were very close, especially since Do-saeng's husband was in Japan doing factory work. These days about a quarter of all Jeju people lived in Japan, because a ferry ticket cost half the price of a single bag of rice here on our island. Do-saeng's husband had been in Hiroshima for so many years that I didn't remember him. My mother helped Do-saeng with ancestor worship, and Do-saeng helped my mother when she had to cook for our family when we performed our rites. "You're no longer an apprentice. You'll be with us today. Are you ready, girl?"

"Yes, Auntie," Mi-ja responded, using the honorific, bowing and backing away.

The other women laughed, causing Mi-ja to blush.

"Stop teasing her," my mother said. "These two have enough to worry about today."

As chief of this collective, Mother sat with her back against the part of the stone wall that had the best protection from the wind.

15

Once she was settled, the other women took spots in strict order, according to each one's level of diving skill. The grandmother-divers—those like my mother, who'd achieved top status in the sea even if they had yet to become grandmothers on dry land—had the best seats. The actual grandmothers, like mine, didn't have a label. They were true grandmothers, who should be treated with respect. Although long retired from sea work, they enjoyed the companionship of the women with whom they'd spent most of their lives. Now Grandmother and her friends liked to sort seaweed that had been washed ashore by the wind or dive close to the beach in the shallows, so they could spend the day trading jokes and sharing miseries. As women of respect and honor, they had the second most important seats in the bulteok. Next came the small-divers, in their twenties and early thirties, who were still perfecting their skills. Mi-ja and I sat with the baby-divers: the two Kang sisters, Gu-ja and Gu-sun, who were two and three years older than we were, and Do-saeng's daughter, Yu-ri, who was already nineteen. The three of them had a couple years' diving experience, while Mi-ja and I were true beginners, but the five of us were ranked the lowest in the collective, which meant that our seats were by the bulteok's opening. The cold wind swirled around us, and Mi-ja and I scooted closer to the fire. It was important to warm up as best we could before entering the sea.

Mother began the meeting by asking, "Does this beach have any food?"

"More food than there are grains of sand on Jeju," Do-saeng trilled, "if we had an abundance of sand instead of rocks."

"More food than on twenty moons," another woman declared, "if there were twenty moons above us."

"More food than in fifty jars at my grandmother's house," a woman who'd been widowed too young joined in, "if she'd had fifty jars."

"Good," Mother said in response to the ritual bantering. "Then let us discuss where we will dive today." At home, her voice always seemed so loud. Here, hers was just one of many loud voices, since the ears of all haenyeo are damaged over time by water pressure. One day I too would have a loud voice.

The sea doesn't belong to anyone, but every collective had assigned diving rights to specific territories: close enough to the shore to walk in, within twenty- to thirty-minutes' swimming distance from land, or accessible only by boat farther out to sea; a cove here, an underwater plateau not too far offshore, the north side of this or that island, and so on. Mi-ja and I listened as the women considered the possibilities. As baby-divers, we hadn't earned the right to speak. Even the small-divers kept quiet. Mother struck down most proposals. "That area is overfished," she told Do-saeng. Another time, she came back with, "Just as on land, our sea fields also follow the seasons. To honor spawning times, conch can't be picked from the ocean floor from July to September, and abalone can't be harvested from October through December. It is our duty to be keepers and managers of the sea. If we protect our wet fields, they will continue to provide for us." Finally, she made her decision. "We'll row to our underwater canyon not far from here."

"The baby-divers aren't ready for that," one of the grandmother-divers said. "They aren't strong enough, and they haven't earned the right either."

Mother held up a hand. "In that area, lava flowed from Grandmother Seolmundae to form the rocky canyon. Its walls provide something for every ability. The most experienced among us can go as deep as we want, while the baby-divers can pick through those spots close to the surface. The Kang sisters will show Mi-ja what to do. And I'd like Do-saeng's daughter, Yu-ri, to watch over Young-sook. Yu-ri will soon become a small-diver, so this will be good training for her."

Once Mother explained, there were no further objections. Mothers are closer to the women in their diving collective than they are to their own children. Today, my mother and I had begun to form that deeper relationship. Observing Do-saeng and Yu-ri together, I could see where my mother and I would be in a few years. But this moment also showed me why Mother had been elected chief. She was a leader, and her judgment was valued.

"Every woman who enters the sea carries a coffin on her back," she warned the gathering. "In this world, in the undersea world, we tow the burdens of a hard life. We are crossing between life and death every day."

These traditional words were often repeated on Jeju, but we all nodded somberly as though hearing them for the first time.

"When we go to the sea, we share the work and the danger," Mother added. "We harvest together, sort together, and sell together, because the sea itself is communal."

With that final rule stated—as though anyone could forget something so basic—she clapped her hands twice on her thighs to signal that the meeting had ended and we needed to get moving. As my grandmother and her friends filed outside to work on the shore, Mother motioned to Yu-ri to help me get ready. Yu-ri and I had known each other our entire lives, so naturally we were a good match. The Kang sisters didn't know Mi-ja well and probably wanted to keep their distance from her. She was an orphan, and her father had been a collaborator, working for the Japanese in Jeju City. But whether or not the Kangs liked it, they had to do what my mother ordered.

"Stand close to the fire," Yu-ri told me. "The faster you get undressed and ready, the faster we'll be in the water. The sooner we go into the water, the sooner we'll return here. Now, follow what I do."

We edged closer to the flames and stripped off our clothes. No one showed any inhibitions. This was like being together in the communal bath. Some of the younger women were big with babies growing in their bellies. Older women had stretch marks. Even older women had breasts that sagged from too much living and giving. Mi-ja's and my bodies showed our age too. We were fifteen years old, but the harshness of our environment— little food, hard physical work, and cold weather—meant that we were as skinny as eels, our breasts had not yet begun to grow, and just a few wisps of hair showed between our legs. We stood there, shivering, as Yu-ri, Gu-ja, and Gu-sun helped us put on our three-piece water clothes made from plain white cotton. The white color would make us more visible underwater, and it was said to repel sharks and dolphins, but, I realized, the thinness of the fabric would do little to keep us warm.

"Pretend Mi-ja is a baby," Yu-ri told the Kang sisters, "and tie her into her suit." Then to me, she explained, "You can see that the sides are open. You fasten them together with the strings. This allows the suit to tighten or expand with pregnancy or other types of weight gain or loss." She leaned in. "I long for the day when I can tell my mother-in-law that my husband has put a baby in me. It will be a son. I'm sure of it. When I die, he'll perform ancestor worship for me."

Yu-ri's wedding was set for the following month, and of course she was dreaming of the son she would have, but her sense of anticipation seemed unimportant to me right then. Her fingers felt icy against my skin, and goosebumps rose on my flesh. Even after she'd tied the laces as tight as possible, the suit still bagged on me. Same on Mi-ja. These suits have forever marked the haenyeo as immodest, for no proper Korean woman, whether on the mainland or here on our island, would ever bare so much skin.

The whole time, Yu-ri continued talking, talking, talking. "My brother is very smart, and he works hard in school." My mother may have been the head of the collective, but Do-saeng had a son who was the pride of every family in Hado. "Everyone says Jun-bu will go to Japan to study one day."

Jun-bu was the only son, and the gift of education was bestowed on him alone. Yu-ri and her father contributed to the family's income, although they still didn't earn as much as Do-saeng, while my mother had to raise all the money to send my brothers to school without any assistance from my father. They would be lucky to go beyond elementary school.

"I'll need to work extra hard to help pay for Jun-bu's tuition *and* provide for my new family." Yu-ri called across the room to her mother and future mother-in-law. "I'm a good worker, eh?" Yu-ri was known throughout our village as a chatterbox. She seemed worry free, and she *was* a good worker, which was why it had been easy to find a match for her.

She turned her attention back to me. "If your parents love you greatly, they'll arrange a marriage for you right here in Hado. You'll maintain your diving rights, and you'll be able to see your natal family every day." Then, realizing what she'd said, she tapped Mi-ja's arm. "I'm sorry. I forgot you don't have parents." She didn't think long enough before she spoke again. "How are you going to find a husband?" she asked with genuine curiosity.

I glanced at Mi-ja, hoping she hadn't been hurt by Yu-ri's thoughtlessness, but her face was set in concentration as she tried to follow the Kang sisters' instructions.

Once we had on our suits, we put on water jackets. These were for cold weather only, but I couldn't see how, since they were the same thin cotton as the rest of the outfit. Last, we tied white kerchiefs over our hair to conserve body heat and because no one would wish for a loose tendril to get tangled in seaweed or caught on a rock.

"Here," Yu-ri said, pressing paper packets filled with white powder into our hands. "Eat this, and it will help prevent diving sickness—dizziness, headaches, and other pains. Ringing in the ears!" Yu-ri scrunched up her face at the thought. "I'm still a baby-diver, and I already have it. *Ngggggg*—" She imitated the high-pitched sound that apparently buzzed in her head.

Following the examples of Yu-ri and the Kang sisters, Mi-ja and I unfolded the paper packets, tilted our heads back like baby birds, poured the bitter-tasting white powder into our mouths, and swallowed. Then Mi-ja and I watched as the others spat on their knives to bring good luck in finding and harvesting an abalone—a prized catch, for each one fetched a great price.

Mother checked to make sure I had all my gear. She focused particularly on my tewak—a hollowed-out gourd that had been left to dry in the sun, which would serve as my buoy. She then did the same with Mi-ja. We each had a bitchang to use for prying creatures from their homes and a pronged hoe to pick between the cracks and embed in the sand or on a crag to help pull us from place to place. We also had a sickle for cutting seaweed, a knife for opening sea urchins, and a spear for protection. Mi-ja and I had used these tools for practice while playing in the shallows, but Mother made a point to say, "Don't use these today. Just get accustomed to the waters around you. Stay aware of your surroundings, because everything will look different."

Together we left the bulteok. We'd return several hours later to store and repair our equipment, measure the day's harvest, divvy up the proceeds, and, most important, warm up again. We might even cook and share a little of what we'd brought back in our nets, if the harvest was bountiful. I looked forward to it all.

As the other women boarded the boat, Mi-ja and I lingered on the jetty. She rummaged through her basket and pulled out a book, while I brought out a piece of charcoal from my basket. She ripped a page from the book and held it over the written character name for the boat. Even tied up, it bobbed in the waves, making it nearly impossible for Mi-ja to keep the paper steady and for me to rub it with the charcoal. Once I was done, we took a moment to examine the result: a shadowy image of a character we couldn't read but knew meant "Sunrise." We'd been commemorating our favorite moments and places this way for years. It wasn't our best rubbing, but with it we'd remember today forever.

"Hurry along," Mother called down to us, tolerant but only up to a point.

Mi-ja tucked the paper back in the book to keep it safe, then we scrambled aboard and took up oars. As we slowly rowed away from the jetty, my mother led us in song.

"Let us dive." Her gravelly voice cut through the wind to reach my ears.

"Let us dive," we sang back to her, our rowing matching the rhythm of the melody.

"Golden shells and silver abalones," she sang.

"Let us get them all!" we responded.

"To treat my lover . . ."

"When he comes home."

I couldn't help but blush. My mother didn't have a lover, but this was a much-beloved song and all the women liked it.

The tide was right, and the sea was relatively calm. Still, despite the rowing and singing, I began to feel sick to my stomach and Mi-ja's usually pink cheeks turned an ashen gray. We brought up our oars when we reached the diving spot. The boat dipped and swayed in the light chop. I attached my bitchang to my wrist and grabbed my net and tewak. A light wind blew, and I began to shiver. I was feeling pretty miserable.

"For a thousand years, for ten thousand years, I pray to the Dragon Sea God," Mother called out across the waves. "Please, ocean king spirit, no strong winds. Please no strong currents." She poured offerings of rice and rice wine into the water. With the ritual completed, we wiped the insides of our goggles with the mugwort we'd picked to keep them from fogging up and then positioned them over our eyes. Mother counted as each woman jumped into the water and swam away in twos and threes. With fewer women on board to help weigh down the boat, it rocked even worse. Yu-ri steadied herself before finally leaping over a swell and into the water. The Kang sisters held hands when they jumped. Those two were inseparable. I hoped their loyalty would now expand to include Mi-ja, and they'd watch out for her in the same way they did each other.

Mother gave some final advice: "The sea, it is said, is like a mother. The salt water, the pulse and surges of the current, the magnified beat of your heart, and the muffled sounds reverberating through the water together recall the womb. But we haenyeo must always think about making money . . . and surviving. Do you understand?" When we nodded, she went on. "This is your first day. Don't be greedy. If you see an octopus, ignore it. A haenyeo must learn how to knock out an octopus underwater, or else it could use its arms against you. And stay away from abalone too!"

She didn't have to explain more. It can take months before a beginning haenyeo is ready to risk prying an abalone from a rock. Left alone, the creature floats its shell off a rock, so that the sea's nourishing waters can flow in and around it. When surprised—even if it's only by the shift in current caused by a large fish swimming past—it will clamp itself to a rock so that the hard shell protects the creature inside from all predators. As a result, an abalone must be approached carefully and the tip of the bitchang inserted under the shell and flipped off the rock in one swift movement before the abalone can clamp down on the tool attached to a diver's wrist, thereby anchoring her to the rock. Only years of experience can teach a woman how to get loose and still have enough time left over to reach the surface for air. I was in no hurry to attempt such a hazardous activity.

"Today you follow in my wake as I once followed in my mother's wake," Mother went on, "and as one day your daughters will follow in your wakes. You are baby-divers. Don't reach beyond your abilities."

With that blessing—and warning—Mi-ja took my hand and together we jumped feetfirst into the water. Instant, shocking cold. I hung on to my buoy, my legs kicking back and forth beneath me. Mi-ja and I looked into each other's eyes. It was time for swallowing water breath. Together we took a breath, a breath, a breath, filling our lungs to capacity, expanding our chests. Then we went down. Light filtered turquoise and glittery close to the surface. Around us, others descended—with their heads directed to the ocean floor—through the canyon Mother had described, their feet pointed to the sky. Those women were quick and powerful, plunging a body length, another body length, deeper and deeper into darker blue water. Mi-ja and I struggled to achieve that straight angle. For me, the worst part was my goggles. The metal frames, responding to the water pressure even at this shallow depth, cut into my flesh. They also limited my peripheral vision, creating yet another danger and forcing me to be even more vigilant in this ghostly environment.

As baby-divers, Yu-ri, the Kangs, Mi-ja, and I could only go down about two body lengths, but I watched as my mother disappeared into the inky chasm of the canyon. I'd always heard she could reach twenty and sometimes more meters on a single breath, but already my lungs burned and my heart thumped in my ears. I kicked to go up, my lungs feeling like they were about to explode. As soon as I broke the surface, my sumbisori erupted and scattered on the air. It sounded like a deep sigh—*aaah*—and I realized it was just as Mother had always said it would be. My sumbisori was unique. And so was Mi-ja's, which I learned when she split the water beside me. *Wheeee*. We grinned at each other, then swallowed more water breath and dove again. Nature told me what to do. The next time I surfaced, I had a sea urchin in my hand. My first catch! I put it in the net attached to my tewak, took another series of deep breaths, and went back down. I stayed within sight of Yu-ri, even if we resurfaced at different intervals. Every time I looked for Mi-ja, I found her not more than a meter away from one of the Kang sisters, who themselves stayed close together.

We repeated this pattern, pausing occasionally to rest on our buoys, until it was time to return to the boat. When I reached it, I easily hoisted my net—noticeably light compared to those of others—and carried it across the deck so that the woman behind me and her catch could board. Mother oversaw everything and everyone. One group of women secured their nets, tying the tops so nothing precious could escape, while Do-saeng and some others gathered around the brazier, sending warmth into their bones, drinking tea, and bragging about what they'd caught. Four stragglers still paddled toward the boat. I could sense Mother counting to make sure everyone was safe.

Yu-ri giggled at our shivering, telling us that eventually we'd get used to being cold all the time. "Four years ago, I was just like you, and now look at me," she boasted.

It was a beautiful day, and everything had gone perfectly. I felt proud of myself. But now that the swells were rising, and the dipping and swaying of the boat was getting worse, all I wanted to do was go home. Not possible. Once our arms and legs were rosy with heat, we went back in the water. The five baby-divers stayed together—with one or another of us popping back up for air. Never before had I concentrated so hard—on my form, on the beating of my heart, on the pressure on my lungs, on *looking*. I can't say that either Mi-ja or I found many sea creatures. Our main goal was not to embarrass ourselves as we tried to perfect the head-down dive position. We were pathetic. Acquiring that skill would take time.

When Mother sounded the call that the day was done, I was relieved. She looked in my direction, but I wasn't sure if she saw me or not. I glimpsed Mi-ja and the Kangs swimming to the boat. They'd be the first three on board, so they'd get to listen as the other women breached the waters and let out their sumbisori. I was about to start paddling when Yu-ri said, "Wait. I saw something on my last dive. Let's go get it." She glanced around, taking in how far the grandmother-divers were from the boat. "We can do it before they get here. Come on!"

Mother had said I was supposed to stay with Yu-ri, but she'd also called for us to return to the boat. I made a split-second decision, took a few deeps breaths, and followed Yu-ri. We went to the same shelf where we'd been harvesting sea urchins. Yu-ri dragged herself along the craggy surface, pulled out her bitchang, jabbed it in a hole, and yanked out an octopus. It was huge! The arms must have been a meter long. Such a catch! I would get some credit for it too.

The octopus reached out and looped an arm around my wrist. I wrenched it loose. By the time I'd done that, some of its other limbs had grabbed on to Yu-ri. One had latched on to my thigh and was drawing me toward it, while another was slithering sucker over sucker up my other arm. I struggled to pull them off. The octopus's bulbous head moved toward Yu-ri's face, but she was so busy fighting the other arms that were reeling her closer into its grip that she didn't notice. I wanted to scream for help, but I couldn't. Not underwater.

Before another moment passed, Yu-ri's face was covered. Instead of fighting or resisting, I swam closer, linked my arms around the octopus and Yu-ri, and kicked as hard as I could. As soon as we breached the surface, I yelled, "Help! Help! Help us!"

The octopus was strong. Yu-ri's face was still covered. The creature was trying to pull us back under. I kicked and kicked. Suckers loosened from Yu-ri and came to me, sensing I was now the greater threat. They creeped along my arms and legs.

I heard splashing, then arms grabbed me. Knives flashed in the sun as suckers were pried from my skin, chunks of the octopus cut off and tossed through the air, discarded. Buoyed by the others, I lifted a leg so they could remove the suckers. When I caught a glimpse of my mother's face, fierce in concentration, I knew I'd be safe. Women worked on Yu-ri too, but she didn't seem to be helping them. Do-saeng pulled her arm back, her knife in her fist. If I were her, I would have used all my strength to stab the octopus's head, but she couldn't. Yu-ri was *under* there. Do-saeng went up under the octopus's head, running the blade parallel to her daughter's face. Despite the support from the women surrounding us, I could feel in my legs that I was the one keeping Yu-ri afloat even as the octopus continued to try to drag us under. The limpness of Yu-ri's body in my arms told me something the others hadn't yet realized. As strong as I wanted to be, I began to cry inside my goggles.

The women worked their way up to the thicker parts of the octopus's appendages. That, combined with the repeated jabs and pokes to the octopus's head from the tip of Do-saeng's knife, thoroughly weakened the creature. It was either dead or close to it, but like that of a lizard or a frog, its body still had impulses and strength.

Finally, I was free.

"Can you swim to the boat?" Mother asked.

"What about Yu-ri?"

"We'll take care of her. Can you make it alone?"

I nodded, but now that the battle was over, whatever had caused me to fight so hard was dissipating fast. I made it about halfway to the boat before I had to flip onto my back to float and rest for a moment. Above me, clouds traveled quickly, pushed by the wind. A bird flew overhead. I closed my eyes, trying to draw on deeper strength. Waves lapped against my ears—submerging them one moment, then exposing them to the worried sounds of the women still with Yu-ri. I heard a splash, then a second, and a third. Arms once again supported me. I opened my eyes: Mi-ja and the Kang sisters. Together they helped me to the boat. Gu-ja, the strongest of us, heaved herself up and over the side. I placed my arms on the side of the boat and began to hoist myself up, but the ordeal had left me too weak. Mi-ja and Gu-sun each placed a hand under my bottom and pushed me up. I slipped onto the deck like a caught fish. I lay there panting, my limbs like rubber, my mind exhausted. I pulled my goggles from my eyes, and they clattered to the deck. The whole while, the three girls babbled nonstop.

"Your mother said we should stay in the boat—"

"She didn't want us to help—"

"Baby-divers would only cause more problems—"

"In a rescue—"

I could barely take in what they said.

Other women began to arrive. I forced myself to sit up. Mi-ja and the Kangs went to the edge of the boat and reached down their arms. I joined them and helped grab Yu-ri. She felt heavy—a dead-weight. We pulled her up and over, and we fell back to the deck. Yu-ri lay on top of me, not moving. The boat pitched, and she rolled to the side. Do-saeng came next, followed by my mother. They knelt next to Yu-ri. As the other haenyeo clambered aboard, Mother lowered her cheek to Yu-ri's mouth and nostrils to feel if any breath escaped.

"She's alive," Mother said, sitting back on her heels. Do-saeng and some of the other haenyeo began to rub Yu-ri's limbs, seeking to bring life back into them. Yu-ri didn't respond. "We should try to empty her of water," Mother suggested. Do-saeng edged out of the way. Mother pressed hard on Yu-ri's chest, but nothing came out of her mouth. Unsuccessful, Mother said, "We must consider that the octopus saved her life by covering her face. Otherwise she would have inhaled water . . ."

The other women circled back in for their massaging.

Mother suddenly turned her attention to Mi-ja, the Kang sisters, and me. She regarded us, considering our actions. We were supposed to stay together. Mi-ja and the Kangs had, but they looked embarrassed. Mother didn't have to say a word before the excuses began to sputter out.

"I saw her the last time I came up for air," Gu-sun stammered.

"We were never out of Yu-ri's sight," Mi-ja choked out. "She watched over us all day."

"She said she saw something big," I mumbled.

"And the two of you went. I saw you go, even though I'd sounded the call."

I couldn't bear that Mother would think I'd been partly responsible for what had happened to Yu-ri, so I said, "We didn't hear you." I lowered my gaze and shivered—from shock, sadness, and now shame that I'd lied to my mother.

Mother shouted for everyone to take her place. We picked up our oars. The boat lurched as it began moving over and through the white-capped waves. Do-saeng remained by her daughter's side, pleading with her to wake up. Yu-ri's future mother-in-law took responsibility for leading our song. "My shoulders on this icy night shake along with the waves. This small woman's mind shivers with the grief of a lifetime." It was so mournful that soon we all had tears running down our cheeks.

Mother placed a blanket over Yu-ri and another over Do-saeng's shoulders. Do-saeng wiped her face with a corner of the rough cloth. She spoke, but her words were carried away by the wind. First one woman then another stopped singing, each of us needing to hear Do-saeng. Yu-ri's future mother-in-law kept our rowing rhythm going by beating the wooden handle of a diving tool on the edge of the boat.

"A greedy diver equals a dead diver," Do-saeng lamented. We all knew the saying, but to hear it from a mother about her own daughter? That's when I learned just how strong a mother must be. "This is a haenyeo's worst sin," she went on. *"I want that octopus. I can sell it for a lot of money."*

"Many things exist under the sea that are stronger than we are," Mother said.

She wrapped an arm around Do-saeng, who then expressed her worst fear. "What if she doesn't wake up?"

"We have to hope she will."

"But what if she remains like this—suspended between this world and the Afterworld?" Do-saeng asked, gently lifting her daughter's head and placing it in her lap. "If she's unable to dive or work in the fields, wouldn't it be better to let her go?"

Mother pulled Do-saeng in closer. "You don't mean that."

"But—" Do-saeng didn't finish her thought. Instead, she smoothed strings of wet hair away from her daughter's face.

"None of us yet know what the goddesses have planned for Yu-ri," Mother said. "She may wake up tomorrow her usual chatterbox self."

————

Yu-ri didn't wake up the next morning. Or the morning after that. Or the week after that. In desperation, Do-saeng sought help from Shaman Kim, our spiritual leader and guide, our divine wise one. Although the Japanese had outlawed Shamanism, she continued to perform funerals and rites for lost souls in secret. She was known to hold rituals for grandmothers when their eyesight began to fade, mothers whose sons were in the military, and women who had bad luck, such as three pigs dying in a row. She was our conduit between the human world and the spirit world. She had the ability to go into trances to speak to the dead or missing, and then transmit their messages to friends, family, and even enemies. Do-saeng hoped Shaman Kim would now reach Yu-ri's soul and bring her mind back to her body and her family.

The ritual was held in Do-saeng's home. Shaman Kim and her helpers wore colorful hanboks—traditional Korean gowns from the mainland—instead of Jeju's usual drab trousers and jackets. Her assistants banged on drums and cymbals. Shaman Kim spun, her arms raised, calling out to the spirits to return the young haenyeo to her mother. Do-saeng openly wept. Jun-bu, Yu-ri's brother, who was just beginning to develop peach fuzz on his cheeks, tried to hold in his emotions, but we all knew how much he loved his sister. Yu-ri's future husband was pale with grief, and his parents did their best to comfort him. It was painful to see their sorrow. Still Yu-ri didn't open her eyes.

That night, I told Mi-ja my secret—that Yu-ri had asked me to disobey my mother, and I had. "If I hadn't agreed to go down one more time, Yu-ri wouldn't be the way she is now."

Mi-ja tried to comfort me. "It was Yu-ri's duty to watch over you. Not the other way around."

"I still feel responsible, though," I admitted.

Mi-ja mulled that over for a few moments. Then she said, "We'll never know why Yu-ri did what she did, but don't tell anyone your secret. Think of the pain it will bring to her family."

I also thought of the agony that would be added to my mother's heart. Mi-ja was right. I had to keep this a secret.

———

After another week, Do-saeng asked Shaman Kim to try again. This time the ceremony was held in our bulteok—hidden from the prying eyes of the Japanese. In fact, no men attended. Not even Yu-ri's brother. Do-saeng carried her daughter to the bulteok and laid her next to the fire pit. An altar had been set up against the curved stone wall. Offerings of food—so scarce—sat in dishes:

a pyramid of oranges, bowls holding the five grains of Jeju, and a few jars of homemade alcohol. Candles flickered. Mother had offered to pay Jun-bu to write messages for Yu-ri on long paper ribbons. He did it for free. "For my sister," he told me when I went to his family's house to pick them up. Now the ends of the ribbons had been tucked into the wall's rocky crevices, their tails flapping in the breeze that squeezed through the cracks.

Shaman Kim wore her most colorful silk hanbok. A sash the tint of maple leaves in spring tied closed the bright blue bodice. The main part of the fuchsia gown was so light that it wafted about her as she moved through the ceremony. Her headband was red, and her sleeves gleamed the hue of rapeseed flowers.

"Given the dominance on Jeju of volcanic cones, which are concave at the top like a woman's private parts, it is only natural that on our island females call and males follow," she began. "The goddess is always supreme, while the god is merely a consort or guardian. Above all these is the creator, the giant Goddess Seolmundae."

"Grandmother Seolmundae watches over us all," we chanted together.

"As a goddess, she flew over the seas, looking for a new home. She carried dirt in the folds of her skirt. She found this spot where the Yellow Sea meets the East China Sea and began to build herself a home. Finding it too flat, she used more of the dirt in her gown, building the mountain until it was high enough to reach the Milky Way. Soon her skirt became worn and tiny holes formed in the cloth. Soil leaked from it, building small hills, which is why we have so many oreum. In each one of these volcanic cones, another female deity lives. They are our sisters in spirit, and you can always go to them for help."

"Grandmother Seolmundae watches over us all," we chanted.

"She tested herself in many ways, as all women must," Shaman Kim told us. "She assessed the waters to see how deep they were, so that haenyeo would be safe when they went to sea. She also searched ponds and lakes, looking for ways to improve the lives of those who worked the fields on land. One day, attracted to a mysterious mist on Muljang-ol Oreum, she discovered a lake in its crater. The water was deep blue, and she could not begin to guess its depths. Taking one big breath, she swam straight down. She has never returned."

Several of the women nodded appreciatively at the good telling of this story.

"That's one version," the shaman continued. "Another says Grandmother Seolmundae, like all women, was exhausted by all she did for others, especially for her children. Her five hundred sons were always hungry. She was making them a cauldron of porridge when she became drowsy and fell into the pot. Her sons looked everywhere for her. The youngest son finally found all that remained of her—just bones—at the bottom of the pot. She had died from mother love. The sons were so overcome that they were instantly petrified into five hundred stone outcroppings, which you can see even today."

Do-saeng silently wept. The story helped one suffering mother to hear of another suffering mother.

"The Japanese say *if* Grandmother Seolmundae existed and *if* that oreum was the water pathway to her underwater palace," Shaman Kim went on, "then she abandoned us, as have all our goddesses and gods. I say she never left us."

"We sleep on her every night," we recited. "We wake on her every morning."

"When you go into the sea, you dive among the underwater ripples of her skirt. She is the great volcano at the center of our island. Some people call it Mount Halla, the Peak That Pulls Down the Milky Way, or the Mountain of the Blessed Isle. To us, she *is* our island. Anywhere we go, we can call to her and weep out our woes, and she will listen."

Shaman Kim now directed her attention to Yu-ri, who had not once stirred.

"We are here to help Yu-ri with her traveling-soul problem, but we must also worry about those of you who've suffered soul loss, which happens any time a person receives a shock," she said. "Your collective has experienced a terrible blow. None has suffered more than Yu-ri's mother. Do-saeng, please kneel before the altar. Anyone else who is in anguish, please join her."

My mother knelt next to Do-saeng. Soon the rest of us were

on our knees in a circle of anguish. The shaman held ritual knives in her hands from which white ribbons streamed. As she sliced through negativity, the ribbons swirled around us like swallows through the air. Her hanbok ballooned in clouds of riotous color. We chanted. We wept. Our emotions flowed from us accompanied by the cacophony of cymbals, bells, and drums played by Shaman Kim's assistants.

"I call upon all goddesses to bring Yu-ri's spirit back from the sea or wherever it is hiding," Shaman Kim implored. After making this request another two times, her voice changed as Yu-ri inhabited her. "I miss my mother. I miss my father and my brother. My future husband . . . *Aigo* . . ." The shaman turned to my mother. "Diving Chief, you sent me here. Now bring me home."

The way Yu-ri's voice came out of Shaman Kim's mouth sounded more like blame than an entreaty for help. This was not a good portent. Shaman Kim seemed to acknowledge this. "Tell me, Sun-sil, how would you like to respond?"

My mother rose. Her face looked taut as she addressed Yu-ri. "I accept responsibility that I sent you into the sea, but I gave you a single duty that day: to stay with my daughter and help the Kang sisters as they looked after Mi-ja. You were the eldest of the baby-divers. You had an obligation to them and to us. Through your actions, I could have lost my daughter."

Perhaps only I could see how deeply affected Mother was by what had happened. I was both awed and humbled. I hoped one day I could prove to her that I loved her as much as she loved me.

Shaman Kim swiveled to Do-saeng. "What do you wish to tell your daughter?"

Do-saeng spoke sharply to Yu-ri. "You would blame another for the results of your greed? You embarrass me! Leave greed where you are and come home right now! Don't ask someone else to help you!" Then she softened her tone. "Dear girl, come back. Your mother and brother miss you. Return home and we will drench you in love."

Shaman Kim chanted a few more incantations. The helpers banged their cymbals and drums. After that, there was nothing left to say or do.

The next morning, Yu-ri woke up. She was not the same girl, though. She could smile, but she could not speak. She could move, but she limped and sometimes jerked her arms. Both sets of parents agreed that a marriage was no longer possible. Mi-ja and I hung on to my secret, which made us closer than ever. In the weeks that followed, after we'd worked in the dry or wet fields, we visited Yu-ri. Mi-ja and I talked and giggled, so Yu-ri would have the sense she was still a young girl with no worries. Sometimes Jun-bu joined us and read aloud the essays he was writing for school or tried to tease us as he had once teased his sister. On other days, Mi-ja and I helped Do-saeng wash Yu-ri's body and hair. And when the weather grew warm, Mi-ja and I took her to the shore, where we sat in the shallows to let the smallest wavelets lap against her. We told stories, we patted her face, we let her know we were there, and she would reward us with a beautiful smile.

Every time I visited, Do-saeng bowed and expressed her gratitude. "If not for you, my daughter would have died," she'd say as she poured buckwheat tea or presented me with a dish of salted smelt, but her eyes sent a darker message. She may not have known exactly what part I'd played in Yu-ri's accident, but she certainly suspected that it was more than I'd let on, either to her or to my mother.

How Do We Fall in Love?

(before)

When Mi-ja and I first met, we were such opposites. I was like the rocks of our island—jagged, rough, all edges, but useful and no-nonsense. She was like clouds—drifting, melting, impossible to catch or fully understand. Even though we both became haenyeo, I would forever be of the earth in the sense that I was practical and concerned always for my family. Mi-ja was more like the sea— ever changing and occasionally tempestuous. I was tied closely to my mother and longed to follow her into a life in the sea; Mi-ja had no memory of her mother but missed her father terribly. I had the love and respect of my brothers and sister, while Mi-ja had only an aunt and uncle who didn't care for her. I worked hard, hauling water, carrying my baby brother on my back, doing farmwork, and gathering dried manure for heating, but Mi-ja worked harder still, completing chores for her aunt and uncle, in our fields, and for the collective. I could not read or write my name. Mi-ja could write her name and still remembered a few Japanese characters. And, as steady as I appeared to others, inside I was often fearful; as evanescent as she seemed from the outside, her inner fortitude seemed to be as strong as bamboo—able to withstand almost any force or weight. On Jeju, we had a saying: *If there is happiness at age three, it will last until you reach eighty.* I believed this to be true. Mi-ja, on the other hand, often said, "I was born on a day with no sun and no moon. Did my parents know how hard my life would be?" We could not have been more different, and yet we were very close.

How do we fall in love? The first time you see your husband's face on your engagement day, you don't know how your emotions will evolve over time. The moment your baby is wrenched from your insides, love may not be what you feel. Love must be nurtured and tended to in the same way we haenyeo care for our fields under the sea. With arranged marriages, many wives fall in love with their husbands quickly. For some, it can take years. And for others, decades of marriage will always be filled with loneliness and sadness, because we never grow the connection to that person with whom we share our sleeping mat. As for children, every woman knows the fears and sorrows. Joy is a delicious luxury that we experience most cautiously, for tragedy conceals itself around every corner. How different it is with friendship. No one picks a friend for us; we come together by choice. We are not tied together through ceremony or the responsibility to create a son; we tie ourselves together through moments. The spark when we first meet. Laughter and tears shared. Secrets packed away to be treasured, hoarded, and protected. The wonder that someone can be so different from you and yet still understand your heart in a way no one else ever will.

I remember clearly the first day I saw Mi-ja. I had recently turned seven. I lived a happy, if simple, life. We were poor, no better or worse than our neighbors. We had our wet fields in the ocean and our dry fields on land. We also had a small home garden next to our kitchen, where Mother grew white radishes, cucumbers, sesame leaf, garlic, onions, and peppers. While the vastness of the sea would suggest endless bounty, it was an unreliable source of food. The island had no natural harbors. The seas were rough. Our Korean kings had long barred our men from fishing in any significant way, and now, under Japanese rule, fishermen were allowed only rafts, with a single seat and a sail. (Or they could work on the large Japanese fishing vessels or in their canneries.) Many Jeju men were lost to rough tides, high waves, and strong winds. Long ago, Jeju's men had been divers, but the Korean monarchs imposed such a high tax on their work that it was eventually given to women, who were taxed at a lower rate. It turned out that women had an aptitude for the work. Women, like my mother, were patient. Women understood suffering. Women had more fat, so they were better suited to endure the cold. Still, it was hard for Mother—or any woman—to make a meal hearty enough for a large family from sea urchin roe, turban shell, sea snails, and abalone alone. Besides, those creatures were not for us. They were for the wealthy—or, at least, wealthier—people on the mainland, or in Japan, China, and the USSR. All this meant that for most of the year my family lived on the millet, cabbage, and sweet potatoes that we grew in our dry field, while the money Mother earned from diving paid for clothes, house repairs, and anything else that required cash.

It was a wife's social and familial duty to birth a son, who would lengthen her husband's lineage. But every family in the seaside villages of Jeju was most grateful for the birth of a daughter, because she would always be a provider. In this regard, our family was not so fortunate, because we only had four females in our household: Grandmother, Mother, me, and Little Sister, who, back then, was only eleven months old and too young to help. Still, one day, she would work with me to help our parents pay their debts, chip in to build a better home for their old age, and possibly even contribute to sending our brothers to school.

On the summer day eight years ago when I first met Mi-ja, Father stayed home, as he usually did, to take care of my siblings. Mother and I set out to our dry field to weed. She looked like a misshapen melon. Her stomach bulged with what would soon be my third brother, while her back was bent under the weight of a basket stuffed with tools and fertilizer. I carried a basket filled with drinking water and lunch. Together we walked through the olles. In the village, the stone olles around houses were high enough to prevent neighbors from peeking inside. Once outside the village, the olles were about waist-high. Each plot of land was also surrounded by stone walls, which had less to do with limning a family's property than with blocking the relentless wind, which could snap long-stemmed crops in two. No matter what their use, the olles were made from volcanic rocks so large they must have required at least two of our ancestors to put each one in place.

Just as we reached our land, Mother stopped so abruptly that I bumped into her. I feared we'd stumbled upon Japanese soldiers, but then she yelled, "You! There! What are you doing?"

I stood on my tiptoes to peer over the stone wall and saw a little girl crouched among our sweet potato plants, her hands digging into the earth. If Jeju was known for its Three Abundances of wind, stones, and women, it was also acknowledged for lacking three other things: beggars, thieves, and locked gates. But here was a thief! Even from afar, I could see her making calculations. She couldn't escape through the opening in the wall, because that would put her in the olle with us. She leapt up and galloped to the far side of the field. Mother pushed me and yelled, "Catch her!"

I dropped my basket and dashed along the olle that edged the field. I turned left into the neighboring plot, galloped across it, scrambled over the far stone wall, and dropped to the other side. When I reached the next wall, I climbed to the top, and there she was on the opposite side below me, scurrying like a rat. Before she could sense me, I jumped on top of her and wrestled her to the ground. She fought hard, but I was far stronger. Once I'd pinned her wrists, I could see her face. Clearly, she was not from our village, because no one here was that pale. It was as if she'd been kept inside her entire life. Or she was a hungry ghost—a type of spirit who restlessly roams the earth and causes trouble for the living. Under any other circumstances, I would have been petrified. Instead, my heart thumped in my chest. The chase. The capture.

"Let me go," she cried piteously in Japanese. "Please let me go."

That's when I got scared. We all had to speak Japanese for the colonists, but this girl's tones were perfect. What if I'd tackled a Japanese girl? Then I registered the tears that ran down her cheeks toward her ears. What if I was caught *torturing* a Japanese girl?

I was about to free her when Mother's voice floated down from above us. "Bring her to me."

I looked up and saw Mother gazing down at us from over the stone wall. I carefully lifted myself off the girl, but I kept a firm grip on her arm. I pulled her to her feet and pushed her ahead of me. She didn't have a choice but to climb over the wall. Once we were both on the other side, Mother slowly scanned the girl from head to toe and back again. Finally, she asked, "Who are you? Who do you belong to?"

"My name is Han Mi-ja," she said, wiping away her tears with the heels of her hands. "I live with my aunt and uncle in the Sut-dong section of Hado."

Mother sucked air in through her teeth. "I think I know your family. You must be Han Gil-ho's daughter."

Mi-ja nodded.

Mother stayed silent. I could tell she was upset, but I had no idea why. At last, she spoke. "Go ahead then. Tell me why you would steal from us."

The words flooded out of Mi-ja's mouth. "My mother died when I came out of her. My father died two months ago. Heart attack. Now I live with Aunt Lee-ok and Uncle Him-chan, and—"

"And they don't feed you," Mother interrupted. "I understand why—"

Defiance skittered across Mi-ja's features. "My father was not a traitor. He worked for the Japanese in Jeju City, but that doesn't mean—"

Mother cut her off to recite a familiar aphorism. *If you plant red beans, then you will harvest red beans.* This meant that a child's character and behavior came from what the parents planted. "No one likes a collaborator," she said matter-of-factly. "The people in all seven villages of Hado were ashamed when your mother and father chose that life. And consider your given name. Mi-ja. So Japanese."

Even at my young age, I knew my mother was taking a risk speaking so openly against the Japanese and those who supported them.

Mi-ja's hands and face were smudged with dirt. Her clothes were finer than any I'd seen before, but they were filthy. At some point during her escape, she'd lost her scarf, and her hair looked matted, as though no one had put a comb through it in weeks. But what struck me most was how thin she was. She was pitiful, but Mother didn't let up.

"Let's see what's in your pockets," she demanded.

Mi-ja searched through her clothes, making sure she showed Mother everything. She held up a lump of coal, then she put it back in her pocket. She carefully wiped her dirty hand on her shirt, reached up under her sleeve, and pulled out a book. It was the first one I'd seen, so I couldn't be impressed or unimpressed, but Mother's eyes widened. In her nerves or out of fear, Mi-ja dropped it. Mother bent to pick it up, but Mi-ja grabbed it first. She gave Mother another defiant look.

"Please. It's mine," she said, quickly secreting the book back up her sleeve. She reached into her last pocket, pulled out a closed fist, and then dropped a handful of baby sweet potatoes barely bigger than pebbles into Mother's palm. Another long silence hung over us as Mother rolled them back and forth, examining them for damage. When she next spoke, her tone was still loud, as it always was, but kinder.

"You're a lucky girl," she said. "If I were someone else . . . But I'm not. You're coming back to our field, and you're going to replant these. When you're done, you're going to help us. If you do a good job, we'll share our lunch with you. If you don't run away, if you obey, if you follow my orders, I'll let you come again tomorrow. Do you understand?"

I didn't fall in love with Mi-ja on that first day—not when I was riled from the chase, confused by my mother's reaction to her, and mad that I had to share part of our lunch with a thief. Here's what did happen: Mi-ja listened to everything Mother told her to do, but she followed what *I* did. I showed her how to plant the tubers, then stomp on the soil to keep it from flying away in the wind. We spent the rest of the time pulling weeds and aerating the soil with a three-pronged tool. As the light changed and the sky began to glow crimson, she helped us pack.

Mother said, "I will see you tomorrow. No need to tell your aunt and uncle."

Mi-ja bowed very low, several times. With that acknowledgment, Mother set off. I was about to follow her when Mi-ja held me back.

"I want to show you something." She pulled the book out from under her sleeve. Her eyes met mine. With two hands and a formality I'd only seen during ancestor worship, she offered it to me. "You can hold it if you want." I wasn't so sure I wanted to do that, but I took it anyway. It was a slim volume, bound in leather. "It's all I have left of my father," she said. "Open it."

I did. The pages were made from rice paper. I assumed the writing was Japanese, but it could have been Korean. A couple of pages in the middle of the book stuck out unevenly. I turned to that section and discovered that they'd been torn out. That seemed disrespectful, but I noticed Mi-ja was smiling.

"Look what I've done," she said, taking back the book. "Here is a rubbing I did of a carving we had in our apartment in Jeju City. This one I made of the ironwork hinges on Father's coffin. I made this one the day Auntie Lee-ok picked me up. It's the pattern of the floor in my old room. It was the only way to save my memories."

The whole time I was trying to imagine what her life must have been like, living in the city, with a room of her own, surrounded by books.

"Auntie sold our things. She said no one in Hado wanted to see reminders of my father. She also said she would use the money to feed me and send me back to school. Now that I'm here . . ." She jutted her chin. "You don't have a school for girls. Auntie had to know that. She thinks my father was a bad man, so she only gives me seaweed and kimchee to eat. My father's money has gone to buy pigs and . . . I don't know . . ." After a long pause, her darkness evaporated. "You and your mother are the nicest people I've met since coming here, and this is the best day I've had since Father died. Let us, you and me, make a memory of it. Of this place. So we will always remember today."

Without waiting for me to agree, she tore a page from the book, placed it on one of the rocks at the entrance to our field, pulled out her lump of coal, and rubbed it on the paper. Rocks were nothing special to me. They were everywhere I looked. But when she put the rubbing in my hand, I saw the rough stone pattern of my birthplace, while the unintelligible words beneath the picture were part of a world I would never know or understand. Tiny pinholes where the coal and rock had punctured the paper seemed like the endless possibilities that the stars in the night sky promised. I felt like I'd been given something too special for me to keep, and I said so.

Mi-ja considered that, and then pursed her lips, gave a tiny nod, and tucked the page in the book with the others she'd made. "I'll

LISA SEE

keep it," she said, "but it's *our* memory. No matter what happens, we'll always know where to find it."

————

When you're seven, you can say you'll be best friends forever. It rarely turns out that way. But Mi-ja and I were different. We grew closer with each passing season. Mi-ja's aunt and uncle continued to treat her terribly. To them, she was like a slave or a servant. She slept in their granary—barely bigger than a meter in diameter—between the main house and the latrine, with its pigs and smells. I showed her how to do chores and taught her the songs for grinding millet, knitting horsehair hats, netting anchovies, gathering pig excrement for our fields, and plowing, planting, and pulling weeds, and she rewarded me with her imagination.

We have many sayings on Jeju Island. One of them is *Wherever you are on Jeju, you can see Grandmother Seolmundae.* But we also say, *Grandmother Seolmundae watches over all of us.* No matter where Mi-ja and I went—going to the fields, walking to the shore, running the few minutes between her neighborhood and my neighborhood within the larger confines of Hado—we could see her reaching for the sky. Her peak was covered with snow in winter. Chores were hardest then: hauling water in the bone-cold mornings, walking on ground white with frost or snow, wind so sharp it cut through our clothes as if we were wearing nothing.

In the first and second months, Mi-ja and I helped Mother weed our millet and rapeseed crops, because it's a well-known fact that men's knees are too stiff for this work, and they are shy around sickles and hoes. Jeju was known for its five grains—rice, barley, soybean, millet, and foxtail millet. Rice was for the New Year celebration, but only if Mother had saved enough money to buy it. Barley was for the rich, who lived in Jeju City and in the mid-mountain area. Millet was for the poor. It was the food that filled our stomachs, while we could extract oil from rapeseed, so both crops were extremely important to us.

That first winter, Mother also hired Mi-ja to work in the collective. "I'll allow you to share the communal meal after the other haenyeo and I return from the sea," Mother said. "Keep the fire hot and your mouth shut, and the others won't bother you." So Mi-ja entered the bulteok long before I did. She gathered firewood, kept the flames in the fire pit steady, and helped sort sea urchins, conch, and the agar-agar and kelp that the haenyeo brought to shore.

This did not sit well with Grandmother, who said, "No one can ever remove the stain of her father's activities for the Japanese, which is why no one other than you will hire her to do chores as they might another orphan."

But on this matter, Mother took a strong stand. "When I look at that girl," she said, "I see someone who will always eke by on her wits and the hunger that drives her."

In spring, azaleas beamed magenta, purple, and crimson even from afar on Grandmother Seolmundae's flanks. Fields of rape-seed gleamed as yellow as the sun. We harvested our crop of grain, plowed the field by hand, and planted red beans and sweet potatoes. At the end of spring, every family across the island stripped the thatch off their roofs. Mi-ja's aunt and uncle made her haul away the old thatch, bring in new thatch, and do the best she could to pass stones up to the men to weigh down the thatch and keep it in place. When she was done, she came to my house, where Mother allowed her to help me sort through our old thatch to search for insect larva, which Mother boiled for us to eat.

Summer brought the coolness of green to Grandmother Seol-mundae's slopes, but everything else was hot, humid, and rainy. Mother gave me my first tewak, which she'd made herself. I was so proud of it, and I didn't mind sharing it with Mi-ja one bit. Since she'd lived in Jeju City, and without a mother's wake to follow, she didn't know how to swim. I took her to the tide pools where I'd played when I was three and four. We went on the very hottest days of summer to a shallow cove to splash and frolic with other Hado children. The Kang sisters were always there, and we loved to listen to them fight and make up. Yu-ri used to come with her brother, Jun-bu, who joined other boys his age to dive over the protective wall of rocks into the open and unprotected sea. We loved watching those boys. Especially Jun-bu. We wondered how someone so studious could laugh in such a carefree way.

Sometimes Mother and the other haenyeo returned to shore at

midday to nurse their babies. They would watch us, calling out to tell us to kick harder or to take a deeper breath to build our lungs. But mostly the mothers didn't have time to come to shore during their workday, and the afternoon air was filled with the sounds of babies yowling in hunger and fathers murmuring soothing, but useless, words, for only a mother has the milk. By the end of our second summer, Mi-ja was swimming well, and we were beginning to practice diving down a meter or so to hide something under a rock for the other one to find or to touch an anemone to watch it close in on itself.

Of course, summers were not just for play. During the sixth month in the lunar calendar, we harvested barley and dried it in the courtyard between the big and little houses. We helped Mother slaughter a rooster in a special ceremony; then we cooked it and served it to Grandmother so she would remain free of old-age illnesses. We learned how to mix ashes with seaweed to make fertilizer, which we carried to our field. We planted buckwheat, and weeded, weeded, weeded. And always, around 7.7 in the lunar calendar and August in the Western calendar, we made gal-ot, a special kind of cloth dyed in unripe persimmon juice. The tannin from the fruit prevented the cloth from holding odors or giving off sour smells, which meant we could wear it for days and weeks at a time without it stinking. It was also water resistant and worked as a mosquito repellent. Barley bristle didn't stick to this type of cloth, and, because the persimmon juice strengthened it, our clothes didn't rip, not even when we brushed against thorns. We used gal-ot for everything. Even Mi-ja, who'd outgrown her fancy city clothes, wore trousers, shirts, and jackets made from it. My clothes were passed down to my brothers and sister, but Mi-ja saved hers. "When I have children," she said, "I'll use the softened cloth for blankets and diapers." The thought had not yet occurred to me that I might have a baby one day.

Every fall, Grandmother Seolmundae's slopes were aflame with leaves in yellow, orange, and red. At this time of year, Mi-ja and I liked to climb oreum, the smaller parasitic cones Grandmother Seolmundae had given birth to when she erupted. We'd sit together—walled-in fields spreading out below us like a quilt, the sky cloudless, the ocean glittering in the distance, the taller oreum topped by ancient watchtowers, where beacon fires once warned islanders of approaching pirates. We'd talk and talk and talk. I loved hearing about Jeju City. To me, every story seemed more fantastic than the last.

One day she mentioned that Jeju City had electricity. When I admitted that I didn't know what that was, she laughed. "It lights up the room without burning pinesap or oil. There are lights on the streets. Colored bulbs brighten shop windows. It's . . ." The space between her eyebrows creased as she thought about how best to describe the intangible to me. "It's Japanese!"

Mi-ja and her father had also owned a radio. She said it was a box with voices coming out of it, made in Japan. I couldn't imagine that either. And it confused me to think that the cloven-footed ones could have so many marvelous creations.

She talked about her father's car—*car!*—and how he drove all over the island on roads that the Japanese had built, when all I had ever seen were pony-pulled carts and the occasional truck that came to our village to pick up haenyeo for leaving-home water-work in other countries. "Father managed road construction crews for the Japanese," Mi-ja explained. "With his help, they connected the four parts of the island for the first time!"

All I knew was Hado.

"My father was well respected," she told me. "He loved me. He took care of me. He bought me toys and pretty clothes."

"And he fed you." I egged her on, because I loved to hear about all the dishes she'd eaten that I'd never tasted—buckwheat noodles with pheasant or spiced and grilled horsemeat from the mid-mountain area. To a little girl who had only tasted pig meat and sea creatures, it all sounded preposterous but delicious. And then there was sugar . . .

"Imagine eating something that makes you smile so hard your face aches. That's what it's like to eat candy, ice cream, and pastries, or *wagashi* and *anmitsu.*"

But when would I ever have a Western or Japanese dessert? Never.

In Jeju City, Mi-ja had "playmates," which were another thing I could not comprehend, not even when she described tag and hide and go seek. Who had interest in games that weren't teaching you something practical like how to dive for top shell or gather seaweed? It was hard to imagine, as well, living in a house with its own attached garden with fruit trees and a pond in which the servants raised fish for the household, making it an impossibility that Mi-ja could ever go hungry.

Mi-ja was aware of all she'd lost, so while talking about her past was fun for me, sometimes it made her feel low. That's when I would suggest she bring out her father's book. We'd sit side by side, turning the pages. It was a manual that her father had used in his travels around the island. In the beginning, Mi-ja could still remember the meaning of a character here and there—*oil, east, road, mountain, bridge*—but as the months passed, with no one to remind her, her ability to read waned. Still, there was something mysterious, magical even, about the characters on the page, and she liked to run a finger down a vertical line and "read" to me stories of goddesses and mothers that she made up.

The saying *You aren't aware your clothes are getting wet in the rain* suggests a gradual change and can be interpreted in two ways, one positive, the other negative. A positive story might involve friendship, which grows over time. First you are acquaintances, then friends, then a closer relationship develops, until you realize that you love each other. A darker example might be about a criminal. A person steals a small thing, then a larger thing, until finally he's become a thief. The point is, you're not aware just how wet you're getting when the drizzle starts. Unlike most people, though, Mi-ja and I had physical proof that we were growing closer, because, as she had said on that first day, we were capturing moments with our rubbings. As precious as her father's book was to her, she was never shy about ripping out one of the pages so we could make a rubbing together. One of us would hold the piece of paper and the other would rub the lump of coal over it so we could capture the ridged outline of a shell won in a swimming contest, the pattern of the wooden door to my house the first time she was allowed to spend the night, the surface of her first tewak, which Mother made for her, as though she were an actual daughter.

When we turned nine, the haenyeo of Hado helped plan an island-wide anti-Japanese demonstration. Mother had started attending the Hado Night School. As far as I could tell, she didn't acquire much in the way of reading or writing, but she and her friends learned how to weigh their catches so they wouldn't be cheated. She also learned about her rights. Inspired by a young male teacher—an intellectual and a leftist, Mother called him—a group of five haenyeo banded together to fight against rules that were being forced upon women divers by the Japanese. My mother wasn't part of that core group, but she repeated what she'd picked up from them.

"The Japanese don't pay us a fair price. They take too high a percentage for themselves. Forty percent! How are we supposed to live with that? And some of their officials—collaborators—sneak our harvest of agar-agar through Jeju City's port for their own gain."

Collaborators. Mi-ja shrunk into herself, pulling her shoulders up around her ears. Mother put a hand on the nape of Mi-ja's neck to reassure her.

"Resist," she went on. "We have to resist."

News passed from one woman's mouth to another woman's ear, from one collective to the next, all around the island. Hearing so many complaints, the Japanese said they would make changes.

"Except they lied to us!" Mother spat out. "Months have gone by—"

Grandmother, who hated the Japanese more than anyone I knew, warned, "You must be careful."

But it was too late for that, because a plan had already been set. On a morning when the village of Sehwa held its five-day market, the haenyeo from Hado would march to the market, where they would gather even more haenyeo. From there, they would continue on to the district office in Pyeongdae to present their demands. Everyone was excited but nervous too, because no one could guess how the Japanese would respond.

The night before the march, Mi-ja stayed at our house. It was early January and too cold to be outside gazing at stars, but Father had taken Third Brother out to see if he could walk him to sleep. Mother asked us to join her and Grandmother in the main room.

"Do you want to come tomorrow?" Mother asked me.

"Yes! Please!" I was thrilled to be asked.

Mi-ja kept her eyes cast down. Mother liked Mi-ja and had done many things for her, but maybe an invitation to an anti-Japanese rally was too much to expect.

"I spoke to your aunt," Mother informed Mi-ja. "What a disagreeable woman."

Mi-ja looked up, pathetically hopeful.

"I told her that if you accompany us it might do much to bleach the stain you carry of your father's past actions," Mother went on.

"*Ieeee,*" Mi-ja squealed with joy.

"Then all is settled. Now listen to Grandmother."

Mi-ja nestled next to me. Grandmother often told us stories she'd heard from her grandmother, who'd heard from her grandmother, and so on. It was through her that we learned about the past but also about what was happening in the world around us. Mother must have wanted to remind us of some of these things before the march.

"In the long-ago days," Grandmother began, "three brothers—Ko, Bu, and Yang—bubbled out of the earth to become the founders of Jeju. They worked hard, but they were lonely. One day, three sisters—all princesses—arrived in a boat heavy with horses, cattle, and the five seed grains, which had been given to them by Halmang Jacheongbi, the goddess of love. Together, these three couples created the Kingdom of Tamna, which lasted one thousand years."

"Tamna means 'Island Country,'" Mi-ja recited, showing how much she'd absorbed from past tellings.

"Our Tamna ancestors were seafarers," Grandmother continued. "They traded with other countries. By always looking outward, they taught us to be independent. They gave us our language—"

"But my father said the Jeju language also has words from China, Mongolia, Russia, and from other countries too," Mi-ja interrupted again. "Like Japan. Fiji and Oceania too. We even have

Korean words from hundreds, maybe *thousands,* of years ago. That's what he said . . ."

Mi-ja's voice trailed off. She could be enthusiastic, and she sometimes liked to show off the knowledge she had learned in Jeju City, but Grandmother never liked being reminded of Mi-ja's father. Tonight, instead of hissing her disapproval, Grandmother simply went on. "The Tamna taught us that the outside represents danger. For centuries, we've been in a struggle against the Japanese, who've had to pass by us on their way—"

"To loot China," I said. I hadn't heard of Fiji or Oceania, but I knew some things.

Grandmother nodded, but her look of irritation made me decide to keep my mouth shut from then on. "Around seven hundred years ago, the Mongols invaded Jeju. They raised and bred horses in the mid-mountain area. They called the island the Star Guardian God of Horses. That's how much they loved our pastures. The Mongols also used Jeju as a stepping-stone to invade Japan and China. We can't hate them too much, though. Many of them married Jeju women. Some say it is from them that we gained our strength and perseverance."

Mother poured hot water into cups for us to drink. Once everyone was served, she picked up where Grandmother had left off. "Five hundred years ago, we became part of Korea and were ruled by kings. We were mostly left alone, because every king saw this as a place to exile aristocrats and scholars who opposed him. They brought with them Confucianism, which taught that social order is maintained through—"

"The self, the family, the country, and the world," Mi-ja recited. "They believed that every person on earth lives *under* someone else—all people beneath the king, children beneath their parents, and wives beneath their husbands—"

"And now we have the Japanese." Grandmother snorted. "They've turned us into a stepping-stone again, building airfields on our island so their planes can take off to bomb China—"

"We can't stop everything they do," Mother interrupted, "but maybe we can force some change. I want you girls to be a part of that."

The next morning, Mi-ja was waiting for us in her usual spot in the olle. The air was frosty, and steam mushroomed from our mouths. We continued walking through the olles, picking up Do-saeng, Yu-ri, and other women and girls, all of us wearing white diving kerchiefs to mark us as past, present, and future haenyeo.

"Hurray for the independence of Korea!" we shouted.

"Stop unfair labor practices!" our voices rang out together.

The five-day market in Sehwa was always crowded, but, on that day, it was even more so. The five leaders from the Hado Night School took turns making speeches. "Join us in our march to the district office. Help us deliver our demands. We're strongest when we dive together. We're even stronger when the collectives come together. We'll make the Japanese listen!"

Top-level haenyeo led us, but it was the presence of grandmothers, who remembered the time before the Japanese arrived, and girls like Mi-ja and me, who'd lived our entire lives under Japanese rule, that reminded everyone of our purpose. This wasn't just about the forty percent discount price that the Japanese were imposing on the haenyeo. It was about freedom and our Jeju independent ways. It was about the strength and courage of Jeju women.

Mi-ja's eyes glittered in a way I'd never seen. She often felt alone, but now she was part of something much larger than she was. And Mother was right. Mi-ja's presence did seem to make an impression on the women in our group, because several of them came up to walk by her side for a while so they could hear her shout, "Hurray for the independence of Korea!" I was excited too, but for very different reasons. This was the farthest I'd been from home. I had Mi-ja by my side. We held hands, while raising our other arms, fists clenched, to shout the slogans. We'd been growing closer—between all the things I'd taught her and all the imagination, stories, and joy she'd given me—but in this moment, we were one person.

By the time we reached Pyeongdae, thousands of women had come together. Mi-ja and I linked arms; Mother and Do-saeng walked shoulder to shoulder. We entered the district office's compound. The five organizers climbed the steps of the main building and began addressing the crowd. The speeches were more or less the same as the ones they'd made earlier, but they seemed to generate more energy with so many people listening and reacting, with shouts echoing what had just been said.

"End colonization!" Kang Gu-ja called out.

"Freedom for Jeju!" Kang Gu-sun roared.

But no one could top my mother's voice. "Independence for Korea!" For everything Mother did in her life, and for all the ways she protected and inspired the women in her diving collective, this was the moment of which I was most proud.

Japanese soldiers came to stand between those making speeches and the front door to the district office. Other soldiers took positions on the edges of the crowd. The situation felt tense, with so many people shoved together. At last, the door opened. A Japanese man stepped out. Out of habit, out of fear, the five Hado women bowed deeply. From her low position, the one standing in the middle extended her hands to present the list of demands. Wordlessly, the man took it, went back inside, and shut the door. We all looked at each other. *Now what?* Now nothing, because there would be no negotiations that day. We all walked back to our villages.

Before we left, Mi-ja and I had to make a remembrance. I pointed to a Japanese character etched on a door to one of the buildings in the compound. Mother was speaking to her friends, and, now that the excitement was over, the soldiers had lost interest too, so no one paid us any attention as we walked to the door and began our ritual. It may not have been the best idea, though, because two things happened simultaneously: four guards ran over to see what we were doing, and Mother yelled at us. "Get away from there right now!" Mi-ja, with the piece of charcoal securely in her hand, and I, with the completed rubbing tight in mine, dashed through the milling women to Mother's side. *Hyng,* but was she angry! But when we looked back at the soldiers, they were bent over, hands on their knees, laughing. It was many years before we learned that the character we'd chosen for our treasure said *toilet.*

———

The march was one of the three largest anti-Japanese protests ever to be held in Korea, the largest led by women, and the largest for the year with seventeen thousand supporters. It inspired another *four thousand* demonstrations in Korea over the following twelve months. The new Japanese governor of Jeju agreed to some demands. The discount ended, and a few crooked dealers were removed from their posts. All that was good, but other things also happened. We began to hear of one arrest, and then another. Thirty-four haenyeo—including the five original leaders from the Hado Night School—were arrested. Dozens of others were detained during a crackdown to stop additional protests. Rumors spread that some of the teachers at the Hado Night School were socialists or communists, and many of them went into hiding or moved away. None of that stopped Mother from attending classes.

"I wish you two girls could learn to read, write, and do basic math, because it will help you if, in the future, one of you becomes chief of a haenyeo collective," she told us. "If I can save up enough money, I'll pay for the two of you to come to school with me."

That sounded far more dangerous than marching in a demonstration, because the women who'd been arrested were being held precisely because of what their education had inspired them to do. But I wanted whatever Mi-ja wanted, and she wanted to go very much. My mother was her only hope.

Eight months after the Hado-led demonstration, Mother, Mi-ja, and I were once again doing farm tasks in our dry field. Weeding is awful—bent over all day, being wet to the bone from rain or sweat or both, the tediousness of the precision required to pull out the intrusive plants without damaging the roots of those we were growing. Mother led us in a call-and-response song to keep us distracted from our discomfort, but with Mi-ja by my side I could never complain too much. She'd become adept at fieldwork after toiling so long with us. Mother paid her in food, which she always asked Mi-ja to eat in our presence. "I don't want your aunt and uncle consuming the results of your labors," Mother said.

We weeded and sang, not paying attention to the world outside the stone walls that surrounded our field. Mother's hearing wasn't good, but her peripheral vision was sharp, and she was alert for all dangers. I saw her leap up, with her hand hoe held before her. Then she dropped the tool, collapsed to the ground, and rested her forehead on her folded hands. All this I registered in seconds.

Beside me, Mi-ja stopped singing. I started to tremble, petrified, as a group of Japanese soldiers strode into the field.

"Bow down," Mother whispered.

Mi-ja and I fell to the ground, imitating Mother's supplicant position. Terror heightened my senses. Wind whistled through cracks in the stone walls. A few plots over, I could hear singing as other women did their farm chores. The soldiers' boots crunched through the field as they approached. I tilted my head so I could peek at them. The sergeant, recognizable by the polish of his boots and the insignia on his jacket, flicked the stick he was carrying, slapping it into the palm of his other hand. I lowered my eyes back to the dirt.

"You're one of the troublemakers, aren't you?" he asked my mother.

My mind scrambled. *Maybe they've come to arrest her. But if they knew about her involvement with the demonstrations, they would have come for her already.* Then my mind spiraled to a darker possibility. *Perhaps one of our neighbors turned her in.* These things were known to happen. The right piece of information could bring a family a sack of white rice.

"Let the girls go home," Mother said, which, it seemed to me, was hardly a proclamation of innocence.

It may have been something else, though. I was only ten, but I'd already been cautioned about what soldiers could do to women and girls. I peered up again, needing to get a sense of when I should run.

"What are you growing here?" The sergeant nudged Mother with the toe of his boot. Her body stiffened in what I first took to be anger. She'd proved her strength by becoming a haenyeo chief, so inside she must have been getting ready to fight them one by one. But then I saw the way her clothes vibrated on her body. She was shaking with fear. "Answer me!" He raised the stick above his head and brought it down on her back. She swallowed a scream.

Behind the sergeant, other men yanked up plants and shoved them in satchels looped over their shoulders. This invasion wasn't about my mother's activities. Or doing bad things to Mother, Mi-ja, and me. It was about stealing our food.

The sergeant raised his stick and was about to bring it down again when I heard Mi-ja whisper in Japanese. "Please don't take our plants by their roots."

"What's that?" The sergeant pivoted toward her.

"Pay no attention to her," Mother said. "She doesn't know any better. She's an ignorant—"

"I'll cut some leaves for you," Mi-ja said as she started to rise. "That way the crop will continue to grow, and you can come again."

Silence grabbed the men's throats as they took in what she'd said and how she'd spoken. Her Japanese was clear in tone. She was lovely in the way we'd heard the Japanese liked—pale, delicate features, with a natural subservience. In a flash, too quick for Mi-ja to tighten her muscles or try to move out of the way, the sergeant struck her bare leg with his stick. She dropped to the dirt. He raised the stick above his head and brought it down again and again. Mi-ja screamed in pain, but my mother and I didn't move. One of the soldiers fingered his belt buckle. Another one, biting his upper lip, retreated until his back was against the stone wall. My mother and I remained completely still. When the sergeant's fury had worn out and he finally stopped whipping Mi-ja, she lifted her head.

"Stay down," Mother mouthed.

But Mi-ja kept moving, pulling herself to her knees and raising her palms upward. "Please, sir, let me harvest for you. I will pick the best leaves—"

The men were suddenly as paralyzed as Mother and I were. They watched, as still as the ancient stone grandfather statues that could be found dotted around the island, as she struggled to her feet, then bent to peel off the outer leaves of a cabbage. With her head bowed, she offered the leaves to the sergeant with both hands. He wrapped his hands around her wrists and pulled her closer.

The sharp metallic trill of a whistle cut through the air. The seven men turned their heads in the direction of the sound. The sergeant released Mi-ja, spun on his heel, and marched toward the break in the wall. Five of the soldiers followed right behind him. The sixth one, who'd shied away earlier, grabbed the leaves, stuffed them in his satchel, and took off after the others, preceding up the olle, going farther inland.

Mi-ja collapsed, whimpering. I crawled to her side. My mother scrambled to her feet and whistled a series of notes—high and shrill like a bird's call—to warn others working in their fields. Later, we heard two women were arrested, but right then we had to care for Mi-ja. Mother carried her back to our house, where she used warm water to help peel Mi-ja's clothes from her broken skin. I held her hand and mumbled, "You're so brave. You saved Mother. You protected all of us." Those stupid words couldn't possibly have lessened Mi-ja's pain. She kept her eyes clamped shut, but tears leaked from them anyway. And they didn't stop until long after Mother had applied salve to Mi-ja's wounds and wrapped her legs in clean strips of cloth.

The next day, a different group of soldiers came to our house, marching through the rain and mud. This time it seemed certain they'd come for Mother. Or perhaps they wanted retaliation against my family. My oldest brother took as many of the young ones as he could gather, and they ran out the back and climbed over the wall. I sat on the floor next to Mi-ja's mat. She was in so much pain that she seemed unaware of the commotion in the courtyard. No matter what happened next, I wouldn't leave her side. Through the lifted slats on the side of the house, I watched as the soldiers spoke to my father. Our house was owned in his name, but he was not in charge of our family. He could comfort a crying baby better than my mother could, but he was unused to adversity or danger. Surprisingly, they treated him courteously. Rather, courteously for occupiers.

"I understand damage was done to your crops and some things were . . . taken," the lieutenant said. "I can't return what's already been eaten."

The entire time the lieutenant spoke, his eyes flicked around the courtyard. The pile of tewaks against the side of the house, the stone Father liked to sit on to smoke his pipe, the upside-down stack of bowls we used for our meals, as though he were counting how many people lived here. He focused his greatest attention on Mother, seemingly assessing her.

"I apologize for the misbehavior of the women in my household," Father said in his fumbling Japanese. "We always want to help—"

"We are not bad people," the lieutenant interrupted. "We've had to crack down on troublemakers, but we are husbands and fathers too."

The lieutenant sounded sympathetic, but there was no way to trust him. Father bit a thumbnail. I wished he didn't look so scared.

The lieutenant motioned to one of his men. A bag was dropped on the ground. "Here is your compensation," he said. "From now on, try to do as we do. Keep your women home."

That was an impossible request, but Father agreed to it.

After that day, Mother stopped attending classes and meetings. She said she was too busy running the haenyeo collective to stay involved in demonstrations, but she was only trying to protect us. What had happened seemed frightening and demeaning. We believed that these were the worst times we would experience— Japanese rule, resistance, and retaliation. As for Mi-ja, the way she'd stepped forward to protect my mother forever changed our friendship. From that day on, I believed I could trust her with my life. So did my mother. Only Grandmother's heart refused to soften, but she was an old woman and stuck in her ways. All of which meant that by the time Mi-ja and I turned fifteen—and Yu-ri had become a different person—we were as close as a pair of chopsticks.

Life Bubbles

Our routines didn't change after Yu-ri's accident. Even Do-saeng returned to the bulteok. We dove for two periods during the lunar month, for six days each, following the crescent moons when waxing and waning. Over the next seven months, my swimming skills improved. I could dive straight down now, even if I still couldn't go that far. If I took several shallow dives, then I could risk a deeper one. I now understood how carefully Mother had orchestrated Mi-ja's and my education. When I'd turned ten, Mother had given me an old pair of her goggles, which I'd shared with Mi-ja. When I'd turned twelve, Mother had taught us how to reap underwater plants without damaging their roots so that they would grow back the next season, just as we did in our dry fields. Now my ability to read the seabed for things I could harvest increased daily. I could easily recognize the differences between brown algae, sea mustard, and seaweed, while my skills at sensing prey—the poisonous bite of a sea snake or the numbing sting of a jellyfish—improved too.

"You're not only painting a map of the seabed in your head," Mother instructed me on a bright fall morning as we walked to the bulteok, "you're learning where you are in space. You need always to be aware of where you are in relation to the boat, the shore, your tewak, Mi-ja, me, and the other haenyeo. You're learning about tides, currents, and surges, and about the influence of the moon on the sea and on your body. It's most important that you always be mindful of where you are in that moment when your lungs begin to crave breath."

I grew more accustomed to the cold, shivering less, and accepting this aspect of haenyeo life, which could not be remedied. I was proud of my accomplishments, but I still hadn't found, let alone harvested, an abalone, while Mi-ja had already brought five onto the boat.

Mother lapsed into silence as we neared the spot in the olle where we picked up Mi-ja. We never knew if she'd be there. If her uncle or aunt wanted her to do something, then that took precedence, and Mother couldn't interfere. If Mi-ja were sick, if they beat her, if they asked her to haul water from two kilometers away just because they could make this cruel demand, we wouldn't know in advance.

We came around the curve in the olle, and there she was. "Good morning!" she called.

Beside me, Mother's shoulders relaxed.

"Good morning," I said, smiling as I reached Mi-ja.

"We should enjoy these next six days," Mother commented, "because the water is still bearable. Soon winter will be here . . ."

Mi-ja gave me a sidelong glance. It was obvious to anyone who knew my mother that she was different after Yu-ri's accident, and it kept people from teasing her too much about the fact that I had yet to harvest an abalone. Still, on occasion, a diver might mock her: "What kind of mother are you, if you can't . . ." Or "A chief needs to teach her daughter to . . ." The question or sentence would never be finished, because another diver would poke that first woman in the ribs or quickly change the subject to husbands, tides, or the estimated time of arrival of a coming storm. Everyone tried to protect my mother—until some other haenyeo would get caught up in a moment of exuberance and say something thoughtless again—because the responsibility for the collective now weighed heavily upon her. This was worrisome, because who hadn't heard the stories of haenyeo haunted by the injuries or deaths of other divers? Whether from ghosts, guilt, or sorrow, a diver could easily be lulled into making a mistake. We all knew of the woman who lived on the far side of Hado. She began to drink fermented rice wine after her friend died and became so disoriented she let a surge push her onto a sharp rock. It sliced deep into her leg, shredding her muscles, and she was never able to dive again. Or the neighbor whose son died of fever, and she let herself be carried away by the waves. Or the unlucky one whose monthly bleeding had attracted a swarm of sharks.

Now, when I looked at my mother, her body seemed worn from worry, from the pain of being under the sea, and from caring for so many others. She never had a chance to rest, because when we went home after our wet- or dry-field work, she still had much to do, including nurse Fourth Brother, now a chunky baby of eight months. The sun rose in the morning, mouths needed to be fed, and life went on, but laboring from before dawn until after dark was taking a toll on Mother.

When we reached the bulteok, she put on the face of a haenyeo chief. She dropped her basket next to the others and took her honorary spot by the fire. She told us where we would dive and how we'd be divided into groups. After we changed, the grandmother-divers went by boat with Mother to an area far offshore, the small-divers swam out with their tewaks to a spot a half kilometer from the beach, and the actual grandmothers and baby-divers, like Mi-ja and me, tended a nearby cove. It was every haenyeo's duty to nurture our wet fields by cleaning and caring for them for future seasons and generations. The work was easy. I was happy, and I liked spending time with my grandmother.

When our group returned to the bulteok for lunch, Father and another man were waiting for us. Each carried a baby on his hip. Around their legs were other sons and daughters under five. The babies were crying, sounding like piglets held upside down by a single hoof. Father handed me Fourth Brother, who nosed at my nothing breasts. I didn't have what he wanted, and his pink mouth became one long howl of frustrated craving. When the boat came to shore, the two mothers agilely leapt from the deck and ran over the rocks to us. They took their wailing babies into the bulteok, and in seconds the only sounds that remained were the rhythmic laps of small waves and the laughing of the remaining haenyeo as they made their way into the bulteok. Father and his friend walked off a few meters with their other sons and daughters straggling behind them. The two men sat on rocks, lit pipes, and spoke in voices too low to hear.

Mi-ja nudged me. "Let's eat!"

Delicious aromas greeted us when we entered the bulteok. Although we'd been doing cleaning duties, Grandmother had spotted a sea cucumber, which she'd boiled, seasoned, and sliced for everyone to share. Another grandmother had gathered some sand crabs, which she stewed with beans. The sun was high, and it poured down on us through the roofless bulteok as we ate.

After lunch, we returned to work. During the afternoon, we repeated the activities we'd done in the morning. All groups met back at the bulteok three hours later. The fathers once again waited for us to arrive, crying babies slung over their shoulders. These were given to their mothers to nurse, while the rest of us changed into land clothes, warmed by the fire, and ate squid that had been cooked. But our labor wasn't finished. We sorted what we had in our nets—abalones from conches, sea cucumbers from sea urchins, crabs from sea snails, sea squirts from sea slugs.

We then prepared our catch for sale: opening sea urchins and scooping out the roe, hanging squid to dry, and placing some creatures in buckets of seawater, so customers could see they were buying merchandise so fresh it was still alive. On some days, all this could take as little as twenty minutes. Other days, we were there for another two or three hours. So, while mornings in the bulteok were serious, the end of the day was filled with laughter, relief that everyone had returned safely, and bragging about what each haenyeo had caught. We were a collective, but not everything was divided equally. Algae and seaweed were weighed together, and the profits divided into equal shares. The money earned for harvesting shellfish belonged to the haenyeo who brought it in. How many kilos of top shell did a single woman have in her gathering net? The diver who found an abalone? That was a very lucky person!

The accepted ritual was for women to complain, and they did. The banter was loud, our ears still clogged from being under the water with all its pressure.

"My husband drinks my earnings."

"Mine gambles away the allowance I give him."

"All mine does is sit under the village tree to discuss Confucian ideals, as though he were a successful farmer. *Ha!*"

"Men," huffed another. "They can't help it. They have weak and idle minds. Men always put things off . . ."

"It's true. They have puny thoughts. That's why they need us."

These were such common grievances that sometimes the women seemed competitive about whose husband was worst.

"I had to let my husband bring home a little wife," another diver announced, "because I couldn't give him a son. She's a widow— pretty, young, and with two sons. Now all she does is whine."

Mi-ja and I had talked about it, and we agreed we didn't think we could bear it if either of our future husbands started a relationship with a little wife—a widow or a divorced woman who enchanted another woman's husband into setting up a separate household for her. Or worse, if he went to live with his little wife in her home. These arrangements seemed too much about men having fun and too little about their responsibility to their first families. But one woman took a different view.

"Two wives mean two purses," she recited, expressing how handy a second wife could be.

"A little wife can bring in cash, if she's a haenyeo," the first diver grudgingly agreed. "She can even be better than a daughter in some cases. But not this one. She doesn't even give our husband pocket money!"

"The only way to prevent a husband from taking a little wife is to bear a son. You are nothing but someone's servant if you don't have a son who can perform ancestor worship for you one day."

The women mumbled their acknowledgment of this basic truth.

"But what woman on earth wants her husband to bring home someone younger and prettier?" one of the older haenyeo asked, cackling loudly, bringing humor into the conversation.

"I do all the work. She gets to have a fun life."

"Fun? What fun?"

The women chortled at the idea.

"We all know the saying," my grandmother said. *"It's better to be born a cow than a woman."*

"Who should eat more—a man or a woman?" Do-Saeng called out, trying to change the subject.

The bulteok shouted in unison: "A woman!"

"Always a woman." Do-saeng beamed. "Because she works harder. Look at me! I have chores in the sea and in the fields. I take care of my son and daughter. And where is my husband? A factory job surely must be easier than what I do."

"At least your husband sends money home!"

Do-saeng chuckled. "But he's too far away to stir the pot."

I turned red. *Stir the pot.*

The woman who would have been Yu-ri's mother-in-law returned to Do-saeng's original question. "How can a man enjoy a meal when he contributes so little?"

"Let's not be so hard on our men," Mother cautioned, bouncing my brother on her lap. "They take care of our children when we're underwater. They make dinner for us. They wash our clothes."

"And they always ask us for money—"

The women roared with laughter.

"Not that I have much to give," someone said, which set the other women to chattering again. "And the money I have, I'm not going to let run through his fingers—"

"Everyone knows that women are better with money—"

"Because we don't turn it into liquor to pour down our throats—"

"You can't blame our men for drinking," Mother said. "They have nothing to do and no purpose to push them through the day. They're bored. And think how it must be for them to *live in a household that depends on the tail of a skirt*." She paused to let the women consider the aphorism and absorb the reality of what it might mean for a man to rely entirely on his wife. "At least we have the sea," she went on. "For me, it is a second home, even my preferred home. I know more about it—its rocks and boulders, fields and canyons—than I will ever know about the interior of our island, let alone the interior of my husband's mind. The sea is where I'm most at peace."

The other women nodded.

When our work was finished—our harvest sorted, tewaks piled, and nets repaired—sand was thrown on the fire. In the same way we'd crossed the jetty together on our way to the sea, we strolled in a long line along the beach, up an embankment, and onto the pathway that edged the shore. Some women walked alone. Others were in groups of two or three—mothers-in-law with their daughters-in-law, mothers and daughters, and friends like Mother and Do-saeng or Mi-ja and me. Do-saeng lived right on the shore. She said her goodbyes, and we continued on, going inland. We passed through Hado's main square, and sure enough a group of men sat under the tree, playing cards and drinking. A couple of women peeled off to grab their husbands and take them home. For me, when Mi-ja turned off at the olle that led to her aunt and uncle's house, the day ended.

———

The next morning, Mi-ja wasn't at her spot in the olle. When we got to the bulteok, Do-saeng wasn't there either. "We'll have to dive without them," Mother said and then made her assignments. The true grandmothers and baby-divers would work the area at the end of the jetty. "Everyone else, we'll swim out a kilometer. Since Mi-ja and Do-saeng aren't here today, my daughter will dive with me. It's time for her to harvest an abalone."

I could barely believe what I'd heard. It was an honor far beyond anything I deserved as a baby-diver. As we changed into our water clothes, a couple of women congratulated me.

"Your mother taught me everything I know about the sea," one of them said.

"You'll get your abalone. I'm sure of it," said another haenyeo.

I could not have been happier.

Once we were ready, we filed out, tewaks and nets slung over our shoulders, our sea-farming tools strung in satchels from our waists, our spears in hand. One by one, we dropped into the sea. The baby-divers and elders, including Grandmother, swam together to the right. The small-divers, actual grandmother-divers, and I looped our arms over our tewaks and began paddling away from the shore, following my mother to our designated spot. The sun spilled gloriously on our faces, arms, and shoulders. The water was cerulean blue. The swells were gentle, giving us nothing to fight against. I wished Mi-ja could see me.

"Here we are," Mother yelled loud enough for her voice to

reach the others over the wind and waves. She spat on her bitchang to bring good luck. I did the same. Then together we dove down. The water wasn't too deep, and we wove in and out between large rocks, with Mother pointing out sea urchins and other creatures we could come back for later. First, though, an abalone for me. How fortunate I was to have my mother teach me this skill.

Back up for breath, then down again. I had years to go before I'd have my mother's lung capacity, but she didn't complain. She was patient. Back up for breath, then down again. She spotted a boulder dotted with abalone. They could camouflage themselves so well, no wonder I hadn't seen them before. Now that I had, I would always know what to look for—a grayish blue or black bump, not all that smooth, rising from the cragged contour of an algae-covered boulder. Back up for a breath.

"Remember everything you've been taught," Mother advised. "I'll be right by your side, so don't be frightened."

We each took several deep breaths, then down again. We approached slowly so as not to disturb the waters. As fast as a snake striking its prey, I thrust my bitchang under the lifted edge of the abalone and flipped it off its home before it had a chance to clamp down. I grabbed it as it started to fall to the seabed. Seeing I was successful and having more air than I did, Mother thrust her bitchang under another abalone just as I started to kick for the surface. I broke into the air with my prize raised above my head. My sumbisori sounded triumphant. The haenyeo, who were resting on their tewaks, cheered for me.

"Congratulations!"

"May this be the first of many!"

Following tradition, I slowly rubbed the abalone on my cheek to show my affection and gratitude and then carefully placed it in my net. I was ready to dive down again, eager to harvest another abalone, when I realized my mother still hadn't come up for air. She could hold her breath a long time, but she should have surfaced by now. A breath, a breath, a breath, and then under ...

As soon as I set myself in the head-down position, I could see Mother still at the boulder, exactly where I'd left her. She was struggling to reach for something in the sand below her. Filtered sunlight caught the edge of her knife lying just out of reach. I gave two more strong kicks and glided next to her. That's when I saw that her bitchang was trapped under the abalone. She had needed her knife to cut off the leather strap. *Never panic* was the greatest safeguard under the sea, but I was terrified. I concentrated hard as I pulled my knife from my belt, afraid I might drop mine as Mother must have dropped hers. By now, though, my lungs were already pressing hard against my chest. Mother had been underwater far longer. She had to be in agony. I pulled myself closer and tried to slip my knife under the leather loop, but it had tightened in the water as it was meant to do. My heart pounded. Blood throbbed in my head. I needed air, but Mother needed it more. I didn't have time to go to the surface for help. If I did, by the time I got back . . .

Now we were both desperate. She grabbed my knife and tried to slice through the leather. In her rush, she slit a deep gash in her forearm. The blood turned the water murky, making it even harder to see where she was cutting. Her legs began to kick frantically, trying through sheer strength to free herself from the abalone's grip on the bitchang. I pulled on her arm, trying to help. I couldn't last much longer . . .

Suddenly, Mother stopped struggling. She calmly set the knife on the boulder and placed her now free hand over my wrist, getting my attention. Her pupils were dilated—from the darkness, from terror. She stared deeply into my eyes for a second or two, taking me in, remembering me. Then she released her breath. Her life bubbles burbled up between us. Another second passed. She still held my wrist, but I placed my other hand on her cheek. A lifetime of love passed between us, and then my mother sucked in water. Her body jerked and flailed. I badly needed air, but I didn't leave her side until she was gone, floating peacefully, still attached to the rock.

———

Since my mother's body was easily retrieved and brought to shore, she would not become a hungry ghost. This was the only comfort I could offer to my grandmother, father, and siblings when I told them that Mother would never again breathe and her body would never again be warm. When pressed, I told them about her final moments. We all wept, but Father didn't reproach me. Or, if he did, it was nothing compared to how I cursed myself. The suspicion that I was the cause of her death ate at me like lye. I was filled with misery and guilt.

Mi-ja came to my house the next morning. She had deep circles under her eyes, and her cheeks were hollowed from a day and night of stomach ailments. She listened as I explained what had happened through gasping sobs. "Maybe I startled the abalone with my kicking to the surface. I was so excited and proud of myself, but maybe I stirred the waters too much and the abalone clamped down on Mother's bitchang—"

"Don't blame yourself for things that *maybe* happened," she said.

Even if she was right about that, I saw no way to remove my guilt.

"Why didn't I retrieve her knife and just give it to her? If I'd done that, she could have worked on the strap herself. And worse," I cried, "I didn't know how to handle my knife effectively."

"No one expects a baby-diver to have such presence of mind. That's why we train."

"But I should have saved her . . ."

Mi-ja had lost her mother and father, so she felt my pain in a way no one else could. She refused to leave my side. She held my hand when my father announced the official beginning of our family's mourning by taking the last tunic my mother had worn to the roof, waving it above his head, and shouting three times into the wind, "My wife, Kim Sun-sil, of the Gul-dong section of Hado Village, has died at age thirty-eight. I inform you of her return to the place she came from."

Mi-ja stayed at our house, woke up early, and helped me haul water and gather fuel for the fire. She assisted me when I washed my mother's body, placed buckwheat kernels in her palms and on her chest to feed the spirit dogs she would encounter on her journey to the Afterworld, and then wrapped her in cloth. This act is a daughter's greatest honor and her greatest desolation. Mi-ja dressed my younger brothers and sister in mourning white. She helped me cook sea urchin soup and other required dishes for the funeral.

Mi-ja walked by my side during the procession through Hado. She bounced Fourth Brother on her hip to keep him from crying. I carried my mother's spirit tablet and took care never to look over my shoulder for fear she might return to this world again. The women from the bulteok followed behind us, helping us clear the road for the passage of the dead to her grave. Behind them, twelve men carried my mother's casket. Many people lined the olles. Everyone wanted to be a part of my mother's journey to the Afterworld.

The coffin was brought back to our house. Friends and neighbors placed offerings—sticky rice cakes, bowls of grains, and rice wine—on the altar. My mother and father's marriage photo held the center spot. She was pretty when she was young—long before the sun, wind, salt water, worry, and responsibility had creased her face and turned it the color of saddle leather. But all I could think about was how she must look now: tinted permanently blue from the chill of the sea and iciness of death.

Mi-ja sat with me on the floor just before the altar, her right knee touching my left knee, as our neighbors offered their condolences and respects. When the coffin was lifted again, Mi-ja accompanied my family to the field the geomancer had told Father would make a propitious burial site for Mother. It was surrounded by stone walls to keep the wind from washing over her and animals from walking on her. Mi-ja stood by my side when the grave was dug. Together we watched as food was distributed first to the older men, then the younger men, then the little boys. Next came women, from old to young. Mi-ja, Yu-ri, and I barely got anything to eat. Some girls, Little Sister included, received nothing, which caused some of the haenyeo to shout in their loud ocean voices that it wasn't fair. But what about death is fair? Mother was lowered into the ground in a position in harmony with the land itself, then some men helped position a stone carved with her name atop the grave. Forever after, I would come here to remember my mother, weep for her, and place offerings in thanks for bringing me into this life.

"You see?" Mi-ja whispered. "She'll always be protected by the stone walls that surround us. You'll always find her here." She gave me a gentle smile. "Every March we'll go to the mountains to pick bracken to give as an offering."

After bracken is picked nine times, it will sprout again. The saying *Fall down eight times, stand up nine* reminds us of this and symbolizes the wish for the dead to pave the way for future generations. We would have many opportunities throughout the year to make different types of offerings, but later that day, after a permanent memorial altar with a spirit tablet for my mother had been set up in our home, Mi-ja was the first to place a tangerine on the table. When I think of the money she must have spent on that . . .

That night, Mi-ja lay next to me on my mat and comforted me as I cried. "You're not alone. You'll never be alone. You'll always have me." These three sentences she repeated until they became a mesmerizing rhythm in my head.

But my mother's journey was not yet complete. Over two days of twelve hours each, Shaman Kim performed a special no-soul ritual for the haenyeo collective to cleanse the spirit of my mother and guide her peacefully to the land of the dead. In addition, the shaman would attend to the living, because so many of us had been touched intimately by Mother's death: I, for witnessing it; Do-saeng and Mi-ja, for being the vehicles that caused my mother to decide to help me get my first abalone that day; the other haenyeo, who helped free her and bring her to shore. The shock we'd experienced caused us all to be affected by soul loss.

The ceremony was held in an old shrine tucked inside a natural outcropping of stones on the shore. Women and girls came from neighboring villages, bringing vessels of cooked fish, rice, eggs, and liquor, which they placed on the makeshift altar next to a photo of Mother. It was not from her wedding day but was a more recent one showing her and a dozen of her classmates posed before the Hado Night School. To honor her diving partner, Do-saeng had her son write messages on white paper ribbons, which fluttered festively in the wind. This was not the only touch of liveliness. Even though it was a sad occasion, Shaman Kim brought with her rainbows of color and a cacophony of sound. Her hanbok was sewn in great bands of magenta, yellow, and blue. She twirled red tassels. Two assistants clanged cymbals, while another three beat drums. All this was accompanied by wailing and crying. Soon we were a mass of bodies swaying in dance. Then we began to raise our voices in prayer and song.

As the sun set, we walked to the water's edge, where Shaman Kim made offerings to the sea gods. "Release Sun-sil's spirit," she entreated. "Let her come back with me." She tossed one end of a long piece of white cloth into the waves, then slowly hauled it in, bringing my mother's spirit with it.

The next morning, the winds were violent, making it impossible to keep the candles lit. Today would be about release: for my mother to be released from this plane and for us to be released from our links to her and from our torments. We began with the same pattern of weeping, wailing, dancing, and chanting, until Shaman Kim finally asked us to sit. Around me, I saw faces filled with sadness but also excitement.

"I greet all goddesses," Shaman Kim declared. "You, esteemed ones, are welcome here. Please know every woman in Sun-sil's collective has been touched by misery. We must heal those most in need. The spirits ask Sun-sil's eldest daughter, mother-in-law, Do-saeng, and Mi-ja to kneel before me."

The four of us did as we were told, bowing three times to the altar. Shaman Kim began with my grandmother, gently touching her chest with a tassel. "You were a good mother-in-law. You were kind. You never complained about Sun-sil."

The mourners crooned appreciatively at these compliments.

Shaman Kim's tassel came to rest on Mi-ja's chest. "Do not condemn yourself for being sick that day. Fate and destiny took Sun-sil from this world." At these words, Mi-ja sobbed. I'd been so consumed by my own sorrow, I hadn't realized how Mi-ja might feel.

"She was the only mother I ever knew," Mi-ja choked out.

Next came Do-saeng . . .

Hearing Shaman Kim console Do-saeng was perhaps the hardest part of the ceremony. She had already lost the lively daughter she had once known, and now her closest friend was gone. Shaman Kim used knives strung with long white ribbons to cut the negativity that surrounded Do-saeng. "Take away this woman's shock and sorrow. Let the collective elect her as its new chief. May she lead her sea women with wisdom and caution. Please allow no more tragedies to befall this group."

Finally, Shaman Kim turned to me. The touch of her fingers along my spine caused my back to relax. Her forefinger tapping my forehead opened my mind. The swish of the tassel across my chest exposed the depth of my anguish. "Let us repair this girl's spirit," she said. "Let her fly from grief." Then she shifted away from me, directing her attention to the Afterworld. "I call upon the Dragon Sea God to bring Sun-sil's spirit to us one last time."

Before my eyes Shaman Kim opened her heart completely, and I heard my mother's voice speak of her life, as was customary. "When I was twenty, I was matched in marriage. This was the same year of the cholera epidemic that killed my mother, father, brothers, and sister. I was an orphan and a wife. My marriage was not particularly harmonious or inharmonious. Then I became a mother."

I needed Mother to say I wasn't at fault. I needed her to tell me to be strong. I needed advice on how to care for my brothers and sister. I needed special messages of love for me alone, but spirits are under no obligation to say or do what we want. They are in the Afterworld now and have their own entitlements. It's up to us to read the deeper meaning.

The shaman's voice rose. Hairs prickled on the back of my neck as I was enveloped in love. "My life has been in the sea, but my heart has been with my daughters. I love my oldest daughter for her courage. I love my youngest daughter for the sound of her laughter. I will miss them in the coldness of black death."

With that, Shaman Kim came out of her trance. It was time for more singing and dancing. Then we shared a meal from the sea— slivers of octopus, sea urchin roe, slices of raw fish. My mother had died in the sea, but we could never forget that it gave us life.

That night, Mi-ja stayed with me again, curling her body around mine. "Every year you will mourn a little less and release a little more," she whispered in my ear. "In time, your sadness will melt away like seafoam."

I nodded as though I understood, but her words offered little comfort when I knew she had never freed herself of the grief she felt for the loss of her own mother and father.

———

They say, *When the hen cries, the household will collapse.* But we don't have a saying for what happens when the hen dies. As the eldest daughter, I had always been responsible for my younger siblings. Now I had to provide their food and clothing and be a second mother to them. My father was no help. He was a kind man, but he shuddered under the added responsibility. Too often I found him outside, alone with his sadness. No man was built to shoulder the full weight of feeding and caring for his family. That was why he had a wife and daughters.

If family worries were not enough, the Japanese colonists gripped us ever tighter in the months after my mother's death. She had once hoped to earn enough money to send my brothers to school, if only to age ten. The extra income I earned might once have helped pay their way. But even if we could have relied on my extra income, it was too dangerous, when those "lucky" boys who attended schools around the island were suddenly being forced to build underground bunkers to hide Japanese soldiers.

I felt pressured from every direction. I sought courage and inspiration in the ways my mother had. *Wherever you are on Jeju, you can see Grandmother Seolmundae.* I walked on the goddess's flesh, I swam over and through her skirts, I breathed in air she had exhaled. I also had two living people I could rely on: Mi-ja, who was a survivor, and my grandmother, who loved me very much and had also suffered tragedies; and they trusted me to do my best for the family.

"Parents exist in children," Grandmother said to bolster my confidence. "Your mother will always exist in you. She will give you strength wherever you go."

And on those days when we walked to the sea and found Mi-ja waiting at her usual spot in the olle, Grandmother recited common sayings in hopes of comforting us two motherless girls. *"The ocean is better than your natal mother,"* she said. *"The sea is forever."*

Day 2: 2008

The morning after the encounter with the family on the beach, Young-sook wakes early. She's had a nearly sleepless night. All through the darkness, her mind was troubled, thinking about the foreign woman, her husband, and their children. She remembered all the rumors she'd heard about Mi-ja over the years: she was in America, living in a mansion, driving her own car, and sending money to her part of the village. But there were other stories too: she had a small grocery store in Los Angeles, she lived in an apartment, she was lonely because she was too old to pick up the language. Having met Mi-ja's family, Young-sook isn't sure what to believe.

She pads to the kitchen, heats water, stirs in tangerine marmalade, and sips the tart, citrusy drink. She goes to her kitchen garden to pick chives and garlic to add to her morning bowl of little-crab porridge. Then she returns to her room to get dressed, put her bedding away, and eat her breakfast. Dawn still hasn't arrived.

When she was a girl, a haenyeo officially retired at age fifty-five. Those who continued breathing the air of this earth didn't want to stay home, so they did water work on the shore. Times have changed. When she joins her grandson and his family in the big house for breakfast, she often announces, "I get lonesome at home by myself. I think I'll go down to the sea." What she means is she gets bored sitting around the house with her youngest great-grandchildren. Yes, she should enjoy those special times with the babies—something she wasn't able to do with her own children—but they don't have stories or tease or joke around. And working in the dry fields has never been, as her great-grandchildren put it, "her thing," with all that stooped weeding, hoeing, planting, and harvesting. For her, life is better when she can live in harmony with nature—the wind, the tides, and the moon.

Young-sook can do what she wants, because she's financially self-sufficient. No one ever paid her way, and no one ever will. She considers the sea to be her bank. Even if she didn't have checks or credit cards, she could make money underwater. She'd always felt healthiest when she dove too, always felt healed in the water. Whenever she had problems in her life, she went diving. Of course, it's dangerous, but every day something pulls her to the sea. When her body isn't underwater, her mind is.

"I hear the ocean calling," she tells her grandson this morning, and he isn't about to fight her, and neither will anyone else in the household. Even long after she could have retired, she was one of the best haenyeo, with the most hard-won experience of tides, currents, and surges, the deepest knowledge of the nesting grounds for octopus, and her ability to hold her breath. How strange that these days it's hard to find a haenyeo *under* fifty-five. They say that in another twenty years, the haenyeo will be extinct.

She has constant pain and ringing in her ears from decades of water pressure. She gets headaches, vertigo, dizziness, and nausea—as if she were always on a rocking boat. Her hips ache from carrying the weights she wore around her waist to drag her to the ocean floor when she started wearing a wet suit and the effort it took to fight against them when she needed to resurface. Those weights were in addition to paddling back to a boat or to shore with her net as heavy as thirty kilos with a day's catch, and then dragging it onto dry land and back to the bulteok. Still, the unrelenting sea . . . It beckons her . . .

As she walks to the shore, Young-sook sees the remnants of the old stone bulteok and bathing enclosures, where these days young people go to meet in secret, listen to music, and smoke cigarettes. Such a waste. She veers left and joins other old women as they enter the new bulteok. It has individual shower stalls, changing rooms, air-conditioning, a stove, and a huge tub that can fit at least a dozen women, so they can rinse away salt water and warm up at the same time. It doesn't have a fire pit, but it has a roof, and area heaters can be pulled out when needed. All these amenities, along with healthcare, have been given by the government as a thank-you for the work the haenyeo have done.

The women peel off their clothes. Breasts that long ago fed babies and gave husbands pleasure droop down to belly buttons. Once flat stomachs now ripple with rolls of insulating fat. Hair that was once lustrous black has dulled to white. Hands that have seen a lifetime of work are knobby, wrinkled, and scarred. Next to Young-sook, the Kang sisters yank and stretch their black neoprene pants up and over their sagging bottoms. Then they pull over their heads their regulation orange neoprene tops, which will make them more visible to passing boats.

Young-sook squeezes her skull through her cap, positioning the small opening above her eyebrows and just below her lips. As she looks around the bulteok, she sees the weathered faces of friends she's known her entire life squishing through their own small openings. The characters of the women—and their histories of goodness, generosity, stinginess, and callousness—are centered in those few centimeters. Each line tells a story of underwater journeys, births and deaths, survival and triumph. The deep grooves around Kang Gu-ja's mouth bloom outward like a child's drawing of the sun. Creases streak from the corners of her eyes down her cheeks. Kang Gu-sun will forever be the younger sister. Despite her losses, kindness radiates from her eyes. Some women are toothless, cheeks pressed forward, amplifying furrows of sorrow and joy. Now, almost as one, they pull their face masks onto their heads, but each woman wears hers in a unique manner—over her brow, on top of her head, or on the side at an angle. A few women add homemade floral vests over their neoprene tops, wanting to show off their individuality.

The grannies leave the bulteok—with their tewaks, nets, fins, and other tools—walk down some steps, and set out across the jetty to the boat. They're taken to a cove off a nearby island known for its abundance of top shell. Once the boat reaches its destination, Young-sook and the other women take a few moments to make offerings of rice and rice wine to the Dragon Sea God and pray for an abundant harvest, a safe return, and peace of mind.

Young-sook's life by now can be summed up in three words—pray, pray, pray—for all the good those prayers have done her.

Then, *whoosh* . . . Into the water. It's been about thirty years since she and other haenyeo started wearing rubber clothes. "You'll be covered head to toe," an official from the government had told them. "This will finally put an end to the criticism that haenyeo are immodest and show too much skin. And you'll be helping with our tourism industry!" (He'd been talking about tourists from the mainland, and he'd been right about that. But no one back then could have predicted the *foreign* tourists, that they'd love to come to the shore to watch ancients like her enter the sea, or that they'd enjoy seeing "re-creations" at the new Haenyeo Museum, where hired girls wore traditional water clothes and sang rowing songs in daily shows.) When Young-sook first started using a wet suit, she'd been able to stay in the water longer, because she was protected from the cold. It had also protected her from jellyfish stings and water snake bites. (It did not protect her from other dangers: fishing lines or speedboats bearing tourists.) Weights and fins had helped her reach a greater depth too. The result: she was safer, her catches were larger, and she'd earned more money. But when people suggested the haenyeo start using oxygen tanks, she, along with other divers around the island, refused. "Everything we do must be natural," she'd told the collective, "otherwise we'll harvest too much, deplete our wet fields, and earn nothing." There, again, balance.

As she settles into the feeling of weightlessness, her aches and pains melt away. And, on a day like today, when her mind is in turmoil, the vastness of the ocean offers solace. She kicks down, going headfirst, shooting her body deeper and deeper. She hopes the pressure on her ears will squash the thoughts of the past. Instead, it feels as though they're being pushed out—like toothpaste from a tube. The image troubles her. She needs to concentrate—always be aware—but her mother and grandmother, and, lurking in the shadows of her mind, Mi-ja, keep pushing against the backs of her eyes.

Young-sook's mother used to say that the sea was like a mother, while Young-sook's grandmother said that the sea was better than a mother. After all these years, Young-sook knows her grandmother to be the most right. The sea *is* better than a mother. You can love your mother, and she still might leave you. You can love or hate the sea, but it will always be there. *Forever.* The sea has been the center of her life. It has nurtured her and stolen from her, but it has never left.

On her third dive, her mind begins to relax. She tunes in to the *thrum* that connects her to the earth, to those she's lost, to love. The way the blood pounds in her head makes her feel alive. When she's in the sea, she's in the womb of the world.

And she forgets to be cautious.

Young-sook dives deeper than she's gone in years. The water pressure is harder on her now. She remembers when she could go down twenty meters . . . Deep enough to crush a plastic bottle. But that was before plastic bottles . . .

Returning to the surface . . . *Aaah.* Her sumbisori sighs out across the swells. She takes in several panted breaths. She's making many short dives in a narrow time span, releasing her sumbisori, then gulping in air for her next dive. She knows better, but the water feels so good. On her next dive, she'll try for her old twenty meters, just to see if she can. One last intake of breath, then head straight down, kicking hard. Down, down, down she goes. She's aware of other haenyeo watching her, which makes her bolder. Finally, for a few precious seconds, she's able to forget the family she met on the beach, their photos, and their daughter, who looked so much like Mi-ja. But in those moments of forgetting, she loses track of the most important thing—air. Now she must return swiftly to the surface. She can see it . . . Then things start to go black . . .

Her friends are waiting for Young-sook by her tewak when, unconscious, she breaks the surface. Together, they pull her to the boat. The boatman grabs Young-sook by the back of her wet suit, while the women lift her up from below. Once everyone is on board, the boatman pushes the throttle. One of the women calls for help on her cellphone. Young-sook is aware of none of this—her eyes closed, her body limp.

An ambulance waits for them at the shore. Young-sook, awake now, already berates herself for being so foolish.

The doctor in the emergency room is a woman, young, pretty, and born on the island to a haenyeo mother. Dr. Shin's questions are nonetheless pointed and embarrassing. She ticks off a list of symptoms and possible causes. "Perhaps this is what you haenyeo call shallow-water blackout. It could have been caused by hyperventilation before your dive. I've seen several deaths from this. You take too many rapid inhales to expand your breath-holding capacity, but this type of hyperventilation lowers your carbon dioxide levels. This, in turn, can cause cerebral hypoxia."

The technical terms mean nothing to Young-sook, and it must show on her face, because the doctor explains, "When the brain stem forgets to send the signal that you need air, you pass out in the water. But you keep breathing . . . Water . . . If people hadn't been there . . ."

"I know. Quiet drowning," Young-sook says, using the haenyeo expression for what happens when a diver loses her thinking capabilities and takes a breath as normally as if she were on land. "I wasn't taking proper care with my breathing, but that's not what happened."

"How do you know?"

"I just know."

"All right," Dr. Shin says when it becomes clear that her elderly patient has nothing more to add. Then she goes on, musing to herself. "We can rule out a heart attack, but should we consider nitrogen narcosis? Deep diving can cause general physical impairment but also a feeling of euphoria—loss of judgment aggravated by forgetfulness that comes from exultation, for example. Some say these moments of bliss are what addict the haenyeo to the sea." She purses her lips, nods sharply, and returns her focus to the woman before her. "Did you *forget* about breathing and the distance to the surface, because you were feeling elation, ecstasy, and joy—like you weren't in your own body anymore?"

Young-sook is barely listening. She aches all over, but she doesn't want to admit it. *How could I have been so stupid?* she asks herself, sure the doctor thinks the same thing.

"What about the cold?" Dr. Shin asks. "The human body cools very quickly in cold water."

"I know that. I dove in winter. In Russia—"

"Yes, I've heard this about you."

So, Dr. Shin knows Young-sook's reputation . . .

"You should be more careful out there," the doctor says. "You have a dangerous job. I mean, do you see men doing it?"

"Of course not!" Young-sook exclaims. "The world knows that the cold water will cause their penises to shrivel and die."

The doctor shakes her head and laughs.

Young-sook turns serious. "Actually, I've seen haenyeo die the moment they hit cold water."

"Their hearts stop—"

"But it wasn't very cold today—"

"What does that matter?" Dr. Shin asks, letting her impatience come through. "At your age, even diving in warm weather is dangerous."

"I have some numbness on the right side of my body," Young-sook suddenly reveals, but what she's feeling is much worse than that. The aches have turned into burning agony.

"Strokes are common for women who've been diving as long as you have." Dr. Shin stares at her, assessing. "You look like you're experiencing pain."

"I hurt everywhere."

The doctor's eyes light with understanding. "I should have recognized this right away, but it's hard when patients aren't forthcoming. You're a breath-hold diver. I think you've got decompression sickness—"

"I didn't go down *that* far—"

"You haenyeo learned from your mothers and grandmothers, but what they taught you is the worst thing you can do. All those short breaths, followed by a deep dive, where you hold your breath for the entire time, and then the quick rise to the surface. And then you do it again and again and again? It's terrible and very dangerous. You've got the bends. You're lucky the air bubbles in your veins and lungs haven't reached your brain."

Young-sook sighs. She won't be the first haenyeo on Jeju to spend time in a hyperbaric chamber. Still, she worries. "Will I be able to dive again?"

The doctor examines her stethoscope, refusing to meet Young-sook's eyes. "There comes a point when you can no longer cheat the limits of the human body, but if I told you no, would you stop?" When Young-sook doesn't respond, the doctor goes on. "What happens next time if you fall unconscious underwater? Sudden death at your age would not surprise me."

Young-sook shuts out the doctor, not wanting to hear the lecture.

She closes her eyes as she's wheeled through the corridors to another room. Nurses help her into a tube that looks like a coffin with a window that allows her to look out. She's told she'll have to remain in the hyperbaric chamber for several hours.

"Do you want us to play music?" a nurse inquires.

Young-sook shakes her head. With that, the nurse dims the lights. "I'll be right here. You aren't alone."

But in the chamber, Young-sook is alone. *In the past, before we had modern medicine, I would have died. But in the past, I would have had Mi-ja to protect me.* Things spiral from there, and all the thoughts she's been trying to avoid since meeting that family yesterday crowd in around her.

PART II

Love

Spring 1944–Fall 1946

Leaving-Home Water-Work

"Did my mother give birth to me only so I would have callused hands?" Mi-ja sang.

"Did my mother give birth to me only to have future prosperity?" we sang back to her.

"Look at how well our boatman goes!" Mi-ja trilled.

"Money, money that doesn't speak," we responded, matching her rhythm. "Money, money that I take home. Go, boatman, go."

I much preferred this type of song to the usual laments the Kang sisters led about mothers missing their children or how difficult it was to live under a mother-in-law. Those two girls had changed since they'd become wives and mothers, and they weren't nearly as much fun. They seemed to have erased from their minds that once they used to whisper about how they met boys in underground lava tubes or kissed someone atop a volcanic cone. They'd forgotten what joy it was to sing for pleasure. Every one of us could complain, but would that make our situation emotionally easier or physically more comfortable?

It was February, and the morning was still dark. The boat bumped over choppy waves off the coast of Vladivostok. The four of us huddled around a brazier, but its heat wasn't enough to reach that place at the core of my body that shivered. None of us wanted to waste our earnings on tea, so we sipped hot water. I was hungry, but I was always hungry. The work combined with constant shivering—whether on land, on the boat, or in the sea—ate whatever stores I had in my body faster than I could replenish them.

I wished I could be home on my island, but that wasn't possible. When I turned sixteen, my youngest brother died from a fever that took him after three nights. Four times my father had been able to tie a golden rope strung with dried red chilies across our doorway to signal that a son had been born, and twice he'd tied pine branches to alert our neighbors that daughters—providers—had been born. If the family had been whole, Mother would have overturned Fourth Brother's cradle before Halmang Samseung's shrine to symbolize her release of him. But with Mother gone from us, this ritual was left to me. After Fourth Brother's death, the faces of my remaining siblings went slack with grief and hopelessness. My sister, just eleven, was still too young to help. Without school to attend, my brothers lazed about the house or ran through the village and got into trouble. My father kept the house, visited men under the village tree, and refrained from bringing in a new wife, which meant only I could do something to change our destinies.

After watching my mother die, I never wanted to see the ocean again, and I certainly didn't want to dive in it, but I couldn't avoid it either. Do-saeng had been elected head of the collective. No one could have felt guiltier than I already did for what happened to my mother, but Do-saeng made her views about me and the roles I assume she suspected I'd played in my mother's death and Yu-ri's accident known by assigning me to barren areas of a cove or reef. And still I *needed* to bring home money for us to buy food and other necessities. Fortunately, I had options. By now, a quarter of Jeju's population had moved to Japan. The men worked in iron and enamel production; the women worked in spinning and sewing factories. Some, of course, were students. The only other legitimate way to leave the island was for women to work as haenyeo, diving from boats in other countries. I wasn't a student and I didn't think I could adapt to indoor factory work, so five years ago, when the recruiter came to the village in a flatbed truck looking for haenyeo to hire for a season of "summer earning," I signed up for leaving-home water-work.

"I'm coming too," Mi-ja announced.

I begged her not to do it. "The trip will mean hardship for you."

"But what would I do on Jeju without you?"

We joined the Kang sisters, Gu-ja and Gu-sun, who had sons at home and had labored away from home for two seasons already.

The four of us climbed onto the back of a truck—a first for me—
and were driven to other villages until the recruiter hired enough
haenyeo to fill many boats. Then we went to the Jeju City port,
boarded a ferry, and chugged across five hundred kilometers of
rolling seas to China. The following year, we traveled three hundred kilometers east over monster waves to reach Japan. The year
after that, we bumped and rolled through the Strait of Jeju one
hundred kilometers to the Korean mainland, where we boarded
another ferry to take us to the Soviet Union. We'd heard it was the
best for earnings. The last two years, Mi-ja and I had hired out for
"summer earning" *and* "winter earning" in Vladivostok, which
meant that we were gone for nine months and returned to Jeju for
the August sweet potato harvest.

So, for a total of five years Mi-ja had signed her name and
I'd placed my thumbprint on contracts saying we agreed to be
away from home. During that time, the world—and not just our
island—was shaken. For decades, Japan had been a stable—if
wholly hated—power on Jeju. Korea had been an annexed colony
for thirty-four years. Yes, we had tensions. Yes, the Japanese colonists could abuse us without consequence. Yes, they could take
advantage of us. Our only recourse had been strikes and marches,
but the Japanese always triumphed in the end. Then, three years
ago, Japan—not content with Korea as a colony or with invading
China—had launched attacks across the Pacific. America entered
the war and fighting erupted all around us.

Mi-ja and I picked up news where we could—passing by the
village tree when we were in Hado and overhearing the men in
their discussions or listening to our dormitory's radio in Vladivostok. When we were on Jeju, we saw with our own eyes that
there were even more Japanese soldiers. They'd always been a danger to young, unaccompanied women, but they began to threaten
women of all ages. They gave grandmothers, who'd once gathered
on the shore to gossip and have fun, compulsory quotas of seaweed to collect and dry, because it was used as an ingredient in
gunpowder. The risks for men and boys were perhaps the greatest
as they were rounded up and conscripted into the Japanese army,
sometimes without being given a chance to notify their families.

Now here we were—on a boat off the shore of Vladivostok. I'd recently turned twenty-one, and Mi-ja would celebrate her birthday in a few months. I hadn't once stopped being grateful for her companionship, her beautiful singing voice, or her bravery. There was a time we'd thought we would eventually grow accustomed to Vladivostok's cold on land and in the sea, because the air temperature on Jeju could go very low. On our home island in winter, snow lay in drifts around the tide pools and our diving clothes froze when we laid them on the rocks to dry. But it turned out conditions on our home island were nothing compared to those in Vladivostok. Mi-ja and I told each other it was worth the discomfort, because we had reached the age when we needed to save enough money to get married and start our own households.

The boatman turned off the engine. Our vessel bobbed in the waves like a piece of driftwood. Mi-ja, the Kangs, and I peeled off our coats, scarves, and hats. We were already dressed in our cotton water clothes with the lightweight cotton jackets to keep us warm. The others wore white, but I had on my black diving costume, because I had my monthly bleeding. Seventeen was a common age for bleeding to start, but it had been delayed for all of us by the daily cold and other hardships we experienced. We tied our kerchiefs over our hair, then stepped outside the cabin and into biting wind. I couldn't see land in any direction.

I made a personal offering to the Dragon Sea God, as I did every time I left the hard earth for the watery realm, following the custom for any woman who'd lost a relative to the ocean. I quickly grabbed my gear. Then, one by one, we jumped off the side of the boat. No place had colder waters than Vladivostok, where only the salt kept the sea from freezing. The constant shiver that always hid deep in my chest overtook my entire body. I forced my mind away from the physical torment. *I'm here to work.* I took a breath, pointed my head down, and kicked. I was aware of the boat engine starting and felt the change in the current as the boatman pulled away, leaving the four of us alone in the sea. The old man was not our safety net. He was only our driver. He stopped not too far away—within earshot—but not close enough to help if one of us got into trouble. He usually dropped a fishing line or net just to keep from being bored.

Up and down I went. Mi-ja was always near, but not so close that she could grab something I already had my eye on. We were competitive but respectful of each other. We were also alert. We didn't mind dolphins, but sharks were another matter, especially when I was bleeding into the sea.

A half hour later, we heard the boat slicing through the water toward us. An octopus I'd spotted in a crevice retreated into the dark hollows from the vibrations. I'd come back for it later. We returned to the surface and swam to the boat, where the old man hauled up our nets. We climbed the ladder—the brutal wind slicing through our wet cotton suits—and hurried into the cabin. The brazier was going, and the boatman had prepared a trough filled with steaming hot water for us to soak our feet. Mi-ja's thigh rested against mine. Our flesh had goosebumps and our veins looked so thin and sad it was as if the blood within them had shrunk and slowed from the ruthless cold.

"I found five sea urchins." Gu-sun's words got lost in the clattering of her teeth.

The cold had an even worse effect on Gu-ja's voice. "So? I found an abalone."

"Lucky you, but I got an octopus." Mi-ja grinned, proud of herself.

And on it went, because it was a haenyeo's right and duty to brag.

Despite, or because of, the dangers, hardships, and sacrifices, each of us was striving for one thing: to become the best haenyeo. We all knew the risks in prying loose an abalone, but catching an octopus was a bigger triumph—and a bigger risk. However, if one of us could reach the level of best haenyeo on this boat, then the captain would reward her with a new pair of shoes and a pair of underwear.

"There is no impossible place for me in the sea," Mi-ja crowed. Then she nudged me with her thigh, encouraging me to speak up.

"I'm so good in the sea that I could cook and eat a meal underwater," I boasted. None of them could deny it or top me, because

I could go deeper and stay down longer than anyone else in our group. Back home, people speculated that it was because I'd waited with my mother until her death, expanding my lungs beyond the usual capacity of someone of my age and experience.

When our half hour was up, we went back outside, grabbed our tools, and dove into the water. Once again, the boatman pulled away, so as not to disturb the creatures living on the seabed as we hunted for them. A half hour in the water, a half hour to warm up, back and forth. Some days we came to this site because it had a variety of things to catch. Other days we went to a rich abalone plot or to an abundant sea cucumber field. We'd even gone out at night, because it's a known fact that you can find more sea urchins then.

During our fourth dive, the water began to reverberate with deep pulses. A ship was coming. The sea creatures retreated into caves and crannies. We wouldn't be able to harvest again until the waters had calmed, but that didn't mean we couldn't profit. We'd been told that Japanese soldiers couldn't get by without a daily ration of sea urchin roe, while the Chinese wanted dried squid, fish, and octopus to carry in their knapsacks. The Soviets were indiscriminate. They'd eat anything.

The boatman picked us up, and we put on our coats to cover our near nakedness from whoever was coming. The Soviets, who weren't participating in the Pacific War, were considered relatively harmless. If it had been a Japanese ship, then we would have needed to get back in the water and let the old man handle business, because the cloven-footed ones were known to steal young women and take them to special camps to be used by their soldiers as comfort women. This ship, however, had an American flag.

Our small boat pitched as the destroyer neared. It was long but not that tall. Dozens of sailors bunched together against the railings, staring down at us and calling out. We didn't understand the words, but they were young men away from home with no women on board. We could guess at their loneliness and their excitement. One man, wearing a different hat than the other sailors, gestured for us to come closer. A rope ladder was thrown down, and Gu-ja grabbed it. Five men moved like spiders down the webbing until they reached us. As soon as the first one was aboard our vessel, he drew a weapon. This was not uncommon. Four of us raised our hands; Gu-ja still held on to the ladder.

The man with the special hat barked orders in English to his men and pointed to different spots on our boat that they should search. They found no weapons. Once they understood that we were just an old man and four haenyeo, the man with the special hat shouted up to his ship, and in moments another man came scrambling down the net. He wore a grease-stained apron. The cook yelled at us, as if that would help us comprehend him. When it didn't work, he bunched his fingers and thumb together and tapped them on his lips. *Food.* Then he tapped his chest followed by his open palm. *I'll pay.*

Gu-sun, Mi-ja, and I opened our nets. We showed him our sea urchins. He shook his head. Mi-ja held up the octopus she'd caught. The cook drew a hand across his throat. *No!* I motioned him over to another net that had already been sorted and held sea snails. I took one, brought the opening to my lips, and sucked out the meaty morsel. I grinned at the cook, trying to convey how delicious it was. Then I scooped up two handfuls of the snails and offered them to him. *Take, take.* "Good price," I said in my dialect. The cook pointed a finger at the snails, then the men, and finally down his throat as if forcing himself to throw up. He didn't have to be that insulting.

The cook put his palms together and wove his hands from side to side. He looked at me questioningly. *Do you have fish?*

"I have fish!" the old boatman said, not that the cook could understand the words. "Come. Come."

The American cook bought four of the old man's fish. Great. He'd been sitting on his boat idling away his time, while we were in the water. And now we'd wasted a half hour of diving.

After the Americans climbed back up their webbed ladder, our two vessels drifted apart, leaving us heaving and yawing in the ship's wake as it churned away from us.

It was time for lunch. The boatman gave us kimchee. The hotness from the chilies warmed us from the inside out, but a bit of fermented cabbage was not enough to replace the energy we'd expended or minimize our disappointment.

"My sister and I are still hungry," Gu-ja complained loudly.

"Too bad," the boatman said.

"Why not let us cook the fish you didn't sell?" Gu-ja asked. "My sister and I can make a pot of cutlass fish soup—"

The old man laughed. "I'm not wasting it on the four of you. I'm taking it home to my wife."

Mi-ja and I exchanged glances. We didn't hate the old man. He was responsible in many ways. He made sure our day did not last longer than eight hours, which included the travel time back and forth from the harbor. He was vigilant about the weather, probably caring more for his vessel than for our safety. But Mi-ja and I had already decided we wouldn't sign up for another season with him. There were other boats and other boatmen, and we deserved to be fed properly.

———

We lived in a boardinghouse for Korean haenyeo tucked in an alley down by the docks. On Sunday, our one day off, the landlady made us porridge for breakfast. The servings were small, but once again, we were warmed by the chilies. As soon as our bowls were empty, the Kang sisters disappeared behind the curtain that gave us privacy in our room. They'd sleep away the rest of the day.

"Can you imagine doing that?" Mi-ja asked. "I'd never waste the hours of light in the darkness of slumber."

Plenty of times I would have wanted to stay on my sleeping mat all day, especially when I was bleeding and my stomach and back ached, but Mi-ja wouldn't allow that, just as she never allowed homesickness to overtake me. She always organized our excursions. After five years of traveling to different countries, electric lights (not that our boardinghouse had them), automobiles (not that I'd been in one yet), or trolleys (too expensive!) didn't impress me any longer. It's funny how quickly you can get used to new things, though. Mi-ja remembered "sightseeing" with her father, and now we had our own adventures. We liked to walk along the wide boulevards, lined with multistoried buildings— old, ornate, and unlike any we had on Jeju. We hiked up Vladivostok's hill to reach the fortress, which had been built decades ago to defend the city from Japanese raids. We commemorated each experience not by writing in diaries or sending letters back home—neither of which we could do—but by making rubbings of the things we saw: the solid base of a filigreed candelabra that stood just inside the entrance of a hotel, the raised brand names of automobiles on fenders or trunks, a decorative iron plaque embedded in a wall.

On that morning, we weren't in a hurry. We dressed in the better sets of the two pairs of clothes we'd brought with us, I stuffed my underwear with cotton rags, we put on our mufflers, coats, and boots, and we went out into the streets. The morning was crisp and the sky clear. Steaming air escaped from our mouths with each breath. We saw a few men staggering back to their ships or rented rooms. A couple of them had women with painted faces hanging on their arms. Ours was not a good part of town. It could be rough, and the smell—from men who relieved themselves on walls or vomited their alcohol in the alleys after the wild release of a Saturday night, combined with the pervasive odors of fish, oil, and kimchee—made for a foul stew. The alleys grew into lanes, then into streets, and finally into boulevards. Families walked past us, the fathers pushing babies in strollers, the mothers holding hands with older children, many of whom wore matching coats, hats, and mittens. Of course, many of them stared at us. We were foreign in our skin coloring, eyes, and clothing.

We didn't want to waste a page of Mi-ja's father's book, so we looked for something unique. We entered a park, strolling the pathways until we came to a statue of a woman who looked like a goddess. Her white marble gown flowed about her, the expression on her face was serene, and she carried a flower in her hand. Her other hand was open, the palm reaching out to us. The lines across her palm were so real that they seemed to match those on my own flesh-and-blood hand.

"She's too beautiful to be Halmang Juseung," I whispered to Mi-ja. This was the goddess who, when she touches the flower of demolition upon the forehead of a baby or child, causes its death.

"Perhaps she is Halmang Samseung," Mi-ja said, also keeping her voice low.

"But if she's the goddess of fertility, childbirth, and young children, then why is she carrying the flower?" I asked tentatively.

Mi-ja chewed on her bottom lip as she thought about this. Finally, she said, "Either way, when we come here after we're married, we'll bring offerings, just to be safe."

With that settled, I spread a piece of paper over the goddess's palm, and Mi-ja rubbed coal over the paper. We were both concentrating so hard, watching the lines of the goddess's palm limn pathways across and over the words, that we didn't register the sound of footsteps coming near until it was too late.

"Koreans! You!" When the policeman began to yell other things we couldn't understand, Mi-ja grabbed my arm and we ran as fast as we could out of the park. We dashed through the families that crowded the sidewalks and down a side street. Our legs and lungs were strong. No one could catch us. After three blocks, we stopped, hands on our knees, panting, laughing.

We spent the rest of the day wandering. We didn't enter any of the cafés that lined the central square. Instead, we sat on a low wall and watched people coming and going. A little boy with a blue balloon in his mittened hand. A woman in high heels clickity-clacking down the street, a fox fur stole draped carelessly over the shoulders of her wool coat. Rich and poor, young and old. Sailors were everywhere too, and they tried to talk to us. They smiled, they cajoled, but we didn't go with any of them. Some of those boys were awfully handsome, though, and they made us giggle and blush. We may have been stupid Korean country bumpkins in our homemade clothes dyed with persimmon juice, but we were young, and Mi-ja was extremely beautiful.

Another two sailors approached. They wore heavy wool trousers, thick sweaters, and identical caps. One had a grin that twisted up on the left side of his mouth; the other had a thick and unruly mop of hair that sprouted from under his cap. Of course, we couldn't understand a word they said, so they gestured, grinned, and bobbed their heads at us. They looked nice enough, but Mi-ja and I were steadfast in our rules about Soviet boys. We knew too many haenyeo who'd gotten pregnant away from home. Those girls were ruined forever. We'd never let that happen to us. That said, we were haenyeo—

strong in our own ways—but we were still girls, and a little flirting wouldn't hurt us. Through much finger pointing and laughter, we determined that one was Vlad and the other was Alexi.

Alexi, the boy with the messy hair, trotted into one of the cafés, leaving Vlad to stand guard over us. A few minutes later, Alexi returned, carefully balancing four ice cream cones interlaced between his fingers. Mi-ja and I had seen people eat them, but we never would have treated ourselves to such an extravagance. Alexi handed out the cones, then he and his friend sat on the wall on either side of us.

Mi-ja's tongue tentatively darted out, touched the creamy ball, then just as quickly withdrew. Her face was very still, perhaps remembering the desserts of her childhood. I didn't wait for her commentary. I stuck my tongue out all the way—like I'd seen other people do—and took a big lick. The air was already cold, but this was so cold! It froze the top of my head just as intensely as diving off the boat into icy waters, but while the ocean was salty, this was sweeter than anything I'd ever tasted. And the texture! I ate my ice cream too fast and had the pain of watching the three of them finish theirs. As soon as Mi-ja was done, she jumped off the wall, waved, and set out in the direction of the docks. I would have liked to stay with Alexi longer—maybe he'd buy me another cone or some other treat—but I didn't want to be separated from my friend. When I slid off the wall, both boys groaned theatrically.

Vlad and Alexi followed us, perhaps thinking they might have a chance, perhaps even thinking we might not be as innocent as we looked. But just as we were about to enter the red-light area, we turned and entered the Korean district. The boys stopped, unwilling to go farther. Soviets were known to be tough, but our men were far better fighters, and they would protect us now that we were in the Korean quarter. When we looked back at Vlad and Alexi—was Mi-ja tempting them to follow us?—they shrugged, clapped each other on the back—*we gave it a try*—and set off. My feelings were mixed. I wanted to get married, which meant I couldn't be a girl who got in trouble. At the same time, I was intrigued by boys—even foreign boys. Yes, we should have been more like the Kang sisters—staying inside, not taking risks, and guaranteeing that our reputations remained intact—but where was the adventure in that? Either Mi-ja and I were walking a fine line or we were tempting fate.

"I thought you'd like the one with all that hair," Mi-ja commented.

I giggled. "You're right. I don't like it when a man's head is too close shaven—"

"Because you think it makes him look like a melon."

"What about you and the way you ate your ice cream? Those poor boys!"

This is how we were: we affectionately teased each other. We knew these foreign men meant nothing to us. We wanted to marry Koreans. We wanted perfect matches. Last year when we went home for the harvest, Mi-ja and I visited the shrine of Halmang Jacheongbi, the goddess of love. Her name means "wants for oneself," and we were clear about what we wanted. We made sandals from straw to give to our future husbands as engagement gifts. We also began buying things to take into our new homes: sleeping mats, chopsticks, pots, and bowls. My marriage would be arranged. The wedding itself would take place in the spring, when cherry blossoms swirled through the air, fragrant, pink, and delicate. Some girls knew their future husbands for a long time, having grown up in the same village. If I were lucky, I would get to exchange a few words with my future husband at the engagement meeting. If I were less fortunate, then I wouldn't see him until the day of our ceremony. Either way, I dreamed of loving my husband at first sight and of a union between two people fated to be together.

When we entered the boardinghouse, Gu-ja and Gu-sun were sitting on the floor, bowls in hand, their stockinged feet tucked to their sides. We took off our coats, mufflers, and boots. The landlady handed us bowls of millet porridge flavored with dried fish. It was the same meal that we'd had the night before and the night before that and almost every night before that.

"Will you show us your rubbing from today?" Gu-sun asked.

"Please tell us what you saw," Gu-ja added.

"Why don't you come with us one of these days?" Mi-ja suggested. "Find out for yourselves—"

"It's dangerous, and you know it," Gu-ja replied tartly.

"You're just saying that because you are now an obedient wife," Mi-ja remarked.

I knew Mi-ja meant it as a joke—in what circumstance could a haenyeo be called obedient, after all?—but Gu-ja must have heard it as an insult because she shot back, "You only say *that* because no one will ever marry you—"

In just a few sentences, a mild inquiry had turned hostile. We all knew that Mi-ja's prospects for an arranged marriage were challenging, but why deliberately hurt her when we had to dive tomorrow? The simple explanation was that we spent too much time together, our lives were in each other's hands six days a week, and we were all homesick. The damage was done, however, and Gu-ja's comment—so thoughtless—brought added darkness to the already dim room. Trying to shift the mood, Gu-sun repeated her initial question. "Will you show us what you made today?"

Mi-ja silently pulled out her father's book. "You show them," she said.

I took the volume from her and stared from it to her questioningly. We both knew the rubbing we'd made today was still in her pocket and not yet tucked into the book for safekeeping. Mi-ja was silently letting me know she didn't want to show Gu-ja and Gu-sun our new image. Now she shifted her body so that her right shoulder blocked the view of her face from the rest of us. In the crowded room, this was her way of finding a little privacy so she could nurse her hurt feelings.

"Here," I said, opening the book and leafing through the pages to show the sisters different rubbings from the world just outside this dreary enclave. "This is from the foot of a statue outside a government building. This is from the side of a toy truck we found left in a square. I like this one a lot. It's the bumpy metal siding of a bus that we rode one day to a mountain park. Oh, and here's one of some bark. Do you remember that day, Mi-ja?"

She didn't respond. The two sisters weren't interested either.

"Do you know the fortress we can see up on the hill when we sail out of the harbor?" I asked. "This shows how coarse the walls are—"

"You've shown these to us before," Gu-ja complained. "Are you going to show us what you saw today or not?"

"Maybe if you were a little nicer," Mi-ja said, her back still to us. "Maybe if you could be a single drop nicer."

Her words were sharp, and Gu-ja went quiet, realizing perhaps that she'd gone too far. But what this exchange showed me was how much Gu-ja's comment about my friend's marriage prospects had stung. I understood with sudden clarity that Mi-ja might long to be married even more than I did. If she were married, she could create her own family with a mother, father, and children.

Later, we sat together under heavy quilts on our sleeping mats, sharing body warmth and whispering so as not to disturb the Kang sisters, who huddled together on the other side of the curtain on their sleeping mats. Mi-ja and I quietly examined the rubbing we'd made that day, comparing it to our others. We'd been friends since we were seven, and we'd been collecting rubbings for fourteen years. Commemorations. Remembrances. Celebrations. Memorials. We had them all, and they eased our loneliness and homesickness. And our worry too, since we couldn't know when Jeju might be bombed or invaded.

As usual, the last rubbing we looked at was the first we'd made: the rough surface of a stone in the wall that surrounded my family's field. My fingers smoothed the paper, and I whispered to Mi-ja a question I'd asked her many times before. "Why didn't I make a rubbing on one of the days of my mother's funeral or memorial rite?"

"Stop punishing yourself for that," Mi-ja answered in a low voice. "It only makes you melancholy."

"But I miss her."

Once my tears started, Mi-ja's came too.

"You knew your mother," she said. "All I can do is miss the idea of a mother."

On the other side of the curtain, the oil lamp went out. Mi-ja tucked the papers back in her father's book, and I turned down our oil lamp. Mi-ja wrapped her body around me, pulling me tighter than usual. She tucked her knees against my knees, her thighs against my thighs, her breasts against my back. Her arm draped over my hip, and she rested her hand on my stomach. The next day we would wake early and be dropped into the bitterly cold sea again, so we needed to sleep, but the unevenness of her breath on my neck and the alertness in her body made me realize she was wide awake and listening hard. Across the room, I sensed the Kang sisters listening to us equally hard. But it wasn't long before Gu-sun began her light, buzzing snore. Soon her sister was lulled by that familiar sound, and her breathing deepened and lengthened.

Mi-ja's body relaxed, and she whispered in my ear. "I want my husband to be filled with grit and mettle." She clearly had not let go of Gu-ja's comments. "He doesn't have to be handsome, but I want him to have a strong body to show he's a good worker."

"It sounds like you're talking about a mainland man," I said. "How are you going to find one of them?"

"Maybe the matchmaker will bring one to me," she answered.

Marriage arrangements were made either by matchmakers or when a relative of high regard made inquiries. It was doubtful, at least from my perspective, that Mi-ja's aunt and uncle would pay for a matchmaker, and Mi-ja had never spoken of a relative of high regard who might bring a proposal. Most important, mainland men saw Jeju women as ugly, loud, and boyish in shape, with our lean bodies and strong muscles. They considered us to be too darkened by the sun. Mainland men also had strict ideas about how women should behave, because they followed Confucian ideals far more than Jeju men did. A woman was supposed to be gentle in her speech. Mi-ja had a lovely voice, but if she kept diving, her hearing would eventually go and she'd shout just as loudly as any other haenyeo. If she married a mainland man, she'd need to maintain a peach complexion. How was that going to happen if she spent her days under the sun, in salt water, buffeted by winds? A mainland husband would want a wife who dressed modestly, but haenyeo were considered to be half naked all the time. A wife should have red lips, shiny eyes, and a quiet disposition . . . All these ideas about women were set in stone in the minds of mainland men. Jeju husbands might have been indolent, but they would never triumph in a battle about what a woman could or could not do, say or not say. I mentioned none of this, however.

"I don't care about looks so much," I offered.

"You do too!" Mi-ja exclaimed.

Across the room, Gu-sun's snoring snagged, and her sister rolled over.

"All right," I admitted quietly after the Kang sisters settled once again. "I do. I don't want someone who's as thin as chopsticks. I want him to be dark skinned to show he's not afraid of laboring in the sun."

Mi-ja gave a throaty laugh. "So we both want men who will work."

"And he should have a good character."

"Good character?"

"Mother always said a haenyeo should not be greedy. Shouldn't that be true for a man too? I don't want to see greedy eyes or be around greedy hands. And he has to be brave." When Mi-ja didn't comment, I went on. "The most important thing is to marry a boy from Hado. That way I can continue to see and help my family. If you marry one too, we'll both maintain our diving rights. Remember, if you marry out, then you'll have to be accepted into *that* village's collective."

"More important, if I marry out, we'd no longer be together," she said, pulling me even closer until nothing could separate us, not even a piece of paper. "We must stay together always."

"Together always," I echoed.

We drifted into silence. I was getting sleepy, but I had a few last thoughts I wanted to share with her. I whispered some of the biggest complaints about Jeju men that I'd always heard. "I don't want a husband with puny thoughts. I won't tolerate a husband who needs scolding—"

"Or requires constant attention to know I care for him," she added. "He can't drink, gamble, or desire a little wife."

There, in the nighttime shadows, we could dream.

When Thoughts Turn to Weddings

July–August 1944

When the season ended in late July, the Kang sisters, Mi-ja, and I boarded a ferry from Vladivostok to the Korean mainland and then took a second ferry down the east coast to Busan. Before catching the boat to Jeju, we went shopping. We were careful to speak Japanese in public as the colonists required. The Kangs quickly made their purchases and headed home. Mi-ja and I didn't have husbands and babies who missed us, which allowed us to spend an extra day wandering the alleyways and open-air markets.

We patronized a stall that sold grain and came away with burlap sacks stuffed with barley and low-grade rice. One by one, we heaved them onto our shoulders and took them back to our guesthouse. A cloth peddler sold us quilts, which we rolled up tight to reduce their bulk and make them more portable. These we would take into our marriages. I spent a week's earnings on a radio, thinking this would make a good present for my future husband in the event our village got electricity one day, while Mi-ja chose a camera for her future husband. I bargained hard for practical gifts for my siblings: a length of cloth, needles and thread, a knife, and the like. Father would receive a pair of shoes, and for Grandmother I bought socks to keep her warm on winter nights. Mi-ja and I chipped in to buy material to make scarves for Yu-ri, which we planned to sew on the trip home. Mi-ja also procured items for her aunt and uncle. Several times I spotted her standing motionless, staring into the distance, trying to remember all the things they'd asked her to bring home. On a few occasions, we went our separate ways, but for the most part we stayed together, haggling for better prices, smiling at merchants if we thought it would help, shouting in our loud haenyeo voices if it looked like they thought we were mere factory girls.

"We'll buy six bags instead of two for me and three for her," Mi-ja might say, her near-perfect Japanese conveying the steel in her heart, "but only if you give us a good price."

When we were done, we still had enough money to pay for our room, buy deck-only tickets on the Jeju-bound ferry, share a simple meal, and have enough left over to help with wedding celebrations that had yet to be arranged. Getting everything to the dock took time. We didn't want to leave our goods unattended, so one of us carried bags and boxes from the security of our room to the dock, while the other stood guard over our growing pile. Then we took turns moving everything from our pile up the gangplank and into a sheltered corner we'd found on the deck near a group of haenyeo, who were also returning home. One haenyeo wouldn't steal from another. We didn't need to worry about strangers trying to get our things off the boat when we were at sea either.

The crossing was rough, but the skies were clear. Mi-ja and I stood at the prow of the ferry, holding on to the railing, bouncing across the waves. Finally, far in the distance, Grandmother Seolmundae—Mount Halla—came into view. I was eager to be on my island. My desire made me impatient, though, and it felt like the crew took an eternity to bring the ferry past the breakwater and into the man-made harbor.

From the deck, we could see that the past nine months had brought many changes. There were far more—yes, absolutely, more—Japanese soldiers than we'd seen on the mainland, and certainly more than we'd seen before in Jeju City's harbor. Some of them stood at attention at each point of entry, exit, and transaction. Others marched in formation, with their bayonet-tipped rifles propped on their shoulders. A few were apparently off duty, and they lounged against walls or sat on crates with their legs swinging. We'd been on our own in Vladivostok, and we were accustomed to men whistling at us or calling out words we couldn't understand, but it had all seemed harmless enough. This felt different. The soldiers' eyes followed us as we took turns unloading our belongings and purchases, with one person staying on the dock and the other doing the carrying. They couldn't do anything to us when there were still so many passengers greeting families, businessmen striding purposefully through the crowd, and others unloading their trunks and suitcases. Most haenyeo unloaded faster than we did, however, and within minutes, Mi-ja and I were the last women left on the dock.

Three more things struck me. First, our port smelled just as bad as any other I'd visited—fetid with diesel fuel and fish. Second, the local boys, who usually crowded the docks looking for work when ships and ferries landed, were not in evidence. And third, seeing all the Japanese soldiers, sailors, and guards recalled the time the patrol came into our field. But we were older now—twenty-one—and we must have looked attractive to them. Mi-ja seemed to have noticed their interest too, because she asked, "What are we going to do? I'm not about to leave you here by yourself."

"And I won't let you walk alone to the recruiter's stand."

I caught sight of a soldier eating a piece of fruit a few meters away. The way he leered at us . . .

"You appear to need help. Is there something I can do for you?" a voice asked in Japanese. Mi-ja and I turned. I expected to see a Japanese man, but he clearly wasn't. (What a relief.) And I doubted he was a native-born Jeju man, because he wore trousers, a white shirt with a collar, and a jacket that zipped in front. He wasn't much taller than we were, but he was stocky. It was hard to tell, dressed the way he was, whether his bulk was from hard work or too much food.

Mi-ja dipped her chin as she explained the practicalities of getting our possessions to the pickup spot. The whole time she was speaking, he stared at her attentively, which gave me a chance to get a better look at him without either of them noticing. His hair was black, and his skin wasn't too tanned. He was handsome in a way that was familiar to me—not like those Soviets, and not at all like a Japanese. I started daydreaming . . . I wondered who he was. My thoughts turned to weddings. I blushed, and I worried that the expression on my face might give me away, but the two of them weren't paying attention to me.

When Mi-ja reached the end of her explanation, he leaned in close and whispered to us in the Jeju language. "I am Lee Sang-mun." His breath was warm and sweet, as though he'd been eating oranges. This was another indication that he was from a good family and not just a farmer's son, who lived on common foods like garlic, onions, and kimchee. He straightened and announced rather loudly in Japanese, "I will help you."

The reaction around us surprised me. Many of the Japanese soldiers lowered their eyes or shifted them away from us, which gave me another piece of information. Sang-mun was important in some way.

He snapped his fingers, and three dockworkers trotted to us. "You will carry these things for . . ."

"I'm Kim Young-sook," I blurted. "And this is Han Mi-ja."

"Boys, please follow Miss Kim to the place where the haenyeo get picked up. You know where it is." His fluency in Japanese and his accent were nearly as perfect as Mi-ja's. "One of you stay with her there. The other two, return to me so you can carry the rest and escort Miss Han to her friend."

When I tried to pick up a bag to sling onto my shoulder, he said, "No, no, no. My boys will handle everything."

I felt like a goddess to have such help. As I set out with the dockworkers jogging behind me, I held my head high and my back straight, sure that Sang-mun's eyes would follow me until I was out of sight.

When we reached the assigned corner, two of the dockworkers went back to the wharf as Sang-mun had ordered, while the other sat on his haunches to wait with me. Did that ever get a rise out of the haenyeo!

"Look! A haenyeo has her own servant!" a woman teased me.

"Are you looking for a bride?" one of them asked the dock-worker.

"You'd better watch her. She might run away!"

The man wrapped his arms around his knees, hung his head, and tried to ignore their comments.

Thirty minutes later—an eternity—a new procession came into view. This time, the two helpers pushed wheelbarrows heaped with goods. Mi-ja and Lee Sang-mun walked side by side. I could hear him laughing even from a distance. That's when I realized he'd sent me away so he could be alone with Mi-ja. I was sure of it. Now, as they approached, I saw that Mi-ja was as pale as a jellyfish. No wonder he was attracted to her. Not in many years had I felt jealous of Mi-ja, but I did now, and it was unsettling. I smoothed my hair and tried to freeze the same type of reserved mask that Mi-ja wore on my own face. I could do nothing to make myself into her perfection, but I could be clever in my own way.

Trucks with different destinations came and went, but none was going in the direction we needed. While we waited, I asked Sang-mun questions, which he easily answered. He'd been born in Jeju City and educated in Japan. "You know," he said, "so many of us have gone to Japan to study that Jeju now has more educated people than anywhere else in Korea!"

Maybe this was so, but it didn't reflect my experience.

"My father manages a cannery here in the port," Sang-mun went on. This had to mean his father was a collaborator, since all canneries were owned by the Japanese. I should have immediately lost interest. Or not. My closest friend was the daughter of a collaborator. Maybe my husband could be the son of a collaborator too. Besides, his expression was so charming and his smile so infectious that all I could think about was how handsome he was.

I asked more questions. Every answer showed him to be unlike anyone I'd ever met. Through it all, Mi-ja stared down the road, ignoring the conversation. Her disinterest gave me even more confidence.

"I grew up following the comings and goings in and out of the harbor," he explained. "I anticipate I'll take over for my father one day, but for now I work for the Jeju City government. I oversee their food warehouses and other stockpiles." This was another confirmation of his status: he was not just a collaborator but a high-ranking one. Working for "the Jeju City government" meant that he was employed by the Japanese military. "I'll admit it," he said. "I have big dreams. My job may not seem very important, but you have to start somewhere."

A flatbed truck pulled up. The driver leaned out the window

and shouted that he'd be heading east on the coastal road, passing through many seaside villages, including Hado, before reaching his final destination of Seongsan, where the remaining haenyeo could take a last ferry home to the small island of Udo just offshore. About a dozen women peeled away from the crowd and began throwing their bags on the truck.

"Come on," Mi-ja mumbled. "This is us." She promptly got to work, wordlessly tossing our belongings up onto the flatbed. Sang-mun and I helped too, but we were still trying to exchange as much information as possible.

"In which part of Hado do you live?" he asked.

"I live in Gul-dong," I answered. I tried to look modest, but it was hard. He wouldn't make an inquiry about where I lived if he wasn't interested in me. Then, because Mi-ja was standing there and I didn't want to appear overeager, I added, "My friend lives close by in Sut-dong." She responded by closing her eyes and bringing a closed fist to her heart. If she thought that made her look dainty, she was right. I fought another wave of jealousy.

I thanked Sang-mun for helping us. Mi-ja climbed onto the truck, reached down a hand, and helped pull me up. The driver ground the gears, the truck lurched, and we started rolling. I waved goodbye to Sang-mun, but Mi-ja had already turned her back and joined the circle of haenyeo seated on the flatbed. She unfolded a kerchief in which she'd packed some fruit. I opened a basket and pulled out rice balls. The other women added dried cuttlefish, jars filled with homemade pickled turnip and kimchee, and a bunch of green onions. One woman passed around an earthenware jug filled with drinking water. Another opened a jug of fermented rice wine. Mi-ja took a swig and squinted in response to the taste. When the liquor poured down my throat, my chest burned with the taste of my birthplace.

Ordinarily, Mi-ja and I would have picked apart every detail of the encounter with Sang-mun, just as we had with Vlad, Alexi, or any of the other boys we'd met in this or that port. Not this time. When I commented that it was lucky that Sang-mun had come along when he did, she replied defensively, "I never would have let you stay alone on the dock."

"Did he ask about me?"

"He said nothing about you," she answered tersely. "Now let's not talk about it anymore."

After that, she wouldn't answer a single question I asked, so we gossiped with the other women. The food, wine, and knowledge that we were home buoyed everyone's spirits.

Each kilometer of the bumpy ride revealed another familiar or beloved vista. We passed through Samyang, Jocheon, Hamdeok, Bukchon, and Sehwa, stopping at each to let off a woman or two. The low stone walls of the olles snaked along the hillsides. They also surrounded fields, creating a patchwork of colors and patterns. Flocks of crows lumbered across the sky. In the sea, we spotted pods of haenyeo, their tewaks bobbing. And always in sight at the center of the island loomed Grandmother Seolmundae. As beautiful and welcoming as it all was, I couldn't stop creating images in my head: Maybe Shaman Kim could conduct the rituals for my marriage celebration. Maybe I could wear my mother's wedding clothes. Or maybe Sang-mun would give me fine cloth to make my own. Or maybe he'd prefer for me to wear a Japanese kimono and have a Japanese ritual, as was required by the colonists. Yes, that was probably it. No shaman, but yes to a Japanese kimono. Maybe Father would pay for banquets in Hado and Jeju City, although I didn't see how.

"We're almost there," Mi-ja said and began to gather the bags. The few people who were working in the fields lifted their heads when the truck stopped. We jumped off. The loud island voices of our neighbors greeted us.

"Mi-ja!"

"Young-sook!"

A mother sent one of her children to run to my house to announce my arrival. Women on the truck threw our belongings down to us. We were about half done unloading when whoops and calls began to reach my ears. There, running up the olle, were Third Brother and Little Sister. They looped their arms around my waist, burying their faces into each of my shoulders. Then Little Sister pulled away, hopping about in excitement. She was sixteen now and already working as a haenyeo in Do-saeng's collective.

Our lives would be easier now if the Jeju saying held true: *A family with two daughters of diving age will have no problems borrowing money or paying their debts.* I was so happy to see her! But not everyone had come, and I looked down the olle for the rest of the family.

"Where's Father? Where are First and Second Brothers?"

Before they could answer, the truck driver yelled out the window. "Hurry up! I can't wait here all day!"

With my siblings' help, Mi-ja and I caught the rest of our things as they were tossed to us. Third Brother picked up what he could and started down the olle toward home just as Mi-ja's Aunt Lee-ok and Uncle Him-chan appeared. Mi-ja bowed deeply to them, but they barely noticed, so focused were they on what we'd brought home.

"Young-sook has arrived with more than you," Mi-ja's aunt nitpicked. "She's thinner too. Did you eat your earnings?"

I tried to intervene. "I bought different sizes of things. My pile only looks like more—"

But Mi-ja's aunt ignored me. "Did you buy white rice?" she asked Mi-ja.

"Of course not!" I objected, trying again to protect my friend. "Mi-ja is always practical—"

"Yes, Auntie Lee-ok, I have brought white rice."

I was stunned. Mi-ja must have purchased it when I wasn't with her. She worked so hard and gave so much of herself. She shouldn't have been buying them something so frivolous. This wasn't the time to ask her about it, though, and I couldn't have inquired anyway, because Third Brother came running back to help Little Sister and me. In minutes, I was trailing after my siblings, leaving Mi-ja alone with her aunt and uncle.

The sounds of my sandals echoing in the olle and the waves rhythmically crashing to shore felt reassuring and welcoming. I was home! But as soon as we stepped through our gate, I sensed something was wrong. The space between the main house and the little house, where Grandmother lived, looked untidy. The side slats to Grandmother's front wall were raised and sitting on bamboo poles. She slowly struggled from the floor to stand. She ducked under the slats and joined us. Even when I was a small child, she had looked old to me, but these last nine months had diminished her vitality. As I glanced questioningly to my brother and sister, a feeling of dread shuddered through me. Their greeting just minutes ago, I realized, had been less about happiness than about relief, for my sister especially. It had been her job to shoulder responsibilities for the family while I was away.

Once again, I asked, "Where is Father? Where are our brothers?"

"The Japanese took our brothers," Little Sister answered. "They were conscripted."

"But they're only boys!" Or were they? First Brother was nineteen and Second Brother was seventeen. Many soldiers in the Japanese army were far younger than that. "When were they taken?" I asked, thinking that if it had happened recently I might have a chance to get them back.

"The Japanese grabbed our brothers just after you left," Little Sister answered.

So nine months ago.

"Maybe I can trade some of the food and other provisions I bought in exchange for their release," I suggested, trying to be positive.

They looked at me sadly. Despair washed over me.

"Have you heard any word of them?" I asked, still trying to find something auspicious in my homecoming, but the three of them stared at me woefully. "Are they here on Jeju?" That would mean only hard labor.

"We haven't heard anything," Grandmother said.

My family had been reduced yet again, and I hadn't known. Whatever happiness I'd had coming back to Jeju—meeting Sangmun, anticipating the joys of reaching home, and seeing my siblings' faces—melted away, leaving my insides blackened by sadness. But I was the eldest in our family. I was a haenyeo. It was my purpose to be a provider of goods and stability. I formed what was surely a thin smile and tried to reassure my siblings.

"They'll come home. You'll see," I said. "In the meantime, let's sell some of the things I brought home. We can use that money to send Third Brother to school for a while."

My sister shook her head. "It's not safe. He's barely fourteen. The Japanese will take him to help build one of their barricades or send him to battle. I've told him he needs to stay hidden at home during the day."

I was pleased to see that my sister had good judgment. This trait would serve her well as a haenyeo. Still, all this sorrow was hard to take in. But the news about my brothers wasn't the worst shock. That came when my father staggered home very drunk long after midnight.

———

On my first morning home, the weather was miserable. Thick clouds blanketed the island. The hot and humid air felt oppressive. A downpour would begin soon, but it wouldn't refresh. It would just be more warm liquid to mix with my sweat. I spent the day bent over, digging up sweet potatoes without damaging the skins, then dividing the tubers into three bins: what we would eat soon, what we would sell to the refinery to be made into alcohol, and what we would slice, dry, and store—another tedious chore—for winter eating. I would have much preferred to be under the sea.

I felt unsettled. It wasn't that I missed honking cars, buses, and trucks, or the roar of factories, canneries, and refineries. Rather, I missed hearing Jeju's whistling wind, which was drowned out by the rumble of Japanese planes as they took off without stop from the three air bases they'd built on the island. The roar of the engines of those birds of death was an endless reminder of Japan's intentions for the Pacific.

So, above me, images of death. Beneath me, the soil. Beside me, Mi-ja, as always. Next to her, Little Sister, who wouldn't stop talking about boys. She was more interested in them than we were, and she kept asking about when *she* would get married.

"Custom says I should wed first," I said. "Whining won't change that. You're too young anyway!" I tried to soften my tone. "You're a pretty girl, and if you turn out to be a hard worker, Grandmother will easily find a match for you."

"Easily?" Little Sister echoed as she dug deep into the earth with her spade, lifted out a sweet potato, and gently shook away the loose dirt. "There aren't many Jeju men left. Haven't you noticed?"

I recited the usual excuses: "Our men have died at sea in typhoons and other storms. They were killed or exiled by the Mongols, and now—"

"Now they're being conscripted by the Japanese," my sister finished for me. In her concern for her own nuptials, she didn't seem to care that she was talking about something that had happened to our own brothers. "I've seen lots of girls my age already go into arranged marriages, but no proposals have come for me."

"I haven't received one either," Mi-ja said. "Maybe it's because we don't have mothers to make the connections."

My sister's eyes gleamed. "Or maybe it's because we haven't been willing to share love—"

"Be quiet and do your work!" I had to stop this chatter, because I remembered how the Kang sisters used to brag about sneaking off to be with boys. Those girls were lucky they didn't get pregnant. Come to think of it, hadn't the younger sister's marriage come a little too soon after her older sister's wedding? Gu-sun's first son was born . . .

"You know what they say," my sister continued dreamily. "Having sex is 'sharing love.'"

Sharing love. Now the Kang sisters liked to talk about sharing love with their husbands and how wonderful it was and how much they missed it and their men when we were away.

"I'm not so sure about marriage," Mi-ja said. "*When a woman gets married, she has the best food for three days. That must last her a lifetime.* If that's not so, why would our elders say that?"

"Why are you so gloomy today?" I asked. "You've always said you want to get married. We've talked about what we desire in our husbands—"

She cut me off. "Maybe being with a man is what we're *supposed* to wish for, but maybe it just brings misery."

"I don't understand your change of heart," I said.

Before Mi-ja could respond, Little Sister rang out, "Sharing love! That's what I yearn to do."

I smacked her hand. "Let's hear no more talk about sharing

love! Just do your work. We still have three more rows to finish before we go home."

Mi-ja and Little Sister fell silent, leaving me to my own thoughts. Mi-ja and I both needed to get married. This was the normal path. We were clearly thinking about it all the time, even if we didn't always discuss it. I already had my heart set on an impossible choice—Sang-mun. I hadn't yet told my friend about my feelings for him, because I was waiting until she set her heart on someone. But her new attitude confused me. How could she suddenly *not* want to get married when we'd spent the last months saving money so we could buy wedding necessities?

———

Three mornings later, after we'd reestablished our household routines, I sent Little Sister to haul water and collect firewood. Father was still asleep, while Third Brother had tucked himself against the back wall of the house, hidden from prying Japanese eyes. I'd just gathered my tools and burlap sacks when Mi-ja surprised me by coming to pick me up. We were about to set out for the field when Grandmother beckoned to us from the little house. "Come sit for a minute. I have things to discuss with you."

We slipped off our sandals and entered.

"The groom builds the house, and the bride fills it," she recited.

I smiled. Here I was, on only my fourth full day home, and I was hearing the traditional words for a wedding and happy years of marriage. Mi-ja, though, kept better control of her emotions.

"Your lives have always been entwined," Grandmother continued. "Therefore, it would be best that you marry at the same time."

"You will easily find a husband for Young-sook," Mi-ja said. "But who will marry me after . . ." She hesitated, searching her mind for what she wanted to say. "I mean, with my troubled background?"

"Ah, girl, this you have wrong. Your aunt told me that she has received interest in an arrangement for you. She asked me to speak for your family, since you were like another daughter to Sun-sil. Didn't your aunt tell you?"

I couldn't have been more surprised or happier, but Mi-ja's brow darkened.

"Auntie Lee-ok will finally be rid of me."

"In some ways your circumstances will be much improved," Grandmother said.

I wasn't sure what that meant, and Mi-ja didn't ask. She looked far from joyous. I was about to start asking questions when Grandmother went on: "And you, my dear Young-sook, will be married in the same week as your sister in heart. Your mother would have been pleased to know that."

With those words, all concern for Mi-ja evaporated. "Who will be my husband?" I asked, excited.

"And who will be mine?" Mi-ja's voice sounded as heavy as lead.

"I didn't see my husband until the day of my wedding," Grandmother said gruffly, "and I was afraid to look at him for many weeks after that."

Was she warning us that we wouldn't be happy with our husbands? Mi-ja gripped my hand. I squeezed back. No matter what happened, we'd always have each other.

———

The next day, again, dawned heavy with heat and humidity. I was used to working in the water, so I was accustomed to having my body washed clean every day. Now, for the sweet potato harvest, I had to be grateful that my clothes didn't show as much dirt as was already on them or would be added today and that the persimmon-juice dye kept them from smelling as bad as they could, but my face twisted at the unpleasantness of it all as I stepped into my trousers and pulled a tunic over my head. After my father, grandmother, and brother were fed and settled, my sister and I started toward our dry field. We met Mi-ja at her usual spot in the olle.

"Auntie Lee-ok and Uncle Him-chan told me I have to do chores for them today," she said. "But can we meet at the seaside for a talk and swim tonight?"

Already sweat trickled down the back of my neck, so I readily agreed to her plan. After a few more words, Mi-ja walked away, and my sister and I continued to our field. We pulled up sweet potatoes, sweated, drank water, and repeated the whole routine again and again. Every time I straightened my back, I saw the ocean in the distance, shimmering and inviting. I looked forward to tonight's swim with Mi-ja. Or maybe we'd just sit in the shallows and let the waters swirl around us. Healing. Soothing. Reviving. Without a drop of energy spent.

At the end of the day, my sister and I, feeling tired and filthy, were walking along the road toward home when we heard the sound of an automobile. So rare! It slowed and pulled up next to us. The car had a driver. In the backseat were two men. Sitting on the far side was Sang-mun, wearing a Western-style suit. My stomach practically swallowed my heart.

The man closest to me—he had to be Sang-mun's father—was dressed similarly. He rolled down the window and leaned his elbow on it as he peered out at me. I bowed deeply and repeatedly. I prayed that through my humility and respect my future father-in-law would see that I was more than just a girl with a dirty face and hands. He would see a hard worker, who would care for his son, help with family finances, and make a good home. At least I hoped so. I peeked at my sister. Now that she'd finished bowing, she stared slack-jawed at the two men with their foreign clothes, their car, and their driver. She'd never been out of Hado, so she was just as unsophisticated as I once had been. Still, I felt a wave of shame. I noticed, though, that Sang-mun stared straight ahead and had not acknowledged me, as was proper for a young man on an engagement mission.

Feeling that no introductions were necessary, my future father-in-law addressed me. "Girl—"

Nervous and still embarrassed by my appearance, I blurted, "Let me take you to my grandmother and father."

Sang-mun started, looking at me in curiosity. His father was more discreet, hiding his surprise. He didn't laugh at me or sneer, but his expression left me deeply humiliated. "I have come to meet the family of Han Mi-ja," he said smoothly. "Can you guide us to their home?"

Mi-ja? Of course. My lips tightened, and my heart dropped down to my bowels. She was more beautiful. She'd grown up in Jeju City. Her father was a collaborator, so this was to be a like-to-like marriage. It all made sense, but how stung I was by Mi-ja's secrecy and my grandmother's treachery. I hadn't told Grandmother of my feelings for Sang-mun, but surely through her arranging she'd learned that he and I had met. It was all I could do to keep from bursting into tears, but I couldn't lose any more face than I already had.

"You'll need to leave your automobile here," I said, "and walk the rest of the way."

The driver parked by the side of the road, and then came around to open the father's door and then the son's. Sang-mun still didn't acknowledge me. It was a hot day, and each house we passed had one wall propped up and open on bamboo poles in hopes of catching a breeze, so everyone on our route witnessed our procession. When we reached Mi-ja's home, her aunt and uncle also had their wall open and were sitting cross-legged in the main room. On one side of them sat my grandmother, wearing her cleanest and best-kept trousers and tunic. On their other side, Mi-ja sat Japanese-style with her bottom resting on her heels and her hands placed delicately on her knees. She wore a cotton kimono printed in a peony pattern. Her hair had been teased and pinned in the Japanese fashion. Her face was nearly white, not from Japanese makeup but from something else. Sadness? Guilt? Perhaps only I could see that her eyes were rimmed pink, as though she'd been crying. The four of them rose and bowed deeply to the strangers. Sang-mun and his father bowed in return but not as low.

"I am Lee Han-bong, Sang-mun's father."

"Please join us," Mi-ja's uncle said. "My niece will serve tea."

Father and son slipped off their shoes, then ducked their heads as they stepped under the overhang and into the house. I was not invited inside, but I wasn't asked to leave either. I edged away, sat on my knees in the sun, and hung my head.

We didn't have a bride price on Jeju like they did on the mainland, but there were other formalities that needed to be negotiated, which Grandmother arbitrated with little dissent or argument from either side. The geomancer had already been hired to examine the years, months, days, and times of Sang-mun's and Mi-ja's births, and he'd announced a date five days from now for the wedding to take place. Although the groom's family was clearly well off, they preferred that the ceremonies be kept to one day instead of the traditional three.

"It is not typical for someone from the mid-mountain area to marry someone from the seaside," Sang-mun's father explained. "Their ways are too different. Nor does someone from the western side of the island wish to marry someone from the eastern side of the island."

What he meant was that mid-mountain men were more sophisticated compared to haenyeo brides, while men from the western side of the island didn't like the snake-worshipping women from many eastern villages. Clearly, he was building to something with his double meanings. I lifted my head to see how the others were taking his comments. The eyes of Mi-ja's aunt and uncle had fallen to half-mast, shielding their reactions, while my friend stared straight ahead. Her body was there, but it was as if her mind had flown out of the house and was soaring high above the sea. But I knew Mi-ja too well. She wasn't feigning being a delicate and modest bride in the Japanese model, nor was she hiding her feelings of sadness or worry that she'd be marrying Sang-mun. She was trying to ignore *me*. Grandmother, meanwhile, had a most disagreeable look on her face. She'd been given a position of privilege and respect, but I worried what she would say.

"It is good for a city boy to be matched with a city girl," Grandmother remarked, when what she could have said was that the sons and daughters of collaborators deserved each other.

"Exactly," Sang-mun's father agreed. "We don't need to have families traveling back and forth between Jeju City and here."

At last, I understood. Lee Han-bong didn't want to have anything to do with Mi-ja's family or the village she'd called home for the last fourteen years. What a disgusting man. And what a terrible loss of face for Mi-ja's aunt and uncle. But they didn't say anything. They may have spent years being cruel to Mi-ja, but now they could benefit from the Lee family's influence. They were showing their usual hypocrisy.

"You will find that Mi-ja has not lost her city ways," Grandmother went on smoothly. "In fact, she has lived and worked abroad. She has much experience—"

"I knew the girl's father and even her mother," Lee Han-bong interrupted. "I'm guessing the girl doesn't remember me, but I remember her very well." Even at these words, Mi-ja didn't glance in his direction. "She always wore a big white bow in her hair." He smiled. "She looked pretty in her little boots and petticoats. Most people prefer to bring in a daughter-in-law who has grown up in a large family, because it shows that she has the skills to get along with everyone."

"And work hard—"

"But my son is an only child as well. Sang-mun and Mi-ja have this in common." He went on to discuss other benefits of the match, which had less to do with the idea of sharing provisions than it did with Mi-ja's and Sang-mun's physical characteristics. "Neither of these children has skin too dark," he commented. "I'm sure you're aware how surprising this is for a sea woman. But once Mi-ja is married to my son, her days of working in the sun will be over. Her face will return to that of the girl I once knew."

I listened to all this with a breaking heart. I watched the formal exchange of gifts. I knew Mi-ja had bought her future husband a camera, but I couldn't tell from the shape of Sang-mun's family's gift what it might be, except that it wasn't a traditional roll of cloth for her to make wedding clothes. (But why would Japanese collaborators give her such a Korean gift?) As soon as the negotiation ended and small glasses of rice wine had been poured for the men to cement the deal, I slowly rose, backed out of the yard, and ran through the olle toward home. Tears poured down my cheeks until I couldn't see. I stopped, covered my face, and wept into the rock wall. How could I have had such ridiculous dreams? Sang-mun never could have been interested in me, and I shouldn't for one instant have wanted to marry the son of a collaborator.

"Young-sook."

I cringed at the sound of Mi-ja's voice.

"I understand why you're sad," she said. "I couldn't even look at you back there for fear I would begin to weep. We wanted to marry boys in Hado, so we would always be together. And now this . . ."

In my jealousy and hurt, I hadn't absorbed that Mi-ja would be leaving Hado for good. How could I have let one short encounter with a man with a handsome face and an enchanting laugh so sway me away from my friend that I hadn't thought about what the consequences of a marriage to him—whether hers or mine—would mean to our friendship? Mi-ja and I would be separated. I might see her if I was going through the port for leaving-home water-work, but otherwise no responsible wife would spend money frivolously on a boat ride around the island or a truck carrying produce to a five-day market just to see a friend. I had been disconsolate before, but now I was devastated.

"I don't want this marriage," she confessed. "Auntie and Uncle would sell the hairs off my head to profit from me, but what about your grandmother? I begged her not to do this."

I found my emotions shifting yet again. "You had to know how I felt about him," I said reproachfully.

"I'd guessed," she conceded. "But even though I knew your feelings doesn't mean I had a say in what happened. I told your grandmother everything. I begged her . . ." She faltered. Finally, she resumed. "You're lucky you don't have to marry him. Anyone can see he is not a good man. You can tell by the strength of his arms and the curve of his jaw."

Her observations shocked me. Just as I felt heat creeping up my spine, Mi-ja burst into tears.

"What am I going to do? I don't want to marry him, and I don't want to be away from you."

And then we were both crying and making promises neither of us could possibly keep.

Later, back home, I sobbed into Grandmother's lap. With her, I could speak more freely about my confused emotions. I'd hoped to marry Sang-mun, I told her. I was disappointed, but I was also angry at Mi-ja. Maybe she hadn't stolen him, but she'd won him nevertheless, and it stung. She would be a city wife—enjoying paved roads, electricity, and indoor plumbing. "Sang-mun might even hire a tutor for her!" I wept, outraged, jealous, and still so very hurt.

But Grandmother wasn't interested in comforting me. Instead, she poured out her disgust with Lee Han-bong, Sang-mun's father.

"That man! He comes here with his oily words, talking about a one-day marriage, and acting like he's trying to save Mi-ja's aunt and uncle from having to travel. He was saying they're too poor to hold a proper wedding, and he didn't want his friends to see it. He pretended he wants a pretty wife for his son—a girl that he and his friends remember from better circumstances—but *he* was trying to save face among *his* friends. He didn't care at all for what this might do to Mi-ja's aunt and uncle."

"But you've never liked them—"

"Liked them? What does that have to do with anything? When he insults them, he insults everyone in Hado! He's a collaborator, and he has too much Japanese thinking in him."

This was about the worst thing she could say about anyone, since she so hated the Japanese and those who helped them. I rubbed my eyes with my palms. I was thinking too much about myself.

Next to me, Grandmother still stewed. "Mi-ja said his hands are smooth."

"Lee Han-bong's?"

"Of course not." She snorted. "The son's hands."

I asked the obvious questions. "How do you know? Who told you?"

"Mi-ja said he grabbed her when they were walking from the port."

"He *grabbed* her? She would have told me—"

"That poor girl was doomed to tragedy from the moment she sucked in her first breath," Grandmother went on. "You must pity her when you have such good fortune. Don't forget I've been working on an arrangement for you too."

I was such a girl—swept up in a swirl of feelings I was too young to understand—and I struggled to make my heart and mind change course. *I* had wanted Sang-mun. Mi-ja had told me she didn't want to marry him, and maybe the reason Grandmother gave was true. But if it were true, Mi-ja would have told me. I was sure of it. Maybe everything Grandmother said was to make me feel better that I wasn't as pretty, as pale, or as precious—with white bows in my hair—as Mi-ja. Every twist made me doubt my friend when we'd always been so close.

"I can't tell you who he is, but I know you'll be happy," Grandmother declared. "I would never arrange a marriage for you with someone you wouldn't like. Mi-ja is a different story. Her choices were always limited, and she deserves what she gets." Then a mischievous look passed over her face. "Your husband is arriving by ferry tomorrow."

"Is he a mainland man?" I asked, knowing that this was what Mi-ja had wanted for herself.

Grandmother smoothed the hair from my face. She stared into my eyes. Could she see the pettiness in them? Or maybe she saw deeper, to my feelings of sorrow and betrayal. I blinked and shifted my gaze. Grandmother sighed. "If you are on the dock tomorrow . . ." She slipped a few coins in my hand. "Here's enough to pay a fisherman to take you by boat to the city. I'm giving you this gift—a modern gift of a glimpse of the man you will marry before the engagement meeting. I caution you, though, to stay out of sight. You don't want him to see you! There's modern, and then there's tradition."

My insides swirled with emotions. Again, I sensed Grandmother assessing me.

"When you're a wife," she went on, "you'll learn how to deprive your husband of a little of his allowance—'My harvest wasn't plentiful this week,' or 'I had to pay extra dues to the collective for more firewood'—so that you'll have money to spend on yourself. You and Mi-ja will be separated, but a free day and a little cash will always bring the two of you together."

On the Sleeping Mat

August–September 1944

The next morning, Mi-ja and I rode on a wind-driven raft to the harbor. We sat on the seawall and waited. We'd always been so close, but there was tension between us now. I didn't ask what Sang-mun did or didn't do to her, and she didn't volunteer the story. We were looking for my husband now. Grandmother hadn't told me which ferry he'd be coming in on or given any clues about what he looked like. He could be tall or short, with thick or thinning hair, with a prominent nose or one that was wide and flat. If he were from the mainland, he might be a farmer, fisherman, or businessman. But really, how did Grandmother expect me to pick him out of a crowd?

Mi-ja peered through the eddies of Japanese soldiers looking for her husband-to-be. I tried to reconcile this in my mind. Did she want to see him or was she afraid to see him? If she saw him, would she speak to him? Would she let him hold her hand? Or would he grab her, as Grandmother said had happened? If Sang-mun and Mi-ja were found talking now that their wedding had been settled, it would soil her reputation, not his.

The ferry from Busan arrived. As crewmen secured the vessel, Mi-ja and I scanned the deck. Was my future husband the one with the bushy eyebrows? He was handsome! We watched another young man come down the gangplank. He was so bowlegged, I looked away for fear of laughing. I had to hope Grandmother wouldn't match me with a man who would stir even more mockery than the typical lazy husband. (Besides, she'd told me I'd be happy.) In the end, there were few passengers, and none of them looked like a potential husband. Maybe he wasn't a mainland man, after all. A disappointment. But Grandmother had also told me my match was better than the one she'd made for Mi-ja. I vowed to stay optimistic.

Mi-ja and I ate a simple lunch of cooked sweet potatoes that I'd brought from home. We ignored the looks and comments from the soldiers and dockworkers. After a couple of hours, the ferry from Osaka arrived. Important male passengers disembarked first. We saw Japanese soldiers, of course, and a few Japanese businessmen in fine suits, with bowler hats and walking sticks. These men were followed by women wearing kimonos, taking tiny steps as they balanced on their wooden platform sandals. Those women could never trot over prickly rocks to the sea or haul in a catch. They were put on earth, it seemed, to look beautiful, as were the other Japanese women, who were dressed in the Western style, their hems brushing their calves, and small hats pinned to their heads. Then the men from Jeju, who'd been working in Osaka, began to trail down the gangplank, carrying bags and boxes of things they'd purchased for their families—or maybe their brides—in the same way Mi-ja and I had done when we returned from Vladivostok. Most of them looked thin and dirty.

I spotted a familiar face. It was Jun-bu, Yu-ri's brother. He hesitated at the top of the gangplank. His gaze arced across the wharf. He wore a Western-style suit. His eyes were as dark as charcoal. His hair, cropped short, was the color of chestnut bark. Wire-rimmed glasses rested on his nose, a reflection of all the reading and studying he'd been doing since we were kids. I lifted my arm to wave, but Mi-ja grabbed it and pulled it down by her side.

"You can't meet your future husband like this!"

I laughed. "He's not my future husband! His mother would never allow it!"

She dragged me into the shadows anyway. "You know what your grandmother said. Under no circumstances should the two of you see each other before the engagement meeting."

We watched until every person had disembarked. I saw no one else who might be a potential husband.

"How lucky you are to marry someone you've known your entire life." On the surface Mi-ja sounded happy for me, but underneath I heard the black dread of her coming circumstances, which I still didn't understand.

"But we already know each other," I said. "What difference will it make if he sees me?"

Nevertheless, Mi-ja kept me out of sight as Jun-bu threaded his way to the fishing boats to catch a ride home. "He's a scholar and so smart. Lucky, lucky, lucky!"

I was thinking that he still had one more year of college, which meant that at least I wouldn't have to live with him for very long before he went back to Japan, but I had other concerns too.

Hours later, after we returned to Hado, Mi-ja and I walked together to our customary spot in the olle and said our goodbyes. I watched her disappear around the corner, and then I ran home. The lantern light burning in the little house told me Grandmother was still awake. When I peeked in the door, she motioned me inside. I asked if she'd matched me to Jun-bu; she answered yes.

"But how could his mother ever want me?" I asked. "I'm a reminder of what Do-saeng lost. Yu-ri—"

"It's true. Your mother-in-law will look at you and see tragedy, but now you can help care for Yu-ri."

"I suppose you're right." This wasn't what I was hoping for.

Grandmother ignored my despair. "On the good side, your mother was Do-saeng's closest friend. Your presence will bring your mother closer to Do-saeng."

"But doesn't she blame me for—"

Again, Grandmother didn't let me finish. "What other complaints do you have?"

"Jun-bu's educated."

Grandmother nodded somberly. "I discussed this with Do-saeng. You can now help pay for his schooling."

"When I haven't been able to help my own brothers?"

"Jun-bu is going to be a teacher—"

"*Aigo!*" I moaned. "I'll always seem a fool to him."

Grandmother slapped me. "You are a haenyeo! Never for one moment believe you are unworthy."

I gave up trying to persuade her, and I hadn't even mentioned that marrying someone I'd known my entire life felt more like marrying a brother than like gaining a husband to lie with and share love.

———

Do-saeng and her son came to the house the next day for the engagement meeting. I wore clean clothes and sat on the floor, staring straight ahead much as Mi-ja had done. Curiosity snuck up on me, though, and I peered over at Jun-bu a couple of times. He'd changed from his Western-style suit into homemade trousers and tunic. His glasses caught the light from where the side slats of the house were propped open, so I couldn't see his eyes. Nevertheless, I could tell from his stillness that he was doing as good a job as I was at keeping his emotions hidden.

"Young-sook is a hard worker," Grandmother began. "And she has bought or made the items needed to establish a home."

"Her hips are like those of Sun-sil," Do-saeng observed. The meaning was clear. She had only been able to bring two living babies into the world, while I might birth as many children as my mother had. "The little house in which the husband and wife will reside will give them the privacy needed to make their own meals and get to know each other."

"Then let us proceed quickly to have the geomancer select a propitious date."

Gifts were exchanged. I gave Jun-bu the radio I'd bought and the pair of straw sandals I'd made. Looking at them, I saw that the first gift was pointless—a product of my wishful thinking—while the second would be well used. I wondered what he thought about them. He placed several lengths of cloth on the floor. They were not colorful. I'd be dressed in traditional persimmon-dyed clothing for my wedding ceremony. I'll admit this was another disappointment.

With that, we were formally engaged. Mi-ja's new family wanted her to move quickly into her new life; Do-saeng wanted things to happen rapidly too, because Jun-bu would return to college in Osaka in mid-September. As a result, Mi-ja and I traveled on swiftly moving, but distinctly different, currents.

To begin, two days after my engagement meeting, Mi-ja and Little Sister helped me carry the sleeping mats, blankets, bowls, chopsticks, and cooking utensils I'd acquired through my hard work to Do-saeng's compound by the shore. The courtyard between the big and little houses was neat. Do-saeng's diving gear was piled in a corner, and several overhead lines were hung with squid to dry in the sun. Yu-ri stood in the shade, a rope wrapped around her ankle to keep her from wandering away from home. This was the first I'd seen her since returning from Vladivostok. She smiled, possibly recognizing me, possibly not. Jun-bu was not there. The little house had one room and a small kitchen area. By the time we finished putting my things away, women and girls from the village began to arrive to see for themselves what I'd bought in my travels. That night, I stayed alone in my new house. The next morning, I went back to my father and siblings.

The following morning, just ten days after arriving back on Jeju, I helped Mi-ja pack her things. She made no attempt to be happy. I felt equally miserable. Whatever jealousy I'd once carried had been washed back to sea. Now all I could think about was that I would no longer see Mi-ja every day.

"I wish there was a way I could still share my heart with you," I confessed.

"That we will be apart is too much to abide," she agreed, her throat hitching.

I struggled to help her see the happiness of her situation. "You'll go back to living as you did when you were a child. You'll have electricity. Sang-mun's family might even own a telephone."

But even as I said these things, I thought how hard all that change would be for her. On one side, she'd lived in Hado for too long. On the other side, Jeju City was nothing compared to Vladivostok or the other big cities we'd gone to for leaving-home water-work.

"How will I know what you're doing?" Her voice trailed off, and her eyes glistened with tears. "We can't exchange letters. I don't remember how to write apart from my name, and neither of us knows how to read—"

"We'll send each other rubbings." I squeezed her arm reassuringly. "Our pictures have always told our stories."

"But how? I can't write your address."

"We'll have our husbands do that." But my suggestion was

just another reminder that I was illiterate and beneath my future husband.

"Will you promise to visit me?" she asked.

"Maybe if I go through Jeju for leaving-home water-work . . ."

"You won't have to do that now. You'll be married."

"The Kang sisters are married and have children," I pointed out. "They still go."

"But not you." She seemed convinced. "Do-saeng wants you to help with Yu-ri, so promise you'll visit me."

"All right. I promise." But I'd never be allowed to spend money on a boat trip to the main port—not with Do-saeng watching over me and collecting the money I earned to pay for Jun-bu's education.

"I can't imagine not seeing you every day," she said.

"Nor I you."

This was the bitter truth. We were two brides filled with sorrow, unable to change our fates. I loved her. I would always love her. That was far more important than the men we were to marry. Somehow we would need to find a way to stay connected.

She changed into the kimono sent by Sang-mun's family. Once she was dressed, she picked up the straw sandals she'd made for the man who would be her husband.

"What use will Sang-mun have for these?" she asked.

It was hard to imagine.

The groom and his parents arrived. They presented Mi-ja's aunt and uncle with a case of rice wine. My friend's future father-in-law didn't give her a piglet to raise and care for. She was told she wouldn't need one in Jeju City. Mi-ja's aunt and uncle gave the new in-laws three quilts. Sang-mun then handed Mi-ja's aunt and uncle a box wrapped in silk to represent good fortune and tied with a cord to symbolize longevity. Inside lay the letter of declaration and a few gifts. Mi-ja and Sang-mun signed their names. Shaman Kim didn't attend. No banquet was held, but two formal portraits were taken: one of the bride and groom, the other of the entire wedding party. Within an hour, the wedding celebration was over.

A smattering of villagers joined the procession to the road, where Mi-ja's belongings were packed in the trunk of her father-in-law's car. We didn't have a chance for last words. She got in the backseat. Mi-ja waved to all of us, and we waved back. As the car pulled away, Grandmother said, "That girl has left Hado as she arrived—the daughter of a collaborator." She sounded strangely triumphant, as though she'd finally won. She headed home with her chin raised, but I stayed on the road, watching until all I could see were clouds of dust.

My chest felt empty. I could not imagine what lay ahead for Mi-ja, but then I couldn't imagine my life either. She'd sleep with her husband tonight. Soon I'd be sleeping with Jun-bu. Mi-ja and I would not be able to share a single thought or emotion about any of these things. I'd been devastated by my mother's death, but now, without Mi-ja, I felt completely alone.

My wedding was more traditional but still condensed. Eleven days after Mi-ja and I returned home and one day after she left Hado, my father slaughtered one of our pigs. The meat was roasted on skewers, and we shared the meal together with our friends and family. Jun-bu and his mother didn't attend. They were writing the letter of declaration and celebrating with their own family and friends. Since we were both from the same part of Hado, people came and went between the two houses. My father drank too much, but so did a lot of other men.

On the second morning, I made offerings to my mother and other ancestors, knowing that Jun-bu, his mother, and sister were doing the same to their ancestors. Grandmother helped me put on the trousers, tunic, and jacket I'd made from the cloth Jun-bu had given me. Little Sister combed my hair and pinned it into a bun at the back of my neck. I pinched my cheeks to bring color into them, then we waited in the open space between our big and small houses for Jun-bu and his family to arrive.

In the distance, I heard the groom's procession coming closer and then stop at the village tree where Shaman Kim and her helpers beat cymbals and drums. The racket quieted, and Do-saeng's loud haenyeo voice rang out: "My son is smart. He works hard. He is of good health. He follows the rituals and trusts in the gifts of the sea." I'd seen this ceremony many times, so I knew what came next. Shaman Kim would take a special rice cake and throw it against the tree. I held my breath, listening for the reaction from the crowd. If the cake stuck to the tree, then my marriage would be blessed. If it fell, I would still have to marry Jun-bu, but we would forever be unhappy. Cheers rose up, and the drums and cymbals blared. My marriage would be a lucky one.

The banging and clanging got louder until finally Jun-bu came through the gate, with the wedding box on his outstretched arms. He wore a tunic that reached midcalf over several layers of ritual undergarments, all of which were tied shut with a strip of cloth wrapped several times around his waist. A dog fur headdress hung low on his forehead and draped over his shoulders. A section of the headdress rose above the back of his head and was tied with a band of bright ribbon. Even dressed as he was in thick layers, anyone could tell he was thin, but his face was round and smooth. His black eyes were set below full brows that arched as if in question. His fingers were long and slim like spider legs, and his hands were startlingly pale—showing that he'd never worked in the sun, not even in his family's plot.

Since Jun-bu's father remained in Japan, Do-saeng fulfilled his duties by presenting me with a two-month-old pig. In a year, if it survived, it would have grown three times in value. I held the pig for a few minutes before handing it to someone to carry back to Jun-bu's family home and place in their stone enclosure with the latrine and other pigs. More wedding gifts were exchanged: quilts bought on the mainland, homemade rice wine, as well as money in envelopes to help both sides pay for wedding expenses.

After Jun-bu signed his name to the letter of marriage, he handed me the pen. "Here," he said. This was the first word he'd spoken to me. I blushed and looked away. Remembering who and what I was, he poured a little ink into his palm. I dipped my thumb in it, touching his skin. This was our first meeting of flesh since we were children playing in the shallows. Wordlessly, I made my mark on the paper. As we faced each other, I saw that he was not much taller than I was. He didn't hesitate to search out and hold my eyes. He gave me a smile so small that I was sure I was the only one who could detect it, but that tender act reassured me.

The wedding procession now went back to Jun-bu's family

compound. People sat on mats in the courtyard between the big and little houses for the feast. Do-saeng and her friends had prepared many small dishes, including pickled turnip, salted fish, and kimchee. They presented a porridge of small birds stewed in Jeju's five grains. Do-saeng had also killed one of her pigs for the banquet, so she served pork sausage with vinegar soy sauce and seasoned bean paste on the side, and grilled pork belly, which guests wrapped in lettuce leaves. Do-saeng and Jun-bu sat down to eat, and I was ushered into a small room in the main house that overlooked the granary. Yu-ri limped in followed by baby-divers from Do-saeng's collective and a gaggle of little girls. The baby-divers had brought food, but custom required I give most of it to the children in a gesture that was said to promote a bride's fertility. Yu-ri, who under normal circumstances would have been considered too old to partake in this tradition, ate her rice cake with relish.

Later, I was escorted back outside so Jun-bu and I could pose for a wedding photograph. Finally, the time came for the "big bows"—which I made to show my respect and obedience to my mother-in-law, to Yu-ri, to various uncles, aunts, and cousins in Jun-bu's family, and then to all the elders in my family.

I was now officially a wife.

I returned to my special room. I tried to soak in the most vital meanings of good fortune, happiness, luck, and fertility. Outside, people continued to drink, eat, and share good cheer. I opened the cupboard, pulled out two sleeping mats, laid them side by side, and covered them with the quilts I'd bought for my marriage. Hours later, Jun-bu entered.

"I've known you my entire life," he said. "If I had to be married to a village girl, I'm glad it was you." Even to his ears this must not have sounded like much of a compliment. "We always had fun together in the water. I hope our marriage nights are as happy."

I'd never been shy about taking off my clothes in the bulteok or on the boat during leaving-home water-work, and I tried not to show embarrassment now. And, unlike men on the mainland or in the mid-mountain areas of Jeju, Jun-bu had seen women—including his mother and sister—mostly naked in their diving clothes. Beyond that, having helped take care of his sister since the accident, he had to know everything about a woman's body. As a result, I was the one who had to overcome *his* modesty to peel off his clothes. His flesh rose in goosebumps at my touch. It turned out we both knew what to do, though. A man is a thinker and weak during the day, but he's always in charge on the sleeping mat. A woman may risk her life to provide for her family, but on the sleeping mat she must do all she can to help her husband become the father of a son.

When we were done and I was dabbing at the bloody mucus that ran down my thighs, my husband said softly, "We will get better at this. I promise you."

To be honest, I wasn't sure what he meant.

The next morning, I woke long before dawn and went to the latrine to do my business. I climbed the stairs, entered the stone enclosure, dropped my pants, and squatted, wary of what centipedes, spiders, or even snakes might live in this unfamiliar place. The stench coming up from the pit stung my eyes, and the family's pigs snuffled below me. I would get used to this new latrine, as all brides must. Once I was done, I came back down the ladder and checked over the stone wall. A small area had been cordoned off to protect my piglet. He was wide awake and eager for food. In time, his day-to-day purpose would be to eat what came out of the family's behinds. I would then gather what came out of my pig and carry it to the fields to be used as fertilizer. Many years from now, my pig would be slaughtered for a wedding, funeral, or ancestor worship. It was a constant circle, with the pigs relying on us and us relying on them. I gave my piglet some of the food I hadn't eaten or given away last night, said a few cooing words, and then went to search for dung for the fire and to haul water. I hoped that in the coming days I'd be allowed to split my time, helping my natal family and Do-saeng's family finish their sweet potato harvests. I'd prove myself to be a good wife and daughter-in-law, starting now.

Later, after everyone had dressed and eaten breakfast, Jun-bu, his mother, sister, and I made one last procession back to my family home. My sister made a meal, which we all shared. Afterward, Do-saeng and Yu-ri returned to their home, but Jun-bu and I spent the night with my family. This last tradition—unique to Jeju—told the world that a haenyeo would always be tied to her birth family. I went to sleep early, but my husband, father, and brother stayed up late, playing cards and talking.

—————

"You will be diving with our collective again," Do-saeng said on my seventh morning of married life. "Even though we still have some dry-field work, we need to eat, and the tides are right."

"This makes me happy," I said. "It's wonderful to be back in Hado, where I can be close to my family—"

"And help pay your father's drinking debts."

I sighed. Yes, this was so, but I went on with my original thought. "And I can help my sister now that she's a baby-diver."

Do-saeng frowned. "I'm sure your mother would have preferred that I be responsible for her. After all, not everyone has good fortune when they dive with you."

Her words hit me like a slap to my face. Was this how it would always be, with Do-saeng reminding me of my family's shortcomings and blaming me for what had happened to Yu-ri?

"Of course you're responsible for Little Sister, as you are for all the haenyeo in your collective," I said. "She's lucky to have you to guide her. I just meant—"

"Will you be wearing your black water clothes this month?"

The further from the latrine and the house of the mother-in-law, the better. I found it especially hard to live within Do-saeng's fence. Grandmother had told me I would get used to my situation, but if I was humiliated all the time, I wasn't so sure. On the current matter, Jun-bu was doing his best to plant a baby, and I was working hard to make sure it found a warm home in my body. Jun-bu had been right that we would get better at our night activities. Sometimes he even had to put a hand over my mouth to keep the sounds of my pleasure from drifting over to the big house. Still, it had only been a week.

"You will know when I know," I answered at last.

131

So, I worked even harder to help Jun-bu plant his seed before he returned to Japan. I liked how he made me feel between my legs, but the practicalities of marriage were, to my mind, not so great. My husband heated water for me to warm myself when I came home from the sea, but mostly he read books, wrote in notebooks, or joined other men by the village tree to discuss philosophy and politics. The only real ways his life had changed were that he prepared dinner for me to eat in our little house and had me next to him at night. As for me, I dove with Do-saeng's collective, worked in the fields, and cared for Yu-ri—brushing her hair, cleaning her behind when she had accidents, washing those dirty clothes, making sure she didn't harm herself by getting too close to the fire in the kitchen, looking for her in the olles if she got loose from her tether when her mother and I were in the sea. For the most part, Yu-ri was good humored, but she could be querulous at times. It wasn't like dealing with an angry or unhappy child, because she was a full-grown woman—strong, obstinate, a typical haenyeo, even though she would never dive again. My heart went out to her, and I would happily take care of her for the rest of her life, but sometimes it all felt overwhelming. That's when I longed for Mi-ja the most. I missed running out in the morning to meet her. I missed talking, laughing, and diving with her.

———

Twelve days after the wedding, Do-saeng and I were sitting in the courtyard, repairing nets, when Jun-bu came out of the little house. Like all mothers, Do-saeng regarded him with eyes of love. "If you don't need your daughter-in-law," he said, addressing her, "I'd like to borrow my wife." What can a loving mother do with a request like that? In minutes, Jun-bu and I were walking through the olles, side by side, but not touching in public.

"Where are we going today?" I asked.

"Where would you like to go?"

Sometimes we went to the water's edge. Sometimes we strolled through the olles. Other times we'd climb an oreum, stare out at the view, talk, and sometimes do nighttime activities in the broad daylight. I liked that a lot, and so did he.

I suggested that we visit the shadow side of an oreum not too far off. "It's a hot day, and you might find it cooling to sit on the grass."

He grinned, and I started to run. He followed close on my heels. He was a man, but I was faster. We snaked through the twists in the olles, broke into a field, and began to climb the steep cone. We lifted ourselves over the top and dropped down to the shady side. Soon we were rolling together in the grass and flowers. I still marveled at his pale skin next to my sun-browned flesh. He ran his hands over the muscles in my arms and the firmness of my bottom. The softness of his arms and torso seemed a physical manifestation of how gentle and nurturing he was. Later, after we'd pulled our trousers back on, we lay on our backs, staring up at the clouds as the wind pushed them across the sky.

I liked my husband. He was as warm and kind as he'd been when he was a skinny boy playing with us at the shore. He was also willing to share his knowledge with me. And it turned out I wasn't as ignorant as I thought. I'd gone out for leaving-home water-work and had seen many places, while he'd only been to Hado and Osaka. He'd read lots of books, but I'd learned by listening and observing. I understood the seafloor, and he never stopped asking me questions about it; he had a better sense of the war and the world, which fascinated me. So, while at first I thought we'd have nothing to talk about, we had plenty of things to share and explore, each of us with our different perspectives on Jeju and the world beyond. He liked to talk about the long-ago time when Jeju was its own independent kingdom. I always felt confident with this subject, because Grandmother had taught me a lot about the Tamna. He also revealed to me things he'd learned about the Moscow Conference and the Cairo Conference, where Allied leaders had spoken about the future independence of Korea. I hadn't imagined that world leaders would be talking about my country or that independence was possible.

"At college, I've met people from China and the USSR who say life can be different," he said. "We should strive to make our own destiny for our country. The big land and factory owners should share their wealth with those who bleed their souls into the soil and into their work. Boys—and girls—should have compulsory education. Why should mothers, sisters, and wives work so hard and sacrifice so much?" He fell silent. Hadn't we been married so I could help his mother pay for his tuition? "What I'm telling you, Young-sook, is we should want our sons and daughters to read, understand the world, and think about what our country can be."

When he spoke like this, he reminded me of my mother in the days leading up to the haenyeo march against the Japanese. These things made me love him for the father he would be one day. And with that thought, I reached over and slipped a hand along his belly and under his trousers. He was young, and it turned out I could be persuasive.

———

On the first of September, Mi-ja's mother-in-law arrived in Hado to speak to my mother-in-law. Madame Lee got straight to the point. "Mi-ja is not yet pregnant. What of your daughter-in-law? Is she with child yet?" When Do-saeng answered matter-of-factly that my monthly bleeding had not yet come since the wedding— and imagine how I felt hearing these things being discussed as though I weren't in the room serving them tea—Madame Lee said, "Perhaps it is time for the daughters-in-law who've married into our families to visit the goddess."

"They've only been married two weeks," Do-saeng said.

"But your daughter-in-law is from village stock. I understand her mother was quite fertile."

I didn't like Madame Lee's tone, and neither did Do-saeng, who must have also smarted at being reminded of her own infertility.

"There is only one way to make a baby," Do-saeng said with a snort. "Perhaps your son hasn't been able to—"

"I understand your son will be going back to Japan in two weeks. A baby needs to be planted before he leaves, don't you think?"

Since I too wished for this, I was pretty sure that Do-saeng did as well. That was her job as Jun-bu's mother and my mother-in-law.

Madame Lee pressed her case. "The local government is sending my son to the mainland to learn how better to oversee warehouses. I'm told he'll be gone for a year." She let my mother-in-law consider this information. If Sang-mun didn't plant a baby in Mi-ja soon, it would be at least a year and nine months before Madame Lee would get a grandson. "My daughter-in-law may be from Jeju City, but your sea-village ways have seeped into her. She believes in your shaman and your goddesses." The woman jutted her chin. "Since this is so, I will send her to Hado every other day, if your daughter-in-law will take her to visit the proper goddess."

"The Japanese punish those who follow traditional island ways," Do-saeng reminded her.

"This may be so, yet we hear you sea-village people do it all the time."

"It's dangerous," Do-saeng insisted, but my whole life I'd seen her make offerings. I hoped she wouldn't bargain too hard, because I really wanted Mi-ja to come.

"Which is why I will pay you for your troubles."

Do-saeng, now sensing her advantage, waved off the idea as though it were a bad smell. "Mi-ja has an aunt and uncle living in another part of Hado. Let her stay with them."

"I think we can both agree that a happy wife is more receptive to baby making."

"But I'll have another mouth to feed. And if your daughter-in-law is here, then how can my daughter-in-law perform *her* duties?"

The negotiation went on like this until a deal was struck. Mi-ja would come to Hado every other day until Sang-mun went to the mainland; his mother would pay for her food, with a little extra thrown in for Do-saeng's trouble.

The next day my friend arrived, wearing a skirt, a little jacket, and a hat with a veil that came down over her eyes. She looked beautiful. She bowed. I bowed. Then we hugged. The first words out of her mouth were "They will send a car to get me later, but at least they let me come."

She borrowed trousers and a tunic made from persimmon cloth. Once she'd changed, she looked like the girl I'd grown up with and loved with my whole heart. I had so much to tell her, but she chattered nonstop as she unpacked the basket she'd brought with her. "Kimchee, fresh mushrooms, white rice. And look! Tangerines! Oranges!" She giggled, but her eyes had the bottomless blackness of those of a dying octopus.

She wanted to visit my mother's grave before going to the shrine for Halmang Samseung, the goddess of fertility and childbirth. I was so happy to see her that I didn't question why. Together, we made a meal for my mother, walked to the burial site, and had lunch with her spirit. After we'd eaten, Mi-ja and I leaned our heads together and began to share our hearts as we always had. I was eager to hear what Mi-ja had to say about her wedding night and all the nights—and maybe days—since.

"It's fine," she said. "It's what wives and husbands do."

I took from this that she didn't like sharing love. "Have you tried tilting your hips up so he can—"

But she wasn't listening. From her pocket she pulled out a piece of silk, which she slowly unfolded. Inside was a simple gold bracelet. Not so long ago I wouldn't have known what a bracelet was, but I'd seen women in Osaka, Busan, and Vladivostok wear them on the street, on ferries, in buses. "They're for decoration," Mi-ja had explained. Only later, after I'd walked past jewelry store windows and understood a bit about the value of gold and silver, did I come to view the idea of "decoration" as a senseless extravagance.

"Did Sang-mun give it to you?" I could imagine that he'd want his wife to be ornamented.

"It belonged to my mother," Mi-ja said, her voice tinged with awe. "I didn't know it existed. Auntie Lee-ok gave it to me on my wedding day."

"Your aunt?" I asked in disbelief. "I can't believe she didn't sell it."

"I know. All the work she made me do . . ."

"Will you wear it?"

"Never. It's all I have of my mother. What if I lost it?"

"I wish I had something that belonged to my mother."

"Oh, but you do. Her tools. Her . . ." She took my hand. "You have her spirit, while I know nothing about my mother. Am I like her in any way? Do I have her smile? Did she feel the same way about my father as I feel about my husband? I don't even know where she's buried. Never have I been able to do the things for her that you do for your mother—like this." She gestured around the field, then looked at me earnestly. "If my husband plants a baby, what if . . ."

"You aren't your mother. You won't die in childbirth."

"But if I do, will you visit my grave? Will you make sure Shaman Kim performs the rites?"

I promised I would, but I couldn't begin to contemplate what she was suggesting.

We packed up our baskets and walked to Halmang Samseung's shrine. As we neared, Mi-ja held me back. "Wait. I'm not sure I want to go."

When she wasn't more forthcoming, I asked, "Is it still because of what happened to your mother?"

"It's not that. I mean, it is, but it's also . . . I'm not sure I want to have a baby." This from the girl who'd saved worn-out persimmon cloth to make into baby clothes and blankets long before I'd thought about becoming a mother myself? My surprise must have shown on my face, because she said, "Things are not good with my husband." She hesitated, chewing tentatively on the side of her forefinger. Finally, she admitted, "He's rough when we're on our sleeping mat."

"But you're a haenyeo! You're strong!"

"Look at him the next time you see him. He's stronger than I am. He's spoiled. And he likes to be in control. We don't share love. He takes it."

"But you're a haenyeo," I repeated. Then, "You have every right to leave him. You're barely married. Get a divorce."

"I'm a city wife now. I can't."

"But, Mi-ja—"

"Never mind," she said in frustration. "You don't understand. Forget what I said. Let's just do this. Maybe if I have a baby planted in me, things will change."

This was the moment I might have said something that could have made a difference, but I was young, and I still didn't understand very much. Oh, I understood life and death, but I didn't yet have a true comprehension of all that could happen between your first and last breaths. This was a mistake I would live with for the rest of my life.

We made our offerings and prayed that we'd get pregnant quickly.

"Not just pregnant," I begged, "but pregnant with sons."

When Mi-ja added, "Who will be born healthy and have loving mothers to nurse them," I convinced myself she'd turned a corner in her mind.

———

Over the following week, Mi-ja and I visited the goddess every other day. She always arrived in her city clothes, changed into a persimmon-dyed outfit, and then back into her city clothes to return to Jeju City. As soon as she was gone, my mother-in-law would push Jun-bu and me out of the big house "to be alone." Whether during the day or at night, we found plenty of ways to sleep together without ever closing our eyes on our sleeping mats.

In the middle of the second week, I asked Mi-ja to invite her husband to pick her up so we might have dinner together. She agreed, and the next time she came, we quickly made our offerings and hurried home to prepare the meal. The kitchens to the big and small houses opened to the courtyard, so we kept our voices low, aware that my mother-in-law—even with ears damaged from years under the sea—would try to listen to all we said.

Mi-ja had seemed happier since that first visit, and I asked her if she enjoyed being back in Jeju City. Her response told me that I'd read her wrong.

"When you're a child," she said, "everything looks big and impressive. Coming to Hado as a little girl was like stepping back in time, making life with my father seem even grander than perhaps it was. But you and I have seen so much more than this island. I love the beauty of Grandmother Seolmundae and that the sea stretches forever, but Jeju City seems small and ugly to me now. I miss Hado. I miss diving. I miss visiting other countries. Most of all I miss you."

"I miss you too, but maybe this is what it means to be married."

Air hissed through Mi-ja's clenched teeth. "I'm a haenyeo, not some Confucian wife. My husband and his parents are unfamiliar with our ways. They believe, *When a daughter, obey your father; when a wife, obey your husband; when a widow, obey your son.*"

I tried to laugh away the idea. "What haenyeo would ever do that? Besides, I always thought following Confucius meant that men needed to think big thoughts all day under the village tree."

Mi-ja didn't giggle or even smile at the ridiculousness of the sentiment. Rather, a troubled expression passed over her features. Before I could say anything, my husband entered the courtyard. Mi-ja put a pretty smile on her face and whispered, once again between clenched teeth, "We must remember that our marriages are steps up for both of us. Each of us has a husband who can read and do sums."

While Jun-bu washed up, Mi-ja and I walked to the road to wait for her husband to arrive. Finally, a pair of headlights appeared, coming through the darkness. Once they reached us, Sang-mun parked and exited his father's car. He was dressed in the same casual style as the day we first met. Mi-ja and I bowed to show our respect.

"Where are your clothes?" he asked gruffly.

"I didn't want them to get dirty," Mi-ja answered, her voice a bare whisper.

I could have taken this as an insult, but I was more concerned with the humbling change in Mi-ja.

I stepped forward and bowed again. "My husband is looking forward to meeting you."

Sang-mun regarded Mi-ja out of the corner of his eye. She was frozen in place. She was, I realized, afraid of him.

"I'm looking forward to this too," he said at last. "Shall we go then?"

When we got to the house and Sang-mun slipped off his shoes and entered, he seemed to relax. Dinner was another matter. Men! What is it about their natures that they feel compelled to gain ground and debate points over which they have no power or control?

"The Japanese will always be in power," Sang-mun maintained. "What need do we have to resist them?"

"The Korean people, especially here on Jeju, have fought against every invader," Jun-bu reasoned. "Eventually we'll rise up and expel the Japanese."

"When? How? They're too powerful."

"Maybe. But maybe they're fighting too many battles in too many places," Jun-bu countered. "Now that the Americans are in the war, the Japanese are sure to lose territory. When they begin to retreat, we'll be ready."

"Ready? Ready for what?" Sang-mun shot back "They'll conscript any and every man, no matter his age, education, marital status, or loyalty!"

This wasn't an idle threat. My own brothers had been taken. We still didn't know where they were or if we'd ever see them again.

"And consider this, my friend," Sang-mun went on. "What will happen to people like you when the Japanese triumph, as they surely will?"

"Like me? What does that mean?"

"You're studying abroad. You've picked up foreign ideas. It sounds like you're an instigator, but are you a communist too?"

My husband laughed long and hard.

"You laugh now," Sang-mun said, "but when the Japanese win—"

"*If* they win—"

"They'll kill traitors and people who speak traitorous words. You need to be careful, brother," Sang-mun warned. "You never know who might be listening."

Mi-ja squeezed my hand to reassure me, but her husband had sown seeds of uncertainty in me.

———

September 14 arrived, and it was time for my husband to return to Japan for his final year of study. Our last night together was filled with kisses and words of love. The next morning, when he boarded a small motorboat to take him to the main port, I surprised myself by weeping. This girl, who'd been so disappointed in her match, had grown to love her husband after barely four weeks of marriage. In this I was lucky—as Grandmother and Mi-ja had pointed out even before the wedding—for not all brides had amicable feelings toward the men with whom they shared their sleeping mats. I would miss Jun-bu, and already I worried about him being far from me when war raged all around us.

The next day, still following our routine, Mi-ja arrived. I took her to visit the goddess, but what good would it do me when my husband was away? We made our offerings and then on the way home sat together on a hill overlooking the sea.

"This will be my last visit for a while," she confided. "My husband leaves in two days. He will travel the length of Korea to make sure the Japanese military convoys get where they need to go. Supervising loading and unloading, as you've heard. The Japanese trust him, and he says this is a big promotion. My mother-in-law has decided I don't need to visit the goddess if he isn't here to plant a baby."

These few weeks had been a gift, but now we were to be separated again. I felt lonely and alone already.

A Golden Rope

October 1944–August 1945

"I come to you as leader of the collective," Kim In-ha, a woman from the Seomun-dong neighborhood of Hado, said to my mother-in-law. "I'm looking to fill a big boat with twenty haenyeo for leaving-home water-work. We'll be going to Vladivostok for nine months and returning, as usual, in time for the August sweet potato harvest."

It was the end of October, and my husband had been gone for six weeks. Do-saeng and I had arrived early at the bulteok and found Kim In-ha waiting for us. Now the two of them sat across from each other on opposite sides of the fire pit. A young apprentice had already gotten the flames going, and a pot of water sat on a grill. I'd been sorting through my gear, but I stopped when I heard the word Vladivostok. I'd earned good wages there the last couple of years.

"Twenty haenyeo. Impressive," Do-saeng said. "How can I help you?"

"I'm looking for young married women, who don't yet have children," In-ha answered. "Yes, they get homesick sometimes, but they're still too inexperienced to suspect their husbands might start sharing love with a village woman or look for a little wife. They aren't worrying if their children are sick or getting into trouble. I believe it's important to have haenyeo whose emotions are calm and not troubled by thoughts of menfolk."

It was a long-winded way of saying she'd come for me. I felt pleased and excited. It would be fun to go again. Doing chores for my mother-in-law and obeying her orders in the bulteok—as good and wise as they were—grated against me. Taking care of

Yu-ri in the afternoons, when she was fussy and fitful, was always hard. And not having my husband to love me or Mi-ja to comfort me had left me in a restive and ill-humored mood. But when my mother-in-law said exactly what I wished her to say—"May I suggest my daughter-in-law?"—a black rock crushed the pit of my stomach. Do-saeng was *too* willing to let me go.

"In terms of age, she's a baby-diver," she went on. "But her skills are good enough to qualify her as a small-diver." This was the first time I'd been officially called a small-diver, and a part of me was honored, but the black stone didn't melt away. "She's a hard worker, but the best thing I can say about her is that her husband is away, so she won't miss him any more than she already does. And it seems she and my son were not together long enough for baby making to occur."

That's when I wondered just how deeply Do-saeng didn't want me around. Grandmother had been wrong, and I was right. Do-saeng would always blame me for the roles she suspected I'd played in Yu-ri's accident and my mother's death. If I could help pay for my husband's education, so be it, as long as I was gone from her sight. All right, then. I didn't want to live with her either.

―――――

Five days later, when it was still dark, I packed a bag, picked up my sea-woman tools, and walked by myself to my family home, where I gave advice to Little Sister: "Stay close to others when you're diving. Learn with your ears. Learn with your eyes. Most of all, stay safe." I warned Third Brother: "Obey your sister. Stay in the house. Don't let yourself be seen by the Japanese." I said goodbye to my father, but I wasn't sure if he'd remember by the time the sun rose. Then I walked out along the jetty and boarded the boat to take me and a couple of other young brides from other parts of Hado to the port. I felt my spirits rise.

I found In-ha and the rest of the divers she'd hired waiting by the gangplank to the ferry. I spotted one or two girls I knew from other visits abroad, but the rest were strangers to me. I was surreptitiously looking from girl to girl, trying through subtle signals to figure out who I'd want to partner with—who had strong legs and arms hidden under her clothes, who looked responsible or like a risk taker, who seemed like she might talk too much or keep too quiet—when I spotted Mi-ja, gazing straight at me, patiently waiting for me to find her, a bemused smile on her face.

"Mi-ja!" I ran to her and dropped my bag and other gear at our feet.

"I'm coming with you," she announced.

"Your mother-in-law is letting you go?"

"My father-in-law received a letter from Sang-mun, who says he's learning a lot and won't be coming home for longer than we expected. I can't dive in the city, so I'm just another mouth to feed while my husband is on the mainland."

Sending Mi-ja away for leaving-home water-work didn't make a lot of sense to me, because Sang-mun hadn't married my friend for her diving skills or her ability to earn money for him and his family, but so what? We were going to be together again. She started to laugh, and I joined in.

Over the next couple of days, we got to know the other girls. They were nice enough, although most of them had come less to earn money than to leave the dangers of where they lived on Jeju.

"I was diving with my collective when bloated bodies, like a school of fish, drifted into our field," a girl with round cheeks recounted. She shivered in disgust. "They'd been in the water a long time, and their eyes, tongues, and faces had been eaten."

"Were they fishermen?" I asked.

"Sailors, I guess," the girl answered. "Their corpses were burned. From the war."

"Japanese?" I asked.

She shook her head. "Not their uniforms."

Another girl, whose eyes were set so far apart she looked disconcertingly fishlike, had lost three sisters. "They went to gather firewood one morning, and they never came home," she told us.

It was said Japanese troops wouldn't dare kidnap a haenyeo to take her to be a comfort woman, but who knew? If a haenyeo or any woman from Jeju was abducted and used for sex by Japanese soldiers, the loss of face and the depth of shame would be so great that she would never be able to return to our island home.

"At least we'll be in Vladivostok and away from the Japanese occupiers," someone said. "The USSR is fighting in Europe and has ignored Japan."

"It's more like the Japanese have ignored the Soviets," the girl with the round cheeks responded knowingly.

Mi-ja and I never talked about the war; it cut too close to her family's past. We never considered why we'd always felt safe in Vladivostok, but our haenyeo senses told us we were safe enough not to question what might be lurking behind every corner. We'd learned from our husbands more about world conferences, battle strategies, and the plans being made about our country in rooms far from our influence. Even so, we seemed less informed than these girls.

Mi-ja and I had our favorite boardinghouse in Vladivostok, but this time all twenty of us, plus In-ha, stayed in a dormitory. The room was long and narrow, with a lone dingy window smeared with soot and port grime at the far end. Some of the girls claimed beds on the three-tiered bunks. Mi-ja and I preferred to lay sleeping mats on the floor, so we could be next to each other.

The following morning, we rose, gathered our gear, and made our way to the dock. The boat wasn't terribly big—there wasn't enough room for us all to sleep on the deck or gather inside if bad weather befell us—but the captain was Korean and seemed reliable. Beyond the protection of the port, the boat rode up a wave before slapping down on the other side. My stomach rose and fell. The engine was strong, but the sea is infinite and powerful. Up ... Down ... Up ... Down ... I felt a little seasick, but I couldn't have been as pale as Mi-ja. Neither of us complained, however. Rather, we put our faces into the wind and let the salty mists spray our faces.

When the captain shut down the motor and the boat bobbed in the whitecaps, we stripped out of our street clothes. Mi-ja tightened the ties on my water clothes, and I checked hers. We put on our tool belts, wedged our small-eyed goggles into place, threw our tewaks overboard, and then jumped into the water feetfirst. Bracing cold swallowed me. I kicked my feet beneath me to stay afloat. Still, the water was rough enough to smack my face. A breath, a breath, a breath, then straight down. Enveloping silence. My heart beat in my ears, reminding me to be careful, stay alert, remember where I was, and forget absolutely everything else. I wouldn't be greedy. I'd take my time. For now, I simply looked around. I counted, one, two, three turban shells I could easily harvest on my next breath. I would make a lot of money today! I was just about to go back to the surface when I spotted a tentacle creeping sucker over sucker out of its rocky den. I held that spot in my head, then swam quickly to the surface. My sumbisori—*aaah!* I detached my net from my tewak, took some quick breaths, and went back down. When I got to the crevice, I saw not one but two octopuses, roiling together. I jabbed one and then the other in the head to stun them. Before they could waken, I stuffed them in my net and kicked to the surface. *Aaah!* Triumphant on my second dive!

———

Mi-ja discovered she was pregnant first. I expected her to cry and worry, and she did.

"What if I have a son who's like his father?"

"If there's a son inside you, he'll be perfect, because you'll be his mother."

"What if I die?"

"I won't let you die," I vowed.

But no matter what I said, Mi-ja remained gloomy and apprehensive.

A week later . . . Joyous! That's how I felt, even though I was hanging my head over the boat's railing and throwing up. I too had a baby growing inside me. And Mi-ja and I weren't the only ones on the boat. Most of us had been married for a year or less. And look! Eight of us were pregnant. Surrounded by so much happiness, Mi-ja's spirits lifted. She was one of many. Of course In-ha wasn't too thrilled.

Children bring hope and joy, but naturally every single one of us wished for a son. A couple girls had secretly known they were pregnant when they left home. This meant that babies would start to arrive within five months. Mi-ja and I figured we'd have our babies—if we were right in our counting—in mid-June. But we had to get through the first rough weeks of morning sickness. Each dawn, as we went to sea, all we needed was one haenyeo to throw up to trigger the rest of us. The boat captain didn't mind if what came out of our stomachs went directly into the sea, while In-ha changed course and decided that each woman with a child growing in her belly would be even more motivated to have a large daily harvest.

We ate abalone porridge with all the organs nearly every day, knowing this was the most nutritious meal we could eat and that it would also train our babies to love the taste. Soon our stomachs began to swell, and we loosened the ties that closed the sides of our suits. We hoped our babies would be born "right in the field," meaning they would take their first breaths on the boat or slip out when we were in the sea.

Pregnancy brings changes not only to a woman's body but also to her mind. Things Mi-ja and I had once done in Vladivostok seemed silly now. We no longer dashed from place to place to make rubbings. We'd already captured those memories. Instead, we were growing our babies. By the time the bitter months of winter arrived, Mi-ja's morning sickness was completely gone. It lingered for me, but I found the frigid waters brought instant relief. The moment of submersion into that cold seemed to calm my baby, put him to sleep, freeze him in place. As the months passed and our bellies grew, water offered new comforts. As soon as I was submerged, my aches were massaged, and the weight of my baby was buoyed. I felt strong. Mi-ja did too.

The first babies began to arrive. Mothers had no one onshore to care for their infants, so each baby was put in a cradle with a single rope securing it to the deck. As soon as we were in the water, the captain would leave us, as was the custom, but go not too far away. Newborns sleep a lot, and the rocking of the boat kept them calm. Nevertheless, as the morning wore on and we came back to the surface after a dive, we would hear not only the individual and unique sounds of each woman's sumbisori but also the individual and unique cries of each baby. Lunches were lively and busy. The new mothers nursed their infants while shoveling millet and kim-chee into their own mouths. The rest of us bragged and gossiped. Then it was back into the water.

In mid-June, Mi-ja went into labor in the sea. She kept working until the final hour, when In-ha and I joined her on the deck for the delivery. After all her foreboding, that baby practically swam out of Mi-ja. A boy! She named him Yo-chan. It was through the ancestral rights he would perform in the future that Mi-ja would be able to stay in contact with her family on earth when she went to the Afterworld. Once we got back to the dormitory, she made offerings to Halmang Samseung and Halmang Juseung—one a goddess who protects babies and one a goddess who can kill them with her flower of demolition—while I prepared a pot of buck-wheat noodle soup for her to eat, since it's known to cleanse a woman's blood after childbirth. We did not have Shaman Kim here to bless the special protective clothes an infant wears for his first three days of life, but on his fourth morning Mi-ja packed away her worries.

I would have preferred to have gone into labor in the ocean and had my baby born in the field, but eight days after Yo-chan's arrival, my water broke in the middle of the night. My labor was even easier than Mi-ja's. What came out was a girl. I liked the name Min and added to that *lee* for her generational name, which Min-lee would share with her future sisters. I still needed to have a son, but what a blessing it was to give birth to someone who would work for Jun-bu and me and help make money to send our future son or sons to school in the years to come. Mi-ja made me the spe-cial mother's soup, we made offerings, and then we waited three days to make sure Min-lee survived. To honor this most import-ant moment in our lives, we traced the babies' footprints on pages from Mi-ja's father's book.

The four of us were back on the boat within days. The babies lay side by side in their cradles, linked with all the other cradles. When we came back to the boat to warm up, we opened the tops of our water clothes, exposed our breasts, and let our babies latch on to our nipples. I was raised to follow the aphorism *A good woman is a good mother*. I'd learned how to be a good mother from my mother and then from being a second mother to my siblings, so I loved my baby from the moment of her first breath. Motherhood shouldn't have come naturally to Mi-ja, but her connection to her son was instant and deep. Whenever she nursed Yo-chan, she whispered into his face, calling him ojini, which means "gentle-hearted person." "Eat well, ojini," she'd coo. "Sleep well. Don't cry. Your mother is here."

When our contracts ended, at the end of July, our babies were six and five weeks old. We took the ferry to Jeju. Our arrival was both frightening and hopeful. My entire life I'd seen Japanese soldiers, but now there were many more of them on the wharf. Hundreds, maybe even thousands, coming off ships, milling about, marching to and fro. It was stunning enough that Mi-ja, curious as ever, asked a pair of dockworkers, "Why so many?"

"The tide of the war has changed," one of them answered in a low voice.

"The Japanese might lose!" the other exclaimed, before dropping his eyes so as not to be noticed.

"Lose?" Mi-ja echoed.

We'd all hoped something like this would happen, but our occupiers were so strong it was hard to believe.

"Do you understand the idea of a last stand?" the first dockworker asked. "The colonists say the Allies will have to come *through* Jeju to reach Japan. This is where the greatest land and sea battles will be! We've heard there are over seventy-five thousand Japanese soldiers living underground—"

"And there are more than that aboveground. They say another two hundred and fifty thousand men—"

"The Allies will step on us, crush the Japanese here, and then take one more step to Japan."

I remembered how Grandmother used to talk about the Mongols using Jeju as a stepping-stone to invade Japan and China. More recently, Japan had used the island as a base for bombing raids on China. If these men were right, then we were to be a stepping-stone again, this time leading *to* Japan.

"Ten Japanese army divisions are here—many of them hiding! In caves! In lava tubes! And in special bases they've built into the cliffs right at the shoreline!" Fear had clearly pushed the second dockworker into his overwrought state. "They'll charge their torpedo boats directly at the American navy ships. You know how the Japanese are. They'll defend the island until all are dead. They'll fight to the last man!"

Mi-ja raised the back of her hand to her mouth. I hugged Minlee closer to my breast. The idea that the war would come to our island was terrifying.

"What should we do?" Mi-ja asked, her voice quavering.

"There's nothing any of us can do," the first dockworker said. He scratched his face. "It's lucky you weren't here three months ago—"

"The Japanese were going to move all women to the mainland and use the remaining men to help them fight—"

"But then the Americans started bombing us—"

"They bombed Jeju?" I asked, my concern turning immediately to my family.

"And they have submarines offshore," the first dockworker said.

"They sank the *Kowamaru*," the second one added.

"But that's a passenger ship!" Mi-ja exclaimed.

"*Was* a passenger ship. Hundreds of Jeju people died."

"Now the Japanese want every Jeju person to fight the Americans when they land—"

"Every Jeju person," Mi-ja repeated.

"You should go home," the second dockworker said. "Hope for the best."

The pain of separating from Mi-ja and her son was made harder by the frightening news, because she would return to her husband's home here in Jeju City, which surely would be the first target in an invasion. Mi-ja, who'd probably come to the same conclusion, had gone white. Sensing his mother's nerves, Yo-chan began to howl. Urgency propelled us each to hire a boy to help with our things. Once Mi-ja's boy had her purchases in his wheelbarrow, she turned to me.

"I hope I see you again."

"You will," I promised, but I was unsure.

I touched Yo-chan's cheek. Mi-ja cupped her palm over Min-lee's head. We stayed that way for a long moment.

"Even when we're separated," Mi-ja said, "we'll always be together."

She slipped into my hand a folded piece of paper. I opened it and saw some written characters. "Before we left, my father-in-law gave me the address for my married home in case anything happened to me," she said. "I give it to you now. I hope you will visit me one day." With that, she flicked a finger at the boy to get him started and then followed him through the banks of soldiers. I watched until she disappeared. She never glanced back.

On the truck ride to Hado, every curve brought a new vista of change. It felt like the entire island had become a fortress. Soldiers were camped on every field and hill. From a distance, I saw outposts at the base of each ancient beacon tower on the crest of each oreum. For centuries, these lookout towers perched atop volcanic cones had been a way for the people of Jeju to send defense communications across the island. Now, cannons pointed out to sea. Even the crows, which were so common on Jeju, felt ominous.

When I got home, my fears about what might happen to our island turned personal and immediate. I learned Little Sister had died the previous winter from "chill." My father hadn't received word about my first and second brothers either. But I didn't have a chance to feel much sadness when Father, Grandmother, and Third Brother were so happy to meet my baby. Do-saeng was beyond pleased to have a granddaughter, and she recited the traditional words when she saw us. *"When a girl is born, there is a party. When a boy is born, there is a kick to the hip."* She hung a golden rope with pine branches on the front door to let our neighbors know the joyful news that I'd given birth to a daughter who would help provide food for our family one day. Yu-ri couldn't stop beaming, but I needed to be watchful that she never be alone with Min-lee. Yu-ri wouldn't do intentional harm, but I couldn't count on her to be gentle always.

The person I most wished to see—my husband—wasn't there. Jun-bu had returned safely from Japan and had been immediately hired to teach at the elementary school in Bukchon, which was about sixteen kilometers from Hado. He was there now, setting up our new home. I wanted to walk there right away, but Do-saeng told me that they'd agreed I should help her with the sweet potato harvest and then join him at the beginning of September, when classes started. Until then, I needed to settle back into Hado village life.

Of course, we were all terrified. If bombs started dropping from the sky or landing boats filled with foreign soldiers came to shore, we had nothing with which to defend ourselves except for the shovels and hoes we used in our dry fields and the hooks and spears we used in our wet fields. There's nothing like a baby, however, to remind you that life goes on. While I'd been away, one of the Kang sisters, Gu-sun, had given birth to a baby girl, Wan-soon, who was the same age as my daughter. The four of us spent many hours together. Often Gu-sun would purr about how our babies would be as close as she and her sister were or as Mi-ja and I had always been: "Min-lee and Yo-chan might marry one day, but they can never be friends the way that Min-lee and Wan-soon will be." I never argued with Gu-sun about this. Instead, I accepted her friendship more out of necessity than out of love or like minds. Our babies needed to be nursed, burped, washed, changed, comforted, and put to sleep. I was happy for Gu-sun's company.

Fortunately, Min-lee was a good baby, which meant my hands could stay busy. When I was in the little house, I used my foot to rock her cradle, so I could repair my nets, sharpen my knives, and patch my diving outfit. When we went to the sweet potato fields, she stayed in her cradle, which I draped with cloth to protect her from the sun. When I dove with Do-saeng and the collective, my father took care of Min-lee. He met me outside the bulteok when we came back for lunch and at the end of the day so I might nurse her. He'd always been good at caring for babies, and he was drinking less.

All that—the real life of a grown woman, wife, mother, and haenyeo—lasted exactly one week. The men sitting under the village tree heard the news first. That day, August 6, the United States dropped an atomic bomb on Hiroshima. We didn't know what an atomic bomb was, but as we heard the reports of an entire city flattened . . . We thought of my father-in-law, who was in Hiroshima . . . If my husband had come home to perform rites with Shaman Kim, then we would have had to accept my father-in-law was dead. But Jun-bu didn't come. Still, Do-saeng wept many tears of worry and sadness, not knowing if her husband might have survived but suspecting the worst. Then, two days later, we heard that the Soviet Union had officially declared war on Japan. Now another world power might want to use Jeju as a stepping-stone. The day after that, America dropped its second atomic bomb, this one on Nagasaki. If the United States could reach Japan by air, they could very easily reach Jeju, where we had so many Japanese troops. And what would the Soviet Union do?

But a bomb never came and neither did a land-and-sea invasion, because the Japanese emperor surrendered six days later. We had always named historic events by their dates. This one became known as 8.15 Liberation Day. We were free from the Japanese colonists at last! We'd also been liberated from the massive number of deaths an invasion would have caused. We went to bed feeling exhilarated, but the next morning every single Japanese person—whether soldier or civilian—was still on Jeju. We were told that Korea would be supervised under a joint trusteeship controlled by four nations: the United States, the Soviet Union, the United Kingdom, and China. Another set of men living on the other side of the world had also divided our country along the Thirty-eighth Parallel. This meant—although none of us understood the practicalities—that the USSR would oversee Korea above the line and the United States would oversee Korea below the line as we transitioned to independence and formed our own country. We thought we were free, but so far the only difference in our lives here on Jeju was that the Japanese flag was lowered, and the American flag was raised. One colonizer had been replaced by another.

The Tail of a Skirt

September 1945–October 1946

Two weeks later, I prepared to move to my husband. Do-saeng helped, and after the last of my belongings was packed, she said, "You and my son are newlyweds and you have a baby, who Jun-bu has never seen, but I beg you to take Yu-ri. You have always been good with her, and it will be only for a short while." I knew Do-saeng worried about her husband's fate in Japan. To ease her burden, I accepted. So, on September 1, Father led my pig, while Grandmother and Third Brother—who no longer had to hide—carried my sleeping mats, quilts, clothes, and kitchen goods to the olle, where they loaded everything onto the back of the horse-drawn cart I'd hired. Do-saeng, always so strong, walked arm in arm with Yu-ri to the cart with tears running down her cheeks.

"Take good care of her," Do-saeng said.

"I will," I promised.

"Come back for the lunar New Year's Festival," Father said.

"I'll come back for more than that," I replied. "Bukchon is not so far. I'll be able to return here on occasion." But I was also thinking about how I might visit Mi-ja in Jeju City, which was about twenty kilometers farther on past Bukchon. These distances I could walk.

The driver was eager to get started, so we had no extra time for tears, but a feeling of unease made the parting hard. As the cart began bumping along the dirt road, I kept my eyes on my family. Even Do-saeng stayed put until we were out of sight.

A few hours later, we arrived in Bukchon. I left the driver on the road to watch over Yu-ri, the pig, and my other belongings, then walked through the olles, past stone houses with thatch roofs, to the shore. Bukchon was built around a small, well-protected cove. The beach had more sand than Hado, but it still had plenty of lava rocks to step on as I made my way to the bulteok. With my baby in my arms, I entered. Three women sat by the fire pit, the sun shining down on them through the roofless structure. I bowed deeply several times as they scrambled to their feet. They shouted in their loud haenyeo voices, "Welcome! Welcome!"

After I introduced myself, I said, "My husband is the new teacher in your village. Can you tell me how to find the home of Yang Jun-bu?"

A woman in her forties, with muscled thighs and arms, stepped forward. "I'm the chief of our collective. My name is Yang Gi-won. Your husband told us you were coming. We hear you are an experienced haenyeo. We would like to offer you diving rights in our village."

I bowed several more times in gratitude, but I had to add a condition. "I have to see what my husband says. He works, as you know."

Mine was not a situation with which they were familiar, and they laughed good-naturedly.

"You and the baby must be tired," Gi-won said. "Let us take you to your house." Then the corners of her mouth turned up, and she added, with plenty of insinuation in her voice, "Your husband has been eager for you to arrive."

The others howled. I blushed.

"No need to be bashful with us. You didn't get that baby by just looking pretty."

She motioned for me to follow, but the others came along too. We threaded through another series of olles. Up ahead I caught sight of the school. To the right was a series of small houses, each behind its own stone wall.

"All the teachers live in these," Gi-won said. "Here is yours."

One of the other women yelled, "Teacher Yang, your wife is here!"

With lots of giggling, the three women pushed me through the gate. Then they sauntered back down the olle, leaving Jun-bu and me to greet each other privately. When I saw his silhouette in the doorway, all the worry of these last months—being separated, caring for a newborn without her father, the impending battle on our stepping-stone of an island—drained out of me. I was a haenyeo—independent and resilient—but I'd missed my husband. He rushed to me, stopping a meter away so we could bow and exchange endearments.

"I missed you."

"I'm glad you're safe."

"You look well."

"You look thin."

"Your daughter. I named her Min-lee."

He peeled back the piece of persimmon cloth that protected her face from the sun. He smiled. "A beautiful girl. A beautiful name."

"I have Yu-ri in the cart," I said.

A shadow passed over his features. Perhaps this was not the reunion he'd anticipated, but then his expression shifted. "Let's go get her and everything else," he said.

The driver lugged my things. Jun-bu escorted his sister. I prepared a place for her next to the warmth of the kitchen wall. Jun-bu and I put away my belongings. Min-lee fell asleep in her cradle. Without eating the dinner my husband had prepared, we lay out our sleeping mats. He was hungry for my flesh. I was hungrier still for his. We did not worry about Yu-ri watching or hearing us. When we were finished, and I curled myself into the crook of his arm, I sent a prayer to Halmang Samseung. *Plant a son in me tonight.*

The next day, the emperor of Japan signed the agreement officially ending the war, which sent many soldiers on Jeju out of their caves and tunnels like ants flooded from their homes. They didn't wait for military transport. They just booked passage on ferries and left. But thousands of soldiers remained, still camped on the hillsides. Barely a week later, the cycle of the moon told me that the month's first period of diving had almost ended. I stood in my doorway, Yu-ri sitting at my feet, as haenyeo from other parts of Bukchon made their way past my house to the sea. Many of them called out, "Join us" or "Come to the bulteok." I just waved and watched them go. In the afternoon, after I'd swept the courtyard, washed Yu-ri, and pickled vegetables for winter, I watched them come home—happy, loud, and strong. I found myself missing the company of Kang Gu-sun and Wan-soon, the comforts and companionship of the bulteok, and so much else.

On September 10, the Committee for the Preparation of Korean Independence met for the first time in Jeju City. The members had all led or participated in anti-Japanese movements. The goals, of course, were to have true independence for the island and all Korea and to have our first-ever elections. Eventually, this organization became the People's Committee. On Jeju, every village started its own chapter to create youth clubs, peacekeeping units, and women's associations. With the help of these committees, every village instituted literacy efforts. All boys were to be educated, but women and girls were also encouraged to attend classes.

"Village leaders want to instill political awareness in women like you," Jun-bu said. "I hope you will go."

"My mother wanted me to be literate, and she surely was political," I responded.

"Now you can be an inspiration to our daughter as your mother was to you."

But I wondered what use I would have for an education when all I wanted to do was dive.

———

Ours was not a traditional marriage. Jun-bu went to work every morning, which meant someone had to take care of Min-lee, which, in turn, meant I couldn't dive. In addition to baby chores, I had to make sure Yu-ri didn't wander off. I cleaned the house and washed clothes. Jun-bu came home tired and still having to grade his students' work, which meant I had to cook dinner. He kept encouraging me to go to the night school to learn to read and write, so I went. I didn't have a gift for reading and writing, though. My skills were in the sea, but I was trying to be a traditional Korean wife. I sowed seeds in my kitchen garden. On a rare hot fall day, I made my husband a chilled soup with shredded cucumber and homemade soybean paste in raw damselfish broth. When my husband caught a cold, I stirred for him bean-powder porridge with tofu and wrapped rice in young bean leaves. For his part, my husband did not sit under the village tree, make and feed our baby abalone porridge, gamble, or drink. Our lives were upside down and contrary to the nature of Jeju. I thought we'd be fine. Then, as the moon moved across the night sky and I saw that the next diving period was coming, I felt the pull of the sea very strongly. I had made it a little over three weeks.

One night—after the baby and Yu-ri fell asleep and Jun-bu and I had made love—I gathered my courage to speak. "We've been living under the same roof for only a short time after almost a year of separation. Before that, we were together for only a few weeks—"

"And we still don't know each other very well," he finished for me. "I want to know you better and not just on our sleeping mats." He leaned over and kissed my cheek. "Have I hurt your feelings in some way? I hope you know how grateful I am for all you do. Taking care of my sister alone . . . But please, tell me how I can be a better husband."

"You're a wonderful husband, and I want you to be happy always," I said. "But I miss the sea."

He turned toward me, a confused expression on his face. "I don't want to be the kind of man to live in a household that depends on the tail of a skirt."

"I'm not saying you are." I tried to explain it to him in a way he'd understand. "I love the way you touch me and the time we spend together on our sleeping mat, but being a haenyeo—"

"Is dangerous."

I corrected him. "Being a haenyeo is who I am. There are parts of it I need. I long for the water and the triumph I feel when I find something valuable. I miss the company of women." I didn't add that I loved how women could speak and laugh in the bulteok without fear of hurting a man's sensitive ears. "Most of all, I miss contributing. I've worked my entire life, why should I stop now because you're a teacher?"

"I had hoped to keep you safe after what happened to your mother and Yu-ri, but it's clearly important to you, and I won't fight you on this matter. I am my mother's son. She didn't quit diving when my sister had her accident, and she hasn't given up now that my father is . . ."

Even Jun-bu couldn't say what had to be true—that his father was a hungry ghost, roaming the shattered ruins of Hiroshima.

"We already have a daughter," he said, quickly changing course. "If Halmang Samseung is good to us, maybe we'll have many more children. Whether they are boys or girls, I want them to be educated, just as I want you to have the opportunity to learn."

Send a daughter to school? I wasn't sure I could do that, despite my husband's passion for education. Even if a girl could attend public school, I wouldn't want to spend the fees to send her there. And the idea that we would send a daughter to a private school . . . Jun-bu must have sensed my thoughts.

"We can decide together what's best for our children. The sea is important to you, and education is important to me, but on what I earn, I could never pay the tuition to send five, six, or seven children to school. I'll need your help."

"Seven?" I tried to calculate the school fees in my head. Impossible.

We both laughed, and he pulled me toward him.

"Even if we have only our daughter, I want her to have the same opportunities my mother gave me. She'll go to school and—"

"But not if we have seven children! I'll need her help to take care of the younger ones and later help put her brothers through school."

"Brothers *and* sisters," he reminded me.

I patted his back. So much wishful thinking, but what else can you expect from a man?

The next morning, I went from door to door, looking for a young girl or a grandmother I could hire to take care of Yu-ri and Min-lee. I found an older woman, who'd recently retired from life in the sea. Granny Cho agreed to work for five percent of what I pulled from the ocean floor for her home eating. That night, I rummaged through my belongings to gather together my water clothes, goggles, tewak, and other harvesting tools.

The following day, Granny Cho arrived early. The baby went to her easily. Yu-ri didn't seem to care one way or the other that we had a stranger in the house. Every mother must leave her children to work, and every mother suffers, but we do it. After goodbyes, I picked up my gear and walked down to the bulteok.

"We wondered how long it would take you to come," Gi-won shouted her greeting. "A woman is not meant for the household!"

Sometimes village collectives are unwilling to let a new wife join them. Perhaps their fishing grounds are small or have been over-fished through bad management or greed, or they don't care for the new wife, or her husband's family has been a source of ill feelings or grudges, or her skills are not good enough to adapt to new waters. This was not the case for me.

"Hey, your husband is my son's teacher," a woman yelled. "Come sit here with me!"

"I live very close to you," another woman called out. "My name is Jang Ki-yeong. That's my daughter." The woman pointed across the circle to a young girl, who waved, encouraging me to come over. Ki-yeong just laughed. "Stop it, Yun-su. You and the others are only baby-divers. Young-sook looks to be a small-diver."

"We will see," said Gi-won. "For now, sit with Ki-yeong. You'll dive with her today. She'll test your skills, and tomorrow I'll let you know with which group you'll sit." As I made my way to Ki-yeong, Gi-won addressed the group. "Now, where shall we dive today? I was thinking . . ."

Later, we rowed out to sea. A long pull through the water's resistance, then a heave of the oar over the swells, then the dip back into the sea, followed by another hard pull. For the last few years, I'd worked as an itinerant laborer on a boat powered by a motor. I hadn't lost all the strength in my arms, but I'd surely be sore tomorrow. What a good feeling that was!

We didn't go too far out, and our dives took us down only ten meters. But even in these relatively shallow waters, the seafloor was abundant with life. For a woman who'd never entered new waters and only knew the wet fields where she'd dived with her mother, sisters, cousins, and haenyeo of her natal village's collective, the experience might have been daunting. But I'd dived in the Sea of Japan, the Yellow Sea, and the East China Sea. Every new diving spot is different, because the ocean—while one vast entity—is varied and complex. Just as on land, it has mountains, canyons, sand, and rocks. Also, just as on land, it has different types of animals: some predators, others prey, some loving the sun, others preferring the dark safety of a cave or crevasse. The plants, too, tell us that the land and sea are but mirror images of each other—with forests, flowers, algae, and so much more. I may not have been here before, but I was in my truest home, and it showed. Gi-won was impressed, and she rewarded me with a seat between the small-divers and the granny-divers.

"Even though Young-sook is barely married, her skills are very advanced," Gi-won explained to the collective. "Young-sook, we welcome your sumbisori."

Two weeks later, as we rowed to sea, a wave of nausea washed over me. I knew immediately what it meant. My smile was big and wide, and then I had to pull in my oar, lean over the side of the boat, and throw up my breakfast. It was as hot with chilies coming up as it had been going down. The other haenyeo cheered for me.

"Let it be a girl!" Gi-won shouted. "One day she will join our collective!"

"Let it be a son!" Ki-yeong exclaimed. "Young-sook still needs one."

"Let it be healthy," my husband said, when I got home.

"No woman can ever underestimate the sentimentality of a man," Gi-won averred the next day, and we all agreed.

———

At the end of September, a group of American officers arrived on Jeju to accept the surrender of those Japanese who'd remained on the island, hidden underground. We were told the Americans would bring democracy and quash communism, but most of us didn't know the difference between the two. We wanted to be left alone to have control over our own lives. We didn't even want mainlanders to interfere. Meanwhile, the Americans dumped Japanese rifles and artillery into the sea, exploded tanks, and set aircraft on fire. The booming woke the elderly from their naps. The acrid smoke—blown about by Jeju's erratic winds—stung our eyes, burned our lungs, and soured our tongues.

"It is not a diving period now. Perhaps you should take a day to visit your friend in the city," Jun-bu suggested. "The air might be better for you and Min-lee."

It was a perfect idea, but I didn't want to leave Jun-bu alone. Still, he insisted. For days, I scavenged for gifts to bring: mushrooms picked on the side of an oreum, mugwort gathered shoreside in case Mi-ja needed to clean glass, and seaweed so she might flavor her husband's soup. All these things I packed into a basket. Jun-bu gave Mi-ja's address to the cart driver, and I was off to see my friend.

When Min-lee and I arrived in Jeju City . . . *Hyng!* The streets were barely passable. Thousands of Japanese soldiers—as well as Japanese businessmen, merchants, and their families—filed in long lines toward the harbor to board ships; coming the other direction were thousands upon thousands of Jeju people returning home from Osaka and other places in Japan, where they'd done migrant work. Unemployed men and women milled everywhere, because the Japanese-owned factories and canneries had closed. And then there were the refugees, who'd fled south and to our island after the country had been divided at the Thirty-eighth Parallel. The past few weeks had been frightening, but the crowds and chaos deeply unsettled me.

I was still troubled when the driver pulled the cart to a stop in front of a Japanese-style house. I knocked, and Mi-ja greeted me at the door, her baby on her shoulder, his neck wobbling as he lifted his head to look at me. She hadn't known I was coming, but she didn't seem excited by my unexpected appearance at her home. I wrote her reaction off as surprise. When she wordlessly glided deeper into the house, I slipped off my shoes and followed her. The house was even bigger and more elegant than I'd imagined. Everything was clean and tidy. A vase of flowers stood on a windowsill. The floors were polished teak instead of the worn planks I'd grown up with. The cushions we sat on were made of silk. The room was eerily quiet even with two babies not yet four months old. We laid them side by side. Mi-ja's son sucked on his fist. My daughter slept. Mi-ja and I would have to wait a long time before we'd see them play together, let alone negotiate a marriage match. *Children are hope and joy.* A sense of peace, of everything being right—something I'd never felt, as nice as they were, with Gu-sun and Wan-soon back in Hado—sank into my bones, but when I took in Mi-ja, my perceptions forcibly shifted. She looked as pale and scared as when we'd said goodbye on the dock. I asked the first question that entered my mind.

"Where is everyone?"

Her eyebrows rose on her forehead like two caterpillars. "You would think that collaborators like my father-in-law would have been punished. Instead he's been hired by"—and here she struggled with the words which were new to all of us—"the transitional American government to help the U.S. Army with logistics."

The words and concepts were foreign to me, but it was the way she spoke them that was unnerving. She whispered, even though we were alone.

"The Americans want the island to be kept running as smoothly as possible," she went on, almost as if she'd memorized what she felt she had to say. "They plan to restore the businesses and enterprises that shut down when the Japanese left. And are still leaving . . . My father-in-law says there could be riots with so many of our citizens out of work. He says more than one hundred thousand migrants have returned home from Japan." Those would be some of the people I'd seen loitering on the streets coming here. "Men—and women—will do desperate things when they're hungry."

"We've always been hungry on Jeju," I allowed.

"This is different. Too many people and not enough food." She sighed. "My father-in-law was a collaborator for the Japanese. Now he's a collaborator for the Americans. I will always have that label associated with me."

Was that true? Was she unable to shift her fate? No matter how many offerings we make to goddesses, it's nearly impossible to change our destinies. I tried to steer the conversation in a new direction.

"My mother-in-law is not a bad woman," I said. "I have great respect for her water skills, but I'm happy not to be living in her compound. How are things with your mother-in-law?"

All brides talk about these issues, and I expected Mi-ja to share her heart with me as she always had.

"Madame Lee went to the five-day market," Mi-ja answered, and that was that. Her eyes drifted to the window. I had the sense she was longing for the sea, but how odd that she wasn't inquiring after me, my husband, or the people we knew. And not a single question about Hado.

I tried a different approach. "Is your husband well?"

Her body had such lightness to it. She could have lifted right off the floor and out the window. "The last time Sang-mun wrote to his parents was five months ago," she answered. "He was in Pyongyang, above the Thirty-eighth Parallel, visiting warehouses and learning to better manage shipments and storage. We've not heard from him again."

Maybe this wasn't the worst news. Still, I hesitated before responding. I placed a hand on her knee and tried to sound positive. "You must not worry. One Korean would never hurt another Korean."

But as the afternoon wore on, I understood there was no point in trying to comfort my friend. She was paralyzingly unhappy. She needed to leave this place.

"You could go back to Hado," I suggested.

"And live with Aunt Lee-ok and Uncle Him-chan? Never."

"You could come to Bukchon and rent rooms near me—"

"I couldn't live in a village as though I were a widow. I would be nothing."

"Not as a widow," I answered, hurt. "As my friend."

All in all, it was a disheartening visit.

Before I left, Mi-ja gave me money to hire Shaman Kim the next time I went to Hado, so she could perform a ritual to retrieve Sang-mun's lost and wandering soul. I returned to Bukchon feeling grateful for my husband, our home, and the stability of my life, which—while completely different from anything I'd previously known—was secure, peaceful, and happy. I worked as a haenyeo, and Jun-bu taught his classes unfettered by Japanese occupiers. He spoke to his students entirely in our native tongue, and they used their Korean names and spoke in the Jeju dialect without fear of punishment. We could do these things, because we were free from the colonists at last, although we still didn't know what life with the American occupiers would be like.

When Jun-bu and I took the family to Hado for a visit, I sought out Shaman Kim, who conducted the ceremony for Sang-mun.

"Where is the husband of Mi-ja?" she asked the gods. "Bring him home to his wife. Bring him home so he might show respect to his parents. Bring him home so he might meet his son."

In June, a baby boy easily slipped out of me. We named him Sung-soo, with the *soo* as his generational name, which all sons born to Jun-bu and me would share. I dressed Sung-soo in the special outfit for him to wear during his first three days of life from good-luck material given to me by Gi-won. Bukchon's shaman blessed him. Her powerful spirit infused his spirit. He not only survived his first three days but turned out to be a strong baby with big lungs and a lusty appetite for my milk.

When he was four months old and fall colors blazed on Grandmother Seolmundae's flanks, Jun-bu, Yu-ri, Min-lee, and I took a boat to Hado to help my father perform ancestor worship for my mother, my sister, my fourth brother, and my two brothers who had not returned home after the war ended. As soon as we arrived and were settled in my natal home, Jun-bu fetched his mother. Do-saeng beamed with joy when she entered my father's house. "A grandson!" she shouted. But beyond the guarantee that ancestral rites would be performed for her for another generation, she was happy to see her daughter, although Yu-ri didn't seem to remember who she was. Together, Do-saeng and I worked side by side to prepare the ritual foods. This year our ingredients were minimal, but we were able to make soup with tilefish, white radish, and seaweed, a bowl of seasoned bracken, and turnip and green onion buckwheat pancakes, since ancestors are known to have a fondness for these dishes.

My father was chasing Min-lee, who was fifteen months old and a master walker, when we heard a honking horn. I knew only one family who owned an automobile. I dried my hands and ran through the olles to the main road. Indeed, there was Sang-mun's family car. Mi-ja stood by the open back door, leaning in. She straightened, pulling out Yo-chan. She set his feet on the ground. She wore a Western-style dress and a hat decorated with a long pheasant feather. Yo-chan, whose plump cheeks made him into a miniature image of his father, had grown a lot this past year.

"Have I ever missed marking this day with you?" my friend asked. "Sun-sil was like a mother to me."

Just then, the sedan's other door slowly swung open, and Sang-mun emerged. I hadn't seen him in two years, and I might not have recognized him if he had not been with Mi-ja and her son. He'd turned to skin and bones. His eyes and cheeks were sunken. He also wore Western-style clothes, but on his feet were the straw sandals Mi-ja had made as a traditional wedding gift. His feet were covered with open sores.

"My husband escaped from the north," Mi-ja explained, speaking for the broken man beside her. "When he first came home, we thought he might not live. Now we are here to ask Shaman Kim to thank the gods and spirits who worked on his behalf. I think he can heal here."

We ended up staying together in Hado for a week. Jun-bu made bowls of sea urchin porridge—known to help the elderly and ailing babies—which Sang-mun slurped down. Each morning, my husband helped Sang-mun to the shore, so he could soak his feet in salt water. The two men watched our children, while Mi-ja and I went diving with Do-saeng's collective. In the early evenings, the four of us sat on the rocks, watching the sun set, drinking rice wine, and doting over our children, who'd stand, fall, grab on to a rock, pull themselves up again, totter over the uneven surface, and fall again.

One day Sang-mun took photos of Mi-ja and me with his wedding camera as we stepped out of the sea in our diving clothes. I took that as a sign he was feeling better, except that his mind remained both bitter and terrified. Like many of those who'd escaped from the north, he hated communism and was distrustful of the direction Jeju and the rest of the country might take, while my husband was idealistic about our new nation and what it could become. By the time we all needed to return to our own homes, the two husbands were barely speaking.

Day 3: 2008

Young-sook has another fitful night. She lies on her sleeping mat, staring at the ceiling, and listening to the sound of waves hitting the rocks. She punishes herself for the bad judgment she showed during her dive yesterday and if it's a hint that worse might be coming. She frets about her children, grandchildren, and great-grandchildren. She agonizes over what will happen if the north decides to invade South Korea again. She worries about the current president of South Korea. She wonders if maybe it's better to have the corrupt leader you know . . . If eighty-five years have taught her anything, it's that governments come and go and that whomever and whatever comes next will eventually become rotten.

These things clutter the front of her mind, and she's grateful in some way, because deeper, more persistent memories of screaming and begging keep floating into view. She counts forward and backward. She scrubs an imaginary eraser against the inside of her skull. She relaxes each toe, then her arches, then her ankles, then her calves, slowly working her way up to her forehead, and back down again. She does everything she can to push the bad pictures out of her head. None of it works. It never does.

When dawn finally comes, Young-sook gets dressed, eats breakfast, and considers what will come next. Some of her friends find company in television soap operas, but the troubles of the characters are of no interest to her. No, she is not the kind of old woman to sit inside and watch television. However, today—and she hates to admit it—she feels worn out. How pleasant it would be to go down to the shore and rest in the pavilion. There, she could look out to the sea, watch the haenyeo bobbing up and down not far offshore, and listen to the lilting, haunting cries of their sumbisori. Or she could doze. No one would bother her, because she's an ancient who's earned the respect of everyone in Hado.

Instead, habit takes her to the cement building with the tin roof that is now Hado's bulteok. Women sit outside on their haunches. They wear long-sleeved shirts with floral or checkerboard prints. Their faces are protected from the sun by big straw hats or broad-brimmed bonnets. Their feet, covered in droopy white socks, are tucked into plastic slippers or clogs. The man in charge of the cooperative talks to them through a bullhorn. She can't decide what she dislikes more—that they're being ordered around by a man or the whining sounds of his bullhorn. "Today you will do a job as old as haenyeo tradition—but with a new title—working as guardians of the sea." It used to be said that the sea's gifts were like a mother's love, unending, but parts of the sea are turning white, where coral, algae, seaweed, and sea creatures have perished. Some of this has been caused by the change in climate, some by overfishing, and some by human disregard. Therefore, the haenyeo will dive for a harvest of Styrofoam, cigarette filters, candy wrappers, and bits of plastic. The man from the cooperative ends his orders with "Young-sook and the Kang sisters will gather litter on the shore today." He's trying to let her save face for the mistake that almost led to her death yesterday, but she wonders how long it will be before she's allowed to dive again, even in the shallows.

The younger women—noticeably fewer than even ten years ago—grab their gear and climb on the back of the truck to be taken to the boat. The Kangs and Young-sook gather their nets and cushions, then begin hobbling down to the beach. The sisters start in right away.

"Hey, old woman, thank you for this special treat!" Kang Gu-ja gripes.

"We love sitting in the hot sun!" Kang Gu-sun chimes in.

Young-sook should bite back at their teasing, but she's noticed that half-and-half girl, Clara, perched on a rock. She wears a tank top and shorts that barely cover her crotch. Her bra straps show. Once again, she's wearing earbuds. Young-sook's great-grandchildren bob their heads when they listen to their music. Not this girl. She has a somber look on her face.

Young-sook changes course and walks straight to the girl. She keeps her Jeju words simple. "You here again?"

"I could say the same to you," Clara says with a smile as she pulls out an earbud and lets the wire drip down her chest.

"I live here!"

"I'm visiting. I couldn't take another day of sightseeing. I just couldn't. Mom and Dad let me take the bus out here."

"By yourself?" Young-sook asks, but inside she's relieved the whole family didn't come.

"I'm fifteen. What were you doing when you were fifteen?"

The old woman juts her chin. She's not going to answer that.

Except for the clothes, Clara has Mi-ja's eyes, legs, and manner. Young-sook should look away or leave or something. Instead, she says what she thought the first time she saw the girl. "So you're Mi-ja's great-granddaughter."

"Great-granddaughter, yes," Clara answers. "We shared a room, and she only spoke the Jeju dialect to me. She could speak English. I mean, she had to, right, having the shop and all? But her English was superbad. And you know how old ladies are. Talk, talk, talk. I had to learn it if I was going to understand her."

The girl's been speaking in the past tense. That must mean Mi-ja is gone. Young-sook focuses her eyes on the shell of a dead sand crab, which helps her control her emotions. Clara stares at her, though, waiting for her to say something. Young-sook settles on "Where have you gone? These sights—"

Clara flips a few strands of hair over her shoulder. "We hiked around Mount Halla Park. We climbed the Seongsan Ilchulbong Oreum to watch the sunrise. We toured Manjanggul—'the world's largest lava-tube cave system in the world.'" She sighs.

"Lots of natural beauty," Young-sook says, but she remembers when people weren't allowed on Mount Halla, when an oreum was for sitting on when you talked with a friend, and when the caves were places of hiding and death. "Mount Halla. We call it Grandmother Seolmundae—"

"But that's not all," Clara rushes on. "We've visited lots of museums or things they call museums or shrines or something. We went to where Jeju's three founding brothers climbed out of a hole in the ground. And guess what. It's just a hole in the ground! We went to a stone park. It had a bunch of stones. *Stones!* Then we went to this place to celebrate the life of some woman, Kim Something, who saved the people of Jeju during a famine."

"Kim Mandeok."

"That's the one. They treat her like a god too."

"Goddess."

"And what's with all the Swiss stuff? You know, like the Swiss Village and all the Swiss restaurants and the Swiss houses and—"

"Do all American girls complain?" Young-sook asks.

Clara shrugs, remains silent for a moment. Then she recites the new marketing slogan that's been plastered on the sides of buses and on billboards in English and Korean. "*The World Comes to Jeju, and Jeju Goes to the World!* What's that all about?"

"Tourism? The future?"

"Well, that's dumb. Because it's not like the world is coming here. It wouldn't be at the top of *my* list." Clara wrinkles her nose. "If it's about the future, that's even more lame. I mean, like, Jeju people seem to live in the past and not in the present. And certainly not in the future."

How can Young-sook explain what she feels about all that to a fifteen-year-old? The past *is* the present. The present *is* the future.

The girl breaks into a grin. "Don't get me wrong. I love to travel."

"Me too," Young-sook admits, glad to be on safer ground.

Clara's eyes widen, as if she hadn't thought of this possibility. "Where have you gone?"

Is it curiosity or impudence?

"I'd gone to three countries by the time I was twenty—Japan, China, and Russia. I went back to China last year. I've gone to Europe. The United States too. I liked the Grand Canyon and Las Vegas. What about you?"

"Oh, the usual places. We live in Los Angeles, so it's easy to go to Mexico or Hawaii on vacation. But we've also gone to France, Italy, Switzerland—"

"Switzerland? I've been there!"

"Figures. Switzerland and all—"

"Have you read *Heidi*?" Young-sook asks.

The girl tilts her head like she's a bird and gives Young-sook a quizzical look. "I was *named* for a character in the book."

"Clara, of course."

"I'm not in a wheelchair, though. Don't you think it's . . ." She breaks off for a moment, trying to find the right Jeju word. Finally, she says, in English, "Weird?" Young-sook has heard her great-grandson use this word, so she recognizes it. "Weird," Clara repeats before switching back to the Jeju dialect, "to be named for a character who's disabled?"

Suddenly, a memory of hearing the story read aloud shears through Young-sook's brain. She wants to go home, swallow some white diving powder, lie down, and close her eyes. "But Heidi helps Clara recover," she manages at last. "The Alps. Goat milk. Grandfather."

"You seem to know a lot about it," Clara says.

Young-sook changes the subject. "I have to work."

"Can I help?"

Young-sook surprises herself by nodding.

They pick their way over the rocks until they find a patch of sand. Young-sook straps her cushion to her behind and lowers herself until she's sitting with her knees drawn up to her shoulders. The girl squats, and those shorts . . . Young-sook averts her gaze.

"You work pretty hard for a grandma," Clara says.

Now it's Young-sook's turn to shrug.

Seeing she's not going to get more of a response, Clara prompts, "So you travel . . ."

"A lot of haenyeo my age travel together. See those two women? They're sisters. We've gone lots of places."

"But you're still working. Don't you ever want to treat yourself? With something other than travel, I mean."

"How do you know I don't treat myself?" But the truth is the idea seems foreign to Young-sook. She worked to help her brothers and sister, support her father until his death, grow vegetables, and bring home seaweed and turban shells for her children, grandchildren, and great-grandchildren to eat. She fills the lengthening silence. "We have a saying: *The granny who weaves on a loom as her work has five rolls of cloth in her old age, but the granny who dives all her life doesn't even have proper underwear.* I began with empty hands. I'll never forget the memory of being hungry, but the saying is wrong. I was able to help my children go to school and buy them houses and fields." She glances at the girl, who stares back at her, still wanting more. "I have plenty of underwear too!" This brings a smile to Clara's face, and Young-sook goes on. "I couldn't be more content than I am now."

"There must be something you've wanted—"

Young-sook finds herself trying to answer. "I wish I could have had an education. If I'd learned more, then I could have helped my children more." She glances over to Clara to see how the girl is taking the response, but her head is bent as she picks through seaweed dotted with bits of plastic. She's fast, efficient in her movements. When she doesn't come back with a follow-up question, Young-sook answers the one she wishes Clara had asked. "So maybe I did more than I'll admit, because my children and grandchildren have accomplished a lot. My son owns a computer business in Seoul. I have a grandson who's a chef in Los Angeles, and one of my granddaughters is a makeup artist—"

This brings forth a spiral of giggles.

"Why is that so funny?" Young-sook asks.

Clara leans forward as if to confide. "Someone's tattooed your eyebrows and lips."

That stings, because all haenyeo Young-sook's age have done this. Her great-grandson called it, in English, a fad. Just as her dyed and permed hair is a fad.

"*Hyng,*" Young-sook bristles. "Even an old woman wants to look beautiful."

The half-and-half girl giggles. The old woman knows what she's thinking: *Weird!*

Young-sook's patience evaporates. "Why are you here anyway?"

"Here?"

Young-sook spells it out. "On my beach."

"My mother sent me. You've got to know that."

"I can't help her."

"Can't or won't?"

"Won't."

"That's what I told her."

"Then why are *you* here?"

It's a simple question, but the girl goes in a different direction. "Your kids and their families, who live in other places, do you see them often?"

"I already told you I've gone to America. My grandson has me come every other year—"

"To Los Angeles—"

"Yes, Los Angeles. And I go to the mainland to visit the family who live there. Then every spring, the whole family comes here. It's been my privilege to introduce each of my grandchildren and great-grandchildren to the sea."

"How deep can you go?"

"Now or back when I was the best haenyeo?"

"Now."

Young-sook spreads her arms out wide. "Fifteen times this."

"Would you ever take me in the water? I'm a good swimmer. Have I told you that yet? I'm on the swim team at my school . . ."

PART III

Fear

1947–1949

The Shadow of a Nightmare

March–August 1947

Immediately after the war, we had great hopes for independence, but the Japanese colonists had merely been replaced by American occupiers through the United States Army Military Government in Korea. We heard Americans speaking in their language and others translating for them. They seemed to have come to the same conclusion that the Japanese had reached long ago: Jeju had a great strategic location. The island was now an American stepping-stone, only this time it led to the USSR, so instead of Japanese regiments, we had the Americans' 749th Field Artillery, the Fifty-first Field Artillery, the Twentieth Regiment of the Sixth Division, and the Fifty-ninth Military Government Company. The commander of the government group, Major Thurman A. Stout, became Jeju Military Governor Stout. He ruled side by side with Park Gyeong-hun, who'd been appointed as the Korean governor. The People's Committees opposed this, since neither man had been elected, but they were powerless to make a change. Governor Stout made lots of speeches, but the newspaper also ran interviews with Captain Jones, Captain Partridge, Captain Martin, and captain, captain, captain. One day, Governor Stout announced, "In the interests of a peaceful and effective transfer, we're asking officials from the former administration to return to their jobs. We also welcome all former policemen to work with us."

"But every one of them is a former collaborator!" Jun-bu fumed. He wasn't the only one to be upset. Most people took these moves to mean that the Americans were siding with the right-wingers and that the administration of the island—and small villages— would shift away from the People's Committees to the police and constabulary. It was as if the Americans didn't understand what they'd inherited.

But anger can be dangerous and have unintended consequences. The relationship between Governor Stout and the People's Committees continued to sour. At the same time, recruitment posters for the Ninth Regiment of the Korean Constabulary were distributed to every village. Jun-bu read one of them to me: "The Korean Constabulary is neither a right-wing nor a left-wing organization. It is a patriotic military agency for youngbloods who love their comrades and are willing to die for their country. We are not the hunting dog of a certain country. We are not the puppet of a certain political party. We are simply the bulwark of the state, which tries to pursue Korea's independence and defend our beloved homeland." The constabulary's actions, however, sent a clearer message. Its troops, many of whom had served in the Imperial Japanese Army, moved into the barracks at the former Japanese Navy Air Service air base in Moseulpo, which sent outrage around the island.

Through it all, people struggled to understand what the other side was saying. So much so that the U.S. military government opened an English academy. Men who'd been conscripted by the Japanese, had worked as collaborators, or had been educated abroad, were encouraged to sign up, which Jun-bu and Sang-mun did. As Jun-bu explained his decision to me, "How can I help change things if I sit by and do nothing?" I thought of my husband as being very smart, but he did not excel in learning this new language. Every night, he struggled with the lessons. Even the children and I picked up the basic sentences faster and better than he did, reciting the lines back and forth to each other like a call-and-response haenyeo song. *Hello . . . Hello! What is your name? My name is . . . Do you have . . . Yes, I do . . . Where is . . . Turn right at . . .*

Sang-mun, whom I did not respect, grasped the language so quickly that the Americans hired him to do almost the same job he'd done for the Japanese. He managed their supplies, making sure they were delivered from the port or airfield to the proper base or warehouse. They gave him a house to live in at their facility in Hamdeok, which was only three kilometers from Bukchon. He was on the road a lot, often staying away for nights at a time. Perhaps this is why Mi-ja did not become pregnant again, while I was just getting over another bout of morning sickness. No one could believe my belly had a third baby in it already, when Min-lee was about to turn two and Sung-soo was only nine months old. Sure, the haenyeo I dove with teased me, but I felt proud. I wished, though, that Mi-ja and I could be pregnant again together as we'd been during leaving-home water-work. I'd felt so close to her then and was certain Min-lee and Yo-chan would always be close as a result.

During Sang-mun's long absences, Mi-ja walked through the olles to Bukchon with her son, and I'd veer toward Hamdeok on my way home from the bulteok so we could meet halfway— almost as we had done in Hado when we were young girls.

"I brought in two nets filled with sea urchins today," I might say.

And she might respond with "I made kimchee." Or washed clothes, dyed cloth, or ground grain.

Sometimes I'd come around the bend and see her with her arms resting on top of the stone wall, staring out to sea.

"Do you miss diving?" I might ask.

"The sea will forever be my home," she always answered.

Once I saw bruises above her wrist. A man does not change with marriage, and I had my suspicions about Sang-mun, but I was hesitant to ask about him directly. One day I gathered my courage and made a more general inquiry. "Are you happy?"

"You and I are finally living with our husbands," she replied. "We know things about them we didn't know in those first few weeks of marriage. Sang-mun snores sometimes. He farts when he eats too much turnip. Often, when he comes home, I can tell he's been drinking. It's not our rice wine, but something he has with the Americans. I can't stand the smell."

These were nothing answers. She knew it. I knew it.

"I should be going home now," she said, then called to her son. I watched them walk up the olle until they were out of sight.

———

As a haenyeo, wife, and mother, I focused on diving, my husband, my two children, Yu-ri, and the new baby to come. *We enter the netherworld to earn our living and return to this one to save our children.* We haenyeo are ruled by the moon and tides, but we're also affected by various sets of three: The abundance of wind, rocks, and women. The lack of thieves, gates, and beggars. The three-step farming system that gives our pigs food from our behinds, fertilizer for our dry fields from the pigs' behinds, and a pig that can eventually be eaten. We didn't talk about it often, but Jeju was also known as the Island of the Three Disasters—wind, flood, and drought. Wind, again, always, and forever.

Now we had a new set of Three Disasters. First, another cholera epidemic broke out. Grandmother died. It hurt to lose her. It hurt even more that I hadn't been able to care for her in her final hours. Mi-ja also lost her aunt and uncle. Second, the fall harvest was extremely poor. The crops that sustained us—millet, barley, and sweet potatoes—failed. We were instructed to go to American distribution points to pick up bags of grain, but the former Japanese collaborators, who'd been put in charge of rationing, stole these provisions to sell on the black market. Within forty-five days, the price of rice doubled, not that we could ever afford to buy rice for more than the New Year's celebration. At the same time, the price for electricity—in those few places on the island that had it—jumped fivefold.

And third, people began to go without other staples. Jeju's population had doubled with those who'd returned from Japan since liberation and refugees from the north since the division of the country, but the Americans forbade us to trade with our former occupiers, which meant haenyeo families had no money to buy food. There were days when we squeaked by on a mixture of seaweed and barley bran. Other families subsisted on the potato pulp usually given to pigs, so even those beasts had to get by on less. On the mornings when I didn't dive, I strapped Sung-soo to my back and—with Min-lee and Yu-ri trailing behind me—joined other mothers on the rocky shore to search for sand crabs to make into love-from-a-mother's-hands porridge. Anytime one of the children found one, a squeal would ring out almost like a sumbisori.

ncentrating so hard that when Sang-mun grabbed Mi-ja's
jerked her away from me, we were completely startled.
reamed in Mi-ja's face. "How could you put my son in

wasn't in danger," she replied calmly. "I was holding him
e horse bolted—"
t about the bullets?" His hands were clenched into fists.
was as red as if he'd drunk a bottle of rice wine. "Did you
anger in that?"
a ran into the square. He visibly relaxed when he saw that
en and I were safe. He jogged over just as Mi-ja admitted,
expect that the police would fire on us." After a slight
e asked, "Did you?"
nun slapped Mi-ja. She staggered back and fell over
and Min-lee. I rushed to her side. Jun-bu pulled Sang-
y. My husband would lose in a fistfight, if it came to that,
as taller and he carried the authority of a teacher.
had landed on her bottom. Red welts in the shape of
n's hand had already begun to rise on her cheek. Yo-chan
cared but not particularly shocked or surprised. That's
ealized that this couldn't have been the first time he'd
ather hit his mother. I felt terrible, sick with worry and
My grandmother had made this match—the daughter of
rator to the son of a collaborator—but Mi-ja and her
could not have been more mismatched in their temper-

un stuffed his hands in his pockets, whether hiding the
he'd used against my friend or keeping them ready for
ime, I couldn't tell. When he looked away, I leaned in
or the first time, whispered to Mi-ja, "You could come
s. Divorce is not uncommon for a haenyeo."
ok her head. "Where would I go? What would I do? We
e house on the base. My son is well fed, and he's picking
a from the soldiers."
n't have to lay out the rest. My husband and I lived in a
e with our children and Yu-ri, and it was clear that we
e enough to eat. If it had been me, though, I would have

I spent long afternoons picking the meat from those tiny shells to
make the porridge.

Mi-ja and I agreed to stay out of political discussions even
as events roiled around us. Colonel Brown, a new American in
charge, gave a speech in which he told us that the long-range goal
for Jeju was "to offer positive proof of the evils of communism"
and "to show that the American way offers positive hope."

"Only one problem," Jun-bu grumbled. "They want us to
accept *their* form of democracy, with an American-backed dictator who can be controlled, while the people of Korea—especially
here on Jeju—want to hold *our* own elections, with *our* own slate
of candidates, so we can vote *our* own way. Isn't that what democracy is *supposed* to be about?"

He took this a step further when Mi-ja and her family came to
visit. "We should shove out the Americans like we did the French
missionaries," he stated, sure of his position.

"That was a small rebellion decades ago," Sang-mun argued
back. "The Christians are still here, and more are coming now
that the Americans have arrived."

"But we should be independent! If we don't stand up for what
we believe, then we are guilty of collaborating in our hearts."

Collaborating. That word again.

On one matter Sang-mun appeared to agree. "At the very least
we should have free elections." But then he warned, "Free elections or not, let me tell you something, friend. You should be careful. You're a teacher. Too much trouble gets stirred up in schools.
Remember what they did to the women organizers from the Hado
Night School and to their teachers?"

They were all dead, but I didn't worry because my husband
wasn't an organizer, and he wasn't going to lead a revolt. Besides,
we had more practical things to worry about, like how we were
going to feed our children.

One thing led to another, though, and people—organized by
the newly formed South Korean Labor Party—began to plan a
nationwide demonstration to take place on March 1, 1947, nineteen months after the war ended and on the same date that my
countrymen had once held gatherings to promote independence

from Japan. Here on Jeju, no matter what side people were on—rightist, leftist, or none-ist—they came from across the island to the starting point at an elementary school in the city.

The sky was bright, and the spring air felt fresh. Jun-bu carried Min-lee, and I had Sung-soo tied to my back. (Yu-ri stayed home with Granny Cho.) Mi-ja and Sang-mun brought Yo-chan. Our husbands had arranged a meeting spot, so we easily found each other, even though the crowd was larger than the one my mother had taken Mi-ja and me to fifteen years ago. Instead of Japanese soldiers watching us, hundreds of policemen kept us under observation. Many of them rode horses.

Our husbands wandered off to join a group of men, while Mi-ja and I stayed with the children. Yo-chan and Min-lee toddled together through the crowd, never getting too far from us. Yo-chan had the sturdy legs of his mother. My daughter was already dark from the sun, but she was wiry like her father.

"A boy and a girl," Mi-ja said, smiling. "When they marry—"

"We'll both be very happy." I looped my arm through hers.

We saw people we knew: the Kang sisters and their families, and haenyeo with whom we'd done leaving-home water-work. I said hello to some women from the collective in Bukchon; Mi-ja introduced me to a few of her neighbors in Hamdeok.

When the speeches started, our husbands returned to us. "Let's move closer to the stage," Jun-bu said. "It's important the children hear what's said."

But even I could have recited the speeches. Korea should be independent. We should reject foreign influence. North and south should be reunited, so that we'd be one nation. The last speaker called for us to march, but getting twenty thousand people to walk in the same direction at once takes time. We finally began to move, with the mounted policemen herding us. We lost sight of Sang-mun and Jun-bu. I picked up my daughter, and Mi-ja carried her son. Just ahead of us a little boy—although later I heard it might have been a girl—about six years old jumped and laughed, excited by all that was happening around us. When his mother reached for him, he twirled away, straight into the path of one of the mounted police. The rider yanked the reins. The horse reared. The mother

screamed, "Look out!" The boy fell. T
down.

The policeman, up so high, pulled s
to turn the animal. As a crowd, we reali
mount to offer help, even though what
an accident. A chorus of voices called
him!" People threw stones, which furt
rider kicked the animal's withers. It da
ing to make its way through the crowd
"He's heading to the police station!"
"Don't let him get away!"
The chants turned to "Black dog! Bl

We came around a corner and into a
on the broad steps leading to the entran
bayonets thrust threateningly before th
had happened. All they saw was an a
them. The demonstrators near the fron
and flee, but we were in a raging sea,
that. We heard several popping sound
eerie moment of silence, with everyo
ing. Then the screams began. People s
Amid the chaos, Mi-ja pulled the ki
As the crowd thinned, we saw little i
square. At the center of each group, ly
Some wailed in agony from their wou
others. An infant's cries hiccuped thr
looked at each other. We had to help.

With our children still in our arm
of the sound. We reached a woman,
had entered her back. Her body lay
set down Yo-chan and Min-lee next
lift the dead woman's shoulder an
Her mouth was a pink hole from
squawked out. Her eyes were squee
see where she'd have wrinkles one

Mi-ja and I rose together. I put
patted her, while Mi-ja checked to

both co
arm and

He s
danger?

"He
when th

"Wh
His face
not see

Jun-b
the chil

"I didn
pause, s

Sang-
Yo-char
mun aw
but he w

Mi-ja
Sang-mu
seemed
when I
seen his
horror. I
a collabo
husband
aments.

Sang-
weapons
the next
and, not
live with

She sh
have a ni
up Englis

She dic
small hou
didn't hav

taken my children as far away as possible. I could work and support us, just as Mi-ja could provide for her son, if she wanted to.

———

Six people died in front of the police station—all but one of them shot in the back as they'd tried to flee. Another six were taken to the provincial hospital. Police posted there were so agitated—having heard the gunshots from the march—that they fired indiscriminately into the air and killed two passersby. A curfew was declared.

The next morning, my husband read to me the contradictory reports in the newspaper. "Some onlookers claim the boy was killed instantly by the horse. Others say he died later from his wounds."

"That's awful."

"But listen to this," Jun-bu went on, incensed. "The U.S. Twenty-fourth Corps has taken an entirely different view. They're reporting that a child was *slightly injured* when he *inadvertently ran into a policeman's horse.*"

I shook my head, but Jun-bu wasn't done.

"Then the police department sent someone out to say the shootings in the square were justified as a matter of self-defense, because people armed with clubs had attacked the station."

"But there was no attack, and no one carried anything other than a child or a placard mounted on a bamboo pole!"

"You don't have to tell me." Jun-bu shrugged in disgust. "They're labeling the shooting 'unfortunate' and 'inconsiderate.'"

It was all very upsetting, but Jun-bu went to the school and I went to the bulteok.

At the end of the day, when we were rowing back to shore, haenyeo on another boat hailed us. We rowed closer to trade gossip.

"Police have taken into custody the organizers of the demonstration, as well as twenty-five high school students," their chief told us. "We've heard they're beating the kids."

We couldn't believe it.

That night, in violation of the curfew, people pasted posters on walls across Jeju. The South Korean Labor Party was asking all islanders to protest the U.S. military government and fight against American imperialism. They asked for money to help the victims who'd survived and for the families of those who hadn't. They demanded that the police who'd fired the shots be brought to trial and sentenced to death. They requested the immediate removal of any Japanese sympathizers or collaborators from the ranks of the police. Last, they implored all Jeju people to join a general strike on March 10.

The leader of this movement was twenty-two years old and a teacher. Jun-bu told me he did not know him.

———

Farmers, fishermen, factory workers, and haenyeo joined the strike, as did policemen, teachers, and post office workers. Businessmen came out of harbor offices, banks, and transportation companies. Shopkeepers shut their doors. The strike was an immediate and overwhelming success, but people very high up labeled it red-influenced. This caused the American military government to side with the hard-liners and the government on the mainland to send members from the Northwest Young Men's Association to help maintain order.

I went to the bulteok not to work but to trade information. Everyone had something to say, none of it good.

"Most of the men from the Northwest Young Men's Association escaped from north of the Thirty-eighth Parallel. They're the worst!" Gi-won seethed.

Sang-mun had also managed to flee from the communist-held territory, so I had an idea of what that experience could do to a man.

"A lot of them are delinquents, thugs, and criminals," Jang Ki-yeong, my neighbor, said. Then she added another set of three almost like a chant. "They're fierce, violent, and unforgiving."

"I heard that too," Gi-won agreed. "They arrived here with nothing. That's how quickly they had to leave their homes. Now they're being told to live off the land. Just you watch. They're going to be even more ravenous than the Japanese when it comes to stealing our food and other resources."

But it was Ki-yeong's daughter, Yun-su, who relayed what had to be the most frightening piece of information. "A friend told me that they're like rabid dogs when it comes to communism. They hate Jeju, because they think we're red in our thinking. I've heard they've labeled it Little Moscow. They call Jeju the island of nightmares."

A few nervous chuckles erupted, then just as quickly disappeared.

A grandmother-diver, who'd been quiet up to now, spoke. "My daughter married out to a village on the other side of the island. Over there, they have a saying about these new men. *Even a baby stops crying when it hears the words Northwest Young Men's Association.*"

It was a warm day, with the sun shining down on us in the bulteok, but a chill went through me, and it seemed to hit the others as well.

She went on in a low voice, and I sensed all of us leaning in to hear her. "My daughter says that the people in her husband's village call those men the shadow of a nightmare." She tipped her head in Gi-won's direction. "Our chief says those men will steal our food and other resources. Think about what that might mean. People are already learning the answer on the other side of the island. What's our most valuable resource? Our daughters. Those of you who have them should quickly arrange marriages. In my daughter's village, girls are being married out as young as thirteen."

This news produced some gasps.

"We didn't even do that when the Japanese were here," Gi-won said.

The grandmother-diver gave our chief a steely gaze. "This is difficult. Tradition says that Korean men won't rape a married woman, but what if that's wrong? What if—"

A deep silence fell over us as we considered what could happen to us or the unmarried girls in our families.

That evening when Jun-bu came home, I told him about the gossip from the bulteok. He didn't try to dismiss any of it. Instead, he said, "I've heard some of this too."

I didn't question why he hadn't told me earlier. Maybe he didn't want me to worry. The truth is, I wasn't nervous or scared that someone would attack me. I felt sure I could take care of myself. But what about Yu-ri?

"Your sister might not be right in her brain, and in ordinary times she might easily be ignored as an old miss past her prime, but we can't take any chances." As I stared at him, I realized he needed me to decide what to do. "We will no longer let her roam the village by herself. She will have to stay within our gate or be with Granny Cho at all times."

Of course, Yu-ri didn't like this one bit. She still had the spirit of a haenyeo, and she chafed at being tied to her tether. But that was just too bad.

Meanwhile, we heard that, high on Mount Halla, four thousand self-defense groups had hidden themselves in old Japanese fortifications. It was rumored that they'd found caches of weapons left by the Japanese and undiscovered by the Americans when they'd first arrived to dump abandoned munitions in the sea.

When I told Jun-bu what had been repeated in the bulteok, he remarked darkly, "Once more, it is islanders against outsiders."

Then, in response to the strike, the police arrested two hundred people in Jeju City in two days. After that, they arrested another three hundred officials, businessmen, Jeju-born policemen, and teachers, including one from the school where Jun-bu taught. Frightened, lots of people went back to work, but not Jun-bu and me. We believed in the power of the strike. That changed, however, when Jun-bu's colleague came to the house after being released from detention. The two men drank cups of rice wine and spoke in low voices, while I listened.

"They kept thirty-five of us in a cell just three by four meters," Jun-bu's friend recounted. "Policemen from the mainland pulled us out one by one. We heard screaming and begging. A few hours later, they'd drag that person back to the cell—unconscious or unable to walk. Then they'd select someone else. When my turn came, they beat me, and I wailed like all the rest. They wanted me to name the organizers of the strike."

"And did you?"

"How should I know who they are? The policemen beat me some more, but what happened to me was not as bad as what went on elsewhere. They had women too. The way they screamed . . . I will never forget it."

"What will you do now?"

"I'm going back to Japan. My family and I will be safer there."

To hear a Jeju person say he would rather live among the cloven-footed ones than on our birth island? It was beyond shocking. The next day, Jun-bu—without speaking to me about his decision—returned to his classroom. His timing was good, because the following morning the teachers who were still on strike were replaced by men who'd defected from North Korea. I begged Jun-bu to be careful. As someone who'd been educated abroad and been exposed to different ideas about equality, land reform, and education for all, he would automatically be suspect.

"Don't worry," he said. "They're just afraid of communism. They see it everywhere."

But how could I not be worried when a sea change was happening all around us, as though a tsunami was washing over our island and sucking all we knew and cherished back out to the ocean? More people were rounded up. Trials were held by U.S. Army officers, which meant that communication between the Koreans accused and the American judges was limited. People went to prison. Clashes between villagers and the police became more frequent and increasingly heated. More posters and leaflets were hung or handed out, and more people were rounded up, while far, far away from us, the United States and the Soviet Union continued to dispute the fate of our homeland. Their squabble felt like it had nothing to do with us, but here on Jeju, the police went on what they called emergency alert.

I couldn't stop thinking about my mother's last moments and the way the bitchang had tightened around her wrist underwater. She had fought to free herself, I'd tried to help, but the outcome had been inescapable. I felt as though a version of that was happening to us now, only on dry land, and yet we just wanted to live our lives. Jun-bu drilled his students on their lessons. Granny Cho took Yu-ri and the children on short walks to the sea when the days seemed long and quiet. I went diving with the collective and began training a baby-diver. I was so busy—and I guess Mi-ja was too—that the three kilometers between Hamdeok and Buk-chon now seemed a great distance. After the march, I didn't see her again for five months.

And still events closed in around us.

———

It was August 13. Sweet potato harvest season. Yu-ri, my children, and I went early to our fields. I was eight months pregnant. My stomach was large now with my growing baby, and my back ached from being bent over. Sung-soo had just begun to walk and his sister wasn't yet old enough to keep him out of trouble, so I had to keep an eye on the three of them as I did my work. By 10:00, it was raining so hard I decided we should go home and wait until the weather settled. I tied Sung-soo to Yu-ri's back, took Min-lee's hand, and we headed to the village. My clothes stuck wet and prickly against my skin, and my feet and legs were muddy. Along the way, we ran into my neighbor Jang Ki-yeong; her daughter, Yun-su; and their other female relatives as they walked back to Bukchon from their field.

"You have many burdens," Ki-yeong complimented me as I herded my children and Yu-ri.

"I'm a lucky woman," I responded. To return her praise, I said, "Your daughter follows in your wake. She's a good baby-diver."

"Your daughter will do the same one day."

"That will be the greatest gift she can give me."

We entered the village. Up ahead, someone passed out leaflets.

"Here. Take one," the young man said.

"I can't read," I said.

The young man tried to press his wares into the hands of Ki-yeong and Yun-su.

"We can't read either," Yun-su admitted.

Just then two policemen came around a corner. When they saw the boy, one of them shouted, "Halt!" The other yelled, "Stop right there!"

The color drained from the boy's face. Then his eyes hardened. He tossed the leaflets and took off. The policemen sprinted after him—toward us. I picked up Min-lee, put an arm around Yu-ri, who had Sung-soo on her back, and together we moved toward the square. In the confusion, Yun-su came with me instead of with her mother, sisters, and grandmother. Gunfire—the same horrible popping sounds we'd heard in the square during the demonstration—burst around us. Next to me, Yun-su stumbled and fell. She rolled over and stood up. Blood oozed from her shoulder. It looked like a surface wound, but I didn't wait to examine it.

"Yu-ri, hold on to me!" My sister-in-law, horrified, grabbed the hem of my tunic in her fist. Min-lee was crying so hard she could barely breathe. I shifted her weight and then wrapped my other arm around Yun-su's waist. We were five people moving as one. When we got to the square, we collapsed to the ground. Min-lee still screamed. Yu-ri, white with terror, hunkered next to me. Yun-su's blood dripped everywhere. I ran my shaking hands over Yu-ri, Min-lee, and Sung-soo. They hadn't been hurt.

A siren rang through the village. Neighbors burst from their homes—some of them armed with farming tools—to chase the two policemen who'd shot at us. I didn't stay to see what would happen. I gathered my group, and together we went to Yun-su's house. Ki-yeong and the other relatives stood in their courtyard, looking frantic. When they saw Yun-su, they leapt into action. One person put water on to boil. Another shook out a length of clean persimmon cloth and ripped it into strips to use for bandages. But when Ki-yeong appeared with a knife, scissors, and tweezers, the poor girl went limp in my arms, her legs collapsing beneath her as she lost consciousness. She was hurt, but her injuries weren't life threatening. Once the smell of blood was gone from her wound, she'd be able to dive again.

I had to get my family home. We retraced our steps to the square, where villagers had the two policemen in ropes. People yelled and cursed. Someone kicked the smaller policeman.

"Jabbing him with your old sandal is not enough!" an old man railed. "Let's take them to the police outpost in Hamdeok! We'll make sure they're punished!"

The crowd roared its approval. I should have followed my plan and gone home, but I roared along with everyone. My terror had turned to fury. How could other Koreans—even if they weren't from Jeju—shoot at us? We were innocent people, and this had to stop! So we joined the throng as they dragged the two police-men through the olle and along the shore the three kilometers to Hamdeok. Barely an hour had passed since my family and I left our dry fields.

"We want to lodge a complaint against these two!" one of the elders from Bukchon called out when we reached the small police station. "Let us tell you our grievances."

The Japanese had listened when we complained, but not our own people. Instead, I watched in horror as some policemen came out on the roof, ran to a mounted machine gun, and, without warn-ing, began to fire. It took a moment to realize they'd fired blanks, but we'd already scattered like bugs on the floor of a latrine when startled by the light of an oil lamp. Hiding behind some barrels, I snuck a quick look to see if it was safe. There, in the window of the police station, staring out, was Sang-mun. I fell back out of sight. My heart dropped to the pit of my stomach. My eyes had to be lying, but when I peeked out again, there he was. Our eyes met.

I didn't stop to visit Mi-ja on my way back to Bukchon. I didn't know what I could possibly say to her. For the first time in our many years of friendship, I wasn't sure I could trust her.

My husband was waiting for us at the front gate when we got home. Wordlessly, he took me in his arms. I sobbed out what I'd seen.

"You're safe," he said. "That's all that matters."

But I was deeply ashamed that I'd let the anger and confusion of the moment put my children and Yu-ri at risk. I promised myself I'd never let that happen again. Not as a mother. Not as a wife.

The next day, the newspaper reported that the police had "needed" to crack down on those distributing leaflets, but that the culprit in Bukchon had gotten away. Two days after that, a report leaked from the U.S. Twenty-fourth Corps also made the front page. My husband read the story:

"Two women and one man were wounded in a wild gunfight between leftists distributing leaflets and police in Bukchon—"

"But that's not what happened!" I cried, indignant.

Jun-bu returned to the article. "A mob of approximately two

hundred attacked the police station in Hamdeok," he read. "Police reinforcements were required to disperse the mob."

"But that's not what happened," I repeated. "How can they change what I saw with my own eyes into something so different?"

He didn't have an answer. I watched the muscles in his jaw move as he read the final words: "All political rallies, marches, and demonstrations are now banned. Crackdowns will occur for any street gatherings, and the posting or handing out of leaflets is forthwith illegal." He folded the newspaper and laid it on the floor. "From now on, we must be very careful."

I'd watched my mother die in the sea. I'd seen Yu-ri go into the sea one person and come out another. I understood the sea to be dangerous, but what was happening on dry land confused and scared me. In the last few months, I'd witnessed several people get shot in front of me. I'd seen people on both sides beaten. Those who'd been killed or injured were all Korean—whether from the mainland or Jeju—and the perpetrators had all been our countrymen. This was unfathomable to me, and I couldn't stop shaking from fear, not even when my husband held me tight and told me he would keep us safe.

The Ring of Fire

March–December 1948

The year following the March 1 demonstration was filled with family and work, and I didn't once see Mi-ja. She had to be struggling with her situation, and I felt terrible about that. But as much as I loved and missed her, I needed to take precautions. She lived in Hamdeok, where the military was headquartered. Her husband was, I believed, on the wrong side, and he was unpredictable. I couldn't risk that in a moment of rage or suspicion he might turn against Jun-bu or me. Of course, there were times I questioned why Mi-ja didn't seek me out and what that might mean. I wondered too if she thought about me or if she was as occupied with work and family as I was.

My children were doing well. Min-lee and Sung-soo would soon have birthdays. They'd turn three and two. Jun-bu and I had been blessed with a second son, Kyung-soo. He was a docile baby, and it pleased me that Min-lee was already learning to take care of her brothers. My husband was respected by his students, and I was well established as a small-diver in the Bukchon collective. Despite our good fortune, we had our disagreements. Jun-bu remained clear that he wanted all our children to be educated, and at least once a week we had nearly the same conversation.

"Let me remind you of the old saying," he said one afternoon after he'd had to punish a boy in his class for cheating. *"If you plant red beans, then you will harvest red beans."* My mother had often recited this aphorism, and it explained that it was up to the parents to plant, grow, and nourish their children, so they became good and useful adults. Then he added, "You should want Min-lee to have the same opportunities as our sons."

"I understand your wishes," I responded. "But I continue to hope that if I have another baby, it will be a girl, who will help her older sister pay for her brothers' learning. After all, it took three women—your mother, your sister, and me—to put you through school. When Sung-soo is ready to go to college, Min-lee will be nineteen and earning money by doing leaving-home water-work. But by the time Kyung-soo goes to college, Min-lee will surely be married. I'll need at least one other haenyeo in the household to help pay for the boys' school fees."

Jun-bu just smiled and shook his head.

To me, all this showed that, as much as I loved and respected him, he was still only a man and didn't have the larger worries I had. When he was at home or at school, I was in the world. I had to be practical and think ahead, because everything was unstable around us. Here we were a year after the demonstration and acts of retaliation continued. If village elders filed complaints that members of the Northwest Young Men's Association had demanded money or bags of millet as bribes, they would not be seen again. If a group of leftists came down Mount Halla and shot a policeman, squads of policemen combed the mountain in search of the perpetrators. If the culprits couldn't be found, the police shot innocent villagers as a lesson.

The U.S. military government decided to make some changes. Our first Korean governor was replaced by Governor Yoo, who was reported to wear sunglasses twenty-four hours a day and sleep with a gun. Even the U.S. authorities labeled him an extreme rightist. He purged all Jeju-born officials and replaced them with men who'd escaped from the north and were as anti-communist as he was. He swapped many Jeju-born police and police captains with men from the mainland, who'd never liked or had sympathy for the people of our island. He banned all People's Committees and called those like my family and me, who'd benefited from them, extreme leftists. I was not an extreme leftist. I wasn't even a leftist. No matter. There would no longer be classes for women or any of the other activities that the village chapters had organized.

We had only one newspaper on the island, but by the time a copy reached Bukchon the news might have been old, or it could have been wrong in the first place. Still, Jun-bu read all he could. One night he said rather glumly, "I think the newspaper is controlled by the rightists, who, in turn, are controlled by the Americans. We have the gossip and rumors that pass from village to village, but can we trust anything we hear?"

I didn't have an answer.

The Americans announced that on May 10 those of us living south of the Thirty-eighth Parallel would finally have our own elections. My husband's spirits momentarily lifted.

"The Americans and the United Nations have vowed we will be free to vote as we wish," he told me. But then reality brought him back to earth. "The Americans support Rhee Syngman as their preferred candidate. His biggest backers are former Japanese collaborators. Anyone who is against him is automatically labeled a red. Anyone who wants to punish former collaborators is labeled a red. That means that just about everyone on Jeju—including us—will be labeled a red."

I worried about Jun-bu's increasingly dark frame of mind.

Visitors from Jeju City, who had access to electricity and owned radios, told us about a broadcast from a station above the Thirty-eighth Parallel that offered an invitation to leaders from the south to go to Pyongyang to discuss reunification and write a constitution that would solve all our problems. In response, the U.S. military government and Governor Yoo strengthened their anti-communist crackdown on Jeju. Former Governor Park, originally appointed by the U.S. military, was the first to be arrested. He was famous, and people were shocked. Then the body of a young man was pulled from a river. He was identified as a protester. A witness to one of the torture sessions reported that the student had been hung from the ceiling by his hair and his testicles pierced with awls. There could not have been a mother on the island who did not imagine the grief she would feel if this boy had been her son.

In the early hours of April 3, we were roused from sleep by the sounds of gunfire, yelling, and people clattering through the olles.

Jun-bu and I protected our children with our bodies. I was terrified. The children whimpered. The commotion seemed to last forever, but maybe it only felt that way because the night was so dark. Finally, Bukchon fell silent. Had arrests been made? How many people were shot, and how many had died? The gloomy shadows revealed no answers. Then we began to hear shouts.

"Hurry!"

"Come quick!"

Jun-bu got up and slipped on his trousers.

"Don't go out there," I begged.

"Whatever happened is over. People may be hurt. I must go."

After he left, I held the children even closer. From outside, I heard men speaking in urgent voices.

"Look at the hills! They've lit the old beacon towers!"

"They're sending a message around the island!"

"But what's the message?" my husband asked.

The men muttered back and forth about it for a while longer but arrived at no conclusions. Jun-bu returned and lay down next to me. The children fell back asleep, curled around us like piglets. When dawn streaked the sky with pink hues, I quietly got up, changed into day clothes, and went outside. I was about to go to the village well when Jun-bu joined me.

"I'm coming with you. I don't want you going alone."

"The children—"

"They're still asleep," he said, picking up a water jar. "It'll be safer to leave them here for a few minutes than to take them with us."

We went to the front gate and peeked out. The olle was empty except for a few abandoned bamboo spears. We hurried to the main square, where we discovered that rebels had broken into the village's one-room police station. Furniture littered the cobblestones. Papers drifted across the ground, pushed by the wind. A few uniformed men scrambled to pick them up. One man had a bandage on his head. Another limped. Some villagers had gathered under the tree to peer at a poster tacked to it. Jun-bu and I pushed our way to the front.

"Tell us what it says, Teacher," someone said.

"Dear citizens, parents, brothers, and sisters," he read, his eyes moving over the written characters. "Yesterday one of our student-brothers was found killed. Today we come down from the mountains with arms in hand to raid police outposts all over the island."

The crowd murmured, confused, scared. Some voices of support rose for the rebels. Retribution had been exacted for the boy who'd been tortured and killed.

Jun-bu continued to read: "We will oppose country-dividing elections to the death. We will liberate families who have been separated by a line. We will drive the American cannibals and their running dogs from our country. Conscientious public officials and police, we call on you to rise up and help us fight for independence."

I didn't care for the language, but the sentiment was real to all of us. We wanted our own unified country. We wanted to choose our own future.

"Fight! Fight! Fight!" men shouted, their arms raised. Soon women's voices joined in. But Jun-bu and I had learned to be wary. We returned home to continue our own lives as word passed from mouth to mouth. By the time we'd eaten breakfast, gotten Granny Cho settled with the children and Yu-ri, and I'd made my way to the bulteok, every haenyeo seemed to have another piece to add to the night's story.

"The South Korean Labor Party was behind the attacks," Gi-won said once we were settled around the fire.

"No! It was rebels, plain and simple," Ki-yeong said, scratching an ear.

"I heard five hundred insurgents came down Grandmother Seolmundae—"

"It was a lot more than that! Three thousand people joined the rebels as they went from village to village. That's how they hit so many police stations at once."

"And that's not all. They blew up roads and bridges."

"With what?" someone asked, dubious.

Before an answer could come, another diver exclaimed, "They even cut telephone lines!"

This was serious. None of us had telephones in our homes, so the line in the police station was the only way a village could call for emergency help from Jeju City.

"It looked to me like they were armed with little more than what we take into the sea," Gi-won said.

"You looked?" Ki-yeong asked in awe.

"You think anyone would dare do something to me?" Gi-won jutted out her chin to make her point. "I went to my front gate. I saw men—and some women—carrying sickles, scythes, shovels, and—"

"They sound like farmers, not haenyeo," Ki-yeong speculated.

"They *are* farmers," her daughter said.

"And some fishermen too."

"This isn't about all that leftist and rightist stuff men talk about," Gi-won said. "It's about not wanting to be told what to do by another country—"

"And reunifying the country. I have family in the north."

"Who here hasn't been touched? First, we had the Japanese. Then the war. And now all the problems of living and eating—"

"Was anyone killed?" I asked.

The bulteok quieted. In the excitement, no one had stopped to consider who might have gotten hurt or how badly.

Gi-won knew the answer. "Four rebels and thirty policemen were killed around the island—"

The woman next to me groaned. "Thirty policemen?"

"Hyun!"

"Aigo!"

"And two officers were lost in Hamdeok," Gi-won added.

That was only three kilometers away. *Mi-ja.* Maybe I should have been more scared for her, but ever since seeing Sang-mun that day in the police station, I had to figure she was safe.

"Lost? What does *lost* mean? Did they desert?"

"They were kidnapped!"

Fear played across the faces of the women around me. Attack and retribution had become a way of life for us, and we were all anxious.

"No one died in Bukchon," Gi-won said. "We can be grateful for that."

The relief was unmistakable. If no one was killed here, then we might not experience reprisals. We could hope that *nothing* would happen.

Once in the sea, I pushed aside thoughts of dry land. By the time we returned to the bulteok a few hours later to eat and warm up, our worries about last night's events had diminished. If we could go back to boasting about what we'd caught, then maybe others would shrug off the raids as well.

The U.S. colonel in charge was also dismissive. "I'm not interested in the cause of the uprising," Colonel Brown told a reporter that night. "Two weeks will be enough to quash the revolt." But he was wrong. This day, April 3 — *Sa-sam* — came to be called the 4.3 Incident, although we did not yet know that this date would be so important in our lives.

Two days later, Jun-bu told me that the U.S. military government had created something called the Jeju Military Command. A more stringent curfew was set in place.

"But how am I supposed to stay in our home between sunrise and sunset, when water needs to be hauled, fuel gathered, and pigs cared for?" I asked my husband.

Jun-bu ran his hands through his hair. He had no solution.

The next day, Jun-bu read in the newspaper that the commander of the Ninth Regiment of the Korean Constabulary was trying to negotiate peace: "I've asked for the complete surrender of the rebels, but they're demanding that the police be disarmed, all government officials be dismissed, paramilitary groups — like the Northwest Young Men's Association — be sent away, and that the two Koreas be reunified."

Naturally, neither side could agree to those conditions. After that, the constabulary brought in nearly a thousand men to strengthen their force on Jeju. Some of those men were sent to guard villages along the coast like Bukchon, Hado, and Hamdeok, for which, I'll admit, I was grateful. Then — and all this we heard about either from the newspaper or through gossip — the constabulary climbed Mount Halla and attacked the rebels. By the end of April, Jeju City was completely cordoned off, and police were conducting house-to-house searches to weed out what they were calling communist sympathizers. But many people in the constabulary and the police were from Jeju. When they could no longer bear what was happening, they defected to the rebels in the mountains. We even had a few people leave Bukchon to join the renegades.

Major General Dean, the U.S. military governor now in charge of Korea, came to our island to "assess the situation." He repeated a rumor that the North Korean Red Army had landed on Jeju and now commanded the rebels. This was followed by rumors about North Korean naval ships and a Soviet submarine circling the island. These false stories cemented a hard-line policy. Major General Dean sent another battalion to Jeju. And while the order was that the U.S. Army should not intervene, it kept track of Korean operations by using reconnaissance aircraft. When I worked in the dry fields, those planes passed overhead, hunting for their prey. At night, I saw cruisers out at sea using searchlights to scan the horizon. When I went to the five-day market, vegetable peddlers from the mid-mountain area told me they'd come across American officers riding in jeeps or on horseback on Korean-led missions. By the end of six weeks, four thousand people had been arrested.

At the beginning of the seventh week, Jun-bu invited the women from the collective who didn't know how to read or write to our house to teach us how to vote. Even if the election was rigged, we wanted to take this opportunity to try to have a voice in our government. "You don't have to recognize the written characters for the candidates' names," he explained. "All you need to know is where he comes on the ballot. Is he number one, two, or three? It's *your* choice. Then you mark the number of the person you want."

But when we went to the polling place, a group of men barred us from entering. "Turn around. Go home," they told us.

Once again, my news came from the bulteok as the haenyeo jabbered like chickens the next morning. In Bukchon, we hadn't been allowed to vote, but that was nothing compared to what had happened elsewhere.

"The police, the constabulary, and the Northwest Young Men's Association blocked—"

"Jeju's main road going east—"

"And west—"

"So rebels wouldn't be able to pass."

Not for the first time, Ki-young's daughter, Yun-su, seemed to have a clearer sense of what had transpired. "None of that mattered," she said, and I heard something like pride in her voice. "Nothing stopped the rebels. They raided polling places and burned ballot boxes. They kidnapped election officials. They cut more telephone lines—"

And then the others were off again.

"Destroyed bridges—"

"And blocked the very roads they weren't supposed to pass."

In the end, no votes were counted from Jeju, and the Americans' choice, Rhee Syngman, was elected president, although we hadn't yet officially become a country.

The next morning, when I returned to the bulteok, yesterday's nervous twittering had been replaced by anxiety. Surely, the government would punish us for the troubles of election night.

"I'm chief of our collective," Gi-won said, "but as a woman, I have no choice in what happens next."

"No woman has a say."

"No child has a say. And the elderly?"

"They have no authority either," Gi-won answered for all of us.

Most of our fathers and husbands had spent their days thinking grand thoughts and taking care of babies, so they were powerless too. But everyone—even the innocent, even the young and the elderly, even those who did not have a husband to read the propaganda to them from the newspaper, or those, like Yu-ri, with no comprehension of what was happening—was forced to take a side.

———

In late May, Mi-ja arrived one day at my door. She was alone. She'd lost weight and her color was bad. I invited her in, but I couldn't help being apprehensive. While I made citrus tea, she visited with Yu-ri. "Have you been good?" she asked. "I've missed you." Yu-ri smiled, but she didn't recognize Mi-ja.

"I've missed you too," she said when I came with the tea.

"You stopped coming to the olle," I replied.

"You could have visited me."

"I have the children—"

"A girl this time?" She scooted toward the cradle, where Kyung-soo slept.

I held up a hand. "A boy." As she slid back to her original spot, I finished my excuse. "The children and Yu-ri are too much for me to take to Hamdeok. It's not easy—"

"Or safe."

"Or safe most of all," I agreed.

Silence hung between us. I couldn't fathom what she wanted. She took a breath and let it out slowly. "Sang-mun planted a baby in me not long after the march. I was sick, so I couldn't come to see you."

A pang of guilt. Of course, there had to be a reason.

"A boy or a girl?" I asked.

She lowered her eyes. "A girl. She lived two days."

"*Aigo*. I'm so sorry."

She regarded me, hurt. "I needed you."

Whatever caution I'd felt disappeared. I'd failed my deep-heart friend.

"Your husband," I ventured. "Has he been good to you?"

"He was gentle when I was pregnant." Before the true meaning of her words could sink in, she went on. "You can't know how hard it is for him. He goes from meeting to meeting and from place to place all over the island. The Second Regiment's Third Battalion is now stationed in Sehwa nearby, but they're headquartered in Hamdeok. It's a lot of pressure."

"That must be difficult—"

She sighed and looked away. "Many people, when they envision being faced with hardship, believe they will fight back. But when I was a child and had to live with Aunt Lee-ok and Uncle Him-chan, I learned what really happens. They didn't feed me, as you know. By the time I wanted to fight back, I was too weak."

I struggled to find something to say to boost her spirits. "That terrible situation brought us together. For me, it will always be a happy result."

But her mind was not on friendship. "Some women imagine

committing suicide, but how can that be a path for a mother?" Her eyes glistened with tears. "I have Yo-chan. I must live for him."

I'd known Mi-ja a long time, and I'd never seen her so melancholy. Not only was she experiencing the turmoil around us but she'd also had the cataclysm of losing her child. And then there was her husband. She didn't look bruised, but I wasn't seeing her naked or in her water clothes. I put a hand on her arm.

"Women live quietly," I said. "However angry or broken a woman might get, she does not think about beating someone, does she?"

"My husband is married to a bad person."

Her comment baffled me. "How can you say that?"

"I failed him. I lost the baby. I don't bring home food. I don't keep the house the way his mother did—"

I cut her off. "Don't defend him or justify his actions as though what he does to you is *your* fault."

"Maybe it is."

"No wife asks to be hit."

"Your mother was more understanding of men than you are. She said we should have sympathy for them. She said they have nothing to do and no purpose to push them through the day. They're bored and—"

"But your husband can't use those reasons! He works. He has his own life."

This didn't stop Mi-ja from continuing to make excuses for him. "He went through so much to come home." Then she set her jaw. "His violence and cruelty are the way of the island these days."

But he'd been violent long before our current troubles . . .

Helplessness settled over me. "I wish we could go back to the way things were when we visited in the olle every day—"

"But it's not safe. We both need to protect our children." So, we'd circled back to the beginning of the visit. After a moment, she added, "I hope our separation doesn't last so long this time."

"And I hope the next time I see you, a baby will be suckling at your breast."

I walked her to the gate. Even as we said our goodbyes, I suspected I didn't know just how bad things were for her.

On August 15, the Republic of Korea was formally established in the south. One month later, Kim Il-sung, with help from the USSR, founded the Democratic People's Republic of Korea in the north. Although the armies of neither the Americans nor the Soviets left completely, the division of our country appeared to be settled. It seemed like life had calmed down, and I'd be able to see Mi-ja again. But all through early fall, the different factions continued to fight on Jeju. The military was armed with machine guns and other modern weapons supplied by the U.S. Army, while the rebels protected themselves with Japanese swords, a handful of rifles, and bamboo spears. Then, on November 17, 1948, President Rhee placed Jeju under martial law and issued the first order:

ANYONE FOUND NOT WITHIN FIVE KILOMETERS
OF THE COAST WILL BE UNCONDITIONALLY
SHOT TO DEATH.

It was to be called the ring of fire. Anything and anyone found violating the order would suffer a scorched-earth policy.

When I went to the bulteok, we discussed what this might mean for us.

"Where will all the mountain people go?" one of the women asked.

"They're being sent to the shore," Gi-won told us.

"But there's nowhere to put them," another diver said.

"That's the point," Gi-won replied. "No one can hide at the sea's edge."

I asked the question I felt sure we were all thinking. "Are we in danger?"

Gi-won shrugged. "We already live on the safe side of the ring of fire."

The next day, the rain poured down as though the heavens were weeping. Men in the Korean Constabulary, Jeju police, and U.S. military troops herded the first few hundred mountain refugees to the outskirts of Bukchon. The women and children did not look like troublemakers to me. Apart from little boys and a few old men who walked with their heads bent, I saw few males in the trail of anguish. I could only come to one conclusion: most men were already dead. The children did not talk or sing to make the burden of their situation less heavy. Families carried whatever they'd been able to salvage from their homes—quilts, sleeping mats, cooking utensils, bags of grain, earthenware jars filled with pickled vegetables, dried sweet potatoes—but they'd been forced to abandon their livestock. They made camp as best they could, building lean-tos from reeds and pine branches.

In Bukchon, we were ordered to use the stones that lay in our fields to build a wall around the village. Men, so unused to hard labor, suffered. Jun-bu came home with blisters on his hands, and his back ached. The job also pulled women from working in either their wet or their dry fields. Even children had to help. Once the wall was finished, we were forced to stand guard day and night, armed with homemade spears.

"If you let someone in who is proven to be a rebel," a police officer warned us, "then you'll all be punished."

The refugees soon ran out of the food they'd brought with them. At night, moans of hunger drifted over the moonlit fields, through the rocky walls, and into my house. Whenever the wind shifted, the bad odors of unwashed bodies and no sanitation soured our nostrils, eyes, and throats.

One day as I was walking past the camp a woman beckoned to me.

"I'm a mother. You look like a mother too. Will you help me?"

Although mid-mountain people had always looked down on the haenyeo, our hurt feelings had moved to pity as we witnessed what had happened to them. So of course I asked what I could do.

"I'm not a diver," the woman said. "I don't know how to harvest from the sea. Can you teach me?"

I was willing, but when I learned she didn't even know how to swim, I had to decline. When she started to weep, I whispered, "Come to my field tonight. I will leave a basket for you with sweet potatoes and some other things."

As I gave her directions, she wept even harder. Soon I heard about other women in Bukchon who left food in their fields or by the wall to the camp. But after one of my neighbors was caught doing this, taken away, tortured, and killed for her charity, I did not take the risk again.

The refugees living outside Bukchon and other seaside villages had obeyed and come to the shore, but others—some fearful, some obstinate, and some rebels—fled inland and tried to hide in remote mountain villages or make new homes in caves or lava tubes. This was the worst thing they could have done. Grandmother Seolmundae couldn't protect them, and the ring of fire became literal as entire villages were burned. Soldiers set fire to Gyorae. When people tried to escape, they were shot and thrown into the flames to destroy the evidence. Some of the victims were babies and children. In Haga, soldiers killed twenty-five villagers, including a woman in her last month of pregnancy. Then they burned the village. Nearly every day, when we rowed to the day's diving spot, we saw plumes of smoke wafting from our great mountain and out over the sea.

I went to the five-day market, but there was nothing to buy. The woman in the dry-goods stand passed along what she knew. "U.S. ships have blockaded the island," she said. "No supplies can be brought in to help those in hiding or provide food to the tens of thousands of refugees now living inside the ring of fire."

She was clearly knowledgeable, so I asked, "What about food for us?"

The woman grunted. "No one on the island—not even those of us on the right side of the ring of fire—will be able to buy goods anymore."

Worse—so much worse—there came a day when we were told that haenyeo could no longer dive. Japanese soldiers had once stolen our food and horses, but now our own countrymen were starving us. My husband and I each got by on a single sweet potato a day, so we could give more food to our children. But they lost weight, their hair turned dull, and their eyes began to sink into their heads.

When someone told me that the haenyeo collective in Gimnyongree had gotten permission to open a restaurant to serve police and army troops, I passed the information on to Gi-won. She called for a meeting in the bulteok.

"The haenyeo in Gimnyongree are hoping to prevent police violence, but we will not dive for the very people who are killing our own," Gi-won said, adamant. "Wouldn't we be truer to our island if we offered shelter, food, and clothing to the insurgents? These are our people. They could be our sons, brothers, or cousins."

"We'd be killed if we were caught!" Jang Ki-yeong exclaimed.

"It's better to go hungry together than to die," Yun-su added.

"Why should we help them?" someone else asked. "The rebels steal food and kill those who try to protect what they grew. I'm afraid of bears as well as tigers."

This saying had recently sprung up, and it meant that the police and the constabulary were to be feared as much as the rebels and insurgents.

"I don't care who started what or when," Ki-yeong said. "I just want peace."

Not one person agreed to Gi-won's suggestion. It was the first time we'd turned against our leader, and it showed that we'd lost all sympathy for the rebels.

————

More news filtered through the stone wall that protected Bukchon. In Tosan, soldiers killed all men between the ages of eighteen and forty. One hundred and fifty died. In Jocheon, two hundred villagers turned themselves in to the military to prevent being killed in a battle against the insurgents. All but fifty of them were executed anyway. We tried to tell ourselves that none of this could be happening, but it was. A third of Jeju's population had been forced to relocate to the shore, and so many people had been killed that no one could guess the count. The skies were black with crows, who flew from one scene of death to the next. Picking at the dead made them stronger; they mated, and hatched even more crows. The flocks grew bigger and blacker. I couldn't look at them without feeling ill.

American soldiers found nearly one hundred bodies in a mountain village, while another group of their soldiers stumbled across the execution of seventy-six men, women, and children in a different village. The Americans may not have actively participated in the atrocities, but they did nothing to prevent them either.

"Is *not* doing something their way of sending us a message about their real intentions?" Jun-bu asked.

Once again, I had no answer.

After men and young boys were killed in yet another set of mountain villages, the survivors—women, children, and the elderly—were housed in military tents set up by American soldiers in the playground of Hamdeok Elementary School. When there was no more room, the Korean Constabulary executed the surplus of people at the edge of a cliff, so they'd fall into the sea.

I was able to anticipate my husband's question before he asked it. "Did the Americans with their tents and surveillance planes not see that?"

It worried me to see my husband's frustrations growing, but the person I thought about most when I heard what had happened in Hamdeok was Mi-ja. She *lived* there.

We'd grown up with the Three Abundances, but we weren't prepared for the Three-All Strategy—kill all, burn all, loot all—of the scorched-earth policy. The impact was hard for us to absorb. You hear about an incident but don't see a mother, a child, a brother. You don't feel the individual suffering, but we began to hear those stories too: A family was dragged from its home. The daughter-in-law was made to spread her legs so her father-in-law could mount her. When he couldn't finish the deed, both were killed. I heard of a soldier who heated his revolver in a fire, then shoved it inside a pregnant woman just to see what would happen. Widows and mothers of sons who'd been killed often went mad and threw themselves off cliffs, sailing to their loved ones in the Afterworld. In one village, the girls were kidnapped, gang-raped for two weeks, and then executed, along with all the young men from that village. Wives were forced to marry policemen and soldiers, because marriage was a way to seize property legally. Some haenyeo sold off their dry fields to buy a husband or son out of jail. The most unfortunate women agreed to marry police officers in exchange for the release from jail of a husband, brother, son, or other male relative. Too often, those loved ones were killed anyway. These things I wished I could erase from my mind, but they would never, ever, go away.

I wanted our family to return home to Hado, where we could be with Do-saeng, my father, and my brother, but Jun-bu felt we should stay in Bukchon. "I need to keep teaching," he said. "We need the money."

Schools had remained open to keep boys and young men occupied. Jun-bu had struggled with his part in this, but he was right that we needed the money when we haenyeo weren't allowed to dive. We were all hungry and getting weaker every day. My children didn't have the energy to cry, but they whimpered at night. All I could do was make meager offerings to Halmang Samseung in the hope she would prevent my breast milk from drying up. If it did, I wasn't sure how I would nourish Kyung-soo.

Life-Giving Air

January 16–17, 1949

Winters can be long and dreary on Jeju, and the January of 1949 was particularly so. One night, the wind seemed to blow worse than ever through cracks in the walls of the house. My children could barely move, because their clothes were so padded that their arms and legs stuck out from their bodies like branches. Jun-bu and I laid out our sleeping mats, all of them touching. Min-lee and Sung-soo crawled off their mats and snuggled close to us, seeking extra warmth. I held Kyung-soo in the crook of my arm. Even with the oil lamps off and the room in utter darkness, the children fidgeted from cold and hunger. We didn't know how to explain our misfortune to them when we were having a hard time understanding it ourselves, but I knew that if I could calm Min-lee, then Sung-soo would quiet as well. A story might help.

"We're lucky that our island has so many goddesses to watch over us." I spoke softly, hoping my lowered voice would bring tranquillity. "But we have one real-life woman, who was as brave and persistent as any goddess. Her name was Kim Mandeok, and she lived three hundred years ago. She was the daughter of an aristocrat, who'd been exiled here. Her mother was . . ." I was not going to say *prostitute*. "Her mother worked in Jeju City. Kim Mandeok did not follow in her mother's wake."

Jun-bu smiled at me in the darkness and squeezed my hand.

"Kim Mandeok opened an inn and became a merchant. She sold the great specialties of Jeju—horsehair, sea mustard, abalone, and dried ox gallstones. Then came the Most Horrendous Famine. People ate every dog. Soon, only water was left over, and our island doesn't have much water. Kim Mandeok had to help. She

217

sold everything she owned and then paid one thousand gold bars to buy rice for the people. When the king heard what she'd done, he offered to repay her, but she refused. He said he would give her *whatever* she desired, but her single request was bigger than the moon. She asked to make a pilgrimage to the mainland to visit sacred sites. The king kept his word, and she became not only the first native-born islander but also the first woman in two centuries to leave Jeju to go to the mainland. It is through Kim Mandeok that the inconceivable became conceivable. She paved the way for your father and so many others to leave Jeju."

"Kim Mandeok was a woman with a generous heart," Jun-bu whispered to Min-lee. "She was selfless and only thought of others. She was, little one, like your own mother."

The children drifted off to sleep. I placed the baby between his sister and brother and moved into my husband's arms. It was too cold to remove all our clothes. He pulled his pants down over his rump. I wiggled out of mine. Our hunger and desperation—and all the death and destruction around us—drove us to do the very thing that created life, that said there would be a future, that reminded us of our own humanity.

Not many hours later, we were awakened by what we'd come to recognize as gunfire. This was not uncommon in those days. The jolting to consciousness. The moment of terror. The instinctual gathering of my children. Jun-bu wrapping his arms around us all. Footsteps echoing through the olles. Shouts and gruff whispers insinuating their way into our room. Followed by silence. Soon, the baby dozed off, and the tension in my other children's bodies melted as they returned to the limpness of slumber. Jun-bu and I lay awake together, listening, until we too fell back asleep.

When dawn broke and Min-lee and I went outside to gather dried dung and haul water, we found Mi-ja standing in the small courtyard in front of my house. She looked better than when I'd seen her eight months earlier. The sheen of her hair caught the morning sun's rays. Her eyes were bright. She'd gained a little weight. Air puffed in clouds from her mouth. She was alone.

"What are you doing here?" I asked, thoroughly surprised but also a little wary. I was relieved to see she was all right, but a part of me felt I had to be careful, knowing the side her husband had taken.

Before she could answer, Min-lee squealed, "Where's Yo-chan?" The two children would turn four in June. They were old enough to remember each other despite our infrequent visits.

Mi-ja smiled at her. "He went with his father to see his grand-parents in Jeju City. It wasn't far out of their way to drop me off. For now"—she turned her gaze to me—"I'm visiting my oldest friend."

I had many questions, but first the required pleasantries. "Have you eaten? Will you spend the night?" Inside, I was wondering what I could feed her, where she would sleep in our small teacher's house, and how her husband would respond.

"No need. They'll be back for me this afternoon." She tilted her head. "Give me a jar. Take me to the village well. Let me help."

Min-lee skipped away to find another jar. Mi-ja put her hands on my cheeks. I couldn't tell if she was taking in all the changes that hardship had brought to my face or was memorizing it to sustain her until the next time we saw each other. Either way, I felt love passing through her fingers and into my flesh. How could I ever have doubted her?

Min-lee returned with a water jar nestled in a basket. Mi-ja put this on her back, then looped an arm through mine. To Min-lee, she said, "Lead the way."

Mi-ja moved with such ease. She had a frail quality to her steps that served as a camouflage for the strength of her body and mind.

I heard a commotion up ahead. I wanted to go back home, but it's the duty of women and girls to fetch water for their families. Bukchon's well was in the square, so that's where we had to go. If my daughter and I were no longer terrified by the sound of gun-shots in the night, I can also say—with sadness—that we were no longer horror-struck by the sight of a dead body, but when we reached the square and found two soldiers, identifiable by their uniforms, lying on stretchers, Mi-ja gasped loudly. Both men had been shot in the chest. Their blood had seeped through their shirts in the shapes of grotesque flowers. About a dozen elders stood over the lifeless forms, arguing.

"We need to take them to the military headquarters in Hamdeok," one of the old men said. "That way we can prove we had nothing to do with this."

"No," another responded indignantly. "All that will show is that we let them die here."

"How did we *let* them die? They were here to protect us from the insurgents—"

Mi-ja had gone as white as seafoam. I took her elbow, and the three of us pushed through the men to the well. We filled our jars and then retreated, hoping to return home quickly.

"If we take them to Hamdeok, the military will retaliate."

"If we *don't* take them, the military will retaliate."

"But we didn't do anything!" another elder shouted, as though his raised voice would bring back the two lives.

Once in the olle, Min-lee babbled happily, as if nothing had happened. "Is Yo-chan good at counting? Has he learned any characters yet? Look how I can count! One, two, three . . ."

But what had become normal to us was horrifying to my old friend, who still looked shaken and hadn't spoken since we'd first reached the square.

"Maybe you should go home," I said. "Trouble could be coming. Jun-bu can walk you."

"No, I'm fine," she mumbled. Then, a little louder, "I agree with the elder who said they should take the bodies to Hamdeok. The military will recognize innocence when they see it."

On the surface, this was how it had been our entire lives. Her lightness; my earthiness. Her cleverness; my simplicity. But things had changed. Now I thought she was acting willfully ignorant. The military was stationed in Hamdeok. Refugees lived in the school yard. People had been killed there. Her husband's position probably protected her, but that shouldn't have made her blind to the realities. Still, I didn't argue with her. I wanted to see her as my friend and not as her husband's wife.

We entered the courtyard before my home. She set down

her water jar and basket, slipped off her shoes, and entered the house. Min-lee and I followed wordlessly behind her. Jun-bu held Kyung-soo. Mi-ja rushed forward, her arms outstretched. "Let me see him." I sensed my husband's hesitancy. The last time we'd all been together hadn't ended well between him and Sang-mun, but then the moment passed and Jun-bu allowed Mi-ja to take the baby. I suggested again that Jun-bu walk her home, but she waved off the idea. All this took only seconds.

"Then I'll go to the school," my husband said. To me, he added, "Our sons are dressed and fed. Granny Cho will be here shortly. I'll come back at lunch." With that, he ducked out the door.

Mi-ja, still holding Kyung-soo, glided across the floor to where Yu-ri was playing with a pile of shells and kissed her on the top of her head. My sister-in-law didn't react, but that was expected. Mi-ja set Kyung-soo on the floor, and in a series of swift movements, she pulled a scarf from her pocket, untied the one that covered Yu-ri's hair, and replaced it with the new one.

"My husband bought this for me," she said. "But from the moment I saw it, I knew it could only be for you. And see? The green and purple pattern looks pretty next to your face."

Yu-ri drew her hand up under her chin to show her pleasure. Next, Mi-ja peered around the room. I couldn't tell if she liked it or not, and she didn't give me a chance to ask, because her eyes came to rest on me. "You look thin," she said, "and I've never seen you so pale."

I was not the kind of woman who sought the reassurances of a mirror, but my fingers went reflexively to my face. Now that I thought about it, I was paler than Mi-ja.

"You're the mother of three children," she chastised me. "You need to be strong for them. Every mother gives the best morsels to her young, but you need to eat too."

I honestly couldn't say if I was hurt because she didn't have sympathy for me or stunned because her life had so changed that she didn't recall the desperation of an empty stomach. "On the day we met—"

Ignoring me, she pointed in the direction of the sea. "Your wet fields are right there. Let's dive."

"Maybe you don't know that the haenyeo have been forbidden—"

She held up her hands in the same innocent gesture she'd used in Vladivostok when we got in trouble. "We aren't diving as haenyeo," she explained to the invisible person who might catch us. "We're just two friends swimming together."

"In January?" I asked, dubious.

She smiled in return. I decided to trust her.

By the time Granny Cho arrived, Mi-ja and I had already changed into clothes we could wear into the sea. Not water clothes, which would mark us as haenyeo, but mere undergarments for me and an old sleeping shirt for Mi-ja. Over these, we wore our day clothes. We were so intent on looking innocent as we strolled toward the shore that we barely paid attention to the procession of elders carrying the two dead soldiers on their stretchers in the direction of Hamdeok. We simply pressed our backs against the rocky wall of the olle and pretended to whisper to each other, as friends do.

We didn't dare enter the bulteok. Instead, in plain view, we stripped off our outer clothes and walked hand in hand into the shallows. We didn't wear our small-eyed goggles, which might also telegraph our intentions. If a villager saw us, he or she might think it strange that we would swim in the frigid water—for fun—at this time of year, but that person might also see two friends who'd enjoyed the sea together since childhood. If a soldier decided to make a fuss, I planned to share what we'd harvested with him.

Since haenyeo had not been allowed to dive, the area just offshore was extra-rich with top shell and conch. These we snatched up and put into small nets. We were not greedy. We could not look greedy if we were caught. We were breaking a rule as tightly enforced as the curfew, but under the sea I felt that what I was doing was completely right. This was *my* world. How could I have let anyone tell me I could not visit it to feed my children? Beside me, I had Mi-ja, who gave me added courage.

Around 11:00, after we'd gathered enough ingredients to make a porridge flavored with sea urchin roe and a stew of top shell and dried sweet potatoes, Mi-ja and I swam back to shore and quickly put on our clothes. We stuffed our nets into our baskets and covered them with pieces of cloth. We were hiding what we'd done but only in a minimal way, sure that any deliberate tricks or ploys would make us seem guiltier if someone stopped us to investigate. As we walked back toward my house, we saw people going about their daily lives with cautious peacefulness. Most of the men had gathered under the village tree, with the smallest children and babies in their care, yet I spotted none of the elders who'd taken the bodies to Hamdeok. Girls, many with younger brothers or sisters strapped to their backs, ran errands for their mothers. We saw women our age and older, bundled up against the cold and sitting on their front steps, doing what haenyeo who are not permitted to dive do—mending nets, sharpening knives and spears, repairing tears in their water clothes or sewing new ones for their daughters. Everyone wanted to be ready when the diving ban was lifted.

The quiet was shattered—without a single shout or rumble of warning—by the sounds of trucks, gunfire, and running footsteps. Instant chaos. It was as if demon gods had descended on us all at once and from all sides. Fathers snatched up babies and toddlers. Brothers grabbed their siblings' hands. Women, who'd been at home, bolted into the olles, searching for their children, grandchildren, and husbands. Mi-ja and I ran too. I had to get home to my children and Yu-ri. Mi-ja stayed at my side. We couldn't be separated. I needed her, but, being away from home, she needed me even more. She was a stranger in Bukchon. No one would take her in if we got separated, because, for all they knew, she could be an insurgent or a spy.

I smelled smoke and heard the crackle of fire before I saw it. When we darted around a corner, burning balls careened toward us. They were rats on fire! Behind them, flames shot up from thatch roofs, with several houses already engulfed. Men in uniforms and carrying torches jogged from house to house, igniting more roofs.

"Come! There's another way!" I shouted.

We turned and sprinted back the way we'd come, pushing through those who were coming toward us. But soldiers were everywhere. We were quickly surrounded.

"Do not move!" one of them shouted at us.

"Do not run!" another yelled.

But my children! I looked frantically in every direction. I had to get home. Another dozen or so people ran into the same trap that had caught Mi-ja and me. Surely every one of us wanted to flee—out of a desire to live or to find our families—but with rifles pointed at us and flames heating our backs, we had to obey. If I was shot in this olle, I could not help my children, and I wouldn't find my husband and my sister-in-law. The haenyeo in me was filled with righteous anger. *I will survive for my family. I will protect my family.*

The soldiers herded us like cattle, pushing us forward. Other soldiers with more captives flowed into our group.

Mi-ja held my upper arm in a fierce grip. "Where are they taking us?" she asked, her voice tremulous.

I had no answer. Mi-ja and I were in the middle of the pack. Bodies pressed against us on every side. We were funneled around another turn and came into the olle with the row of teachers' houses, where I lived. I squeezed through the press of humans until I reached the edge. The gate to my courtyard was pulled open. Yu-ri's tether lay limp and useless. The door to the house was ajar. It seemed like no one was there, but I shouted anyway. "Min-lee. Sung-soo. Granny Cho." No answer. I hoped Granny Cho had taken the children to a secure place—whether to her own home or to the fields. But deep in my heart, I knew that wasn't likely. I was sick with terror, but my blood felt like molten steel. I let myself be pulled back into the crowd.

"The school." I did not recognize the voice that came out of me. "They're taking us to the elementary school."

"Jun-bu—" Mi-ja said.

"Maybe he already has the children."

We were steered through the school's main gates. Husbands, brothers, and fathers were separated and pushed to the left. Many of them still carried babies and small children in their arms. The rest of us, including old men, were shunted to the right. At the point of separation, the ten Bukchon elders, who'd taken the two dead soldiers to Hamdeok in an attempt to avert reprisals, were stretched out like seaweed to dry on the playground. They'd each been shot in the head.

"Keep moving! Keep moving!" soldiers yelled at us.

My limbs bumped into those ahead of me. I was shoved from behind. Mi-ja clung to my arm. There was comfort in having her with me. At the same time, I fought the urge to shake her off. I had to find my children.

I rose on my tiptoes, hoping to see Jun-bu and the children, but the entire population of Bukchon seemed to be here. Having heard of whole villages being wiped out—burned to the ground, all inhabitants killed—I was terrified, thinking what the soldiers might do to us.

We came to an area with another group of soldiers, who had new orders for us. "Sit! Sit! Sit!"

In an undulating wave, we dropped to the ground. Around me people sobbed. Some prayed to goddesses. One old woman chanted a Buddhist sutra. Babies wailed. Older children cried for their mothers. The old men hung their heads. A few people, weak or sick, lay crumpled on the ground, too exhausted to move. Opposite us, across a barren stretch of dirt, sat the men and teenage boys of Bukchon. Above us, black crows circled. Their dinner was coming.

Soldiers stood with their legs spread to anchor themselves to the ground. Their weapons swung back and forth, roaming over us, searching for anyone who might try to bolt. Smoke clogged the air, making it hard to breathe. The whole village, except for the school, seemed to be on fire.

The screeching whine of a bullhorn cut across the school yard, and a man stepped forward. "I am the commander of the Second Regiment of the Third Battalion. If there are among you any family members of the police, the military, or those who work for us, please step forward. You will not be harmed."

Mi-ja fell into this category. "Go," I whispered.

"I won't leave you," she whispered back. "If I stay here, maybe I can help you. When Sang-mun comes, I'll make him gather all of us. He'll save us. I know just how to ask him."

I bit my lip, torn. I doubted he would put himself forward to help me and my family. More important, I doubted Mi-ja had influence over him. But I tried to believe her.

The commander repeated his announcement, adding, "I promise you'll be safely delivered to your families." At that, a few people stood. Policemen and soldiers gathered their relatives and guided them away from whatever was going to happen to the rest of us. Once they were out of sight, the commander addressed us again. "We're looking for the insurgents who killed two of my men in the early morning hours of this day."

My family was asleep when that happened, as were probably all the other families.

"We're also looking for those who've aided the enemy, and informants who've whispered of our movements."

I'd done neither. But . . . More than a year ago, I'd left food in my fields to help that mother and her children who'd been pushed from their mountain home. I'd whispered gossip with members of the collective when we were still allowed to work and with my neighbors in recent months. And I'd heard my husband bitterly condemn what was happening around us.

"If you step forward now and confess, we will be more forgiving," the commander shouted. "If you don't step forward, then your family and friends will suffer."

No one accepted the offer.

"Already we've gone to the villages surrounding Bukchon," he went on. "We have rid Jeju of three hundred people, who claimed to be farmers."

Rid had to mean killed. But again, no one volunteered.

"All right, then." The commander motioned to the soldiers nearest to him. "Take any ten men you choose."

The soldiers waded through the sea of fathers, husbands, brothers, and sons, who sat in the dirt across from us. As the soldiers made their choices, I followed them with my eyes, searching for Jun-bu. The first ten men—mostly in their teens and twenties—were escorted from the playground into the elementary school. On our side of the yard, the mothers, wives, sisters, and daughters of those men began to sob. All I could feel was relief that the soldiers hadn't taken Jun-bu.

Soon enough, Jeju's relentless wind carried screams to our ears as the men were tortured. I was frozen with fear. I prayed to Halmang Jacheongbi, the goddess of love, who is independent, determined, and unafraid of death, but the men were not returned to the yard. Another ten men were gathered and taken inside. Again, their womenfolk keened with grief, followed by wails of agony, then eerie silence.

I met Mi-ja's eyes. I could not fathom what she was thinking.

"If I'm going to die here," I announced, "then it's going to be with my children."

After the next group of men was taken inside, I began to scoot on my bottom through the crowd. Mi-ja came with me.

"Have you seen my children?" I asked those around me every few meters. "Have you seen Granny Cho?"

I was not the only one making inquiries.

During one of our hazardous ventures to the perimeter, we came close—too close—to an ambulance. The back doors were open, and we could hear men inside arguing.

"I fear we're going to need to kill everyone here," rasped a man.

"That's impossible." I recognized the commander's voice and felt a shard of hope. Then he went on. "But if we let them live, how will we provide their necessities—clothes, food, and housing—after burning everything?"

"And we can't have witnesses."

"But it's—what?—a thousand people," the commander asked.

"Not that many, sir. Only a few hundred . . ."

Just then, the ambulance driver opened his door, lurched to the edge of the yard, and vomited. A moment later, the commander and his officers poured out the back of the ambulance. As they strode away in V formation, Mi-ja and I scooted back into the crowd. We didn't tell people what was coming. Panic wouldn't help.

I'd been reduced to an animal wanting to protect its young, acting from instinct as old as the earth. Mi-ja and I approached the front of the gathering, going to the one area we'd most feared. We were getting close to the soldiers with their weapons when Mi-ja choked out in a half whisper, half cry, "Look!"

A few meters ahead of us, through the heads of about a dozen people, I saw Granny Cho and Yu-ri. My daughter, Min-lee, sat safely tucked between them. Yu-ri held Sung-soo, my eldest son, in her lap, while their little brother, Kyung-soo, was asleep on Granny Cho's shoulder. Relief swept through me. My three children were safe. Now all I had to do was make my way to them without attracting attention. And then find my husband.

Mi-ja and I had almost reached them when the commander marched once again to the open space between the two groups.

"We take your men, but you don't care. Let us see what happens when we ask questions of one of your daughters."

He reached out and grabbed the closest person who met his requirements. It was Yu-ri. Sung-soo fell from her lap, stood, and was about to run when Granny Cho grabbed the tail of his tunic and held him back.

Someone shouted, "That girl is dumb! She won't be able to help you!"

I buried my face in my hands, realizing the voice belonged to my husband. He was alive, and he was here.

"Who said that?" the commander demanded. "Who knows this girl? Step forward now! Give your life for hers."

"No," I wailed.

Yu-ri groveled on the ground, terrified. When the commander flicked his wrist and several men strode to her, my husband did the only thing he could. He rose to his feet.

"That girl is my sister. She does not speak. She will not be able to help you."

The commander turned to my husband, his eyes gleaming. "And who are you?"

"I am Yang Jun-bu. I am a teacher in this school."

"Ah! A teacher. The worst of the instigators."

"I am not an instigator."

"Let's see what your sister has to say about that."

The soldiers moved on Yu-ri and began ripping at her clothes. They did not have torture in mind. My husband tried to run forward, but the strong arms of our neighbors held him back, pulling on his legs from where they sat. He screamed in anger. I used the distraction to rise to a crouch and go the final distance to Granny Cho and my children. I swooped my daughter into my lap. I felt Mi-ja drop down next to me. My eyes shot between Yu-ri, my husband, and the commander.

Goddess, any goddess, help us. My sister-in-law was in the hands of the soldiers. I couldn't allow my brain to consider what they might do to my husband, when, seemingly out of nowhere, Mi-ja's husband came running across the yard.

"Commander! Commander!"

Sang-mun carried Yo-chan, dressed to visit his grandparents in a sailor suit.

Sang-mun frantically gestured to the commander. He knew Jun-bu, but he seemed unaware that my husband was right there.

"My wife is here. Let me find her!" he implored. "She's in the protected category!"

He said not a word about Jun-bu. Inside I was sending a message: *Look!*

In my lap, my daughter struggled, wanting to run to Yo-chan.

"Mi-ja!" Sang-mun shouted. "Come!"

I grabbed Mi-ja's arm. "Take my children."

"I can't," she said without a moment's hesitation.

Those two words felt like a knife turning in my belly.

"You must."

"They know I have only one child. And Yo-chan is already with his father."

"These are my babies—"

"I can't."

"They're going to kill us. Please," I begged. "Take them."

"Maybe I can take one . . ."

But what was she thinking? Earlier she'd said she could help us. Taking one child was not helping us!

"Mi-ja!" Sang-mun yelled again.

She hunched her shoulders like a beaten dog.

Before us, Yu-ri had been stripped naked. My sister-in-law, who'd never hurt a soul and didn't understand what was happening, scrambled to her knees. A soldier kicked her down.

"One," Mi-ja repeated. "You will need to choose."

My insides were being ripped apart. Rage and disappointment in Mi-ja. Hope that somehow she'd still be able to help us. And desperation, because how could I possibly make the decision she was demanding of me? Save my daughter, who would one day join me in the sea? Save Sung-soo, my oldest son, who would be able to provide for all of us when we reached the Afterworld? Save Kyung-soo, who was his father's favorite?

"It has to be Sung-soo," I said, "for the rest of us will die here today. Take him. Make sure he performs ancestor worship for us in the years to come."

Next to me, Min-lee whimpered. She was old enough to understand I hadn't chosen her. I would need to comfort her during our final moments together, but before I could begin, Mi-ja said something that soured my blood.

"I'll need to speak to Sang-mun first and see if he agrees."

Speak to him first? See if he agrees?

"I have to protect my son, too, you know" was the last thing she said to me before rising. Rifles and pistols swung in her direction. The movement caught Sang-mun's attention, and he pointed Mi-ja out to the commander, who again flicked his wrist, this time allowing her to pass. Everyone watched as she walked, her beautiful gait slowed even more by terror. With attention momentarily focused on Mi-ja, my husband broke away from the arms that held him and rushed toward his sister. The soldiers seized him, using their strength to subdue his struggles. Behind them by just two meters, Mi-ja whispered into her husband's ear. I watched and waited.

"You want to mount her instead?" the commander asked Jun-bu.

The soldiers now shoved Jun-bu forward. I wanted to cry out, but I had to protect my children too. I looked toward Mi-ja. Sang-mun seemed puzzled, just now taking in what was happening. And what was Mi-ja doing, taking her son into her arms when she should have been pleading mercy for my family?

"People can be made to do all sorts of things," the commander said.

"Perhaps," my husband said, his voice as thin as thread. "But I will not."

I tried to cover my daughter's eyes, but I wasn't fast enough. Another flick of the wrist from the commander, and a soldier lifted and shot his pistol. My husband's head split apart like a melon being broken open with a rock.

And then everything, again, seemed to happen at once. My husband toppled. Sang-mun put his palm to his forehead as he realized what had happened. Granny Cho must have loosened her grip, because Sung-soo suddenly broke loose and ran toward his father. Another shot rang out. Dust skipped up at my son's heels.

"Don't waste the bullets," the commander shouted. "You'll need them later."

So that soldier picked up my boy by an ankle. Sung-soo fought and kicked, until the soldier grabbed hold of his other ankle. Then that man swung my son back like he was going to throw a net into the sea, only it was my son who sailed through the air until his little body came up against the wall of the school. He went completely limp. The soldier lifted what I already knew was dead-weight and repeated the action three more times.

Sang-mun grabbed Mi-ja's arm and began to walk away.

"Mi-ja!" I screamed. "Help us!"

She kept her face turned, so she didn't see what happened when the soldiers decided to stop wasting their time with Yu-ri. She had not been able to speak for all these years, but she screamed when they cut off her breasts. Her agony was my agony. Then she stopped screaming.

Within a matter of seconds, I lost my husband, my son, and my sister-in-law, for whom I'd felt responsibility since my first dive as a haenyeo. And Mi-ja, my closest and oldest friend, had done nothing to help.

I stopped breathing, holding in air longer than could be possible, as if I were in the deepest part of the sea. When I couldn't hold it any longer, I sucked in not the quick death of seawater but instead unforgiving, unrelenting, life-giving air.

And then the shooting began.

The Village of Widows

1949

There are those who say no one survived the Bukchon massacre. Others say that only one person lived. Still others will tell you that four survived. Or you'll see accounts that say 300 people died. Or maybe it was 350, or 480, or 1,000 people . . . Some will tell you about the group of one hundred *or so* survivors, who were herded to Hamdeok, where they ended up being "sacrificed." So, yes, there were those who lived. One grandmother wrapped her grandson in a blanket and tossed him in a ditch. He crawled out under cover of darkness. Some families managed to live through the first night and escape past the wall that marked the ring of fire. And then there were the wives, parents, and children of police officers and soldiers, who were protected in the rice-hulling room until the massacre ended.

I will tell you this. More people died in Bukchon than in any other village during all the years of the 4.3 Incident. Those who survived the three days of torture and killing—whether in the school or in one of the small villages nearby—were forced to help deal with hundreds of bodies. Disposal—some might call it covering up the evidence—turned out to be a logistical problem. We dug a huge pit. Then we dragged the bodies of our neighbors and loved ones to the edge and dumped them in. Only after the soil was replaced were we released. We were told we were the lucky ones.

When I left the school yard with Min-lee and Kyung-soo, we joined a trail of people paralyzed by what we'd witnessed. We had nothing to return to, since every house in Bukchon had been burned, but the need for survival brought us together. We repaired tumbled stone walls. We gathered thatch to put roofs over our heads. In the meantime, we slept in tents provided by the American military. We scavenged through every burned-out house for any foodstuffs that might have survived the flames. We ate what we could of the pigs that had been roasted alive in their sties. I found a cabbage that hadn't already been stolen. Since I didn't have salt, I used ocean water and a few red chili flakes to make kimchee, soaking the mixture in a stone bowl for two nights and then putting it in earthenware jars. I did whatever I could to feed my children, even if that meant sneaking out at night to dive. And that was the only time I could be by myself, for Min-lee—knowing I was willing to give her up in favor of a brother—now stuck to me like an octopus on a rock.

No solace came from knowing I was not alone in my misery. So many men had been killed in Bukchon that it was now called the Village of Widows. I was filled with grief, but my mind raced like a rat trapped in a cage. That rat for me was Mi-ja, and she skittered and scratched back and forth inside my skull. Rightly or wrongly, I held her responsible for what had happened to my family. If she'd stepped forward when we were first herded into the yard, then she could have spoken directly to the people in charge, as the wife of someone who worked with them. Or she could have waited until her husband came and approached him thoughtfully and with purpose. Instead, everything she'd done was to protect herself. And maybe her son and husband, although I could not bring myself to believe they had at any point needed help. What I'd witnessed was the daughter of a Japanese collaborator safeguarding herself first and foremost.

I burned with the knowledge that I'd always known this fact about her but had not given it enough weight. *You aren't aware your clothes are getting wet in the rain.* Day by day, year by year, I'd been deceived by Mi-ja. Now I could see as clearly as the fires that incinerated more villages on the slopes of Mount Halla that Mi-ja's sacrificial act all those years ago to save my mother when the Japanese soldiers came to our dry field was motivated solely by self-preservation. After that, Mother had made sure Mi-ja was fed. She'd given Mi-ja a job. She'd allowed Mi-ja to become a haenyeo in her collective. Most important, Mi-ja's behavior that day in the fields blinded me to the truth about her. I'd seen only what I wanted to see, when what she'd done was designed to benefit her alone.

If there were moments that my mind fought with itself—telling me I must have read her actions and heard her words incorrectly—her absence from my life reminded me every day that I had to be right. If she were innocent, she would have come to see how I was, brought food for the children, or held me in her arms as I cried. She did none of those things. I considered that Sang-mun had been at fault, having more power over her than I imagined. Maybe he'd seen Jun-bu and had chosen to do nothing. Maybe he'd whispered to the commander to murder Jun-bu. Maybe he'd nudged the soldier to kill my little boy. But none of that had happened, which left my soul feeling as though it were drowning in a vat of vinegar.

My grief over the loss of my husband, son, sister-in-law, Granny Cho, and many neighbors and friends was so deep and so terrible that when the black water clothes time of month didn't arrive, I paid no heed. The next month, when it didn't come again, I blamed it on the tragedy and not enough food. When I missed my third month, my dark pit of mourning wouldn't allow me to acknowledge my aching breasts, my deep fatigue, and the terrible nausea that came every time I thought of my husband's head exploding, my son being bashed against the wall, or Yu-ri's howls of terror and pain. The following month—and we were still living like animals—I understood at last that my husband had planted a baby inside me before he died.

At night, when I couldn't shut my eyes for fear of what I'd see on the backs of my lids, I thought of my husband in the Afterworld. Did he know that he'd given me another baby? Was there a way he could protect us? Or would it be better if the thing growing inside me—traumatized by the anguish I'd experienced—was squeezed out of me before it could breathe the bitter and dangerous air of the pitiless world? I was exhausted—from the growing baby, from not sleeping, from living in dread that teams from the military, police, Northwest Young Men's Association, or rebels would come again. I couldn't let my baby be born in the Village of Widows. For days I mulled over what to do. Grandmother

Seolmundae offered many places to hide—caves, lava tubes, the cones of the oreum—but all of them were inside the ring of fire. If we were seen, we would be shot—or worse, I now knew—on the spot. My only hope—and it was a huge risk—was to try to make it back to Hado.

I gathered what food and water I could carry. Beyond that and my two children, I didn't have anything to pack. I didn't say goodbye to anyone. I slipped out in the darkest part of night and creeped barefoot through the village, with food and water strapped to my back, Kyung-soo tied to my breast, and holding Min-lee's hand. I'd stuffed her mouth with straw and tied it shut with a rag so she couldn't make a sound until we were safely out of the village. We walked all night, skirting refugee encampments with their foul odors and pathetic cries. We slept during the day, curled together in the shadow of a rock wall surrounding an abandoned field. As soon as darkness fell, we started again, staying far off the dirt road that circumnavigated the island, hugging the shore, and avoiding anything that warned of human habitation—houses, oil lamps, or open fires. My entire body ached. Kyung-soo slept on my chest, but I now carried Min-lee on my hip in addition to the strain of the pack on my back.

Just when I felt I couldn't go another step, the outline of Hado came into view. Suddenly, my feet flew across stones. I longed to find my father and brother, but my duty was to go straight to my mother-in-law's home. I ducked into the courtyard between the little and big houses.

"Who's there?" came a quavering voice.

I'd lived through so much, yet it hadn't occurred to me that Do-saeng, one of the strongest women I would ever know, could be so cowed by fear.

"It's Young-sook," I whispered.

The front door slowly opened. A hand reached out and pulled me inside. Without the aid of glittering light from the stars, I was unbalanced, waiting for my eyes to adjust. Do-saeng's rough palm stayed closed over my wrist. "Jun-bu? Yu-ri?"

I couldn't bring myself to say the words, but my silence told my mother-in-law the answers. She choked back a sob, and in the darkness I felt her fight her body's impulse to collapse in anguish. She reached up, touched my face, and ran her hands down my body, before caressing Min-lee—her hair, her sturdy little legs, and her size. Then she felt the baby on my chest. When her hands didn't find a little boy, she learned that I'd lost a son too. We stood together like that, two women bound by the deepest sorrow, tears running down our faces, afraid to make a sound in case someone might hear us.

Even with the door and side wall used for ventilation pulled shut, we moved like a pair of ghosts. Do-saeng unfolded a sleeping mat. I lay Min-lee down first, then unwrapped Kyung-soo. With that, the cold air bit through the front of my tunic and pants, which had been soaked through with his urine. Do-saeng undressed me like I was a small child and wiped down my breasts and stomach with a wet cloth. Her hand paused for a moment on my lower belly, where Jun-bu's child was just beginning to make his or her presence known. No words could express the grief and hopefulness that passed between my mother-in-law and me in that moment. Still feeling her way, she drew a shirt over my head and then whispered, "We'll have time for talking later."

I slept for hours. I was aware of things happening around me as dawn broke. Padding feet going in and out of the house. My mother-in-law prying Min-lee away from my side to take her to the latrine or perhaps to fetch water and firewood. Kyung-soo making a couple of squawks, and my being conscious enough to feel hands lift him from the sleeping mat and carry him to a distance far enough away that I would be neither terrified nor wakened. I heard men's voices—low and worried—and knew they belonged to my father and brother.

When my eyes finally blinked open hours upon hours later, I saw Do-saeng sitting cross-legged about a meter away from me. Kyung-soo was crawling nearby, exploring. Min-lee was setting pairs of chopsticks on the rims of bowls that had been put on the floor. The room smelled of steaming millet and the tanginess of well-fermented kimchee.

"You woke up!" I heard in my daughter's voice the fear that I might leave her or give her up. The poor child helped me to a sitting position and handed me one of the bowls. The food smelled delicious—giving off the fragrance of home and safety—but my stomach lurched and twisted.

"After the bombing of Hiroshima," my mother-in-law said, unprompted, "I couldn't accept what had happened. I didn't have my monthly bleeding for six months, but my husband hadn't blessed me with another life to bring into the world. I finally had to acknowledge that he'd died alone, without me or any family to care for him. The worst part was wondering if he died immediately or if he suffered. Like you, I couldn't eat. I couldn't sleep—"

"I thank you for your worry."

Do-saeng smiled at me sadly. *"Fall down eight times, stand up nine.* For me, this saying is less about the dead paving the way for future generations than it is for the women of Jeju. We suffer and suffer and suffer, but we also keep getting up. We keep living. You would not be here if you weren't brave. Now you need to be braver still."

This was her way of telling me that even though nothing had yet happened in Hado, terror could be visited upon this place, whether by the insurgents, the police, or the military.

My mother-in-law continued in a gentle tone. "Young-sook, you need to look forward. You need to eat. You need to help the baby inside you grow. You need to live and thrive. You need to do these things for your children." She hesitated for a moment. Then, "And you need to start preparing in earnest to be the next chief of the collective."

There was a time when I would have wished this above all else. Now, not only was my desire gone but the idea seemed an impossibility. "Chief of the collective? Even if we were allowed to dive, I couldn't do it. I'm not strong enough."

"When the string breaks while working, there is still the rope. When the oars wear out, there is still the tree," she recited. "You feel you can't go on, but you will." She waited for me to respond. When I didn't, she went on. "Have you never wondered the real reason that I allowed you to go out for leaving-home water-work when you were barely married to my son? I wanted to increase the speed of your training to become chief. What if something happened to me?"

But this was opposite to everything I'd believed about her. "I thought you blamed me—"

"Once I would have wanted Yu-ri to become chief," she said, speaking over me, "but we both know she did not have the judgment for it. On that day . . ." Even after all these years, it was hard for her to talk about what happened. "You showed courage, even though it was your first dive. Becoming a haenyeo chief is what your mother planned for you too. She was a good mother to you, and she trusted you. You have been a good mother to your children, but now you must be an even better and stronger mother. *Children are hope and joy.* On land, you will be a mother. In the sea, you can be a grieving widow. Your tears will be added to the oceans of salty tears that wash in great waves across our planet. This I know. If you try to live, you can live on well."

I used to think mothers-in-law are difficult the world over, but on that day I came to understand that they're simply unknowable. Their motives. The things they say. Who they choose for their sons or daughters to marry. Whether they share the way they make kimchee with you or not. But one thing was clear: for all the losses Do-saeng had suffered, which were at least equal to mine but perhaps far worse since she had no son left to care for her when she went to the Afterworld, she'd continued to live. Yet again I was faced with the most basic truth, the one that I'd learned when my mother died: when the end comes, it's over. Plain and simple. There's no turning back the clock, no way to make amends, no way, even, to say goodbye. But I also remembered how my grandmother had said, "Parents exist in children." Jun-bu existed in our unborn baby, in all our children. I now had to follow my mother-in-law's advice and draw strength from the things I'd learned, if only to protect this tiny bit of my husband I carried in my belly. I would live because I could not die.

When July came, the seas, wind, and air went hot and still. My pregnancy was now unmistakable. At six months, my belly ballooned out bigger than for any of my previous pregnancies, even though I had less to eat. And whatever I was lucky enough to put down my throat came right back up. The vomiting I should have had in the early months came full force in the final months and wouldn't leave. It felt like I was on choppy seas but couldn't get off the boat. Not ever. I threw up in the latrine, with the pigs fighting beneath me to get what fell from my mouth. I threw up in the *olles* when I fetched water or gathered dung for the fire. I threw up outside our neighbors' houses and *in* their houses. And still my stomach grew.

"Perhaps this is because you can't go in the sea," my mother-in-law speculated. It was true. I was too awkward to sneak out at night, scurry across the rocks, let alone lug a net heavy with harvest on my back, which meant I could find no refreshing chill of the water, no buoyancy, no quiet.

My father and brother laughed whenever they saw me, and they tried to revive my spirits by gently teasing me. Our neighbors offered home remedies to relieve my discomfort. Kang Gu-ja said I should eat more kimchee; Kang Gu-sun said I should avoid kimchee. One said I should sleep on my left side; the other said I should sleep on my right side. I tried all but one suggestion.

"You need to get married again," Gu-sun said. "You need a man to stir the pot."

"But who would want to marry me and stir my pot filled with another man's child?" I asked, going along with the idea even though I would never do it.

"You could become a little wife—"

"Never!" Jeju, which had never had enough men, now had far fewer. There had to be many women like me—widowed, with children, particularly from the mid-mountain areas—who would need a man to give them security, but not me. "I'm a haenyeo. I can take care of myself and my children. A time will come when I'll be able to dive again."

Beyond all that, I'd loved Jun-bu. He wasn't as replaceable as a broken diving tool. No, I could never become a wife or a little wife.

Anyway, I had a different theory for why I was so big. My muscles, which had always been so strong, had been stretched beyond their limit by what I'd experienced and by what was still happening around me. Since the first of the year, dozens of villages had been burned to the ground, and more of the population had been killed. Among them were many innocents. I felt like I carried all of them inside me. My mother-in-law and I made spirit tablets for Yu-ri, Jun-bu, and Sung-soo, and we bowed to them every day and made offerings, but nothing soothed my discomforts. My back and legs ached constantly. My feet, ankles, face, and fingers swelled. I couldn't get comfortable on my sleeping mat. In fact, it was hard for me to get up from and down onto the floor. Min-lee complained that I would no longer pick her up. I felt damp and sweaty in every crevice. My tears, for the most part, had dried, but there were times I still thought about dying. I could swim out across the path of moon shadows late at night until I wouldn't have the strength to return to shore. I could drink poison, throw myself in the well, or slice open my wrists with my diving knife. I so much wanted to find peace.

In August, the weather changed as winds stirred on the East China Sea and raced unobstructed across the waters until they smacked into Jeju, telling us a typhoon was coming. Do-saeng promised we'd be safe. She said that her husband's great-grandfather had built these houses and that they'd withstood every typhoon that had passed over the island. Still, I was frightened and longed to move inland to my family home. The typhoon that hit us wasn't the worst we'd ever experienced, but we were all so much weaker in our bodies and minds that the impact was just one more remorseless blow. Lashing winds and savage gusts whipped the island. Massive waves roiled over the shore and into houses. Violent rain came in horizontally. Boats were smashed on the rocks. Those few families that had crops saw them drowned or washed away. Once the rain stopped, the churning seas settled, and the sun came out, I saw that Do-saeng was right. Many people had lost their homes or had their roofs ripped off, and a wall of the bulteok had collapsed, but we were unscathed. I helped my neighbors gather the stones from fallen walls and cut thatch for their roofs. All the members of the collective worked together to rebuild our bulteok, bathing enclosures, and the stone wall that created the pool in the shallows we used for catching anchovies.

We received yet another setback in September, when insurgents entered Hado and burned the elementary school. Fortunately, it happened at night and no kids were there. At the beginning of October, the hillsides climbing Grandmother Seolmundae went aflame not with another village being burned but with the fiery colors of the season. This was a reminder to us that whatever was happening between men would pass, and nature would endure with her cycles and beauty. People in Hado were still working hard, seeing what, if anything, they could plant for the winter months, and mending nets and other sea tools in hopes that the haenyeo would be allowed back in the water at some point. This was not a display of optimism. We were just trying to stay alive.

There came a day when I noticed that Do-saeng was being unusually quiet. No joking. No bossing. No nothing. I told myself she was unused to having small children in her life, and their laughter, crying, and demanding ways were heartbreaking reminders of the son and daughter she'd lost. My father and brother came to help me with the children. Only instead of taking them to the village tree, as they once did, they played with them in the courtyard. They said they wanted to keep the family close in case the Ninth Regiment should arrive. When my brother, father, or Do-saeng offered to fetch water from the well, I agreed. What could an immensely pregnant woman—who had about as much swiftness in her as a stranded whale—do to protect herself if military men or insurgents decided they wanted to rape or kill her? For the first time in my life I let others take care of me. Then one day it all became clear.

I was in my ninth month and home alone. My mother-in-law had gone to the five-day market in Sehwa to see what staples she could buy. My father and brother had taken the children to my old family home, so I could nap. But as soon as they left and silence fell over the house, my mind got itchy with images and memories. To distract myself, I swept the courtyard. Then I decided to wash the children's clothes and let them dry in the sun. I tied their garments in a piece of cloth, grabbed the bucket, washboard, and soap, and carefully picked my way across the rocks to the shallow area enclosed by rocks where we could wash clothes and our bodies without being seen. Stepping inside was like entering a bulteok: I never knew who would be there, but I looked forward to hearing the gossip. This time, a lone woman sat in the water, naked, scrubbing an arm and humming to herself. I recognized who she was by the curve of her spine. My insides spasmed protectively around my baby.

"Mi-ja."

Her back stiffened at the sound of my voice. Then she slowly tilted her head to the side to peer at me out of the corner of her eye. "You're as big as everyone says."

That's what she had to say to me?

"What are you doing here?" I choked out.

"My son and I live here now." After a long pause, she added, "In my aunt and uncle's house. Our home in Hamdeok and my in-laws' house in Jeju City were destroyed by the typhoon. My husband has gone to the mainland. He's working in the government. I—"

A second spasm hit me with such ferocity that I doubled over. I dropped my bucket and the other things I'd brought and steadied myself by holding on to the rock wall.

"Are you all right?" Mi-ja asked. "Can I help you?"

She started to rise. Water ran down her breasts and legs. Her skin rippled with goosebumps. As she reached for her clothes, I turned and staggered out of there. Another spasm. I bent at the waist, barely able to walk. I saw Do-saeng standing outside the house, scanning the beach. When she saw me, she let her shopping bags fall and scuttled as fast as a crab over the rocks to me. She put her arm around my midsection and hurried me up to the house. Mi-ja did not follow us, but I was weeping with anger, sadness, and pain.

"How can she be here?"

"They say her husband's house was destroyed in the typhoon," Do-saeng answered, confirming what Mi-ja had just told me.

"But there are other places she could go."

"Hado is her home, and her husband—"

"Was sent to the mainland," I moaned, finishing for her. "Why didn't you tell me she was here?"

"Your father, brother, and I thought it best. We wanted to protect you."

"But how can she be *here*? How can anyone let her live here after what she did?"

Do-saeng set her lips in a grim streak. This was painful for her too.

Another contraction gripped me. I was sure the baby would slip out easily, since I'd never had problems giving birth in the past. I was wrong. This baby had been difficult from the first moment I knew of its presence. Did it not want to come out? Or did *I* not want it to come out? All I know is that the baby took three days to push its way into the world. I threw up the entire time. I cried. I screamed. I thought about all I'd lost. I felt hate for Mi-ja and love for my baby. I felt the loss of Jun-bu, my son, and Yu-ri even as I brought a new life into the world. At last, Do-saeng pulled the baby from between my legs and held it up for me to see. A girl. I named her Joon-lee.

Do-saeng recited the traditional words. *"When a girl is born, there is a party,"* but I was exhausted, my body ached, and I couldn't stop weeping. Joon-lee, worn out from her three-day journey, was too sleepy to take my breast. I flicked my fingernail on the bottom of her foot. She blinked and then closed her eyes again.

Mi-ja came several times to the house, bringing gifts for the baby, packets of tea, and bags of tangerines—all such extravagances. I relied on Do-saeng, my father, and brother to turn her away:

"Young-sook is sleeping."

"Young-sook is nursing the baby."

"Young-sook is not here."

Some of those excuses were real; others were not. If I was home, her voice insinuated itself through the cracks in the walls:

"Tell Young-sook I miss her."

"Tell her I would love to hold her baby girl."

"Tell her I'm happy that such goodness came from such tragedy."

"Tell her I will be her friend forever."

Sometimes I peeked out to watch her walk away. She'd returned to Hado with a limp, which I hadn't seen that day in the bathing enclosure. I heard people speculate about how she'd come to have it and what a shame it was that she'd lost her lovely gait. I didn't care. I told myself that whatever had happened to her she probably deserved. Otherwise, I managed to avoid her. She went to the well early; I had a baby, so Do-saeng took Min-lee to fetch water. Like all little girls, Min-lee ran through the village to do errands for me and began caring for her younger siblings. "In this way, you are learning to be a wife and mother but also an independent woman," I told her. "You need confidence and self-respect to lead your own household one day." But having Min-lee out and about was also a way for me to elude Mi-ja.

At night, after the baby was asleep, Do-saeng and I would go down to the bulteok to talk about the responsibilities that lay ahead for me. "You will sit where I am now," she said. "You will need to listen deeply. You know how we praise Shaman Kim for her eye sensitivity and her ability to read a group's mood? These characteristics you need to nurture in yourself." She made me memorize breeding seasons for different sea creatures. She taught me new ways to tie knots and the importance of keeping the bulteok neat: "A haenyeo does not need mess around her," she explained. "Too much clutter in the dry world has the ability to litter the mind when it needs to be clean and aware in the wet world."

Many of these things I'd already absorbed without knowing it, but to have them planted so directly gave me purpose. Over time, she turned to advice on how to settle an argument, how to calm the natural jealousy and envy that arose when some divers were better than others, and how to stay alert to dangers that might affect the collective.

"You must keep track of the blood cycles for every woman. Sometimes a woman forgets that her time is coming, but you can whisper a reminder. Our local waters are usually safe, but a shark can smell blood from very far away. One shark, a collective can fight off. But a swarm of sharks . . ." She shook her head. Then, "One of the most difficult duties you will have is to tell a woman who has reached fifty-five that it is time for her to go home to her children and grandchildren." When I pointed out that she was nearing that age, she said, "Exactly."

Finally, the diving ban ended. Do-saeng and I returned to the bulteok, and my father and brother came to the house to care for the children. Mi-ja dove with the collective in her part of the village, which was the group she would have joined if my mother hadn't taken her in. So much malevolence and fighting existed all around us that it came as no surprise that the different enclaves in Hado would take sides. The people of Gul-dong, the section of Hado where I lived, stood with me; the people of Sut-dong, where Mi-ja's aunt and uncle had cared for her, now felt sorry for her. This, after all the years of thinking her the daughter of a Japanese collaborator. But these were the times we lived in, where villages, families, and friends were divided, and you couldn't trust anyone. The women's fishing grounds, which had always been assigned, were now ferociously guarded by the women of the two factions. The sea became a place of territorial battles, old resentments, and continued bitterness. Home became my refuge, the place where I could shut out problems and focus love on my children.

———

A year passed and the first anniversary of the massacre at Bukchon arrived. Kyung-soo, not quite two and a half years old, was far too young to hold ancestor worship for his father, aunt, and brother, but his grandfather and uncle helped him. Do-saeng and I cooked for days, and then removed ourselves so the men could have their ceremony. Father guided my son, and together they placed offerings before the three spirit tablets that represented Jun-bu, Yu-ri, and Sung-soo. Neighbors paid their respects, with much weeping.

In a separate ritual, the women in my family and collective went to the field where my mother was buried, since there were no graves for the other people I'd lost. Shaman Kim tapped me with her tassels. I hoped for messages from the dead that would calm my heart, but Jun-bu, Yu-ri, and Sung-soo remained silent. I was terribly disappointed. When the ceremony ended and I rose from my knees and turned to face my neighbors, I saw Mi-ja standing by the entrance to the field. Anger washed through me, flushing my face and constricting my breath. I suspected that her presence was why my loved ones had not sent messages. I walked straight to her.

"You have not allowed me to visit," Mi-ja said as I neared. "You've never given me a chance to explain."

"There's nothing to explain. My husband is dead. My sister-in-law is dead. My firstborn son is dead."

"I was there. I saw." She shook her head as if trying to drive out the memories.

"So was I. You told me you had to protect your own family! You wouldn't even take my children!"

Muted gasps rose up around us. Mi-ja turned red—whether in anger or in humiliation, I couldn't tell. Then her body stiffened, and her eyes went cold.

"Every family on this island has suffered. You are not the only victim."

"You were my friend. We were once closer than sisters."

"What right do you have to accuse me of not saving your family?" she asked. "I'm only a woman—"

"And a haenyeo. You could have been strong. You could have—"

"I ask you again. Who are you to condemn me? Look at your own deeds. Why didn't *you* stop Yu-ri from diving down again—"

I staggered back. This woman, whom I'd loved, and who had—through her own actions and inactions—destroyed my family, was using a secret I'd confided to her against me. And she wasn't done.

"And what about your mother's death? She was the best haenyeo. She went down with you and didn't come back to the surface alive. Your kicking caused the abalone to clamp down on her bitchang. And you admitted you were inept with your knife—"

Do-saeng, who for so long I'd believed saw me in a bad light for all the things I was being accused of now, stepped forward. On either side of her were Gu-ja and Gu-sun. They made a powerful trio.

"This is a day of mourning for our family." Do-saeng's voice held the authority of a chief haenyeo. "Please, Mi-ja, leave our family alone."

Mi-ja held still for a few long moments. Only her eyes moved, slowly passing over the faces of people she'd known from childhood. Then she turned, limped out of the field, and disappeared behind the rocky wall. I did not speak to her again for many years.

Big Eyes

Five months later, on June 25, 1950, the north invaded the south. We called this the 6.25 War. Three days later, Seoul fell. On Jeju, the police demanded that all radios be turned in. I did not want to give them the wedding gift I'd bought for my husband, even though he'd never been able to use it. I considered all the places to hide it. Maybe in the granary. Maybe in the pigsty or the latrine. But those ideas were tossed aside when I saw neighbors not only had their carefully hidden radios seized but were arrested and not heard from again. I turned in the radio, and another piece of my husband disappeared.

I didn't know what was happening elsewhere in the country, but here on Jeju, in addition to the tens of thousands of refugees we had from the mountains still living in camps outside villages, we received more than a hundred thousand refugees from the mainland. Food became even scarcer. Human filth lay everywhere. Diseases spread. And more people were rounded up. Anyone suspected of being a communist—or having ever attended a meeting that might be considered leftist—plus their wives, husbands, brothers, sisters, parents, and grandparents—was detained. It was said over one thousand were now in custody on Jeju, including some from Hado. We never saw them again either.

Those who'd been held in custody since the beginning of the 4.3 Incident were sorted into groups and labeled A, B, C, or D, depending on how dangerous they were perceived to be. On August 30, Jeju's police were instructed to execute by firing squad the people in the C and D categories. The only good news in all this was that most members of the Northwest Young

Men's Association joined the army to fight against the northern regime.

And still we haenyeo rowed, sang, and dove. When we'd first been allowed back into the sea, Do-saeng had paired me with a woman named Kim Yang-jin, who had married, as a widow, into our part of Hado. She was my age. She kept her hair cropped short. She had bowlegs, which gave her an amusing style of walking, but they didn't seem to hinder her underwater.

"As I enter the sea, the Afterlife comes and goes," Do-saeng trilled as we headed to the open waters. "I eat wind instead of rice. I accept the waves as my home."

And we sang back to her. "Ill fate, I do have. Like a ghost underwater, diving in and diving out."

"Here comes a strong surge," Do-saeng called. "Let us ignore it and keep diving."

"Our husbands at home, smoking and drinking, do not know our suffering. Our babies at home, crying for us, do not see our tears."

Far to our right, we spotted a boat filled with haenyeo. First, we had to make sure they weren't from Sut-dong and that Mi-ja wasn't among them. Several women grabbed their spears, knives, or prying tools, holding them low and out of sight in case we had to fight for our territory. Once we saw they weren't our rivals, we rowed closer. I didn't recognize any of the women on the boat. I glanced at my mother-in-law. She was ready for a confrontation, if these were poachers, but also ready to exchange information, if they were friendly.

We pulled up our oars as we neared. The two vessels glided toward each other, rising and falling over the swells, until we were close enough that we had to use our oars as prods to keep the boats from crashing into each other. The chief of the other collective spoke first.

"We're sorry if we're trespassing into your wet fields," she said. "We decided to row away from home for a few days. We didn't want to be followed back to our families."

"Where are you from?" Do-saeng asked.

"We live to the east of Jeju City, near the airport."

They'd rowed more than thirty kilometers to get here. Something or someone had frightened them not just out of their territory but very far from home. The women on the boat, all physically strong, were clearly shaken. None would meet our eyes.

"What happened?" Do-saeng asked.

The other chief didn't respond. Sound travels far across the water, and wind can carry voices even farther. I reached out and grabbed the tip of an oar from the other boat. The women holding that oar grabbed mine. A couple of other paired women did the same until we were close enough to hear low voices but not so close that we'd damage our boats. Now we could share information without fear that it would be heard by the wrong ears onshore.

"We saw them dumping bodies in the sea," the chief's gravelly voice rasped.

"In the sea?" Gu-ja, who was sitting at the back of the boat with her sister, blurted, too loud.

"So many men . . ." The chief shook her head.

Do-saeng asked a practical question. "Will they wash ashore?"

"I don't think so. The tide was going out."

Yet again, there'd be no proof of what had happened. But it also meant—and this was so disconcerting that my stomach flipped—the sea had become like our home latrines. Only instead of the cycle starting from our bottoms, going into pigs' mouths, and then later our eating the meat from their bodies, which would later fall out of our bottoms, it was starting with our own people, who were even now being consumed by fish and other sea creatures, which we would harvest and eat.

"What have you heard?" the chief on the other boat asked.

My mother-in-law then revealed something that she hadn't told me or the collective in the bulteok. "The haenyeo chief in Sehwa says that her cousin saw several hundred people shot near the airport. They've all been buried there."

I began to shake. Why, why, why did my countrymen have to turn on each other? Wasn't the ongoing 4.3 Incident enough? Now we had an invasion and bloody war. To me, it was multiples upon multiples of sorrows and tragedy for families on both sides. We, the survivors, were linked together in an intricate web of grief, pain, and guilt.

Do-saeng offered to let the women spend the night in our bulteok. "But in the morning, you'll need to leave."

Over the following months, I found myself making offerings to different goddesses every day. I counted the ways I was lucky. One, my son was too young to fight. Two, the war never came directly to Jeju. That was it—One and Two—because in every other way these continued to be sad times. Those who'd participated in the uprising on Jeju and had been moved to mainland prisons were executed in case North Korean troops pushed far enough south to free those prisoners to fight by their sides. And right here on Jeju, high on Grandmother Seolmundae, rebels were still holed up, making weaker and weaker raids, unable to recruit new followers or resupply. The police continued to search and destroy camps and kill whomever they suspected of being rebels, even if that included a farmer, his wife, and his children. What I'm saying is that killing happened on both sides here on Jeju and on the Korean mainland. Guilty and innocent died every day across our country. This had been happening for years now. Imagine that for a moment. Day after day. Month after month. Seeing and smelling death, while mothers still tried to feed, clothe, and comfort their children.

Six months into the war, Do-saeng turned fifty-five. Everyone in the bulteok knew what that meant, but I took on the responsibility of saying the words.

"My mother-in-law has led us for twelve years," I said. "We have not had a single death or injury under the sea during her leadership. Now it is time for her to gather algae and seaweed and spend time with her grandchildren."

"Let us have a vote to elect our new chief," Kang Gu-sun proposed. "I nominate my older sister, Gu-ja."

I did my best not to glance in Do-saeng's direction. We'd earlier agreed that someone other than she should nominate me, and she'd been quietly working on my behalf, so this came as a surprise. A betrayal, even.

"Gu-ja has always lived in Hado," Gu-sun went on. "My sister did not marry out or move away. Most important, she has not been touched by grief."

Do-saeng asked for other nominations. None came. She called for a vote, and Gu-ja won unanimously. Every moment was colored by sadness for me in those days, but I think the other haenyeo took my subdued reaction for humility.

"I will always be here to help Gu-ja," Do-saeng said. "The deep-sea fields are gone from me, and I'll miss them."

Later, when we returned home, Do-saeng handed me something wrapped in a piece of faded persimmon cloth. "I had hoped things would go differently today," she confessed. "While it's not the custom, I even bought you a present."

I peeled back the folds of the cloth and found a piece of glass surrounded by black rubber with a strap hanging from the back.

"We've all suffered with our small-eyed goggles," Do-saeng explained. "The metal rims press against our faces, and the sides limit our vision. This is something new. The Japanese call them big eyes. You'll see better, and they'll cause no pain. You may not be the chief, but you're the first haenyeo on Jeju to have big eyes."

I thought of Mi-ja then with anger and confusion, as I often did. I wondered how long it would be before she got big eyes too.

The next time we went to sea, the other haenyeo in the collective were impressed, crowding around to look at my mask. I put it on, jumped in the water, and headed down. Looking through my big eyes, I began to forget the things I'd seen and the people I'd lost. My mind cleared and steadied as I searched for abalone and sea urchins. In just these few seconds, I understood that this mask would also be a way for me to protect myself from feeling anything about the woman who had once been my friend or from letting my emotions escape, if only by accident.

Day 4: 2008

Young-sook wakes up, folds her sleeping mat and blankets, and stacks them out of the way. Her wet suit and face mask hang from hooks, and her flippers lean against the wall, but she won't be diving today. She steps outside and pads around the corner of the little house to the bathroom she added on to the exterior eight years ago. (She wasn't quite the last person in Hado to sell off her pigs and buy a toilet, but she was close.) Once her business is done, she picks flowers from her garden and then heads for the kitchen. Standing at the sink, she trims leaves and thorns. She puts the ends of the stems in a small plastic bag, pours in a little water, and then seals it as best she can with a rubber band. Then she binds the bouquet with wrapping paper and ribbon. One task done.

She takes a sponge bath at her kitchen sink, changes out of her night clothes into black slacks, a flowered blouse, and a pink sweater. Instead of her usual bonnet, she puts on a visor she bought the previous week at the five-day market. She packs her purse with the things she'll need today, carefully cradles the bouquet, and leaves her house. She wishes Do-saeng were here to be a part of this day, but she died fourteen years ago at the age of ninety-five. There'd been other losses as well: Young-sook's father back in 1980 from cancer and her third brother just last year from an aneurysm. She wishes they too could accompany her today.

Young-sook's friends from the collective are already gathered on the main road by the time she arrives. Hado still has more haenyeo than any other village on Jeju, but they're disappearing every day. Today there are only four thousand haenyeo on the island. More than half of them have passed their seventieth birthdays. Many, like Young-sook and the Kang sisters, are well beyond that. No one is following them into the sea. The daughters of Young-sook and others like her traded their wet suits for business suits and hotel uniforms. Now, as Young-sook looks at the aged faces around her, she thinks, *We are but living myths, and soon we will be gone.*

Each woman is dressed in her best. The Kang sisters have gotten new permanents and dye jobs. One woman wears a bright green sweater with blue and white pom-poms decorating the collar. Several wear dresses. Some carry bouquets. Others have baskets hanging from the crooks of their arms. The current head of the collective pins a white chrysanthemum to honor the dead on each woman's lapel or sweater. They've waited sixty years for this day to arrive, and each has chipped in to rent a bus. The women should be subdued—somber even—when they climb aboard, but they're haenyeo. Their voices are loud. They tease each other and make jokes. But some, it's easy to see, weep through their laughter.

The road that skirts the coast is paved. At every village, Young-sook sees people boarding buses—some public, others private—but plenty of cars, vans, and motorcycles also head in the same direction. When the bus passes Bukchon, Young-sook closes her eyes. It hurts her to see the hotels and inns that rise along the shoreline. Next comes Hamdeok. As always, Young-sook revisits her pain, as she thinks of the olles between the two villages and the person she used to meet there. But it's not just that. Both villages are ugly now, as are most across Korea, including her own. The New Village Movement caused that—replacing many stone houses with stucco boxes and all thatch roofs with tiles or corrugated tin. It's supposed to be an improvement, making villages safer from fires and typhoons, but much of the island's charm has diminished.

The driver turns inland, and the bus begins to climb. Horses nibble grass in fields. Pine trees sway in the breeze. Grandmother Seolmundae—dignified yet immutable—watches over everything. Young-sook has now flown on planes, seen the sights in Europe and across Asia, even gone on safari in Africa. The Kang sisters on the other hand ... They're always telling her about this or that museum, park, or attraction they've visited. "Right on our island!" they'll burst out in unison. The Museum of Greek Mythology, the Leonardo da Vinci Science Museum, the African Museum. "Why would I go to those places when I've seen the real thing?" Young-sook has asked indignantly. When the Kang sisters brought up the Jeju Stone Cultural Park, Young-sook waved it off. "I've lived in and among stones my entire life. Why do I need to go to a park to see those?" (This question initially stumped the sisters, until Gu-ja said, "They have things you don't see anymore. Stone houses like we used to live in, stone barrels for holding water, stone grandfather statues . . .") They suggested the Museum of Sex and Health. "I don't want to hear about it!" Young-sook exclaimed, putting her hands over her ears. They tempted her with Chocolate Land and the Chocolate Museum, debating the pros and cons of each. They offered to take her to see natural vistas and lookouts. "Jeju is a UNESCO World Heritage site! Do you want to be the only old woman on Jeju who hasn't seen the sunrise on Seongsan Ilchulbong Oreum peak?"

The bus pulls into a driveway that leads to a complex of buildings and gardens. The main structure stands immense and majestic, like a giant offering bowl. Attendants wave buses forward so they can drop off their passengers. Young-sook and her friends fall silent, awed at last by the grand solemnity of the occasion. They're here for the opening of the Jeju April 3 Peace Park, which will commemorate the years-long massacre and honor the dead. Young-sook's knees tremble. Feeling very old and very weak, she sticks with her friends, but they look just as wobbly as she feels. Again, attendants direct them. The women walk around the side of the museum and along a paved path toward the memorial hall. On the huge lawn between the two structures, row after row of folding chairs have been set up. Thousands of people are expected. Signs with village names mark each section. The women wander the aisles until they find the sign for Hado. Here, they see friends and neighbors. Young-sook's entire family is present, and she's grateful for that, but she sits with the haenyeo anyway.

The program begins with speeches and musical interludes. One speaker comments on the beautiful scenery, and Young-sook agrees. If she keeps her eyes open, that's what she sees: beauty. But she's afraid to close her eyes for all the dark images that are coming back to her. "Who can name a death that was not tragic?" the speaker asks. "Is there a way for us to find meaning in the losses we've suffered? Who can say that one soul has a heavier grievance than another? We were all victims. We need to forgive each other."

Remember? Yes. Forgive? No. Young-sook can't do that. Being allowed to speak the truth? Too, too long in coming. Thirty years ago, back in 1978, a writer named Hyun Ki-young published a story called *Aunt Suni*. Young-sook couldn't read it. She never did learn to read, but she heard it was about what happened in Bukchon. The author was taken to the national spy agency, where he was tortured. He wasn't released until he promised never to write about the 4.3 Incident again. Three years later, the guilt-by-association system finally came to a close. This program had devastated many families across the island. If someone had been accused of being an insurgent or someone had been killed, then the rest of his or her family might not be hired, receive a promotion, or travel abroad. When the program ended, it was said that police stations destroyed their files, but people kept their mouths shut, just in case. Eight years later, in 1989, a group of young people hosted a public commemoration of the events of the 4.3 Incident. Young-sook didn't go, because what difference would it make when the government insisted no proof existed that anything had happened on Jeju? Yet again, silence fell across the island.

A new speaker addresses the assembly. "Every person I know— from old to young—suffers from mental scars," he tells the crowd. "There are those who experienced the massacre directly, those who were witnesses, and those who've heard the stories. We are an island of people suffering from post-traumatic stress syndrome. We have the highest rates of alcoholism, domestic violence, suicide, and divorce in Korea. Women, including haenyeo, are the greatest victims of these problems."

Young-sook pushes the speaker and his statistics out of her head, returning to her own memories. Sixteen years ago, eleven bodies were discovered in the Darangshi Cave, including those of three women and a child. Strewn around them were not rifles or spears but the items people had carried from their homes: clothes, shoes, spoons, chopsticks, a pan, a pair of scissors, a chamber pot, and some farming tools. They'd sought refuge in the cave but were discovered by the Ninth Regiment. Soldiers heaped grass at the entrance, lit it on fire, and sealed the cave. Those inside suffocated. Here, at last, was the tangible proof the government could no longer deny, except President Roh Tae-woo ordered the cave to be once again closed. The evidence was literally covered up.

Then, in 1995, the island's provincial council published a list—the first of its kind—with the names of 14,125 victims. The list was far from complete, however. Jun-bu, Yu-ri, and Sung-soo were not among the thousands, but Young-sook had considered it too dangerous to step forward. Then came the fiftieth anniversary, in 1998. More memorial services were held, as well as an art festival and religious activities, all tied to 4.3. The following year, the Republic of Korea's new president, Kim Dae-jung, promised that the government would give 3 billion won to build a memorial park. "We cannot carry forward the twentieth-century incident into the twenty-first century" became the slogan. At the end of that year, the National Assembly passed a Special Law for the Investigation of the Jeju 4.3 Incident and Honoring Victims. The investigation committee planned to interview survivors on Jeju, as well as those who'd moved to the mainland, Japan, and the United States. Materials—such as police and military reports and photographs long hidden in institutions and archives in Korea and the United States—were found and examined. But only in 2000 was speaking about the massacre finally decriminalized. Investigators came to Young-sook several times, but she refused to see them. They sought out her children and grandchildren, who approached her with the same message. "It is the duty of the next generation to bring comfort to victimized souls," her grandson said. "We'll do that, Granny, but only you can tell your story. It's time." But it wasn't time for her. Even now, she's too accustomed to her anger and sorrow to change.

A new speaker steps to the podium. "Three years ago, the central government announced its intention to declare Jeju an Island of World Peace. And here we are." He pauses to let the applause die down. "In that same year, Hagui, which after the incident was divided into two separate villages, declared forgiveness. There would no longer be a village for victims and one for perpetrators. There would be no more labels of reds and anti-communists. Together, the people petitioned to reunite the two villages. It would once again be called Hagui. They built a shrine of reconciliation, with three stone memorials: one to remember those who suffered during Japanese colonialism, one for the brave sons who died in the Korean War, and one for the hundreds of people on both sides who died during the Four-Three Incident."

Nausea tumbles Young-sook's stomach. A monument will never change how she *feels*. It's unfair that victims should have to forgive those who raped, tortured, and killed, or burned villages to the ground. On an Island of World Peace, shouldn't those who inflicted terrible harm on others be forced to confess and atone, and not make widows and mothers pay for stone monuments?

"We still have many questions we must ask ourselves," the speaker continues. "Was this tragedy a riot that got out of hand? Was it a rebellion, a revolt, or an anti-American struggle? Or do we say it was a democratic movement, a struggle for freedom, or a mass heroic uprising that showed the independent spirit that has flowed in the blood of the people of this island since the Tamna Kingdom?"

He receives a long round of applause, for all native-born Jeju people cherish that self-reliant part of themselves that came from the Tamna.

"Should we blame the Americans?" he asks. "Their colonels, captains, and generals were here. Their soldiers saw what was happening. Even if they didn't directly kill anyone, thousands of deaths occurred under their watch, but they do not take responsibility. And not once did they intervene to stop the bloodshed. Or do we accept that they were trying to suppress the very real threat of communism at the early stages of what would become the Cold War? Was the Four-Three Incident America's first Vietnam? Or was it a fight for people who craved reunification of north and south and wanted to have a say in what happened in our country, without interference or influence from a foreign power?"

At last, the speeches end. Village by village, people are led past headstones that commemorate the victims whose bodies were never recovered. Young-sook pauses for a moment. She remembers when the mass grave in Bukchon was dug up and people came to tell her that her husband, sister-in-law, and son had been identified. She and her other children were finally able to bury them in a propitious site chosen by the geomancer. Jun-bu, Yu-ri, and Sung-soo now forever lie side by side, and Young-sook visits their grave site daily. Others are not so fortunate.

She gives herself a small shake, looks around, hurries to catch up to the rest of the Hado group, and together they enter the memorial hall. Here, on a long, curved marble wall, are engraved the names of at least thirty thousand dead. Offerings of flowers, candles, and small bottles of liquor are heaped on a ledge that serves as an altar and runs the entire length of the room. Young-sook splits off from her haenyeo friends when her family approaches. She has enough flowers and offerings for them to present as a family, but she's pleased that they've each brought something too. Min-lee, Young-sook's oldest daughter, holds a bouquet of flowers wrapped in cellophane. Kyung-soo—paunchy and dull, Young-sook must admit—carries a bottle of rice wine for his father, a bag of dried squid for Yu-ri, and a bowl of cooked white rice for his older brother. These were things Young-sook's husband, sister-in-law, and son liked six decades ago, but have their tastes changed in the Afterworld?

Min-lee's eyes are swollen from crying. Young-sook takes her daughter's arm. "It will be all right," she says. "We're together."

The hall is packed, and people push and shove, eager to find the names of those they lost. People yell at each other to make room or get out of the way. Min-lee doesn't shy away from using an elbow to jab those blocking their passage. They reach the wall. The rest of the family is right behind them. If this weren't so important, Young-sook would feel desperate to escape the crush of bodies, the lack of oxygen, her sense of claustrophobia. Edging along the wall, Min-lee searches for the Bukchon section. Some villages have only a handful of victims. Others list name after name in row after row. People around them shout their discoveries. Others wail laments.

"Bukchon!" Min-lee cries. "Let's find Father first." Min-lee is sixty-three now. She was three and a half the day her father, brother, and aunt died. She's strong by any measure, but she's now so pale that Young-sook worries her daughter might faint. "Mother! Here!" Min-lee exclaims, her index finger resting on the engraved marble. The family parts to let Young-sook through. She reaches up to meet the spot her daughter has marked. Her fingers graze over the etched characters. *Yang Jun-bu.*

"Look, here are Auntie Yu-ri and First Brother." Min-lee is crying hard now, and her children stare at her in concern.

Young-sook feels strangely calm. She reaches into her bag and pulls out a piece of paper and a nub of charcoal. It's been decades since she made a rubbing, but she hasn't forgotten what to do. She places the paper over the names of those she lost and rubs the charcoal back and forth. She's about to tuck the paper inside her blouse next to her heart when she feels the eerie chill of people—strangers—staring at her. Suddenly self-conscious, she glances around. Her children and grandchildren are occupied making their offerings. But as they bow together, she sees that foreign family . . .

She sends a message with her face. *Leave me alone.* Then, without saying a word to Min-lee or the others, she dips back into the crowd, loses herself in the sea of people as she makes her way to the exit, and then hobbles down a path. She comes to a platform set above something that looks a bit like a bulteok with a low wall built of stones. Looking down into it she finds a bronze statue of a woman hovering protectively around her baby. A length of white cloth is draped around her legs and pulled to the side of the pit. Young-sook recognizes the image from all the memorials for lost or dead haenyeo she's attended over the years. None of those ceremonies was more important to her than the one for her mother, and she remembers the way Shaman Kim tossed the long cloth into the water to bring Young-sook's mother's soul back to shore. Young-sook is so lost in her pain—with so many deaths and tragedies on her mind—that she startles when she hears a voice speaking the Jeju dialect in an accent tinged by Southern California and the luxury and benefits of limitless freedoms.

"My mom asked me to follow you. She wants me to make sure you're all right."

It's that girl. Clara. She's dressed suitably, for a change, in a dress, but of course she still has wires leading to her ears, feeding her music.

PART IV

Blame

1961

Years of Secrecy

February 1961

Jeju had always had a surplus of women, but with so many men and boys killed—with entire posterity lines wiped out—the imbalance was even greater. For the last eleven years, we women had forced ourselves to do even more than we had in the past. Those of us who ran our own households learned we could gather more wealth without husbands to drink or gamble it away. We contributed funds to rebuild schools and other village structures. We donated money to repair old roads and construct new ones. None of this would have been possible if we hadn't been completely free to dive again. And to dive, we needed to remain safe, which was why on the second day of the second lunar month we washed our minds of all trivialities, and then met Shaman Kim for the annual ceremony to Welcome the Goddess.

We gathered on the beach, totally exposed, and the back of my neck prickled. What we were doing was against the law. Although the Japanese colonists had sought to ban Shamanism, the new leader of our country decided to end it once and for all. President Park Chung-hee had come to power during a military coup, and he approached his new job in the same manner. There were more kidnappings and instances of torture, disappearances, and deaths. He ordered all shrines to be dismantled. Shaman Kim had been forced to break her drums and burn her tassels. Things that were difficult to destroy—her cymbals and gongs—were confiscated. This came at a time when we all needed—*wanted*—to be cleansed of the blame and guilt we felt for being survivors. Some turned to the Catholic missionaries for help. Others sought comfort in Buddhism and Confucianism. But even though Shamanism had been outlawed, Shaman Kim, and so many like her across the island, did not abandon us.

We typically took precautions and hid our activities as best we could, but this annual event was too large to be held in private. Not just my collective but all the collectives from the different villages that made up Hado had come together. Unlike the Jamsu rite, which was for haenyeo alone and honored the Dragon King and Queen of the Sea, this ceremony included fishermen. The women wore padded jackets, scarves, and gloves. The handful of men stamped their feet, seeking warmth in movement.

"I call on all the gods and goddesses of Jeju," Shaman Kim beckoned. "We welcome Yeongdeung, the goddess of the wind. We welcome all ancestors and spirits who accompany her. Enjoy the peach and camellia that are blooming. Embrace the beauty of our island. Sow the seeds of the five grains on our land. Sow seeds into the sea, which will grow into underwater crops."

Offerings of fruit, bowls of rice, dried fish and squid, bottles of homemade liquor, and hard-boiled eggs spilled across the makeshift altar. Every woman and girl from our collective was here. Kang Gu-ja sat in a prominent spot. Her sister, Gu-sun, sat nearby, with her sixteen-year-old daughter, Wan-soon, beside her. Min-lee and Wan-soon had become friends when we moved back to Hado. Min-lee tended toward melancholy, for which I blamed myself, so to see the two girls giggling together was wonderful. Do-saeng and Joon-lee, who would turn twelve in the fall, sat together. Yang-jin, my diving partner, was next to me. At the far end of the gathering, as far as she could be from me, Mi-ja sat with her collective. Everyone had bathed and wore clean clothes, yet she somehow managed to look fresher than the rest of us.

Shaman Kim swirled in her hanbok. Her helpers had made a new drum from a gourd, since only the sounds from this instrument can reach the ears of spirits, and hammered flat a cooking vessel to use as a gong to waken the spirits of the wind and waters. Shaman Kim rang a bell, which she'd hidden during the raid of her home, to rouse the spirits who live on the earth. Her tassels were now made from shredded pieces of persimmon cloth. We feared for her, because if she was caught with any of these things, she would be arrested.

"I pray to the goddess of the wind to look after the haenyeo," Shaman Kim implored. "Don't let a tewak drift. Don't let tools break. Don't let a bitchang get stuck or let an octopus pin a haenyeo's arms."

We knelt and prayed. We bowed. Shaman Kim spat water to keep evil spirits at bay. She commented on the weather and tides, cajoling the goddess of the wind to be gentle in the coming months. "Let our haenyeo be safe all season. Prevent our fishermen from being lost to a typhoon, cyclone, or tempestuous seas."

When the ceremony ended, we ate some of the offerings and then threw the rest of the food into the sea for all water and wind goddesses and gods to enjoy in hopes they would show us favor. Then it was time for dancing. Min-lee and Wan-soon held hands as they swayed. They looked free and happy. Last year, when Min-lee turned fifteen, I'd given her a tewak made of Styrofoam. Wan-soon was given one as well. Gu-sun and I had taught our daughters to dive, but their destinies lay elsewhere. I'd thought Jun-bu crazy when he'd said he wanted all our children to be educated, but now I did everything possible to respect his wishes. *If you plant red beans, then you will harvest red beans.* Min-lee was in high school, Kyung-soo in middle school, and Joon-lee in elementary school. My two eldest children were only so-so students, but Joon-lee was truly her father's daughter. She was smart, diligent, and studious. Each year, her teachers proclaimed her the smartest person—boy or girl—in class. Gu-sun had also saved money to send Wan-soon, her youngest child, to school, so our daughters only dove with us if their free days corresponded with the right tides. Since they worked so little, Gu-sun and I had told them they could use their earnings to buy school supplies, but they mostly treated themselves with ribbons for their hair or candy bars.

For the next two weeks, while the goddess of the wind was on Jeju, we'd remain idle. We wouldn't dive and fishermen wouldn't board their boats or rafts, since the winds the goddess brought with her were particularly fierce and fickle. No other chores could be done either. It was said that if you made soy sauce at this time, insects would hatch in it. If you repaired your roof, it would leak. If you sowed grains, a drought would come. Hence, this was a time to visit neighbors, talk long into the night, and share meals and stories.

———

"Mother, come see!" Joon-lee called.

I peeked out the door as she came into the courtyard with the water she'd drawn from the village well. Through the open gate, I saw men filing past, one right after the other like a string of fish.

"Hurry here!" I cried, fearful. Joon-lee left the jar on the ground and ran to my side. I pushed her protectively behind me. "Where's your sister?" I asked.

Before Joon-lee could answer, Min-lee came through the gate. She set down her water and jogged over to us. "They're strangers," she whispered. Of course they were. They wore black trousers with sharp creases. Their shoes were made of leather. Their jackets were unlike any I'd seen before, making them look puffy and awkward. Some of them were Korean. They had to be from the mainland. But there were also Japanese and white men. I automatically took them to be Americans, because they were tall and sandy-haired. Not one of them wore a uniform. They weren't armed either, as far as I could tell. At least half of them wore glasses. My initial anxiety was replaced by curiosity. The last man strode past. Friends and neighbors, chattering, pointing, and craning their necks to get a better glimpse, trailed behind him.

"I want to see who they are," Joon-lee said, grabbing my hand. She was too young to understand terror, but for some reason I wasn't afraid, and neither was Min-lee. I even called to Do-saeng to join us.

We stepped into the olle and were swept along the shore road.

"Who are they?" Joon-lee asked.

Her older sister asked the more important question. "What do they want?"

More women came out of their houses. I saw my diving partner, Yang-jin, up ahead, and we rushed to catch up to her.

"Are they going to the village square?" I asked.

"Maybe they have business with the men," she replied.

But we didn't turn inland toward the village square. Instead, we spilled onto the beach. Once there, I saw that there weren't so many of us after all. Maybe about thirty women and children. The strangers turned to us. With their backs to the sea, the frigid wind ruffled their hair and flapped through their trousers. A small, compact man stepped forward. He spoke in standard Korean, but we were able to understand him.

"My name is Dr. Park. I'm a scientist." He motioned to the men around him. "We're all scientists. Some of us are from the mainland, but we also have scientists from around the world. We're here to study the haenyeo. We've just spent two weeks in a village near Busan, where many haenyeo go for itinerant work. Now we've come to the native home of the haenyeo. We hope you will help us."

We had six haenyeo chiefs—one for each of the sections that made up Hado—but not one of them was with us. I nudged my mother-in-law. "You're the highest ranked among us," I said. "You must speak to them."

She set her jaw, determined, and then stepped out of the crowd and crossed halfway to the men. "I am Yang Do-saeng. I'm the former chief of the Sut-dong collective. I'm listening."

"We understand you have just greeted the goddess of the wind and will be free from activity for the next two weeks—"

"A woman is never free from activity," she said.

Dr. Park smiled at her comment but chose not to address it. "You may not know this, but the cold-water stress that the haenyeo endure is greater than for any other human group in the world."

This was met by indifferent looks. We didn't know about "other human groups" or "cold-water stress." We only had our own experiences. When Mi-ja and I had dived off Vladivostok in winter, we didn't see any people in the water with us apart from other haenyeo. We considered our ability a gift that allowed us to help our families.

"We're looking for twenty volunteers," he went on. "We would like ten haenyeo and ten nondivers."

"What are they volunteering for?" Do-saeng asked.

"We'll be testing women in and out of the water," Dr. Park answered.

271

"We don't enter the sea when the goddess of the wind is here," Do-saeng said.

"You don't enter the sea, or you don't harvest?" he inquired. "We aren't asking you to harvest anything. That's why we came now—when you aren't busy. If you aren't harvesting, the goddess won't be angry."

But what did he know about our goddess or how strong she was? Still, he had a point. No one had ever said it was forbidden to enter the water during this time.

"We'll be taking your temperatures," he continued, so sure of himself. "We'll—"

"Can I help?" Joon-lee chirped.

People on both sides laughed. Those who knew Joon-lee expected something like this from her, while the strangers clearly thought she was cute. She ran to her grandmother. Dr. Park squatted so he was face-to-face with her. "We're studying the basal metabolic rate of the haenyeo compared to nondiving women. We'll come in each of the four seasons. Is your mother a diver?" When she nodded, he continued. "We're going to set up a lab on this beach. We'll take women's temperatures before and after they go in the water. We want to study their shiver index. We're wondering if a breath-hold diver's ability to withstand cold is genetic or a learned adaptation. We—"

Joon-lee turned and stared at me with her soot-black eyes. "Mother, you have to do this. Granny too! And you too, Big Sister." She swung back to Dr. Park. "That's three. Oh, and Kim Yang-jin will do it too, won't you?" When my diving partner nodded, Joon-lee gave Dr. Park a resolute look. "I'll help you find the others. We don't have many households without haenyeo, but there's a widow who grinds and sells millet, a woman who makes charcoal, and another who's known for her weaving." She cocked her head. "When do you want them to start?" And then she took in the other men's faces. "Where are you going to put your lab?"

Lab. I didn't know what that was. That's how far my daughter had come already.

Finding volunteers was not easy, though. These were still the years of secrecy, and we had reasons to be cautious. On September 21, 1954—after seven years and six months—the last of the insurgents were caught or killed, and the shoot-on-sight order for Mount Halla was finally lifted. The 4.3 Incident—although how something that lasted more than seven years could qualify as an "incident" didn't make sense to me—was officially over. We pieced together information in a variety of ways. What we learned was staggering. Three hundred villages had been burned or razed, forty thousand homes destroyed, and so many people killed that not one family on Jeju had escaped untouched. On the mainland, Koreans were told not to believe stories about the massacre. The people of Jeju had always been suspicious of outsiders. Now we were even more so. As a result, our island had become more closed off. It was as if Jeju had once again turned into an island of exiles, all of us wandering souls.

Reminders of what had happened were everywhere. The man who walked on crutches because his knee had been shattered by a pickax. The girl, with burns on most of her body, who grew to marriageable age but received no proposals. The young man who'd survived months of torture roamed the olles, his hair uncut, his face unshaven, his clothes uncleaned, and his eyes unfocused. We all suffered from memories. Nor could any of us forget the throat-choking smell of blood or the crows that had swarmed in great clouds over the dead. These things haunted us in our dreams and during every waking moment. But if someone was foolish enough to speak a single word of sadness or was caught shedding a tear over the death of a loved one, then he or she would be arrested.

The list of restrictions was long, but none were more terrifying for me than those that limited access to education. No matter how bad things got, I had to do my best to make sure Jun-bu's dreams for our children became real. This meant that while the idea of total strangers poking and prodding me had no appeal, I agreed to participate—and made my older daughter and mother-in-law participate too—because Joon-lee was interested in the project, and those men might help her in some way I couldn't conceive.

We were told to eat a light supper, wear our diving clothes under our land clothes, and report to the laboratory the next morning without having eaten breakfast. Wan-soon and Gu-sun picked up my mother-in-law, two daughters, and me. The six of us walked down to the beach, where two tents had been set up. Between my daughter's efforts and the team's inquiries, they'd managed to find ten haenyeo—including the Kang sisters and my diving partner, Yang-jin—and ten women who did not work in the sea.

Dr. Park introduced us to the others on his team: Dr. Lee, Dr. Bok, Dr. Jones, and so on. Then he told us, "You will begin the day with thirty minutes of rest."

Do-saeng and I exchanged glances. Rest? What an idea. But that was exactly what happened. We were escorted into the first tent, where we lay down on cots. Joon-lee stayed at my side, but her eyes darted from cot to cot, table to table, man to man. Although I could understand their Korean words, much of the meaning was lost on me.

"I'm using a nine-liter Collins spirometer to measure oxygen and convert that to kilocalories to establish a basal metabolism rate as a percent deviation from the DuBois standard," Dr. Lee intoned, speaking into a tape recorder.

It sounded like gibberish, but Joon-lee seemed to soak up every word and action.

The next step was conducted by Dr. Bok, who put a glass tube in my mouth. He reported that I had a normal temperature of 37 degrees Centigrade and 98.6 degrees Fahrenheit. Across the aisle, my older daughter giggled when one of the white doctors placed something on her chest that had tubes running up to his ears. I did not like that one bit, nor did I like the idea that he would do the same to me. I was about to take my girls and walk out of there when Dr. Park cleared his throat.

"Yesterday I told you something you must know already. You have a greater tolerance for hypothermia than any other humans on the planet. In Australia, aborigines walk naked, even in winter, but their temperatures rarely fall below thirty-five degrees Centigrade. Men and women who swim across wide channels lose a lot of body warmth, but even they rarely drop below thirty-four point four degrees Centigrade. Gaspé fishermen and British fish filleters spend their days with their hands immersed in cold salt water, but it is only their hands. And then there are Eskimos. Their temperatures stay within the normal range. We believe that's because they have a diet high in protein, and they wear so many clothes."

The way he spoke was strange, but his animated bearing was even more foreign. Still, I wasn't a fool, and I suspected he was using his energetic manner to distract us from what the other doctors were doing to us. One of them put a band around my upper arm and squeezed a rubber ball, which caused the band to swell and press into my flesh. What happened next was so swift that none of us had the time to process it fully. Gu-ja had the same type of band around her arm, but the scientists didn't like what they were seeing. "Her blood pressure is too high to qualify her to be in the study," I overheard one of the men say. Before anyone could object, our collective's chief was escorted from the tent.

Dr. Park didn't acknowledge what to me seemed stunning. He just kept talking. "We want to see how long you can stay in the water and what that immersion does to your body temperatures. We hypothesize that your shiver index is a latent human adaptation to severe hypothermia that is rarely, if ever, experienced in modern man or, in this case, woman."

Of course, we had no idea what he was talking about.

"Could this ability have something to do with your thyroid function?" he asked, as though we might actually know the answer. "Does something in your endocrine system allow you to perform in the cold as well as small animals do on land and in water? Could you be like the Weddell seal that—"

"Tell that man to stop touching my daughter!" Gu-sun sat up on her cot and glowered so fiercely at a white doctor that he raised his hands and backed away from Wan-soon. "You need to tell us exactly what you're doing or we're leaving."

Dr. Park smiled. "There's nothing to be afraid of. You and the others here are helping to create science—"

"Are you going to answer my question?" Gu-sun asked as she swung her legs off the cot. A few others did as well. Haenyeo or non-haenyeo, we didn't like these men touching our daughters.

Dr. Park clasped his hands together. "I don't think you understand. We respect what you do. You're famous!"

"Famous to whom?" Gu-sun asked.

He ignored the question and went on. "All we're asking is that you go in the water, so we can measure your shiver threshold."

"Shiver threshold," Gu-sun echoed. She snorted and jutted her chin, but I could tell she didn't plan on leaving. By staying in the study, she had something over her sister, who'd been dismissed. None of this was to say *I* was comfortable. My desire to protect myself and Min-lee fought against my desire to help my younger daughter.

"Is there a way you can do the tests without . . ." I was a widow and hadn't been touched by a man since the Bukchon massacre.

Dr. Park's eyes widened in understanding, and his enthusiasm disappeared. "We're doctors and scientists," he said stiffly. "You are our subjects. We don't look at you like that."

But every man looked at women like that.

"And even if we did, we have this little girl here," he added. "We need to protect her from anything improper. Her presence protects you too."

Joon-lee blushed, but it was obvious she enjoyed being singled out.

"She helped bring you here," he said. "Let's see how else she can help."

With that, the men went back to conducting their tests. They didn't let Joon-lee handle a single instrument, but they used her to explain to us—in words we could understand—what they were doing. It turned out our average age was thirty-nine years. We averaged 131 centimeters in height and fifty-one kilos in weight. (Or, as one of the American scientists put it, "A little over fifty-one inches tall and one hundred and twelve pounds.") About fifteen minutes later, the doctors asked us to remove our land clothes. The haenyeo among us had never been shy about showing our bodies. We'd all seen each other naked, and we'd lived for generations with the stigma of nakedness. Still, despite Dr. Park's sentiments about the team being doctors and scientists, it was embarrassing to step out of our trousers and jackets in front of them. The women who weren't divers were the most uncomfortable. They'd probably never worn so few clothes in front of a man apart from their own husbands, and it proved too much for one woman, who decided to drop out of the study. Now the haenyeo and non-haenyeo were equal again, with nine women on each team.

This was the coldest time of year, which was why we chose this period to Welcome the Goddess. Even so, a haenyeo is accustomed to freezing temperatures, while the nondiving women squealed and yipped as they tiptoed across the rocks, the bitter wind raising goosebumps and turning their skin blue. Joon-lee sat on the sand and hugged her knees to her chest to keep warm. The rest of us entered the water and paddled about ten meters offshore. Do-saeng and I dove down together. We knew this area well. The water wasn't too deep, and light filtered to the ocean floor. Spring was coming, and what happens on land—leaves sprouting and flowers budding—also happens in the sea. Seaweed grows with the warmth of the sun. Sea creatures mate and have babies. When I came up for breath, I swam to Gu-sun to ask her to tell Gu-ja, her sister and our chief, about an area I'd spotted with many sea urchins we'd be able to harvest in the coming weeks.

Within five minutes, the nondiving women went to shore. As they disappeared into the tent, I headed back down. I managed to stay in the water for a half hour—the same amount of time as when Mi-ja and I used to dive in Vladivostok. The scientists wanted to see shivering. This I could give them.

When I returned to the tent, the nondiving women were on their cots, having a repeat of the earlier tests. Joon-lee went from cot to cot, talking to each woman, trying through small talk to distract her from her various levels of discomfort—the cold, the men, the way they spoke, the instruments, the foreignness of it all.

Dr. Park approached me. "I hope you'll permit me to do your tests."

I nodded, and he slipped the glass tube into my mouth. I tried to assess him without being too obvious about it. He seemed young, but maybe that was because he hadn't spent a life outdoors. His hands were soft and surprisingly white. As had happened earlier, he spoke into a recording device. Again, I understood very little of what he said.

"Today the water was ten degrees Centigrade, fifty degrees Fahrenheit. Subject Six remained submerged for thirty-three minutes. Her postdive skin temperature, five minutes from exiting the water, has dropped to twenty-seven degrees Centigrade, eighty point six degrees Fahrenheit, while her oral temperature is thirty-two point five Centigrade, ninety point five Fahrenheit." He met my eyes. "That is a remarkable level of hypothermia. Now let's see how long it takes you to return to normal."

He then moved on to Do-saeng. A different doctor took my temperature every five minutes. I returned to "normal" after a half hour. "Would you go into the sea again at this point?" he asked.

"Of course," I answered, surprised he would ask such a stupid question.

"Remarkable."

Do-saeng met my eyes. *Remarkable.* This was beyond our comprehension.

———

The next day, the doctors performed the same tests. On the third day, they asked Joon-lee to bring towels and blankets to us when we came out of the ocean. By the fourth day, we'd grown more accepting of their peculiar ways. And they were so easy to tease. We repeated the words they used in singsong voices, making them laugh. Min-lee and Wan-soon were the biggest instigators, and the doctors loved them. On the morning of the fifth day, our little group was just about to enter the tent when I spotted Mi-ja standing on the seawall. Her son straddled a bicycle next to her. By now everyone in the village knew about the science experiment, and many people had come to the wall to gawk and point. I could imagine Mi-ja wanting to be a part of the study. Maybe she even felt jealous that I had this opportunity. Surely this was Mi-ja's reason, because by bringing Yo-chan and his bicycle she was showing off what she could give her son.

Joon-lee interrupted my thoughts by pulling on my sleeve and exclaiming, "Look, Mother! Yo-chan has a bicycle! Can I get one too?"

"I don't think so."

"But I want to learn how to ride—"

"That's not something girls do."

"Please, Mother, please. Yo-chan has one. Shouldn't we have at least one for our family?"

Her excitement disturbed me. First, of course my daughter would know Yo-chan and his mother, but that didn't mean I liked it. Second, we were only here because I'd wanted to give Joon-lee an opportunity, but now it seemed she'd completely forgotten about the study in favor of the bike's shiny metal.

Up on the seawall, Mi-ja abruptly turned and limped away, but the boy remained where he was, staring in our direction. I realized he wasn't looking at me but at Min-lee and Wan-soon. The three of them attended the same school and had many of the same classes together. All three were sixteen, old enough to get married, old enough to get in trouble. I nudged the girls' shoulders to make them move along.

Yo-chan was gone by the time we exited the tent in our diving costumes. The water was just as freezing as it had been all week. Once again, the dry-land women lasted only a few minutes, while the rest of us stayed in the water until we were shivering badly. When I came out, Joon-lee was there with my towel.

"Mother," she said, "can I have a bicycle? Please?"

My youngest daughter could be fickle, but she could also be determined.

"Do you want to be a scientist or a bicycle rider?" I asked.

"I want to do both. I want—"

I cut her off. "You *want*? We all *want*. You complain when I put a sweet potato in your lunch for school, but I had years when my only meal of the day was a single sweet potato."

Unfortunately, this pointed Joon-lee in another—but sadly familiar—direction. "Other kids get white rice, but the food you give us makes it look like we're living a subsistence life."

"I buy white rice for the New Year's Festival," I said, stung. Then, defensively, "I often put barley in your lunch—"

"Which is even more embarrassing, because that means we're *really* poor."

"What a lucky child you are to say that. You don't know what poor means—"

"If we aren't poor, then why can't I have a bicycle?"

I wanted to tug her hair and remind her that the money I saved was for her and her siblings' educations.

That night, after dinner, Wan-soon came over, as she usually did, and the three girls went out for a walk. I made citrus tea and took two cups across the courtyard to Do-saeng's house. She was already on her sleeping mat, but the oil lamp still burned.

"I was waiting for you," she said. "You seemed upset all day. Did one of those men do something to you?"

I shook my head, sat on the floor next to her, and handed her the cup of tea.

"You were a good mother to Jun-bu," I said. "You sent him to school when many haenyeo didn't."

"Or couldn't. Your mother had many children," she said wistfully. "But look what you're doing now. Three children in school. That's more than any other family in the village."

"I couldn't do that without your help."

She tipped her head in acknowledgment. Then, after a long pause, she said, "So tell me. What's wrong?"

"I saw Mi-ja and her son today."

"Don't think about her—"

"How can I not? She lives a ten-minute walk from here. We do our best to avoid each other, but Hado is small."

"So? In every village, victims live next door to traitors, police, soldiers, or collaborators. Now killers and the children of killers run the island. Is this so different from when you were a girl?"

"No, but she knows everything about me—"

"Who doesn't know everything about you? As you said, Hado is small. Tell me your real concern."

I hesitated, then asked, "What future can I give my children when we have the guilt-by-association system?"

"Those we lost were not guilty of anything."

"That's not how the government sees it. Anyone who died is considered guilty."

"You could do what others have done and claim your husband died *before* April Three," Do-saeng suggested.

"But Jun-bu was a teacher! He was known to everyone in Bukchon—"

"He was a teacher, true, but he was not an instigator, rebel, insurgent, or communist."

"You say that as his mother." Then I allowed myself to voice my deepest fear. "Could he have had secrets we didn't know about?"

"No."

It was a simple answer, but I wasn't so sure. "He read the posters. He read the newspaper."

"You told me he read the posters from *both* sides, so he could tell people what was happening," Do-saeng said. "He read the newspaper for the same reason. The authorities probably think he was just a typical Jeju husband—"

"Who taught?"

"I was always proud of him for becoming a teacher. I thought you were too."

"I was. I am." Tears welled in my eyes. "But I can't stop being afraid for my children."

"Whatever my son did or didn't do, you know that Yu-ri and Sung-soo did *nothing* wrong. They were victims. Those of us who are left are victims. But unlike many others, I don't feel like we've been targeted." She held my gaze. "We haven't been forced to report to the police every month as some families have."

"That's true."

"And have you ever had the sense we're being watched?"

I shook my head.

"All right then," she said decisively. "Just keep your focus on the good in our lives. Your son performs the rites for the ancestors, and he's learning family duties like cooking. Min-lee is turning out to be a good diver, while Joon-lee . . ."

As she went on talking about the virtues of each of my children, I felt myself becoming calmer. My mother-in-law could be right.

That we hadn't been called to the police station or followed had to mean something. That didn't mean we weren't on a list somewhere, though.

———

By day six, the nondiving women had become more accustomed to being in their water clothes in front of the men. The scientists had gotten bolder too. At first, they'd taken care not to stare at us as we filed down to the shore, but now they gazed at us in the manner men do. I was particularly concerned about the way they gaped at Min-lee and Wan-soon. They were beautiful girls, slim, with happy faces and pretty skin. Looking at them together, I couldn't help but think of Mi-ja and myself when we were that age. Or when we were older in Vladivostok. We hadn't always realized the impression we were making, although we tried to be careful when we were on the docks. Our fears were concentrated more on what Japanese soldiers might do to us than on the looks we received from the men of Jeju or elsewhere. But Min-lee and Wan-soon weren't old enough to remember the Japanese, and Wan-soon had seen nothing like what happened in Bukchon here in Hado. A saying my mother and father often recited came to my mind: *For a tree that has many branches, even a small breeze will shake some loose.* The meaning had always been clear to me. With children, there will be many conflicts, griefs, and problems. It was my job as Min-lee's mother to prevent any of those things from happening.

Two days later, Dr. Park and his team left Hado. They promised to return in three months. Two days after that, on the fourteenth day of the second lunar month, exactly two weeks after we'd welcomed the goddess of the wind to Jeju, it was time to send her away. Once again, haenyeo and fishermen cautiously gathered at the shore. Kang Gu-ja took a prominent seat as chief of our collective. On this occasion, however, her sister and niece did not sit with her. Although the Kang sisters had bickered since childhood, the fact that Gu-sun and Wan-soon had gotten to participate in the study irritated Gu-ja in a way that none of us could have predicted, as if our swimming in frigid water for no money had somehow threatened her position and power. It could be an hour, a day, or a week before Gu-sun and Gu-ja warmed again to each other.

We made offerings of rice cakes and rice wine to the goddesses and gods. Then it was time for fortune-telling. The old women who traveled from village to village to fulfill this purpose sat on mats. Min-lee and Wan-soon sought out the youngest fortune-teller. I approached a woman whose face was dark and wrinkled from the sun. She didn't remember me, but I remembered her because my mother had always trusted the futures she foretold. I got on my knees, bowed, and then sat back on my heels. The old woman filled her palm with uncooked rice kernels and tossed them in the air. I watched as my destiny rained down. Some kernels fell back onto the old woman's hand; others fell to the mat.

"Six grains will mean you'll have good luck," she said, quickly covering the back of her hand. "Eight, ten, and twelve are not as good but good enough. Four would be the worst number I could tell you. Are you ready?"

"I'm ready."

She removed the hand covering the kernels and counted. "Ten," she said. "Not too bad, not too good." With that, she flicked away the kernels, and they dropped through the spaces between the rocks around us.

I sighed. I would now make extra offerings and pray more. Others got bad readings. Some women cried at their prophecies; others laughed them off. Min-lee and Wan-soon both received sixes. Their fortune-teller asked them to swallow the kernels so they might carry their good luck.

Finally, under Shaman Kim's watchful eyes, we wove miniature straw boats, each about a meter in length. We filled them with tributes and offerings, attached small sails, invited the goddesses and gods to board, and then sent the vessels out to sea. We tossed more rice wine and handfuls of millet and rice into the water. With that, spring officially arrived.

The day after the farewell rite, I started to cut sweet potatoes to mix with barley to make my children's lunches appear more substantial when I remembered what Joon-lee had said about us looking poor. I opened an earthenware jar and dipped into my supply of salted anchovies to put on her barley. I expected her to thank me when she got home from school, but her thoughts were elsewhere. She ran in, opened her satchel, and pulled out a new book. The jacket showed a little girl wearing a ruffled skirt, apron, and ankle boots. Blond curls framed her face. She held an old man's hand. Goats nibbled on grass. Behind them rose snowcapped mountains that seemed plentiful in number and awesome in height.

"She's Heidi," Joon-lee announced, "and I love her."

Supplies of the book had been delivered to schools across the island. Why? We never learned, but every girl her age had received a copy. Now my daughter, who only days earlier had been fixated on learning to ride a bicycle and days before that had proclaimed her desire to become a scientist, became obsessed with *Heidi*. Wanting to encourage her, I asked her to read the story to me. Then Heidi, Clara, Peter, and Grandfather possessed me too. Next Do-saeng and Min-lee became consumed by the story. Min-lee got Wan-soon to read it. Then Wan-soon read the book to her mother. Soon houses across Hado were lit by oil lamps at night as daughters read the tale to their mothers and grandmothers. Everyone wanted to talk about the story, and we visited each other's houses or gathered in the olle to discuss it.

"What do you suppose bread tastes like?" Wan-soon asked one afternoon.

Her mother answered, "When you go to Vladivostok for leaving-home water-work, you'll have an opportunity to taste it. They have a lot of bakeries there."

"What about goat's milk?" Min-lee asked me. "Did you drink it when you went out for leaving-home water-work?"

"No, but I tasted ice cream once," I answered, remembering licking cones on a street corner with Mi-ja and two Russian boys.

One person loved Clara's grandmother. Another loved Heidi's grandfather. Many of the baby-divers, whose thoughts were turning to weddings, adored Peter. Wan-soon even said she wanted him for her husband. Min-lee said she preferred the Doctor, because he was so kind. But again, no one was more bewitched by the story than Joon-lee. Her favorite character was Clara.

"Why would you choose her?" I asked. "She's injured. She can't help her family. She cries. She's selfish."

"But she's healed by the mountains, the sky, the goats, and their milk!" After a pause, she stated, "I'm going to Switzerland one day."

When I heard that, I knew I had to steer her in another direction. No matter what Do-saeng said, having three victims in our family—one of whom was a teacher—guaranteed that we were tainted by the guilt-by-association system. Joon-lee would never receive permission to go to the mainland, let alone Switzerland. Since she was still too young to understand all that, I asked the first thing that came to my mind. "How can you go to a fairy world?"

Joon-lee just laughed. "Mother, Switzerland is not a fairy world. It is not a land of goddesses either. I will leave Jeju just as Kim Mandeok did. And I'll buy myself a bicycle."

The Vast Unknowable Sea

August–September 1961

Three months after the first visit, Dr. Park and his team returned, as promised. Then three months after that, at the end of August, they came again. For two weeks each visit, the same group of eighteen women—nine divers and nine nondivers—had light suppers, rested on cots in the mornings, and were tested. This time, though, we were driven by boat to the underwater canyon where Mi-ja and I had taken our first dive. The scientists selected the site for the very reason that my mother had chosen it: the geography allowed the nondivers to hover above the rocks that came nearly to the surface, while the divers could go down twenty meters into the coldness of the canyon. The nondivers still couldn't last more than a few minutes, but with the warmer weather, we divers went back and forth for at least two and a half hours before returning to the boat. We learned that our temperatures didn't drop as much as they did in winter, which seemed obvious to us. But now Dr. Park had the precise measurement he desired: 35.3 degrees Centigrade in water that was 26 degrees or 95.5 Fahrenheit in water that was almost 79 degrees. "Very impressive," he said to us. "Not many people can function as well as you do when their temperatures fall so far below normal."

The scientists added a new dimension: food. They came to our houses three times a day to measure everything before we put it in our mouths. They asked us the same question we often joked about in the bulteok. "Who should have more food—a man or a woman?" We knew the answer, but their tests proved it. A haenyeo not only needed 3,000 calories a day compared to a non-diving woman, who typically ate 2,000 calories a day, but also ate more than any man they tested in Hado. "We have not seen this magnitude of voluntary heat loss in any other human," Dr. Park effused, "but look how you make up for it!" But he was studying us at a very different point in our lives. I remembered back to when Mi-ja and I were girls just learning to dive, later when we were in Vladivostok, and later still in the lean war years. We'd never had enough to eat, and we'd both been very thin.

Every woman—diver and nondiver—wanted to be hospitable. Each woman prepared her best dishes, so she could offer a meal to the scientist who came to visit. In my household, Do-saeng, Min-lee, and I pushed aside Kyung-soo, who usually did the cooking, so we could make the types of dishes we ate in the bulteok: grilled conch, steamed blue abalone, small crabs stir-fried with beans, or octopus on skewers. As the scientist of the day sat on our floor, eating, Joon-lee asked endless questions. What was it like in Seoul? What university did he attend? Was it better to be a research scientist or a medical doctor? Those men answered Joon-lee's questions, but they watched her older sister whenever she crossed the room.

When Dr. Park finally came to my house, I invited him to sit and poured him a bowl of rice wine. The low table was already set with side dishes: kimchee, pickled beans, lotus root, boiled squash, sliced black pig, salted damselfish, spiced bracken, and boiled, sea-soned, and slivered sea cucumber. Just as we were about to start eating, Joon-lee's teacher came to the door. Teacher Oh bowed and then made an announcement.

"Your daughter has won an island-wide contest for fifth graders," he said. "Joon-lee will now represent our side of Mount Halla in an academic competition in Jeju City. This is a great honor."

Joon-lee jumped to her feet and hopped around the room. Her sister and brother congratulated her. Do-saeng cried happy tears. I couldn't stop smiling. After Dr. Park said, "The daughter is smart because the mother is smart," I really couldn't stop smiling.

I invited Teacher Oh to join us. Space was made for him, and more rice wine was poured. When Dr. Park inquired about the competition, Teacher Oh responded, "Joon-lee is not just a bright girl. She's the brightest student in our elementary school. The children from schools in Jeju City will have received better opportunities, but I believe she has a good chance of winning the entire competition."

These words of praise should have humbled my daughter. Instead, they encouraged her to ask, "If I win, Mother, will you buy me a bicycle?"

My answer escaped my mouth too quickly. "Riding a bicycle is not for you. Everyone knows that riding one will give a girl a big butt."

Dr. Park raised his eyebrows, and my argument didn't sway Joon-lee one bit. "But if I win," she said, "don't you think I should be rewarded?"

Rewarded? Impatience flushed my face. The scientist politely changed the subject. "Did you catch this squid yourself?" he asked. "If so, can you tell me about the drying process?"

After dinner, Wan-soon came to collect my daughters for their nightly walk. Teacher Oh left with them, and Do-saeng returned to the little house, taking Kyung-soo with her. I inquired about Dr. Park's life in Seoul; he tried to delve deeper into my life as a haenyeo. It all went about as well as could be expected, which is to say fine. He was just leaving when Min-lee burst through the door.

"Mother, come quick!"

I slipped on my sandals and ran after her. Dr. Park trotted behind me. We followed Min-lee to the main square. There in a heap lay Joon-lee, her arms and legs tangled with a bicycle. She was crying softly. Yo-chan crouched over her. Of course. Yo-chan. His bicycle. My daughter. A wave of anger washed over me.

"Get away from her," I said.

The boy backed off but didn't leave. I squatted next to Joon-lee.

"I think I broke my arm," she whimpered.

I started to lift the bicycle. She yelped in pain.

"Here, you steady her arm," Dr. Park said. "Let the boy and me move the bike."

He motioned to Yo-chan, who stepped forward. "It's my fault," he said.

"Don't worry about that now," Dr. Park told him. "Let's just work together to help her. All right? Are you ready?"

While we pried the bike off Joon-lee, her older sister wept and muttered, "I'm sorry, I'm sorry, I'm sorry." Not far from her, Wan-soon stood with her back against the village tree. She looked as pale as the moon.

"I'll drive her to the hospital in Jeju City," Dr. Park said once Joon-lee was free.

"I'm coming too," I said.

"Naturally. And the others can tag along too if they want," he said. "There's room."

I motioned for Min-lee and Wan-soon to follow us. Before we left the square, I turned back to look at Yo-chan. His head was bent, and his shoulders were hunched.

———

I hadn't been to Jeju City's hospital before. The electric lights glowed brightly. The nurses and doctors were all dressed in white. Joon-lee was put in a wheelchair. "Like Clara," she said and smiled weakly. Then a nurse pushed her down a hallway and out of sight.

"It's not a compound fracture," Dr. Park said. "You can be happy about that."

I closed my eyes so I could concentrate on finding tranquillity. He couldn't possibly know how it felt for me to see my little girl hurt and to understand that Mi-ja's son was somehow involved. What made it worse was that Yo-chan had probably taught Joon-lee how to ride a bike to get to her older sister. All those times Mi-ja and I had dreamed that her son and my daughter would marry one day burned in my chest. *Never.*

It wasn't long before the nurse came to the waiting room and took us to see Joon-lee. Her arm was in a plaster cast. Her cheeks were wan. The doctor tried to make sense of our group: a man clearly not from Jeju dressed in Western-style clothes, two sixteen-year-old girls, a younger girl, and me in our persimmon-dyed island pants, tunics, and scarves.

"Joon-lee tells me she comes from a haenyeo family," the doctor said. "Please be assured that her injury will heal well. She'll be able to dive with you when the time comes."

During the drive back to Hado, the emotions in the car were

so heavy that it felt as though it were weighted down by rocks. I stared out the window. The streets were nearly deserted, but a few women strolled with their men. Neon lights lit up bars and stalls that served barbecued pork. The city seemed much more modern now, although most of the houses were still made from traditional stone and thatch.

Dr. Park drove as close to my house as he could get. When he turned off the motor and opened his door, I said, "Thank you for your kindness and help, but we can make it the rest of the way ourselves. I'll see you in the morning at the usual time."

Joon-lee cradled her arm. Min-lee and Wan-soon walked ahead of us hand in hand. When we reached our house, Wan-soon said, "I'm sorry."

"I'll discuss things with your mother tomorrow," I informed her.

Wan-soon and Min-lee exchanged glances. As Wan-soon padded away, I felt a stab, remembering what it was like to have a friend so close.

When my daughters and I entered our courtyard, we found my son and mother-in-law sitting on the steps of the little house waiting for us.

"Yo-chan came to tell us what happened," Do-saeng said. "Are you all right, little one?"

"I'm fine," Joon-lee answered, her voice sounding small and tinny.

"Can Kyung-soo stay with you tonight?" I asked my mother-in-law. "I need to talk to the girls."

My son jumped to his feet. "But I want to hear—"

His grandmother pulled him back down beside her.

Once my girls and I were in the big house, I addressed Min-lee, keeping my declaration short to see how she'd respond. "You kept a secret from me."

"It would have stayed a secret too, if Joon-lee hadn't fallen," she admitted.

"Are you blaming your little sister?" I asked.

Before Min-lee could reply, Joon-lee said, "We like Yo-chan, and I wanted to learn—"

"*We?*" I turned back to my older daughter, who turned red to the roots of her hair.

"Joon-lee's the one who wanted to learn how to ride a bike!" Min-lee exclaimed defensively. "She asked Yo-chan to help her."

"She's a child," I said, "but you're old enough to know better. When I say no, I mean no. But this goes far beyond a bicycle, does it not? I don't want you to see Yo-chan again."

She laughed. "How's that supposed to happen? It's a small village and—"

I cut her off. "You've been given so much. Food. Schooling. You've had such an easy life that even your monthly bleeding has come early." I gave her the sternest warning I could. "If you share love with Yo-chan, you could get pregnant." I followed up with the worst curse a mother can give her daughter on an island with no beggars. "You'll end up a girl who's going to beg."

She cocked her head. I felt like I was watching her think.

"It's not like *that,*" she said at last.

"He's a boy. You're a girl—"

"I've known Yo-chan my entire life. He's like a brother to me."

"But Yo-chan is not your brother. He's a boy—"

"Mother, we are not having sex."

I blinked, stunned. I was hinting at this certainly, but I never expected her to be so blunt, especially in front of her little sister. Trying to regain my footing, I turned my attention to Joon-lee. "Yo-chan is not your brother either. And he's not your friend. Stay away from him."

Joon-lee lowered her eyes. "I'll do my best."

"Best is not enough," I said. "So you understand how serious I am, tomorrow you will not be allowed down by the tents."

"But—"

"Keep talking. For every word, you'll stay home another day."

The next morning, Joon-lee moaned a bit about her punishment and how unfair it was, and I told her she should have thought about that before getting on a bicycle. Then Min-lee, Do-saeng, and I left the house together. We met Gu-sun and Wan-soon in the olle. Wan-soon apologized once more for her part in last night's accident. Her eyes were swollen from crying and the color of her usually rosy cheeks had drained to an off-green. Acknowledging her suffering, I said, "Thank you, Wan-soon. I appreciate that you've taken greater responsibility for what happened than my own daughters."

"And I've made her promise she won't be a part of anything having to do with Yo-chan or his mother in the future," Gu-sun reported.

Again, Wan-soon and Min-lee exchanged glances, wordlessly sending messages back and forth. Again, I thought of how Mi-ja and I had once done the same thing, which further convinced me that Gu-sun and I would need to keep an eye on these two.

When we got to the laboratory tents, Dr. Park inquired after Joon-lee. I let him know she wouldn't be coming today.

"I hope to see her tomorrow," he said. "She should be exposed to things that will put her ahead of the city children."

He was right, of course. The next day, I let Joon-lee return to the lab, where it seemed Dr. Park had confided to the others the news about the competition to which she'd been invited. For the first time, she was allowed to put a thermometer in a woman's mouth and pump the cuff that went around her arm.

———

Two days later, Dr. Park and his team packed up their instruments and left Hado. They would return in another three months. I worked in my dry field, while my children started their fall semester. After school let out, when her brother and sister went to the shallows to visit friends and cool off, Joon-lee sat in the main room to do her homework, study for the competition, and read.

The next diving period arrived on a Sunday, which meant that Wan-soon and Min-lee were able to come. It was a particularly blustery day, and wind pressed our clothes tight against our bodies. Waves frothed and sprayed as though pushed by a storm. Once inside the bulteok, Gu-ja took her honorary position. The rest of us sat according to our skill levels. Gu-ja was peevish. The recent visit from Dr. Park and his team reminded her how irritated she was that she'd been dropped from the study, but I figured she'd return to her normal irascible self after a day in the water.

Forgoing the usual pleasantries, Gu-ja began. "Today is going to be hot—"

"And it's certainly gusty," Gu-sun interrupted. "We'll need to be careful where we dive—"

Irritated, Gu-ja waved off her sister. "I'm willing to hear suggestions for where we should go. Anyone?" she asked.

Although it seemed apparent that she was deliberately not asking her sister, Gu-sun offered the first idea. "Let's walk to the cove north of us. The cliffs protect that area from the wind."

"It's too hot to walk that far," Gu-ja said.

Gu-sun tried again. "We could stay here and dive off the jetty."

"Did you not notice how the wind is pushing the surf?" Gu-ja scanned the faces in the circle, but her sour mood invited no other proposals. "All right then. Let's row straight out to sea to the plateau. Hopefully the waves will be milder than what we're seeing from shore, and the deeper waters will be colder."

Next to me, Yang-jin muttered under her breath, "This is not good."

I agreed. Gu-ja was the chief, but she'd made her decision just to be contrary.

We changed into our water clothes, strapped our face masks on the tops or sides of our heads, gathered our gear, and filed out to the boat. Gu-ja's mood may have been off, but she was right that on this unseasonably hot day the deeper and cooler waters would feel refreshing. We took our places on the boat. Min-lee and Wan-soon sat across from each other. Soon we were bending over our stomachs and pulling back, dipping our oars into the water together. The girls' voices sounded clear and fresh as we sang. A single wisp of a cloud raced across the sky, seagulls soared and swooped, and just as Gu-ja had predicted the sea was uneasy but not as bad as at the shore. Nevertheless, ruffling whitecaps were not welcomed by those with weak stomachs. A haenyeo pregnant with her fourth child pulled in her oar, threw up, and then resumed rowing. We cheered for her and then went back to our singing. I noticed, though, that Wan-soon's complexion had faded to an even more unsettling green. She didn't look well, but in the year and a half she'd been diving with us I hadn't known her to get seasick.

Gu-ja raised an arm, signaling us to stop. After the anchor was dropped, she made the traditional offerings to the sea gods. When she was done, she said, "Together, let us scour the ocean floor." With that, we pulled our face masks from our foreheads, rubbed mugwort on the glass, and positioned them over our eyes and noses. Each woman double-checked her tools. Then two by two, women threw their tewaks into the water and jumped in after them. Gu-sun and Gu-ja went down together. I told Min-lee to be careful, as I always did, and then she and Wan-soon dropped over the side of the boat. I nodded to Yang-jin, and together we entered the sea.

We were far from shore, as Gu-sun had wanted, but the under-water geography made it ideal for divers of all levels. Unlike the spot my mother had chosen for my first dive, which had a deep canyon, here a wide plateau rose up—high, flat, easy to reach but deep enough not to scrape a boat's hull, and so wide it presented a vast field of opportunity. In the murky waters, I couldn't see the full circumference, but if the baby-divers stayed together, they'd be fine.

Down I went. Yang-jin and I stayed within sight of each other but not so close that she would invade my territory or I hers. I went up for sumbisori and to put what I'd harvested in my net. The water felt wonderful. Down. Up. Sumbisori. Down. Up. Sumbisori. The concentration involved to stay safe, grab as much as I could, and forget the troubles of land created the pattern of my life.

Once our nets were full, Yang-jin and I returned to the boat. We stored our gear and began to sort what we'd harvested. As Gu-ja, Gu-sun, and the other women came in, we helped them haul their nets into the boat. Many of these women also sorted their harvests, while others drank cups of tea. A few propped themselves against their full nets and allowed the rocking of the boat to lull them to sleep. I kept an ear tuned to the sumbisori of the haenyeo still in the water, always relieved when I heard Min-lee's distinctive *hrrrr*. She was still learning how to dive, but I trusted her skills. That said, my shoulders relaxed when I saw her loop her arms over the side of the boat. But when she didn't try to push her net on board or hoist herself up, I knew something was wrong.

"Has anyone seen Wan-soon?" she asked.

At these words, Gu-sun's head snapped up.

"I saw her out that way," a woman said, pointing off the bow.

"So did I," Yang-jin added. "When we came up for sumbisori at the same time, I told her to dive closer to the boat."

"Then where is she now?" Gu-sun asked, turning to her older sister.

"Don't worry," the chief responded. "We'll find her."

A couple of stragglers paddled toward the boat. Gu-sun shouted to them, but no, they hadn't seen Wan-soon either. Gu-sun and Gu-ja stood, rooting their feet to the deck as the boat bobbed in the swells.

"There!" Gu-ja shouted. "Her tewak."

I knew this area well—all the grandmother-divers did—and seeing that the tewak had drifted farther out to sea was concerning.

Those of us on the boat picked up our oars and began rowing, leaving several divers in the water. We wanted to get to Wan-soon's tewak quickly, but to be efficient we had to keep our rhythm. When we reached the tewak, Gu-sun and Gu-ja dropped their oars and stood. Gu-sun yelled at us to be quiet, so we could listen for Wan-soon's sumbisori, but it was nowhere on the wind. Slowly turning in circles, the sisters scanned the swells. They must have tried for five minutes, far longer than a haenyeo could stay underwater. The aunt looked terrified and desperate, while the mother looked sad and resigned.

"Everyone," Gu-ja said, "we need to get back in the water. Hurry." Then she spoke the words no one wanted to hear. "We must find Wan-soon's body before it's lost to the sea and she becomes a hungry ghost."

Face masks were fitted back into place, and everyone leapt into the water. Those who were already in the sea were coming closer. Gu-sun called to them. "We're looking for Wan-soon. Search the area where you are."

The baby-divers, including my daughter, fanned out across the plateau. If an abalone had grabbed Wan-soon's bitchang or if her hair or clothing had somehow gotten caught on a rock, they'd find her body. The small-divers and grandmother-divers swam down the sides of the plateau. Nothing. Every time I resurfaced, women yelled questions across the cresting waves, which were growing larger now. *Did you search here? Did you search there? Nothing here. Nothing there.* Down again.

The next time I surfaced, I spotted Min-lee with her arms draped over Wan-soon's tewak. I was not much younger than she was now when Yu-ri had her accident, so I knew the guilt and remorse my daughter had to be feeling. I swam over to her.

"Wouldn't she need to be near her tewak?" Min-lee asked before sucking in her lips to hold in her emotions.

"Hopefully," I said. "Let's look together."

I took her hand, and we swam down directly beneath Wan-soon's float. I was immediately alarmed by what I saw and felt. We were at the farthest edge of the plateau. The current was strong here, and the vastness of the sea grabbed at us, but my daughter was too focused on the search to notice. I let her set the pace and depth, conscious that Wan-soon wouldn't have been able to go faster or deeper than my daughter. We had not yet reached two body lengths when Min-lee stopped. Together we righted our bodies. Min-lee couldn't hold her breath for much longer, but I needed to show her something. I held up my free hand to stop her from returning to the surface. Then I let go of her. The suck of the sea was so strong here that she was immediately pulled away from me. A look of terror passed over her face with the knowledge that she too might be drawn into a current that could take her body hundreds, if not more, kilometers away. I grabbed her hand and with the strength of many years of diving, I guided her away from danger and up to the surface.

Our search was over. We would not find Wan-soon today.

Once everyone was back on the boat, Gu-ja addressed us. "When we reach shore, I'll send word to the haenyeo chiefs in the neighboring villages." She put a hand on her sister's shoulder, but Gu-sun shrugged it off. "By the end of tomorrow, word will have circled the island and reached every haenyeo and fisherman. Let us pray to the Dragon Sea God and every goddess who has sway in the sea to bring Wan-soon's body to shore."

Gu-ja picked up her oar, and the rest of us took our places. I couldn't imagine what was going through her mind. Dealing with an accident or death is every haenyeo chief's greatest torment. She must lead, even as she feels grief and culpability. My mother had not been responsible for Yu-ri's greed or her encounter with the octopus, and yet the burden of what happened had weighed heavily upon her. This situation was different. Gu-ja couldn't have anticipated this calamity, but the fact remained that she'd chosen this spot to dive out of jealousy and spite. That anyone died was terrible, but Gu-ja had to feel even more sorrowful because the victim was her niece.

———

It is said that after experiencing the vast unknowable sea, a daughter comes to know her mother and understand her for the first time. Indeed, on the day of Yu-ri's accident I'd seen my mother in a new way. Now Min-lee saw me differently too. Every child should know that a parent will love, teach, and protect her, but during the Bukchon massacre my daughter had experienced something quite different. Now, for the first time, she absorbed deep into her marrow the love I felt for her. Still, the days that followed were hard. Min-lee was sick with heartache and regret.

"If I hadn't looked away from her—"

"There was nothing you could have done," I soothed. "You felt the current. You aren't strong enough yet to have pulled her out of it."

"But if I'd stayed with her—"

"You would have drifted away with her. I would have lost you."

Once, in frustration, she blurted, "But I just don't see how this could have happened. You were there for the fortune-telling. She received six rice kernels—"

I nodded in understanding. "We talk sometimes about fate and destiny," I said. "And we like fortune-tellers to tell us our futures. Then we ask ourselves why Wan-soon received a good fortune and died, while other women received bad fortunes but are still with us. Even I have doubted. I've often questioned why the rice cake that Shaman Kim threw against the village tree during my marriage ceremony stuck, foretelling happiness, when so much adversity was coming. I have never found an answer."

Min-lee buried her face in my lap to cry. I patted her back.

"But I wonder," I went on tentatively, "if Wan-soon had a reason to be careless."

Min-lee's body stiffened under my hand. I wanted to say more, but Joon-lee came in to try to lift her older sister's spirits. She sat on the floor next to us, opened her copy of *Heidi,* and began to read. Tonight, the story made Min-lee weep all the harder.

"Heidi and Clara were such good friends," she managed to get out. "Wan-soon and I were like that. Now I've lost her."

I tried my best to provide solace to my daughter, but I was also dealing with my own shaky spirits. When I wasn't contemplating the plain truth that Min-lee could have been the one sucked into the depths, I was nibbling on the thoughts I'd had about Wan-soon in her last days: how white she'd been when Joon-lee broke her arm, which turned to sickly green the next morning, until she'd looked like she was going to throw up on the boat. When I wasn't wondering whether I was the only person to suspect Wan-soon might have been pregnant—and if my daughter knew who the father was—I was pestered by thoughts of Mi-ja and how I could no longer turn to her for advice or consolation. When I wasn't dwelling in that familiar shadowy abyss, I worried about Gu-sun and Gu-ja. One had lost her daughter; the other would be held responsible for the accident. The sisters had always squabbled and had bouts of jealousy, but they'd also been inseparable. I couldn't imagine what they were feeling toward each other or what words could be said to bring forgiveness. This again brought Mi-ja to mind. I had once consoled her. She had once consoled me. Min-lee had now lost that. Gu-sun and Gu-ja may have lost that too. Then, in a moment of unsettling understanding, I saw how nearly all these occurrences had come as a result of Dr. Park's study. His presence—and that of the other scientists—had rippled out, changing us and how we saw each other. We would not recover from Wan-soon's death quickly, but other petty things—like Mi-ja buying her son a bicycle and Joon-lee breaking her arm—might still ripple out in ways I didn't want to imagine.

After ten days, Wan-soon's corpse still had not been found. With that, she turned from a tragically dead girl, who should have been buried properly, into a hungry ghost, who can cause illness and trouble for the living, but we also had to acknowledge the realities of the situation. Since word of the effort to find Wan-soon's body had passed from haenyeo village to haenyeo village around the island, lots of people had to know we'd be holding a ritual, which was illegal. A total stranger could report us to gain favor from the authorities. We needed to stay especially alert and wary, so only those in our bulteok were notified of the date, time, and location. We met in a seaside cave about a twenty-minute walk from Hado. Gu-sun looked haggard, but her older sister seemed to have aged ten years. They stood together, wedded in grief. Do-saeng and I had Min-lee between us. Shaman Kim rang a bell in four directions to open heaven's door and invite the spirits to join us. She slashed her sword through the air to expel any evil spirits that might try to attend.

"A woman who dies alone in the water has no one to hold her hand or stroke her forehead," Shaman Kim began. "Her skin grows cold with no one to warm her. She receives no comfort from friends or family. But we also know that when the dead express concerns about the living, then it is accepted that they have become free of their grid of sorrows. Let us see what Wan-soon has to say." Shaman Kim was known for her ability to sweet-talk, compliment, and negotiate with spirits. Now she addressed Wan-soon directly. "If you were unhappy for some reason, tell us, so we can help you."

The assistants clanged their improvised cymbals and drums. The aromas from the offerings filled our noses. Shaman Kim twirled in her colorful hanbok. Her handmade tassels flew. Suddenly she and her assistants halted in midmovement. Silence fell over us, like the pause between hiccups. The cause: Mi-ja had entered the cave and was standing with her back against the jagged wall. She was dressed modestly, and she cradled offerings in her arms. She'd known Wan-soon since she was a baby, but her presence was thoroughly unsettling.

The banging and clanging resumed. Shaman Kim slashed her knives through the air even more ferociously. She slowed, came to a stop, and went into a trance. When she next spoke, her voice seemed to come at us from far away. Wan-soon had arrived.

"I am so cold," she said. "I miss my mother and father. I miss my aunt and uncle. I miss the haenyeo in our bulteok. I miss my friend."

The shaman changed back to her regular voice. "Tell us, Wan-soon, of your grievous miseries."

But in those days even spirits had to be careful what they said, and Wan-soon's spirit refused to impart another word. This seemed terribly disconcerting. Then something even more unnerving occurred. Shaman Kim twirled in my direction and stopped in front of me.

"I nearly lost my life in the sea," Shaman Kim said in a different voice as another trance came over her. "I was greedy."

Yu-ri! How many times had I asked Shaman Kim to look for her, my husband, and son, only to be given silence?

"I suffered for many years," Yu-ri said through the shaman's mouth. "Then came my last day of life. *Aigo!*"

The agony in that sound was chilling. Do-saeng sobbed for her daughter.

Then a small voice spoke. "I miss my mother. I miss my brother and my sisters."

I collapsed. *Sung-soo.*

Min-lee knelt beside me and put an arm around my shoulders. Others also fell to their knees and lowered their foreheads to the cave's floor. We had come for Wan-soon, but *I* was the one being contacted.

Shaman Kim could never sound like my husband, but I recognized his cadence and careful way of speaking. "It's crowded in this grave, but I'm grateful for the company. We share our anguish together."

Then it was as if the three people I'd lost were fighting to find space in Shaman Kim's mouth to relay their thoughts.

"I was a child who only wanted his father. I was innocent, they killed me, but I have found forgiveness."

"I was a girl who once longed for marriage. I was innocent, they killed me, but I have found forgiveness."

"I was a husband, father, and brother. I was innocent, they killed me, but I have found forgiveness."

Then Shaman Kim sang the things I'd long wanted to tell them. "To my son, I wish I could have protected you. To my sister-in-law, I'm sorry for your years of affliction. And to my husband, I say a baby was growing inside me even when I wished to die. We could not give any of you a proper burial, but at least I know you're together."

Now Shaman Kim returned to herself to address the spirits directly. "The three of you are not hungry ghosts in the sense you were lost at sea, but you died terribly and away from your ancestral home." Then she shifted her attention back to the person who'd brought us here today. "Please, Wan-soon, find comfort in the presence of the others from Hado." Addressing all of us, she said, "Let us together allow our tears to flow as I ask the Dragon Sea God to help Wan-soon's spirit travel to the Afterworld, where she can reside in peace."

The ceremony continued, with offerings, music, tears, and singing. It was not our way to question the shaman or who might send messages through her, but I did wonder at the reason the people I'd lost had chosen this occasion to visit. To hear the voices of those I'd loved stirred my soul. I was grateful. At the same time, I could taste the bitterness I felt toward Mi-ja. When I looked for her, she was gone. *Why* had she come?

─────

Haenyeo have no choice but to provide for their families, so the next day Do-saeng and I returned to the bulteok. Min-lee had school, so she didn't come, which was just as well. Gu-ja took her usual place, and her sister sat beside her. Gu-sun looked as if she hadn't slept in a month. This was a part of mourning I understood well. But Gu-ja's appearance was shocking. The tragedy had caused her sun-etched wrinkles to cut even deeper, making her look older than my mother-in-law. Her hands shook, and her voice trembled when she spoke.

"Long ago our collective had an accident, and our chief was haunted by it. Sun-sil should have stepped aside. She didn't, and months later she died in the sea." Those old enough to remember my mother nodded gravely at the memory. "As chief of this collective, I accept responsibility for what happened to Wan-soon. For this reason, I now ask for nominations for a new chief."

Her sister's reaction was so swift that not one among us didn't recognize the depth of her condemnation of her sister. "I nominate Kim Young-sook for the very reason that I didn't nominate her years ago," she said. "No one understands loss better than someone who has lost. Of all of us, Young-sook has lost the most. This will make her cautious in her decisions. She will look out for everyone."

No one else was nominated, and I received a unanimous vote. If there were others who wanted my place, I never heard about it.

I solemnly gave my first instructions and assignments. "Today we will enter the sea with caution. Let us be prudent for the rest of this diving cycle. Our spirits are worn, and we do not know what the goddesses and gods desire of us. We will make extra offerings. The baby-divers will stay close to shore. The small-divers and grandmother-divers will watch over them. We want to make sure everyone is safe the next time we go to deeper waters."

My orders meant that all of us would earn less money for a while, but no one disagreed.

"As for diving partners," I went on, "I ask Gu-sun if she would like to dive with me."

Gu-ja stared down at her folded hands, afraid to glance at her sister.

Gu-sun gave an unexpected answer. "My sister and I have gone into the sea together since we were small children. I will be safer with her than with anyone else."

A few women audibly gasped. For myself, a person who had held so much blame and anger within me, I could not understand her thinking, but I said, "If this is what you wish." I ended our meeting with something my mother used to say. "Every woman who goes into the sea carries a coffin on her back. In this world, in the undersea world, we tow the burdens of this hard life." Then I added a few words of my own. "Please be careful today and every day."

———

I settled into my responsibilities quickly. All the training that had come to me from my mother and mother-in-law now flowed naturally from me, and I like to think I was respected for my judgment from the first day. *Chief of the collective.* I wondered what Mi-ja thought when she heard the news. Maybe she didn't think anything, because she had problems of her own.

Gossip spread about Wan-soon's last day of diving. "She was sick that morning," the butcher's wife told me knowingly. The woman who ground millet commented, "Who among us has not been ill in the first months of pregnancy?" "She spent too much time with Mi-ja's son," the weaver whispered when I came to buy muslin to make a dress for Joon-lee. I absolutely did not start these rumors. I'm not proud to admit this, but some days I wished I had. No act of retaliation would ever erase the pain Mi-ja had caused me, but this might have been a start. A good part of Hado had never trusted Mi-ja—the daughter of a Japanese collaborator and the wife of someone who had worked for the Americans and currently lived on the mainland. Now she had another black mark against her as the mother of the boy who might have gotten Wan-soon pregnant. "Maybe the girl was afraid to tell her mother," the butcher's wife said. "Maybe Yo-chan told Wan-soon he wouldn't marry her," the woman who ground millet speculated. Everyone had a theory, and they ranged from Wan-soon being distracted by her troubles to the idea that she deliberately let herself be swept away out of shame that she was pregnant.

My daughters remained surprisingly silent about the gossip. Joon-lee may have been too young and embarrassed to repeat the rumors to me, and I didn't want to have a conversation about sex with her just yet, but I finally asked Min-lee if they were true.

"Oh, Mother," she said, "you'll always think the worst of Yo-chan and his family. He and Wan-soon were friends. The three of us just wanted to help Joon-lee learn to ride a bike. That's all."

I didn't know if I could believe her or not.

The day arrived when Teacher Oh took Joon-lee on a bus to Jeju City for the competition. They returned three days later with wonderful news. Joon-lee had won. I bought her a bicycle, thinking it would prevent any future meetings between her and Yo-chan.

This is not to say I didn't have misgivings. "You really are going to get a big butt," I warned her, but she just laughed and pedaled away. Then, as she disappeared around the corner, I realized the terrible mistake I'd made. She might not need Yo-chan to give her lessons any longer, but now the two of them could ride together and I couldn't do anything about it except rely on the gossip of others to tell me what my daughter was up to.

A week after the competition, Teacher Oh paid another visit. "A happy day!" he announced. "Joon-lee has been selected to go to Jeju City Middle School."

I should have been joyous, but my first thought was practical. "It's too far for her to travel back and forth every day."

"No travel will be required. She will board with a family."

This was even worse. "She's only twelve," I objected. "I don't want us to be separated."

Teacher Oh jutted his chin. "But all haenyeo daughters go out for leaving-home water-work. Even you—"

"But I didn't leave Hado until I was seventeen. And I *had* to go."

"If Joon-lee does this," he went on, almost as though he'd practiced his response, "she might be able to go to college or university on the mainland. Or"—his eyes gleamed—"maybe even to Japan."

But he'd gotten ahead of himself.

"How can she leave Jeju for the mainland, let alone leave the country?" I asked. "The authorities would never allow it."

"Why? Because your husband was a teacher?"

"We're stained by the guilt-by-association system. We—"

"I prefer to think the authorities know you now as a haenyeo chief. Your mother and mother-in-law were also haenyeo chiefs. Maybe that will be a help. And it's not as though she's a boy who could cause trouble in the future. I've heard of many cases where sons are not admitted to school or military academies, while daughters have gone to the mainland for university and jobs."

"Maybe that's true for some, but I lost three family members during the Four-Three Incident."

"I don't think you understand," he said. "The higher-ups have already decided to look the other way in Joon-lee's case."

This took me aback. "How can that be?"

He shrugged. "She's exceptionally smart. Maybe Dr. Park put in a good word . . ."

But now he was telling me another story. I spoke bluntly. "Which is it? The higher-ups will look the other way or Dr. Park helped? Or she's smart enough? Or she's not a boy?"

"Does it matter? She's been given an opportunity that few will ever receive." He scrutinized my face before adding, "Best of all, you won't have to worry about her bicycling in the olles with a boy who's older than she is."

He didn't need to say another word.

———

We packed Joon-lee's clothes and her few books. The entire family walked her to the bus stop, where Teacher Oh waited for us. The road was busy with people walking to market. Women wore white scarves and carried baskets over their arms. Men had their pants rolled up to midcalf and horsehair hats pulled down over their ears. One farmer led a donkey, whose back was piled high with bulging burlap bags. As far down the road as I could see in either direction, there wasn't a car, truck, or bus. Do-saeng, Min-lee, and I couldn't stop weeping. My father, brother, and son stood off to the side, trying to camouflage their feelings. Joon-lee wasn't sad, though. She was excited.

"I'll come home for every holiday and festival," she babbled breathlessly. "I'll ask if I can come when Dr. Park next returns. I promise to work hard."

I saw so much of her father in her—her love of family combined with an eagerness to learn, and her sense of responsibility combined with a desire to try new things—but when the bus came into view, her eyes finally got misty.

"You're a brave girl," I said, but inside my heart was aching. "We're all proud of you. Do well. We'll all be here when you come home."

The bus ground to a stop, and the door swung open. As dust swirled around us, I brought my daughter into my arms, and we held each other tight.

"I'm not going to wait here forever," the bus driver shouted out the door. "I have a schedule to keep."

Teacher Oh picked up Joon-lee's satchel. "I'll make sure she gets settled."

Joon-lee let go of me, bowed to me and the rest of the family, and then climbed the steps. The driver pulled away before she had a chance to sit down. My last glimpse was of her walking down the aisle.

Three days later, Mi-ja and Yo-chan departed on the morning bus. Some said they'd left because Mi-ja couldn't stand hearing the gossip about her son. One rumor had her joining her husband in Seoul, while another had the entire family moving to America. Others said she was never coming back, using the fact that she'd sold her pigs to the butcher as proof. After all, no one could live a civilized life without the three-way cycle of latrine, pigs, and food. A few people pointed out that if she were never coming back, then she would have tried to sell her aunt and uncle's house, sleeping mats, chests, and cooking utensils. None of the gossip made sense to me.

For the first time in many years, I walked to the Sut-dong part of Hado, where Mi-ja had lived. I opened her gate and entered. The courtyard was tidy, and the straw roof was well kept. A stack of empty earthenware jars filled a corner. The granary, where Mi-ja had slept when she was a girl, was empty. A vine with magenta flowers creeped along a wall. Cucumbers, carrots, and other vegetables flourished in a patch next to the kitchen. The door was unlocked, and I walked in. It was just as people had said. She'd left all her furniture in place. Mi-ja may not have been here, but her spirit infused everything. Idly, I opened a chest in the main room. Inside, I found her father's book. I couldn't believe she'd left it behind.

Weeks, then months, went by. Mi-ja and Yo-chan did not return. The house remained unlocked. Nothing was stolen. Perhaps people were following the aphorism that we have no robbers on Jeju. Or maybe they were afraid they might find me, because I went there every day. I found I missed glimpsing Mi-ja from afar. I missed having her to blame. When that missing grew too strong, I walked to her house, where I touched her things and sensed her all around me. The house became the scab I could not stop picking.

Day 4 (continued): 2008

"I'm fine," Young-sook confesses, although she can't imagine why she does to Mi-ja's great-granddaughter, of all people. "It's just hard to be here."

Clara thinks that over. Then, "Have you been inside the museum yet? Don't go." She pauses for a moment before adding, "I mean, I just learned that our plane *landed* on a mass grave. A lot of the bodies have been dug up and reburied, but still. How gross is that?"

Clara is a nuisance. No doubt about it. But Young-sook feels compelled to caution her. "You may be a foreigner, but be careful in what you say. These are still dangerous times, perhaps even the most dangerous."

Clara cocks her head and pulls out an earbud. "What?"

"Never mind. I should get back to my family," Young-sook says.

"Why? So you can see all the names of the dead? Or what's inside the museum? I'm telling you. Don't do it."

Nevertheless.

Young-sook gives a last glance to the statue of the mother, cradling her baby and being draped by the white cloth, and then begins to walk away. Clara follows along. "Halmang Mi-ja always said—"

"You called her Halmang Mi-ja?" Just hearing her name that way leaves Young-sook unaccountably shaken.

"I usually called her Granny, but she preferred Halmang. She definitely didn't like to hear the word *great*. She said it made her sound old. Anyway, she always said she had a hard life. I never met my great-grandfather, but Granny Mi-ja said he was a bad man. He beat her, you know. A lot. That's why she had the limp. Did you know that?" Clara stares at her intently, waiting for a response. When one doesn't come, she goes on. "He terrified her. He had total control over her."

Young-sook gazes into the distance. Many women are beaten, but they don't betray their closest friend. She doesn't say this, suspecting the American girl wouldn't understand.

Clara continues. "When she first moved to Los Angeles . . ." She shrugs. "It's not easy being an immigrant. I learned that in school, and it was true for Granny."

Young-sook stumbles, and Clara takes her arm. "We'd better sit down. Mom will get really mad at me if something happens to you."

They find a bench. Young-sook tries to calm her racing heart. Clara looks worried. Young-sook needs to get her talking again.

"So Mi-ja had a shop," she prompts.

"In Koreatown. A mom-and-pop grocery. Only minus the pop. You know what I mean?"

"Of course." Although she doesn't really. "Did Mi-ja have more children?"

"No."

"Her son and his wife—"

"My grandparents."

"Yes, your grandparents. Did they have more than just your mother?"

"My mother is an only child."

"Didn't Mi-ja have her daughter-in-law make offerings and pray to Halmang Samseung?" Young-sook asks, perplexed.

"Who's Halmang Samseung? Is she another one of my great-grandmothers?"

"*Halmang* means granny *and* goddess," Young-sook explains. "Halmang Samseung is the goddess of fertility and childbirth. Surely, Mi-ja would have taken her daughter-in-law to visit the goddess—"

"I never met my grandmother. She died not long after she moved to the States. Breast cancer."

The girl doesn't seem to notice how white Young-sook has gone, because she keeps chattering.

"Yeah, I'm pretty sure no one went to visit the goddess. They wouldn't have made offerings either. We don't believe in things like that. Especially not Granny Mi-ja. She was the biggest Christian of them all—"

"But your grandmother—"

"I already told you. I never met her. After she died, Grandpa Yo-chan brought Granny Mi-ja to L.A. He needed someone to take care of my mom, who was only a baby. Later, when I was born, Granny Mi-ja took care of me. And then my brother. She lived with us."

Being here at the memorial opening makes these stories even more agonizing, and Young-sook can't help being distrustful of Clara. Because why is this girl so persistent? Why do her parents keep sending her to talk to Young-sook? Why can't they all just leave her alone?

"I know the pain Granny Mi-ja caused you and your family," Clara says. "But after what happened, she did everything she could to help you and your family."

"You don't know anything about it!"

But, horrifyingly, the girl seems to know *all* about it. "You and Granny ran through the olles. You were trapped in the schoolyard. You begged Granny to take your children. She said she could only take one. She made you choose. Then she didn't take him. The soldiers killed your husband, your first son, and the one they called Auntie Yu-ri. Granny told me so much about her."

Clara regards the wizened face of the sea woman. "For as long as I can remember," she says, covering Young-sook's hands with her own, "I've had to think about the dark shadow side of friendship. This is the person who knows and loves you best, which means she knows all the ways to hurt and betray you." A fleeting wisp of sadness crosses her face. "And surprise! I don't have any friends. Mom and Dad worry about it. They keep wanting to put me in therapy. I'm not going to therapy!" She shakes her head, realizing she's gone off-track. "Granny Mi-ja hurt you. Every single day, she tortured herself. You should have seen the way she cried at night. And the nightmares."

Young-sook stares into the girl's eyes. The green flecks must come from her white father, but otherwise they're Mi-ja's eyes. What Young-sook sees in the depths of those eyes is pain.

"Granny always asked me the same question. 'What would Young-sook have done if our positions were reversed?'" Clara says. "Now I'm asking you. Would you have sacrificed your life or the lives of your children to save Sang-mun or Yo-chan? Somewhere inside, you have to know that she wasn't aware—"

"Of how severe the consequences would be," Young-sook finishes for her.

Clara releases Young-sook's hands, removes her earbuds, and places them in Young-sook's ears. There's no music. Instead, someone is speaking. The voice belongs to Mi-ja. Tears have pooled in Clara's eyes. She knows what's on the recording, but each word hits Young-sook like sleet—icy and sharp.

"Every day I've forced myself to accept what I did by *not* doing," Mi-ja says. Her voice is old, soft, and quavering. It does not carry the strength or volume of a haenyeo who's been diving for sixty or more years. "I've prayed to Jesus, the Virgin, and God to grant me forgiveness—"

Young-sook yanks the wires from her ears. Clara takes her hands again and recites, *"To understand everything is to forgive."*

"Who said that?"

"Buddha."

"Buddha? But you're Catholic."

"My parents don't know everything about me." She lets that hang in the air for a moment. Then she repeats the saying. *"To understand everything is to forgive.* Now, put these back in your ears."

Young-sook sits as still as a heron. The girl puts the earbuds back in place. Again, Mi-ja speaks.

"I tried so many ways to atone, becoming a Christian, making my entire family go to church and Sunday school, volunteering. I did what I could for Joon-lee . . ."

On the recording, Clara asks, "If you saw your friend today, what would you say to her?"

"Read my letters. Please, please, please, read my letters. Oh, Clara, if she would do that, then she would know what was in my heart."

"But I thought you said you guys didn't know how to read—"

"She'll understand. I know she will. She'll open them and know . . ."

Young-sook pulls out the earbuds. "I can't. I just can't." She stands, steadies herself, and then, drawing on the strength that's seen her through so much, she puts one foot in front of the other, leaving the girl on the bench.

PART V

Forgiveness

1968–1975

Born a Cow

We sat on our haunches outside the bulteok as a man bellowed at us through a bullhorn. "Today the grandmother-divers will go out two kilometers for deep-water work. I'll have the captain drop the small-divers in a cove that's ripe with sea urchins. We have no baby-divers today, so we don't need to worry about them. I keep telling you we need more baby-divers. Please continue to encourage the young women in your families to join the collective."

It was galling enough to have a man tell us what to do, but shouting at us through the bullhorn made matters worse. We may have been hard of hearing, but everyone had always been able to understand me when we sat around the fire pit and discussed the day's plan. I was still the chief of our collective, though, and the other haenyeo looked to me to put this man straight.

"How are we supposed to bring in baby-divers when you changed the rules about who can dive?"

"*I* didn't change the rules," he yelled, indignant.

"All right. *You* didn't," I agreed. "Politicians somewhere far from here passed a law, but what do they know about our practices and our traditions?"

The man puffed his chest. It truly wasn't his fault, but the law that said one diver per household went into effect six years ago—without asking our opinion—and had been a terrible blow to all families who relied on grandmothers, mothers, and daughters for family income.

"It's always been the case that if a woman married out or moved away, she lost her rights to that village," he said.

"So? Years ago, when I married and moved to another village, I was readily accepted into that collective. Now, a woman can only apply for a license after living in a new village for sixty days. And if her mother- or sister-in-law is already a diver, then—"

"The point is," Yang-jin cut in, "if only one diver can be licensed per household, how are we supposed to bring our daughters to the sea?"

"And even if I could bring them," I asked, adding to the point my diving partner had made, "why would I?"

"Am I to hear about Joon-lee now?" the man queried with a pronounced sigh.

Yes, because I knew it irked him. "My younger daughter attends university in Seoul."

"I know. I know."

"While not all daughters are as lucky or as smart as Joon-lee, every young woman now has opportunities that are far less dangerous than diving," I went on. "Look at my older daughter. As her mother, I can say Min-lee was never the cleverest girl, but she helps provide for her family by selling postcards, soda pop, and suntan oil to tourists."

The women around me nodded knowingly, but not one of us had heard of soda pop or suntan oil until recently.

"Why dive when you can be safe on land?" Yang-jin asked.

The man didn't bother to answer. He wasn't risking *his* life entering the sea.

"So who does that leave? You see around you women who've been diving together for many years." I chuckled. "The Kang sisters, Yang-jin, and I—most of us here, actually—are getting close to retirement age. What will you do when that happens?"

He shrugged, pretending indifference, which made us laugh, which made him turn red. He brought the bullhorn back to his mouth. "I run the Village Fishery Association. I'm in charge. You're to do as I tell you."

We laughed even harder then, and more blood rushed to his face. He didn't realize he'd given us another Jeju set of three: he used his line, we laughed at him, and he flushed. Every diving day, the same thing.

Jeju had always been the island of the Three Abundances. We

still had plenty of wind and rocks, but we women were being forced to conform in ways we hadn't before. I can't say if this is a fact or not, but I believed that the Fisheries Cooperative Act came about because of the shortage of men caused by the 4.3 Incident, the 6.25 War, and the new industrialization on the mainland, which lured men away for factory jobs. We had yet another struggle between Shamanism, which was primarily for women, and Confucianism, which favored men. Confucius didn't care much for women: *When a girl, obey your father; when a wife, obey your husband; when a widow, obey your son.* But when I was a girl, I obeyed my mother; when I was a wife, I had equal say to my husband; and now that I was a widow, my only son had to obey me. This was not the case in many households. I was glad I wasn't a daughter or wife now, and that my son knew better than to test me.

The most important and startling of the changes was that men now oversaw the Village Fishery Association. We still had our own collective and met in the bulteok, but the man told us who could work and for how long. He tried to control us—as other men did with every haenyeo collective around the island—so we felt less free to be ourselves or determine our futures. He even made us pay fines if we exceeded catch limits or harvested something in the wrong season. Fines! This I had managed to prevent as chief, so the women in my collective did not have to pay penalties. If you put it all together—men telling us what to do, daughters going to school and getting dry-land jobs, and, especially, rules forbidding more than one woman in a household to work as a haenyeo—no wonder there were fewer of us. Add to that what happened after President Park came to visit. He looked around our island and decided that it wasn't practical to build factories here, but, since the weather was good, he declared that the *only* way to earn a living was by growing a type of tangerine called gamgyul. So people, including many haenyeo, started growing tangerines on the other side of the island. The first time Dr. Park came, there were about twenty-six thousand haenyeo on Jeju. When he came last year—to measure our tolerance to holding our hands in ice water—we'd dropped to eleven thousand haenyeo. Eleven thousand! He made me a bet that within another five years we'd lose another half to retirement.

The only good thing about the Village Fishery Association, as far as I was concerned, was that we could keep whatever we'd harvested beyond our "required quota." These items I took to sell on the streets of Jeju City. The income had paid for my children's educations and Min-lee's wedding and would help me with the banquet and other festivities attached to the forthcoming marriage of Kyung-soo and a girl he'd met on the mainland during his mandatory military service. Soon I would have four generations living within the same fence: my mother-in-law, me, my son and daughter-in-law, and the children they would have.

"Hurry up now!" the man shouted. "Gather your gear!"

We did so, and then climbed onto the back of his truck. He drove us to the dock, where a large motorboat waited for us. Once we were aboard, the captain headed to sea, first dropping the small-divers in a cove and then steering through the churning waves to the deep sea. When we arrived, I took charge.

"Mind your tewaks," I said. "Stay close to the boat. Come in when you get cold. And please watch out for each other."

Life on land had changed, but the sea remained the same. A breath, a breath, a breath, then down . . . The water here was crystal clear to a great depth. Black volcanic rocks stood in contrast to the pearly sand. To my left, a forest of seaweed swayed as if blown by a gentle wind. As always, my above-sea concerns melted away when I began to concentrate, searching the rocks for creatures to put in my net, my senses heightened to watch for dangers.

Four hours later, we arrived back at shore and were returned to Hado, where a few men waited for the truck to pull to a stop. Husbands still spent the day in the village square, minding babies and toddlers, but they helped their wives in ways once unimaginable. We haenyeo are strong, and we had always done our own hauling. Since our men were unaccustomed to physical labor, it typically took two of them to carry what a haenyeo brought ashore. "When you accept our help," the man in charge had explained, "you become more profitable." Of course, I didn't have a husband, and my son was on the mainland. Today, my net was so heavy with my harvest that I had to bend over so that my face was nearly parallel to the ground to bear the weight. The burden—the tangible, physical proof of my labors—felt like money, opportunity, and love.

We still weighed our catches together, but the man in charge oversaw sales and the distribution of monies earned from our sea harvests. Once that was done, we entered the bulteok, warmed by the fire, got dressed, and shared a meal. At least that man didn't come inside. That would have been one insult too many.

"I hear Joon-lee's coming home today," Gu-ja said.

"For the summer," I answered.

"Have her thoughts turned to marriage yet?" Gu-sun asked.

I put a hand on her shoulder, knowing how hard it had to be for her to ask questions that involved a daughter and the unfolding of her life. "You know how Joon-lee is," I answered. "Her thoughts seem to be only on books. I'm lucky Min-lee has already given me twin grandsons."

"Very lucky," Gu-sun agreed. "Now you have the security of another generation of boys to provide for you in the Afterworld."

We left the bulteok together but parted ways almost immediately. I headed to my home perched on the shore. Do-saeng, now sixty-nine, still lived in the little house, but I found her in the kitchen of the big house preparing Joon-lee's welcome-home meal. A wall was stacked with earthenware jars, filled with homemade pickled radishes, sauces, and pastes. To me, those jars were like stacks of gold bars, representing how far I'd brought my family.

"Joon-lee has always liked pork sausage," Do-saeng said. "I've sliced this thin, so each person can have several pieces."

After so many years, I knew my mother-in-law very well, and she wasn't speaking a pure truth. Having Joon-lee return home from her first year at university was a big occasion, and I'd agreed to slaughter one of our pigs. We'd use every part of the animal for the celebration tonight, but the sausage wasn't for Joon-lee. It was for the twins. Do-saeng loved to spoil her great-grandsons.

"What else have you made?" I asked. "And how can I help?"

"I used pork bones, bracken, and spring onions to start the broth for the stew. You can stir in the powdered barley to thicken it, if you'd like. Just remember to—"

"Keep stirring to keep it from getting lumpy. I know."

"Min-lee should be here soon. She's promised to bring tilefish for us to grill. And you brought things from the sea too, I hope."

"I have a basket of baby abalones to grill. This I know Joon-lee loves."

"She is our greatest hope," Do-saeng said with a smile.

But, *aigo,* for the past seven years I'd never had a day when I hadn't missed her. When she was at the all-girls middle and high schools in Jeju City, I only got to see her on special occasions. She even stayed in the city for summer school. "I want to improve my chances of getting into a better college," she'd often repeated on those few days she visited. I thought perhaps the city had twisted her mind to have such a big dream, because to me it was miraculous enough that she was going to her special private schools. I should have known better, because whenever she came to Hado, she showed no desire to join me in the sea. Instead, she wanted to visit the new Village Fishery Association! The government on the mainland had sent books to create small libraries for each association so that a haenyeo like me could "improve her level of literacy." But I wasn't literate to begin with, so this gift felt like another insult. Joon-lee, however, loved those books. She systematically read every one. When the time came, she did so well on the entrance exam that she won a scholarship to Seoul National University—the top school in the country. I was stunned and very proud. Her attitude about it was different.

"During the war, half the students went missing," she'd said when she received the acceptance letter. "They were either killed in battle or moved to the north. Just like here on Jeju, the mainland has fewer men. They need girls like me to fill the slots."

Her older sister said what I felt. "You worked hard for this. Don't dismiss it by acting like you didn't earn your spot."

I couldn't predict what would happen in the future, but even now twice as many boys as girls went to middle and high school. Competition would become ever fiercer as those boys moved forward, but I would make sure all my grandchildren would go to high school, and maybe even college or university, even if it meant their parents and I would be separated from them for most of the year. Sometimes you must experience heartache to have a treasured result.

I heard Min-lee call, "Mother! Granny!"

Do-saeng and I ran outside.

"Look who I found in the olle," Min-lee said. She carried her sister's suitcase in one hand and a basket in the other. Next to her was my younger daughter, who looked completely different than when I'd waved goodbye to her on the dock nine months ago. That day Joon-lee had worn a skirt that came midcalf and a long-sleeved blouse—both made from persimmon cloth. Her hair had hung down in two braids. Now she wore a sleeveless dress with a hem many centimeters above her knees. She'd cut her hair in such a way that her new bangs hid her eyebrows. The rest of her hair had grown several inches and it swung loose and straight almost to her waist. Her twin four-year-old nephews held her hands. Her smile was big. She did not have a big butt. I'd been wrong about that, for which we were all thankful.

———

"No, Mother, I can't go with you to the sea," Joon-lee told me two weeks later, when the next diving cycle arrived.

"Don't worry about the law—"

"I'm not worried about that. I can't go, because I have to study."

"Can't I even get you into the sea to cool off?"

"Maybe later," she said. "I need to finish this chapter."

Maybe later. I already knew what that meant. *Never.* It was always the same two excuses. Either she had to study, or she needed to write letters.

This was the longest she'd been home since she was twelve, and it wasn't going well. I loved my daughter, but she couldn't stop complaining. She didn't like to go in the ocean, because she didn't have a shower to rinse the salt from her skin. She didn't like to wash her hair in the bathing area, because her conditioner didn't work well with salt water. She was unaccustomed to chores and didn't get up early to help me or her grandmother haul water or gather firewood, but she would go by herself to the well to bring back a bucket or two of water to wash her hair. (I had her do it behind the little house so our neighbors wouldn't see how wasteful she was.) She saved her worst complaints for the latrine: "It stinks! The pigs are groveling around right under me. And the bugs!"

We still had another two and a half months to go before she returned to Seoul.

"Tell me about the book," I said, trying to find a way to connect. "Remember when you read *Heidi* to me. Maybe you could read this one—"

She looked at me with annoyance that turned to sadness. "Mother, you wouldn't understand it. I'm trying to read ahead for the sociology class I'm taking next semester."

Sociology. It wasn't the first time I didn't know what she was talking about.

"All right," I said, turning away. "I'm sorry. I won't bother you again."

"Oh, Mother, don't take it that way." She put the book down, crossed the room, and put her arms around me. "I'm the one who should be sorry."

She stared into my face, and I was taken aback, as I always was, by how much her delicate features reminded me of her father. I smoothed tendrils of hair behind her ears.

"You're a good girl," I said. "And you make me proud. Go back to your studying."

But inside, I hurt. I thought of her like seafoam—drifting farther and farther from me—and I couldn't figure out how to change its course.

————

Gu-ja, of all people, told me what sociology was. "It's the study of how people get along. Gu-sun and I have a second cousin who does that work in Jeju City."

That the Kang sisters had an educated relative in the city surprised me, but this also told me that I needed to adapt better to the changing conditions around me as I did, without thinking, to those in the sea.

"Do you mean how friends or family get along?" I asked.

"I suppose," she answered, "but I think it's more like what happens in our bulteok."

For days I mulled over what Gu-ja had told me. Gradually an idea began to form in my mind. When the second diving period of summer arrived, I invited Joon-lee to come to the bulteok with her grandmother and me. "Not to go in the sea," I explained, "but to learn about haenyeo society." I was thrilled when she said yes.

Once in the bulteok, Joon-lee sat quietly, listening to the other divers and me as we changed clothes. "Is there food on this beach?" I asked the collective. As the typical boasting answers flew at me—"More food than rocks in my fields, if I had any fields" and "More food than the liters of gasoline it would take to fill my car, if I had a car"—she jotted them down in a notebook. When Do-saeng and her friends went to the beach to collect the algae that had washed ashore, Joon-lee joined me and the other haenyeo on the back of the truck to the dock. She hadn't tied up her hair, and it blew here, there, and everywhere. Even as she waited on the boat while we dove, she didn't properly cover her hair. Hours later, during our return to shore, she asked questions about what we were doing, but they only made me look like a bad mother.

"Haven't you taught her anything about diving?" Gu-ja asked me.

When I let the years scroll across my mind, I could see I'd tried, but it hadn't taken. As a young girl, Joon-lee had never been interested in taking the tewak I'd given her into the sea. She'd never borrowed my big eyes, nor had she asked me to make her a set of water clothes. When she turned fifteen, she was already living in Jeju City, so I couldn't train her for sea work as my mother had trained me. I couldn't help but be embarrassed in front of the collective, but my daughter came to my defense.

"Don't tease your chief," she said lightly. "She's worked hard to give me this life. You've done the same for you daughters too, right?"

They had, but of course none of those girls had done as well as Joon-lee.

Once in the bulteok, we did as we usually did: warmed ourselves by the fire, cooked a meal, and talked about problems in our families. Joon-lee blossomed in front of me, asking all sorts of questions about our matrifocal society. This was the first time any of us had heard this label—a culture focused on women—and it intrigued us.

"You make the decisions in your households," she explained. "You make money. You have a good life—"

Gu-ja waved off the idea. "We think of ourselves as being independent and strong, but all you have to do is listen to our songs to know our days are hard. We sing about the difficulties of living under a mother-in-law, the sadness of being separated from our children, and lament how difficult this existence is."

"My sister's right," Gu-sun said. "*It's better to be born a cow than a woman.* No matter how stupid or lazy a man is, he has the better hand. He doesn't have to supervise the family. He doesn't have to wash clothes, manage the household, look after the elders, or see that the children have food to eat and mats to sleep on. He doesn't have to do hard physical work in the wet or dry fields. His only responsibilities are to take care of babies and do a little cooking."

"In other places, he would be called a wife," Joon-lee said.

This made us laugh.

"So if you were a man," she prompted, "how would your life be different?"

From my youngest days as a baby-diver, conversation in the bulteok had often centered on men, husbands, and sons. I could remember my mother leading a group as they discussed whether it was better to live as a man or a woman, but my daughter's question sent the haenyeo in my collective in new directions.

Gu-ja answered first. "If I were a man, I wouldn't worry about chores or responsibilities. I'd sit under the village tree, like they do, and contemplate big thoughts."

"I've wondered sometimes if it would be better to be my husband," Gu-sun admitted. "Ever since our daughter died, he drinks too much. I've asked him to find a little wife and share her home. His response? 'Why should I do that when you already house and feed me?'"

I knew each woman's story. Whose husband drank too much. Or gambled. Or beat her. Whenever a woman came to the bulteok with bruises, I told her the same thing I'd once told Mi-ja. *Leave him!* But they rarely did. They were always too afraid for their children, and maybe afraid for themselves.

"Drinking and gambling are the hardest," one of the women commented. "Once my babies were old enough to be taken care of by their older siblings, my husband became purposeless. I felt sorry for him, but what would have happened if *I'd* started drinking and gambling?"

"I was a slave in my first husband's family," Yang-jin confessed. "My husband and father-in-law beat me. It's true! I wouldn't want to be a man who did something like that. I'm happier as a woman."

"Someone will always take care of a man," a woman said. "Ask yourself if you know a man who lives alone."

No one could think of even one man in Hado who lived alone. He resided with his mother, his wife, his little wife, or his children.

Do-saeng finally joined the conversation. "Not many men can do without a wife, while all women can do without a husband."

My daughter looked up from her notebook. "It seems to me that what you're saying is you're in charge, and yet you aren't. When husbands die, houses and fields pass to sons. Why is it that men own all the property?"

"You know the reason," I answered. "A daughter cannot perform the ancestral rites, so all property must go to sons. It is how we thank them for caring for us in the Afterworld."

"It's not fair," Joon-lee said.

"It's not," I agreed. "Many of us lost sons in the war or during"—I lowered my voice—"the incident, which is why some here have adopted sons. But there are others of us, like myself, who've bought fields to give to our daughters one day."

"You bought fields for me?" Joon-lee asked with a curious look on her face. Until this moment, I hadn't considered the possibility that she might not want land on Jeju, that she might not return at all.

"I don't know why you're all talking about how your husbands do all the cooking and taking care of the children," one of my neighbors said. "In my house, cooking, cleaning, and washing are women's work. *My* work. I keep it simple. Barley porridge. A soup with pickled vegetables."

"I know what you mean," someone else agreed. "My husband

longs to be the master of our family, but I do everything. I consider him only a guest in my home."

"It's better to have a guest in your home than have no husband at all," I said. "I loved my husband, and I will love him forever. I would give anything to have him with me."

"But Jun-bu was different than other men," Gu-sun said. "We all grew up with him, and—"

"I had two wrong husbands," Yang-jin interrupted. "My second husband did nothing for me. Now that he's dead, I'll never think about either of them again."

"I lost my husband too," one of the small-divers said, "and I also don't miss him. He never helped our family. He couldn't dive. Men are weak under the sea, where we face life and death every day."

"You're being too severe." I paused for a moment to see how I could say this so they'd understand. "Times are changing. Look at my son. He didn't seek permission to marry. His future wife is not a haenyeo. I love my son, and I know every single one of you loves your sons. Sons grow up to be men."

"It's true," Gu-ja agreed. "I love my sons."

"I lost Wan-soon," her sister admitted, "but I would die if I lost one of my sons."

"I'm teaching my great-grandsons to cook," Do-saeng boasted.

"Already?"

"They're never too young to start learning," Do-saeng said. "I'm teaching them how to make porridge."

"Me too!"

And suddenly the conversation shifted as the women began to speak of their love of their sons and grandsons. Joon-lee kept writing, but I wasn't sure she was getting the information she'd hoped for. As for me, I was troubled. She'd made me see things in a different way. We lived on an island of goddesses. One for childbirth, one for child death, one for the hearth, one for the sea, and so on, with gods serving as their consorts. Our strongest goddess was Grandmother Seolmundae—the embodiment of our island. Our strongest *real* woman was Kim Mandeok, who'd saved the people during the Most Horrendous Famine, but we'd been inspired by made-up women and girls too. Every single person in the bulteok had either read or had read to her the story of Heidi. But as strong as we were and as much as we did, not one of us would ever be chosen to run the Village Fishery Association or be elected to Hado's village council.

———

In August, when our sweet potato crop was ready to harvest, Joon-lee came with Do-saeng and me on the first day to help. She lasted exactly one hour before sitting in the shade of the rock wall that edged the field. She pulled out a transistor radio and a notebook from her backpack. The music she played? *Eeee.* It hurt my ears, but it kept away the crows. She began writing. It had to be another letter.

"Who are you writing to this time?" I asked.

"A friend. In Seoul."

Do-saeng glanced over at me. She'd kept quiet about my daughter, but I could tell she disapproved of the way Joon-lee acted.

"Every day you write," I said. "You take your letters to the post office, but I never see you receive anything in return."

"That's because everyone's so busy," she replied, not even looking up from her notebook. "Seoul isn't like Jeju. The magic of Seoul is that boredom is impossible. There's culture, history, and creativity everywhere."

When she was a little girl, her inquisitiveness had gotten her into trouble on occasion, but it had also taken her to where she was now. I should have been exulting in her accomplishments, but all I felt was sadness.

———

Then too fast—although in many ways it wasn't fast enough—it was time for Joon-lee to go back to her university. Do-saeng and I packed dried fish, sweet potatoes, and jars of kimchee for her to take to her dormitory. I prepared an envelope with money for her to spend on books and other supplies. I'd even re-dyed one of her persimmon-cloth outfits to make it stronger, although I had a feeling she'd never wear it in Seoul.

When Joon-lee entered the room, she was already dressed in her traveling outfit—a sleeveless white blouse and what I'd learned was called a miniskirt. What she said startled me more than anything else she'd said or done all summer.

"Mother, before I leave, will you take me with you to Yo-chan's house?"

I took a breath, hoping to slow my racing heart, then asked, "Why would I take you there?"

She lifted a single shoulder. "You go every day. I thought you could take me with you."

"You haven't answered my question."

She looked away, avoiding my eyes. "Yo-chan asked me to get something for him."

Beside me, Do-saeng hissed between clenched teeth. I stared hard at my daughter, but I tried to tread carefully.

"You're in contact with Yo-chan?"

"We've known each other since we were kids," she said, as if I didn't know that.

"They moved away—"

"But we met again in Seoul."

"That you even know him is a surprise," I admitted, while keeping my voice as steady as possible.

"I saw him on campus one day. We recognized each other right away. He invited me to a restaurant to see his mother—"

"Mi-ja—"

"They've been kind to me. He's attending the Graduate School of Business right on campus, and—"

"Joon-lee, don't hurt me this way."

"I'm not hurting you. We're friends. That's all. They take me out for dinner sometimes."

"Please stay away from them." That I had to beg my daughter for this seemed incomprehensible to me.

She stared at me in frustration. "*You* go to her house every day."

"That's different."

"*Deep roots remain tangled underground,*" she recited. "Yo-chan's mother says that about the two of you, and I guess she's right."

"I'm not tangled with Mi-ja," I said, but I wasn't speaking truthfully. I don't know why I felt compelled to visit her house every day, but I was drawn there nevertheless. I watered the flowers she'd left behind. I washed her floors when they got dirty. I went to the city office every year to make sure the taxes were paid. (They were.) If Mi-ja ever came back, I'd be ready for her. For now, though, I had to convince my daughter to avoid Mi-ja and her son. "It would bring me solace to know that when you're far from home you won't see them. Can you please promise me that?"

"I'll do my best."

"You said the same thing years ago when you broke your arm, and yet here we are."

Defiance flared in her eyes, but she said, "I promise, all right? Now will you let me get the thing Yo-chan needs from his house? I said I'd bring it to him. After that—"

"What is this *thing*?"

"I don't know exactly. He said it's in a chest that sits against the wall in the main room."

I knew everything in that house, and what was in that chest did not belong to Yo-chan. It belonged to Mi-ja. It was her father's book.

"You know," my daughter went on, "I could have gone over there any day this summer and picked it up. I didn't have to ask you."

But of course she did, because I would have noticed if anything was missing.

"I was showing you respect," she insisted.

This I had to believe.

"The sooner this is behind us, the better," I said. "I'll take you."

Joon-lee rewarded me with her father's smile.

But I was still hurt. These past few years, I'd been obliged to accept orders from the man from the Village Fishery Association, but my consolation had come from knowing I was giving my daughter the best education possible. She was smart and ambitious. She knew things I would never know. But now I saw other realities: You can do everything for a child. You can encourage her to read and do her math homework. You can forbid her to ride a bike, giggle too much, or see a boy. I'd just asked her to promise she wouldn't see Yo-chan or Mi-ja again. She'd done so grudgingly. Sometimes everything you do is as pointless and as ineffective as shouting into the wind.

A Guest for One Hundred Years

1972–1975

"Sit. Sit," I said in heavily accented English to the American soldiers. I squatted on my haunches, surrounded by plastic tubs filled with abalone, sea cucumber, sea squirt, and sea urchin. I also had a basket stuffed with paper plates, plastic spoons, and napkins. These servicemen on leave from battles in Vietnam looked young to me, but some of them had a haunted look I easily recognized. Or they were drunk. Or using drugs.

"What are you selling today, Granny?" a local boy the servicemen had hired asked.

"Here's sea squirt—the ginseng of the sea. It will help these men below the belt."

The boy translated this. A couple of the soldiers laughed. One turned bright red. Two others pretended to gag. Young men. Even when they're embarrassed they try to outdo each other. I could profit from that. I reached into a tub and pulled out a sea squirt.

"See how it looks like a rock," I said, with the local boy quietly repeating my words in English. "Look more closely. It's covered in sea moss. Does it look familiar yet?" My knife slit open the underside and spread the creature apart. "What does this look like now? A woman's privates! That's right!" I switched to English. "Eat."

The soldier who'd blushed earlier now turned crimson, but he ate it. His companions slapped him on the back and shouted I-don't-know-what. I poured homemade rice wine into abalone shells. The soldiers held the shells to their lips and swilled down the white liquid. I next sliced abalone, which they dipped into chili sauce. When they were done, I pointed to an octopus, still alive, and curled at the bottom of one of my tubs. I grinned, poured more rice wine into their shells, and encouraged them to drink. I watched as they egged each other on. Finally, the boy they'd hired said, "They'll try it."

Soon sliced suckers writhed and twitched on a plate. "Be careful," I warned in English. Then I switched to my native tongue. "The squirming bits are still alive. Those suction cups can grab your throat. You've had a lot to drink. I don't want you to choke and die."

Hoots of daring. More rice wine. And soon the pieces of octopus were gone. These men were so different from the ones I'd met during my itinerant work. I remembered that time the chef climbed down the rope ladder to our boat and refused anything and everything except what was most recognizable to him: fish.

The tallest of the soldiers pulled out a stack of postcards. He showed them to his friends, who nodded appreciatively. Then he held one out to me, pointed, and spouted a string of English words.

"Tell us, Granny," the Jeju boy said, translating as best he could, "where can they find girls like these?"

I examined the image, which showed young women—their legs and arms firm, wearing form-fitting water clothes with bare shoulders, their hair hanging loose about their shoulders—in provocative poses. The mainland government had decided that the haenyeo might be a good tourist attraction, so now we were being advertised as the Sirens of the Deep and the Mermaids of Asia. I had no idea who the girls in the postcard were, but I was glad none of them worked in my collective.

"You tell them I'm a haenyeo," I said. "You tell them I'm the best haenyeo on Jeju!"

That wilted their enthusiasm. I looked good, but I was forty-nine years old and only six years away from retirement.

Every Saturday afternoon was like this. I brought my catch in from the sea, Min-lee helped me load everything onto a bus, and then I rode into Jeju City, found a street corner near the area with all the bars and girls, and sold my wares. My customers were mostly American servicemen. Here on leave, they rappelled off ocean-facing cliffs, swam in our wet fields, and raced each other up Mount Halla. I had other American customers too. They were from the Peace Corps, but rumors circulated that they actually worked for the U.S. government and were keeping tabs on "red" activity. It was hard to tell what was true or just more gossip, but all those people were so young and inexperienced that I often spooned out sea urchin roe and dropped it directly into their open mouths like they were baby birds.

I sold the last of my goods, and the soldiers wandered down the street and into a bar. I emptied my tubs, stacked them, and walked to the bus stop. Along the way, I passed women wearing tight dresses. Men in untucked T-shirts and shorts or jeans sauntered up to those young women and exchanged words. Sometimes a deal was struck, but most of the women continued on their way, ignoring the eager attentions.

When I was a girl going in and out of the port for leaving-home water-work, Jeju City had seemed so much more advanced than Hado. It still was. Jeju City had the largest five-day market on the island, where I could buy just about anything, but the city also had souvenir shops, photo studios, beauty parlors, and places to buy or repair toasters, fans, and lamps. Cars, motorcycles, trucks, buses, and taxis moved through traffic that also included horse- and donkey-pulled carts, as well as hand-pushed wheelbarrows piled high. The air was thick with cigarette smoke, perfume, diesel and gasoline exhaust, and dung from the dray animals. Raw sewage still ran through the gutters down to the harbor, where ships spewed oil and fish waited to be off-loaded to canneries. The alleyways were chockablock with bars serving our local rice wine, beer, barbecue, and girls. I had to be careful as I passed those places, because customers liked to throw chicken, pork, and beef bones out the door to the sidewalk, where poor kids scurried and darted to scavenge these discards and take them home to their families.

By the time I boarded the bus, the sun had set. Outside the window, lights sprawled to infinity—from cafés and houses, to the port, and then offshore to the squid and shrimp boats, which dotted the sea all the way to where the ocean met the star-filled sky. The road circling the island had been paved the previous year, and the ride was smooth and fast. I got off at Hado and walked home through the olle. Oil lamps glowed here and there, but the old quiet was gone. People were frugal, so they didn't always use their new electricity to light their homes, preferring instead to play radios and record players.

I heard the racket from my house even before I reached it. I sighed. I was tired and didn't want to face a crowd. I entered the gate, and the entire courtyard was filled with people, sitting with their backs to me. The new sliding doors into the big house had been pushed open. More people sat on the floor inside the house. Whether inside or outside, everyone faced the television like they were in a cinema. They'd all brought food too—buckwheat pancakes with shredded turnip and stews filled with rice cakes and fish floating in spicy red sauce and topped with fried chilies. The television picture was in black and white, and the reception was fuzzy, but I recognized the show right away. Maybe tonight Marshal Dillon would finally kiss Miss Kitty. I spotted Min-lee, her husband, the twins—now eight—and her daughters, five and two. Min-lee's husband rubbed her back. Their fifth child was due in six weeks, and Min-lee stood on her feet all day in the gift shop in the hotel where she worked. They all lived in the big house now.

I picked my way through the crowd to the little house that Do-saeng and I—two widows—now shared. I put away my tubs and added the cash I'd earned today to the tin box where I kept my savings. When I was done, Do-saeng said reproachfully, "They've been peeing in the courtyard again."

"Tell them to use the latrine next time."

"Do you think I didn't?"

Not only were we the first in Hado to get a television, but our compound had been among the first to be affected by Saemaul Undong—the New Village Movement—which the regime had recently inaugurated. We'd been told we couldn't promote tourism without upgrading the island. We were to have indoor plumbing, electricity, telephones, paved roads, and commercial airlines. This meant, among other things, that thatch roofs had to be replaced with those made of corrugated tin or tile. We were told tourists wouldn't like our three-step farming system, and that we had to get rid of our pigsty latrines. Tourists wouldn't want to see or smell pigs, and they certainly wouldn't want to put their rear ends above the pigs' greedy snouts. I didn't know one family willing to tear down its latrine, and I'd continue to keep mine for as long as possible. So much change so fast was unsettling, and it undermined our way of life, our beliefs, and our traditions.

"You spoiled your children, and now you're spoiling your grandchildren with that television," Do-saeng complained.

I absorbed the criticism. Yes, I gave a spoonful of sugar to Min-lee's twins and to her two daughters whenever I saw them, which was every day. I didn't begrudge my grandchildren their treats, but the television had clearly been a mistake.

"Look at it this way," I said. "You get to see your great-grandchildren every day, and you're healthy enough to enjoy them. Not every woman your age can say that."

At seventy-three, Do-saeng was in remarkable shape. Her braids had gone gray, but her body was strong. Even though she was well past retirement age, she'd begun diving again. That broke the rule of having more than one diver per household, but the man in charge of the Village Fishery Association let her join us from time to time because we needed her, and women like her, since it was impossible to find baby-divers these days. This, more than giving sugar to children, would have been unimaginable back when my own grandmother was alive.

"Tomorrow is going to be a big day," she reminded me. "You need to tell everyone to go home."

"You're right," I agreed. "But I think I'll join them for a while first."

"*Hyng!*"

I took some tangerines from a bowl and tucked them in my pockets. Then I waded through the courtyard and into the big house.

"Granny!"

"Granny!"

I sat with my legs tucked under me, my bottom nestled between my feet. My granddaughters climbed into my lap, and my grand-sons cuddled close.

"Did you bring us anything?" the oldest girl asked.

I pulled out a tangerine. I unpeeled it in one long string. Once I was done, I rolled the peel back into its tangerine shape and set it on the floor. The children loved when I did that for them. I gave them each a couple of wedges, then repeated the process three times.

How lucky I was to have such beautiful grandchildren. How fortunate I was that Min-lee had married a teacher like her father, who taught right here in Hado. I missed Kyung-soo and his family, though. When he'd sent word that he was getting married, I'd thought the wedding would happen here. But when the goddess brought him home, he was already married to his mainland wife. I'd participated in no discussions about matching birth dates or seeking help from the geomancer for a propitious day to hold the wedding. Naturally, my feelings were injured, but I let all that go when I met my daughter-in-law for the first time and saw she was big with a baby in her belly. After they returned to Seoul, she gave birth to a son, giving me another grandson. Now she was pregnant with a second child, and Kyung-soo worked at his father-in-law's electronics company. I wished my only son didn't live so far away, but there was nothing I could do about it.

I missed Joon-lee most of all. For the last four years, she'd also been in Seoul. In the fall, she'd attend the Graduate School of Public Health at Seoul National University. Tomorrow she'd be coming home for a short visit. The note she'd written to Min-lee had said, "I have a surprise for everyone." My guess was she'd won another award.

"Do you have more tangerines?" the five-year-old asked. I turned out my pockets to show they were empty. She sucked her bottom lip in disappointment. I kissed her forehead.

Do-saeng was right. I did spoil these little ones. I gave them and their parents everything—fixing up our houses to meet the new standards, buying tricycles and bicycles, getting the television so they could learn more about our country and the world—and it had left them soft. Children these days wanted easy lives. They didn't have the physical or emotional strength of their grandmother or great-grandmother. That said, I loved them and would sacrifice anything for them, even if it meant selling seafood to American soldiers on a street corner.

I'd been a widow for twenty-three years, but I considered myself to be a fortunate woman. I squeezed the twins, they squealed, but no one seemed to mind the noise. Everyone was too focused on the shoot-out happening on the screen.

———

The next day, our diving was good. I was the last to leave the bulteok and was just crossing the beach toward my house when a motorcycle came bumping along the shore road and pulled to a stop. A man wearing a black leather jacket and a helmet that hid his face sat in front. Joon-lee sat behind him, holding his waist. She waved and called, "Mother! It's me! I'm home!" She jumped off the bike and ran down the steps and across the beach to me. Her long black hair flew behind her. Her short shirt fluttered in the wind. When she reached me, she bowed.

"I thought you weren't coming until later," I said. "The bus—"

"We rented the bike." With that, her initial burst of enthusiasm ebbed, and she stood with such stillness that I was immediately concerned.

"We?"

She took my hand. "Come, Mother. I couldn't wait to tell you. I'm just so happy." Her hand was soft and warm in mine, but her voice was far too somber to be expressing anything close to joy.

I kept my eyes on the man with the motorcycle. He didn't have to take off the helmet for me to know who he was, because he was in nearly the same spot where he'd been perched on his new bicycle many years ago to see what was happening on the beach with Dr. Park and his team. When I said his name in my mind— Yo-chan—my stomach fell so hard and fast that for a second the world went black. I blinked a few times, trying to bring back light. Up on the roadway, Yo-chan set the kickstand, took off his helmet and hung it on one of the handlebars, and watched us approach. He put his palms on his thighs and bowed deeply when we reached him. As he rose, he offered no greetings or small talk. Instead, he said, "We've come to tell you that we're going to get married."

The inevitability of this moment seemed obvious and predictable, and yet it was still agonizing. I hesitated awhile, too long, really, before I asked, "What does your mother say?"

"You can ask her yourself," he answered. "She's coming in a taxi."

I felt as though I were suspended in gelatin, watching as he turned to the bike and pushed it the last few meters to my house, with Joon-lee following behind him.

———

We aligned in two pairs: my daughter next to me facing Yo-chan, who sat next to his mother, who faced me. Teacups sat on a small tray on the floor between us. I could hear my granddaughters crying across the courtyard in the little house, where Min-lee had taken them so I could have this meeting in the big house. I hadn't seen Mi-ja in eleven years. When she'd entered, I saw that her limp was much worse, and she used a cane. She looked far older than I did, even though her life had to be easier than mine. Her clothes were loose. Her hair had gone completely gray. Looking into her eyes, I sensed a deep well of unhappiness. That was not my problem, however.

"We have not consulted a geomancer to determine if this is a good match," I said, keeping my sentences and attitude as formal as possible. "We haven't brought in an intermediary. No one has asked if our family gives permission—"

"Oh, Mother, no one does those things anymore—"

I spoke right over my daughter. "No one has set an engagement meeting or—"

"Let us consider *this* the engagement meeting," Mi-ja said.

I addressed my daughter. "I did not know your thoughts had turned to marriage."

"Yo-chan and I are in love."

I barely knew where to start. "Four years ago, I asked you to promise you wouldn't see him again. Then you kept this"—I searched for the right word and settled on—"affiliation a secret from me, your mother."

"I knew how you'd react," Joon-lee admitted. "But I also wanted to make sure in my own heart. I didn't want to hurt you."

"This cannot happen."

"We're happy," she said. "We love each other."

She could be stubborn, but I would never back down. I could

have dredged up the nasty gossip about Yo-chan and Wan-soon, but even I didn't believe it, so I went straight to my deepest argument. "For you to show such disrespect to the memory of your father—"

"I'm sorry, but I have no memory of my father."

This was too painful. I closed my eyes as the horrifying images came flooding back. No matter how much I fought against them, the details were as vivid and brutal as in the moments they'd happened: Mi-ja touching her husband's arm . . . Yo-chan in his little uniform . . . My husband when the bullet hit his head . . . Yu-ri's screams . . . My little boy being snatched away . . . I would never heal or forget.

Mi-ja quietly cleared her throat, and I opened my eyes. "There was a time when you and I wished for this day." She allowed herself a small smile. "Although we thought it would be Min-lee and Yo-chan. Still, this day has come. *A son-in-law is a guest for one hundred years,* meaning forever. It is time for you to put aside your anger, so these two, who have no responsibility for the past, can be wed. May you accept my son as part of your family for one hundred years."

"I—"

She held up a hand to keep me from speaking. "As your daughter said, they do not need our permission any longer. We can only give them what they want. I had no desire to return to Jeju, but I did because Joon-lee wants to be surrounded by her family on her wedding day. I've made arrangements for them to be married in the Catholic church in Jeju City."

I gasped. Christianity had grown on the island, and those people were even more fanatical than our government when it came to Shamanism. Joon-lee lowered her head as her hand went to finger the small cross hanging from her neck, which I'd been too stunned by Yo-chan's presence and Mi-ja's arrival to notice until now. That she was not just hurting me but also abandoning the traditions of our haenyeo family was more than I could absorb.

Mi-ja went on, unfazed. "The ceremony will be followed by a banquet and party here in Hado."

Resentment bubbled to the surface. "You've taken so much from me," I said to her. "Why do you have to take Joon-lee too?"

"Mother!"

In response to my daughter's outburst, Mi-ja said, "Perhaps it would be best if the two mothers speak alone."

"We want to stay," Yo-chan said. "I want to make her understand."

"Believe me," Mi-ja said mildly. "This will be best."

Yo-chan and Joon-lee were barely out the door before Mi-ja said, "You've never understood a single thing. You've carried your blame and hatred without ever asking me what really happened."

"I didn't have to ask you. I saw with my own eyes. That soldier picked up my son—"

"Do you think I don't see that in my mind every single day? That moment is burned in my memory."

She looked tortured, but what did that mean? I waited to see what she would say next.

"After my cowardice, I needed to atone," she said at last. "When my husband began to travel and I knew he wouldn't miss me"—an emotion flitted across her face, but she buried it before I could read it—"I moved back to Hado. I wanted to see if I could help you."

"I saw no help from you."

"I had to wait a long time. I thought there was no hope for me. Then Wan-soon died."

"You came to the ritual rite. No one wanted you there."

"You may not have wanted me, but the spirits of those you lost did. They spoke to me—"

"They spoke to *me,*" I corrected her.

"You change what happened, because you only see evil when you look at me." Her quiet calm was having the opposite effect on me. She must have sensed this, because she kept her voice low and steady, like she was trying to lull me into believing her. "Consider what actually happened: Shaman Kim went into her trance. Yu-ri spoke first—"

"Yes, she spoke to *me*. I'd been waiting so long to hear from her. From any of them."

"But they only spoke when *I* was there." Mi-ja, perhaps sensing my doubt, went on. "They never came to you again, did they?"

My head throbbed as I thought about what she'd said. This couldn't be right.

"Each of them said the same thing," Mi-ja continued softly. "They had found forgiveness. Who was that message for, if not for me?"

I was innocent, they killed me, but I have found forgiveness.

I began to tremble. Maybe they *had* come for her.

"If the dead can forgive me, then why can't you?" she asked.

"You could never understand, because you haven't suffered the losses I have."

"I've suffered in my own ways."

I suspected she wanted me to question her, but I didn't.

The moment lengthened until she finally said, "Even though you refuse to accept it, I've tried to make amends to you in every way I can. When Joon-lee won the competition, Teacher Oh came to me—"

"No, he didn't—"

"Yes, he did. He explained that she'd been offered a place at a fine school in Jeju City but that the guilt-by-association system had tainted her. I took a ferry to the mainland and met with my husband. I told him I was willing to do whatever he wanted if he would see that she got her place. I reminded him how you and your family had helped bring him back to health after he escaped from the north. He still had those scars, you know, inside and out."

"But he did nothing that terrible day to stop—"

"He didn't know you were there, and then it was too late. When he found out . . . He'd beaten me before, but not like that. I ended up in the hospital. I stayed there for weeks, which is why I couldn't come to you right away. Most of my injuries healed, but my hip has never been the same."

"Am I supposed to feel sorry for you?"

The corners of her mouth turned up into the barest smile. "All that matters is that Sang-mun said he'd have Joon-lee erased from the guilt-by-association records so she could go to school. In exchange, I'd have to move to Seoul and live with him again. He told me that this was the only way *he* could remove the stain of *my* actions from *his* face. I accepted Sang-mun's terms, which meant I would also have to accept the way he'd treated me from the day we met on the dock. Of course, I didn't trust him, so I stayed in Hado until Teacher Oh confirmed Joon-lee was settled at her school."

I wasn't sure what she wanted me to feel. Pity? Maybe I did pity her in my own way, but what she'd told me made her sound even worse than I'd thought. For her own husband to blame her . . .

"So," she said, breaking another long silence, "I did what I could for Joon-lee. Yo-chan and I visited her in Jeju City when we came to the island to see Sang-mun's parents. When she arrived in Seoul—"

"You had Yo-chan hunt her down."

"*Hyng!* It was far from that! They bumped into each other on the campus. I never expected them to fall in love, but they did. I saw it on their faces the first time he brought her to the apartment. It was fate, don't you see?"

"Do Catholics believe in fate?" I asked.

She blinked rapidly. She could accept my hatred, but she wouldn't allow me to mock her faith. Interesting.

"Joon-lee's been on her own a very long time," she said. "I've tried, when possible, to be a second mother to her. I love Joon-lee, and I've done my best to help her."

"You mean you tried to steal her from me."

Mi-ja's cheeks colored, and she shook a finger in front of my face. "No, no, no."

Good, I'd finally gotten to her. Maybe now she'd speak truthfully. But then she took a breath, her cheeks paled, and she returned to the unnerving calm she seemed to have perfected.

"There's no point in trying to share my heart with you," she said. "Your anger has poisoned you. You've become like Halmang Juseung. You touch everything with the flower of demolition. You're killing all that is beautiful—our friendship, your love for Joon-lee, the happiness of a young couple." She rose and padded across the floor. When she reached the door, she turned back to me. "Joon-lee told me that you've been taking care of my house. Why?"

"I thought . . . I don't know what I thought," I confessed, because my years of believing that I'd be *ready* when she came back had turned out to be false. I hadn't been prepared for any of this.

"I thank you anyway." She lifted her chin as she added, "The ceremony will be tomorrow at the church, as I told you earlier. The banquet will be at my aunt and uncle's home. You are welcome to attend. The children would love to have you with them on their joyous day."

But as much as I loved my daughter, I couldn't go to her wedding. First and foremost, it would have been disrespectful to her father, brother, and aunt. On another level, I was too hurt by Joonlee's years of lies and broken promises even to want to see her face. I would have to overcome a lot within myself to break through the barriers that now separated us. So, the next day, I stayed with Min-lee—who also refused to attend the wedding—and her family through the long, hot hours until night finally fell. They rolled out sleeping mats in the main room, so we could all be together. The children fell asleep. Min-lee's husband snored lightly. But Min-lee and I went outside, sat on the step, held hands, and listened to the music, songs, and laughter that wafted from the other side of the village.

"So many bad memories," Min-lee whispered. "So much pain."

I patted her back as she quietly wept. She and I would never be the same after what we'd seen and lost twenty-three years ago, but that could also be said for most people on the island. On this night, I couldn't take my mind from Jun-bu, what he'd wished for our children, and what he'd feared for them. *For a tree that has many branches, even a small breeze will shake some loose.* We had grown a tree with many branches. One son had died too soon, but we now had grandchildren who would ensure our family's line. But wherever Jun-bu was, could he be disappointed in Joon-lee and even more disappointed in me for how I'd raised her? For me, the pride of my life, my youngest daughter, was the branch who'd broken off in a way I never expected. By joining Mi-ja's family, she had shattered my heart.

———

Fourteen months later, on a sultry fall morning, I walked my twin grandsons to school. They usually went with their father, but he'd needed to leave the house early to attend a meeting. We saw other children in the olles. The girls wore school uniforms: a dark blue skirt, white blouse, and wide-brimmed sunhat. The boys wore blue pants and white shirts. We met a teacher as we neared the school. Jun-bu had always worn traditional clothes made of persimmon-dyed fabric to teach, but these days the instructors wore their own version of a uniform: slacks, white shirts, and ties. We bowed to show our respect. The teacher nodded to us and continued purposefully in the direction of the high school. When we reached the elementary school, I gave each grandchild a tangerine. These days, teachers in Hado expected to find tangerines placed in a neat stack on their desks every morning, and I was proud that my grandchildren could participate in that. I watched them run inside, and then I went back home. Min-lee waited for me much as I'd left her, sitting on a low stone wall, holding an envelope in her hand. This was the first letter Joon-lee had sent since her wedding.

"Are you ready?" she asked.

"Open it."

Min-lee slit open the envelope. Money fluttered out of it, which we quickly gathered. Then she began to read: "'Dear Mother and Sister, I've given birth to a baby girl. She's healthy, and I'm fine. We've named her Ji-young. I'm hoping you've softened toward me and my husband these past months and will come to Seoul to meet her. I've enclosed money for your travel expenses. We'll be moving to America in December. Yo-chan will be working at Samsung's office in Los Angeles. I'm hoping to become a student at UCLA, so I can finish my degree. I'm not sure when we'll be back, so you must come see us. Mother, you've always said that children are hope and joy. Ji-young is hope and joy to us. I hope she will be to you too. With love and respect, Joon-lee.'"

Min-lee's voice trailed off. She studied me, trying to get a sense of my feelings. I was ripped up inside. I had a new grandchild. Such a blessing. But that child was also the grandchild of the woman who'd nearly destroyed my life.

"If you want to go," Min-lee said tentatively, "I'll take time off from work and come with you. Would you like that?"

"You're a good daughter," I said, "but let me think about it."

A flash of hurt crossed Min-lee's face.

"Don't misunderstand," I said. "If I go, I'd love for you to come with me. You've always been a perfect daughter, and I'd need you. But I'm not sure if I'll go."

"But, Mother, it's Joon-lee. The baby . . ."

I slowly rose. "Just let me think for a bit."

All that day and all that night I tortured myself with what I should do. In the deepest hours of darkness, I realized I needed advice from Shaman Kim. I followed the proper customs to prepare myself. I gave myself a sponge bath and dressed in clean clothes. I searched my mind for any contaminating activities I might have participated in and found none. I hadn't drunk rice liquor recently, nor had I argued with friends, family members, or women in the bulteok. I no longer had my monthly bleeding. I wasn't sharing love with anyone. I hadn't butchered a pig, chicken, or duck, nor had I harvested any marine creatures in the past week.

The sun had not yet risen when I put on my white kerchief and left the house with a basket filled with rice cakes and other offerings over my arm. I found Shaman Kim and her daughter at a makeshift shrine for Halmang Yeongdeung—the goddess of the wind. Shaman Kim was quite old now, and her daughter was training to take her place.

"*Visiting the goddess is like visiting one's grandmother,*" Shaman Kim recited when she saw me. "It's always best to arrive at a goddess's shrine close to dawn, when she is sure to be in residence. You can say anything, and she will listen. You can cry, and she will console you. You can complain, and she will be patient." Shaman Kim motioned for me to sit. "How can we help you?"

I gave her the news of the birth of my newest granddaughter and told her of my conflicted emotions.

"You should go to Seoul, of course," she said when I was done.

But my mind was too divided to accept this simple direction. "How can I? I'll look at the baby and see—"

"Everyone lost people, Young-sook," Shaman Kim said, not unkindly. "And you know you want to forgive. If you didn't, well, then, explain to me why you've never taken the opportunity to retaliate against Mi-ja. You cared for her house all these years when you could very easily have set fire to the roof."

"I stopped visiting it after she came last year," I pointed out. "It's scheduled to be demolished."

"Ah, but how do you know that information? It's because you make it your business to know everything about her."

I veered toward the subject that had been eating at me since the last time I saw Mi-ja. "She said that Jun-bu, Yu-ri, and Sung-soo spoke only when *she* appeared. She said their messages were for *her*. She said they'd forgiven her. But how can any of that be?"

Shaman Kim's eyes narrowed. "Are you questioning my abilities to let the dead speak through me?"

"I'm not doubting you or what they said. I just need to know if they were speaking to her or to me."

"Maybe they were speaking to you *and* Mi-ja. Have you considered that?"

"But—"

"You waited a long time for them to come to you, but did you actually *hear* what they said? You should be grateful. They've found forgiveness. Why can't you?"

"But how can I forgive Mi-ja after what happened to them? I live with that every day."

"We all see that in you, and we all feel sorry for you, but everyone on the island was hurt in those terrible years. You more than some but also less than others. *They did this to me. They did that to me.* A woman who thinks that way will never overcome her anger. You are not being punished *for* your anger. You're being punished *by* your anger."

I listened, but Shaman Kim wasn't telling me anything I didn't already know, because of course I was being punished by my anger. I lived with that every day as well.

I left my offerings and, dissatisfied, walked to Gu-sun's house. It was still early, but she had already built a fire and heated hot water. We sat together, drinking tea. I felt I could be direct, so I got straight to the point.

"How did you forgive Gu-ja for Wan-soon's death?"

"What else could I do?" she asked me right back. "Gu-ja is my sister. We share our mother's and father's blood. Gu-ja may have been at fault, but maybe it was Wan-soon's fate to be carried away. Maybe it was even her choice. I've heard the rumors."

"Not that it matters, but I don't think they were true."

"Do you say that because Yo-chan is now your son-in-law?"

"Hardly. I say it because I believed what my daughters told me."

"Min-lee I might trust," Gu-sun said. "But Joon-lee? She *married* Yo-chan."

All these years, I'd never had a sense of Gu-sun's feelings about Yo-chan. She'd kept them very well hidden.

I surprised myself by saying, "I still believe my daughters. Whatever happened had nothing to do with Yo-chan."

A faraway look came to her eyes. "I guess you know I was full with child before I was married."

"People gossiped."

"Before my husband agreed to marry me, I wanted to die, so I understand if that's what happened to Wan-soon."

"Maybe it was just an accident. That day the current was too strong for a baby-diver—"

"Maybe. But if she was pregnant, I wish she would have come to me. I would have told her that once her father and I were married and I gave him our first son, we were both happy. I would have wished that for her. But I understand it's my destiny never to know what happened to Wan-soon, or why."

The sadness of that lay in the silence between us.

Finally, I said, "About Gu-ja . . ."

"I will tell you this," she said. "There are days when I think my sister has suffered more than I have. She will never forgive herself. How can I not love her for that?"

"Mi-ja blames herself too," I admitted, but I didn't go into all the ways she'd tried to help Joon-lee. "But that's not enough. I must know *why*. How could she have turned on me that way? How could she have been willing to let all of us die? I begged her to take my children, and she did nothing."

"Then accept that, and go and meet your granddaughter. She is the baby of your most beloved child. Once you hold her, you will love her. You know that as a halmang."

I let out a long breath. She was right, but I just couldn't do it.

"I can't see that baby, let alone touch her," I confessed. "If I looked at her, all I would see is the grandchild of a collaborator and perpetrator."

Gu-sun's face filled with compassion as she stared at me. It pained me to know I couldn't change and I couldn't forgive, but I had to hold on to my anger and bitterness as a way of honoring those I'd lost.

About six months later, the mailman delivered the first letter from America, unsealed, with the stamp torn off.

"It looks like Joon-lee's handwriting," Min-lee said when she brought it to me.

"It has to be." I shrugged, pretending I didn't care. "Who else would be writing to us from there?"

Min-lee pulled the letter from the envelope. I peered over her shoulder when she unfolded it. Most of the written characters had been blacked out.

"The censors," Min-lee said, stating the obvious.

"Is there anything you can read?"

"Let's see. 'Dear Mother and Sister . . .'" My daughter's finger traced each row, allowing me to follow along. "'We've been here for . . . Yo-chan's job is . . . The air is brown . . . The food is greasy . . . The sea is right here, but they get nothing from it . . . No sea urchin . . . No top shell . . . Their abalone is fished out . . .'" Then several lines were completely crossed out. The next paragraph began "'I went to the doctor and . . . Wish it was slow . . . Fast . . . Time . . . This foreign land is not home . . .'" Min-lee stopped reading to say, "It's like they only want negative things about America to come through."

"I was thinking the same thing. What about this part?" I put my finger on the last paragraph, which seemed to have the fewest characters inked out.

"It says, 'All mothers worry. I worry about what will happen and how Yo-chan will get by. I wish you . . . Please . . . If I could be home on Jeju . . . You would . . . Always remember I love you, Joon-lee.'" Min-lee looked at me. "What do you think it means?"

"She sounds homesick." But the letter was more troubling than that.

"What should I write back?"

"What does it matter what you write back, if the censors are only going to black it out?"

My daughter set her jaw. "I'm going to write to her anyway."

I nodded. "Do what you must."

———

The next month, we received another letter. Again, the envelope had been opened, the stamp taken, and most of the letter inked out, but the handwriting was different. Min-lee read, "'Dear Mother Young-sook, This is Yo-chan. I write for my mother.'" That's as far as she got before I rose and walked away. Later, Min-lee told me that there was no real news. Just a word or phrase here and there. "It's like trying to understand the ocean floor by seeing only ten grains of sand," she said. This time, Min-lee did not write back.

After that, a letter came around the first of every month. In those days, they always arrived unsealed, but I didn't pull them from their envelopes. I hid them in a small wooden box. It comforted me to know that whatever lies Mi-ja and her son wished to send me were hidden in the dark, where I wouldn't have to hear them. It made me feel that I'd won.

In spring, the rapeseed fields bloomed yellow, stretching from the mid-mountain area all the way to the gnarled coastline. The ocean kept its relentless movement. The deep blue waters frothed one moment and became almost serene the next. I did my farming work and went to the sea. When I dove I was able to push my daughter and granddaughter from my mind. Often I was reminded of Dr. Park and his search for the mystery of why the haenyeo could withstand cold better than any other humans on earth. I think I now knew the answer. Not only did I have a coldness at my core that would not thaw but it had become as hard as ice. I could not do what Shaman Kim, Gu-sun, and so many others had told me to do. If I could not forgive, then at least I could wrap my anger and bitterness in an icy shell. Each time I sank into the sea, I stretched my mind outward, away from that shell. *Where's my abalone? Where's my octopus? I need to make money! I need to make a living!* I would continue to strive to be the best haenyeo, even if I knew it wouldn't last.

Day 4 (continued): 2008

Young-sook doesn't go back to the memorial hall to find her family or her friends. Instead, she makes her way to the parking lot, waits for a taxi to drop off another group of visitors, and then hires the driver to take her home. Listening to Clara and hearing Mi-ja's voice on the recording have opened something in Young-sook. *What if I was wrong all these years? Or, maybe, not wrong completely, but what if I didn't understand some of what happened?* Her mind returns again and again to the questions posed by the man who spoke earlier today: Who can name a death that was not tragic? Is there a way for us to find meaning in the losses we've suffered? Who can say that one soul has a heavier grievance than another? We were all victims. We need to forgive each other.

Young-sook knows she's old, but for the first time she has a deeper understanding of what that means. Life moves fast, and the sun of her life is setting. She doesn't have much time left to love or hate or forgive. *If you try to live, you can live on well.* How often did her mother-in-law recite that aphorism? And it turned out to be true. Young-sook worked all day and had body aches all night, but she would do it all again for her children, because life without them is meaningless. And yet, she'd let Joon-lee slip away. Young-sook's anger had convinced her she didn't care what her daughter, Yo-chan, or Mi-ja might have to say to her, but she should have tried to look them up after the guilt-by-association system ended and she'd finally gotten a passport. She'd traveled to Los Angeles to visit her family plenty of times. Just once she should have asked to be driven past the house attached to the return address on the envelopes, if only to peer at the inhabitants from the car window.

The taxi hugs the curves of Hado's shoreline until it stops at the gate to her beachside compound. She pays the driver—the ridiculous extravagance not registering in her mind—and hurries inside. She pulls out the box with the letters from America and hobbles down to the beach. She looks around, but with the opening of the memorial, there are no haenyeo on the sand, and even the tourists are staying away.

To understand everything is to forgive. With Clara's words in her mind, she reaches into the box, pulls out the stack of letters from America, and flips them over, so she can start at the beginning. She runs a finger over Joon-lee's handwriting on the first envelope. She remembers what it said. Then come the ones in Yo-chan's script. The first group arrived once a month. After six months and up until a year ago, Young-sook had received two letters a year: one on the anniversary of her mother's death, and the other on the anniversary of the deaths of Jun-bu, Yu-ri, and Sung-soo. In the early years, each had been opened by the censors, but Young-sook's stubbornness had kept her from pulling out the letters. Now she reaches inside the first envelope and unfolds the letter written by Yo-chan on his mother's behalf. The censors had been active with this one, so very few characters remain. She wonders how Mi-ja could have thought she'd "understand." She pulls the letter from the next envelope, unfolds it, and this time finds another piece of paper tucked inside. Again, the letter has writing on it, most of which has been blacked out. The other paper she recognizes right away. It's a page from Mi-ja's father's book. It's old and yellowed. Young-sook's hands tremble as she unfolds it. Here is the first rubbing she and Mi-ja made together: the rough impression of a stone they created on the day they met.

She reaches for the next envelope: again unsealed, with a letter folded around another page from Mi-ja's father's book. *Toilet,* made the day of the big haenyeo march. The next envelope: *Sunrise,* the name of the boat on their first dives together. Each envelope reveals another rubbing that commemorated for two girls the places they visited and the events of their lives: the surface of a scallop shell from this very beach, a carving they'd liked in Vladivostok, the outlines of their babies' feet. Maybe the letters that

Yo-chan wrote for his mother offer words of apology or regret, but Young-sook doesn't need to hear them. These treasures of their friendship mean so much more.

When she comes to the last rubbing she remembers making with Mi-ja, she looks at the remaining stack of letters—all of them sealed, marking that they came after censorship ended—and wonders what could be inside. The first one has another letter she cannot read. This time, however, the page from Mi-ja's father's book is folded around a photograph. The page from the book shows a baby's foot. In the photograph, Joon-lee sits propped in a hospital bed, a newborn in her arms. The next letter has a rubbing on a much larger piece of paper. Young-sook can't read it, but she recognizes the pattern of letters and numbers and realizes that it's from her daughter's headstone. Young-sook chokes back a sob.

Once she's reined in her feelings, she opens the rest of the letters. Each one is accompanied by a rubbing and a photograph, showing some aspect of the life of their shared granddaughter, Janet: smiling, with her hair clipped with brightly colored barrettes, standing on the steps to a house, with a lunch box in her hand, at a holiday sing-along, graduating from elementary school, junior high, high school, and college. A wedding photo. Another baby footprint: Clara. Later, another footprint: Clara's brother. Mi-ja had tried to tell Young-sook everything that was happening, and everything that she missed.

Young-sook's concentrating so hard and her emotions are so strong that she's unaware of the woman and girl who've approached.

"She wanted you to know us," Janet says in her poor Jeju dialect. "And she wanted us to know you."

Janet and Clara have changed out of the clothes they wore to the opening of the Peace Park and are now dressed almost identically in shorts, T-shirts, and flip-flops. Clara's iPhone with the wires and earbuds dangles from her hand.

"She wanted," Clara says, putting stress on every word, "for us to hear your story, your side. But you must hear her too. I taped Great-Granny Mi-ja for hours—"

"It started as a school project," her mother explains.

"I've set this to the most important part," Clara says. "Are you ready?"

Yes, finally, Young-sook is ready. She takes the earbuds, puts them in her ears, and nods. Clara pushes a button, and there comes Mi-ja's old-woman voice.

"Young-sook always said I should divorce my husband, just as she always told the women in her collective who had similar experiences to mine. She was always so understanding of them when they couldn't leave their husbands, but she could not think the same way when it came to me."

"That was selfish of her," Clara says on the recording.

"Not selfish. I loved her, and she loved me, but she never fully understood who or what I was." Mi-ja gives a knowing snort. "And neither did I. It took me many years to see that I *was* different from those other women. I mean, of course, I was afraid of Sang-mun, as they were afraid of their husbands. I was in constant terror of what he might do to me. What made me different from the other haenyeo, whose husbands could be violent, was that I deserved Sang-mun and the punishment he gave me."

"Granny, no one deserves what he did to you."

"I did. My husband was married to a bad person."

On the recording, Clara tries to tell her great-grandmother that she isn't a bad person, and this gives Young-sook time to remember when she too had tried to argue this point with Mi-ja. Why hadn't she *heard* what Mi-ja was truly saying? Why hadn't she asked more questions? Even more painful is that this conversation had happened back when her heart had still been open to Mi-ja, or so she thought.

"I was a bad person," Mi-ja now insists in Young-sook's ears. "I killed my mother when I entered the world. I was the daughter of a collaborator. I let Sang-mun ruin me. But my greatest disgrace came when I didn't stop what happened in Bukchon. From my birth to that moment, I lived a life of shame."

In the recording, Young-sook hears Mi-ja weeping and Clara comforting her. Again, Young-sook is racked by memories, only they are of her own shortcomings. There's a click, then another click, and the voices come back. Mi-ja is once again composed.

"To be ruined," Mi-ja said. "You know what that means."

"Granny, you've told me many times. You forget sometimes—"

"Forget? No! I will never forget. Young-sook and I were so happy. We'd just returned to Jeju from leaving-home water-work. Everything was so different on the dock. Scary. Sang-mun offered to help us. He looked man-beautiful, but he was evil. I don't know why Young-sook didn't see that right away, but she didn't. I hated him from the first moment I saw him, and he must have seen in me the weakness of my bloodline. I was a person who would give in. He knew he could take advantage of that, and I let him. He easily separated us. Once she was out of sight, he took me to his office. When he started touching me, I froze. I let him pull down my pants—"

"You didn't *let* him, Granny. He *raped* you."

"I thought, If I don't move or scream, then soon it would end."

Mi-ja starts to cry again. This is all going back so much further than the events in Bukchon. Even when her own grandmother had hinted at what had happened to Mi-ja, Young-sook had refused to believe it, let alone ask more questions. She'd been too wrapped up in her own misery that Sang-mun had not come to Hado for her.

"I couldn't tell Young-sook what happened," Mi-ja says. "She would have been disgusted with me. Never would she have looked at me the same way."

"Then she couldn't have been a very good friend—"

Mi-ja's voice comes back, surprisingly sharp. "Don't ever say that. She was a wonderful friend and a great diver. She became the best haenyeo in Hado. She learned early on from Yu-ri's accident and the loss of her mother how to protect those who looked to her for security and safety. Not one person died in her collective when she was chief."

That Mi-ja would have known this about Young-sook should perhaps be more surprising. Or not. Young-sook had made it her business to know all about Mi-ja. Maybe Mi-ja had done the same with Young-sook. In the silence that follows Mi-ja's outburst, Young-sook imagines how Clara must have felt in that moment— chastened, maybe even afraid or embarrassed—but for the first time she understands that, for all the anger and blame she's held within her these past years, she herself failed Mi-ja in many ways.

"Young-sook was my only friend," Mi-ja insists. "That's why it all hurt so much." Another long pause, then she continues. "You see, she *liked* Sang-mun. I thought she'd think I was trying to steal him from her."

"Steal him?"

"There was always a part of Young-sook that was jealous of me. That I could read and write a tiny bit. That I got to work in the bulteok before she was allowed to enter it. That I was prettier. You look at me now and see an old face, but once I was beautiful."

The shifting sea that has kept Young-sook unbalanced all day shifts again. She puts her fingers over the earbuds, pushing them farther into her head, trying to block the sound of the wind. Clara and Janet stare at her, watching her reaction.

"So either she would have been disgusted with me or she would have thought I'd gone with Sang-mun to hurt her."

"Oh, Granny—"

"And later? If I'd told her after the killings, she wouldn't have believed me. She would have only heard made-up excuses."

The pause on the tape allows Young-sook to sort through this information. She purses her lips in acceptance of these truths about her own failings.

"I made a choice," Mi-ja continues. "I sought out Young-sook's grandmother and told her what happened. That old woman was fierce. I begged her not to tell anyone, but she went straight to my aunt and uncle. 'What if the girl is pregnant?' she asked them. Auntie and Uncle took the bus to Jeju City and confronted Sang-mun's parents. They said if their son didn't marry me, they would report him to the police."

Young-sook tries to take this all in, seeking to understand things that happened more than sixty years ago. That Mi-ja's aunt and uncle would have let her go into that marriage was one thing, but for Grandmother to arrange it? And then not tell her? With a chill, Young-sook remembers meeting Mi-ja in the olle after her engagement meeting. *I told your grandmother everything. I begged her* . . . And later, Young-sook's grandmother's triumphant demeanor when Mi-ja was driven away from Hado after her wedding. *That girl has left Hado as she arrived—the daughter of a collaborator.* Young-sook had loved her grandmother. She'd taught Young-sook about life and diving, but her hatred for the Japanese—whom she'd called the cloven-footed ones—and for those who collaborated with them had caused Mi-ja to be sent into a cruel and unforgivable situation. But it was Young-sook's own blindness that had kept her from wanting to know the truth, and as a result she'd lost the sister of her heart. And later, Joon-lee and her family . . . But now . . . *To understand everything is to forgive.*

"After that," Mi-ja continues, "it was as I've told you before. Sang-mun was forced to marry me. He considered it his duty to share love with me every night. He needed and wanted a son, and his parents needed and wanted a grandchild. They even sent me back to Hado, so I might visit the goddess with Young-sook. I'd longed to have a family of my own, but now I didn't want to do anything that would help plant a baby in me."

I'm not sure I want to have a baby. Mi-ja had said this directly to Young-sook on that first visit. If only Young-sook had questioned her more. But she didn't. She'd been thinking solely of her own happiness.

"I was in constant fear of him," Mi-ja continues. "When he escaped from the north, he was even worse. Sharing love. *Aigo!* What a lie that is! I didn't know what to do, and I had nowhere to go. Every time I was as frozen as I was the day he first ruined me. And so terrified. He didn't stop with me either. The way he beat your grandfather . . . I did everything I could to protect Yo-chan and raise him to be a good man."

"You should have told Young-sook," Clara says on the recording. "If you had, and if she was truly your friend, then maybe everything would have turned out different."

When Young-sook thinks about how her friend suffered . . . For years . . . How pale Mi-ja had been when she and Sang-mun met Young-sook at the pickup point the first day the three of them met. The bruises she'd covered up over the years. The way she always froze when he came into view. How she made excuses for him. How she dressed for him. That Mi-ja herself had told Young-sook that Sang-mun made her pay for his loss of face before his superiors that day in Bukchon. And still later, how she'd gone back to Sang-mun to help Joon-lee . . .

On the recording, Mi-ja lets out a tortured moan. "Different? I thought we were all going to die that day in Bukchon. I had no hope of survival, but if I had to die, I was grateful it would be with my friend. Then Sang-mun arrived with Yo-chan. I never had a mother to love me, and I missed that always. I couldn't let Yo-chan grow up without me and live alone with his father."

With a chill, Young-sook remembers a visit from Mi-ja. She had talked about how some women chose suicide over living with their husbands. "But how can that be a path for a mother?" she had asked. "I have Yo-chan. I must live for him."

On the tape, Mi-ja adds another reason. "Then, when Young-sook asked me to take her children," she says, "all I could think of was the brutality they'd be stepping into."

"I'm sorry, Granny, but I think it's better to be alive and beaten than, well, *dead*."

"If you could know what it was like that day . . . The screams . . . The crying . . . The smell of fear . . . But you're right," Mi-ja admits. "In the end, everything that happened was my responsibility alone. I couldn't take Young-sook's children into his home. I couldn't even take one. I couldn't bear the thought of what Sang-mun might do to them when I knew what he had already done to Yo-chan and me. And then everything happened so fast." Her voice falters. "Later, when Sang-mun found out what I'd done— *not* done—he was so angry with me. He worried that Jun-bu and the others would come back to haunt him. He said that by making him look like a weakling, I'd threatened his position with the government. Worst, I hadn't stepped forward from the beginning and pleaded with the commander for Young-sook and her family. He looked at me and saw a collaborator, perpetrator, and traitor, but all I'd wanted to do was stay alive for my son."

Young-sook pulls out the earbuds. She looks from the girl, to her mother, and back to the letters. Her heart is cracking open. Maybe she won't be able to bear it. *A good woman is a good mother.* She had tried to live by those words and had prided herself on all she'd done for her children. Now she sees that Mi-ja tried to do the same but with tragic results. She feels excruciating pain as decades of sorrow, anger, and regret she's carried within her begin to shatter and melt.

"My grandmother never stopped loving you," Janet says. "She accepted what she did, and she wanted you to know everything. This we've brought to you."

For years, people have pestered Young-sook to tell her story. Always she's said no. But now . . . The people asking carry within them the blood of Mi-ja and Young-sook. Yes, she'll finally tell her story. She'll tell them about the pain she endured but also about her closed heart that could not forgive.

Clara drops to her knees. "Does this beach have any food?"

This question is as old as the first haenyeo, and Clara must have learned it from her other great-grandma. Young-sook finds herself smiling. How can she not be transported back to the relationship she had with her closest friend, right on this beach, as they'd learned to swim, play, and love together?

"More food than thirty refrigerators in my grandmother's house," she answers, adding, "if she'd had a refrigerator."

"Then will you take us into the sea?" Clara asks. "Will you teach us?"

Young-sook doesn't hesitate. "Have you brought something to swim in?"

Clara grins up at her mother, who grins right back. Each of them shrugs a shoulder to reveal the brightly colored straps of their bathing suits.

A breath,

a breath,

a breath . . .

Acknowledgements

I would not have been able to write *The Island of Sea Women* without the help of three extraordinary women: Dr. Anne Hilty, Brenda Paik Sunoo, and Jenie Hahn. I tracked down Anne Hilty, Jeju's official ambassador of the haenyeo, through her numerous articles in *The Jeju Weekly, National Geographic Traveller,* and other magazines, as well as her book *Jeju Haenyeo: Stewards of the Sea*. Beyond her haenyeo expertise, she's also written extensively about Jeju's geography, shamans, goddesses, Kim Mandeok, food, the April 3 Incident, and death and burial rituals. We had a lively e-mail correspondence and Skype chats in which she answered every question I threw her way. She helped put together my travel itinerary to Jeju, arranged interviews, and introduced me to numerous people who proved to be extremely helpful: Governor Won Hee-ryung, who gave me a warm welcome to the island; Grand Shaman Kim Yoon-su, whom I visited at the Chilmeoridang shamanistic center; Shaman Suh Sun-sil, who shared her experiences with me in her own home; Song Jung-hee, the publisher of *The Jeju Weekly;* Kim Jeyon, Jeju government's international relations coordinator; Professor Lee Byung-gul, director of the Jeju Sea Grant Center; Dr. Choa Hye-gyong, who early on headed a team to study the haenyeo for the Jeju Development Institute and shared with me her recordings and translations of haenyeo songs; Grace Kim, for her translation duties; Kim Hyeryen, who arranged for me to stay at her niece's traditional house in Hado; and Marsha Bogolin, the manager of a guesthouse in the mid-mountain area.

Dr. Hilty also sent me *The Jeju 4.3 Incident Investigation Report*, which outlines the conclusions of the National Committee for the Investigation of the Truth about the Jeju April 3 Incident. From this 755-page document, the result of one of the lengthiest human rights investigations in the world, I garnered details given by survivors and others on both sides of the conflict, as well as from declassified documents provided by the U.S. National Archives and various U.S. and Korean military branches. The report gave me first-person descriptions of the events at the March 1 demonstration, the shooting of the young woman in Bukchon, and how events played out in that village, including the account of an ambulance driver who overheard the plans of what would happen that day. It also provided me with the texts of posters, leaflets, radio broadcasts, speeches, and rallying cries.

Brenda Paik Sunoo, the author of *Moon Tides: Jeju Island Grannies of the Sea,* is a bighearted woman. She arranged for me to stay in her building in the seaside village of Gwakji. She introduced me to Yang Soonja, a fashion designer who walked me through the persimmon-dyeing process; Cho Oksun, a retired haenyeo and neighbor; Kim Jong Ho, a poet, who shared his memories of being a boy during the April 3 Incident; and Kang Mikyoung, the daughter of a haenyeo and expert on domestic abuse on Jeju. Brenda and I also spent wonderful hours with Youngsook Han, a scholar, who translated for me during an especially moving interview with her haenyeo mother, Kang Hee-jeong, who spoke about the first time she saw electric lights, the Japanese occupation, how she became a haenyeo, and what it meant to send her daughter to college. (I'll be thanking other haenyeo shortly, but let me say here that together their stories and memories helped me create the bantering conversations in the bulteok about the nature of men, the benefits of widowhood, and so much more.) Along the way, I had several lively discussions with many of these women about the influence of *Heidi* in their lives and on the island. Last, Brenda and I had a lot of fun with Yim Kwangsook, a nurse visiting from the United States, who translated during various interviews. I won't forget our visit to the traditional Korean bathhouse any time soon.

I met Jenie Hahn at Jeju National University. She translated the oral histories of several haenyeo, including those of Ko Chungeum, Kim Chunman, Kwon Youngae, and Jeong Wolseon, in which they spoke of the day-to-day practicalities of recruitment, ferries, food, and dormitory life for itinerant work in other countries. Jenie also sent me *A Guide to Jeju Spoken in the Language of Jeju and English* by Moon Soon-deok and Oh Seung-hun—which proved to be invaluable with its explanations of food, traditions, and aphorisms—and her translation of Kim Sooni's "The Goddesses, the Myths and Jeju Island." When I needed to confirm facts, Jenie graciously checked with Moon Soon-deok (Jeju Development Institute) and Kang Keonyong (a senior researcher at the Haenyeo Museum) for me.

Allow me to gently shift my thanks to more general categories: the island, cultural traditions, haenyeo, and the April 3 Incident. Jeju is thirty times the size of Manhattan. This lush and beautiful island is home to 25 percent of the entire plant species of Korea. It's the native home of what we commonly call the Christmas tree. The first foreigners believed to visit the island were Hendrick Hamel and his crew of Dutch sailors, who were shipwrecked on Jeju in 1653. They were imprisoned in Seoul, but a few of them, including Hamel, escaped thirteen years later. Once he returned to the Netherlands, he wrote a memoir chronicling his travails, thereby introducing Jeju Island to the West. Hundreds of years later, in 1901, Siegfried Genthe, a German climber, sought and received permission to be the first Westerner to scale Mount Halla. He also wrote of his adventures, and even today Mount Halla is used by many mountaineers as practice for climbing Mount Everest. Jumping to the 1970s, David J. Nemeth did his Peace Corps stint on Jeju. He kept a diary, which was eventually published as *Jeju Island Rambling*. The island also became the subject of his dissertation, *The Architecture of Ideology: Neo-Confucianism Imprinting on Cheju Island, Korea*, and later he wrote *Rediscovering Hallasan: Jeju Island's Traditional Landscapes of Sincerity, Mysticism and Adventure*. For other general information about Jeju, I relied on *Stories of Jeju*, published by the Jeju Development Institute. The Kim Mandeok Memorial Hall gave me insights into the legacy of this early female philanthropist. The exhibits at Jeju Hangil Memorial Hall provided details about the island's anti-Japanese movements. The Folk Village offered a good sense of the varieties of architecture and their purposes on Jeju, while the Jeju

Stone Cultural Park was a great place to learn about the many uses of this natural resource.

As stated throughout the novel, Jeju is quite different from the rest of Korea. The language, for example, is unlike standard Korean. The Jeju dialect is heavily nasal, and many words end abruptly, so they won't disappear into the island's rough breezes. It's completely free from those elements of Korean that stratify tenses and grammar, telling people how to address everyone from the emperor down to a chicken. On Jeju, people greet each other as equals. The matrifocal nature of the island is manifested in its being home to ten thousand spirits and deities, with the vast majority of them goddesses. *Goddesses and Strong Jeju Women,* by Soonie Kim and Anne Hilty, and translated by Youngsook Han, tells the wonderful myths and stories of several of those goddesses. The writings of Chin Song-gi and Gui-Young Hong were also useful as I tried to re-create Jeju's rich landscape of traditions. Every person I met graciously invited me to sample Jeju's extraordinary and delicious cuisine. For a more scholarly look at food, however, I turned to *Top 20 Jeju Local Dishes for Your Life and Health,* published by Jeju National University's Department of Food Science and Nutrition, and once again translated by Jenie Hahn.

As I begin expressing my gratitude to all those who helped me with additional information about the haenyeo, let me first note that this is not what Jeju's sea women call themselves. They use *jamsu, jamnyeo,* or *jomnyeo,* which are all Jeju words. That said, the Japanese word *haenyeo* is how sea women are known internationally. This might be a good place to note that in 2004 a large abalone could fetch about 50,000 won or $60. These days, a haenyeo can make approximately $26,000 a year for part-time work.

One of the first articles I found as I began my research was a piece written in 1967 by Suk Ki Hong and Hermann Rahn in *Scientific American* about a study looking at whether the haenyeo's ability to withstand cold was genetic or an adaptation. This question fascinated me, and down the rabbit hole I went. Through additional articles in *American Headache Society, American Physiological Society, Journal of Sports Sciences,* and the *Undersea and Hyperbaric Medical Society,* I learned invaluable details about breath holding, decompression sickness, energy metabolism, and body temperature for both Korea's haenyeo and Japan's ama. The following are grouped by research paper: Hideki Tamaki, Kiyotaka Kohshi, Tatsuya Ishitake, and Robert M. Wong; Jay Chol Choi, Jung Seok Lee, Sa-Yoon Kang, Ji-Hoon Kang, and Jong-Myon Bae; William E. Hurford, Suk Ki Hong, Yang Saeng Park, Do Whan Ahn, Keizo Shiraki, Motohiko Mohri, and Warren M. Zapol; and Frédéric Lemaitre, Andreas Fahlman, Bernard Gardette, and Kiyotaka Kohsi. The following collaborated in various groupings on multiple papers: N. Y. An, K. A. Bae, D. S. Han, S. K. Hong, S. Y. Hong, B. S. Kang, D. H. Kang, C. Kim, C. K. Kim, P. K. Kim, Y. W. Kwon, I. S. Lee, S. H. Lee, K. S. Paik, S. C. Park, Y. D. Park, Y. S. Park, D. W. Rennie, S. H. Song, C. S. Suh, D. J. Suh, and C. S. Yoon.

I'd also like to acknowledge Choe Sang-hun, Alison Flowers, Priscilla Frank, Gwi-Sook Gwon, AeDuck Im, Kim Soonie, Joel McConvey, Simon Mundy, Lee Sunhwa, and Catherine Young for their magazine articles and academic essays on the haenyeo, shamanism, and Jeju's women in general. For current issues related to the sea, I turned to a survey in *Marine Policy* about production, economics, and management of marine resources conducted by Jae-Young Ko, Glenn A. Jones, Moon-Soo Heo, Young-Su Kang, and Sang-Hyuck Kang. Also informative was a transcript of an interview by Youngmi Mayer with three haenyeo—Jung Won Oh, Ko Jun Ja, and Mun Yeon Ok—for *Lucky Peach: The Gender Issue* and reprinted in *Harper's* magazine, and Ines Min's interview with diver Kim Jae Youn for *COS*. I also found articles about the haenyeo on the following websites: Ancient Explorers, The Jeju Weekly, Culture24, and Utne Reader. I have the deepest admiration for scholars who embed themselves in a culture. Haejoang Cho lived on Udo Island, which is part of Jeju, in the 1970s. Her dissertation, *An Ethnographic Study of a Female Diver's Village in Korea*, provided me with great details about the lives of haenyeo, their views on men, and translations of rowing songs. I visited the Haenyeo Museum several times. The exhibits allowed me to examine haenyeo tools and diving costumes up close. The video-taped oral histories of elderly haenyeo offered wonderful details.

The staff gave me books published by the museum—*Mother of the Sea* and *Jeju Haenyeo*—and introduced me to haenyeo who lived nearby.

In addition to the interviews that were arranged in advance, Grace Kim and I also spoke to haenyeo as they waited to be taken to the sea, gathered seaweed on the shore, or were coming out of the water with their catches. Among these were Kang I-suk, Kim Wan-soon, and Kim Won-seok. I'd like to single out Kim Eun-sil, who worked as a haenyeo on Jeju and as an itinerant diver to help her family, and Yun Mi-ja, who, among other things, shared what life was like for her in Vladivostok. To understand the functions and importance of the bulteok, I relied on the research of Eun-Jung Kang, Kyu-Han Kim, Kyeonghwa Byun, and Chang-gen Yoo. Artist Mikhail Karikis's video and sound installation about the haenyeo and Hyung S. Kim's wall-sized photographic portraits of divers helped me to visualize the physical attributes of the older Young-sook, Kang sisters, and others. I was fortunate to meet Barbara Hammer in New York and talk to her about her documentary, *Diving Women of Jeju-do*. Journal Films' Families of the World series produced a lovely little documentary about a twelve-year-old girl learning to dive on Jeju in 1975.

If you ever find your way to Jeju, I hope you will visit the April 3 Peace Park. It is a beautiful and very moving place. The final accounting of how many people died on Jeju during the April 3 Incident may never be known. There were 300,000 people living on Jeju when it started. Death estimates have ranged from 30,000 to 60,000, although recent research suggests that as many as 80,000 may have been killed. The early months of 1949 accounted for the highest number of deaths, with some estimates as high as 10 percent of Jeju's total population. Another 80,000 islanders became refugees, living with relatives or in community halls, elementary schools, or lean-tos in fields. By the time the incident officially ended, seven years later, 40,000 people had fled to Japan. Since for fifty years people on Jeju could not speak about what had happened under threat of death and other reprisals, it was the exiles in places like Osaka who kept the stories of death and destruction from disappearing entirely. Seventy percent of Jeju's villages had been burned. Many of them were never rebuilt. In the hills, people still come across crumbling ruins of villages, with eighty-four "lost villages" being identified at this date. Today the site of the massacre at Bukchon is a field for growing garlic. It has a small memorial tablet similar to those honoring victims in other villages around the island.

In addition to the aforementioned official report about the April 3 Incident, I found further information in "The Question of American Responsibility for the Suppression of the Chejudo Uprising" by Bruce Cumings; "Crimes, Concealment and South Korea's Truth and Reconciliation Commission" by Do Khiem and Kim Sung-soo; "The Northwest Youth League" by Lauren Flenniken; "Jeju Women's Lives in the Context of the Juju April 3rd Uprising" by Rimwha Han and Soonhee Kim; *The Massacres at Mount Halla* as well as other articles written by Hun Joon Kim; "Healing the Wounds of War" by Heonik Kwon; "The Cheju-do Rebellion" by John Merrill; "The Ghosts of Cheju" by the *Newsweek* staff; "Reading Volcano Island" by Sonia Ryang; and "The 1948 Cheju-do Civil War" by Wolcott Wheeler.

I'm lucky to have many wonderful people who support me as a writer and as a woman. I must thank Ginny Boyce at Altour Travel for once again getting me to where I needed to go, Nicole Bruno and Sara Seyoum for errands and office work, and Mari Lemus for keeping the ship on an even keel. Carol Fitzgerald and her colleagues at the Book Report Network have helped me with my newsletter, while Sasha Stone continues to make my website both beautiful and informative. (Please visit my website at www.LisaSee.com to see videos about the haenyeo, find discussion questions for book clubs, and much more.) My agent, Sandra Dijkstra, and her staff of fabulous women stay attuned to the business side of things. Everyone at Scribner and Simon & Schuster has been kind to me. Kathy Belden edited the novel with a delicate hand. Nan Graham and Susan Moldow encouraged me. Katie Monaghan and Rosie Mahorter carried out publicity duties with abounding energy and kindness. And here's a shout-out to the many others in marketing and sales who astound me daily with their enthusiasm and creativity.

My sister, Clara Sturak, has read every manuscript, and I trust completely her editorial eye. Chris and Rakhi surround me with love. Alexander and Elizabeth inspire me to work hard. Henry fills me with good cheer. And my beloved Richard makes me laugh, reminds me to have fun, and misses me—while still giving unending support—during the times I'm away on a research trip or book tour. I love you all so much. Thank you.

About the Author

Lisa See is the *New York Times* bestselling author of *The Tea Girl of Hummingbird Lane*, *Snow Flower and the Secret Fan*, *Peony in Love*, *Shanghai Girls*, *China Dolls*, and *Dreams of Joy*, which debuted at #1. She is also the author of *On Gold Mountain*, which tells the story of her Chinese American family's settlement in Los Angeles. See was the recipient of the Golden Spike Award from the Chinese Historical Society of Southern California and the Historymakers Award from the Chinese American Museum. She was also named National Woman of the Year by the Organization of Chinese American Women.

I spent long afternoons picking the meat from those tiny shells to make the porridge.

Mi-ja and I agreed to stay out of political discussions even as events roiled around us. Colonel Brown, a new American in charge, gave a speech in which he told us that the long-range goal for Jeju was "to offer positive proof of the evils of communism" and "to show that the American way offers positive hope."

"Only one problem," Jun-bu grumbled. "They want us to accept *their* form of democracy, with an American-backed dictator who can be controlled, while the people of Korea—especially here on Jeju—want to hold *our* own elections, with *our* own slate of candidates, so we can vote *our* own way. Isn't that what democracy is *supposed* to be about?"

He took this a step further when Mi-ja and her family came to visit. "We should shove out the Americans like we did the French missionaries," he stated, sure of his position.

"That was a small rebellion decades ago," Sang-mun argued back. "The Christians are still here, and more are coming now that the Americans have arrived."

"But we should be independent! If we don't stand up for what we believe, then we are guilty of collaborating in our hearts."

Collaborating. That word again.

On one matter Sang-mun appeared to agree. "At the very least we should have free elections." But then he warned, "Free elections or not, let me tell you something, friend. You should be careful. You're a teacher. Too much trouble gets stirred up in schools. Remember what they did to the women organizers from the Hado Night School and to their teachers?"

They were all dead, but I didn't worry because my husband wasn't an organizer, and he wasn't going to lead a revolt. Besides, we had more practical things to worry about, like how we were going to feed our children.

One thing led to another, though, and people—organized by the newly formed South Korean Labor Party—began to plan a nationwide demonstration to take place on March 1, 1947, nineteen months after the war ended and on the same date that my countrymen had once held gatherings to promote independence from Japan. Here on Jeju, no matter what side people were on—rightist, leftist, or none-ist—they came from across the island to the starting point at an elementary school in the city.

The sky was bright, and the spring air felt fresh. Jun-bu carried Min-lee, and I had Sung-soo tied to my back. (Yu-ri stayed home with Granny Cho.) Mi-ja and Sang-mun brought Yo-chan. Our husbands had arranged a meeting spot, so we easily found each other, even though the crowd was larger than the one my mother had taken Mi-ja and me to fifteen years ago. Instead of Japanese soldiers watching us, hundreds of policemen kept us under observation. Many of them rode horses.

Our husbands wandered off to join a group of men, while Mi-ja and I stayed with the children. Yo-chan and Min-lee toddled together through the crowd, never getting too far from us. Yo-chan had the sturdy legs of his mother. My daughter was already dark from the sun, but she was wiry like her father.

"A boy and a girl," Mi-ja said, smiling. "When they marry—"

"We'll both be very happy." I looped my arm through hers.

We saw people we knew: the Kang sisters and their families, and haenyeo with whom we'd done leaving-home water-work. I said hello to some women from the collective in Bukchon; Mi-ja introduced me to a few of her neighbors in Hamdeok.

When the speeches started, our husbands returned to us. "Let's move closer to the stage," Jun-bu said. "It's important the children hear what's said."

But even I could have recited the speeches. Korea should be independent. We should reject foreign influence. North and south should be reunited, so that we'd be one nation. The last speaker called for us to march, but getting twenty thousand people to walk in the same direction at once takes time. We finally began to move, with the mounted policemen herding us. We lost sight of Sang-mun and Jun-bu. I picked up my daughter, and Mi-ja carried her son. Just ahead of us a little boy—although later I heard it might have been a girl—about six years old jumped and laughed, excited by all that was happening around us. When his mother reached for him, he twirled away, straight into the path of one of the mounted police. The rider yanked the reins. The horse reared. The mother screamed, "Look out!" The boy fell. The horse's hooves crashed down.

The policeman, up so high, pulled sharply on the reins, trying to turn the animal. As a crowd, we realized he wasn't going to dismount to offer help, even though what had happened was clearly an accident. A chorus of voices called, "Get him! Get him! Get him!" People threw stones, which further startled the horse. The rider kicked the animal's withers. It danced from side to side, trying to make its way through the crowd.

"He's heading to the police station!" someone shouted.

"Don't let him get away!"

The chants turned to "Black dog! Black dog!"

We came around a corner and into a large square. Police stood on the broad steps leading to the entrance of the station, with their bayonets thrust threateningly before them. They didn't know what had happened. All they saw was an angry mob rushing toward them. The demonstrators near the front tried to stop, turn around, and flee, but we were in a raging sea, being pushed this way and that. We heard several popping sounds. This was followed by an eerie moment of silence, with everyone frozen in place, assessing. Then the screams began. People scattered in every direction. Amid the chaos, Mi-ja pulled the kids and me into a doorway. As the crowd thinned, we saw little islands of people dotting the square. At the center of each group, lying on the ground, a person. Some wailed in agony from their wounds. Death silence hung over others. An infant's cries hiccuped through the square. Mi-ja and I looked at each other. We had to help.

With our children still in our arms, we trotted in the direction of the sound. We reached a woman, who lay facedown. A bullet had entered her back. Her body lay partially atop her baby. We set down Yo-chan and Min-lee next to each other, so Mi-ja could lift the dead woman's shoulder and I could pull out the infant. Her mouth was a pink hole from which the most pitiable cries squawked out. Her eyes were squeezed so tightly shut that I could see where she'd have wrinkles one day. She was covered in blood.

Mi-ja and I rose together. I put the baby on my shoulder and patted her, while Mi-ja checked to see if she was injured. We were both concentrating so hard that when Sang-mun grabbed Mi-ja's arm and jerked her away from me, we were completely startled.

He screamed in Mi-ja's face. "How could you put my son in danger?"

"He wasn't in danger," she replied calmly. "I was holding him when the horse bolted—"

"What about the bullets?" His hands were clenched into fists. His face was as red as if he'd drunk a bottle of rice wine. "Did you not see danger in that?"

Jun-bu ran into the square. He visibly relaxed when he saw that the children and I were safe. He jogged over just as Mi-ja admitted, "I didn't expect that the police would fire on us." After a slight pause, she asked, "Did you?"

Sang-mun slapped Mi-ja. She staggered back and fell over Yo-chan and Min-lee. I rushed to her side. Jun-bu pulled Sang-mun away. My husband would lose in a fistfight, if it came to that, but he was taller and he carried the authority of a teacher.

Mi-ja had landed on her bottom. Red welts in the shape of Sang-mun's hand had already begun to rise on her cheek. Yo-chan seemed scared but not particularly shocked or surprised. That's when I realized that this couldn't have been the first time he'd seen his father hit his mother. I felt terrible, sick with worry and horror. My grandmother had made this match—the daughter of a collaborator to the son of a collaborator—but Mi-ja and her husband could not have been more mismatched in their tempers.

Sang-mun stuffed his hands in his pockets, whether hiding the weapons he'd used against my friend or keeping them ready for the next time, I couldn't tell. When he looked away, I leaned in and, not for the first time, whispered to Mi-ja, "You could come live with us. Divorce is not uncommon for a haenyeo."

She shook her head. "Where would I go? What would I do? We have a nice house on the base. My son is well fed, and he's picking up English from the soldiers."

She didn't have to lay out the rest. My husband and I lived in a small house with our children and Yu-ri, and it was clear that we didn't have enough to eat. If it had been me, though, I would have

Am I Guilty?

JACKIE KABLER

KILLER READS

A division of HarperCollins*Publishers*

www.harpercollins.co.uk

KillerReads
an imprint of HarperCollins*Publishers* Ltd
1 London Bridge Street
London SE1 9GF

www.harpercollins.co.uk

First published in Great Britain by HarperCollins*Publishers* 2019

A catalogue copy of this book
is available from the British Library.

ISBN: 978-0-00-832841-2

Set in Minion by
Palimpsest Book Production Limited, Falkirk, Stirlingshire

Printed and bound by CPI Group (UK) Ltd, Croydon, CR0 4YY

MIX
Paper from
responsible sources
FSC™ C007454

PART ONE

PART ONE

1

THEA

They were staring again. I shivered, curling my fingers tightly around the handle of the pram, and walked quickly past them, my eyes not meeting theirs. It was two women this time, around my age, late thirties, standing outside WHSmith. I'd only stopped for a moment, to adjust my scarf, but I knew instantly that it had been a mistake. *Never stop, keep moving. Keep your head down. Don't give them a chance to recognize you.* I was usually so careful, on the rare occasions I ventured out. Tried to avert my gaze from store assistants, cashiers, other shoppers, looking down into my purse or at the pram, so they didn't get a good look at me. It was easier that way, safer. But today, with the scarf slipping, I'd risked it, just for a moment, stopping to wind the stupid thing back into place. *Idiot.* It was January, the sky a bleak grey, a biting wind whistling down Cheltenham High Street and whipping loose strands of hair across my cheeks, a crisp packet scudding across the road in front of me as I hurried past the shopfront, eyes fixed firmly ahead, not looking at their faces. I heard them, though, their voices sharp and full of disgust. Full of loathing.

'It *is* her, isn't it? Look at her. What a freak,' said one.

'Evil bitch, more like,' said the other.

A sob caught in my throat and I walked faster, suddenly

desperate to get home. I shouldn't have come out today, I *shouldn't*. I'd been feeling all right earlier, almost sprightly, after a good night's sleep for the first time in weeks. Seven hours. *Seven.* I couldn't remember the last time I'd slept for that long and it had done wonders, made me feel that today I could cope, that it would be fine to go out, get some fresh air, pick up a few bits and pieces in town before I started work. I did most of my shopping online now, but it had seemed silly to pay delivery charges when you only needed some cotton wool, wrapping paper, a pack of pens. And sometimes, it was fine. Sometimes I got away with it, and nobody recognized me, nobody stared or commented or shouted abuse across the street. Not often though, and not today, clearly.

It had started to rain now, fat drops spattering the clear plastic cover I'd put over the pram before going out. Beneath it, a white cashmere blanket was pulled up high, but I could picture Zander's sleeping face, his ludicrously long lashes resting softly against his delicious pink and cream cheeks, see in my mind's eye the gentle rise and fall of his little chest as he dreamed his baby dreams, oblivious. At the thought of him, my darling boy, I sobbed again, aching to hold him in my arms, look into his bright blue eyes, hear his adorable chuckle as he reached up to grab my hair, the chuckle that made everything bad in the world simply melt away.

I bent my head against the wind, wiping my tears away fiercely with one hand as I steered the pram round the corner onto the Prom, heading for home. Everything would be fine, I told myself. I'd get back, have a nice cup of tea, something soothing – camomile? – and then get to work. I didn't really like camomile tea, but Isla said it always calmed her down, and Isla knew about these things. She was my best friend, one of the few who had stuck by me.

We were more like family really, me and Isla, discovering soon after we met all those years ago that both of us were only children who'd craved siblings, jokingly offering to be each other's substitute sister, bonding quickly, irreversibly. From day one we hated to be apart for long, and it was the same even now, now that we were both all grown up with homes and jobs and responsibilities, and even though our everyday lives were so different. She was a real party girl, Isla, but she balanced out the excesses of her crazy work and social life, the boozy nights and junk food lunches, by being into all that healthy stuff too – Pilates, meditation, mindfulness, smoothies, funny teas. She'd only managed to persuade me to go as far as the tea, but she was persistent.

'Yoga next!' she'd said chirpily, when she'd rung me before bed as usual to check that I was OK. 'We can have a private lesson, just the two of us, and I'm paying, so no excuses. It will do you good, Thea. Especially now. I know everything is horrible, but you need to chill out a bit. You're too tense, and it's not helping. I'm going to book it, and you're coming, and that's that.'

I hadn't argued, didn't have the energy. And Isla knew me better than pretty much anybody; so maybe she was right, maybe it *would* do me good. I had so much to do, my work more important than ever now that I was a single parent. I didn't even have an assistant anymore, not since November, not since Flora had left, and I hadn't got round to trying to find a replacement, not yet. I doubted I'd find anyone who'd work for me anyway. So, I had to carry on, even if it *was* just me now and the workload was overwhelming.

I'd let things slide recently, there was no doubt about that, and I needed to get the business back on track. The orders had slowed drastically for a while, last autumn. But they'd picked up over Christmas, and I needed to get on top of things again. I had to keep going, no matter how shitty I felt. I needed to show everyone that I could still do something good, something positive, despite everything. That I was still *me*, no matter what I'd done. Still Thea. Still Theodora Alice Ashfield.

I stopped outside GAP as the bloody scarf started to unwind itself again, one end trailing perilously close to the pram wheels. Frustrated, I yanked it off and stuffed it under the plastic cover, catching a glimpse of myself in the shop window as I straightened up again. I paused for a moment, staring. I didn't look good. My long dark hair, unwashed for days, was pulled up into a messy topknot, and even in the hazy reflection I could see the dark shadows under my eyes, my high cheekbones in sharp relief. I'd lost weight recently, and not intentionally.

I dragged my gaze away from the window and started moving again. As I crossed Montpellier Gardens the rain grew heavier, and I walked faster, almost jogging now, the pram bouncing over the uneven path. A park keeper in a luminous jacket, pulling up weeds around the bandstand, paused as I approached, watching me, and my chest tightened, my heart rate suddenly speeding up. *Not again, please. Not today.* But as I got nearer he smiled and waved a muddy hand skywards.

'Nice mornin' for ducks, eh love?'

'Yes. It is, yes.'

I stopped for a moment, bending to adjust the pram cover and push my shopping bags further under it, and smiled back at him before moving off again, the momentary panic subsiding, my breathing steadying. Feeling almost dizzy with relief, I twisted my right wrist round as I walked, checking the time on my vintage Omega. Just after eleven. I had about four hours before Nell would be home from school. Four hours to do some work, drink tea. Eat something. Avoid the gin bottle. Or try to. Try hard to. Keep focused. I lowered my head against the now-torrential rain and headed for home.

4

2

FLORA

I stretched luxuriously, wriggling my toes against the 400 thread count Egyptian cotton bedding, then reached for my phone, which was on the bedside table, tapping it to check the time. Just after eleven. For a moment, I felt a pang of guilt for still being in bed at such a late hour, then shrugged and pulled the duvet back over my head. Stuff it. It was Monday, my day off this week, after all. And the weekend had been hard work: a two-day fiftieth birthday event at a stately home near Oxford. Annabelle had been anxious, and even more needy than usual, and she'd run me ragged. I didn't mind, not really – I enjoyed the job, loved it in fact. But today I was tired, and I deserved the lie-in, I thought.

I'd worked for Annabelle Garrington for nearly two months, as her personal assistant. Bit of an unusual PA job, compared with most – I lived in, like a nanny, and indeed part of my role *was* helping out with the kids, but it was much more than that. It was the second job I'd found through a specialized London agency, and my job was mainly helping Annabelle with her business. She ran an events management company, her clients mainly the Cotswolds set, the glitzy sort, numerous celebrities among them.

In the short time I'd worked with her, I'd helped her throw

5

a flamingo-themed baby shower for a well-known catwalk model, a Christmas party for a flamboyant London hair stylist at his Gloucestershire hideaway, and a fortieth birthday lunch for a slightly neurotic daytime television presenter who, clearly in denial about her age, had banned the word 'forty' from her event entirely, even asking me to quietly destroy several birthday cards and a balloon bearing the dreaded number presented to her on the day by well-meaning friends. Yes, it was hard work, this job, but I was enjoying it thoroughly, and there were some exciting events coming up in the next few months.

The day, though, was all mine, and I planned to spend it doing very little indeed. A run first, obviously. Then a leisurely brunch, followed by a wander around nearby Cirencester to pick up a few bits and pieces, maybe. And then an evening chilling in my room, catching up on some TV or something on Netflix.

I pulled the duvet down so my head was free again and gazed with pleasure around my little home. It was a big, bright room on the top floor of the Garrington house, a rambling but lovingly – and expensively – decorated and modernized Victorian villa, set in three acres of manicured gardens. Two large sash windows gave me a stunning view of rolling countryside and Cotswold stone houses, a church spire visible in the distance. On Thursday and Sunday evenings the bell-ringers did their practising, the peals drifting across the fields as they had for centuries: a sound which had driven me mad at first, but which I'd gradually begun to find oddly soothing.

My room was flooded with light, even on a grey day like today, and the white walls, soft cream curtains and duck-egg blue cushions on the big, squishy sofa gave the space a calmness, a much-needed contrast to the frantic pace of life outside it. The ensuite bathroom was spacious too, with a separate shower and a glorious free-standing claw-foot bath, and Annabelle had made sure I had everything I needed to be self-sufficient up here, if I'd

6

wanted to be. I had the run of the main kitchen downstairs, of course, but there was a little kitchenette in a corner alcove of my room, and she'd also installed a forty-inch television, so I could watch my favourite shows alone, away from the chaos of the family living room.

She was thoughtful like that, Annabelle. She seemed to really like me, and I liked her too, liked the whole family, in fact, and I knew I'd been lucky to land a new job so quickly. It helped that I'd known Annabelle for a while, although only vaguely. Before this job I'd worked in Cheltenham for Thea Ashfield, who ran *Just Enfant*, the children's online clothing company. Thea's daughter Nell and Annabelle's Millie were the same age and went to the same school, so Thea and Annabelle were acquaintances, if not exactly close friends, and I used to chat to the tall, glamorous Mrs Garrington now and again when Thea put me on the school run. When I needed a new job – when I decided back in November that I just couldn't work for Thea any longer – I was amazed when the agency told me about the vacancy at Annabelle's, and she'd seemed equally delighted. Serendipity, we both said.

I never spoke about what happened at Thea's, though, not to Annabelle – not to anyone, to be honest. I just couldn't. It was too awful, too horrific. Annabelle hadn't asked either, not even in the beginning. I supposed it was because she knew all about it already – everyone did really. You couldn't escape it, at the time, and for weeks afterwards – the papers, the television news, and then all that horrible social media stuff – and Annabelle didn't seem to need anymore details, for which I was grateful.

I had *tried* to stay on with Thea, afterwards, but it was never going to work. I just couldn't do it. I managed nearly two months, but then I quit, took a holiday, then came back to start at Annabelle's. I thought about Thea a lot though. I still saw Nell, via Millie, which was nice. Nell and I had been close, still were. But I often thought about Thea, and Rupert, her husband. And

7

about Zander, of course. Zander, the beautiful baby with the bright blue eyes and the winning smile …

Their faces swam through my head and I shivered, even though the room was warm. Then I jumped as there was a gentle rap on my door.

'Flora? Flora, are you up? I've drawn a picture of you. Flora?'

I smiled. I'd never have admitted it to Annabelle, but Sienna, the youngest, was my favourite of her brood. They weren't supposed to bother me, the kids, not on my day off, but I didn't mind. And it was time I was getting up, anyway.

'Come in, Sienna, sweetie, come in and show me,' I called, and threw back the duvet as she ran in, bright-eyed, clutching her drawing to her chest, and leapt onto my bed, giggling. She was three years old, blonde and adorable. I grabbed her, pretending to try to wrestle the picture from her, and she shrieked with delight. I grinned, and she grinned back, her tiny nose wrinkling, blue eyes squinting up at me. They were gorgeous, those eyes – sparkling, cornflower blue. Eyes that reminded me of Zander's. I swallowed hard, my heart aching for a moment, then resolutely pushed the feeling away. *Stop it*, I told myself. *You're with a new family now. Move on.*

'Right, missy. Are you going to show me this picture or not?' I demanded.

Sienna looked coyly at me for a moment, then beamed and pushed her drawing into my hands. I took it and frowned at the scrawl of red and yellow scribbles topped with a vaguely face-shaped blob, then raised my eyebrows at Sienna in mock shock.

'Well, if I look like this, I need a makeover pronto,' I said, then jumped out of bed, scooping the giggling little girl up into my arms. Today, I decided, was going to be a good day. No more thinking about Thea, or about any of them. What was the point? It was over, all of it.

'All over. Done,' I said out loud.

'What?' Sienna frowned, and I laughed and ruffled her fine,

soft hair.

'Nothing, sweetie. Come on, help me choose what to wear.'

I put her down gently and headed for my wardrobe.

3

ANNABELLE

As I loaded the dishwasher, I hummed softly to myself. I had to admit, I felt rather content today, despite it being a damp, chilly Monday morning. The weekend house party that I'd been so anxious about had gone incredibly well – so well, in fact, that several guests had asked for my details for their own parties later in the year – and arrangements for the next few events in the diary were already coming together nicely. Business was, to use a cliché, booming, and I knew that this was thanks in no small part to Flora, my new PA, who was proving to be a bit of a godsend. Personable, efficient, hard-working, a fast learner, she had improved my life immeasurably in the short time she'd been here. I'd never had an assistant before, preferring to juggle everything myself, but at the end of last year my workload had finally got too much, the challenges of running a growing business alongside a home with three demanding children and an equally demanding husband finally beating me. I needed help, and I finally admitted it.

I'd met Flora ages before she worked for me, of course – she often did the school run with my middle child Millie's close friend, Nell. Nell, Thea Ashfields's daughter. I'd actually been a little wary at first about taking Flora on, after what had gone

10

on at the Ashfields. I am anxious by nature, but I'd been silly, really, in retrospect. It had been a sort of superstitious thing, I suppose – the thought that maybe the terrible thing that had happened might cling to Flora somehow, like a fine dust, and that traces of it might end up here, in my beloved home. Stupid, I know.

And it really had been stupid, because Flora had fitted right in pretty much straight away. She'd been a bit reserved at first, still was a little quiet at times – not surprising, really, after what she'd been through at Thea's – but it hadn't taken long for her to come out of her shell. The children loved her, even Oliver, who at eleven was at the age where he didn't much like anyone or anything, except his skateboard and games console.

Flora Applegate … the children even adore her *surname*, I thought, as I stacked plates neatly side by side and slotted knives and cereal spoons into their basket, then reached up to the shelf for a dishwasher tablet and turned the machine on. Cute name, cute face. A wellspoken Surrey girl, she's twenty-five, but looks years younger, her dark brown hair cropped into a pixie cut with a wispy fringe sweeping across her forehead, green eyes sparkling with intelligence and humour. Not beautiful, but definitely very attractive, her petite frame strong and boyish, her skin smooth and blemish free, other than a little scar on her right wrist from some childhood accident.

I like the way she dresses too – sporty, but stylish. Sports-luxe, I think they call it. Completely the opposite to me – I am more of a maxi dress and florals kind of person – more than a decade older and half a foot taller than Flora, blonde hair falling in loose waves past my shoulders. Willowy, my husband Greg likes to call me. His 'willowy blonde' wife.

I smiled at the thought, then grinned widely as shrieks of laughter drifted down the stairs from Flora's room, where I knew Sienna had sneaked off to a few minutes earlier. She was normally at nursery on a Monday morning, but it was closed today for

11

urgent maintenance, and with the other two at school and Flora off duty today, I'd decided to take the day off too and spend some quality time with my baby. She'd be at school, too, come September, so I needed to make the most of these last few precious months.

Sienna is obsessed with animals, birds in particular, and once I'd tidied up I was planning to take her to Birdland, the wildlife park in Bourton-on-the-Water, about half an hour's drive away. We'd look at the birds, grab some lunch in one of the picturesque village's numerous cafés and be back in plenty of time for the afternoon school pick up, I thought.

I rinsed my hands under the tap, dried them on the towel on the hook by the sink, then wandered into the hallway.

'Sienna!' I called up the stairs. 'Flora, can you send Sienna down? We need to go in a minute.'

There was a faint yell from three floors up, then the sound of a door opening and footsteps thundering down the stairs. Moments later Flora appeared, still in her red and white striped pyjamas, hair tousled, a laughing Sienna perched on her back, legs wrapped around Flora's waist, her cheeks pink.

'Sorry, Annabelle! This little monster wouldn't come down unless I carried her. I'll go and get dressed in a minute. Right, you, off you get.'

Flora smiled at me then twisted sideways so that Sienna slid gently to the floor, where she lay in a giggling heap, one hand still clutching onto Flora's leg.

'Gosh, that's fine, thanks for putting up with her on your day off,' I replied, and she shrugged.

'I don't mind. Have fun at Birdland. Now let go of me, trouble. I'll see you later.'

She reached down and peeled Sienna's fingers from her calf, and my daughter stuck out her bottom lip.

'Awwww! Come with us, pleeeeeese!'

'Sienna, leave Flora alone, it's her day off,' I said warningly.

'Oh, it's OK. I don't mind,' Flora said again. 'Go with Mummy, Sienna. I'll see you later. Maybe I can read you a story before bed; sound like a plan?'

Sienna nodded, her petulant expression turning into a beaming smile.

'Yesssss!'

'Good. Now get up, silly.'

Flora poked Sienna gently with a bare toe then turned and darted up the stairs again, and I bent and pulled my daughter to her feet, smoothing her soft hair back.

'Good girl. Shall we go and see the birds then?'

'YES!' she shouted.

'OK, go and get your boots on, and I'll get the coats.'

She ran off into the kitchen, and as I turned to the heavily laden coatrack to find our warm jackets, I wondered for a moment if I *should* have asked Flora if she'd like to come too. So far, she'd appeared to have spent all her days off on her own, going for long runs or walks, shopping, watching TV. If she'd had friends when she'd worked in Cheltenham, she didn't seem too interested in seeing them. I didn't like to ask though, and she seemed happy enough. Maybe she was just one of those people who were happy with their own company. Or, more probably, maybe she just needed time alone to adjust, time to recover.

We'd never really talked about it – I didn't dare ask, not yet – but I knew it must have been horrendous for her, going through what she did in her last job. But I watched her sometimes, noticed that now and again when we were at work, at an event, a sudden stillness would come over her, a look of sadness flashing across her face, just for a few seconds, as if a memory had briefly surfaced in her mind. It never lasted long though, and within moments she'd be smiling again, filling glasses, flitting between tables, wiping up spills and charming the guests. It hurt my heart, imagining her pain, and I hoped that one day she might feel able to talk to me about it. Or that one day I might be brave enough to ask her about it …

'Ready, Mummy!' Sienna had reappeared, boots on and clutching her favourite soft toy, an overstuffed penguin with an incongruously bright pink beak.

'Is Percival coming too? Great idea. He can meet all his penguin cousins there, can't he?'

I helped her with her coat, deciding not to issue Flora with a last-minute invitation after all. I didn't want to put her in an awkward position – spending her day off with her boss and a toddler was probably the last thing she'd want to do, but she was so polite she might feel obliged to say yes. No, I'd leave her be. Maybe next time.

I closed the door behind us and headed to the car, an excited Sienna scampering ahead of me, and hoped Flora would enjoy a peaceful day. But as I strapped my daughter into her car seat, I found myself thinking about Thea Ashfield again, as I did so often – Thea, who one day not so long ago had been having a normal day, just like this, with her family, her children. Thea, who fell asleep, and woke up in hell.

4

THEA

'I don't *want* to do it, Mummy. It's stupid and boring and I don't see the point.'

Nell scowled at me, then slammed her pen down onto the polished wood of the dining table, her dark curls bobbing with the ferocity of the action. At the opposite end of the table, I sighed and closed my laptop.

'The point, Nell, is that you need good grades at school to make a success of yourself in life. And yes, homework can be boring. Lots of things in life are boring, but we still have to do them, OK?'

She scowled harder, her chocolate brown eyes narrowing to slits.

'Well, help me then. Flora used to help me. You never do. You're *rubbish*.'

I flinched slightly, trying to stay calm. Fighting back never worked with Nell – it only wound her up more.

'Flora doesn't live here anymore, does she, darling? I do help you, when I have time, but I'm trying to work right now. And please don't talk to me like that. What would Daddy say? And what would your baby brother think? Come on, let's—'

Nell stood up so suddenly that her chair tipped backwards

15

and crashed to the floor behind her. Her eyes flicked to the pram in the corner of the room and back to mine, an expression on her face that I couldn't read. Anger? Hatred? Something else?

'Well, Daddy's not here anymore either, is he? And who cares what my baby brother would think? Who cares what *anybody* thinks?'

She slapped the table hard with both hands, her face contorted with emotion, then turned and ran from the room. I heard her stomp up the stairs and then a door slammed. I sat motionless for a moment, then sank my head into my hands. Shit. Shit, shit, *shit*. It was getting to the point where I just didn't know how to handle Nell anymore when she was like this. What was I supposed to do, how could I help her? Had I ruined *her* life, as well as my own? She was eight years old, still a baby really, and yet in the past few months she'd changed so much, often seeming more like a raging, hormonal teenager than a sweet little girl. It wasn't all the time, thankfully – I had no idea how I'd cope if this was a daily occurrence. But these outbursts were regular, and becoming more frequent, and it frightened me that I didn't seem to be able to reach her anymore.

I knew exactly what had caused today's, too. I didn't often do the school run these days, not since … well, not *since*. I'd tried to, at first, tried to keep everything as normal as possible for Nell. But I'd had to stop. Too many nasty comments, too many stares, especially in those early days. It upset Nell, frightened and confused her, and I couldn't bear it. Now, some of the other parents took it in turns, had set up a sort of rota, to pick her up in the morning and drop her off at home again in the afternoon. I knew they were doing it for Nell, and not for me, but I was still deeply grateful. There was the odd day, though, where they couldn't fit the detour into their schedules, and on those occasions, I'd have to do it myself. And sometimes, just like when I went shopping, it was fine. They always looked, of course they did, but I was used to that. I could cope with the sideways glances, with the mutterings – it was only really the shouts, the loud name-calling, the vile language, that made my heart pound and my head swim.

But today, one of the fathers, one who'd been particularly abusive in the past, the dad of a little boy in the year below Nell, spotted me. My breath caught in my throat as I spotted him at the same time. I'd grabbed Nell's hand, trying to steer the pram quickly out of the school gate with the other, get her away before he started, but it was too late.

'Oi! Fucking evil cow! Look at her, the fucking weirdo. Should be locked up. Fuck off out of here!'

I didn't look at him, didn't need to. I knew exactly what his expression would be like, his eyes narrowed with hate, his thin lips set in a sneer. I'd seen the same expression so many times, on so many faces, in the past few months.

But Nell had looked, her eyes wide, face reddening, tears beginning to roll as I dragged her down the road, out of earshot. I'd asked her if she was all right, told her not to listen, told her not to worry about it, all the things I'd said to her a hundred times before, and she'd nodded and wiped her eyes, and started telling me about the art class she'd had this afternoon where silly Charlie Wilson had spilled an entire jar of dirty water down his trousers, but I'd known then. I'd known by the set of her jaw and the stiffness of her smile that sooner or later today we'd have another outburst, that she would punish me for what had just happened.

I was making my daughter desperately unhappy, and the thought was almost unbearable. All I wanted to do was run upstairs after her, take her in my arms, tell her everything was going to be all right. But was it? Would everything ever be all right again? Or would that just be a lie, another lie to add to all the others I'd told her? I'm fine, Nell. I won't drink today, Nell. It's just water with lemon, Nell. People will soon forget, Nell. It'll all be OK, Nell. Lies. All of it, lies.

So no, I couldn't go upstairs to comfort my daughter, not yet.

17

She wouldn't let me anyway, would hold herself rigid now if I tried to wrap my arms round her. I knew that if I left her alone for a few minutes she'd calm down, but she'd still be cagey with me for the rest of the day, refusing to let me cuddle or console her, and it broke my heart. I swallowed hard, trying to put her out of my mind for a few minutes, and opened my laptop again.

I *had* to order some new stock, had to arrange a photo shoot, had to keep this business on track, had to concentrate. I'd been running *Just Enfant* for four years, setting it up after Nell started school, and I suddenly found myself with hours of spare time every weekday. I imported children's clothing from all over the world, quirky, unusual pieces – mini kimonos from Japan, dresses with beautiful Masai beadwork from Kenya, little rhinestone-studded cowboy boots from Texas. I'd had some decent publicity when I launched – Isla had helped – and the business had taken off in a big way almost immediately. Within a year I'd needed to hire a small warehouse to house the stock and some casual help to pack the orders; by the end of year two I'd needed a full-time assistant, which was when Flora had come along. Those were the glory days – my life a whirl of work and motherhood and happiness. Not like now, when life was nothing but greyness and pain. Would I ever be happy again? And would Nell?

Before she was born I'd worked full-time in London as a fashion buyer for Normans, the department store chain. I adored it – the travel, the trade fairs, the designers, the shows. But motherhood and that sort of lifestyle really weren't compatible, and so just before Nell was born we left London and moved to the edge of the Cotswolds, to Cheltenham. Rupert's company had offices in the town, and were happy to transfer him, and we thought it a reasonable place to live, a pretty Regency spa town with decent shops and restaurants and a seemingly never-ending stream of festivals – literature, jazz, food, science, horse racing. More importantly for me it was just two hours from London, my friends and social life a short train ride away. Of course, by the time Nell was born, I had new friends, mummy pals acquired during antenatal classes, coffee mornings, parenting groups. I'd grown to love it here, the town, my social network, the beautiful countryside just minutes away.

But everything was different now. Most of my friends had drifted away, the stream of invitations to dinners and parties fading to a trickle and then stopping altogether.

I stared at my screen for a moment then pushed back my chair, stood up and walked to the window. Outside, the street was quiet, the sky already darkening. A man bundled up in a padded jacket, a woolly hat pulled down low over his eyes, was half-walking, half-jogging on the other side of the road, a large black Labrador tugging at the lead he held in his outstretched hand. Even from this distance, I could see that he was smiling, saying something to his eager pet, and I felt a sudden pang of envy.

Everywhere around me, people were going about their lives, feeling happy, enjoying the little things. The normal things. I wondered, would I ever be able to feel like that again? To take pleasure in simple, everyday tasks, without this gnawing pain, this overwhelming guilt, this grief that paralyzed me? Would I ever stop feeling this self-loathing, this disgust every time I looked at myself in the mirror? And what about Nell? How was I going to fix Nell?

I turned from the window, wondering, not for the first time, if I should get her some professional help, a counsellor or something. I was seeing Isla later in the week, as usual – she'd probably know somebody. Isla knows everyone. But what if Nell refused to go? Could I make her? I sighed, my eyes drifting to the drinks cabinet under the mirror, the big one with the elaborate metal scrollwork that I'd loved so much when Rupert and I had spotted it in a junk shop when I was pregnant with Zander, just after the scan where we found out we were having a little boy. Rupert had bought the mirror for me straight away when I said how much I loved it, so excited about the new baby, so thrilled he was getting a son. If only he'd known then, how things were going to turn out. If only *I'd* known.

My eyes flicked again to the drinks cabinet, then I resolutely looked away. I'd been doing so well, hadn't had a drink for two days now. Well, this was day three, so nearly three really, if anyone was counting. I took a deep breath. No, no drinking today. I could do this sober. I had to. I inhaled again, slowly, deeply, blew the air out forcefully, then walked out into the hallway and headed upstairs to Nell's room.

5

ANNABELLE

'Oh, that garden will be perfect for photos! Look Annabelle, how lovely it is!'

Flora, who was standing at one of the three windows of the large drawing room, turned to me, her eyes bright with excitement. I put my notebook down on the arm of the sofa and went to join her. She was right.

'Wow,' I said. 'It really will, won't it?'

We stood there for a moment, shoulder to shoulder, taking in the view. It was Wednesday morning, and we were on a site visit to a house near Wotton-under-Edge. It was owned by Elaine Gorton, a criminal barrister who worked in London during the week and spent her weekends in the Cotswolds, but she'd given me keys this week so I could come and check the place out, put a plan together for our next meeting.

She was getting married in May, at nearby St Mary the Virgin church, and I was in charge of the reception, a relatively small affair for around sixty people, which would be held here at her home, an elegant, Grade II listed, Queen Anne-style villa set in an acre of beautifully landscaped gardens. From a paved patio area outside the window, steps led down to an expanse of lawn, ideal for the marquee I intended to set up, and bordered with

21

shrubs, roses and fruit trees. A curved path led, via an archway covered in some sort of evergreen climber – I'm not bad on trees, but not great on recognizing plants – to a large, white, painted summer house, and behind that a walled 'secret' garden. It had been too wet to venture out yet this morning, but I knew from the photos Elaine had sent me that that would be the perfect spot for pre-lunch drinks, with wooden benches dotted around under magnolia trees, beautifully colour-coordinated beds of herbs and flowers, and a gently bubbling fountain.

'You've got a good eye, you know.' I turned to Flora and she looked at me and grinned.

'Thanks, Annabelle! I'm not much of a photographer myself, but it does look like a garden from a wedding magazine, doesn't it? I can just picture Elaine out there, all slinky in her dress, the sun shining, the roses in bloom … it's going to be fabulous, isn't it?'

Her green eyes shone, and her enthusiasm was infectious. My first thoughts when planning an event like this, which would rely so heavily on good weather, were anxious ones about rain and wind, flyaway marquees and soggy food. But Flora was definitely better at looking on the bright side, and although I still needed to have a wet weather contingency plan, I suddenly felt inspired.

'It is,' I said. 'Maybe we could drape that archway halfway down the garden with some little fairy lights, and do a few more photos out there later on, when it gets dark? And … random thing to say, and tell me if you think I'm bonkers … what do you think about trying to use that horse? The one we saw as we drove in?'

'Oooh yes!' Flora squealed, clapping her hands, and I could see that she'd immediately understood my idea. 'We could make a flower garland for its neck. It would look wonderful! I wonder if it's tame enough though?' She wrinkled up her small nose, pondering.

'Hmm, yes, maybe we should check that out before we suggest

it to Elaine – could go horribly wrong otherwise!'

We both laughed. We'd spotted a white horse in the field adjoining Elaine's garden as we drove in, the animal almost fairy tale in appearance with a long flowing mane and graceful swishing tail, and a haughty, regal stare. I wasn't sure who owned it, but if they were willing, and the horse was a well-behaved one …

'Oh, Flora, I almost forgot.' I turned from the window as something else from my never-ending to-do list suddenly came to mind. She turned too, grabbing her own notepad and pen from the windowsill.

'Yes? Shoot.'

I flicked through my notes.

'Here it is. Isla Laird's been in touch. You know her, don't you? Oh, of course you do, she's a friend of Thea's, isn't she? She's a producer on that late-night chat show, *Yak Yak Yak*? Anyway, Ailsa Levi is appearing on the show in a couple of weeks' time, and as we're doing her book launch on Friday Isla was wondering if we could get a bit of footage for her to use on the show – you know, Ailsa signing books and that sort of stuff? She said the show will pay for it – we just need to sort someone who can shoot broadcast-quality video as well as the stills photographer we've already booked. Can you organize that?'

'Sure, no problem.'

Flora nodded, scribbling away in her book. I watched her for a moment. Was it my imagination, or had she suddenly turned a little pale?

'Are you OK, Flora?' I asked hesitantly.

She looked up, a slightly haunted expression in her eyes, then smiled.

'Fine! I'll get onto that this afternoon. Oh look, it's stopped raining. Do you want to make a run for it now, zoom down and have a peek at the secret garden while the going's good?'

I nodded.

'Great idea. We can roughly measure the lawn too, see how

big we can go with the marquee. She wants a dancefloor as well as dining space. Should be fine, but let's just check.'

As I followed Flora out through the hallway and down into the kitchen to the back door, I mentally kicked myself. I should have dealt with Isla Laird myself, damn and blast it. Why had I passed the job on to Flora? She'd definitely looked a little shaken there for a moment. I should have thought, should have realized that as one of Thea's best friends, Isla was very much a part of what had happened, and that being forced to deal with her now was bound to be very difficult for poor Flora. That had been thoughtless of me.

I knew Isla myself a bit, too, of course – as a showbiz type, who flitted between London and Gloucestershire, she often attended events I'd organized, launches and celebrations and parties thrown by writers, actors, local celebrities. She'd even been to a do at my own house once, a couple of years back, I remembered now – probably the garden party I'd held to mark three years of Big Day Event Planning.

She was quite loud, the sort of person who some would describe as 'fun', I suppose. A bit over the top for me, and I'd sensed that Rupert – he and Thea had been at the same party – found her slightly irritating too. But, by all accounts, she'd stuck by Thea, after what had happened, and that had to be admired, I supposed. I was pretty sure I couldn't have done it. My chest tightened slightly, as it always did when I thought about Thea, and what she'd done, but I swallowed hard, pushing the thoughts away, pulled on my wellies and followed Flora out into the damp garden.

6

THEA

'What time is Daddy coming, Mummy?'

I looked up from my laptop – I'd just been ordering some stunning little brocade jackets from a designer in Iran, which I intended to team on the website with a recently arrived selection of embroidered dresses from Moscow, a modern twist on the traditional sarafan style – and glanced at my watch.

'He said he'd be here about five thirty, darling. So any minute now.'

It was Wednesday, one of Rupert's nights to have Nell. The days varied every week, depending on his work schedule – Rupert worked in field support for an IT company, and often had to travel to repair or install systems – but we aimed for Wednesdays if we could, hoping a regular routine would be better for our daughter. He had her every weekend too, picking her up from school each Friday and returning her on Monday evening, so he had four nights a week with her and I got three. It didn't sound like a lot, but it was more than I deserved, way more, and I was deeply grateful for it.

'Have you got everything? Did you remember your PE gear for school tomorrow as well as your other stuff?'

I got slowly up from the table, trying not to jar my throbbing head. I'd fallen off the wagon again the night before, despite my good intentions for the week, opening a bottle of red, and then another, waking stiff and cold on the sofa at 2 a.m. before dragging myself to bed to toss and turn restlessly until dawn. The nausea had eased now but the headache remained, a dull pounding in my skull. Trying to act normally, I crossed the room to check Nell's overnight bag, rummaging through it. She had a spare toothbrush, other toiletries, books and toys at Rupert's place, so it was really only clothes and school things she needed to bring, and she seemed to have everything she needed. Plenty of packing practice by now, I supposed.

'All present and correct by the look of it, well done!'

I kept my voice bright, but I was already missing her, already dreading the quiet when the front door closed behind her and she was gone from me for another twenty-four hours.

'Of course, what do you expect?' she replied, with a cheeky grin. She was in a good mood today, and I smiled back and reached out a hand to stroke her dark curls.

'Oi, stop it, mum! I've just brushed it!'

She batted my hand away, then squealed as the doorbell rang.

'Daddy! I'll get it!'

She turned and ran out into the hallway. Moments later Rupert was in the doorway of the dining room, tall and broad-shouldered, his head freshly shaven, a hint of dark stubble at his jawline. He was wearing a dark suit with a pale pink shirt, tie loosened at the neck.

'Thea.' His voice was cool, polite.

'Hi Rupert.'

He glanced around the room, eyes resting for a few seconds on Zander's pram, which was sitting next to the window. He shook his head slightly, then looked down at Nell who was bouncing up and down on her heels.

'Ready to go, sweetheart? Thought we could stop for a takeaway pizza on the way home, eat it in front of the telly, that sound

26

OK?'

'*Awesome!*' she said.

'Great. Well, say goodbye to your mum and we'll be off.'

Nell launched herself at me, wrapping her arms around my waist and tilting her head back for a kiss. I dropped one onto her forehead then held on tightly, making 'grrrrr' noises until she yelled at me to get off her and wriggled free.

'Bye, Mummy! See you tomorrow evening!'

She skipped out into the hall, and I turned to Rupert.

'You'll pick her up from school tomorrow, as usual? Or *arrange* to have her picked up, I should say?' he said.

The hint of ice was there in his voice, as always, but I had become immune to it.

'Of course. Oh, and don't let her forget her PE stuff in the morning. It's in a separate bag and you know what she's like.'

He nodded.

'I know. OK, well, see you Friday then.'

He turned and left the room, and moments later I heard the front door slam. He hadn't mentioned Zander, of course. He never did. It had upset me terribly at first, in the early days after he'd left me. Now, I was used to it – his coldness, his lack of emotion. The revulsion in his eyes when he looked at me. My husband, this man who'd been by my side for over a decade, the man I'd married in a beautiful country church on a glorious spring day in Oxfordshire, and thought I'd love and be loved by forever. The man I'd built a home with, a life with, raised children with.

Our marriage wasn't perfect – how many were? – but it had been good, great even, for so many years. And … well, he despised me these days, I knew that. I was even getting used to it, knowing it was only what I deserved. I never got used to Nell being away, though, hated the house without her in it at night, and although I tried to settle back down to some work I couldn't concentrate.

Restless, I pushed my laptop to one side, wishing it was Friday

27

when Isla would be here, when the house would be filled with her, her loud voice, her gorgeous if ridiculously high shoes, her expensive perfume. And, more importantly, her friendship, her love, her hugs. The lights seemed brighter, my home actually physically warmer, when Isla was around, especially now, in these dark cold days.

Rupert had never really understood it, the bond between us – 'obsessive, you two. It's a bit weird, Thea,' he'd said once, in the early days – and he'd been right when he complained too, back then, that Isla resented him, that she'd been reluctant for me to get serious about him. She'd cried, actually cried, when he proposed. She didn't really have many other friends, not in those days, not now really either, if I thought about it. Work colleagues, people she socialized with, had fun with, but not *friend friends*, nobody she was as close to as me. I'd never really been able to work out why, but I supposed some people were just like that, weren't they? After all, how many close friends do you need? And although I'd made other friends over the years, many of whom I'd grown really fond of, it was never like it was with Isla. We were Thea and Isla, Isla and Thea. Thila, we'd joked once, at the height of the Tom Cruise and Katie Holmes 'Tomcat' thing. It was just the way it was.

The nausea was back, and realizing I'd barely eaten today I wandered through to the kitchen and opened the fridge, wondering what to cook for dinner. I had some pasta in the cupboard, but nothing to make a sauce with. Deciding the fresh air would do me good, I manoeuvred the pram out into the hallway, pulled on my coat and walked briskly up to Bath Road, past the bank on the corner and the wine bar with the little front courtyard where, even now, in the dark and the chill of the January evening, people were sitting outside, smoking and nursing pints of beer, huddling under the patio heaters that warmed the space.

At the little Sainsbury's I headed straight for the aisle where the ready-made sauces were, suddenly lacking the energy to make my own. Arrabbiata or carbonara? My hand wavered in front of the shelf, then I picked up the jar of carbonara and put it in the basket I'd rested on top of the pram. Maybe I'd get another couple of jars for the weekend, make life easy for myself, I thought.

As I added a four-cheese sauce and a jar of pesto to the basket, a small girl sidled up alongside me, long red plaits swinging. She peered into the pram, clearly keen, as so many children were, to see the baby within, and my breath quickened. I grabbed the handle and tried to move the pram away, but it was too late. Her eager expression faded, replaced by a frown that crinkled her smooth, pale brow, and she looked up at me quizzically for a moment, then ran down to the end of the aisle to where a petite woman, also with red hair and bundled up in a navy puffer jacket, was leaning on her trolley, scanning a list in her hand.

'Mummy! That lady's got an empty pram. It hasn't got a baby in it. Why hasn't it got a baby in it?' the child hissed.

The woman glanced down the aisle to where I stood, frozen, then back at her daughter. She shrugged and started to walk away.

'No idea, love. Come on, help me choose some soup for dinner.'

The little girl stared back curiously at me for a moment, then followed her mother around the corner.

I stood stock-still, staring into the pram. She was right, of course. It was, as it had been for months, empty. Zander's blanket was still there, soft and white, still smelling of him, very faintly now, the brightly coloured chain of little teddy bears holding hands still strung across the front of the hood. But yes, the little girl had been absolutely right. I *was* pushing an empty pram. Pushing an empty pram around like the crazy, sick woman I now was. Because, of course, there was no baby, was there? Not anymore.

7

FLORA

'Right. Chairs laid out, wine chilled, glasses polished, food all plated up … what time is it, Flora?'

Annabelle looked up from the tick-list on her clipboard, tucking a blonde curl behind her ear. I pulled my phone from my pocket and tapped the screen.

'It's 6.20. Doors will open in ten minutes. We're fine, Annabelle, don't worry. I've had a peek out the window and there's already a queue building. Jenny, the manager, is going to nip downstairs in a minute to man the door. Or woman the door, I suppose I should say …'

I smiled at her and she smiled back, although somewhat distractedly. She was always pretty tense just before an event – probably not the best time for my silly jokes.

'And Ailsa's just nipped to the loo but then she's going to stand at the top of the stairs and greet her guests as they come up,' I continued hurriedly. 'Then there'll be forty-five minutes of milling around with wine and nibbles before we start at bang on 7.15. The two waitresses are here and ready to circulate with nibble trays and top up the drinks, and the photographer and cameraman are just over there checking their equipment. All sorted, I think.'

'Brilliant. Thanks, Flora. OK, well I'm going to go and make sure Jenny is all right and just check everything's looking good downstairs. Back in a mo. Oh – could you just make sure there's a glass of water for Ailsa on her table? And one for the interviewer?'

'Sure, no problem.'

She headed for the stairs and vanished, and I crossed the room, manoeuvring between the long rows of chairs, heading for the drinks table. We were on the first floor of Waterstones in Cheltenham, where the stage was now set for Ailsa Levi's book launch party.

The glamorous, Gloucestershire-born author had topped the *Sunday Times* bestseller list with both of her previous gory crime novels, and tonight's event would launch her third book, a thriller set in 1940's London.

We were expecting about a hundred people, and Annabelle had been on edge all week, knowing there'd be extensive coverage of the evening not only in the trade press but also in a number of celebrity magazines – the photographer hired for the evening was providing stills to *Hello* and *Heat*, among others. Ailsa, unusually for a crime writer, was also a bit of a party girl and tabloid darling, and the gossip mags loved her.

I didn't think Annabelle had anything to worry about though. We'd worked hard on this event, and the place looked fantastic, with piles of Ailsa's novel artfully arranged on side tables, ready for signing later, and delicious looking canapés and cupcakes decorated with edible, miniature replicas of the new book's cover ready to be served. Even the two waitresses looked great, dressed in forties-style uniforms of simple black dresses with neat white collars and cuffs, finished with crisp, snowy aprons and little frilly caps.

There had been a slight blip earlier on – one of the waitresses had called me in a panic at five o'clock, saying that her childcare had let her down and that she would have to pull out of the job unless she could bring her young baby with her. Unwilling to add to Annabelle's stress by asking her if it would be possible to find somebody else to step in at such short notice, I'd taken a gamble and told the woman to bring the child with her and that we would find a quiet spot to put it in, promising that I'd personally go and check on the baby every ten minutes or so while her mum was working. As I filled two crystal tumblers with mineral water, I wondered where exactly Jenny, the bookshop manager, had hidden the child, whose mum was now poised by the food table, ready to begin serving. I needed to start baby watch, so I put the drinks on the table at the front of the room where Ailsa would soon be interviewed and host a Q and A session for her guests, and did a quick tour of the first floor, peering behind bookcases.

'Seen a baby anywhere, Gerry?' I grinned at the photographer, who was snapping a few shots of a poster of Ailsa. He was a short, stocky man of about fifty, dressed in a black leather bomber jacket. He nodded and smiled back at me, showing nicotine-stained teeth.

'Over there. Behind Sci-Fi,' he said. 'It's fine, don't worry – Mark just popped it out of sight for a minute, don't want it in the shots. It's sound asleep, for now … hope it stays that way, eh?'

'Hope so!'

Mark was the videographer I'd hired for the evening, to get footage for the TV chat show at Isla Laird's request. Thankfully, I hadn't needed to speak to her to sort it out – her instructions to Annabelle about what she needed and how to get the footage to her afterwards had been pretty clear, which had been a relief, so all I'd had to do was drop her an email to confirm that all was fine. It wasn't that I didn't like Isla or anything – actually, I liked her quite a lot. She was a good laugh, interesting to talk to, and had always been a great friend to Thea, and after a bit of a shaky start, we'd ended up getting on really well. It was just that, at the moment certainly, I really couldn't face talking to

32

her, or to anyone who reminded me of last year. It was just too recent, too raw ...

'Oh God! Oh *God*!'

As I peered round the science-fiction bookshelf I gasped, my heart suddenly pounding, my legs wobbly. I grabbed onto a shelf for support and stared at the pram for a moment, then looked away and took a deep breath, trying to calm myself. *For goodness' sake, Flora, get a grip.* It was only a pram. And, now that I'd seen it properly, I could see that it wasn't even the same pram. It *looked* a bit like Thea's though. Same make, Silver Cross. It had the same chrome chassis and herringbone fabric, but this one was in a deep berry shade, and Zander's had been grey. Zander. I leaned forward and peered into the pram, gently pulling the soft fleece blanket back to get a better view. The baby, clearly a little girl in a pink dress with a polka dot collar, was indeed sound asleep, making a tiny snuffling noise with each breath. I tucked the blanket back into place and edged away slowly, back into the brightly lit central area of the bookshop, but suddenly in my head I was back at Thea's, in her lovely Regency townhouse on Montpellier Terrace.

She'd started taking the empty pram out about two weeks after Zander died, back in September. I'd been on the phone in the dining room, where we often sat and worked, a gorgeous space with huge windows, Montpellier Gardens just across the road, the sound of children's shrieks and laughter drifting in through the open window from the park's play area. I'd just finished checking that a big delivery had been sent out, when I suddenly saw her, wheeling the pram past the door and down the hallway, leaning over it as she walked, talking quietly. I'd dropped the phone, run out into the hall and grabbed her arm.

'Thea! Thea, what are you doing? Where are you going?'

She'd straightened up and looked at me for a moment, a peculiar expression on her face, the face that was still so beautiful, but so pale today, dark circles like painful bruises under her eyes.

Then she dropped her gaze again, back down to the empty pram.

'I'm just going for a walk. To the park. I need some fresh air. I've been in this house almost twenty-four hours a day for the past two weeks, Flora, and it's driving me mad.'

Her voice was flat and expressionless, her soft Somerset accent barely discernible. She'd begun to move away but I grabbed her again, my hand moving down her arm to cover her hand as it gripped the pram handle.

'I get that but ... but why are you taking the pram, Thea? He's ... he's gone. Zander's gone, you know that, don't you? Why ... why are you pushing an empty pram?'

She took a little gasping breath, her eyes fixed on the vacant space under the pram cover.

'I don't know. I don't know, Flora. I know it looks a bit mental but ... I just ... I just need to feel close to him, and ... well ... it sort of brings me comfort, I don't know why. I did it yesterday too, when you were off? Just for a few minutes, down the road and back. It's something to hold onto, and when I'm walking with the pram I don't feel ... I don't feel so alone, I suppose.'

Tears had started to roll down her cheeks. She'd been drinking, I suddenly realized, a whiff of alcohol on her breath, even though it was barely midday. I stared at her for a moment, my heart twisting, unsure what to do, then I reached into my pocket and pulled out a tissue, pushing it into her hand.

'OK. I'm sorry, Thea, I understand. If that's what you need to do ...'

She nodded, dabbed at her cheeks with the tissue and smiled a small, wobbly smile.

'I'll see you later. Thanks, Flora, I don't know how I'd have got through the last couple of weeks without you.'

And so it had continued. She'd carried on taking that pram, that unbearably sad, empty pram, out with her, time after time. It was as if she'd lost the ability to walk without it, as if it supported her, as if the day she left it at home she would simply crumble.

We were all horrified, mortified for her – me, Isla, Rupert, even Nell – but no matter what anyone said, whether we cajoled or shouted or begged, she would simply nod, tell us quietly that yes, she understood, and she knew it was weird and mad, but that she couldn't stop, she couldn't leave it at home, she *needed* that pram, that comfort. She didn't even stop when somebody put a picture of her with the damn empty thing on Twitter, sneering at her, calling her all sorts of names, and it got retweeted and retweeted and practically went viral …

'Flora! Everything all right?'

Annabelle had returned from downstairs, waving at me from across the floor. I waved back.

'Fine! Just checking everything's shipshape!'

I took a deep breath. It was, wasn't it? Everything was shipshape. The past was the past. No looking back, I told myself. Onwards. Let's get this party started.

8

THEA

I opened my eyes and instantly closed them again, wincing as even that tiny movement, just that miniscule eyelid flutter, caused a fresh wave of pain inside my skull. Why the hell was the room so bright? What time was it? My clock was right there on the bedside table, inches from my face. Could I risk it? *Oh, for God's sake, Thea.* I opened just one eye this time, squinting to minimize the damage. Twenty past eleven. Eleven in the morning? It must be, yes, and I clearly hadn't managed to close the curtains when I'd passed out last night, the sun flooding in as if it were June and not January. I winced again as a passing car honked its horn on the road outside, sending a spasm of pain through my head, then moved my right hand slowly under the duvet, running it cautiously down my body. I was wearing a jumper, jeans … and oh, great. Shoes. Yes, definitely trainers, still on my feet.

My stomach lurched suddenly, and I knew I was going to be sick. Moaning, I pushed the duvet aside and stumbled to the ensuite, the room swaying and swirling around me, and crashed painfully to my knees beside the toilet, my hands shaking uncontrollably as I pushed the lid up and leaned over the bowl.

When I'd finished, I slumped to the floor, the tiles cool against my burning forehead, traces of vomit still on my cracked lips.

Why did I do this to myself? *Why?* What was the point? Because I hated myself, that's why. Because I was constantly filled with shame and self-disgust and pain, and alcohol helped to numb it, to sedate me, just for a while. But I'd clearly gone too far, yet again. Did I really think that drinking myself into oblivion would help? I must have yet again last night, mustn't I? I didn't even remember what I'd drunk, or what I'd done … and what about Nell? Oh shit, where was Nell?

I sat up so suddenly that the room started spinning again, my head throbbing violently, black flashes strobing in front of my eyes. I took a few gasping breaths, trying to calm myself, trying to stop the nausea taking a grip again. Then slowly, I remembered. Isla. Isla had been here last night, hadn't she? And Nell wasn't here. Yesterday had been Friday, and she was with her father. With him until Monday, after school. With him for two more days. That was assuming that today was still Saturday, and that I hadn't been so wasted I'd actually lost a whole day …

I crawled, like a baby, on hands and knees, off the tiles and back onto the soft bedroom carpet, then collapsed again, my eyes shut tightly against the burning sunlight. A few minutes later, thirst and self-loathing taking over, I dragged myself up into a standing position and slowly peeled my clothes off, leaving them on the floor where they fell. I could tidy up later, when I felt more human, I thought, my hand still trembling as I reached for the bottle of water that somehow, miraculously, was sitting on my bedside table. I drank the entire thing down, then staggered back to the bathroom and stood under a hot shower for a long time.

It was nearly twelve thirty by the time I made it downstairs, wearing a clean pair of navy leggings and an oversized, soft blue sweatshirt, my hair still damp. I suddenly felt ravenous, cramming bread into the toaster and cutting chunks from a block of Cheddar I found in the fridge, ramming it into my mouth, the events of last night slowly coming back to me.

37

Isla had arrived not long after seven, escaping London for the weekend as she almost always did. She was based there during the week, working as a producer on the Thursday night chat show *Yak Yak Yak*, the one which interviewed all the most controversial guests – the ex-cons, the kiss and tellers, the unapologetic racists who wanted to close Britain's doors to immigrants. Isla worked long hours during the week, but once the live show had gone out on Thursday night and the Friday debrief was over, she liked to leave the city for a day or two before the madness started again on Monday. And to see me, of course. We talked on the phone pretty much every day, but it wasn't the same as being together in the same room.

We'd met in a backstreet pub in Soho about fifteen years before, not long after I'd left university and moved to London; me, a skinny, quiet country girl from Somerset, trying to make my way in the big city's fashion industry, her a loud, funny Edinburgh lass, all spiky red hair and dark lipstick, already a runner for a daytime TV show and determined to hustle her way to the top.

I'd been in the pub with a couple of people from work, and had only started talking to Isla because I'd somehow managed to trip and spill my cider all down her black T-shirt on my way back from the bar. When I, mortified, had offered this now very damp stranger a tissue to clean up the mess, she'd simply laughed, slapped away the hand that was ineffectually dabbing at her, and told me not to worry about it, and just to buy her a drink instead. And then I'd admired her necklace, a chunky gold lizard on a long shimmering chain, and that had been that. We'd ended up chatting for hours, two young women at the beginning of our careers, our London adventure, sharing our hopes and dreams and realizing that despite our very obvious personality differences, we were both so similar, deep down. Not just the lonely only child thing, but our hopes and desires for the future too, both fiercely ambitious, determined to succeed, both wanting many of the same things out of life.

When Rupert and I had moved to Cheltenham, Isla had come to visit and fallen in love with the place. Three weeks later, she'd rented a cute little bedsit near the hospital, just a few minutes' walk away from our house.

'My Cotswold retreat!' she'd announced. And so Isla had remained an important part of my life, to my joy and delight, although Rupert wasn't quite so keen sometimes. He'd grown to tolerate her, even enjoy her company at times, over the years, despite his initial concerns about our 'obsessive' relationship. But … well, Isla was Isla. You either got her, or you didn't, and Rupert never did, not entirely. For me, though, he put up with her frequent presence, and she in turn gradually thawed towards him too, grudgingly accepting that, for me, my husband was a non-negotiable extra now.

'He's OK, your Rupert,' she'd finally admitted, about a year after we got married. Not exactly gushing, but I'd hugged her anyway.

And so they rubbed along all right, the two of them. Most of the time, anyway. Rupert's biggest issue with Isla was … well, her perennial *singleness*, really. She had boyfriends, of course she did, but few of them lasted more than a few dates, many – the frequent married ones – just one-night flings. While I enjoyed living the wild single life vicariously through my friend, Rupert disapproved.

'She's just so … well, she acts like a twenty-year-old,' he would say. 'She leads you astray. She drinks too much, *way* too much, and so do you, when she's around. And she hates kids. How can you be friends with someone who hates kids?'

She didn't *hate* kids though, not exactly. She'd been brought up in a tough part of Edinburgh by an abusive, single mother, walked out on by a violent father when she'd been just five years old. And she'd vowed, vowed from a very young age, she'd always told me, that motherhood was not for her. She didn't have a strong maternal instinct anyway ('Kids are just so *boring*, Thea'), but her big fear was, she said, that she might cause another child

39

to be hurt the way she'd been hurt. Not because she *herself* had any violent tendencies, far from it. But she was scared that she'd pick the wrong man, and that the child would suffer because of that.

'You know me, I always go for the bad boys, Thea. I'd get it wrong, I know I would. It's not worth the risk. And it's not for me, anyway, being a mum. I really don't like them very much, which isn't exactly ideal. And Christ, I'd be terrible at the whole caring thing. I can barely remember to feed myself most of the time ... can you imagine? I can't even keep a house plant alive.'

And so her decision had been made. As a result, she wished that, like her, I'd chosen to stay child-free, as she put it, too – she didn't like how they 'cramped my style'. The children took up so much of my time, time that I would have normally spent with her, and she definitely hated that, hated that I was often tired and distracted, hated my lack of energy when I was pregnant, and my inability to be spontaneous once I became a mother. She couldn't just whisk me off for an impromptu drunken night on the town anymore, not after Nell arrived, and she'd been pretty horrified when I'd told her I was pregnant again with Zander.

'Christ, Thea, *two*? Wasn't one enough? Are you seriously going to have it?' she'd said, clearly exasperated. It sounded horribly selfish, when I thought back to it now, the way she behaved, the things she said – it sounded like it was all about her, that my wants and needs and feelings didn't enter into it at all. But I knew she wasn't selfish, not really. She was, on the contrary, one of the most generous women I knew, always turning up with gifts for Nell and, later, Zander, even though she didn't have much interest in them, not really; always there on the end of the phone when I'd had a bad day and needed to talk, always ready to drop everything for me.

So no, not selfish. She was just ... insecure, I supposed. Desperately insecure, despite her brash, confident exterior, and terrified that she was going to lose me, her best friend, her surrogate sister, to these tiny, new, needy humans, despite my constant reassurances that that would never happen.

And it didn't. I made sure of that, made sure that, despite Isla's fears, my children didn't really affect our friendship at all. We were too strong for that by then anyway, had too much shared history. When she arrived in Cheltenham after her week in London we'd stay in instead of going out, downing bottles of wine and Prosecco or, on sunny Saturdays, taking Nell and later Zander, too, out with us for long boozy lunches in beer gardens and bistros with pretty outdoor seating areas.

It wasn't perfect – Isla was sometimes irritated on those days, the days I needed to bring the children with me and, if I was really honest, she basically ignored them most of the time, although I thought she'd warmed to Nell in recent months, just a little, as my daughter had grown and developed into the feisty, intelligent little girl she now was.

But in general, I supposed that Rupert was right about her attitude to kids, even mine. They just weren't her thing. It was always OK though, once she'd had a few drinks. A glass of bubbly fixed everything, she always said. Rupert was right about that too, although I hated to admit it – Isla *did* lead me astray, certainly when it came to alcohol. I didn't drink much at all when she wasn't around – not in recent years, not since becoming a mum (although that has rather obviously changed somewhat drastically recently) – but when she was, all bets were off. She'd always denied having a drink problem, as such, although I was fairly sure she'd struggle to give it up for any length of time. But if I ever asked her about it, she'd dismiss my concerns with an airy wave.

'I'm Scottish, Thea. Drinking's in our *blood*. And when have you ever seen me with a hangover? It's stress relief, that's all. Hush. Here, pass me your glass.'

Oh yes, that girl could *drink*, and for some reason when she did, I always joined in. The problem was, as she liked to point

41

out, she could down it by the gallon with, seemingly, no major repercussions, whereas I …

I rubbed my eyes, waiting for the toast to pop up, my head beginning to throb again, and hoped the paracetamol I'd just washed down with half a carton of orange juice would kick in quickly. I'd been able to handle the booze when I was younger, no problem at all, but since having the kids … *serious* lightweight. I'd often offer to be designated driver or, if Rupert and I were walking to one of our numerous haunts nearby, stick to two or three small glasses of wine.

Things had changed, though, over the past few months. Everything had changed. I didn't need Isla to make me drink too much these days. I was quite capable of doing that all by myself.

The toaster finally spat out its browned offerings, making me jump. I slathered on some butter and layered on the cheese, then turned the grill on, put the toast on a tray underneath it and waited again, listlessly wiping surfaces and stacking empty bottles in the recycling box, my stomach growling. As I put the bottle opener back in its drawer I smiled suddenly as I remembered the conversation Isla and I had had last night as I'd wrangled a stubborn cork out of a crisp Sauvignon Blanc.

'So, next week we're interviewing the guy who owns that kids' play park – you know, the one in Leicester where three kids were seriously injured because the equipment was faulty? And he's blaming the parents for not keeping an eye on their offspring, and it's sparked a big debate? Thea?'

Isla had been sitting at the kitchen table, nibbling crisps, filling me in on her week, trying as always to distract me from my thoughts, cheer me up, make me laugh. I'd nodded, struggling with the cork.

'Yeah, yeah, I know. And?'

'Well, I suggested we do it outside in the garden set, stick a bouncy castle behind him, have some kids on it, you know, for atmosphere? Light it up all spooky. It'll look good, I think. Except,

42

of course, the show goes out live, and at eleven o'clock at night legal won't let us use kids, child employment laws, can't allow them to work after 7 p.m., blah blah …'

I'd turned and raised an eyebrow at her.

'I'm not surprised, Isla! Did you have to scrap the idea, then? Pity …'

'Och, no!' She'd slapped a hand on the table, a triumphant look on her face. 'Because I, my dear, am a genius. I've hired a load of midgets instead. They'll just be in the background, dim lighting, so nobody will notice the difference – brilliant, eh?'

I'd stared at her, aghast.

'A load of … do you mean dwarves? Little people? Seriously?'

She'd nodded, eyes bright, and held out her glass for a refill.

'Aye. Dressing them up in kids' clothes. Hey – you don't have any spares knocking around I can borrow, do you?'

I'd laughed out loud then, long and hard, laughed so much I'd first doubled over then slid slowly to the kitchen floor, tears running down my cheeks. Isla had watched me, slightly bemused, for a minute, then joined in, the two of us shrieking like hysterical banshees. She could do it, even now, in these days of such dark despair – make me laugh until I cried, and last night I had needed to laugh, needed it so desperately. Needed it to numb the pain, if only for a few moments. And I needed to do it with Isla, with the friend with whom I had shared so much. So much laughter over the years, so much happiness.

And now, so many tears, so much pain. So much guilt. Oceans of it, guilt so vast and deep and choking that sometimes I could barely breathe. Guilt that I know Isla felt too, just a little. It wasn't her fault – it was me, all me. But she was with me, you see, that day. The day it happened. And we were drinking that day too. The day Zander died. Or, I should say, in the interests of accuracy, the day I killed my baby.

43

9

ANNABELLE

The sound of pounding feet on the stairs, accompanied by shrieks and giggles, made me look up from my laptop and smile. I usually tried not to work on the rare Saturdays when I didn't have any events to worry about, but I was just finishing a quote for a short-notice Valentine's Day party at the home of a young foot-baller and his wife in Winchcombe. Dan Foster plays for league two Cheltenham Town – or The Robins, as they are known, due to their red strip – but his wife, Lara, clearly has her eyes fixed on a premier league lifestyle. It was the third event she'd asked me to organize for her in as many months, and with less than four weeks to go, I needed to get started on planning the evening as soon as possible.

'You two OK?'

I smiled again as Millie skidded into the kitchen, Nell Ashfield close behind her.

'Fine. Nearly finished. We just need a drink. Can we have some apple juice?'

Millie was already heading to the fridge.

'Of course. I made some of those crumbly cookies you like too, look, in that tin on the side, if you want a couple? Take a plate though, Millie. I don't want crumbs everywhere.'

'Thanks, Mum!'

Nell smiled shyly at me and followed Millie across the room. Rupert, who always had her at weekends now, had dropped her off just after lunch, Millie and Nell needing a couple of hours together to finish a school photography project. Between them they had managed to take some rather lovely photos for the 'winter scenes' themed assignment, and today were arranging all their pictures on a large display board, ready to take to school on Monday.

I watched as the two girls poured juice and selected biscuits, chatting happily, Nell's dark curls in stark contrast to Millie's golden blonde bob. It was nice to see Nell smiling, especially as Millie had told me she'd been horribly upset earlier in the week, after another episode of verbal abuse at the school gates.

'It was *awful*, Mum,' Millie had said, her dark blue eyes narrowing. 'Mrs Ashfield just shouldn't pick Nell up from school, especially when she's doing that weird thing with the pram. It's not fair. It's so *embarrassing* for her.'

I'd nodded, agreeing with her. I knew Thea didn't often do the school run now, not unless she had to, but Millie was right. Nell was a sweet little thing, but she clearly wasn't the same child now as she had been before her baby brother died. I'd watch her sometimes, when she was here with Millie, and it chilled me to think about what she had been through, and how it was affecting her. She was quieter now, less raucous than she had been before, although I wasn't sure Millie had noticed. Nell still put on a good act, still played the part of the fun best friend, but I could see it. I'd seen it last weekend when the two of them were sprawled on the sofa watching a DVD, a cartoon baby cooing on the TV screen, and I'd felt an ache in my throat as I saw a shadow suddenly cross Nell's face, pain flashing in her eyes, as if a memory had just surfaced. I wanted to wrap her in my arms, tell her everything would be OK, but I never did, knowing instinctively that what this damaged child needed was what I tried to make sure she got here – normality, ordinary, dull, family time, with no mention of her mother or her brother whatsoever.

I wondered, sometimes, if they still talked about what had happened – Millie and Nell, I mean. Because Millie had been there that day too. She hadn't seen much, though – Greg, who'd been there too, had whisked her away as soon as it had happened, although that hadn't stopped Millie crying for days afterwards. It had been her first experience of death, and it had hit her hard. She hadn't even wanted to see Nell for weeks, told me she couldn't face her, but I made her eventually. Her friend needed her, I insisted. It's not about you, Millie. Harsh maybe, but then life can be, can't it? And she was glad, when I finally insisted and made her invite Nell round. They locked themselves in Millie's room, and came out an hour later all smiles, back to normal. Well, as normal as anyone could be, after that …

'Where are Olly and Sienna, Mum?'

Millie turned to look at me, and I blinked at her, slightly startled, then tapped save on my keyboard, not wanting to lose the email I'd started to compose.

'Ermm … Daddy's taken them into town – Olly needed new school shoes and Sienna went along for the ride,' I said. 'They should be back soon though. Why?'

'No reason,' she said breezily. 'It's just nice and quiet without them. Nell and I have actually had *peace* to do our project …'

'FLORA!' There was a sudden yelp from Nell as the door opened and Flora wandered in, wearing orange patterned leggings and bright coral trainers, a black fleece zipped high under her chin and her nose pink with cold. Nell barrelled across the kitchen and flung her arms around Flora's waist.

'Hey, Nellie-bells! Didn't know you'd be here today. I was out running, I'm freezing, feel!'

Flora flattened her palms against Nell's cheeks and the child squawked.

'Urrrgh, get off!'

Flora laughed, and Nell laughed with her. She stepped back, brushing an errant curl from her forehead, and looked Flora up and down.

'I like your leggings. And your trainers,' she announced.

'Well, thank you very much. Ooh, I've missed your little face.'

Flora reached out both hands as if to squeeze Nell's cheeks, and the little girl ducked.

'Get off!' she said again, but her eyes were shining. They definitely had a special bond, Flora and Nell, and it made me happy to see it, to know that Nell had Flora here in my home as well as Millie. Millie and Flora got on well too – once or twice when Millie had seemed a little down, I'd seen Flora take her to one side, for a stroll around the garden or a chat upstairs, and soon Millie would be smiling and bouncing around again. I felt a little guilty sometimes – it wasn't Flora's job, after all, was it, to counsel my children – but when I was so busy, and she was so good at it …

'We're back!'

I started slightly again as the front door slammed and Greg's voice drifted down the hallway.

'In here!' I replied and shut my laptop with a sigh. I clearly wasn't going to get this finished now, and I needed to start thinking about dinner. There were some nice steaks in the freezer – maybe those with some baked potatoes? Or possibly a moussaka?

'Mummy! Daddy bought me a new colouring book!'

Greg appeared in the doorway, rubbing his hands together, and Sienna pushed her way past him and leapt onto my knee, waving a brown paper bag, her pink woolly hat askew on her head.

'Lovely, darling. Did you get Olly's shoes, Greg?'

I pulled my daughter's hat off, smoothing her hair down, and looked at my husband, who was glancing round the room. His eyes rested on Flora for a moment, then he spotted Nell and winked, and she grinned back at him. He was dressed in a tight blue sweater under a navy quilted gilet, and he looked fit and toned.

Greg is a few years older than me, in his early forties, but he still has a full head of hair, flecked with silver now at the temples and swept back off his smooth forehead. He has a strong jawline, with a hint of stubble, his weekend look.

He looked good, healthy, handsome, and I smiled.

Greg is the only man I've ever loved – the only man I've ever slept with too, something I'm not sure if I should be proud of or slightly embarrassed by. We met at university, and I knew I certainly wasn't the only woman *he'd* slept with. It hadn't bothered me back then, his obvious popularity, the envious looks from other girls when they'd see us out together, arm in arm. I'd enjoyed it, if I was honest – enjoyed the fact that he'd picked *me*, over everyone else, when he could have had anyone. But as the years had passed it had begun to worry me more. It made my anxiety go into overdrive sometimes, having a husband who looked like this, who was attractive and clever and nice and successful, crazy as that sounded.

I worried, frequently, about the women who might want to steal him from me, and I wondered sometimes if my fears were justified. There'd never been anything concrete – a hint of perfume, maybe, on a sweater, a musky scent wafting from the laundry basket as I crouched in front of the washing machine, stuffing the clothes in, trying to pretend I couldn't smell anything. Or the occasional boys' night out which ended in the early hours of the morning, Greg stumbling in through the front door, crashing out on the sofa downstairs instead of coming to bed, a vagueness the next morning about where he'd been until so late when all the bars closed at eleven.

I never pushed it, though, never asked. Greg worked hard, very hard, and he needed a release sometimes, just as we all did. He was moody sometimes, distracted, distant, but that was just how he was.

Recently though, things had been good. Great, in fact. And it was another good day. *Today he's here with me and the children and life is good and there's nothing to worry about.* I chanted the phrase in my head like a mantra, supressing a tiny tremor of anxiety, and smiled at my husband again. Me and my bloody insecurities.

'Got them, yes. And he's actually happy with them, amazingly.'

'They're cool, Mum! I put them upstairs, I'll show you later. Is there anything to eat? Oh, hi, Flora.'

Oliver appeared, stomping across the room, heading for the biscuit tin, the laces of his high-top trainers trailing, jeans so baggy half of his bright purple underpants were on full view. Flora glanced at me and grinned, knowing what I was thinking. I'd moaned to her more than once about my son's scruffy dress sense.

'Hi Olly,' she replied. 'You're seriously going to trip over one of these days you know. Ever think of actually *tying* your laces?'

He looked down at his feet with a puzzled expression, then back at Flora.

'I forgot. Sorry.' He crouched down, fumbling at the laces, tying them, and I looked at my assistant in amazement.

'Wow,' I said. 'Now that's a first. Look, Greg. Or even better, take a photo, go on. Our son, Olly, tying his shoelaces, live right now in our kitchen. It's a miracle.'

'It is. Good grief. Are you feeling OK, son?' Greg's voice was full of mock concern.

'Oh shut up, parents.' Oliver straightened up again, cheeks a little pink, and everyone laughed. Flora beamed and poked him teasingly on the shoulder, and he shrugged her off, his face growing even redder. Sienna wriggled on my knee then buried her face in my chest, joining in with the laughter even though she clearly didn't understand what was so funny.

'And you shut up too, brat.'

Oliver had directed the comment at Sienna, but she ignored

him, as usual. My son and Millie had always rubbed along all right – well, as all right as a brother and sister three years apart in age generally could be expected to – but it was a different story with him and Sienna. It wasn't even just that he had little interest in her: he seemed to actively dislike her, and it bothered me, my concern about it only slightly lessened by the fact that she in return cheerfully disregarded his presence, his verbal hostility towards her mostly going unnoticed.

'Oliver, don't talk to your sister like that,' I said wearily. 'Go on, help yourself to some biccies, if Millie and Nell haven't scoffed them all. And stick the kettle on, will you? I'm sure Daddy and Flora would like a coffee.'

'Oh, thanks, Annabelle, but I'm OK. I'm going for a shower. I'll grab one later.'

Flora smiled at me, waved a hand vaguely at everyone else in the room and left. Millie waited until she'd gone then bounded over to Oliver, a cheeky grin on her face.

'You like Flora! You like Flora!' she chanted.

'Shut up, Millie. I do not. You're an idiot.' Hands full of biscuits, he pushed roughly past her and she giggled, Nell grinning broadly by her side.

'Geez. What is it with you kids?'

Greg rolled his eyes.

'Leave him alone, Millie. Go on, thought you and Nell had schoolwork to do? Get out of here.'

He clapped his hands then gestured towards the door with his thumb and, clutching their drinks and balancing biscuit plates, the two girls followed Oliver to the door, still sniggering. I raised an eyebrow at Greg, shifting Sienna into a more comfortable position on my knee, and he winked, then left the room too, taking his gilet off as he went.

I sat for a moment, arms wrapped around Sienna, thinking. Olly probably did have a bit of a crush on Flora, but that was pretty normal, at his age, and she seemed to take it in her stride, if she'd even noticed. We'd been so busy recently there was every chance she hadn't though, and I suddenly decided I needed to do something to thank her for all her hard work. I'd take her out for dinner, one night this week, somewhere nice in town. Our midweek schedule wasn't looking too bad, so a night out would be nice, and Greg would be happy to stay in with the children.

I might finally ask her, too, I thought. I might ask her if she minded telling me about what happened at Thea's – what happened the day Zander died. I knew a bit, of course, the basics. Millie and Greg had been there, after all, and then there had been all the stuff in the papers. But to hear about it from somebody who was there all the time, living with Rupert and Thea when it happened ... oh gosh, was that really horrible of me? Why did I want to know so much? Why did I have such a morbid fascination with Thea, think about her so often? OK, so I'd think carefully about it first, that's what I'd do. I'd only ask Flora if it felt right, if I could find the right moment ...

'Mummy? I want to colour a picture. Where are my pens?'

Sienna was sitting up straight again, face upturned to mine. I kissed her forehead and gently lifted her off my knee and onto the floor.

'They're in the living room, darling. You go and get them and start, and I'll be in in a few minutes. Daddy will help if you can't find them, OK?'

'OK.' She scampered off, and with a sigh I stood up and started thinking about dinner.

10

FLORA

The closing titles of *Made in Chelsea* rolled and I yawned and picked up my phone to check the time. Just after nine o'clock. I could definitely fit in another couple of episodes before bed, I decided. The show was my guilty pleasure – the antics of rich kids in the wealthy west London borough made me laugh, but it was also aspirational. I wanted that sort of life one day – the carefree existence that money seemed to bring, the endless travel, the designer clothing, the casual sipping of champagne in exclusive clubs.

I picked up the glass of sparkling water from the table in front of me and took a sip of that, instead, for now, wondering how long it would take before I could work my way up into the sort of income bracket that would allow me to afford the Chelsea lifestyle. Or even the Cotswold lifestyle, come to think of it. Houses like the one I was currently sitting in didn't come cheap. Six bedrooms, acres of gardens … I'd checked online on one of those property search websites, just out of interest, shortly after I'd moved in with the Garringtons, and guessed that this place was worth at least a million and a half. Maybe more.

Still, Annabelle and Greg deserved it. They were both locals, from modest backgrounds as far as I could gather, and they'd worked hard – she with her business, him advertising director for a major London agency, running their Gloucestershire branch – and I had no problem with doing the same. I'd get to where they were, one day, and in the meantime Annabelle paid me well, and this room was all I needed, for now at least.

It was at its nicest tonight, curtains snugly drawn against the January cold, a couple of fragrant candles – lime and vanilla, my favourites – flickering on the little side table, and me cuddled up on the sofa with a faux fur throw across my legs and trashy telly to watch, my belly full from the luscious moussaka Annabelle had insisted I share with the family downstairs earlier, the taste of the cinnamon-spiced lamb, aubergine and creamy white sauce still lingering on my tongue.

Yes, I was twenty-five years old and probably should have been out partying somewhere, on the pull like most young single women, but I was content to be right here tonight, safe and cosy in my room, tired after another busy week. I didn't have many friends, not around here – I'd always found it hard to relate to people of my own age, and the sort of stuff they liked to do, which seemed to revolve around shopping, taking selfies and partying. I wasn't much of a drinker anyway, and the kind of men you met in pubs and clubs did nothing for me – young, immature, boozed up, slobbery, wanting only one thing and doing it badly when they got it.

I'd always preferred older men myself, and for a moment I let my mind drift back to earlier in the kitchen, to the look Greg had given me when he'd arrived back from shopping with the kids. It had only been a glance, a quick up and down, but a little shiver had gone through me. He is nearly twenty years older than me, but he is ... well, *hot*, quite frankly. And there was something, sometimes, when we were in the same room ... was *frisson* the word? An exchange of looks, eyes meeting for just a fraction too long. It made my stomach flip, my hands shake a little, my mouth go dry. I blew out hard through my mouth, dispelling the thoughts. I was definitely *not* going to go near Greg, not in that way. No, I wasn't even going to think about it. I'd made that mistake before, elsewhere, and I wasn't going to do it again.

Maybe he had some friends though? Someone he could introduce me to? I leaned back on my cushions, pulling my throw up to my chest, running my fingers across the soft fibres, and idly wondered if I could ask Annabelle if she knew of any attractive, single older men when she took me out for dinner this week. It had been nice of her to offer, and I'd been happy to accept, but I already knew the meal would come at a price. I'd noticed it for a while, every time Nell was around or Thea's name cropped up – the way Annabelle almost seemed to be holding herself back, clamping her lips together, desperate to ask me for the full story but not quite able to bring herself to form the words. She'd do it on Wednesday, though, I knew she would, and I'd resigned myself to it. It would do no harm to talk about it, not now. And there were too many secrets in life, too many things not talked about. So I would tell her, I decided, on Wednesday, if she asked me. *When* she asked me. I'd tell her what she wanted to know, finally. I'd tell her what happened to Zander.

54

11

ANNABELLE

'Marvellous, my dear. Simply marvellous. Do you have a card? I may need you one day myself. I'd love to throw a little party, but never have the time to organize them.'

'Of course. And it was lovely to meet you. I'm glad you enjoyed it.'

I reached into the back pocket of my jeans where I always kept a few business cards when I was working, pulled one out and handed it to the small woman in front of me with the elaborate hairstyle and the rather freakishly smooth face. She must have been at least sixty, judging by the appearance of her hands and neck, but from the chin upwards her skin was tight and shiny, the lips smeared with bright red gloss plump and pouting.

'*Not* a good advert for this place,' Flora had hissed at me as we'd passed in the crowd earlier, and I'd suppressed a giggle, raising my eyebrows at her in agreement. I was, it seemed, one of the few women in the room who was over thirty-five and still had the *ability* to raise an eyebrow. It was Thursday afternoon, and we were just finishing a relocation party for what the owner Sylvia described as a 'cosmetic enhancement clinic' in the centre of Cheltenham. With business on the up, she'd left her small premises on the outskirts of town and taken over two floors of a stately Georgian building on Regent Street. The reopening event was taking place in the reception area, a grand room with enormous windows, beautifully polished floorboards and white leather sofas, framed 'before and after' shots of people – mostly women, I noted – who'd been treated with Botox, fillers and various other injectables and procedures dotted around the walls. The changes were impressive, and when Flora and I were setting up, laying out rows of champagne glasses and trays of dim sum, I'd found myself squinting into one of the large, gilt-framed mirrors that also decorated the space.

'What do you think, Flora? Bit of filler here? Botox here?'

I poked at the fine lines across my forehead and the little creases – did they call them marionette lines? – that ran downwards from the corners of my mouth, frowning. I was thirty-eight. Nearly forty. Was it time to start a little – well, *maintenance*? It was OK for men … Greg looked better and better as he aged, but …

'Oh shut up, Annabelle! You're drop-dead gorgeous! Don't even think about putting that stuff in your face, you don't need it!'

The horror on Flora's face made me snort with laughter. I turned away from the mirror and grabbed her free hand – the other was balancing a wine bucket – and squeezed it.

'Oh Flora, you do make me feel better about myself. Thank you.'

She reddened slightly, pulling her hand free, but she looked pleased.

'Only speaking the truth, boss. Now stop looking at yourself and come and help me with the ice; we have six buckets to fill yet.'

She headed towards the little kitchen area off the main reception and I followed, smiling. I loved it that she clearly now felt comfortable enough to speak to me like that – at first, she'd been quieter, more deferential, but I could see her confidence growing daily and I was enjoying the gentle banter that went on between us when we were working.

'OK, OK, slave driver,' I groaned, and she laughed. I thought how good it was to see her happy today – I'd been worried, after last night, she would be low, but she'd bounced downstairs this morning with a cheery greeting and a wide grin.

We'd spent the evening before together in a restaurant – as planned, I'd left Greg with the kids, and Flora and I had gone for dinner in Cirencester, taking a taxi so we could both have a couple of glasses of wine. It was a little Italian place I liked, family-run, producing delicious meat and fish dishes along with perfect pizza and pasta from a tiny kitchen out back.

At a little corner table near the open fire we'd sipped Pinot Grigio and chatted about work for a while, giggling about an incident the day before when an extremely grumpy man had managed to get stuck in a toilet cubicle at the opening of a new fashion boutique in Chipping Norton.

But once our starters – bruschetta and a fresh *insalata tricolore* – had been devoured, and the mains of *penne arrabbiata* for Flora and some *salmone con spinaci* for me had arrived, I took a deep breath.

'Flora … look, I haven't asked you about this, not really … I didn't want to upset you, not when it was all so fresh. But now … well, it's been a few months, so I wondered … do you feel able to talk about it? That day at Thea's, when … when the baby died?'

Flora, who had just speared a piece of penne with her fork, moved it slowly to her mouth, chewed and swallowed, then put the fork back on her plate.

'I … I suppose so. Yes. What do you want to know?'

'I'd just like to know how … well, how it actually happened, I suppose. How things unfolded that day. It's a while to the trial yet, when it will all come out, and it's just that there've been so many rumours, you know? So many different stories flying

57

around, for months. And all the abuse Thea gets … I mean, I know Greg and Millie were there, but they aren't even sure exactly how it happened – Millie was upstairs playing with Nell, and Greg was out in the garden with Rupert, so they were never able to tell me much, just how horrible and sad and scary it all was. I'd like to know the truth, Flora, so at least then maybe I can put people right if I hear them talking rubbish about it …'

I was looking at her warily, nervous that I'd overstepped the mark, that she'd close up and retreat back into the shell she'd often seemed to be in when she first joined us. But to my relief, she looked back at me, nodding slowly.

'I get that. That's nice of you, Annabelle. And no, I don't mind talking about it, not really.'

And so, she told me. In a low voice, conscious of the other diners, even though the restaurant was half empty and there was really nobody within earshot, she told me the whole, horrible story. Told me how, that day, the fourth of September last year, the weather had been hot, really hot, one of the hottest days of the summer, and unusually hot for the time of year. I remembered it – the fourth had been a Monday, and I'd been rushing around town in the heat, buying pencil cases and lunch boxes, white ankle socks and navy PE shorts, sweating over the last-minute back-to-school buys before term started for Millie and Oliver on the Wednesday.

Thea had been out for lunch in Charlton Kings with Isla Laird, and they'd taken Nell and Zander with them, Flora said – an end of summer holidays treat for Nell, who liked doing grown-up things, a lovely long lunch in the sunshine outside that restaurant out on the London Road, the one with the big garden out back, a nice place to sit in the sun, and enjoy good food and an excellent wine list.

They'd sat there for a couple of hours, Isla and Thea knocking back champagne, celebrating some big interview Isla had landed for her chat show.

'Thea wasn't a big drinker normally, unless Isla was around ... well, not back then anyway. She drank a lot more afterwards, to forget, I suppose,' Flora said. 'But Isla ... well, I like her, you know? I'm not saying I don't. But she ... well, she wasn't a great influence on Thea sometimes, not when they were out together. Isla loves to drink, and she can really put it away, and Thea sometimes just got carried away with it. And well, it's nice, isn't it, sitting in the sun, drinking champagne ... I suppose you can understand why she might have had a bit too much?'

I nodded, reaching for my glass of wine and taking a sip, but secretly thinking: *No. No, not really, Flora. And I don't think you think it's understandable either, you're just being diplomatic. Because it's not OK, is it? Not when you have a young daughter and a baby son with you. Getting drunk in the sunshine, when your kids are there? I can't understand that at all.*

She ate another piece of pasta then continued, telling me how Thea, Isla and the children arrived home around three o'clock, Thea driving, despite having been drinking heavily.

'I didn't know that, of course, at the time – that she'd driven, or even that she'd been drinking so much. I only realized that later, when Isla told me, after ... after ... Anyway, I didn't actually see them come in – I was upstairs, in my room where it was a bit cooler, because I'd kept the curtains drawn. I was sending some emails and sorting some deliveries that had arrived that morning, and I wanted to get it finished so I could go out for a run a bit later on, when the temperature had dropped. But I *heard* them get back – Isla and Nell came in first. They were both shrieking and giggling, yelling that they were desperate for the loo and racing each other. It made me laugh ... Isla isn't that fond of kids, she sort of tolerated Nell as opposed to really getting on with her, you know? Didn't normally pay her much attention. But they seemed to be having fun that day.'

Flora stopped talking, a little sigh escaping her lips. She gazed down at her plate for a moment, then lifted a corner of the white linen napkin that lay on her lap, twisting it around her fingers. Then she took a deep breath and carried on.

'I heard the door slam a minute or so later and assumed that was Thea, bringing Zander in. I didn't come downstairs for about another half an hour, and by then Thea and Isla were crashed out in the sitting room. They'd opened a bottle of wine, and it looked like they'd already downed most of it. Isla was nodding off, just barely awake, and Thea was already sound asleep, all sprawled out on the sofa. I popped my head in, but Isla just opened her eyes for a minute and hissed at me to ssssh. So I took Nell out of the room and told her to go and play quietly upstairs, leave them to it. It didn't seem right, her sitting there with two drunk women.'

Flora stopped speaking again, her fingers plucking at the napkin. My insides had begun churning as I listened, my appetite for the delicious meal in front of me rapidly waning. I knew the outcome of this story, but hearing it unfold like this, step by step, was proving to be harder than I had expected. I suddenly wanted her to get to the end, for this to be over, but I stayed silent, not wanting to interrupt as she relived the nightmare.

'Rupert came home a while later, just before five, and I told him not to disturb them – Isla had totally conked out by then as well, and I thought it might be best to let them sleep it off. The kids seemed fine – Nell was up in her room and … well there was no sound from Zander, so I assumed he was asleep in his pram … I … well, I just did. Isla had gestured towards the pram when she was sssshing me, so I just *assumed* …'

She swallowed hard, even though there was no food in her mouth, her eyes fixed on her plate, then she dropped the crumpled napkin, her left hand moving to her right wrist, rubbing the small scar she had there as if it had begun to ache.

'Flora, honestly …' I started to speak, wanting to say something, to reassure her, to tell her she didn't have to go on if this was too difficult, but she held up a hand, silencing me. My mouth was dry, my fingernails digging into my palms now, my heart pounding, and suddenly I desperately wanted this story to have a different ending to the one I knew was coming, a horror movie with the inevitable imminent shock playing out in front of me.

'Then Greg and Millie arrived. That must have been about five thirty, I reckon. I think Millie and Nell just wanted a quick catch-up before they went back to school – see each other's new shoes and school bags, something like that?'

'Yes, they did,' I said, remembering.

Millie had begged Greg, who was on a half day from work, to take her round to Nell's that day, and he hadn't minded.

'I haven't seen much of her recently,' he'd said. 'We can have a catch-up in the car, and then I can wait for her out in their garden. It's nice and cool out there on a day like this.'

I repeated this to Flora now, and she nodded.

'That's what happened. I'd come down to get some papers from the dining room, so I said hi, and I think Millie ran up to join Nell in her room, and then Rupert took Greg straight out into the back garden. It was still really hot, and it was always cooler out there under the big oak tree than it was in the house. They took a couple of beers from the fridge and went out … they shouted out to me to join them, but as I said I wanted to get my work finished and then go for a run, so I said no …'

Her voice tailed off and she took a deep breath, her fingers still massaging the scar on her wrist, eyes flitting around the room, looking from one occupied table to the next. I followed her gaze, but nobody seemed to be listening. At a window table, an elderly couple were having a semi-heated discussion in hushed voices – a mild dispute over something in their garden, I had gathered, from the odd audible phrase – and a few tables away, a group of six middle-aged women were chatting and giggling over bottles of red wine, engrossed in their gossip. The only other diners were a young couple in the far corner, holding hands over a shared, extra-large pizza.

'It's OK. I'm pretty sure nobody can hear us,' I said quietly.

Flora looked back at me and nodded.

'Well, anyway, that was it, for a while. I finished off what I had to do, then came down to the kitchen to get a cold drink. It was after six by now, but still ridiculously hot. I remember hearing raised voices and looking out into the garden – Greg and Rupert seemed to be having a fairly intense discussion about something, but I couldn't hear what. Probably just football or something, knowing them.'

She gave me a slight smile, and I tried to smile back. *Gosh, this was torture. Come on Flora …*

'Anyway, I went back to the dining room to file away the papers I'd been using, and that's when I heard somebody shouting out on the street. I went to the window, just being nosey really, and there was a couple … well, I don't know if they were actually a couple, but a man and a woman, standing next to Thea's car – she'd managed to find a space right outside the house for once. Doesn't always happen. Anyway, they were sort of peering into the car, into the back window. And the man kept looking round, and shouting "Whose is this car? Who owns this car?", all frantic and kind of scared sounding, you know? And he was waving his arms around …'

She waved her own arms in the air, eyes wide now, as if she was replaying the scene in her head, then continued, her voice low and urgent.

'I had a sudden sick feeling in my stomach. All I could think was, why are they looking in the *back* of the car? And I sort of knew then, you know? I just knew that it wasn't going to be good, when I went out there. I started running … I grabbed the car keys from the hall table as I went … and then I got to the car, and I just pushed past them, the couple – I was shouting something, I don't know what, but I think I was just screaming at them to get out of the way probably – and then I saw it too. I saw what they were looking at. I don't even remember opening the car door, but somehow I did it, and then I was fumbling, my hands wouldn't work properly, fumbling with the seat belt, trying to get him out ... and I knew. I knew straight away. It was obvious ...'

There were tears in her eyes now, and I suddenly felt dizzy, my chest tightening. I gripped onto the edge of the table, wanting to stop her, not wanting to hear the end of this, the horrific outcome of Thea's day out, but I couldn't speak, and anyway she was still talking, the words pouring out of her, as if it was a relief, as if she'd been holding all of this inside her for too long, and now the dam had finally broken and the torrent of pain and anguish and emotion was unstoppable.

'I pulled him out, and I shook him and called his name over and over, but he was completely limp, Annabelle. His eyes were wide open, his little face was bright red, and he looked like a doll, a little floppy doll, not like a baby at all. And he was ... he was so *hot*. His skin was *hot* to the touch.'

The tears were rolling freely down her cheeks, her voice now barely a whisper.

'And that's when I knew for definite. He was dead. Zander was dead.'

12

THEA

'No, that's all right, I understand. Thank you so much anyway.'

I put the phone down and sighed, raking my fingers through my unwashed hair, wiping a bead of perspiration from my forehead, suddenly feeling sweaty even though the room was chilly. Another child modelling agency, another polite refusal to help me. I desperately needed to organize a photo shoot, needed pictures of my new spring stock for the website, but since Zander died, since all the publicity, it was proving nigh on impossible to hire any models at all. The refusals from the places I'd used previously were always gentle, always diplomatic, but the meaning was clear.

'It's just, Mrs Ashfield, in the light of *events*, you know …', and 'It's a little tricky, you see, Thea, to persuade parents to allow it, you understand, after …'

That kind of thing. Parents didn't trust me around their children anymore, and why on earth would they? I asked myself for the hundredth time why I was so determined to keep doing this, why I didn't just close the company, questions that so many people, some I knew, many I didn't, had asked in recent months.

'Who's going to buy clothes for their kids from a woman who killed her baby?'

'You're probably going to be in prison soon anyway. Why bother? Give it up, Thea.'

'Don't you have enough to worry about with the trial coming up? You need time to prepare your defence. You don't have to close it down for ever, just take a break.'

This last comment was from Isla, and I knew she was probably right, but something in me just didn't want to let it go, not now, not unless I really had to. I needed my work, needed the distraction, something other than alcohol to fill the long days when Nell was with Rupert. Something to make me feel that I wasn't just a sick woman who had done something unspeakably evil, that I could still do something good, support myself and my child. And maybe, in some small way, forcing myself to keep the business afloat was another way of punishing myself. I deserved the abuse I got, understood it completely. I wouldn't let someone like me, someone who'd done what I'd done, *near* my child.

I was disgusting, a monster. A child killer. A vile excuse for a mother. A woman who was on police bail, awaiting trial, after being charged with the manslaughter of her own baby. I mean, who the hell would want to even talk to me, never mind work with me? I was amazed the modelling agencies were so civil. I doubt I would have been, in their position.

I ran my fingers over the soft alpaca wool of the poncho that was folded on the table in front of me, a sample just in from Bolivia, trying to calm myself down, then pushed my chair back from the table and walked to the window, staring out at the wet, dull morning. On the pavement outside my front gate, two elderly ladies, one clutching a red umbrella, the other wearing one of those transparent, plastic headscarves, were chatting animatedly. I wondered if they were talking about me, if they realized whose home they were standing outside. The worst mother in Britain. The woman who drank so much champagne she forgot about her baby and left him to die in a hot car.

It had happened in the UK before, but not often, and never

like this. People who were rushing to work, stressed and harassed, forgetting to drop their children off at nursery. People popping into a shop on a scorching day, not wanting to disturb their sleeping baby, intending only to be a few minutes, not realizing that that could sometimes be all it took. But never a case as reprehensible, as abominable as mine. Nobody else had done what I'd done, not here, not like that. I'd spent hours trawling the Internet, for reasons I didn't really understand, looking for similar cases. Trying, maybe, to make myself feel less alone. And then, as I read the details of others, of other lost children, I wished desperately that I'd never started looking. So many people, so much pain. I *wasn't* alone, but knowing that didn't help. Nothing did.

I watched the two old ladies, but they weren't looking my way, not casting their eyes sneakily towards the house. I'd seen people do that, so many times since September. The stand-and-starers, the pointers. Not for a while though – Isla had been right.

'People have short memories,' she'd said. 'It'll pass. Just wait it out.'

She'd said it again when I'd told her how weird it was, just before Christmas, to see business slowly picking up again, after virtually coming to a halt for the three months before that, those dark, terrifying early days, when I thought my life was over.

I'd almost given up then, and not just on the business, my horror at what I had done overwhelming me, making me question whether I deserved to even go on living. But when my legal team urged me to plead not guilty, told me they were planning to mount a defence, that there were mitigating factors they could use, told me there was a chance that if I flung myself on the mercy of the jury I may get a suspended sentence, however unlikely many others around me thought that was, it was as if somebody had turned on a faint, flickering light. I threw myself back into work. It was either that, or throw myself *entirely* down the neck of the gin bottle.

66

First, I removed my name and other personal details from the website, then invested some time and money in foreign advertising, where I hoped people were less likely to have heard about the case. And, to my astonishment, it worked. It took some time, but things slowly started to improve, mainly overseas orders at first, and then a steady trickle of orders from the UK again, mostly new customers. They would probably all dry up again, when the trial started, when the name of my company would be bandied around once more, but for now, at least I had a chance to get some money in the bank. Rupert was paying a decent chunk into my account every month, for Nell, but I couldn't rely on that. I needed to prove to him, to myself, to everyone, that I was still self-sufficient, a competent, successful business woman, and not just a-a whatever I was now. A monster.

I stared blindly out of the window, suddenly feeling nauseous, and tried to drag my thoughts back to the photo shoot. I'd have to use Nell again, for the older girls' clothes, and maybe Millie would like to take part too, I thought. But that would mean approaching Greg and Annabelle, and while they seemed happy enough for now to allow Nell and Millie to continue their friendship – Annabelle had been very, very kind to Nell in fact – I felt certain it would be a step too far to allow their daughter to appear on the *Just Enfant* website.

What I'd do about the boys' and baby clothes I had no idea. I'd done a few shoots recently of just the clothes, laid out artily Instagram-style on white backgrounds, pegged up on clothes lines, hanging from wooden ladders. They were nice photos, but they didn't really show off the clothes to their best advantage. It seemed I had little choice for now, though, and I rested my forehead against the cool glass of the window, thinking.

What else could I do? Maybe my photographer friend, Melissa, who often worked with me on shoots, could help? She had a little boy, a toddler. I'd make some calls later, but it was Friday morning and that meant I needed to go into town, two appointments beckoning.

I glanced in the mirror and decided that today I didn't care that my hair was greasy and that the dark rings under my eyes spread halfway down my cheeks. There had been a time that I wouldn't even have considered going out looking like this, but recently I no longer cared. What did it matter, in the grand scheme of things? And I had so much on my mind today, the anxiety prickling now at the edges of my brain, pinpricking my skin. I headed into the hall, pulled my long black coat off its peg, picked my handbag up off the floor where I must have dropped it last time I came in and grabbed a pair of sunglasses from the drawer in the side table. They would do, in lieu of make-up, I decided, as I slammed the front door behind me and headed for the police station.

It was one of a list of bail conditions that had been imposed when I'd been charged – a weekly trip to report to the police, to prove I hadn't done a runner. Not that I could drive myself anyway, even if I *was* thinking about it – I'd also been charged with drink-driving, of course – and I'd had to surrender my passport until the Crown Court trial, which had been set for the twelfth of March, just over six weeks away.

I'd been terrified, in the beginning, that I'd be jailed until the trial, almost collapsing with relief at what they called my plea and case management hearing, when I'd been told that I could go home.

Rupert left me soon after that, but the joint custody order was swiftly put in place too. At that hearing, I'd agreed to everything he wanted immediately, shaky with fear, incredulous that I was still going to be allowed to share the care of my daughter after what I'd done.

Soon, there'd be another court room, and in the coming weeks I'd have to sit down with my legal team to plan my defence for what I'd done to Zander. And that made me feel sick to the stomach, for what defence did I have?

'We'll go with postnatal depression and issues with alcohol,' they had said. 'That's a good defence, Thea. You weren't yourself, you were ill. It will go in your favour, especially if there are women on the jury. Trust us.'

Desperate to stay out of jail, I'd weakly agreed. But had I had postnatal depression, really? When I, under duress, finally went to see my doctor after Zander died, I'd been able to tick almost every box on the checklist – persistent low mood, feeling tired all the time, trouble sleeping at night, problems concentrating and making decisions.

But I'd been going through some stuff, back then, struggling with a few things that had been going on, and I'd put how I'd been feeling down to stress, anxiety.

In any case, postnatal depression or not, was that really an excuse? I mean, the facts were horribly simple. I got drunk. I got drunk, and I drove home in that state, and then I forgot about my baby, and left him alone in a car on the hottest day of the year. The most terrible, most horrific crime a mother could commit, and I'd done it. I'd killed my own baby. Not with my bare hands, but as good as.

The Crime Prosecution Service rarely decided to prosecute in cases like mine, apparently, normally deciding the loss of a child was punishment enough and that prosecution wasn't in the public interest. Not in my case though.

I shuddered violently as I walked, a fresh wave of nausea washing over me, the words that haunted me flashing through my head: *Involuntary manslaughter due to gross negligence – a breach of duty of care to the deceased, which caused the death of the victim.*

That was the legal description of my crime, but in the days after Zander died the newspapers said it very differently.

WEALTHY BUSINESSWOMAN 'LEAVES SON TO DIE IN HOT
CAR' AFTER CHAMPAGNE BINGE
FACE OF THE BABY WHO DIED IN A SCORCHING CAR AS
HIS DRUNK MOTHER SLEPT
HORROR AS CHILDREN'S FASHION ENTREPRENEUR IS
CHARGED AFTER 'FORGOTTEN' CHILD DIES IN HOT CAR

I swallowed hard and walked faster, sunglasses on, head down, remembering again those early days, the shock, the shame, the grief, the disbelief. The jeers, the taunts, the vile abuse on social media. The horrified reactions of friends and family when they'd heard what I'd done.

It was the only time in my life that I'd been glad that my parents were no longer around. They'd died, both of them, within a year of each other, when I'd been in my mid-twenties. Dad had had a heart attack, collapsing and dying on his beloved golf course. Months later mum had been diagnosed with a late-stage, already terminal pancreatic cancer, and had passed away within weeks.

It had been a terrible, traumatic time, one I'd only managed to get through thanks to Rupert and Isla, and I'd missed my parents desperately ever since, especially since becoming a mother. It was devastating that they'd never had a chance to meet their grandchildren, but when Zander died, I had, for the first time, felt grateful that they weren't here. The thought of the anguish they would have gone through because of what I'd done was simply unbearable.

Rupert's parents were still around, though, and that had been horrendous. They had always been so incredibly kind to me, especially after I lost Mum and Dad, and the fact that I'd always got on so well with them, always loved them, had made their disgust and horror heartbreaking.

I'd lost them too, now. I'd killed their much-longed-for grandson, and they'd simply walked away, and told me they never wanted to see me again.

And then, of course, there was all the stuff about the pram. I still wasn't really sure how it started, taking the pram out with me, that sad, empty pram. But it was a way of feeling closer to him, somehow. A support, something to cling on to, both physically and emotionally.

When I was near that pram, I could still smell my baby, the soft, clean scent of him on the blankets, still see his beautiful face, blue eyes shining up at me, his rosebud lips parting in a glorious smile, and for a few brief moments I could pretend he was still there and everything was all right. Except it wasn't all right, of course, and it never would be again, and I was now the freak, the unhinged mother whose baby was dead but who still pushed his pram around, still talked to him as I did so. Everyone was horrified, of course – Nell, Flora, Isla, Rupert … they took it in turns to cajole, scold, beg me to stop doing it.

'Mummy, *please* don't take the pram out. It's so weird. Please, Mummy, it's *embarrassing*.'

'Thea, are you sure about this? Do you think maybe you should see a doctor, talk to someone?'

'Come on, Thea. Stop doing that. Stay in, open a bottle of wine, take your mind off it that way. We'll get drunk and forget about it for a bit. This isn't right, OK?'

'You look like a crazy woman, Thea. For fuck's sake leave the fucking thing at home, you mental bitch.'

That was Rupert, obviously. I tried to stop, and after a while I only did it occasionally, on the really bad days, the worst days, the days when I felt I couldn't go out on my own, when I needed something to cling to. Days when I missed Zander so much I could barely move, barely cope with the agonizing pain and loss.

Those were the days when gently rearranging the blankets, clutching onto that handle, manoeuvring the Silver Cross around corners and up and down steps and on and off pavements, somehow helped me get through.

It *was* crazy, of course; they were all right about that. And then there was the day when somebody, some stranger in the street, stared at me, recognizing me from the newspaper coverage, and then peered into the pram, and then looked at me again, face contorting in shock and disgust. That evening he posted something on his Twitter account, a horrible sneering remark with a photo of me, and it got retweeted and retweeted, the comments multiplying, hundreds of abusive messages being sent to my own feed, the one I used to promote *Just Enfant*, forcing me to close my account, until it seemed the whole Internet was jeering at me, at the woman charged with killing her baby, who was now so deranged she was pushing an empty pram around Cheltenham.

And even then, I carried on. Who does that? But I just couldn't, couldn't put the pram away, couldn't bear to. Until now. That day at the school, with Nell, had made me realize that it had to end. I'd hurt Nell, damaged her, enough already. And so I'd put the pram away, finally, hidden it out back in the shed, tears running down my cheeks as I shut the door on it, leaving it there in the dark, among the cobwebs and garden tools.

Today, I was out, heading to the police station to report in, on my own. No crutch, nothing to hold on to. And actually, I thought, as I hurried down Lansdown Road – past the Texaco garage where I used to stop sometimes when I was out for walks with Zander, and where the lady behind the shop counter used to tell me he was the ''andsomest baby' she'd ever seen – actually, it was better to be walking on my own, in my circumstances, I realized now. I was less conspicuous, just a frumpy, weary-looking woman with her head down, the sort of woman you wouldn't look twice at. It was safer.

Reporting to the police station done – the usual perfunctory scribble of my signature on a page pushed across the counter by a bored-looking officer – I started walking again, headed for my weekly doctor's appointment. As I walked, I thought about Isla, who'd be coming down from London, as usual, and a ghost of a smile twitched on my lips. She'd insisted on booking us the exercise class she kept going on about for tomorrow morning, and we'd agreed to keep the alcohol to a minimum tonight.

'Well, obviously we'll have a *couple* of glasses. Let's be realistic, it's you and me, and it's Friday night after all,' she'd said on the phone the night before. 'But we don't want to be rotten, not if we have to be there for eleven. I decided on reformer Pilates in the end, not yoga, by the way. We need a bit of reforming, you and me ...'

She'd sniggered, and I'd laughed too, and then immediately felt sick, as I always did now if I ever found a moment's happiness, forgot even for a second what I'd done and what a tremendous mess my life was.

At least I hadn't drunk this week, I thought, not at all, not after the hangover from hell last weekend, and although I probably would have a few tonight, I felt better for the week of abstinence, my head clearer, my eyes a little brighter.

For a week or so after Zander died I'd vowed to never drink again, so devastated was I that my drunkenness had led to me doing something so appalling, so catastrophic. But the pain was so bad that I needed something to help me forget, to take the edge off the agony, and the gin bottle, the wine bottle, the anything-with-alcohol bottle was the only way I knew. I'd gone through phases ever since, days of not drinking and vowing to stop, then crazy binges, and I couldn't blame Isla for all of them. I couldn't blame anyone, for any of it. Even if I didn't remember what happened, I knew that there was only one person to blame, and that was me.

Because that was the thing, you see. I *knew* what happened that day, of course I did. I knew, because everyone had told me, and because the facts spoke for themselves. I got drunk, and fell asleep, and woke up in every mother's worst nightmare, a horror film, the end of my world.

I remembered *that* bit vividly, the bit when the darkness came down, and life changed for ever. But before that, earlier in the day, the lunch with Isla and the children, the drive home, leaving my baby in the car to die? I knew what people had told me. But I couldn't remember anything. I killed my baby, and I couldn't remember a single thing about it.

13

ANNABELLE

It snowed during the early hours of Saturday morning, and I woke up just before eight to shrieks of joy from Millie and Sienna, and the pounding of their feet on the stairs as, still in pyjamas, they rushed outside to dance in the garden, scooping up handfuls of the cold white powder and flinging it at each other. Greg grunted and turned over in bed as I stood at the window watching my children and laughing, their delight contagious.

I hadn't slept well for the past couple of nights, my thoughts returning time and time again to little Zander Ashfield, and Flora's anguished face as she recounted the details of his final hours. Before Wednesday night, before I'd heard all the sordid, alcohol-sodden details, I'd secretly had a tiny shred of sympathy for Thea – I knew what it was like running your own business and having small children to look after, the crazy busyness of every waking hour, the impossibility of keeping on top of everything, the non-stop juggling of work and motherhood.

There'd even been times, just a few, when I'd briefly forgotten my *own* children – well, not forgotten them *entirely*, but been so engrossed in a quote or in planning an event that school pick-up time had come and gone and I'd still been there, head down at my desk or at the kitchen table, until my phone had rung and an icily polite school secretary had asked me if I would be collecting the children today, or was somebody else supposed to be doing it?

Those phone calls would send me into a panic, grabbing my car keys and driving far too fast to Cheltenham, arriving red-faced and sweaty, apologizing profusely to whichever irritated teacher had been given the job of waiting for today's latecomers, Oliver and Millie slumped on hard, straight-backed chairs in the entranceway, bored and grumpy, and fractious all the way home.

So, yes, when I'd initially heard about the dreadful thing that had happened at Thea's, I had felt a tiny bit sorry for her.

'There but for the grace of God ...' I'd said to Greg, who'd shaken his head vehemently.

'You would never, *ever* have done that. *Never*,' he'd said.

And now, having heard what had really happened, that Thea was drinking heavily, driving her children home in that awful state and then passing out with those terrible, nightmarish consequences, I knew that Greg had been right. I would never have done that, never in a million years, and all traces of sympathy for Thea had been completely wiped out. The woman was a monstrosity.

It wasn't as if we'd ever been close, both too busy with work and family to have much time for making new friends, but there'd been, I'd thought, a mutual respect there in the past, a sense that we understood each other, that we were similar in many ways. We'd chat briefly at the school gates, at the occasional party, although much of the conversation was practical, discussions of arrangements between our daughters, plans for weekend play dates and sleepovers.

I liked her, but she intimidated me a little, if I was honest. It was her exotic beauty – those dark eyes and high cheekbones, the leanness of her body, the fullness of her lips. She was sexy, even I could see that, and I'd watch her at social events, envying her confidence, envying the naked lust in the eyes of the men in the room when they looked at her, worrying that Greg would be among them.

People looked at her in a different way now, revulsion replacing the admiration, and finally I was finding myself revolted too.

And yet, there was Nell, the little girl of whom I was so very fond, who was so close to Millie and who I desperately wanted to protect and look after. Nell, Thea's daughter. And that made all this even more difficult, impossible, because I knew I *would* have to maintain some sort of relationship with Thea, for her daughter's sake, and for Millie.

As I watched my beautiful little girls bounding across the snowy lawn, cheeks pink and hair flying behind them, I felt a sudden surge of anger. How could the courts have given Thea joint custody of Nell when she had done such a terrible thing? How on earth did they think she could be trusted with something so precious, when she clearly had so little regard for her children's safety? At the time, Rupert had told us that Nell had desperately wanted to stay with her mother after he left, and that it was for her sake that he hadn't begged the court for sole custody.

'She's in a bad enough way after losing her brother. She was hysterical when she thought she might lose her mother too. And Thea doesn't usually get drunk, not unless Isla's around, so I didn't make it an issue, even though I could have,' he told us, the first time we'd seen him after the residency hearing. 'And to be honest, I can't manage Nell full-time anyway, not with work. I can't even bear to look at Thea right now, but she's only having Nell three days a week, and I get her four. They said even though she did what she did, there'd been no reason for concern about her parenting before that, no police record, no social services involvement, no indication that Nell could come to any harm. It'll be OK, I hope, and if it isn't, if I get even the tiniest hint that Nell's in any danger …'

But it didn't seem right to me. The woman had neglected her

baby and let him die, for goodness' sake. How could anyone guarantee that Nell would be safe with her?

On the bedside table, my phone started to ring and, lost in thought, I jumped. From under the duvet Greg grunted again, clearly irritated, so I grabbed the mobile and hurried out onto the landing, gently closing the door behind me.

'Annabelle? Jessica Evans here from Greyline. Sorry to call so early; can you talk? Just wanted to check a few final bits for tonight.'

'Jessica, good morning! Of course, not a problem. What can I help you with?'

I rolled my eyes as I made my way down to the kitchen, nodding and making appropriate noises as the woman on the other end of the line fretted about that evening's event, reassuring her that everything was in hand but that Flora and I would get there extra early, just to make sure.

Greyline Stationery is a nationwide chain with headquarters just outside Bath, and tonight was their annual staff awards ceremony, which they were holding in a town centre hotel and combining with a late Christmas party. Companies avoiding December's booked-up venues and inflated prices was a growing trend – I'd organized a festive bash for a local firm of solicitors in *July* last year – but even so, Flora and I found it extremely odd and a little tedious later that afternoon to be putting up Christmas decorations in a hotel ballroom so soon after taking the ones at home down and banishing them to the attic for another year.

'Ugh. I'm not the biggest Christmas fan at the best of times. But twice in a month? Yuk. Glad this is the last bloody tree.'

Flora sighed heavily as she picked delicate silver-grey baubles studded with crystals from their padded box and placed them carefully on one of the three ten-foot tall, fake white trees we'd brought in for the event, real trees proving difficult – and therefore extremely pricey – to acquire in late January. I straightened up from where I was bending over the seating plan and smiled, rubbing my aching back.

'Sorry. You know, I wasn't sure about this "fifty shades of grey without the smut" decor idea for Greyline's do. But it's working, isn't it, even if it *is* boring you to tears.'

'Suppose so.'

She looked around the room, and then nodded.

'Actually yes, it looks fantastic, doesn't it?'

It did. The trees looked beautiful, the baubles glittering amidst deftly draped platinumcoloured silk ribbon, snow-dusted pine cones and tiny white fairy lights. Swathes of grey silk had been flung over the tables arranged around us, and the chair seats were covered with charcoal velvet. The overall effect was understated and chic, and for a moment it slightly upset me to think that in a matter of hours this lovely room would be filled with envelope and staple gun salesmen. Then I shook my head, mentally berating myself for my snobbishness. *Honestly, Annabelle*, I thought, as I returned to my scrutiny of the table plan, wondering how I could squeeze six extra seats in as requested an hour ago by the ever-stressed Jessica. *Just because they sell paper and sticky notes for a living doesn't mean they can't appreciate a gorgeous party venue. Don't judge when you've never met them …*

'Mind if we stop for a quick coffee? All the trees are done and I need a few minutes to sit down before I start blowing up the balloons for the doorway, I think. Fancy one? I'll go and order it. I'm sure they won't mind serving us in here?'

Flora was looking at me expectantly.

'Good idea. I'd love one, thanks.'

She grinned and gave me the thumbs up, then headed off to find somebody to order the hot drinks from. I watched her go, her lithe body looking like that of a fit teenage boy from behind. She'd sounded like a grumpy teenager with her moans about the Christmas decor, but it had amused rather than annoyed me, and I suddenly felt a wave of gratitude for how well my decision to employ an assistant seemed to be working. We had a lot of fun alongside the work, and in the car on the drive down here earlier we'd put a Christmas playlist on, giggling and singing along to songs that we'd thought we wouldn't hear again for months in an attempt to get us in the right festive mood for the task ahead.

'Santa Claus is coming to towwwwwwnnnnn!'

I screeched the line in a tuneless falsetto as the latest track came to an end, and Flora laughed and clapped her hands.

'Lovely, Annabelle. Maybe don't give up the day job just yet though, eh?' she said, a wry expression on her pretty face.

'No plans to do that, don't worry.'

I smiled and looked back at the road, thankful that the gritters had clearly been out down this way. The verges were still covered with snow but the tarmac was clear, making the drive a pleasant one, the weak winter sunshine making the hedgerows and trees shimmer an iridescent silver.

'It always reminds me of Rupert Ashfield, that song,' I said, as I saw a red light up ahead and hit the brake.

'You know, "Santa Claus is Coming to Town"? We had a Christmas fete at the school a few years back and he volunteered to dress up as Father Christmas. They played that as he came in. The kids loved it, they went crazy, and Millie and even Nell were completely fooled, never suspected who he really was at all, even when he popped them on his knee and asked them what they wanted him to bring them for Christmas. I suppose they *were* quite young then though, barely five I suppose ...'

My voice tailed off as I glanced at Flora again and noticed that her face had darkened, her eyes fixed on the road ahead.

Darn it, I thought. *Damn and blast. What's wrong with me? Why do I keep bringing the Ashfields up? I'm such a twit.*

'Oh gosh, I'm sorry, Flora. I really shouldn't talk about them. I don't mean to upset you. Sorry.'

I smiled ruefully at her, and she stayed still, rigid almost, for another few moments then took a deep breath and turned to look at me, attempting a smile.

'No, it's fine, honestly. I just don't really like … well, you know …'

'I know, I know, I totally understand and I'm a total idiot for bringing it up. I won't do it again.'

'Oh don't worry, it's just me being oversensitive. I'm OK, I promise.'

She smiled again, properly this time, and picked up my iPod, which was plugged into the car's sound system, scrolling through the tracks.

'Aha! Now if this doesn't get us in the mood, nothing will!' she said, sounding satisfied. A moment later the bell chimes that were the opening bars of Mariah Carey's 'All I Want for Christmas is You' tinkled through the speakers and I nodded slowly, then started bobbing in my seat as Mariah's soulful voice and the bouncy rhythm kicked in. As we both sang along, the brief feeling of tension passed, and I vowed *not* to talk to Flora about the Ashfields in future. The poor girl was trying to move on, and every time I mentioned them I was dragging her backwards, wasn't I? Honestly, I really needed to think before I spoke.

I turned left onto Southgate Street, the honey-coloured stone of the Georgian buildings on either side glowing in the fading light, sales shoppers scurrying along the pavements, bundled up in coats and scarves, laden with bags.

As I halted the car at a pedestrian crossing, I reminded myself that Rupert Ashfield had also apparently moved on now – I'd heard at the school gate earlier this week that he had a new girlfriend, according to the Cheltenham rumour mill. Rupert had left Thea a matter of weeks after Zander's death last September, but even so, it was only January now – fairly soon for him to have found somebody new. I'd been meaning to casually ask Flora if she knew anymore about it, but I couldn't now, could I?

You'll just have to put up with not knowing, you nosey old bag,
I berated myself, then spotted the hotel up ahead.

'Aha. Arrival at venue imminent,' I announced, and Flora
sighed and reached out to lower the volume of the music.

'Right. Let Christmas commence. *Again*,' she said.

14

THEA

'Just another snowy Sunday.'

I sang the words to the tune of 'Manic Monday', trying to remember which Eighties band had sung it, as I shook out the duvet on my bed, then straightened up, satisfied. It was just gone ten, and Isla had popped in to say goodbye on her way back to London, leaving earlier than usual on a Sunday because, as she said: 'Everyone's an idiot on the roads when it's snowy. The M4 will be a *nightmare* later'.

It had been a low-key weekend, but a nice one, just the two of us, and Nell would be back from Rupert's shortly, to spend the rest of the day helping me with the photo shoot I'd finally managed to arrange. I'd been surprised he'd agreed to give her back a day early, but he knew how much she enjoyed a photo shoot, and I was grateful. A quick tidy up here, I thought, then I'd make a start on a Sunday roast for this evening. I wasn't much of a cook, but I could manage roast chicken, which was Nell's favourite.

Still humming, I went downstairs and began to assemble dinner. As I peeled potatoes, though, the brief feeling of contentment faded, the old gnawing sadness and anxiety returning. Isla had been here waiting for me when I got back from the doctor's on Friday afternoon, and we'd had a pleasant evening, just a couple of glasses of white wine with our fish and chips takeaway.

I'd enjoyed our reformer Pilates session yesterday morning, too, just the two of us with an instructor who didn't appear to recognize me, which meant I could relax and enjoy the class, relishing the feeling of my body being stretched and eased into positions I didn't think possible on the torture-chamberesque moving platforms complete with ropes and pulleys. I'd realized that I'd barely done anything other than walking for ages. I was certainly feeling it today, as muscles not exercised with any regularity for months ached and burned in protest, but it was a good pain, a pain earned by hard work, and I liked it.

We'd stayed in again last night, watching a couple of silly romcoms back-to-back, and although Isla downed a bottle of red by herself, I managed to get through the evening on just two gin and slimline tonics.

'You're becoming a right wuss in your old age,' Isla had remarked, but she hadn't pushed it. The result was that instead of a banging hangover, a regular occurrence on a Sunday morning, today I had a clear head, into which kept popping replays of the conversation I'd had on Friday with Dr Evans, my GP.

I had a weekly appointment with her, something she'd insisted on after my diagnosis, to monitor my memory loss. When I'd realized, after Zander died, that my mind, my memory, was completely blank, it had terrified me. I'd always had a good memory, really good. I never forgot anything, and to suddenly have a gap: a huge, gaping, fourthofSeptembershaped hole, made me feel as if I was going mad, losing my mind, my grip on reality. Instead, I was told, I had developed a condition called dissociative amnesia, sometimes known as psychogenic amnesia. I hated the latter term – well, it had the word psycho in it, didn't it? – so I tended to stick to the former, if anyone asked. What it was called, though, was irrelevant. It was what it had done to me that freaked me out. I knew what I'd done, of course I did – the horrific

84

evidence was right there in front of me. But the detail, the order of things, my arrival home, leaving him in the car – it was all a blank. In fact, I couldn't remember anything of that day at all, not a single moment, until the point where Flora came running in from the car, white-faced and trembling, Zander in her arms. Not getting up that morning, not the lunch with Isla and the children. Nothing.

'Your form of dissociative amnesia is called localized,' the psychiatrist I'd originally been referred to had told me. He'd looked at me quizzically with his head tilted to one side as he spoke, little round glasses perched on the end of his nose, as if I was an interesting museum display.

'Your memory loss was triggered by the trauma you've been through, and you're actually lucky, Mrs Ashfield, that it's just affecting a brief period, a day of your life. Others, with other forms, can forget who they are completely, not recognize friends or family. The memories will return, most likely. It's just a matter of time. Be patient.'

'So is there anything at all coming back yet, do you think?' Dr Evans had asked me, gently, on Friday, as we sat in her small, bright surgery. She is a quietly spoken woman in her forties, her face kind and make-up free.

'Anything? Do you remember waking up that day, having breakfast?'

I shook my head. She smiled, and tapped on her keyboard, making a note on my online file. I waited, eyes flitting across her desk. Tissues in a fancy floral box, a half-empty coffee mug, a potted plant. Homely and safe, like she is. She looked up and smiled at me again.

'Well, don't worry about it,' she said. 'As you've been told before, it's just the way your mind is coping with the stress. For some people, dissociation just lasts for hours or days, but with a major trauma it can be months. It's your brain protecting itself by switching off from reality. You'll get there. It might just be the

85

tiniest thing at first, a little flash of memory. And when that starts, the rest should follow. But don't get stressed about it, Thea, OK? Are you all right, otherwise? How's the drinking been this week?'

'I've not had much at all,' I said honestly. 'I've realized it just makes me feel worse, act a bit … well, a bit oddly.' I hadn't mentioned the pram thing to her and decided there was no need to say anything about it now. I'd stopped doing it, and I wouldn't be doing it again. 'So I've cut down, quite dramatically. Only a couple of glasses at a time now, and not every day.'

She nodded, looking pleased.

'Good. That's excellent. And you never know, cutting down might help the memories to come back too.'

I nodded in agreement, suppressing a shudder. Of course I wanted to remember, more than anything, but there were moments when I hoped that if … *when* … the memories returned, they would be just the good ones, the nice bits of that day. I desperately wanted to remember my last hours with Zander, our last cuddles, the last time my lips brushed his cheek. But did I really want to know in full, graphic detail, what happened later … what I did? Everyone said it would be better for me, to have my head clear again, but would it, really? Would I be able to live with it? It was hard enough, agonizing enough, now. How would I cope if suddenly I could relive that day in my head, every single, sick second of it?

Now, potatoes peeled, I tipped them into a saucepan of cold water and started scraping the carrots. Nell loved carrots so much I was sometimes surprised she hadn't yet turned orange, something which could actually happen, I knew – something to do with the betacarotene.

My darling Nell. I knew I spoiled her now, sometimes, but she'd suffered so much. *I'd* made her suffer so much. She hadn't even escaped the police questioning, on the day it happened. I hadn't expected that – the adults, fair enough, but Nell? My beautiful little Nell, taken aside and quizzed about what she knew, what she'd seen. She was just another witness to them, another on the list who had to be interviewed, but there seemed no doubt what had happened, and in the end it was only me who was charged, and that was only fair. It *was* me, wasn't it? It was my fault, and only mine.

And ... well, I admitted it. I *told* the police I had left Zander in the car. The sequence of events was crystal clear – Isla and Nell had run in from the car as soon as I'd pulled up outside, both shrieking about needing a wee, racing each other to the front door, laughing and jostling each other, leaving me to unbuckle the sleeping Zander from his car seat and follow them in. By the time they got back from the bathroom I was sprawling on the sofa, the pram in the corner of the living room as usual, and they *assumed* ... well, they assumed, as everyone did, that he was in it, safe and sound, still asleep. Why wouldn't they?

So we opened some wine, Isla and I, and started drinking again. Shit, as if we *needed* anymore, after all the champagne with lunch, but by then ... and sometime after that, we fell asleep.

I'd gone over it over and over and over again, with the police, with my legal team, just by myself, trying to make sense of it, trying to make the pieces add up to ... well, to some sort of coherent whole. Trying to work out why I had done what I had done, trying to formulate some sort of defence, outside of the alcohol and the possible postnatal depression.

And I couldn't. Other than temporary insanity, I just couldn't. For a start, what on earth possessed me to drive home in such a state? It horrified me. I'd *never* driven drunk before, not ever. I had two children in the car, for God's sake. The memory of why I did was gone too, of course. I remembered none of it, not the drive, or finding a parking space, or parking in it, but I clearly did all of that somehow, the car parked neatly in the spot right outside the door, no indication that its driver had been half pissed in the middle of the day, the worst kind of irresponsible mother, the kind that disgusted me, would disgust anyone.

It was a miracle I didn't kill us all. I did ask Isla why she'd let me drive, afterwards, after the police had released me. Well, I didn't *ask* exactly – I grabbed her by the shoulders, hysterical with grief and fear and anger and horror, and *screamed* at her, shook her violently, told her it was all her fault, that if we'd got a taxi home it would never have happened, if I hadn't driven us home Zander would still be alive and well. That Zander would still be *here*. And Isla, my beautiful, bold friend who never cried, crumpled in front of me, sobbed as if her heart was being torn in two, and told me she was sorry, so desperately sorry, that she didn't *know* how drunk I was, that she hadn't been counting, and that I'd insisted I was fine, that I wasn't drunk at all, that it was only a few minutes' drive, that everything would be OK. And then I'd crumpled too, and the two of us had slid to the floor, wrapped in each other's arms, and cried and cried.

'I'm sorry, I'm sorry, I'm sorry. I know it's not your fault. It was mine, only mine,' I whispered, over and over, my throat raw, my eyes blind with tears, and she'd held me tightly, rocking me in her arms like a baby, murmuring unintelligible words of comfort. And after that, I let it go. I needed her, needed her desperately, and what good would it do, falling out with my best friend, trying to pass some of the blame on to her? I was responsible for this. Nobody else.

We talked about it, though, talked and talked, as I tried to remember, tried to make some sense of it all. Isla had tried to jog my memory, at my insistence – describing for me in detail how we'd chatted and laughed as we drove home, both children dozing in the back of the car, worn out by the heat. How even Zander, who woke easily, had slept throughout the short journey, his long lashes brushing his pink cheeks, tiny snores coming from the baby seat. My darling baby, my son, my little boy. And still, I couldn't remember. Couldn't remember his last hours alive.

Tears pricked my eyelids as the thoughts tumbled through my mind. And then, as I blinked them away, flinching as I ran the peeler over the end of my finger, dropping the carrot, it happened again. A weird, crawling sensation, like a bony hand running up my spine. It had happened earlier today too, first thing this morning while I was still lying in bed, unwilling to leave my warm cocoon. A strange, shivery feeling, that had nothing to do with being cold. A feeling of unease, so intense that it was almost a physical sensation. This morning it had come and gone in a flash, and I'd put it down to being in that odd, semi-awake state but now, as I leaned against the kitchen counter, it stayed, first that shiver up my back, then a sense that something was trying to wriggle its way into my consciousness, a voice far, far too tiny for me to hear trying to make itself audible. I squeezed my eyes tightly shut, trying to listen, but just as quickly as it had arrived, the feeling was fading again, and then it was gone.

I opened my eyes, staring down at the pile of carrots on the chopping board, aware that my finger had started to bleed. What the hell was that? A hallucination? Or could it have been a memory, trying to return, like Dr Evans said it would? But it hadn't been a memory, had it, not exactly. More of a feeling. A weird, unsettling feeling. A feeling I couldn't identify. But as I stood there, watching the blood drip slowly from the end of my finger and pool on the chopping board, I suddenly realized that I knew what the feeling was *about*. It was a feeling that something wasn't quite right. That something was off-kilter. I didn't know what. But I knew, suddenly and with absolute clarity, that it was something about the day Zander died.

15

FLORA

The frozen earth, still covered with a fine blanket of snow, crunched under my feet as I marched along the public footpath that crossed the field behind the house, heading for the woods on the other side. Last night had been a late one – we hadn't arrived back from Bath until nearly 3 a.m. after the Greyline do – but even so, I hadn't been able to sleep past eight, despite today being a day off. Wary of breaking an ankle in my running shoes, I'd decided on a brisk walk this morning instead of my usual fast 5k, wrapping up warmly and slipping a small flask of hot coffee into my backpack before I left, and closing the door gently behind me, the family all seemingly still fast asleep.

It was a beautiful day, frost shimmering on tree branches, the morning sunshine so bright I wished I'd remembered to grab some sunglasses before I left. As I clambered over the stile at the edge of the wood, I felt a sudden wave of happiness wash over me. Life hadn't always been that easy, but I was in a good place, really good – a job I was thoroughly enjoying, a lovely home to live in, nice people around me, and this glorious countryside literally right on my doorstep. I felt … well, *calm* I suppose, at peace, these days, and that wasn't a word I'd been able to associate with my feelings for such a long time that I suddenly laughed out loud, a little bubble of euphoria making me almost light-headed for a moment. A robin who'd been sitting on a low branch flapped his wings, startled, and flew away, and I laughed again.

'Sorry, Mr Robin! I'm just in a VERY. GOOD. MOOD,' I announced, as I headed down the winding path through the trees, the snow thicker here, the sunlight dappled, trees close together, branches entwined high above my head.

I walked for twenty minutes or so, my body warming from the exertion, my breath forming a ghostly cloud around my face as the path wound steeply uphill now, twisting around century-old oak trunks and criss-crossed by gnarled roots.

Finally, I reached my coffee-stop destination, a clearing at the top of the rise where somebody had once had the genius idea of putting a wooden bench for those exhausted by the climb, a few square metres of relatively flat, scrubby ground before the path curved back into the wood again, for the descent to the road a mile or so below.

I slipped my backpack off and brushed the snow off the bench with my gloved hand, then sank gratefully onto it and poured myself a coffee. The first sip burned my tongue, so I carefully put the cup down beside me, balancing it across the wooden slats of the seat, and gazed out across the valley, waiting for my drink to cool.

I could see the church spire from here, standing tall above the cluster of houses which surrounded it, their red roofs which usually glowed softly in the early morning light today covered in snowy blankets. It was so quiet, so peaceful, the twittering of a few birds and the occasional crack of a twig in the woods behind me the only sounds, and I took a deep breath of cold air, closing my eyes for a moment, savouring the near-silence.

I'd been invited to join the family for Sunday lunch later, and I was looking forward to it – (Annabelle is a fantastic cook); I enjoyed being with the kids – but it would be noisy and chaotic as always. It was one of the reasons I'd always relished my solo runs and walks – I needed the short spells of solitude, the moments alone with nature, the time to centre myself, to calm my racing thoughts.

As I opened my eyes again and reached for my cooling coffee, I remembered yesterday and the conversation about Rupert Ashfield. Annabelle seemed to be fascinated by Thea and Rupert and the whole awful story, and I supposed I couldn't really blame her for that – most people were the same when they discovered where I'd worked before this, their eyes widening, hands clapped over mouths, eyes expressing sympathy and curiosity.

Although if pushed, and if I felt in the mood to cope with the telling, I would now and again give the inquisitive a few details of the day Zander died, I'd never given my full account to anyone except Annabelle, the other night in the restaurant. I'd felt I owed it to her, to tell her what she wanted to know, but I doubted I'd talk to anyone else about it in such detail. I didn't feel the need to tell her anymore, though, about the other stuff – didn't feel the need to fill her in about Rupert, and about his and Thea's relationship.

They had been happy, once, or so I believed, but even when I arrived on the scene things were already starting to deteriorate, and while there seemed to be various reasons for that – he was away a lot, she was always working when he was at home, the usual – a lot of it was definitely down to Isla or, more accurately, to Isla and Thea's friendship, and the pressure Isla always put on Thea to go out partying.

It had always seemed quite intense to me, as if Isla wanted Thea all to herself, as if she resented the fact that Thea was now a mother of two with all the responsibilities that entailed, and couldn't simply drop everything to go out and have fun on a Friday night when Isla arrived from London, ready to let off steam after another week of high flying.

I'd heard them arguing, more than once, Thea and Rupert – those low-voiced, spiteful little arguments that took place after the children were asleep: Rupert accusing his wife of being a bad mother, telling her she should never have had children if she still wanted to 'party like a teenager with that vacuous woman'; Thea retaliating in a shaky, tear-filled voice, 'I'm not allowed to have friends then? Not allowed to go out at all? Lock me up then, why don't you? For God's sake, Rupert, it's once a week, if that. I'm trying to juggle the kids and my business every bloody day here, on my own while you're off doing your thing. Surely you can cope for one evening? I'm suffocating here, I *need* this.'

They'd make up, eventually, but sometimes it took days, days when the atmosphere in the house was heavy and tense, the children picking up on it too: Nell irritable and tetchy, Zander whimpering and needy.

It was during one of those times that Rupert had first turned to me. It was a still-chilly evening last March, when Zander was a couple of months old, and I'd been curled up with a pile of magazines and a hot chocolate on the old sagging velvet sofa in the snug, a cosy little room off the kitchen. It had become my sitting room, sort of, Thea and Rupert preferring the main lounge at the front of the house, but that suited me. I had a lovely room upstairs but I liked having my own space downstairs, too, and I loved the snug, with its walls lined with bookshelves and its French doors opening out into the garden. There was no TV in the room, but there was a digital radio which I enjoyed tuning in to obscure French or Italian radio stations, humming along to Europop as I flicked through the pages of *House & Garden*, *Red* or *Cotswold Life*.

That evening I'd been engrossed in an article about the trend for boudoir-style bedrooms – odd how I still remembered that, specifically – when the door opened and Rupert ambled in clutching, rather to my surprise, a beer bottle. It was a Tuesday night and he wasn't a big drinker, not during the week at home anyway. But Thea was out that night, meeting some mums from her postnatal classes, and I'd supposed he was just taking the chance to have a quiet drink alone, the children both in bed by this time.

He'd nodded at me, then slumped down into the armchair opposite my sofa, took a long drink from his bottle and sighed heavily.

'You all right, Flora?' he asked.

I gave him a brief smile, replied 'Yes, fine thanks!' then turned back to my magazine, hoping he wouldn't hang around. I didn't mind Rupert, although weirdly I still didn't know him that well at that point, despite working for Thea for well over a year by then. I still preferred my own company after a long day at work, and it made me a little uncomfortable to be alone with him, especially when I knew his relationship with my boss was not in a good place.

I'd taken up the job in the December, and Thea had fallen pregnant the following April, with Zander arriving at the beginning of January. I lived in their house, of course, like I did now with Annabelle, and in many ways I did, I suppose, become part of the family, certainly as far as Thea and Nell were concerned.

But Rupert was away so much, and on those evenings when he *was* at home I usually made myself scarce, not wanting to intrude on their family time, especially during those long summer months when Thea was pregnant, hot and exhausted, so Rupert and I had never really got to know each other, outside of being basically polite and making small talk.

Of course there'd been times when Thea had insisted I join them, for dinner or barbecues, or Friday night drinks in the garden, and they were fun times, more often than not. When they were getting on, Rupert and Thea were interesting and entertaining company, and generous with their food and wine, taking it in turns to cook and good-humouredly trying to outdo each other. Isla was frequently there too, and although at first she seemed to resent my presence, she gradually accepted that I was part of the household, although it took a while.

'She's protective of me, that's all. Wants to make sure I'm not replacing her with you,' Thea had whispered to me when we went inside to refill our glasses one evening, after Isla had pointedly ignored me when I'd asked her if she was staying in Cheltenham all weekend. I'd nodded and told Thea not to worry, at the same time thinking how peculiar, how strangely juvenile it was to see a grown woman so possessive of her 'best friend'.

But gradually, Isla thawed, seemingly realizing that I was no threat, that she was still the number one woman in Thea's life, that although Thea and I got on well she was really just my employer and landlady, and I actually began to look forward to her visits.

On form, she was hilarious company, full of stories about London and television life, and she made me howl. Even so, I could see that her presence always put Rupert a little on edge, and often he and Thea would exchange sharp words after Isla had finally taken her leave for the evening. Thea once confided in me that her husband thought her best friend was a bad influence, and that he'd be happier if they terminated their friendship.

'He doesn't realize that I quite like being influenced by her. If she was a man, I'd probably have married *her*,' she'd said to me once, and grinned. 'I've never had as much fun with anyone in my life as I've had with Isla. Sometimes I wish Rupert was a bit more like her. He can be so … so *uptight*, you know?'

As he'd slumped in the armchair in the snug that evening, though, Rupert hadn't looked uptight at all. He'd looked … I don't know, *defeated* might have been a better word, his shoulders hunched, one finger distractedly circling the mouth of his beer bottle, his eyes dull.

'Flora – can I ask you something? This may sound odd but – do you think Thea is … well, *happy*? I mean … I don't mean that really, of course she is, generally. But … do you think it's too much for her, the children and the business?'

I looked up sharply, the magazine slipping from my hands and sliding to the floor.

'What? I mean … well it's not really for me to say. I'm just … I'm just her assistant,' I said lamely, feeling horribly awkward. What a strange question, I thought.

He sat forward in his seat, eyes fixed intently on me now.

'Yes, but that's exactly why I'm asking you, Flora. You're the one who spends the most time with her, day after day. Way more time than I do, or even that bloody woman Isla. Do you think she's OK? Do you think she's coping? It's just with all this drinking, these nights out recently …' He sighed again, put the bottle down on the carpet and leaned back in his chair, rubbing his eyes with balled fists, then dropped his hands to his lap and stared at the ceiling, his forehead creasing into a frown.

I swallowed, not sure how to answer. In truth, I thought, Thea was coping pretty well really, considering how busy her business was these days and how recently she'd given birth. She'd only taken a week off after Zander was born, arguing that she worked from home anyway, so it wasn't as if she had to leave her baby, that she had me to help her, and that most of her job involved Internet research, email and phone calls, which weren't exactly strenuous. Any of the heavier stuff, like sorting deliveries and transferring stock to the warehouse, she'd left to me for those first few weeks, and the business had continued to run smoothly, orders flooding in, compliments and five-star reviews being added to the *Just Enfant* website daily by satisfied customers.

Even Nell wasn't a problem back then, a sweet, happy little girl thrilled to have a new baby brother. But it was true that in recent weeks Thea had seemed more stressed, more anxious, and Isla had been quick to step in, whisking her friend off for wild nights out. I had briefly wondered if she might be suffering from a touch of postnatal depression, but I hadn't said anything. It wasn't my place to, and if there *was* something wrong I knew she'd have Isla to turn to, even if she didn't feel she could talk to Rupert.

'She needs to let her hair down, for God's sake, Rupert. Give her a break,' I'd heard Isla snap the previous Saturday evening as she and Thea had headed out yet again, Thea casting a guilty glance at her baby, still wide awake in his bouncer on the lounge floor, Rupert's face tight and angry as he slammed the front door behind them.

Now, though, I took a deep breath, trying to formulate an answer that would placate Rupert without making me feel disloyal to Thea.

'It's probably just a phase, that's what I think, Rupert. She's coping brilliantly, honestly – the website's doing amazingly, she's got fabulous new stock coming in all the time ... I think it's just that, with that, and the *two* kids now, she needs a bit of respite once a week or so. She couldn't drink for nine months, remember, and she's stopped breastfeeding now ... she's probably making up for lost time. I'd be the same!'

I laughed, trying to lighten the mood, but Rupert's expression didn't change.

'She breastfed Nell for nearly a year,' he said, still staring at the ceiling. 'Why has she stopped feeding Zander after just two months? I don't get that either. She said he wasn't getting enough, that he was always still hungry, that it was better for him to move on to the bottle, but ...' He exhaled, the air puffing out his cheeks, then sat up straight again.

'I'm sorry, Flora,' he said. 'I shouldn't be putting this on you, it's not fair. I'll leave you in peace.'

He smiled, a slightly crooked, little-boy-lost sort of smile, and I smiled back, feeling a little pang of sympathy, and ... to be honest, and to my immense surprise, suddenly something more too. He was a handsome man, Rupert, I'd always noticed that, but in a passive sort of way, the way you'd observe a passing stranger in the street as being attractive.

But now, alone in this room with him, I felt a sudden tension, an awareness for the first time that he was ... well, quite fanciable, I suppose, with that closely shaven head, full lips, deep-set dark brown eyes. Those eyes were fixed on mine now, as he stood up and took the few steps across the room to stand next to me. I tilted my head back to look up at him, my breath catching in my throat, my heart suddenly beating faster. He reached out a hand and touched my cheek, just for a second, then turned abruptly and walked away.

'Thanks for listening,' he said, over his shoulder, and then he was gone, the door closing gently behind him. I sank back on my cushions, my breathing still rapid. My God, did I fancy Rupert? Where had that come from? I shook my head like a cow shaking off flies, cross with myself. *Ridiculous, Flora. Don't even go there*, I thought. But it wasn't, of course, going to be quite so simple, was it?

Now, today on my bench, I sat quite still for a moment, remembering, my left index finger running over the old scar on my right wrist; it's a habit I have when I am worried or anxious. Then I slapped my wrist gently instead. Why think about these things now, when I had such a nice day ahead, such a nice life?

I swallowed the last of my coffee, screwed the cup back onto the flask, and shivered, the cold air licking at my face. It was beautiful here, but it was too chilly today to sit still for long. I stood up, stamping my booted feet on the snowy ground to warm them, slung my backpack over my shoulder and rejoined the path, heading downhill through the trees.

Annabelle would be up by now, I thought, preparing lunch, and soon the delicious aroma of roast beef or pork or whatever was on today's menu would be drifting through the house. I salivated at the thought, suddenly ravenous.

I'd been so damn lucky to get this job with the Garringtons. So lucky that they'd taken me in, just like Thea had, made me part of the family, and been so kind, so accepting. That's what made it harder sometimes, my growing friendship with Annabelle, this woman I'd grown so fond of recently. The closer we got, the guiltier I felt. Because I knew something, you see. I knew something I wish I *didn't* know, something that only a small handful of people knew, something that could destroy so much happiness. And something that I had to make sure Annabelle never, ever found out.

made it harder sometimes, my genuine friendship with Annabelle, this woman I'd grown so fond of recently. The closer we got, the guiltier I felt, because I knew something, you see. I knew something. I didn't know something that only a small handful of people knew, something that could destroy so much happiness. And something that I had to make sure Annabelle never ever found out.

16

THEA

'Smile, Nell, come on! You look gorgeous!'

I clapped encouragingly, and in front of the camera Nell grinned, tossing her hair back, one hand on her hip, posing perfectly.

'Brilliant, got it! You're a star, Nell. Want to go and pop that blue jacket on? Over what you're wearing is fine.'

Nell nodded and skipped off to the far corner of the room, where the rail of new season pieces was sitting behind a screen, and I turned to Melissa and smiled.

'Thanks so much, Mel. Finally, *finally* we're getting there, those last few shots looked fantastic. And I'm *so* sorry again about earlier. Honestly, I don't know what to do with her at the moment.'

Melissa, the photographer I'd worked with on several shoots in the past, and who was one of the few who'd still work with me, shook her head, her mousy brown ponytail swinging.

'Forget it, Thea. She's been through a lot. She'll be OK. These things take time, you know? Want a water?'

'Please. And thank you.'

She waved a hand and headed off to the fridge down the hallway, and I wandered over to where Nell was pulling on a sky-blue swing jacket I'd brought in from Switzerland, its bodice hand-embroidered with tiny birds and flowers. She turned to the full-length mirror next to the rail and began to button the coat up, humming along to the current track on the Ed Sheeran album Mel had been playing on a loop since we'd arrived an hour and a half ago.

I leaned on the rail, watching my daughter, and worrying. She seemed fine now, but earlier we'd had yet another meltdown, an explosion so fierce I'd almost abandoned the shoot there and then and packed her off home.

It had started when we'd tried to do a few shots of Nell with Sasha, Mel's adorable eighteen-month-old son who she had, after all, astonishingly kindly agreed to let model a few of my baby clothes.

After thinking about it for a while, I'd chickened out of asking Annabelle if Millie would like to take part in the shoot, deciding that Nell would just have to model all of the older girls' stuff, but it was fantastic to be able to show some of the cuter boys' outfits on Sasha.

Nell, who did quite like the spotlight for herself when she was in the mood to help me out like this, grudgingly agreed to the joint shots at first, and we managed to get a few beauties, Nell sitting cross-legged on a big red chair with Sasha grinning disarmingly up at her from a cushion on the floor, both of them wearing Aran jumpers, his in the traditional ecru and Nell in emerald green. But when, between shots, the toddler stood up, reached out a pudgy hand and grabbed one of Nell's dark curls, the mood suddenly changed.

'Ow! Get off me, stupid baby,' she snapped, pushing him roughly away. Sasha fell backwards, thumping down onto his nappy-clad bottom, sat there in shocked silence for a moment, and then began to bawl.

Dismayed, I ran to pick him up as Mel, who'd been fiddling with her camera and hadn't seen the altercation, looked up, a slightly panicked expression on her face.

'What … what happened? What's wrong, Sasha?'

She ran across the room, grabbing her still-sobbing child from my arms, and I turned to glare at Nell.

'Nell! For God's sake, he's only a baby! He was just playing, why did you have to push him like that?'

'*Push* him?'

Mel turned to Nell, too, frowning, as Sasha buried his face in her shoulder, snuffling. Nell was staring at the ground, cheeks pink, arms folded.

'Mel, I'm so sorry, Sasha got hold of her hair and she pushed him away. It wasn't hard, not really, but he lost his balance and fell down. I think his nappy probably cushioned the fall pretty well … it's just the surprise that's upset him, I think.'

'Oh, it's OK, he's fine now, look. But Nell, really? Please be more careful, all right, love? He's only little.'

Mel's voice was gentle, but Nell ignored her, her face reddening even more, and I marched over to her, temper flaring, embarrassed by her behaviour.

'Nell! Look up when you're being spoken to. And apologize to Mel, right now. You could have seriously hurt Sasha. You should never, ever push another child, especially one younger than you, do you understand me?'

She looked up then, dark eyes flashing.

'And *you* should never ever get drunk and leave a baby on his own in a car, but that didn't stop you, did it?'

There was a gasp from Mel, and I stood stock-still for a moment, mouth open, horrified, emotion suddenly hovering somewhere between anger and awful, terrible shame. She was right, wasn't she? Of course she was. Who was I to judge *her*?

'I-I … that was an accident, Nell,' I stuttered finally. 'I would never, ever have hurt Zander intentionally, you know that …'

Close to tears, I reached out a hand but she batted it away, hard, then turned to the little round table nearby that was serving as an accessories station, and with one enormous shove accompanied by an angry roar upturned it, hairbands, mini handbags and pieces of jewellery scattering.

'Nell!' My admonition was more of a strangled whisper this time, tears pricking my eyelids. In Mel's arms, Sasha began to cry again, startled by the crash, and I turned to my friend, ready to apologize, but she shook her head.

'Thea, don't say anything. Nell needs you, she's clearly very upset. I'll take Sasha upstairs for a few minutes, give you some space, OK?'

'OK. Mel, I'm so—'

'Shhh. It's fine.'

She turned and left the room, Sasha still sobbing, and I looked down at Nell, who was now slumped on the floor, breathing heavily, body crumpled like a rag doll among the ribbons and necklaces. Slowly, I moved towards her and sat down, too, edging closer.

'I'm sorry, Mummy. I didn't mean to do that. I'm sorry.'

Her voice was low, cracking with unshed tears, and my heart broke for her all over again then, broke for this beautiful little girl, this child I loved so much and had hurt so badly. I was disgusting, a revolting, disgusting human being, and I wasn't worthy of Nell, I wasn't worthy to call myself her mother. And yet … I reached out to her again, and this time she didn't push me away but slipped into my arms, and I pulled her close, rocking her like a baby.

'No, Nell. You have nothing to be sorry about. It's me, all me. I'm sorry. So, so sorry, about what's happened. I love you so much, I loved Zander so much. I never meant to … never meant to hurt him; I'd never hurt either of you, hurt *anyone*, not intentionally, you know that, don't you? Please, Nell, I love you …'

I murmured the words into her hair, tears running down my cheeks now, and she nestled into my chest, her breathing slowly steadying. Eventually, eyes wet, she straightened up and looked at me.

'Please don't cry, Mum. I've stopped now, look.'

She pointed to her eyes with both forefingers, a slightly comical gesture that made me smile.

'OK, well I'd better stop too then. Sorry, Nell.'

I fumbled in my pocket for a tissue, dabbed her cheeks and then wiped my own eyes, feeling my mascara smearing on my face but not caring.

'Is it … do you get so angry because you miss him, Nell? Did Sasha remind you of Zander, was that the problem?'

She nodded, fingers plucking at my jumper.

'It's not so bad with girls. But every time I see a little boy I think about him. It's horrible, Mummy. I miss him so much.'

She gulped, her body shuddering, and I pulled her close again, rubbing her back in circular motions, muttering soothing nonsense in her ear, until the door opened and Mel reappeared.

'All OK?' she asked quietly.

'We're fine. Aren't we, Nell?'

'Yep. Sorry, Mel, about …'

Nell sat up and gestured vaguely at the mess around us, and Mel shrugged.

'Don't worry, no big deal at all. It'll only take a minute to pick it all up again, and nothing's broken. I'll put the kettle on and then we can get started with your solo shots, Nell. I've put Sasha down for a nap; he was worn out, poor little chap.'

She smiled at us, then squinted at me.

'Oh and Thea … not sure about the panda look. Hot on the spring catwalks, is it?'

She grinned and headed out of the room again, and I turned to Nell, who laughed.

'You *do* look like a panda, Mummy! Think you need a wet wipe.'

'Oh hush, you. I never remember to buy waterproof mascara. Go on, you start picking this stuff up and I'll be with you in a minute.'

'OK.' She clambered off my knee, and I watched her for a minute as, with a grunt, she righted the little table and began to gather up the fallen accessories. She seemed fine again, but the ferocity of the outburst had frightened me, and I wondered again whether counselling might be the way to go.

After our Pilates session yesterday, when Isla and I had collapsed into comfortable chairs with a complimentary drink, I'd finally remembered to ask her if she knew anyone who might be able to help Nell. She thought for a moment, sucking her green smoothie greedily through a straw, then put the glass down and pushed a tendril of dark red hair, damp with sweat, off her forehead.

'There's a woman Lennie at work saw, when she was having some sort of emotional crisis after her latest break-up. Her name's Karen … Karen Ballington, Basildon, something like that. I'm thinking of her because Lennie said she was amazing, but also because she specializes in kids with emotional problems. Lennie recommended her to a woman we had on the show who was having massive issues with antisocial behaviour in her son. She's in Reading, so not exactly local, but might be worth a go?'

I nodded. Reading was about an hour and a half away, but that might be a good thing. I didn't want anymore local gossip about me than there was already, and if anyone happened to recognize me taking Nell into a therapist's office in Cheltenham, the Twitter trolls would have a field day.

'Brilliant. I think I need to do it, Isla. Nell isn't right, and I need to try and help her. And best to start now. Who knows how bad things will get when the trial starts.'

Isla reached out a hand and stroked my arm, 'I'll get you her number. And don't start worrying about the trial, not yet. It won't do you any good. Worry solves nothing, remember? What's that saying? "No amount of regret can change the past, and no amount of worry can change the future"?'

I smiled at her, but my stomach was twisting. It happened

every time I thought about the trial, the court room, the jury, the TV cameras outside, the media frenzy, for I already knew that was what it would be, knew off by heart the statistics the papers and news bulletins would be full of: seven cases of children left to die in hot cars in a two-year period in France and Belgium; four cases in two years in Israel; thirty-six, on average, every single year in the United States. But rare, so rare in the UK. Rare, until Thea Ashfield got drunk om champagne, and left her baby to die a horrific death. Statistics to shock and sicken, and strike fear into every parent.

Even if I could get through that, somehow survive the shame, the agony of being forced to relive Zander's death in a roomful of people, people who were all judging me, despising me, what then? What if I went to prison? Despite the reassurances from my barristers, the promise to do their very best to stop that happening, the prospect of jail terrified me. Not for myself so much – although I had no idea how I would bear it, cope with being locked up, maybe for years – but for Nell. How would I survive, knowing that she was out here in the world without me, and bearing the stigma of a mother in prison?

I swallowed hard, my orange, mango and pineapple juice turning to acid in my mouth. Suddenly all I wanted to do was run, to take Nell and go somewhere far, far away where nobody would ever find us. I wouldn't, of course, though. Because this was all my doing. My fault. And people who did things like I had done have to be punished. It is just how it is.

Now, as I watched Nell back in front of the camera, looking so beautiful and, for now, so happy again, moving with the music, laughing as Mel called out encouragement, my one bright light in this awful darkness, my reason to keep going, to keep working, to keep living, my eyes blurred, a sudden light-headedness making me grope for the wall behind me for support. Oh God, was it happening again?

My breath quickened, that creeping sense of unease not

crawling but rushing this time up my spine, and then suddenly, without warning, I was back there. Back in September. Back outside the house, the afternoon sun hot on my neck. Isla and Nell running inside, and me unbuckling Zander's seat belt, a little unsteady on my feet, but still able to scoop my slumbering baby out of the car and walk up the path with him. Me, putting him gently into his pram in the cool living room, dropping a kiss on his forehead before gratefully sinking onto the nearest sofa ...

'*What?*'

I gasped out loud, feeling panicky, heart pounding, eyes snapping open now, fixing on Mel and Nell, still happily engrossed in the shoot, oblivious. And then, just as quickly, the picture in my head faded, and I slid down the wall, shaking, sweat beading on my forehead.

What was going on? What was happening to me? What had that *been* – my imagination, a hallucination, a memory? *Could* it actually be a memory, after all this time? But no, it made no sense. That wasn't what had happened. Was I going mad, then? Or, I thought, wiping a hand shakily across my forehead, could that have been a *false* memory, wishful thinking, something conjured up by my sick mind? It had to be, hadn't it? Because it didn't match, didn't match at all what happened later, and I clearly remembered that. The screams, the terror. Flora stumbling into the room with Zander limp in her arms and tears running down her face, people shouting out on the street, sirens blaring. I remembered all that with absolute, nightmarish clarity.

I killed my baby. My son is dead, it was my fault, and I'll be paying the price forever. So that wasn't a memory, then. It can't have been. And yet ...

I stood up slowly, my breathing less erratic now, a strange calm descending. I didn't know why I'd just seen, felt, remembered, *imagined*, whatever, what I had. But now, I had the strongest feeling, the deepest certainty, that something was definitely wrong. Something was wrong with the way it happened. With the way everyone *said* it happened. Something was wrong with the way they said my baby died.

17

FLORA

Annabelle's Sunday lunch was as divine as I expected it would be – perfectly cooked lamb with garlic and rosemary, roast potatoes with crisp, herby outer shells and delightfully fluffy insides, carrots glazed with Dijon mustard, baby leeks with bacon, and the promise of a heavenly sticky toffee pudding to finish.

We ate in the kitchen, the windows steamed up, linen napkins draped across our knees, a basket of warm, fragrant bread rolls in the centre of the big table. Annabelle and Greg were both relaxed and smiling today, a fine Rioja flowing, even the children behaving themselves for once, teasing each other good-naturedly.

But once or twice I caught Greg's eye across the table, and now I was sure I wasn't imagining it, that strange frisson – my eyes drawn repeatedly to his face, only to find him already looking at me; a stare a little too intense when Annabelle's attention was elsewhere, cutting up meat for Sienna or pouring more gravy onto Oliver's plate. Why was he doing that? *Stop it*, I thought. *What are you up to, Greg? And stop responding, Flora.*

I forced myself to look away first, willing myself not to blush, gulping my wine too quickly, my mind racing. Couldn't he see it was making me uncomfortable? I wished that I didn't find him so increasingly attractive, didn't feel that stirring in my groin, that fluttering in my stomach when he looked at me. It was ridiculous, and I was *not* going to go there. I couldn't, wouldn't do that to Annabelle.

The thing was, I was pretty sure he didn't actually have any real feelings for me either, pretty positive in fact that this was just a little game he was playing. He and Annabelle were solid at the moment, I could see that – the loving looks they exchanged, the secret smiles across the table, the occasional entwining of fingers and touches on shoulders as one or other got up to fetch more vegetables from the sideboard or another bottle from the larder.

No, Greg Garrington had no real interest in me, I was certain of that. He might find me attractive, possibly, but I'd come across his type before, the married men with no real intention of being unfaithful, the men who just wanted a little illicit flirting with an attractive younger woman, the ego boost of seeing her respond and redden. That's what Greg was doing with me, because why would he want me when he had a wife like Annabelle, tall and slender, that mass of blonde hair cascading over her shoulders, that sweet and caring nature, but with an innate sexiness she seemed barely aware of?

'Oi, Sienna, give me that back right now!'

I jumped. Oliver's voice was raised, a sudden edge to it. Sitting opposite him at the far end of the table, his little sister's bottom lip was sticking out, a mutinous look in her eyes. She was clutching a roast potato firmly in both hands, squeezing it so hard that the outside had cracked, the soft middle oozing.

'Mum, the little brat just grabbed that off my plate. It's my last one and there aren't anymore in the dish and she'd better give it back to me or ...'

Oliver pushed back his chair and stood up, glowering, and leaned across the table towards Sienna, hand outstretched. She screamed and cowered in her chair, but didn't drop her stolen potato, and Oliver's face darkened.

'Give that back, now, or I'll bloody thrash you,' he yelled.

'Olly, calm down.'

Annabelle was on her feet now, grabbing her son's arm as he leaned further across the table.

'For goodness' sake, she's only a baby. And do you really want it now, after she's squished it all, look? Come on, sit down and I'll get you some more lamb instead ...'

'Yes, Jesus, Olly, leave the child alone.'

Annabelle gave her husband a sharp glance – I'd noticed that, while not at all religious, she disliked anyone using profanities, especially of the non-secular variety – and he grimaced and shrugged.

'Oliver, sit down. You can't possibly still be hungry; you've had more food than the rest of us put together,' he said mildly.

'And Sienna – stealing is never right, OK? You want another potato, you ask for it. You don't just nick it from your brother's plate. You're like that robin in the garden who always grabs the bird food from under the blue tit's nose, aren't you? Little miss tinker.'

Sienna giggled, putting the potato down on her plate, and next to her Millie snorted.

'Errr, birds don't have noses, Dad. Beaks. They're called *beaks*.'

Everyone laughed, the crisis seemingly averted, but I noticed that Oliver, although forcing a smile now, still had a dark look in his eyes. He saw me looking and I winked, trying to cheer him up, and he blushed slightly and smiled at me, a more genuine grin now. Satisfied, I picked up my wine and swallowed the last mouthful. My head was swimming a little, but pleasantly – that soft, woozy feeling you get when you drink a little too much in a warm room, when you're relaxed and happy and know you have nothing pressing to do later.

'Sunday lunch is the best,' I announced. 'And that was absolutely delicious, Annabelle. Thanks so much.'

'You are more than welcome,' she said with a smile, holding

out her glass to clink against mine and then noticing mine was empty.

'Oh, Greg, top Flora up, will you? I'll get dessert.'

'Of course.' Greg reached for the wine bottle and stood up, walking around the table to where I was sitting. As he poured, he leaned against me, ever so slightly, and suddenly I could feel the taut muscles of his stomach against my back, the warmth of his body against mine, and I felt that stirring again, my heartbeat quickening, my nerve endings tingling. *Oh shit*, I thought. *Shit. Stop it. If you keep this up* … I couldn't remember when I'd last had sex, but clearly it was far too long ago, if I was reacting like this.

I clenched my fists, waiting for him to move away, not looking at him, and then the glass was full and the moment had passed, Greg ruffling Millie's hair in an exaggerated fashion as he returned to his seat, making her shriek in faux outrage, Sienna demanding he did the same to her own soft blonde mop.

I relaxed again, not looking at Greg as Annabelle returned, bearing plates of pudding and putting bowls of ice cream and custard on the table to accompany it. As I ate, only halflistening now to the again cheerful family banter, my mind drifted back to my own childhood, when meals like this were an impossible fantasy, something I'd longed for, but never experienced.

I'd grown up in Farnham, one of those Surrey towns often described as 'well-to-do' – less than an hour from central London by train, it attracted wealthy commuters, driven out of the capital by exorbitant property prices but still wanting to be within a comfortable distance of its attractions.

An historic market town, overlooked from the crest of a nearby hill by the twelfth century Farnham Castle, it was generally considered to be a 'nice' place to live, and to rear children – safe, cultured, pretty. I supposed how nice it *actually* was, though, depended on your family, and mine … well, it hadn't been ideal.

I'd been an only child, my mother cold and distant, my father largely absent. Mum worked full-time, and when my father *was* around … I flinched slightly, and then jumped as Millie shrieked with laughter, and everyone else joined in. Having completely missed the joke, I smiled, not wanting to draw attention to myself.

How lucky they were, these kids, I thought. Oh, they'd grow up moaning about their parents like everyone did, but in reality they had no idea how fortunate they were, to be loved and cared for as they were, to grow up in this beautiful house with no money worries, to have parents who would always be there for them. Lucky, lucky, lucky.

And how lucky I was now, too, to have been accepted into a family like this, to have a secure home, a job I enjoyed so much. To feel useful and valued and appreciated. I looked at Sienna, her little face glowing pink, thinking of the way she hugged and kissed me so unselfconsciously, wrapping her little body around mine. Told me she loved me. I was *loved* here. I was lucky, lucky, lucky too, wasn't I?

Lunch over, the family scattered and Annabelle shooed me out of the kitchen when I hung around, offering to help clear away ('It's your day off, Flora, and you've had an incredibly busy week. Go, scoot, vamoose! Watch some TV or read a book or something, chill out, I can do this!'). I wandered into the lounge, looking for the magazine I'd left there earlier. Millie and Sienna were already sprawled on the sofa, their much-loved *Frozen* DVD playing on the TV.

I laughed. 'Girls, how many times have you watched that film? It must be hundreds, and that's only since *I've* been here!'

Mille shrugged. 'Thousands, probably. We never get bored though. We I don't know why it never gets boring, but it doesn't. We both know all the words and everything.'

'I know, I can see!' I gestured at Sienna, who was mouthing the dialogue as, on screen, Anna tried to persuade Elsa to come out of her room to build a snowman.

I sat down, squeezing into the small space at one end of the sofa uninhabited by the girls. If I was honest, I quite liked the movie myself, having watched it three or four times with Nell while I was working for Thea, and it wasn't as if I had anything urgent to do.

Rain was pattering against the windows now, but the room was warm, a log fire crackling in the hearth, and I leaned back on the soft cushions, full and a little light-headed from all the wine, content.

A few minutes later, just as I had started to nod off, the door burst open and Oliver marched in.

'Oh SHIT,' he said, and glared at his sisters, ignoring me. 'Do you two really have to watch that crap again? *Pimp My Ride* starts in five minutes. Come on, turn it off. You two are always hogging this telly. And you've seen that moronic film a million times. Bugger off.'

Millie looked up at him and frowned.

'Can't you watch your stupid car show in your room?' she said.

'I don't *want* to watch it in my room, Millie. My TV up there is tiny. I want to watch it down here, on the good telly, and where it's warm. And this is the family TV, not yours, OK? That means you *share* it. I never get to watch it. So piss off, all right?'

His tone was even, but held a hint of menace now, and his cheeks were reddening.

'Olly, that language isn't ideal. And why don't you just let the girls finish this film and then you can take over the telly for the rest of the afternoon? Does that sound fair?' I said, smiling at him, trying to defuse the situation. I really wasn't in the mood for another sibling row.

He glanced at me, then turned back to the girls.

'Flora, they had it all morning, so no, that's not fair. Sienna, Millie, turn that off NOW.'

Sienna, whose eyes had remained glued to the screen despite her brother's arrival, finally turned to look at him, then slowly reached for the remote control which was sitting on the arm of the sofa, and with one quick movement grabbed it and shoved it under the cushion behind her back.

'NO!' she shouted, and crossed her arms, brows knitted in a determined scowl.

'You little ...' Olly was across the room in two strides, face contorted in sudden fury. He bent down, scooped Sienna up and threw her, hard, onto the floor, where she landed with a thud on the sheepskin rug in front of the sofa. For a second she lay there, in stunned silence, then her face crumpled and she began to scream.

'OLIVER!' Annabelle – who had walked into the room just as her youngest flew through the air – and I shouted his name simultaneously. With Millie open-mouthed with shock next to me, I leapt from my seat but Annabelle got there first, gently checking her howling daughter over for any obvious injuries before bundling her into her arms and standing up.

'Olly, what on earth?' She looked aghast. 'What's wrong with you? She's three years old, you could have seriously hurt her!'

'Well, she should move when I tell her to, then.' Oliver, his face still flushed and angry, was staring at the carpet, shuffling his feet. 'Those two are always hogging the telly, it's not fair. I gave her a chance and she didn't take it, not my fault.'

Annabelle shook her head, looking furious, as Sienna's sobs grew even louder.

'Hush, Sienna, you're all right. Oliver, you never, *ever* use violence against your sisters. Or against anyone, do you understand me? When your father hears about this ... oh, just get out. Go to your room, I can't even look at you. But you haven't heard the last of this, I promise you.'

Oliver looked at her mutinously for a moment then turned and stalked from the room, muttering under his breath. Annabelle shifted Sienna's weight to her other hip and looked at me despairingly.

'Flora, what on earth am I going to do with him? He's a nightmare. He never leaves Sienna alone. Are you all right, Millie?'

Millie nodded. 'Yeah. He's just an idiot boy, Mum. Sienna can be a bit bratty but he's so horrible to her. Can't you send him away to boarding school or something? You know, like those old-fashioned ones in films where the teachers will hit him with sticks and make him eat slugs for dinner? That'd teach him, wouldn't it, Flora?'

She looked at me and I clamped my lips firmly together, trying not to laugh. Then I caught Annabelle's eye and realized a tiny smile was playing on her lips too.

'I don't think boarding school is the answer, sadly, Millie. I wish I knew what was, though. Flora, I hate to ask, I really do, but I just don't seem to be able to get through to him at the moment. I don't suppose ...?'

She raised her eyebrows, and I nodded.

'Sure. I'll talk to him in a bit. Not sure I can do much but I'll give it a go.'

'Thank you *so* much. Look, you two watch your film in peace. Come on, Sienna, your colouring book and pencils are in the kitchen. Shall we go and do a nice picture?'

Face still nestled into her mother's shoulder, Sienna nodded, her crying abating now.

'OK, let's do that then. Thanks again, Flora', Annabelle said over her shoulder as she left the room.

I listened as her footsteps faded down the hall and the kitchen door closed, then sighed. I'd talk to Oliver later, when he'd calmed down a bit. I would have anyway, even if Annabelle hadn't asked me to, but I needed to relax a bit first, let the alcohol wear off.

I turned to look at Millie, who had retrieved the remote control from under the cushion and was rewinding the film, presumably to where it had been when Oliver had arrived.

'I need the loo, Millie. Start watching again, don't worry about waiting for me, but I'm definitely coming back so keep my seat!'

'I will,' she said, and snuggled back onto her cushions, pressing play with a grin.

As I left the downstairs toilet down the corridor off the main hall, wiping my still-damp hands on my jeans, I jumped as Greg suddenly appeared from his study next door.

'Gosh, you scared me!' I said, edging past him, but he held both arms out, blocking my path.

'Flora, I need to talk to you.' His voice was an urgent whisper. 'Come in here for a moment, will you?'

He gestured with his head, indicating the study behind him, and I hesitated, nerves suddenly swirling in my stomach. What did he want? If I went in there …

'Please, Flora.' He glanced down the corridor, checking that we were alone, then raised a hand and touched my cheek, his fingers barely grazing my skin. His touch sent a jolt of electricity through me, my eyes suddenly locked on his deep grey ones, my breath quickening.

'Please. Just for a minute. I can't … I can't stop thinking about you. You must have noticed …'

His voice tailed off, and he moved closer to me, his other hand on my waist now, pulling me in until I could smell the fresh scent of his aftershave, the citrussy fragrance mixing not unpleasantly with the hint of red wine on his breath.

He was quite drunk, I suddenly realized, his eyes glassy, his stance a little unsteady, and the realization brought me to my senses.

'Greg … no, I can't. I'm watching a film with Millie, she'll wonder where I've gone. And Annabelle …'

I placed a hand on his chest and gently pushed him away, and he took a step backwards, releasing me, face suddenly sagging.

'Oh God, I'm sorry. I'm so sorry, Flora. Shit, that was so inappropriate. Can we forget it happened? Really, I was out of order …'

117

He sank his head into his hands and started rubbing his face, groaning.

'It's fine, don't worry. Lunchtime booze and all that! Forget it, honestly,' I said. 'Look, I'll see you later, OK?'

I half turned, ready to walk away, but he grabbed my arm.

'I'd still like to talk to you though, Flora? Just for a moment, please?'

His tone was beseeching, a hint of desperation in his eyes now, and I stared at him for a moment. What was all this about? And then it hit me, a sudden wave of clarity washing over me. Of course. What an idiot I'd been. I knew *exactly* what this was about.

'Look, maybe another time, OK? Maybe you need to sober up a bit? Get a coffee or something? We can talk another day.'

I turned sharply and walked away then, back towards the living room, the scar on my wrist tingling, and even though he was behind me I knew he was still standing there, watching me go.

I'd been right when I'd thought he was playing a game. He wanted to get close to me, yes, but the flirting, the 'accidental' touching, the long glances, none of that meant he really wanted me, desired me, not in that way. What he actually wanted, I'd suddenly realized, was to get me on my own, make me vulnerable, because he suspected that I knew, and he wanted to find out if he was right.

Because it was about him, you see. The secret thing, the thing I felt so guilty about keeping to myself, the thing I had to make sure Annabelle never found out, was *Greg's* secret. I knew what he was hiding. I knew what he'd done.

18

ANNABELLE

'Annabelle! Annabelle! Come here, quick!'

From across the room, where she was signing delegates in at a long table, Flora was waving at me frantically. I took a last glance at the coffee area, where everything seemed to be in order, and hurried across to her, a sudden wave of anxiety rushing over me. What was wrong? Surely there hadn't been a mistake with the name badges or arrival information? I'd checked it all myself at seven this morning when we'd arrived, and there'd been nothing obvious amiss then, so what on earth could have happened … then, as I reached the table, my momentary panic subsided as I realized that Flora's shoulders were shaking with suppressed mirth.

'Flora, what …?'

'Here, look.'

She tapped the list in front of her then waved her pen at me, urging me to come round to her side of the table. Puzzled, I did so.

'What is it? Is something wrong?'

'Hang on. Here you go, enjoy the day.'

She handed a folder to a woman in a sharp navy suit who'd just picked up her name badge, waited until she'd wandered off and then turned to me, eyes shining.

'Yes, something is wrong. Very wrong. Clearly, one of our delegates had very, very cruel parents. Verging on child abuse, this is. Look. *Look* at the name of the company's finance director, Annabelle.'

I peered at the piece of paper on the table, then back at Flora, frowning.

'Huh?'

'Oh Annabelle, you're such an innocent. William Stroker. His name is *William Stroker*. WILLIE STROKER. Get it?'

'Oh!' The word came out as a squeak, and I gave a sudden snort of laughter.

'Oh Flora, stop it! I thought something terrible had happened. You're dreadful!'

I nudged her with my shoulder and she nudged me back, both of us tittering like twelve-year-olds.

'Well, something dreadful *has* happened. How am I going to keep a straight face when Mr Stroker comes to sign in? I mean, seriously? It's all right for you ...'

She groaned theatrically, and I collapsed into giggles again. To think I'd thought today was going to be deathly dull. The weather certainly was – one of those colourless, gloomy January Tuesdays, violent gusts of wind whipping loose twigs from the trees, my feet still damp inside my uncomfortable court shoes after I'd managed to step out of my car right into a deep puddle earlier, soaking my tights.

We were in Worcestershire, running a conference for an IT company at a small hotel on the edge of the Cotswolds. The Trout was a laidback, country retreat sort of place, with a mix of standard bedrooms in the main building and adorable little shepherds' huts perched on the hill above, where guests could huddle in front of tiny log burners and enjoy the sound of the rain pattering on tin roofs from the comfort of luxurious feather beds.

The hotel, known for its Scandi-chic style, had begun outsourcing its conference management bookings the previous year, and this was the third event I had run here. The annual business meeting of GarrowTech was a relatively small affair, with just thirty or so delegates, and it hadn't been a complicated job, especially with Flora on board.

A cosy meeting room, welcome packs and name badges, a sound system and projector for the presentations, and morning coffee, a buffet lunch and a sit-down dinner this evening had all been organized swiftly and efficiently, and once the business part of the day concluded at five this evening we could leave, the hotel manager agreeing to allocate key staff to take care of the delegates until they checked out tomorrow morning. Nice and straightforward, just how I liked it, especially at the moment. I had enough concerns at home suddenly, without work causing me issues too.

I remained sitting next to Flora, absentmindedly straightening the welcome packs and notepads on the desk as she began to cheerily check in the latest wave of arrivals, and began to worry again.

Oliver's behaviour with Sienna on Sunday was one thing that was bothering me. He'd never been that nice to her, even when she was a tiny baby, but recently he'd been more aggressive, nastier, and I hated it. I'd tried to rationalize it in my head, tell myself that sibling rivalry was completely normal and that almost-teenage boy hormones combined with little girl stubbornness was an unfortunate mix, but it was still making me uneasy. To his credit, Oliver *had* come to find me and Sienna that evening, a couple of hours after his outburst, and had apologized, if grudgingly. I was pretty sure it hadn't been his own idea ... I'd heard Flora knock on his bedroom door a short while before that, asking him if she could come in for a chat, and I assumed she'd suggested it might be a good idea to say he was sorry. Even so, the apology had helped, but it still didn't excuse his behaviour.

'Uh oh. There's only three people left on this list to sign in: Stroker and two women,' Flora suddenly hissed.

'And these must be them now, look. Willie alert!'

She gestured towards the door, where a trio of new arrivals were being greeted by Tom Griffiths, the managing director who'd been there pumping hands and pecking cheeks since the meeting room doors opened at eight.

The two women were both small and blonde, one in a pinstriped grey trouser suit, the other in a tight emerald dress and towering red heels. The man was rotund and ruddy faced, belly straining against the buttons of a pale pink shirt.

'Hmmm. Probably finds it quite hard to *find* his willie under that stomach,' Flora muttered.

'*Flora!*'

I took a deep breath, feeling slightly hysterical all of a sudden. As Tom pointed across to where we were sitting, and the three newcomers began to cross the room, I took another gulp of air, willing myself not to start laughing again.

'Flora, you're killing me. *Please* call him William, not Willie, or I'm not going to be able to cope,' I whispered.

Flora winked at me, then turned cheerfully to the three delegates.

'Ladies, good morning. And you must be Will— I mean, Mr Stroker? Good morning to you too.'

Later, as the conference paused for lunch and Flora and I moved slowly through the meeting room, laying out fresh notepaper and bottled water for the afternoon session and putting chairs and tables into the requested rows now instead of in circular groups, my earlier good humour faded and anxiety began to gnaw at me again.

Greg was away this week, working at head office in London, and after a period of feeling secure and happy, for some reason in recent days I'd been back to feeling uneasy about him again too. Things had been good between us – great, in fact – but his occasional distracted moods, I had noticed, had become more frequent in the past few weeks.

After such a nice lunch on Sunday he'd disappeared into his study and barely spoken to me for the entire evening, and when I'd questioned him about it, asked if anything was wrong, he'd mumbled something about work and big new contracts and pressure, and told me not to worry about it, that everything was fine. He'd even dismissed my concern about Oliver's latest assault on Sienna with an exasperated sigh.

'All brothers and sisters fight, Annabelle. Didn't you, with your sister, when you were kids? I know I certainly did. They'll grow out of it, wait and see. They'll be the best of friends in a few years' time. Stop stressing.'

Now, he was away with work until Friday, and I knew that although I'd pretend everything was fine, although I'd be my usual bubbly self on the phone when he called me at night, in reality I'd be a nervous wreck all week, and my sleep would be disturbed by bad dreams, dreams about being abandoned in dank forests or walking alone, terrified, around dark, empty buildings. Classic anxiety dreams, my sister would have said.

Why was I so insecure? Greg was distant at times, but it was just down to work stuff, I knew that. And why did I always, when he was like this, get these stupid worries about other women wanting to steal him from me? This was Greg, my husband, the father of my children, the man I loved.

Even if, worst case scenario, there *had* ever been other women, even if my insecurities were justified, it didn't mean he was going to leave me, did it? They would have just been blips, little dalliances, meaningless, inconsequential.

And he did love me, I was sure of that. He wasn't always good at saying it, but he showed it in a million little ways – a squeeze of my shoulder as he passed my chair, a wink across the table, a kiss on the back of my neck as I stirred a pot on the cooker. The last time he said it, really said it, was when Zander Ashfield died.

He was there, of course, in the house, waiting for Millie, and I suppose that's why he was so desperately upset – that tiny dead body in Flora's arms, the police, the ambulance, the sirens, the panic, the chaos. He had swept Millie out of the house before she saw too much, but he had seen everything, and it destroyed him. He sobbed that night, wept inconsolably in my arms like a small, frightened child, told me that family was the most important thing, the *only* thing that mattered, that me and the children were his world and that he had no idea how he could live without us, without any of us, if something so terrible was to happen here.

'I love you, Annabelle. I don't say it enough, but I love you so much. And I'm sorry, so sorry, if I've ever made you feel that I don't. This puts everything into perspective, doesn't it? Life is so short, and you never know what might happen, what's lying around the next corner. You know I love you, don't you?'

I'd reassured him then, and through the following weeks. It was a horrific thing to happen, and absolutely dreadful to actually be there when it did, but even so I was surprised, and unexpectedly moved, by just how difficult my strong and usually fairly unemotional husband found it to deal with. He seemed to be struggling with it all, with everything that had happened on that shocking afternoon – the proximity of death, the loss of a child, even the questioning by the police, who'd talked to everyone who'd been there that day, everyone who'd witnessed some or any of Thea's movements.

Greg's sadness, his vulnerability, made me reach out to him even more than usual, and in turn we seemed to grow closer, more affectionate, happier. Clearly, nearly five months was enough for him to recover, though, because in recent weeks there'd definitely been a change, a feeling, just occasionally, that he was drifting away from me again, that his mind was elsewhere. Or was I imagining it? Everyone got stressed about work, didn't they? I certainly did, and there was no doubt that Greg's company had landed some huge accounts recently. That was probably all it was, wasn't it?

'They're on their way back in … all shipshape your side?'

Flora's question brought me back to the job in hand. I looked quickly around the room, checking.

'All shipshape. Everything's fine, Flora,' I said.

And it was, I told myself firmly, as the delegates filed back in. Everything was fine. Say it, and it will be so.

They're on their way back in and all shopstage your sides. Blunt question brought me back to the shop in hand. I looked quickly around the room, checking.

All shopshave. Two whisks. five. Four. I said.

And three. I told us all from say, the pelapure. Hold back in the colony on the Surg it, and a line will be so.

19

THEA

'It's the thirty-first tomorrow. Almost February. This year's going quickly, isn't it?'

I looked at Rupert, who was sitting on the sofa opposite mine, and he grunted and shrugged, then turned a page of his newspaper and carried on reading, ignoring me. My attempts at small talk were not going well. I fell silent, tired of trying, and picked up an interiors magazine from the small glass table next to me, half-heartedly flicking through it, my mind elsewhere.

We were in Reading, at the clinic run by counsellor, Karen Ballerton, the woman recommended by Isla to help Nell with her mood swings and anger. Karen, a tall, gangly woman with wiry dark brown hair streaked with grey, large hoops swinging from her earlobes, had gently insisted that it would be better if she and Nell chatted alone, which had left Rupert and I sitting uneasily together in the small waiting room down the hallway.

I'd been surprised that he'd wanted to come – I'd planned to take Nell by train, as I wasn't allowed to drive at the moment – in fact, my car had been sent for scrap back in October, the sight of it an unbearable reminder of what had happened, not so much a car any longer but a wheeled coffin, intolerable. But Rupert had said he wasn't busy today, and that he could afford to take a few hours off to 'try to sort my daughter's head out'. He *had* asked me if he could just take her to Reading on his own, but I'd firmly told him I wanted to be there too – Tuesday was one of my days with her this week, after all – and he'd sighed heavily, given in and grumpily offered to drive us all.

So, here we were, the two of us, sitting together for the first time in months, just a few feet apart in this little overheated room, with its creaking black leather sofas, small TV tuned to a nature programme, the sound muted, and a coffee machine burbling gently away in the corner.

Nell, to my astonishment, hadn't kicked up a fuss about today at all. I'd expected a fight, or a downright refusal from my wilful child to even get into Rupert's car for such an appointment, but when I'd told her where we were going and explained why, she'd thought carefully for a minute then nodded.

'OK. It's a day off school I suppose. Can we get a burger on the way home?'

I'd looked at Rupert, who'd raised an eyebrow and grinned at me before turning to Nell and telling her, yes, of course, whatever she wanted. I couldn't remember the last time he'd looked me in the eye, never mind smiled at me and, for a moment, my heart had leapt. Was he softening towards me, finally? Was this joint concern about Nell, about our damaged, troubled daughter, the thing that might fix us, bring us together again, even as friends?

The hope – in retrospect, pitiful – that my husband might still care, that we could somehow go back to something resembling normality, surged through me, but it didn't last long. The drive to Reading was made largely in a silence filled only by Radio 4, and an occasional outburst of tuneless singing from the back seat, where Nell, wearing headphones, was bopping along to the new Little Mix album on her iPod. I loved my daughter with all my heart, but she could sing about as well as I could play the bagpipes, which was not at all.

There had been one brief conversation though. As we'd sped along the M4 at a steady 75, Rupert had cleared his throat.

'Just for your information – I'm seeing somebody. Mia. She's in accounts, at work. I haven't told Nell yet but I will, soon, when it feels right. I'm just letting you know, in case she mentions it to you.'

The tiny little flame of hope from earlier, which had gradually shrunk as each mile of our silent, awkward car journey passed, dwindled to nothing and went out, and I stared out of the window, my body rigid, tears suddenly pricking my eyes. *Seeing somebody. Already?* OK, so we'd been apart for about four months, but even so …

I took a deep breath, willing the tears not to fall, and glanced over my shoulder. Nell, oblivious, was still humming along to her music, eyes closed, hands tapping her knees.

'Right. Well, thanks for telling me.' My voice was husky, and I coughed and continued. 'If … if Mia is going to be around when Nell is there, I'd like to meet her too, though, at some point, if that's OK.'

Rupert didn't respond for a moment, indicating right to pull out and overtake a slow lorry up ahead. Back in the middle lane, he sighed.

'Whatever. It won't be yet. It's early days, no need for her to meet Nell right now. But yes, OK.'

His voice was cold, and he'd reached out then and retuned the radio to 5 Live, the conversation clearly over. On the *Daily* show they were talking about sexual harassment in the workplace, but the words made no sense to me, a jumble of sounds, background noise to the sudden turmoil inside my head.

It had been inevitable, I supposed, but even so … yes, I'd known, deep down, that my marriage was over. What man would stay with a woman who'd done what I'd done, after all? But I'd still dared, now and again, to hope. Hope that he could forgive me, one day. Hope that, for Nell's sake, we could give things another go. But now …

'I need a coffee.'

I looked up from my magazine as Rupert stood up and stomped across the waiting room to pour himself a drink. He didn't offer to get one for me, and I didn't ask. I had to just deal with this now, I thought. Nell was my first priority, not Rupert, and if I was going to get through this, through the next few weeks, through the trial, I was going to have to toughen up, to harden my heart.

There were several solicitors' meetings in my diary for the coming days, and the thought made me instantly nauseous. The sick fear I'd felt ever since I realized the consequences of what I'd done was worsening by the day. I hadn't just killed my child, filling me with a grief and shame that I would never recover from. There was still so much to come, so much to face. I was terrified, I realized now. Terrified of it all, but most of all about leaving Nell.

She would go to Rupert, of course, if the worst happened – if I was locked up. It was one of the few proper conversations we'd managed to have since he'd left, and even that had been terse.

'Of course. Why would you even need to ask that? She'll come and live with me, and she'll be fine,' he'd said.

But would she, really? A little girl, her mother in prison, being brought up by just her father – and, it seemed now, possibly by some woman called Mia I'd never even met? Would Nell really be fine? The nausea worsened, and I looked around for a door that might lead to a toilet, suddenly feeling that I might actually have to go and throw up.

I didn't allow myself to think about it, not usually, not unless I was in one of my legal meetings – I'd become an expert at banishing the thoughts from my mind, focussing only on the here and now, in recent months. But soon there would be no avoiding it – the trial was a matter of weeks away. Final decisions had to be made: most importantly whether I definitely wanted to continue to plead not guilty, as recommended, and put my faith in a jury, or change my plea, which would spare the expense of a trial and hopefully get me a more lenient sentence – a reduction of up to a third was possible, my solicitors had told me.

It was what the sentence would be that took over my dreams, my nightmares ... the permutations racing through my mind, waking me in those dark, cold small hours and making a return to sleep impossible.

There was, in the UK, no mandatory sentence for manslaughter – it was at the judge's discretion. Life imprisonment, a shorter sentence of up to ten years, suspended imprisonment, community service or even a hospital order – a stay in a mental health hospital. Who knew which way it would go?

I knew already, too, what my judge, this man or woman who held my fate in his or her hands, would take into consideration when deciding my future. Were there any mitigating circumstances? Did I pose a threat to the public? Was I likely to commit another crime? Did I have any previous convictions? *Yes, no, no, no.* But would that be enough? Would the circumstances which surrounded this terrible thing that had happened be enough to keep me out of prison?

I'd tortured myself with far more than thoughts of incarceration since it happened, though, of course. For weeks afterwards, I'd obsessively searched websites, newspaper articles, looking for information, trying to convince myself that Zander might not have suffered, that he may have just fallen asleep. There was no such comfort to be found. The facts appalled me, sickened me, rendered me a howling, sobbing mess of pain and guilt, seared across my heart forever.

The car temperature would have risen ten to fifteen degrees Celsius every fifteen minutes, my baby becoming increasingly distressed, hyperthermia occurring within minutes.

Young children overheat fast, with dizziness, confusion, profuse sweating, agitation ... then, as heatstroke takes hold, headache, seizures, and the beginnings of organ failure, before a slow slip into unconsciousness. It is not a painless death – it is a horrific one.

I swallowed down the nausea as Rupert returned with his coffee, trying to appear normal, trying to stop the sudden tremor in my hands as I turned the pages of my magazine, seeing nothing on the smooth, colourful pages. Instead, the pictures that had begun to so frequently float into my mind since they had first surfaced at the weekend suddenly seemed to dance across the paper. The images of my hands unclipping the seat belt holding Zander in place, slipping under his sleeping body, hefting his weight up onto my shoulder, floated across my vision, and I blinked hard, trying to make them disappear.

Again? What was wrong with me? I was going crazy, I must be. We all knew what had happened that day. So why was I repeatedly now seeing this other version, the one where I *didn't* forget my baby, where I brought him inside as I was supposed to do, made sure he was all right before I lay down to sleep off the booze? It was impossible, a false memory, wishful thinking, my brain refusing to accept that I did this terrible thing. Because if I had brought Zander inside, the rest of the day, the way he died, made no sense whatsoever. I knew that. So why, each time I saw it in my head, was this new version becoming more and more clear, sharpening, as if seen through a slowly focussing camera lens? *This is ridiculous, Thea. Stop it.*

I closed the magazine abruptly, my hands pressing down on the glossy cover, trying to squeeze the images into oblivion. Instead, a new image, that of Flora, drifted into my mind, the shock and anguish in her eyes as she stumbled into the room that day, the pallor of her skin as she held Zander's limp, lifeless body in her outstretched arms.

Flora. She'd stayed afterwards, for a while, tried to keep on doing her job as usual, trying to support me through it, despite her impish little face crumpling with grief every time she passed the pram in the hallway, but she didn't manage it for long. I knew she would leave, and I never blamed her for that. Within a month, she was gone.

I had a sudden urge to see her now, and slowly put the magazine back down on the table, wondering if I had the nerve to give her a call. Would she want to see *me*? Maybe, if she did, I could talk through the events of that day with her, try to clear the confusion that was increasingly fuddling my mind.

I felt the desperate urge to tell somebody about it, and although Isla was the obvious choice, the thought of trying to explain this to her, with her cynical, no-nonsense attitude, made me nervous. She'd dismiss it out of hand, and she was too close to what had happened anyway, whereas Flora … well, Flora would listen, I thought. And if she didn't want to see me, well … what did I have to lose? I'd call her, later this week. Or text her maybe. A text would be easier, give her the chance to think about it before she replied …

'Hi Mum, Dad.'

Nell's voice, chirpy and light. She was standing in the open doorway, Karen Ballerton behind her, both of them smiling.

'Nell! How did it go? Are you OK?'

'Fine. I feel better actually.'

I stood up, and she skipped across the room and into my arms. Rupert and I both looked at the counsellor, and she nodded.

'I'll send you a written report, but I think she'll be all right. She was struggling with feelings of deep sadness, of course, but also of guilt … she seemed to think that she could have saved her brother. I've made her see that it was … well, an accident. Given her some coping strategies for days when she feels low …'

Nell released me from her bear hug and looked up at me, dark eyes seeking mine.

'Yes, bad things happen and we have to move on, Mum. All of us. You can't keep going over and over them in your head, because it's not good for you. You have to think about other things to help you stop doing that. It's OK to be sad, sometimes, but then you must find something to do, like a TV programme or a walk or something to take your mind off it ... that's right, isn't it, Karen?'

'That's right. Very good, Nell.' Karen nodded vigorously, her enormous hoop earrings swinging wildly, and gave Nell a double thumbs-up sign.

Rupert and I exchanged glances, and I felt it again, another brief moment of solidarity, of shared relief. Then he turned to Karen.

'That's fantastic, Miss Ballerton, thank you so much.'

He held out a hand to Nell, and she moved towards him, away from me, grabbing onto his fingers.

'Burger time, Dad?'

He patted her head with his free hand, and grinned.

'Burger time.'

That night in bed, Nell safely tucked up in her room, calmer and more content than I'd seen her in months, I dozed off quickly. I felt a little more relaxed myself tonight, something of my daughter's improved demeanour possibly rubbing off on me.

I'd spent half an hour in a deep, hot bath, scented with orange flower oil, emerging pink and slippery, my very bones seeming to be melting with sudden weariness. Crawling beneath the duvet, I'd fallen asleep thinking about Nell. But when I woke with a start an hour later, there was something very different in my head. I'd been dreaming, or had I? It had been so vivid, more like a memory than a dream. But even so, like the earlier images, they couldn't possibly be true, these brand-new pictures that had just flashed so clearly through my brain, could they?

I sat up, my breath coming in ragged gasps, fingers clutching at the edge of the duvet, trying to order my thoughts. I'd been back there, yet again, back on the fourth of September. Back in the car, with Isla and Nell and Zander, pulling up at our house, expressing surprise and delight that there was an empty space right outside the front door, something which never happened. The car sliding neatly into the space, the engine being turned off, Nell, waking from her slumber in the back seat, shouting at us to hurry up and open her door, because she needed a wee.

All of it, exactly as it happened. Exactly as it happened, except for one small detail. As we pulled up outside the house, as we parked the car, as we laughed at Nell's impatience, it wasn't me in the driving seat. I was sitting on the *inside*, the side closest to the pavement, to the house. The passenger seat. I wasn't driving the car. It was Isla.

20

FLORA

I paced the kitchen floor, up and down, up and down the polished terracotta tiles, pausing during each pass to straighten a tea towel on its peg, pick a crumb from the draining board, wipe a smear from the shiny black kettle. Why was I feeling so ridiculously nervous? It was Saturday afternoon, a Saturday off for once, and all that was happening was that Annabelle had gone out shopping with Greg and Sienna, and Olly was spending the day with a friend, leaving me at home with Millie, who was waiting for Nell to arrive for a sleepover. The issue, though, the thing that had thrown me into this unexpected disarray, was that the person who would be delivering Nell today was ... Isla Laird.

I couldn't put my finger on it, not really. I just didn't want to see Isla, just as I hadn't really wanted to see Greg, not after our encounter last weekend. He'd been away all week, working at head office in London, which had been a relief, and he'd arrived home last night after I'd retired to my room with my latest box set, so other than a quick 'good morning' earlier, I hadn't had to face him. I would, sooner or later, I knew that, but the longer I could put it off the better. There was no putting Isla off, though, and the prospect was proving to be strangely unnerving.

I stopped pacing, poured myself a coffee and sat down at the kitchen table, where Millie, seemingly unconcerned by my odd behaviour, was leafing through *National Geographic Kids* magazine, holding it up every now and again to show me another stunning photograph of a black rhino enjoying a mud bath or a seahorse floating in azure water. Her recent school photography project had clearly inspired her.

'I think that's what I want to do when I grow up. Go to all these faraway places and take pictures of animals. Is that an actual job though, Flora?'

'Wildlife photographer? Certainly is,' I said. 'Maybe you could work on one of those TV shows, you know? Like *Blue Planet*?'

Millie's eyes widened.

'Wow, yes, I could, couldn't I? I'm telling Mum and Dad as soon as they get home!'

'Good for you.'

She turned back to her magazine, and I got up from the table again, bringing my coffee with me, and walked to the window, feeling restless. Why the hell was I so jittery? It was, I supposed, just that I hadn't seen Isla for months, since I'd left Thea's. Other than Nell, I hadn't had any close contact with anyone from that period of my life since I'd been at Annabelle's – I'd seen Rupert briefly once or twice when he'd dropped Nell off or collected her, but we hadn't really spoken – and I preferred it that way, not wanting to revisit that stilltoorecent past, stir up those memories.

Today, though, I knew I wouldn't get away with a simple 'hello, how are you' at the door when Isla arrived. She'd want to talk – she always did – so it was more a matter of how quickly I could get her in and out. A quick coffee, a bit of polite small talk … fifteen minutes? Twenty?

'BRRRRRRRRR.'

Down the hallway, the doorbell rang, making me jump, my coffee splashing over the edge of my mug and down the front of my grey sweatshirt.

136

'Bugger! Oh, gosh, sorry, Millie, you didn't hear that, OK?'

'Hahaha, OK, I didn't hear you saying a *very* rude word!'

Millie ran past me, giggling, heading for the front door, and I swore again under my breath, grabbing a tea towel and dabbing ineffectually at the brown stain creeping across my top, then giving up with a sigh. I'd have to stick it in the washing machine later.

I walked into the hallway just as Millie and Nell were heading for the stairs.

'Flora!'

Nell changed direction and ran towards me, wrapping her arms around my waist, and I hugged her back, dropping a kiss onto her dark curls.

'Hey you! Go on upstairs, Millie's been dying for you to get here. But we need to have a catch up later, OK? And take your bag up with you; we'll all fall over it if you leave it in the middle of the floor like that.'

'Sorry! OK, see you later!'

She released me with a grin, grabbed her bag then ran after Millie, and I turned to look at Isla, who was standing just inside the still-open front door. She looked exactly the same as I remembered her, although of course there was no reason why she shouldn't – tall, her short red hair in soft layers around her face, hazel eyes outlined with a khaki colour which made them look more green than brown today.

'Isla. How nice to see you.'

I smiled at her, trying to quell the sudden rush of nerves that was making my stomach churn, and she smiled back, showing teeth that were white and even.

'And you. It's been a while, Flora. You look well.'

'Thanks. So do you. Look, do you fancy a coffee? I've just made a pot, and it's cold out there. Come on in for a few minutes.'

She nodded immediately.

'Aye, I could murder a coffee actually. Don't suppose there are

137

any of Annabelle's famous biscuits going too, are there? I haven't eaten since breakfast.'

I laughed.

'I'm sure I can find some. Come in.'

A few minutes later, fresh coffee poured and a plateful of apple flapjacks and cranberry oat cookies on the table between us, and chit-chat about our respective jobs and the weather exhausted, Isla swallowed a mouthful of biscuit and leaned across the table, looking at me earnestly.

'Flora, you haven't heard from Thea recently, I suppose? I'm worried about her.'

I shook my head.

'No. I haven't heard from her at all since I left. It wasn't intentional – I'm not avoiding her or anything. It's just that I'm so busy here and, well, she hasn't contacted me either, so ...'

'Oh, don't feel bad about it. I get it, honestly. It's just that the last couple of days she's been a bit abrupt on the phone when I've called her, and last night when I got in from London, she told me she couldn't see me. We were supposed to be hanging out, getting a pizza, you know, nothing exciting. But she told me she was too tired, hadn't been sleeping. She sounded bloody weird, if I'm honest. And then she asked me if I could collect Nell from Rupert's today and take her down here. She was going to do it herself, in a taxi, obviously, as she's off the road at the moment, but she said she couldn't now, because she needed some time alone. I mean, that's strange, right? She has nothing *but* time alone these days. What does she have to do, other than the business?'

I ran a finger round the rim of my mug, unsure how to respond.

'Well, maybe it's to do with the trial. I mean, it's not that far off now, is it? Mid-March? Maybe she needs time to process that, make plans for when ... well, for *if* things don't go her way?'

Isla was silent for a moment, then shrugged.

'Maybe. But she usually talks things like that through with me.

She doesn't usually shut me out. I'm wondering if she's upset about Mia. When I saw Rupert earlier, he told me he'd finally told Thea about her.'

'Mia? Wow. Is that still going on?'

Isla nodded.

'Yep. Who would have thought it? And out in the open now too. Must be serious, eh?'

She raised an eyebrow and reached for another biscuit. I nodded slowly, trying to take it in. *Mia.* It had been Isla who'd told me about Mia in the first place, all those months ago, one night in August when Rupert had been away working and Thea had gone upstairs to try to put a wakeful Zander back to bed. We'd been sitting in the lounge – the 'good' room at the front of the house, not my little snug at the back – sipping wine, the remains of a Chinese takeaway strewn on the coffee table. I'd said something, I couldn't even remember what now, something innocuous about Rupert missing out on a good meal, and Isla had snorted suddenly, tossing an errant red lock back from her forehead.

'He's missing out on nothing, trust me!' she'd said.

I'd frowned, not understanding, and she'd laughed.

'Oh Flora, you're so innocent. This "business" trip he's on?'

She used her index fingers to draw little quotation marks in the air as she said *business*, emphasizing the word.

'What? You mean …?'

'Yes, I *mean*. He's been shagging one of his colleagues on and off for a while. Her name's Mia. Sexy little blonde, or so he says!'

I'd felt my cheeks go hot suddenly, ripples of shock running through me.

'How … how do you know?'

'Greg told me. Greg Garrington? Millie's dad. He and Rupert got pissed at that garden party thing in Montpellier Gardens a few weekends ago and he confessed all. Then I bumped into Greg one night when I was out with a couple of my neighbours and he spilled the beans – he'd had a few drinks; you know what he's like when he's drunk. It started a couple of months ago, June-ish I think. Rupert's a little shit, isn't he? Thea doesn't know, though, and I'm not telling her, not yet anyway. I thought about it, don't get me wrong. She's my best friend, and I'm fucking furious that he's treating her like this. And I'm not keeping quiet to protect him; he can burn in hell for all I care after what he's been up to. But …' She had paused, pushing another strand of hair back off her face. 'I just don't want to upset her. It would kill her, and she's got enough on her plate with the kids and the business, and anyway Greg says he doesn't think it's serious, with this Mia piece. It'll probably blow over. So keep your trap shut, OK?'

I'd nodded, too stunned to speak.

Now, I stared at Isla as she took a gulp of coffee and wiped her mouth with the back of her hand, waiting for her to tell me more.

'He's gone away with her today, to meet her parents, somewhere up in Staffordshire. Taking advantage of a Saturday night without Nell, seeing as she's on this sleepover. Thea doesn't know he started seeing Mia while they were still together, though; he told me that today. He asked me not to say anything, then told me that actually he supposed it didn't matter if I did, as he didn't very much care what Thea thought anymore. I won't though. Tell her, I mean. I decided not to back then, so what would be the point now? They've split up anyway and they're hardly likely to get back together. What difference would it make, in the long-term, except hurt her even more?'

I nodded.

'Yeah. No point.'

Isla sighed, running her hands through her hair, then sank her chin into her cupped hands, elbows on the table, and looked at me intently again. Outside the sun had come out, the kitchen suddenly brighter, and her eyes now seemed flecked with gold. She really was very beautiful, I thought. Thea was beautiful too, or had been before what happened had taken its toll. They must have been a formidable duo, those two, when they were out together, the tall, outgoing redhead and the stylish, sultry brunette with the killer cheekbones. Oh. Killer. No pun intended, I thought, then said out loud: 'He's happy then? With Mia?'

Isla nodded, chin still in her palm.

'Seems to be. Which is good, I suppose. Not enough happiness around these days. You've got to take it where you can, haven't you? And, as we both know, he hadn't been happy with Thea for ages, had he? Before, I mean, not just after … after what happened. They'd had their moments before Zander was born, but after … well, he and Thea just went downhill, argued so much, all the time. You lived with them; I don't need to tell you that.'

I nodded.

She sighed and carried on.

'I mean, he never liked me that much, not in the beginning, but we rubbed along all right eventually, and maybe the man deserves a bit of happiness. What do you think, Flora?'

She stopped talking, her eyes fixed on mine.

'Yes. He does, yes.'

My voice was little more than a whisper. Isla continued to stare at me.

'Because, as we both know, Thea was no angel either, right? Even before she killed that poor baby.'

I swallowed, my mouth dry, my tongue rough against my teeth. 'Right.'

Isla looked at me for a moment longer, then stood up abruptly, her chair legs scraping on the tiled floor.

'I'd better go. Thanks for the coffee, and the chat. Nice to see you again, Flora.'

I showed her out, and as the door closed behind her, my knees suddenly felt weak. I sank down onto the cold floor of the hallway, my armpits damp, hands shaking, and took a deep breath. *Shit.* I shouldn't have agreed to stay here today, I *shouldn't*. Why hadn't

I told Annabelle I was busy, had plans? Seeing Isla had been a mistake, had brought everything flooding back, had cracked the fragile carapace of my happiness. No, Isla, Thea was no angel. She'd done something bad long before Zander died. But what did that matter, in the wake of what had happened? What did that matter now? Yes, Thea had her secrets. But then again, we all had secrets, didn't we?

21

THEA

'OUFF!'

I hauled another box down off the shelf, edged it along the floor with my foot until it rested against the others, then straightened up, breathing heavily. How could boxes of such small garments be so ridiculously heavy? That was the last one though, thank God.

I bent to pick up my bottle of water from the floor and took a long swig. I was feeling a little dehydrated today, and lugging boxes around in my warehouse wasn't helping. Last night, alone at home, I'd succumbed to the wine bottle again, although not excessively, by recent standards. I'd finished one bottle, admittedly, but when I found myself walking to the fridge for a second, something had stopped me. Why cloud my mind, scramble my thoughts, when things were finally becoming clearer, when memories seemed to be finally resurfacing?

So, amazingly, miraculously, I'd put the kettle on instead, making myself a mint tea, and taking it to bed. The wine had done its job anyway, in the quantity I'd already drunk – just for a while, it had taken the edge off the stinging pain I'd begun to feel each time I thought about Rupert and Mia.

I'd thought I was OK, had quietly accepted it when Rupert

had told me. But now I'd had time to process it a bit ... *Mia*. I had no idea what she looked like, but in my head I was picturing Mia Farrow in her younger days, a gamine beauty with an elfin hairstyle and fine bone structure. Stupid, really – Rupert's Mia could have been an Eskimo for all I knew.

I wondered how long he'd known her, how long they'd worked together, when they started to have feelings for each other. But really, what was the point of thinking about that, either? He and I were clearly over, and if he was able to find happiness, comfort, then I should be happy for him. I wasn't there yet, of course ... it would take time to adjust to this new state of affairs and, if I'd suddenly decided that drowning my feelings in alcohol was not the answer, then drowning them in work was the only other way I knew.

Hence, here I was, on a Saturday afternoon, sorting through boxes in my little warehouse on an industrial estate on the northern edge of Cheltenham, alone, pulling out looks for my next shoot and deciding what to order next. I was hoping to organize one more shoot and bring in a little more summer stock before the trial, even though I knew this would be construed by anyone watching me as grossly over-optimistic.

At my meeting with my solicitors this week I'd confirmed that I did want to continue to plead not guilty, meaning the trial would now definitely go ahead. It was a risk I had to take, and while there were no guarantees, certainly not in a case as high profile as mine, there *was* a chance, however small, that I'd be found innocent, Zander's death ruled a tragic accident, and not manslaughter.

Even if I *was* found guilty, the sentence might not be a custodial one. I clung to these thoughts now as I worked, knowing that trying to stay positive was the only way to get through each day, that I couldn't let myself dwell on the unthinkable alternatives. I simply had to carry on, despite everything.

I squatted down on the floor, a shaft of sunlight from the high windows of the warehouse lighting up the boxes in front of me, dust motes dancing in the air. Opening the box, I pulled out a tiny blue-green, Thai silk blouse, held it up and admired it for a moment, then dug back into the box again.

But as I sorted the clothing into sizes and colours on the big trestle table that ran along the side wall, laying the silk blouses out with little indigo jeans and washed denim skirts, arranging them into matching outfits, my mind began to wander again, the sunbeams warming the chill air around me, taking me back to another day, a day when the sun beat down and my life imploded.

I walked backwards and forwards between boxes and table, my footsteps gradually slowing, a strange calmness descending on me. And then, as if in a trance, I suddenly stopped moving, stood completely still, eyes closed, face tilted upwards to the soft yellow light streaming into the room, and there it was again, this time as if I was watching it on a cinema screen, in vivid, high definition, the colours brighter and clearer than ever. Me, climbing out of the passenger seat of the car, smiling, stumbling a little, wearing my long blue T-shirt dress, my strappy flats. Isla leaping from the driver's seat, she and Nell rushing past me, shrieking, giggling.

'I'm going first, out of my way!' Nell yelled as she thundered up the path to the front door.

'Noooo!' Isla, hot on her heels, laughing as she ran. And me still standing there, leaning on the car for a moment, watching them, then turning to open the rear door, to take Zander from his car seat before I went inside too …

'Oh my god!'

My eyes snapped open, and I was back in the warehouse, the pictures gone again as quickly as they had arrived. I ran my hands through my hair, my nails clawing at my scalp. What was going on in my head? Should I go and see Dr Evans, tell her about this? I'd skipped my appointment with her yesterday, telling the receptionist I had an important business meeting that couldn't be rearranged, that I was fine, that I'd come back as usual next week, not wanting to see my GP just as I hadn't wanted to see Isla this weekend, wanting to try to process all this in my own mind first.

Now, I wondered if I should have gone to see the doctor after all. I must be having some sort of breakdown. Why were these thoughts filling my head all of a sudden? Were *any* of them memories, or were they just fantasies, a vision of how I *wanted* the day to have happened? I mean, Isla *couldn't* have been driving, could she? I still didn't remember the journey home, but it was *my* car, she *never* drove it. Never had, not even once. Why would she start that day? Why would I let her? She'd been drinking as much as I had, hadn't she? And if she *had* driven us home, she would have said, wouldn't she? She wouldn't have let the police take my driving licence. She wouldn't have let me think I'd driven home drunk, as well as what happened afterwards. Would she? *Would* she? Of course she wouldn't.

And even if for some weird, inexplicable reason she did, what difference did it make anyway? What did it really matter *who* was driving, in the light of the biggest crime of that day? I was still in charge of Zander. I was his mother. It was still up to me to bring him inside. Isla and Nell were already indoors, racing to get to the bathroom …

I groaned, a sudden sense of panic gripping me, a chill running down my spine. I could *see* it now. I could *feel* it. Zander in my arms, my feet moving unsteadily up the path and through the open front door, the welcome cool of the hallway. And yet, these must be desperate longings, falsehoods created by a subconscious mind which could not accept the truth. Because if Isla did drive the car home, and I did take Zander inside, which was what my brain was now trying to convince me of, what did that mean?

I dropped to my knees on the hard, dusty floor, trying to think clearly. Trying to imagine, just for a minute, the implications if what was in my head was actually true, humouring myself. If my visions, my new memories, whatever they were, were real, and

146

I'd arrived home in the passenger seat of my own car, then that would mean that Isla – and Nell? Nell too? – were both lying to me about who was driving that day. But what would be the point of that?

And if the next bit, the bit where I took Zander safely inside, was true, that would mean ... what would *that* mean? That somebody had taken him back out to the car again without my knowledge, strapped him into his seat, and left him there to die? That's where he was found; but that scenario was obviously ludicrous, impossible, for who would do that?

Nobody would. Everybody adored Zander – well, except maybe Isla, who didn't particularly like anyone under the age of eighteen, but even so ... it was like not liking mice, or dogs. You might not want one in your living room, but that didn't mean you'd go out of your way to harm one. To kill one. It was insane to even think like this. *Stop it, Thea. Get a grip. You're losing your mind.*

I stood up slowly, brushing the dust from my jeans, scooping another bundle of clothing from the nearest box, thinking of my brief phone conversation with Isla last night, when I told her I couldn't see her this weekend. She said she understood, told me to get some rest, but I knew she was hurt, confused. Almost as compensation, to show her that I still needed her, valued her, I'd asked her if she could do me a favour instead, and take Nell to the Garringtons for her sleepover.

But for the first time ever, it was something I'd had to think hard about, the doubts at the back of my mind making me desperately uneasy, making me wonder if Nell would be OK, would be safe, with Isla.

Then I'd angrily pushed the apprehension away. Of course Nell would be all right. This was *Isla*. What was wrong with me? Suddenly, I ached to have my best friend here, to talk everything through with her; but at the same time I knew that taking a break from Isla this weekend had been the right decision, because how *could* I tell her what was going on, truly going on, in my head?

How could I see her, while I was feeling so bewildered? I knew I needed to talk to somebody about all this, though, and soon, or my brain might actually explode. Maybe if I wrote it all down, made a list …

I deposited the armful of clothes on the table and whirled around, looking for my bag. Finding it dumped on the floor by the door, I rummaged through it, pulling out a notebook and pen, then dragged the mini-stepladder I used to access higher shelves over to the table and perched on the top step, using it as a makeshift stool.

Right, a list. Stay calm. Make a list, think about this logically. Who was there that day? Who was there when it happened, in the run-up to it happening? Me, obviously, and Isla. Nell, who'd been upstairs playing with Millie Garrington. Rupert, and then Greg Garrington, who'd dropped Millie off and then hung around, having a beer in the garden. And Flora, who'd been working, and then heard the commotion outside and gone running out …

That was it. Nobody else. I stopped scribbling and looked at the list of names. What was I doing? None of these people would hurt Zander, harm me, would they? These were the people I loved and trusted most in the world, the people I was closer to than anyone else. My family, my friends.

And yet, as I sat there, staring at my barely legible scrawl, I couldn't quell a rising sense of fear inside me, a sudden feeling that I didn't quite know what was real anymore. I sat there for a moment, staring at the notebook, then with one swift movement ripped the page out, scrunched it into a ball and threw it into my bag. It landed on top of my purse, balancing on it neatly, and I glared at it as if it had been a living creature which had just crawled there, uninvited.

I groaned and sank my head into my hands. I needed to stop this insanity. *I* did this, nobody else. *I* killed my child. It was me, of course it was me. Yes, it was an accident, but it was still me. It had to be. Because if it wasn't, that would mean something unimaginable. It would mean that someone else did something too terrible to even contemplate. It would mean that if it wasn't me, killing my baby by accident, then it was someone else, killing him deliberately. And that would mean that one of them – one of my friends, one of my family – was lying about what happened, about all of it. And everyone who was in the house that day, everyone who witnessed it, all said the same thing. So it would mean *everybody* was lying. And that just wasn't possible, was it?

22

ANNABELLE

'WEEEEEEEEEEEEE!'

A small boy, bright red in the face, thundered past, a slab of cake in one hand and, close behind him, a further five screeching boys followed suit, whooping and hollering as they all headed back into the main party room where a lively *Doctor Who* quiz game had just commenced.

I peeled myself off the wall I'd flattened myself against and went in search of Flora, who was in the kitchen brandishing a large knife, frowning at a semi-demolished, four-foot high Tardis.

'Good grief. Sugar high or what?' I said. 'Does it taste OK, that Tardis cake? Looked a bit dry to me.'

She nodded, carefully putting the knife down on the table.

'It's all right, actually. Sort of chocolate-orange inside. There must be so much food colouring in all that blue icing, though. I don't envy the parents this evening. Those kids will be wired till midnight.'

I smiled and sank down into the nearest chair.

'Indeed. Tabitha told me to take some home if I wanted to, but I think I might accidentally forget.'

'Good idea. And I'll accidentally forget to remind you. Don't think any of yours need it. OK, what else? Goody bags all ready to go?'

'All ready. Sit down for a minute, take the weight off. They'll be doing that quiz for a while now, we can take a break.'

'OK. Just nipping to the loo then, back in a mo.'

Flora turned and skipped out of the room, and I closed my eyes and took a few deep breaths, rolling my head from side to side, trying to ease the tension in my neck. Flipping kids' parties. It was bad enough doing them for my own brood, never mind other people's, but it had been a quiet weekend, and this Sunday afternoon job had been easy money, just four hours' work, close to home and not much to organize in advance other than the specialist entertainer, the themed goody bags and the food. The enormous cake had been delivered by the bakery, thank goodness ... my estate car was roomy, but not that roomy.

It had done me good to get out of the house too, I thought, as I moved a precariously balanced bowl of melted ice cream away from the edge of the table, smiling as I heard a roar of laughter followed by cheers and loud applause down the hallway, and a brief blast of the *Doctor Who* theme music. Both Greg and Oliver were continuing to worry me, anxiety nibbling away at the edges of my mind, and being here, having a laugh with Flora, had done wonders for my mood, especially after what had happened this morning.

I'd been alone in the house, Flora out for her run, Greg having taken the kids for a bike ride. Sorting through some plans for upcoming events, getting organized for the next few days, I'd wandered into the spare room where I'd left a box of party poppers and streamers, when a sudden movement at the window caught my eye. I moved closer to take a look, realizing with increasing distaste that something – or several somethings – were wriggling on the windowsill. Ants? Beetles of some sort? Ugh. Not good with creepy-crawlies, I shuddered, keeping my distance, peering at the sill, trying to identify the creatures, their stocky bodies dark grey, familiar. They looked like ... but what on earth?

I moved closer, curiosity replacing my nervousness now, and then my breath caught in my throat. Moving clumsily on the white painted wood were half a dozen or so flies. But flies in name only; flies walking with an ungainly gait, flies with their wings entirely missing, or just filmy remnants where their instruments of flight should be, useless wisps of membranous tissue, translucent in the morning light, the multiple amputations rendering the insects earthbound, helpless. My stomach churned, and I backed slowly out of the room, thinking only one thing. Oliver.

When I had told Flora about it, on the drive to the party, she'd gasped and then remained silent for several moments, a heavy frown creasing her smooth brow.

'That's ... well, that's *horrible*,' she'd said, finally. 'It's kind of sick. But, look, I'm not trying to normalize it or anything, but I've definitely heard of kids doing that kind of thing before. It's not *that* unusual, I think, particularly in boys. Experimenting, trying to see how things work. Maybe he wondered what would happen, if they could carry on functioning, eating and so on, if they couldn't fly?'

'But it's so cruel!' I said, slightly horrified that she could be so rational about it. 'Those poor little things, wandering around looking all lost. It's horrible! I can't stop thinking about them. It made me feel sick to my stomach. It's not *normal*, Flora. What's wrong with him?'

'It *is* pretty unpleasant,' she admitted. 'But assuming it was Olly – and I'm sure you're right, because it certainly wasn't me, and I can't see Millie or Sienna doing something like that ... well, maybe it's a good thing? That he's channelling his anger away from Sienna to something else? I think that last little outburst when they were watching *Frozen* shocked even him.'

I'd thought about that for a minute.

'I suppose so. Maybe. But still ... pulling the wings off flies?

152

Isn't that an early sign of being a psychopath or a sociopath or something? Honestly, Flora, this has totally freaked me out. I'm going to have to talk to him. And goodness knows what Greg is going to say.'

She'd laughed then, and patted me on the arm.

'Annabelle, Olly is *not* a psychopath. He's an almost-teenage boy, it's a phase. It'll pass.'

I smiled too, but felt only slightly reassured.

Now, a few hours later, I was still thinking about it, but a little less obsessively. Maybe Flora was right, and my son *was* just going through an angry, destructive phase. It was only occasional after all, not a daily occurrence. It would be fine, of course it would. Gosh, kids. Who'd have them, eh?

'Cup of tea? I boiled the kettle a few minutes ago, thought you might be about ready for one?'

Flora was back. I nodded.

'That would be lovely. Thanks, Flora.'

She flicked the switch to bring the kettle back to the boil, found two mugs and teabags and made the drinks, then sat down opposite me with a sigh.

'Nightmare, these parties, but I'd have loved it as a kid. I never had a party, you know. Not ever, the whole time I was growing up.'

I swallowed a mouthful of tea and looked at her, surprised.

'What, *never*? That's awful, Flora. How come?'

She shrugged.

'My parents were … well, always busy. Work, you know. Dad was away a lot and … well, it just never happened. Although I didn't really have many friends anyway, so I'm not sure who would have come, even if I *had* had a party.'

She laughed, but there was a sudden stiffness in her body, her eyes downcast, staring into her mug.

'Flora, I … but you're so lovely, so bubbly. Why didn't you have friends?'

She continued staring down at her mug, and I cringed inwardly.

I shouldn't have asked, should I? But it had been her who'd brought it up, after all …

'Oh, I was just shy at school, didn't really fit in.'

She looked up at me, a more normal expression on her face now, thank goodness.

'Some kids just take a while to sort of, well, grow into themselves, don't they? That was me. Once I got to uni I found it much easier to make friends, to find people with the same sort of interests. I didn't keep in touch with many afterwards, but while I was there it was good. I sort of like my own space, you know? Not everyone needs lots of people round them all the time, and I suppose I'm one of those people. It helped me feel less odd, studying psychology – helped me understand myself a bit more, understand other people too. Sorry, I did English and Psychology, at Northampton.' She paused. 'Oh … duh. You know that already, don't you? You've seen my CV.'

I smiled.

'I have, and very impressive it is too. You got a first. Must have been really interesting. The psychology bit, especially. I'm surprised you didn't go into it as a career.'

'I thought about it. I just got a few casual jobs after uni, trying to decide what to do longterm. But then I saw an ad for the agency that recruited me for Thea's and it all sounded quite exciting, working for an Internet fashion business, and well … the rest is history. But it was incredibly interesting, the psychology. Fascinating, actually. Learning how to analyse and understand human behaviour, how the mind works, how our emotions and thoughts can be shaped by other people as well as by ourselves … I loved it.'

She looked relaxed again now, her eyes shining.

'I can tell. Probably why you're so good with my troublesome kids. Pity I didn't do psychology too, might have helped. Especially recently.'

She laughed.

154

'Oh, you do all right, Annabelle. They adore you, I wouldn't worry. I wish my mum had been like you. We were never close, you know? I've probably talked more to you in the past few months than I did in eighteen years with my mum ...'

Her voice tailed off and the sadness was back, the passion fading from her eyes. Pushing my tea aside, I reached out a hand and touched her arm.

'I'm so sorry about that. Do you see your parents often, speak to them?'

She shook her head.

'The odd phone call. I visit maybe once a year. It's enough.'

My hand was still on her arm, and I ran it gently down to her fingers, grasping them lightly.

'Well, you know you can always talk to me, Flora, OK? You're fantastic, and just like part of the family already, and I hope we can continue to work together for a long time. I'd like us to be friends too ... well, not that we're not friendly now, but, well, you know what I mean ...'

She squeezed my hand, and the corners of her mouth turned upwards, ever so slightly.

'I do. I'd like that. You're so kind, Annabelle. I know I can be a bit ... well, unsociable sometimes. I like my own space. That doesn't mean I don't want to be friends though, I ... oh, damn it, who's that?'

In her pocket, her mobile had started beeping. She pulled her hand gently from mine and retrieved the phone, frowning at the screen.

'It's a text. Oh ... it's ... it's ... from Thea.'

Her face had turned pale.

'*Thea?* Gosh. What does she want?'

'Hang on.'

She scrolled down the screen, her body very still, only eyes and thumb moving. Then she looked up at me, eyes wide, an expression I couldn't read on her face.

'She says she's starting to remember things. Things about the day Zander died, and she says they don't really make sense. She wants to talk to me, see if I can help her straighten a few things out in her mind …'

She looked down at the phone again, and now I could see that her hands were shaking, her face even more drained of colour.

'Straighten things out?' I said. 'But everyone *knows* what happened. Even she does. I mean, I know she's supposed to have had some sort of memory loss since it happened, if what I've heard is true, but even so. Are you OK, Flora? Look, you don't have to talk to her if you don't want to, it's not your responsibility, you know that, don't you? She's not being fair … it's not fair on you, raking this all up again, just as you're trying to get over it …'

Flora dropped her phone onto the table, shaking her head. She inhaled sharply, then let the breath out again, and looked at me.

'No, it's fine. I'm fine, Annabelle. She's asked if we can meet up. I'll do it. I'll go and see what she wants. I'll go and see her one more time. I was there, I was part of what happened. I owe her that, at least. I'll go. And then I'll never have to see her again.'

23

FLORA

I first slept with Rupert Ashfield last April. I'd never told anyone about it, not a single person – it wasn't something I was proud of. It was only a few weeks after that evening when he came to talk to me in my little snug, the cosy room off the kitchen at the house on Montpellier Terrace – the evening when I first realized, with a jolt, that I found him attractive.

In the days that followed that – that *awakening*, of sorts, I suppose you could call it – my stomach would flutter every time I heard the front door open, signalling Rupert's arrival home from work. When we were in the same room, I was suddenly hyper-aware of his every movement, my eyes following him as he walked across to pick a book from a shelf or to close the curtains.

It was pathetic, and embarrassing – I felt like a teenager with her first crush – but at the same time it was a rush, that feeling that all of a sudden I was somehow more alive than I had been for months, my senses on high alert.

There was guilt, too, though – this was Thea's husband after all. Thea, my boss, and now my friend too. How could I do this, how could I yearn for Rupert, when he belonged to her? It was wrong, really wrong. Still, though, somehow I convinced myself that it wasn't my fault. It was Rupert who had first come to seek me out, come to talk to me, after all – Rupert who had touched my cheek and looked into my eyes that evening in the snug, and started these unexpected stirrings inside me. Rupert, who in the weeks since, had brushed against me 'accidentally' in the hallway, his hand lingering on my waist as he passed; who let his fingers graze mine when he passed the pepper mill at dinner; who sometimes gazed at me so intently across a room that I would start to become tongue-tied, stumbling over my words as I tried to update Thea on an order, making her laugh, oblivious to what was causing my discomfort. The covert flirting, which I suppose was the best way to describe it, continued until midApril, and then the inevitable happened.

It was a Saturday night, and Isla and Thea had gone out, first for dinner and then on to late-night drinks at a trendy bar opposite Montpellier Gardens. They'd asked me to go with them, saying Rupert was happy to babysit, but I'd declined, feigning tiredness and saying I fancied a few hours in front of the telly and an early night.

It had, in fairness, been a long week, but deep down I think I knew that if anything was going to happen between me and Rupert, it would be that night. We would be alone in the house – well, alone apart from two (hopefully) sleeping children – for hours.

Even so, my feelings of guilt kept me upstairs in my room until after nine o'clock. I couldn't just saunter down there and into the living room and seduce him, could I? If anything was going to happen between us, it would have to be him making the first move.

I soaked in the bath for ages, trying to relax, to quell the butterflies, then rubbed in some of my favourite body butter, slipped into a soft cashmere sweater and leggings, added a touch of mascara and lip gloss then went downstairs, outwardly casual, inwardly quivering. The lounge door was open, and as I walked past, heading towards the kitchen, I saw Rupert standing by the window, beer bottle in hand, staring out into the dark night through the open curtains.

'Flora!'

I turned, and he was already out in the hallway, smiling at me.

'I thought you were hiding from me. Drink?' His voice was warm, his dark eyes crinkling at the corners, the faint musky smell of his aftershave sending sudden little shivers of anticipation through me.

'A drink would be nice, yes. Thanks.'

'There's red wine open in the kitchen. I'll get it for you, hang on.'

He put his beer bottle down on the hall table and stepped towards me. I moved slightly to let him pass, but somehow in the wrong direction, and suddenly we were just inches apart, chest to chest, and I could feel his breath on my cheek, his arm slipping round my waist, pulling me in, and then his lips were on mine, soft and urgent, and I was lost.

Somehow, ripping clothes off as we went, we moved back into the lounge, Rupert flicking off the light switch as we passed it, the lamppost outside spilling its soft orange glow through the tall windows, illuminating our naked bodies. And then it was done, and we lay there, panting, staring into each other's eyes, both of us slightly shell-shocked.

'Shit, Rupert,' I remembered saying.

'I know,' he replied. 'I know.'

We didn't really need to say anymore than that. It was wrong, and stupid, and shameful, and yet we kept doing it. Whenever Thea was out, and we were alone in the house, or at least when Nell and Zander were asleep, we would seek each other out. In my room, in the snug, even in the garden shed one warm night in July, giggling like children, trying to avoid the spiders' webs and almost choking with suppressed laughter when Rupert ended up with one foot in a bag of compost.

For a while, I kidded myself that this could work. That, although it would be horrible and difficult and unpleasant, Rupert might one day leave Thea. I started to believe that this man could bring me the stability and love that had so far eluded me. It's awful, isn't it, what lust can do to you? How it can make you do things you never thought yourself capable of, how it can turn you into a deceitful, lying, cheating bitch. And into an idiot too. What an idiot I was. When Isla told me about Mia, over that Chinese takeaway on that August night, I nearly fainted. The shock made me breathless, dizzy.

He's been shagging one of his colleagues on and off for a while. Her name's Mia. Sexy little blonde, or so he says!

Still feeling sick and shaky the next day when Rupert had returned from his business trip, I'd pulled him aside and told him it was over. His eyes had widened in surprise, full of questions, but I hadn't explained, and after that I simply refused to talk to him, other than basic polite conversation when Thea was around.

He'd tried, once or twice, to corner me, to 'talk about it', but I always wriggled away, and eventually he gave up. I was angry, for a while, and then the rage subsided, simmered and vanished, leaving only a feeling of emptiness. It would never have worked, would it? And he was Thea's, after all. It was what I deserved.

Thea. It was her I was on my way to see now, this Monday afternoon, a day off after yesterday and the chaos of the *Doctor Who* party. Her text had stirred everything up again, brought back all the old feelings I'd had about what had happened with Rupert, and I walked slowly, reluctantly from the bus stop on Cheltenham's Promenade, passing the Queens Hotel and cutting across Montpellier Gardens, heading for the Terrace and Thea's, my feet dragging.

It was a beautiful day, cold and bright, joggers pounding past, dogs bounding across the grass, and I remembered summer days here, throwing a ball to a laughing Nell, Zander gurgling in his pram, fat little fists pumping the air.

I didn't want to see Thea today, didn't want to go back there, to that house, the house with so many memories. But when she'd sent the text yesterday, asking me if I would, how could I say no? I owed it to her, didn't I? I'd slept with her husband. I'd betrayed her trust. I owed her this, at least.

I passed through the pedestrian gates at the edge of the park and waited to cross the road, wondering if Nell would be coming home from school later, or if tonight was a Rupert night. I missed her. We'd been … well, it sounded odd to say we'd been friends, *were* friends, considering the massive age difference, but it was true. We were a little team, me and Nell. Pals, keepers of each other's silly little secrets, and I still felt protective over her.

I'd seen her on Saturday evening, of course, when she'd been sleeping over at Annabelle's with Millie, and we'd found time for a chat, just the two of us, after Nell had had a bath and Millie had gone off to have hers. She'd told me about her visit to a therapist, a woman called Karen something, a visit her parents had insisted on, and how she was feeling better now, about Zander. How this woman had told her she must stop worrying that she could have done something to save her little brother, how it's the parents' responsibility to keep a child safe, how she must let it go now, put her feelings about it into a little red balloon, let the balloon go, watch it float away up into the clouds.

'I did it, Flora. I did it, and it works! Imagine that! Karen said you can do it with any worries. You know, if you're scared in the night, or you think something bad is going to happen, you just push it all into the balloon, in your head, all those horrible thoughts, just shove them in, and watch them float away. And then you feel better. I'm going to tell Millie and Sienna how to do it, because they get scared too sometimes.'

I'd pulled her close then, burying my face in her soft brown curls, inhaling the clean scent of her, filled with relief. Nell was going to be OK.

I could see the house now, the bright blue door, the grey-painted railings, the bay tree in its tall pot by the gate. A space outside, where Thea's car had been, the day I found Zander limp and hot and dead in his car seat inside it. I walked the final few steps, took a deep, slightly shaky breath, and rang the bell.

24

THEA

TICK. TICK. TICK.

I was sitting in the dining room at the front of the house, laptop open in front of me, trying to work, but the clock in the hall was distracting me. It seemed so ... so LOUD tonight, ticking its way into my brain, insisting on being heard. And what sort of clock goes tick, tick, tick anyway? Where was the *tock*? Clocks were supposed to go 'tick TOCK', weren't they? Why had I never noticed that before? I had a disabled clock. Oh, this was ridiculous. I was obsessing about a clock now, instead of trying to keep my business on track, or trying to keep myself out of prison.

I pushed the laptop aside and stood up, paced restlessly around the room a few times and then decided tea might help. It was too quiet here tonight, without Nell, I thought, as I made my way to the kitchen. That had been my choice, though. Rupert wasn't due to have her until Wednesday, but I'd asked if she could stay another night this week. I had yet another solicitors' meeting tomorrow, and I needed time to organize my thoughts, I'd told him.

That was true, more or less anyway. I needed to think, but I was also feeling increasingly unstable, increasingly scared. The memories, real or otherwise, of the day Zander died, were becoming so vivid, so clear now, that they were making me feel unbalanced, terrified that I was spiralling into some sort of madness. I hadn't mentioned them to anyone apart from Flora, not yet, still hadn't made a new doctor's appointment either, but I knew I probably should. I should probably be on some sort of medication too, and yet I didn't want that, for I knew that pills would cloud my mind, and now, more than ever before, I needed to stay away from drugs, from booze. I needed clarity. I knew I would never hurt Nell – never knowingly harm *anyone*, ever – but I was frightened that I was so distracted at the moment that I might not, right now, be the best mother. She was better off with Rupert, just for a day or so, while I tried to straighten things out in my head.

I'd hoped that today, meeting up with Flora, might help. But it hadn't, not really, even though seeing her had been nice. She looked great, fresh-faced and pretty as always, dressed in tight black leggings, a leather jacket, funky red trainers. She'd seemed a little nervous though, for the first few minutes, rubbing at the old scar on her wrist, looking anxiously around the living room, eyes flicking towards the window and back to the corner of the room where Zander's pram used to sit. Understandable, of course. She'd left because the aftermath of what had happened had been too hard for her to deal with, and now I'd asked her to come back, to relive the events of that day all over again. I was surprised she'd agreed, to be honest, but that was Flora – always willing to assist, even if she wasn't really able to help in the end this time, or not much anyway.

She'd looked a little shocked when I'd opened the door, although she recovered quickly, and for a moment I couldn't work out why she'd reacted liked that. But as I'd let her in, and followed her into the living room, I'd caught a glimpse of myself in the hall mirror and realized what was wrong. I looked dreadful. I was even thinner now than I had been a few weeks ago, when

I'd first noticed I'd lost weight, my appetite virtually gone. My cheekbones jutted out beneath the dark circles under my eyes, my skin was deathly pale and free of makeup – free of even moisturizer most days, if I was honest – my hair was stringy and greasy, scraped back in a scraggy ponytail. I hadn't even put clean clothes on today, and my white, lambswool jumper and jeans were both looking less than pristine. I'd always taken care of myself, before, always enjoyed a bouncy blow-dry and a red lipstick, but there didn't seem to be any point, not anymore.

As we sat down, I touched my hair self-consciously, and apologized.

'Flora, I'm so sorry, I look a mess. It's just with all this on my mind, I've neglected the old personal grooming a bit ...'

She held up a hand, shaking her head, her composure returned.

'Don't be silly, Thea, honestly. I totally understand. You look fine. It's nice to see you again.'

I smiled.

'You too.'

I had already prepared coffee and biscuits, expecting that, as usual, she would arrive exactly on time, so I busied myself pouring the drinks and sliding salted caramel cookies onto the saucers, knowing I wouldn't touch mine. Once we were settled, cups in hand, I leaned back in my chair and began.

'Flora, I'm so sorry to ask you to come back here – I know how difficult this must be for you.'

She opened her mouth, probably to protest, but I carried on, the words coming out in a rush now.

'The thing is, and this is going to sound mad, crazy even, but the thing is, Flora, after months of not being able to remember anything, having this amnesia thing, well, over the past little while things have started to come back, memories, about the day Zander ... about that day, but the thing is these memories, thoughts, whatever they are, they're just ... well, they're just weird, because they're telling me that things happened really differently, *totally*

165

differently, to how everyone else says they happened, and I know that can't be possible, but it just seems so real, Flora …

I paused for breath. Her eyes were fixed on mine now, frowning.

'Diff … differently? In what way? What are you remembering?'

I sighed.

'Well, this is the thing, you see. I don't know if I'm *actually* remembering, or if it's some sort of false memory. A sort of wishful thinking, if you know what I mean? My stupid brain not being able to cope with the truth and trying to come up with a more … I don't know, a more palatable version of what happened. So I thought it might help to talk it through, with someone who was there, but I can't talk to Rupert, he hates me too much, and Isla … well …'

I put my coffee cup down on the table in front of me and rubbed my eyes. Flora sat in silence, waiting.

'Isla … well, I've remembered something a bit odd that involves her, so I feel I can't talk to her about this either, not right now anyway. So you seemed the best person. Someone who was there, but someone a little bit removed, you know, from my immediate circle? I'm so sorry to bring you into this, but I feel like I'm going mad, Flora, and it just might help, to run this all past you, if you can bear it? I have another meeting with my solicitors tomorrow, you see—'

'It's fine, it's fine,' she interrupted me, leaning over to put her own cup down too. 'Tell me, Thea. Tell me what you're thinking, and I'll see if I can help.'

'Thank you. Thank you so much.'

And so I told her. I told her that, although I still couldn't remember the actual drive home from the bar that afternoon, that I remembered us pulling up outside the house, and being in the passenger seat. That, in *my* head, Isla and Nell had gone ahead, running into the house, and that I had taken my sleeping baby out of his car seat, up the path, inside. Had put him, still asleep, in his pram in the corner of the living room, before

166

collapsing onto the sofa. How Isla and Nell had returned from the bathroom, and how Isla and I had decided to have a few more drinks and opened a bottle of wine. And then how everything became a blur again, until the only part which was, and would always be, horrifically crystal clear – the part where she, Flora, had come running in, white-faced with fear, my dead baby in her arms.

She listened, eyes flitting between my face and the empty corner where the pram used to be, her expression unreadable. When I'd finished she sat in silence for a moment, then cleared her throat.

'OK. Look, the car driving thing, that's weird. I mean, I was upstairs in my room, which was at the back, of course. So I suppose, thinking about it, I have no idea who drove the car home, because I didn't actually see that. I know I heard the front door open, and slam shut, and then I heard Isla and Nell both shouting and laughing and running. And then a minute or so later, I heard the door open again, and I assumed it was you, bringing Zander in. And then ... well, when the police came and everything, and you were telling them what happened, you told them you couldn't really remember anything, but you did say *you'd* driven home, didn't you? I mean it was your car, and you always drove, so why would Isla be driving that day? Nobody questioned it, didn't even think to question it. I certainly didn't.'

She was looking deeply puzzled, and I nodded.

'I know, I know. And it doesn't really mean anything, not on its own. It doesn't matter who was driving, not really. It was still up to me to bring Zander in. But it's just so odd, don't you think? That I think now that it was Isla?'

'Yes. Yes, it is. I don't know what to say, Thea. I didn't see. I just assumed that it was you. It could easily have been Isla though. Haven't you asked Nell, does she not remember?'

I had asked Nell, eventually, a few days ago, after agonizing about it for ages. I hadn't wanted to stir things up for her, especially not now when she seemed to be feeling a little better, and knowing how any reference to that day could send her into meltdown. But it had got to the point where I needed to, I had to. She was the only other person in the car that day – surely she'd remember who was driving?

'I did ask her. She says she thinks it was me. But she says her head is … well, *fuzzy* is how she describes it. But she'd fallen asleep in the back seat, of course, with her headphones on, and didn't really pay much attention to what was going on in the front. And it's true, kids don't, not really. She says she just remembers opening her eyes when we got home and realizing she was dying for a wee, and jumping out of the car and racing Isla up the path.'

Flora nodded slowly.

'I mean, that's what we all thought happened. I don't know how you could find out for definite, not really, without asking Isla, unless a neighbour or someone passing by saw the car pull up and noticed who got out of the driver's seat? Unlikely, I suppose, though, after this long?'

'Pretty unlikely, yes.'

I'd thought of that too, had even plucked up the courage to knock on a few doors on Saturday morning, asked my bemused neighbours the question. I'd been greeted by blank stares, shrugs, ill-concealed hostility. You weren't friends with your neighbours, not on this road. But they all knew who I was, what I'd done. It had been a waste of time.

I topped up the coffee, offering Flora another biscuit, even though her first two, like mine, were untouched. Then I sat back in my chair again.

'So, the other bit. The most important bit. Why do I think I brought Zander in from the car? Why is that so clear in my head now? Because that bit, that can't have happened, can it?'

Flora turned to look out of the window again. A car was parked outside now, in the space right next to the gate, a blue estate of some sort. She stared at it for a moment, then looked back at me.

'Well, again, I was upstairs when you came home, so I didn't see. But if it did happen like you think, what would that mean, Thea? I found Zander ... I found Zander *dead* in your car, out there. If you brought him in, how would he get back out there again? He couldn't walk, couldn't unlock the car and climb back in by himself, could he? He was eight months old.'

Her voice had an edge to it now, and I glanced down at my hands, suddenly feeling ridiculous, sick.

'I know. I know that what I'm suggesting is impossible, Flora. I'm suggesting that if I did bring him in, somebody else must have put him back out there again. Which is insane, right? Because who would do that? But—'

'Yes, who would do that? Come on, Thea. I want to help you, and I agree with you that the issue of who was driving the car could be up for debate, if you think it wasn't you. But ... well, the rest of it ...' She shook her head. 'I can't help you, Thea, I'm sorry. And I need to get going. I have some shopping to do and I don't want to miss my bus back to Cirencester. I'm sorry, really, but ...'

She shook her head again, sighed and stood up, zipping her jacket. I stood, too, and reached out to touch her arm.

'Don't be sorry. It's just me, clutching at straws. I shouldn't have involved you, I'm really sorry. But thank you so much, for coming up here and seeing me. You didn't have to, and I appreciate it.'

She shrugged.

'That's OK. Good luck, Thea, with the trial and everything. I know you would never have hurt Zander intentionally. I know how much you loved him. I'm so sorry about how it all turned out. You're a great mum. I hope it all ... I hope it all goes your way.'

The unexpected kindness of her words brought sudden tears

169

to my eyes, and I stammered a thank you. But as I saw her to the door and said goodbye, the memory was there again, the blue door, my stumbling feet, the weight of my baby in my arms. I slammed the door shut and leaned my forehead against the cool wood, my brain racing. I was going insane. I was ill. What other explanation was there?

Now, hours later, as I sat in the quiet kitchen cradling my mug of tea, trying to still my churning thoughts, I was still as confused as I had been before Flora's visit. My appointment at my solicitors was at ten tomorrow morning. I had still been undecided about whether to tell them about all this, whether to confess to this sudden, senseless confusion I was experiencing about the events of that day. But now, I suddenly realized that I had to say something, just in case. *Tell us everything*, they had told me at earlier meetings. *Everything you remember, no matter how trivial.*

Oh, you're going to love this, I thought.

170

25

FLORA

'OUCH.'

I rubbed my arm, scowling at the corner of the kitchen worktop, then made my way unsteadily to the sink, reached for a glass on the shelf to the right, and turned the tap on. The water splashed noisily into the sink, and I moved the glass under the stream of water, catching a little before glugging it down and returning the glass for more.

'Flora? You OK? What are you doing in here in the dark?'

It was Greg, and suddenly the kitchen lights blazed.

'Urgh, too bright!' I said, turning to squint at him across the room. He was leaning on the door frame, looking fit and lean in a close-fitting long-sleeved navy T-shirt, looking me up and down with an amused smile.

'You sound like Gizmo. From *Gremlins*? The film?'

He paused, as I stared at him, not understanding. Then he frowned.

'Flora … are you … are you *drunk*?'

I put the glass down and took a step towards him, staggered a little, then stopped again.

'I'm … I'm not drunk, exactly. I may have had a glass of wine. Or … two, or … look, it's allowed, isn't it? I'm not working today.'

Oh dear, I thought. I am drunk, aren't I? What on earth possessed me to open a bottle of wine in my room after I got back from Cheltenham? Greg was right … I was definitely rather drunk.

'Well, yes, of course it's allowed. It's just not like you, that's all. It's not even eight thirty. And I don't think I've ever seen you even remotely drunk before. Are you all right?'

He was crossing the room now, the amusement on his face turning to concern, and suddenly, to my horror, I felt tears sliding down my cheeks. I brushed them away fiercely with the backs of my hands, but he'd already noticed.

'Flora! What is it? What's wrong? Come here.'

With one swift movement he took me by the shoulders and pulled me into an embrace, one arm moving downwards to wrap around my waist, the other gently patting my hair. For a moment I rested my head on his hard chest, enjoying the comforting warmth of him, the soft murmurings of: 'Hey, don't cry, it'll be OK, whatever it is.' Then I pulled away, embarrassed.

'Greg, I'm sorry … I saw Thea today. She asked me to go and see her, to talk through what happened, you know, when Zander … and it's just upset me, that's all. Going back there, remembering …'

'Talk through it? Why? What's to talk about?'

He was frowning now, his face darkening.

'Oh, she says she's remembering things, her memory is starting to come back and she's remembering it differently to how she thought it all happened … she wanted to see if I could help shed any light on it, but I couldn't, not really. Excuse me …'

I turned away, intending to get a piece of kitchen paper from the roll on the wall to wipe my face, but Greg grabbed my arm, pulling me back towards him.

'God, that woman. She's crazy. We all know what happened, and it wasn't fair of her to upset you like this,' he said quietly. He cupped my chin in his hand, tilting my face upwards, and before I could think or move away again he had dropped a quick, soft kiss onto my lips.

'I hate seeing you upset, Flora,' he whispered.

'Dad? What's going on?'

We both jumped as Oliver suddenly appeared in the doorway, and I took a step backwards, shocked. How much had he seen?

'Olly.'

Greg turned and smiled at his son, then gestured at me.

'Flora's just a bit upset. She ... bumped into Thea Ashfield today. It brought back bad memories, you understand?'

There was a suspicious look on Oliver's face, but he looked slowly from his father to me and back again, then nodded.

'Sure. Zander and all that. Sorry, Flora. Hope you're OK.'

'I'm fine, thanks, sweetie,' I said. 'Just a bit embarrassed your dad caught me having a sniffle. I think I'll go upstairs and have a bath and an early night.'

I turned back to Greg, not quite meeting his eyes.

'Thanks, Greg, for being so nice. Goodnight.'

''Night, Flora. Take it easy.'

His tone was light, casual, and I slipped gratefully out of the room, patting Oliver on the arm and smiling at him as I passed. He smiled back, and I was relieved to see that the look of suspicion was gone. Maybe he hadn't seen the kiss, after all? Shit, why had Greg done that? And why hadn't I stopped him? What was it with these bloody men?

Deeply grateful that the girls were in bed and that Annabelle had gone to the cinema with some of her mummy friends, I climbed the stairs to my room, locked the door and ran a deep, bubbly bath. I stayed in it for nearly an hour, topping it up at regular intervals, feeling my muscles finally relax and the tension in my neck and shoulders ease.

I'd have a little chat with Oliver tomorrow, I thought – get him on his own and make sure everything was OK. I was pretty sure that even if it wasn't, even if he had seen something of what had just happened with Greg, I'd be able to make it all right. I knew how to handle Oliver. But Greg … I wasn't so sure how to handle Greg. Keeping away from him was the obvious answer, but it didn't seem to be that easy. I was still pretty certain he didn't actually fancy me, though, despite what he had done tonight. It was like the last time, when he'd got me alone in his study. He wanted to know what I knew. He was scared, and that made him dangerous.

I wriggled my toes against the tap and thought back to the night I found out. It was a Friday night, and Rupert was away on business – or, more likely, away shagging bloody Mia, again – and Thea had called to say she was stuck on a slow-moving train from Glasgow, where she'd been on a buying trip to a kilt factory or sporran shop or some such thing. Isla had arrived early evening anyway, as she did most Fridays, so once the kids were in bed we'd ended up chatting in the lounge, over a bottle of Prosecco. And that's when she told me.

To this day, I don't know why she did – it's not like we were the best of friends – we got on OK by that point, but not to the level of sharing our deepest secrets. I found it weird, how even though she and Thea were so close, obsessively so at times, she would sometimes say really nasty things about my boss. I'd thought about it a lot, trying to apply what I'd learned in my psychology classes at uni to Isla and Thea's relationship, trying to analyse the complexities of it. And I'd come to the conclusion that Isla's feeling of no longer being number one, of coming in fourth in Thea's affections behind Rupert and the children, was sometimes hard for her to handle, and that her way of dealing with this perceived snub, this demotion, was to occasionally let rip at Thea, try to humiliate her. To her face, now and again – I'd heard a few bitchy, vicious remarks being exchanged between them, although their rows never lasted long – but more often, behind her back, to me or even to Rupert, who would be taken aback on occasion to find Isla backing him against her friend. That night, though, she dropped the bombshell.

'We were out, Thea and I, and we were on one of our biggest ever benders. I mean, we can both drink, but that night we were *so* pissed. I mean, properly pissed. Rupert was away, and Nell was at a friend's for the night, and I don't remember where you were. It wasn't long after you'd started working here. Anyway, we were in All Bar One, and …'

And she told me the whole story. How two men had come in, acquaintances of theirs, both out without their wives, and how the four of them had carried on drinking together until closing time, and then somebody had suggested, half-jokingly, that it might be fun to get a hotel room and order room service and have a bit of a party, and how they'd ended up getting not one hotel room but two, and then the obvious had happened. And how Isla had actually ended up dating her guy, Alan, for a month or two afterwards – 'well, I say dating. Having an affair with, more accurately,' she said – but how it had then fizzled out, and she hadn't seen him since. But how things had turned out a little differently for Thea. Because, a few weeks later, Thea had discovered she was pregnant. She'd hoped, prayed, that the baby was Rupert's, even though she'd had a feeling, right from the beginning. But when Zander was born she'd managed to do a sneaky DNA test, and her fears were realized. The baby wasn't Rupert's. He was the child of the man she'd had the one-night stand with. Horrified, she had told nobody except Isla, desperate to stop Rupert finding out, and as far as I knew he still didn't know, still thought Zander had been his baby. She didn't tell the biological father either, Isla said.

'But I'm pretty sure he suspects, Flora. Because just look at him. Look how like his real dad Zander looks.'

And she was right. Zander looked exactly like his real dad. That hair, those eyes. The likeness was, when you thought about it, unmistakable, and it still astounded me that, even now, it seemed that nobody else had ever guessed, or even suspected. How nobody else knew that Zander was, quite, quite obviously, Greg Garrington's son.

26

THEA

'Thea, I'm really not sure what your barrister can do with this information in court. I mean, it's great that you're remembering things, finally. But – I mean, are you *remembering*, really? We'd need proof, you know? And … well, how likely is it, when you think about it? That somebody deliberately put your baby back outside in your car, on one of the hottest days of the year? Who would do that? The house was full of your family and friends. Why would any of them do something so wicked? What would the motive be? It would be murder, plain and simple. And with not a shred of evidence? Unless somebody actually confessed, you'd have a pretty impossible time convincing a jury.'

Bernard Gilchrist grimaced at me, tapping his pen on the legal pad on the desk in front of him. My solicitor was a short, rotund man with cheeks so pink they looked as if he spent several minutes scrubbing them with wire wool every morning. To his left, his colleague Robina Watson was nodding, agreeing with him.

'I feel for you, Thea, I really do. It's a terrible thing you're dealing with. But you took responsibility for your child's death right from the beginning, remember? To change your story now … I mean, the jury just needs to decide whether the mitigating factors – your probable postnatal depression, your alcohol issues

177

at the time – are enough to find you not guilty of involuntary manslaughter. To begin to suggest at this late stage that the baby's death wasn't down to you at all, that somebody *killed* him ... well ...' She sighed heavily. She was in her fifties, an attractive woman with auburn hair in a severe, upswept bun, her skin free of make-up other than a slash of vibrant red lipstick. 'I just don't think it's going to help, to start throwing accusations around, with zero evidence. I'm sorry, Thea.'

I looked from one to the other, a tight knot forming in my chest. I knew they were right, but I'd woken up this morning feeling more convinced than ever that no matter how impossible it was, I had to try to work out why I was so sure now that things didn't happen the way everyone said they did. The fact that my solicitors clearly thought I was crazy was a blow, but I'd half-expected it. I was going to have to do this on my own.

That afternoon, I cleared all my *Just Enfant* paperwork off the dining table and sat down with my notebook. It was raining, one of those raw, early February days when it never seems to get quite bright enough to turn the lights off, the wind making the windows rattle, the sky bruised, grey with angry purple patches.

Nell was coming home later, after school, but I had several hours before she'd be dropped off, and I needed to do this *now*, feeling that if I wrote it all down it might suddenly become clearer. It was probably pointless, but at least I would feel that I was doing *something*. So, how should I go about it? I thought for a moment, trying to separate my own feelings from this, to think about it dispassionately. I needed to think like a detective, I decided – needed to treat it like a crime scene, with an unsolved murder. If I was Poirot or Miss Marple or someone like that, I'd treat everyone as a potential suspect, wouldn't I? And then look for motive. So that's what I'd do.

I began with a list of everyone who'd been in the house that afternoon. Me, obviously, and Isla, and Nell. Flora. Rupert, later.

178

And two Garringtons, Greg and Millie. Seven of us, but only four to consider if I was ruling myself out, and the children too. Eight-year-old girls didn't kill babies, especially as both Nell and Millie had adored Zander so much. He was like a real live doll to those two. I crossed out their names and looked at the list, trying to pretend that I didn't know these people, trying to be objective. Isla, Flora, Rupert and Greg. Shit, if any of them saw that I was doing this they'd think I'd finally lost it, wouldn't they? But I'd started now. I took a deep breath, cracked my knuckles and added a column to the right headed 'Possible Motive'.

Right, Isla first. I wrote down (*did she drive car home?*) in brackets after her name, then paused. I still had no idea what that would signify, but it needed to be asked, and noted. My pen hovered on the motive column. God, this was hard. Then I wrote: *was unhappy about me having children, especially when Zander was born. Resented time I spent with them and not with her.*

Hardly a motive for *murder* though, I thought. Nobody kills a baby just because they're not getting to spend as much time as they used to with the child's mother. Ludicrous. Still, carry on. OK, Flora. I blew out forcefully. This was stupid. I couldn't remotely think of a motive for Flora. She was good at her job, good with the kids, kept herself to herself … I left the line blank for now and moved on to Rupert. Shit. OK.

We hadn't been getting on. He hadn't bonded well with Zander. Possibly suspected he wasn't his father.

I stared at the words. Written down, it looked so callous, so cruel. But, looking back, if I was honest I think Rupert knew, or at least suspected, right from the start. It was just so bloody obvious. Zander looked so … so different, from any of us. I was so dark, my hair such a deep brown it was almost black, Nell's too, our eyes both a matching chocolate. And although Rupert shaved his head, what hair he did have was brown too, not quite as dark as ours but still dark. Then there was Zander – the

179

blondest, most blue-eyed baby ever, his hair almost white, his eyes bright as a summer sky.

I'd been horrified, when I'd seen him, when the doctor first put him on my chest in the delivery room, when Rupert had leaned in to drop a kiss on his new son's head. Well, not horrified, not by Zander, that sounds dreadful – I loved him desperately, almost painfully, from that first second, just as I had Nell. But I'd hoped so fervently, so feverishly, through my entire pregnancy, that my gut feeling was wrong, that this would be my husband's child. That I wouldn't be punished for my one, huge mistake, for getting drunk and sleeping with Greg. That I'd been weak enough, yet again, to be led astray by Isla, and this time with unthinkable consequences.

It had been a moment of madness, something I'd bitterly regretted from the moment I'd crawled out of that hotel room bed, something that had haunted me every day since. But as soon as I saw Zander, in that first second, I knew. I knew he was Greg's, and that a lifetime of deceit and pain lay ahead.

Rupert said nothing, not initially, but I would see him sometimes, in those early days, staring at Zander while he slept, running a finger across that white-blond hair, a slight frown on his face.

I managed to avoid Greg for about two weeks, sending Flora or Nell to the door when he came to drop off or collect Millie, but I knew I couldn't do it forever. And so came the day when Rupert was at home, all of us there together, and Greg brought both Millie and Sienna round, the younger girl desperate to meet this beautiful baby her big sister kept coming home full of stories about.

Zander was in his pram in the corner of the room, and the three Garringtons stood around it, Sienna and Millie cooing and stroking, while I sat rigid in an armchair, waiting for the inevitable, my stomach churning so badly I thought I might actually vomit.

It didn't take long. Greg stared into the pram for a moment, then turned to look at me, his face such a picture of fear and realization that for a moment I was transfixed, unable to move or speak. Then he turned away again and I knew that he knew, and then I looked at my husband and instantly knew that he knew too. His eyes were glued to the little tableau in the corner, flitting between Greg and the white-blonde heads of Millie and Sienna, and there was so much pain in his eyes that my heart suddenly felt as if it was breaking.

And still – and this was almost the weirdest, most bizarre thing about this whole ludicrous situation – nobody said a word. Not ever. I never admitted it, Rupert never asked me, Greg never confronted me. *Why?* Why on earth did none of us ever talk about it? Were we really all happy to live a lie, live out this unspoken conspiracy? It seemed so.

Rupert never spent much alone time with Zander, not like he had with Nell, never truly bonded, but when we were together as a family he was fine, playing with the baby, feeding him, smiling at him. Nobody would ever have known. How crazy was that? He just carried on, and he and Greg carried on acting totally normally when they were together, too. They were never best mates, but on social occasions, at parties, they'd always end up drinking beer together, chatting football or cricket or politics or whatever, and that didn't change.

The way they behaved, both of them, meant that I was able to kid myself, a lot of the time, that it was all OK, that neither of them knew anything at all. And I took that, and I ran with it, because that way I could live with the guilt a little more easily. That way, the shame of what I'd done wouldn't completely destroy me. And so that was how it was, for months. All three of us, living a big fat lie. Four of us, if you count Isla, the only person I'd actually told. All of us, sharing an unspoken secret.

I'd stopped breastfeeding Zander within a couple of months. My milk had begun to dry up, something I was still convinced was a physical symptom of my inner turmoil, and he wasn't getting enough food, waking in the night, crying with hunger. I knew Rupert thought it was strange, uncaring of me, to stop so soon, but how could I explain?

By then, I was as sure as I could be about Zander's parentage, but even so, I needed to know for definite, just in case. So, like in a scene from a soap opera, I furtively rummaged through Greg's jacket in the hall one day when he was drinking coffee in the kitchen while he waited for Millie. I found a comb, which I sent off to one of those online DNA test companies. And of course, the test was conclusive.

Probability of paternity given the DNA evidence is at least 99.9999% compared to an untested random man of the UK population.

I still remembered that there were four 9s after the decimal point.

I started avoiding Annabelle after that, too, making excuses to rush off when I saw her at the school gates or during Millie/Nell exchanges, although I was pretty certain that she, like most people, never suspected a thing. She never even remarked on Zander's colouring, just admired his good looks.

Poor, innocent, sweet Annabelle. I hated myself even more each time I bumped into her, feeling lower and more depressed daily. It was, later on, easy to explain those feelings away as post-natal depression, to use that as an excuse for what happened, but I knew it was the guilt that was predominantly to blame. It was around then that my drinking got worse, my need to escape from what I had done leading me to seek oblivion from time to time, the strain of living with it every day sometimes overwhelming. And still, the secret remained a secret, even though it wasn't a secret at all, not really, because we all knew the truth. Twisted, wrong, perverse, wasn't it? But that was what we all chose to do, to ignore it, to carry on. And so it continued.

I dragged my thoughts back from the convoluted mess my life had become and tried to concentrate on my list. Rupert.

We hadn't been getting on. He hadn't bonded well with Zander. Possibly suspected he wasn't his father.

I crossed out the words 'possibly suspected' and instead wrote 'knew'. He did, of course he did. But was that a motive, really? If you think a child isn't yours, you don't hurt the child, do you? Of course you don't. It's not the child's fault. You're more likely to want to hurt the mother, punish her for being unfaithful. Although ... my breath started to quicken. What would hurt a mother more than to kill her child? And even worse, to kill her child and *make her think she had done it*? It would be the ultimate revenge, wouldn't it – to take away the thing that is most precious to your cheating, lying bitch of a wife, and then get her locked up for years too, as a sort of bonus? Oh my god. Could Rupert ... was it possible?

I flung the pen down onto the table, where it landed with a clatter, and stood up, my whole body suddenly shaking. It was the most logical motive so far, but Rupert? This was my husband, a man who I'd loved and trusted for years, a man who I'd rarely even seen roused to temper until recent months, never mind hurt anyone.

I started to pace the room, my mind racing. Rupert couldn't, wouldn't. And yet, grief and anger and betrayal might do terrible things to someone, might cause them to do things they would never normally dream of. And Zander wasn't, after all, Rupert's son. They were not related, not at all. Could what I had done, my deceit, have made my husband do something so terrible? If it did, then it was my fault after all, that Zander had died. It was all down to me, whichever way you looked at it.

I stopped pacing, trying to calm myself, deliberately slowing my breathing. Stop winding yourself up, Thea, I thought. This is all just speculation. Finish what you're doing first, then think about what it all might mean. I sat down again, reached for the pen and tapped it on the paper next to Flora's name. I needed to write *something* next to it. I thought for a moment, then scribbled:

was sometimes annoyed by his crying when she was trying to work.
It was pathetic, but it was all I had. And it had been Flora who'd found Zander, who'd run frantically inside with my dead baby in her arms, shaking and crying, horrified. You can't fake that sort of shock, that grief. This wasn't Flora. Move on.

Greg.

I looked at the last name on my list:

knew/suspected he was Zander's father. Looked terrified when he realized. Didn't want Annabelle to find out?

But again, would anyone go as far as murdering a child to stop his wife finding out that he'd been unfaithful? It wouldn't really help in any case, not when so many people knew, or suspected, the truth. Annabelle could easily find out, couldn't she, whether Zander was dead or alive? Rupert could have gone to her and told her what he suspected at any time. I was surprised he hadn't, in a way. Wrecking Greg's marriage would be a good way to get revenge on him …

My head was starting to throb. I put the pen down again and stared at my list. That was all I had for now. And, now that it was all there in black and white, the possible motives of three of these people seemed tenuous, at best. Isla, Flora, Greg? No. There was only one person on this list who really had a reason to kill Zander. To destroy my life. To punish me. I felt a sudden rush of nausea, and clasped my hands to my mouth, willing myself not to be sick.

Rupert.

If I didn't kill Zander, if I *did* take him inside, and put him safely in his pram, then the only other person who could realistically have put him back in harm's way, who had a real motive, was my husband. Rupert.

'I think Rupert killed Zander,' I whispered.

27

ANNABELLE

'Wonderful. The velvet looks amazing, thank you.'

I smiled at the two young men on the ladders by the tall windows, and they mumbled an acknowledgement, concentrating on getting the final folds of the deep rose-coloured fabric to fall perfectly to the deep pile, shell-pink carpet below. Draping the windows in great swags like this instead of using formal curtains had been Flora's idea, and it had been a genius one, the perfect finishing touch.

We were basically temporarily redecorating an entire room for this week's biggest event – a pyjama-party-style baby shower for a mum-to-be in Malmesbury. Wife of a wealthy London stockbroker, Octavia MacdonaldBrown had given up her Mayfair art gallery job as soon as she'd fallen pregnant and had begun to nest in the couple's country home. Now, with just weeks to go before the baby, a little girl, was born, it appeared she'd stopped going out at all.

'It's this *bump*, Annabelle,' she'd said to me earlier with a pained expression on her beautiful face. 'I just don't have anything to *dress* it in.'

The pyjama party baby shower had hence been the perfect solution. Octavia had asked me to order twenty pairs of baby pink silk pyjamas – the tops with her guests' names embroidered across the back in fuchsia – with matching faux fur mule slippers.

The pink theme carried through to the food – there would be rosé champagne and pink lemonade, smoked salmon canapés and beetroot hummus, rhubarb fools and raspberry cupcakes. A manicurist who'd been instructed to bring only shades like 'Pink Bubblegum', 'Cotton Candy' and 'Misty Rose' had been hired, and a flashing pink neon sign rigged up above the door of the dining room, pronouncing that 'Girls Do It Better'.

'No gender stereotyping here then,' Flora had muttered sarcastically as Octavia had waved us off after our first visit, and I tended to agree with her. Neither of my girls were particularly into pink, and it wasn't something I'd ever encouraged, not being the biggest pink fan myself. But hey, a well-paying event was a well-paying event, and money definitely seemed to be no object to Octavia, who had declared at that first meeting that none of the nineteen rooms in their stunning Victorian Gothic mansion was right for the party, and asked us if we could redecorate the little-used formal dining room for the occasion.

'We can change it back afterwards. Toby won't care. Probably won't even notice. He prefers to eat in the kitchen most of the time anyway,' she'd said breezily, giving us an eyewateringly large budget for a new carpet, curtains and paintwork.

We'd rented several chaises longues upholstered in orchid chenille, due to be delivered on Friday morning for the party that evening, and the flowers for the tables – stargazer lilies, alstroemeria, gerberas and hydrangeas – were all arranged too. Now, on Wednesday morning, the paint was dry, the carpet in and the windows almost finished, meaning Flora and I could relax and concentrate on a couple of other little jobs before returning here to make sure everything ran perfectly on the day.

Relaxing, though, was not something I was finding easy at the moment. My low-level anxiety of recent weeks had worsened, for reasons I couldn't quite understand, but it seemed as though a strange current of unease was rippling through my home, as if something unnamed was bubbling menacingly under the surface, about to erupt.

We'd talked to Oliver, Greg and I, about the wingless flies, and he'd totally denied any involvement, yelling that he always got the blame for everything, and that it was 'probably that little brat, Sienna'. I'd seen the look in his eyes, though, when we first confronted him, and I knew. I knew he was lying, and maybe I would have too, at his age, in his position, but I still hated it, hated the fact that my baby son, my first born, was lying to me, was acting so oddly, seemed to have such a violent streak, seemed capable suddenly of such nasty things. It scared me, and I had no idea what to do about it.

Then, this morning, something even more horrible had happened, and now I couldn't banish the awful, gripping fear that Olly might be behind that too. I'd been making breakfast, pausing to sip my coffee while I gazed out of the kitchen window, eyes flitting across the garden, making a mental list of jobs to be done out there, when I noticed it, an unmoving reddish mass at the edge of the lawn. What was that? A dead fox, maybe? I'd slipped some outdoor shoes on and walked down the garden to investigate, but as I'd got nearer I'd seen that it was no fox, but something familiar, something so familiar and, in its present state, so horrific, that I'd actually screamed. Frozen to the spot, I stood and pointed as Greg and the girls came running out of the house, and then they saw it too and Millie and Sienna both burst into frightened tears.

'Hamish! Poor, poor Hamish! What's happened to him, Mummy?' Sienna wailed, clinging to my legs, eyes wide and terrified, Millie covering her eyes with her hands, sobbing. Hamish was the big ginger tomcat owned by our nearest neighbours, the Wares, but he'd always spent a lot of time in our garden, and Sienna, in particular, adored him. We'd never had dogs or cats, Greg and I knowing the bulk of the pet care would fall to us and our working hours just too long and erratic to make it fair on the animal, so Hamish had almost been a surrogate, a stand-in pet, Sienna spending hours playing with him on the lawn on sunny afternoons, cuddling him, even on occasion dressing the tolerant cat in her dolls' bonnets and laughing hysterically as he wandered off to climb a tree or chase a bird, looking like a feline Jane Austen taking a turn around the lawn.

Now, we saw, Hamish was very dead, a deep slash across the soft orange and white fur of his throat, his eyes wide open, unseeing. A fox maybe? A dog? But as Greg had swept our weeping daughters back into the house, muttering to me that he would deal with the corpse and break the bad news to the Wares, and I had turned to follow them inside, a movement up above caught my eye. It was Oliver, standing at his bedroom window, staring down into the garden, his face pale, blank. He'd caught my eye, met it for a moment, then turned away, and a chill ran through me that was nothing to do with standing in a windy garden so early in the morning in just a thin sweater and jeans. Olly? Could he? But *why*? Why would he?

I had said nothing to Greg this time, unable to face it, letting the theory of a dog or fox killing Hamish stand. I couldn't confront Oliver again, couldn't listen to him lying to me again. Something had to be done, though, if I was right, if I wasn't being paranoid, for how could we go on like this?

Flora had missed it all, out for her morning run when we'd found Hamish, but as we'd driven down to Malmesbury I'd asked her advice, yet again. She'd listened, raising her eyebrows when I told her about Oliver's silent watching from his window, and then shrugged.

'Annabelle, I just don't know. Killing a cat? Olly can be a bit aggressive with Sienna, and the flies thing was pretty horrible, but that's a whole new level. Are you sure it was him? Why would he? I've seen him stroking Hamish loads of times, talking to him. He loved that cat as much as the girls did, I'm sure he did. Maybe it really was just a fox?'

'Maybe. I don't know. Oh Flora, it's just all getting to me, you know?'

I hit the brake as the lights changed to red up ahead, then carried on talking.

'Olly just seems to have developed this *aggression*. He wasn't always like that, especially with Sienna. It started fairly recently, and I can't figure out why. It worries me, Flora. I'm scared he's going to hurt somebody, one day. Properly hurt somebody, I mean. I just don't know what to do ... telling him off just doesn't seem to make any difference ...'

'Oh, it won't come to that, come on.' Flora's hand briefly covered mine on the gearstick.

'It'll pass, this phase. And Sienna irritates him, that's all. It's the age difference. He's heading into his teens soon and she's still a baby. At least he and Millie have *some* interests in common – some of their games, even TV shows. Sienna is so much younger, it's tricky for him to relate to her. It'll get easier as they get older, wait and see.'

I gave her a sideways glance, but her words made sense, and some of my anxiety began to dribble away. She was right, of course she was.

'We ended up promising to get Sienna a kitten,' I said. 'After we've said for years we didn't have time for pets. It was the only thing that calmed her down. It has to be white, she says. So that she can call it Olaf. After the snowman, in flipping *Frozen*.'

Flora snorted, and I found myself smiling too.

'You'll love it, you know, when it arrives. It'll be good for you. It's a known fact that stroking a pet is very calming. Good for stress relief. Trust me.'

I took a hand off the wheel for a moment to poke her gently on the arm.

'How did you get so wise, Flora Applegate? Honestly, you do make me feel better. It's like talking to a sensible older sister sometimes. I forget that I'm more than a decade older than you.'

There was a second or two of silence.

'Until you look in the mirror, obviously,' she said, then shrieked and ducked as I yelled 'OI CHEEKY!', my left arm flailing at her as I tried to keep the car steady with my right.

We took a diversion to Cheltenham on the way home, me needing to collect a pair of shoes I'd ordered from Cavendish House, Flora wanting to pick up a few bits and pieces in Boots, both of us fancying a quick mooch around the shops.

I parked the car in one of the spaces in front of the municipal offices on the Promenade, agreeing with Flora to meet back there in an hour, and nipped across to Cavendish House, buying some new tights too, before whiling away a good fifteen minutes browsing the shiny shelves of Space NK. As I left, clutching a tiny bag containing an equally tiny but vastly expensive pot of moisturizer, I almost walked straight into Thea Ashfield.

'Annabelle! I'm so sorry, I was miles away.'

I stared at her for moment, shocked not just at her unexpected presence but also at her dishevelled appearance, her hair greasy and pulled back from her thin face, her skin dry, lips chapped, eyes red-rimmed.

Then I mentally shook myself and held out a hand. Being polite wouldn't kill me, I thought, and no matter what I thought about this woman and what she'd done, she was clearly in a bad way.

'Thea, how are you? I wasn't looking where I was going either, don't worry. How are … how are things going?'

She took my outstretched hand and gripped it between both of hers, her black leather bag sliding down her shoulder to rest in the crook of her arm. Her hands were freezing, and reflexively I began to rub them with my own.

'You're so cold! Do you ... do you fancy a coffee? I have to meet Flora, but I have about half an hour.'

Gosh, what was I doing? It was too late now though – Thea was nodding gratefully.

'We could nip up to the Costa in Waterstones? I'd love a coffee, actually,' she said, and I nodded. It was close, and I had my excuse to leave quickly. A quick drink, and I'd be out of there.

It was warm in Costa, and quiet, just a few tables occupied by couples or small groups of elderly women, gossiping over tea and muffins, winter coats draped over nearby empty chairs. The air was aromatic, the scent of coffee mingling with warm caramel. A couple of people looked curiously at Thea as we entered, and I wondered for a moment if this had been a good idea, being seen in public with a woman who had done what she had done, but nobody said anything, and the moment passed. I was here now.

I sent Thea to find a table while I got our drinks, and she chose one in the far back corner, next to the steamed-up windows that looked out onto the wide roof terrace. I sat down opposite her, and we made small talk for a few minutes, chatting a little awkwardly about Millie and Nell, and about work, as if things were completely normal, as if I didn't know that this bedraggled, broken-looking woman had left her baby to die in a hot car, and would soon be on trial for the crime. And then, quite suddenly, she put her mug down on the table and leaned across towards me, gripping my right forearm.

'Annabelle. I don't know what to do.'

She was speaking in an urgent whisper now, her fingers digging into my flesh.

'I've been ... I've been remembering things. About that day, the day Zander ... the day it happened. And I'm scared, Annabelle. I don't think it happened like everyone said it did.'

I pulled my arm from her grip and stared at her. Flora had vaguely mentioned something about this, after she'd met up with Thea on Monday, told me that Thea's memories were coming back, that she was beginning to recall the events of the day Zander died, but she hadn't been specific, and I hadn't asked, too busy concentrating on dinner and trying to make the kids finish their homework.

'What do you mean, it didn't happen like everyone said? I don't understand, Thea? I didn't think there was any question about what happened – I mean, you ... you left him in the car, didn't you?'

I flinched inwardly as I said the words, but she was shaking her head, eyes fixed on mine.

'That's just it. That's what I thought happened, that's what *everyone* thought, or assumed. At least, that's what everyone *said*, at the time. But Annabelle, I remember now. I *remember* bringing Zander inside, putting him in his pram. I remember it clearly. At first I thought I was just imagining it, because I couldn't bear to accept what I'd done. But every day, it's becoming more and more vivid, and I know, I just know, that it's a memory, Annabelle. A real memory, not just my imagination. I *did* bring him in. And that means ... well ... it means something dreadful, doesn't it?'

I shook my head, frowning, unable to grasp what she was getting at.

'That would mean ... well, what? You must have left him in the car, because that's where Flora found him. Otherwise—' I stopped, stunned, as realization dawned. No. Come on. Was that what she was suggesting, really?

'Hang on ... are you really saying that you think somebody put him back there, in the car, deliberately? Seriously?'

She nodded so vigorously that a strand of hair came loose from her messy ponytail, flopping down across her face. She pushed it back roughly, tucking it behind her ear, and suddenly her eyes filled with tears.

'I know, I know, it sounds insane. And I have no idea why I'm telling you this, and I'm so sorry to lay this on you. I have no right. But Annabelle, I *know* now that I didn't do this. And that means somebody else did. And there were only a few other people in the house that day, and now I don't know who to trust, or what to do ...'

A sob escaped her, and a man a few tables away turned abruptly, casting his eyes around the café, clearly trying to see where the noise had come from, before turning back to his companion again. I rummaged in my coat pocket, found a tissue and passed it to Thea, my mind racing.

'Thea, I don't know what to say.'

She shook her head, dabbing at her eyes.

'No, no, you don't have to say anything. I'm so sorry. You must think I'm crazy. Please, don't say anything to anyone, will you? I can't prove anything anyway, so ... look, you need to go; it's getting late; you're meeting Flora. Sorry, Annabelle. Thanks for the coffee.'

She was standing up now, pulling her coat on, fumbling for her bag.

'Sorry,' she said again. 'Put it down to the ramblings of a mad woman. Grief, guilt, all that stuff. But thank you, for listening. And for your kindness, you know, to Nell. I don't know how she would have coped, without Millie and ... well, without you and your family, these past months. I appreciate it more than you know. Bye, Annabelle.'

And then she was gone, moving swiftly across the café and out of the door, a slight figure hunched inside a too-big camel coat. I sat there, staring after her, and then it hit me, like an icy cold wave, making me gasp. Oh my ... GOD. Could this be happening? For months, I had thought terrible thoughts about Thea, and the dreadful, unthinkable thing she had done, and yet now, I had sat in front of her, and looked into her eyes, and there had been something … something in her expression, in the tone of her voice … something which, in a matter of seconds, had changed everything.

I think she's telling the truth, I thought.

28

THEA

Nell was bright red in the face, tears streaking down her cheeks, huge sobs sending spasms through her slender body. I'd tried for a full five minutes now to calm her, to hold her, but she was too angry, too distraught to let me anywhere near her.

The change Karen Ballerton, the therapist, had made in my daughter had lasted precisely eight days, I calculated, trying to give myself something else to think about for a moment, to distract myself – I felt on the verge of joining in with Nell's hysteria, and that would help nobody.

Even worse, Rupert would be here shortly to collect her – he normally picked her up from school on a Wednesday, but today he'd been delayed – and the thought of him arriving while she was in this state horrified me.

I wasn't even totally sure what had precipitated this outburst – she had come home from school in a perfectly normal mood, drunk a glass of milk and eaten two chocolate chip cookies, and then happily sat down at the dining room table to do her homework. My mobile had rung just as I was about to join her, my solicitor calling to clarify a few small points about my case, and I'd chatted quietly to him, moving away to stand by the window, not wanting to disturb my daughter's concentration.

It was only when I finally sat down, too, muttering that I needed to send a follow-up email, that Nell suddenly began to fly into a rage.

'Do it somewhere else, Mum! That tapping noise is SO ANNOYING!'

I'd looked down at my keyboard and back at Nell, surprised. I didn't think I was a particularly heavy-handed typist, and I'd often sat there working while she did her homework across the table from me.

'Sorry, darling. I didn't realize it irritated you, I can—'

'OH, FORGET IT! I DON'T WANT TO DO THIS STUPID HOMEWORK ANYWAY!'

She swiped violently at her school books, sending them crashing to the floor, and then the tears began, as my daughter stomped around the room, kicking chairs and howling, before slumping to the floor in a sobbing heap, refusing to let me anywhere near her.

Now, I stood over her, my gut twisting with misery, fists clenched. What was wrong with her? This wasn't just grief over her brother's death, there was something else going on here. I suddenly wondered if it was the call from my solicitor. Had she been listening in, as we'd chatted briefly about the upcoming trial? Was it that that was frightening her? Could she be that scared of me going to prison? I mentally kicked myself. *Idiot*. Why hadn't I left the room to take the call?

We had talked to Nell about the chances of me going to jail, both Rupert and I, regularly over the past few months, tried to reassure her that it was unlikely, but that if the worst happened that it probably wouldn't be for long (this with crossed fingers – we both knew that if things went wrong, I could get years) and that she would be well looked after by Daddy while I was … while I was *away*. She'd seemed to take it in her stride, but now I thought that maybe my tough-acting little daughter was more affected by the prospect than we had realized. The thought sent a wave of guilt through me, my chest tightening. I wiped a bead of sweat from my top lip and reached for her again.

'Nell, darling, please … come here.'

She lifted her face from her knees, and the pain in her eyes was almost more than I could stand.

'Mummy, I'm scared …'

'Oh Nell. My darling, darling Nell. What is it? What are you frightened of?'

She gulped, and swallowed, wiping a hand across her face.

'I don't want you to go to jail.'

Her voice was little more than a hoarse whisper, and my chest tightened further, a physical pain now. I'd been right, and it was unbearable. I sank to the floor and pulled her towards me, wrapping her tightly in my arms, and now she wasn't resisting, her body shaking with fresh sobs, her face buried in my neck. I rocked gently back and forth, stroking her soft curls, murmuring in her ear.

'Everything will be all right, Nell, I promise you. Everything's going to work out just fine. Don't cry, baby, please. I love you so much, and I'm so sorry. I'm so, so sorry. It will all be OK, Nell …'

But would it, really? As I tried to comfort my trembling daughter, anger began to rise inside me, a hot rush of rage mixed with fear and, now, something akin to despair. Why had I said what I'd said to Annabelle earlier? We weren't even close, so why on earth had I told her what I was increasingly thinking – that someone else, not me, was responsible for all this pain, this grief? She must have thought I was barking mad, and who would blame her, maybe I was. And if I doubted myself – if even *I* didn't entirely believe what I was saying about what happened the day Zander died, then how on earth could I expect anyone else to? I knew, though, that now I'd come this far, in my thought process if nothing else, I had to keep going. I had to think, logically, about that day, about the timescale, timeline, whatever it was called in those TV cop dramas. I had to work out if Rupert would have had *time* …

'Mummy? Mum? I'm OK now. You're squeezing me so hard I can't breathe!'

Nell was trying to wriggle out of my arms, eyes puffy and red but a hint of a smile back on her face.

'Oh darling, I'm sorry, I was miles away! Are you sure …?'

She was standing up now, straightening the tunic of her school uniform, looking down at me and nodding.

'Yes, I'm fine. Shall I finish my homework and then can we watch *Friends*? Please?'

I clambered to my feet and laughed, massively relieved at this sudden return to normality. Nell had only recently discovered *Friends*, and would sit, captivated and giggling, in front of the endless reruns on one of the satellite TV channels for hours if I let her. I didn't mind too much to be honest – I was quite a fan myself, and often joined her if I needed an hour of escapism.

'Of course. I'd love a *Friends* binge actually. I'll take my laptop into the kitchen so you have some peace while you finish off, and then we can eat in front of the telly. Lasagne for dinner? I think there's some garlic bread in the freezer too.'

Nell nodded happily, her outburst seemingly forgotten. She gathered her books from where she'd flung them onto the floor and arranged them neatly back on the dining table, even humming to herself now, and I picked up my laptop and files and left her to it, marvelling at how children could switch from extreme distress to placidity so seamlessly.

As I settled down in the kitchen, though, I wondered if I needed to book another session with Karen Ballerton, and scribbled it on my to-do list. Maybe she could help Nell come to terms with the idea of me potentially going to prison, help her with some sort of extra coping strategies. A shiver ran through me. And maybe Nell could share them with me …

Stop it. *Stop it.* Don't think about going to prison, try to find a way of staying *out* of it, I berated myself. Right, Thea, think. I leafed through the file of legal paperwork until I found the document that included the timeline Bernard Gilchrist, my solicitor, had drawn out for me when I was trying to get the events of the fourth of September clear in my head. He'd put it together based on the timings given in all the statements the police had taken from me and the others, and now I studied it carefully, running my finger down the page, reading the notes attached to each of the marked times.

Approx. 3 p.m. – Thea Ashfield, Nell Ashfield, Zander Ashfield (deceased) and Isla Laird return to Montpellier Terrace.

That had come from Isla's statement, of course, and had probably been verified by Flora, who was the only person in the house when we got back, and the time seemed accurate enough.

Approx. 3.30 p.m. – Flora Applegate enters sitting room to find Thea Ashfield and Isla Laird asleep. Takes Nell Ashfield upstairs to play, returns to work in her room, does not check on Zander Ashfield as hears no noise and assumes is asleep in pram in corner of room.

My stomach flipped, as it had the first time Bernard went through this with me in his office. I knew that Nell had been able to verify to the police that this was what had happened – that she and Flora had gone upstairs together, but that neither of them had checked on her little brother. My first anguished reaction, in those early days, had been tears and rage – why hadn't Flora looked in the pram? *Why?* If Flora had checked, at that point when she was taking Nell upstairs, if she had looked and realized Zander wasn't there, she would have raised the alarm immediately, and it would have meant that my baby would only have been in the car alone for half an hour, and that would have meant ... well, that *might* have meant ... that he would still be alive. If only Flora had looked, had taken those few seconds to walk to the pram and peer in, everything would have been different. *Everything.*

Even so, I never confronted her about it, because I knew I

couldn't. I knew it wasn't fair, or right. She wasn't a nanny, she was my PA, and although she helped out with the children now and again, it wasn't her job to take charge of them. And I knew how much pain she was in, how much she was suffering, as we all were, and how dreadful it would be to try to shift any of the blame onto her when what had happened was entirely down to me. The baby wasn't her responsibility, he was mine, and mine only, but the agony of that terrible *what if* had haunted my dreams for weeks.

Now though, reading the 3.30 p.m. note again, I was thinking something entirely different. Because now, I believed that at 3.30 p.m., Zander *was* in his pram. He was in his pram, safely sleeping, just like Flora assumed he was. He was, because now I remembered bringing him in from the car, laying him there, dropping a kiss on his warm, soft cheek before sinking onto the sofa, The rest of the afternoon was still a blur but that bit, that crucial part, was so clear. So *real*. And now, I still wished that Flora had checked on him, but for a totally different reason. Now, I wished she'd checked, because then she would know too. She would know that at 3.30 p.m., my baby was safe. And yet …

And yet he was still dead, wasn't he? I thought for another moment. What else could have happened during this time period? Isla could have woken up, and taken Zander back outside. But why? Why would she? OK, she didn't coo over him like others did, but we'd just had a lovely afternoon out when, as far as I knew, he'd been no trouble at all. If she ever had an urge to hurt him, it was unlikely to have been then. OK, what else? Flora could have come back downstairs, while we were both asleep, and put him outside. But again, why on earth would she? She just had no motive whatsoever. Those two simply didn't make any sense to me as suspects, but I had to consider them, didn't I? I couldn't trust anyone, believe anyone's story, not while I was doing this. I took a deep breath and read on.

Approx. 5 p.m. – Rupert Ashfield returns home. Flora Applegate calls down to suggest he be quiet as Isla Laird and Thea and Zander Ashfield are sleeping. Checks on his daughter Nell Ashfield in her room and retires to garden.

I read the entry again and swallowed, hard. This was from Rupert's statement. At this point Nell was upstairs playing alone in her room, and Flora was up there too, working. Isla and I were still asleep. Who would see, then, if Rupert had slipped into the sitting room, taken Zander from his pram and carried him out to the car? Nell's and Flora's rooms were both at the back of the house, the car at the front. It would be risky, yes – it wasn't the quietest road, always traffic and pedestrians, and there were houses all the way along, but if he'd thrown a blanket over Zander, if he'd covered him and moved quickly …

I pushed the sheet of paper away, suddenly feeling dizzy. This was crazy. I was ill, I had to be, to even *think* like this, to think my husband, my friends, capable … then I took a deep breath. No. Come on, play the game. This wouldn't work if I was going to start bringing emotion into it. I wasn't accusing Rupert. I wasn't accusing anybody. I was just looking at alternatives, at possibilities, that was all. There was no need to get upset. I needed to do this calmly, dispassionately. Simply look at the timeline, and think about different scenarios, different ways this could have played out, as if I had no connection with the case.

I inhaled again and reached for the list, forcing my body to relax. So, logically then … logically, if Rupert *had* returned Zander to the car at around 5 p.m., and Zander's body had been found at … I ran my finger down the page … approximately 6.15 p.m., that was an hour and fifteen minutes. Was that long enough? It was. I'd learned far, far too much in recent months about the horrors of leaving anyone, animal or human, in a hot car. The temperature on a day like that would have risen to fatal levels inside an hour. *It was long enough.*

The light-headedness was returning, but I made myself read on.

Approx. 5.30 p.m. – Greg and Millie Garrington arrive, let into house by Rupert Ashfield and seen briefly by Flora Applegate who comes downstairs to collect some files. Millie joins Nell upstairs in her bedroom. Greg joins Rupert Ashfield in garden where they remain.

Greg's and Rupert's statements agreed on this sequence of events. But ... I thought for a moment, trying to keep an open mind, to remain impartial, like an outsider. One of them could have been lying. *Both* of them could have been lying. Greg might not have gone straight out to the garden, could have said he needed the bathroom maybe, could have slipped into the sitting room before joining Rupert out back, and taken Zander ... it was still about forty-five minutes before his body was found, would that be long enough? Maybe. I couldn't rule Greg out, not yet. And Rupert could have left the garden at any point ... but why would those two cover for each other, if either of those scenarios were true? Rupert certainly wouldn't cover for Greg, would he? Not if he suspected, as I was positive he did, that Greg might be Zander's father. He'd do anything, surely, to get revenge on him for that, not protect him? Although ... oh God. What about the reverse? Would Greg cover for Rupert? He might, if he felt guilty enough. He might, if he thought it was better for everyone if Zander was no longer around ...

A shiver ran down my spine. Rupert. It all kept coming back to Rupert. Suddenly struggling to fight back tears, I read the final note.

Approx. 6.15 p.m. – Flora Applegate comes downstairs to dining room to file paperwork, hears commotion on street. Rushes outside, finds Zander Ashfield dead in car.

Dead. Dead in car. My baby. My baby, my love, my life. I stood up, pushing the piece of paper fiercely across the polished wood. It slid off the edge, fluttering to the carpet, and I stared at it. Nothing I could do, nothing I could say, would bring Zander back. But it was time to start asking questions. It was time to start confronting these people, my friends, my family. It was time to get to the truth. And if the truth was that I was insane, that it had been me after all who left Zander in the car to die, then so be it. But right now, I was fighting for *my* life. For my freedom, for my sanity, for my daughter's happiness. It was time to speak up, to tell everyone what I was thinking. To tell everyone what I remembered. And I was going to start right now.

PART TWO

29

THEA

I started with Isla. She'd been calling me, leaving messages I'd ignored, for days, since I'd told her I couldn't see her last weekend. So the next morning, Thursday, the morning after I'd gone through the police timeline, I gave her a call at work.

'Isla, I'm sorry. I've had a few tough days, and I shouldn't have cut you out. Are you coming down to Cheltenham this weekend? Please say you are?'

There was a pause on the line, but Isla could never be angry at me for long. She was coming, of course she was, she hated staying in London at weekends, and she'd love to come round tomorrow evening. Nell would be there – Rupert was away again, I hadn't asked where or with whom – but that would be fine. We could eat early, watch some TV, and then chat properly once Nell was in bed.

I was nervous on Friday evening, wandering distractedly from room to room, straightening cushions, lining up the wine glasses on the coffee table, lighting candles and then blowing them out again as Nell watched from her perch on the end of the living room sofa, a rather bemused look on her face.

'You'd think someone really important was coming. It's only *Isla*, Mum. Not Kate Middleton,' she said, as I passed through the

207

room once again, cloth in hand, swiping at imaginary particles of dust. I stopped dead and threw the cloth at her, and she yelped and ducked, then flung it back at me, both of us laughing now, the tension I was feeling ebbing away a little.

It eased further when Isla finally arrived, half an hour later than expected ('bloody Friday night traffic, the 417 was just *crawling*, I almost cracked the wine open in the car I got so desperate'), engulfing me in an enormous hug and brandishing Sauvignon Blanc and – to Nell's immense delight – a bag full of chocolate creme eggs.

'Creme eggs? In February? It's not Easter for yonks, where did those come from? *After* dinner, Nell,' I said, as my daughter tried to slip a surreptitious hand into the bag.

She groaned theatrically.

'They've been in the shops practically since Christmas,' Isla said, wriggling out of her tan-coloured knitted poncho with its dangling pompoms. 'Right, where are the glasses? Ahh, very organized. Well done, Thea. I'll do the drinks, you order the takeaway. I'd kill for Indian tonight, what do you think?'

She poured us two large glasses and joined Nell on the sofa, and as I headed out to pull the Indian restaurant menu from its drawer in the hall cabinet, I listened to their casual chitchat, suddenly wondering how on earth I could ask Isla what I wanted to ask her tonight. Yes, she'd struggled with the fact I'd chosen motherhood, disliked my children, ignored them even, but that had been in the past, in the early days. She and Nell got on fine now – in fact, Isla had made such an effort with Nell since Zander's death that I'd go as far as to say that they were actually quite fond of each other even – and as for Zander ... well, she hadn't exactly been all over him, but ... oh, this was ludicrous! How could I ask Isla – my oldest friend, my closest friend, the friend who knew all my secrets, who knew more about me than anyone, than my own husband – how could I ask her if she'd callously put my baby back into a hot car, one terrible afternoon back in September, and let him die? *How?*

And yet, I had to. I had to, even though it was highly likely, now I had decided to plead not guilty, that she, and Rupert too, maybe others, would be called as prosecution witnesses in my trial. I'd been shocked when Bernard Gilchrist had told me that, had warned me that the prosecution would want to establish my state of mind before Zander died, the extent of my depression and alcohol abuse, would use my friends and family to try to prove that I was a bad mother, neglectful, uncaring. Could I afford to alienate any of them now, with so much at stake? No matter the consequences, though, I had to ask Isla, had to ask all of them, one by one. Had to judge their reactions, had to see if there were any cracks in their stories. I had no choice, not anymore.

The Indian food was delicious, and to my surprise I ate as much as Nell and Isla did, suddenly ravenous, wolfing down naan bread and chicken tikka masala, scooping up dal and matar paneer, washing it back with mouthfuls of cold wine, but with sparkling water too, careful not to drink too much.

When Nell had been finally packed off to bed, shortly after nine, promising to read for just twenty minutes and then turn the light off, I sat down next to Isla on the sofa.

'Isla? I need to ask you something. This is going to sound really weird, OK ...'

I paused, and she looked at me quizzically.

'Weird is your normal, Ashfield. Shoot.'

I smiled, but a nervous flutter had started in my stomach, the food suddenly laying heavily.

'Right, well, it's about September. About the day Zander died. The thing is, I've started remembering things, finally. And ... well, I suppose I'm not sure if I'm really *remembering*, or if my mind's playing tricks on me. I know how things happened – well, I know how everybody *said* they happened. What *I assumed* happened. But these memories, or whatever they are – well, there are some contradictions, I suppose you could call them.'

'Contradictions?' Isla had put her wine glass down on the table as I'd been speaking, and now she turned to face me, frowning. 'What sort of contradictions? What do you mean?'

I put my own glass down too.

'Well, first of all … and this doesn't really make sense, no sense at all actually, but I always assumed I drove the car home from lunch that day. I mean, it was my car, and I always drove it, and obviously I shouldn't have that day, because I was pissed, but I assumed I did, and nobody said any different. I mean, *you* didn't say any different, did you?'

She was staring at me now, eyes wide. Was I imagining it, or had some of the colour drained from her face? She looked paler somehow, her skin milky against the deep red of her hair.

'The thing is, Isla, and this is going to sound mad, but as these memories have started to come back, I keep thinking that I didn't drive home after all. I mean, not that it matters, in the light of what happened after that, drink-driving is the least of it all. But I've got these pictures in my head … these … these *images*, and every time, I see myself in the passenger seat. Not in the driver's seat, Isla. And I don't know why. I mean, tell me I'm crazy, but … well, was I? Was I the passenger that day, and not the driver?'

Isla was sitting very still, eyes fixed on my face, and I definitely wasn't imagining it now – she was so pale her skin had developed a greenish tinge. My stomach lurched. Why was she reacting like that? What was …?

'Holy shit, Thea? Are you serious? Why would … why would I drive your car home? I was just as pissed as you, remember? And you *never* let me drive your car. Why would I suddenly drive that day? I can't believe you're asking me this. What do you think I am? For fuck's sake, Thea …'

She was on her feet now, pacing the room, repeating: 'Fucking

210

hell, are you serious? I mean, for fuck's sake …' over and over. I sat for a moment, watching her, then stood up too.

'OK, OK, I'm sorry. Isla, please, sit down. I'm sorry, OK? It's just an image, in my head … but you're right, it makes no sense. I'm just really confused, OK? I have all these pictures, flooding back, and I don't know how to make sense of them, don't know which are real and which aren't. I'm just trying to sort it all out in my mind, before the trial, you know? I'm sorry. Come on, sit down. Have some more wine.'

I sat down again, picking up her glass, topping it up with more wine and holding it out towards her, and she stopped pacing, stared at me again for a few moments, then came and sat next to me, grabbing the glass from my hand as she did so. She took several gulps, draining the glass, then put it down on the table.

'We're going to need more, if we're going to carry on with *this* conversation. You're a freaking nutter, you know that? Go on then, what other *memories* have come back? Anything else you want to accuse me of?'

She drew air quotes as she said the word 'memories', her tone deeply sarcastic. I looked at her for a moment, relieved that she hadn't walked out, and that her colour had returned to something near normal. Did I dare though, ask her this next question, the most important one? I had to, but the enormity of what I was about to say was suddenly hitting me. It was the sort of conversation that could destroy our friendship forever, and I couldn't bear that. I needed to ask her, but I needed to phrase it carefully.

'There is something else, yes.'

My hand fluttered to my throat, and then back to my lap. Isla was reaching for a new bottle of wine, one she'd popped in the cooler on the table earlier.

'Oh good. Go on then. Can't wait.'

The sarcasm was still there. I sat in silence as she picked up the opener and uncorked the bottle with a practised twist, then refilled our glasses. I took a deep breath. I'd just have to say it.

211

'I have another memory, Isla. And this is the craziest one of all, and please don't laugh. But … well, I know what's supposed to have happened is that I left Zander in the car, and then we fell asleep, and everyone assumed he was in his pram so nobody checked, and then he wasn't in his pram at all … but the thing is, Isla … the thing is, I *remember* now. I remember bringing him inside. I remember putting him in his pram. And *then* sitting down, and falling asleep. And so how can it be, that later he was back out in the car again? If what I remember is right, and every day now I remember it more clearly … if what I remember is right, how can that be, Isla? How did he get there? How did my baby get back into that car, when I brought him in, Isla? *How?*'

I was suddenly aware that I was on my feet again, my voice high-pitched, screaming the words at her, tears rolling down my face, and that Isla was staring up at me, open-mouthed, a look of pure horror on her face.

'Thea? Thea, what are you *talking* about? What are you …?'

And then there was a terrible wailing sound, a primal, guttural howling, and we turned in unison to see Nell, standing in the doorway in her pyjamas, fingers clawing at her hair.

'Nell!'

I reached for my daughter, and she staggered towards me, eyes blank, and collapsed into my arms.

30

ISLA

The wine bar was packed, bodies five deep at the counter, punters waving twenties or leaning provocatively forward in low-cut tops, trying to catch the barman's eye. The air was thick with beer and perfume and a hint of sweat – the smell of Friday night. Miraculously, I'd found a single empty stool at the far end, near the door to the toilets, and sat there, still reeling from what had happened at Thea's.

When Nell had come staggering in, making that hideous noise, sleepwalking or having a nightmare or whatever the hell was wrong with her, I'd simply walked out, left without another word, grabbing my bag and coat from the hall where I'd dumped them and slamming the front door hard behind me.

Once out on the street, I'd hesitated, suddenly unwilling to turn right and go back to my empty bedsit so early on a Friday night, and in desperate need of another drink. So I'd turned left instead, turning my collar up against the cold, walking so fast I was practically jogging, until somehow I found myself pushing open the door of the Montpellier wine bar, wincing as the wall of heat and noise hit me. I stumbled through the throng, the suited after-work crowd, the groups of overdressed women clinking Prosecco glasses, looking hopelessly for a quiet corner, then spotted the bar stool and bulldozed my way towards it.

Now, clutching a double whiskey, I gave the man behind me a further sharp elbow in the ribs as he leaned drunkenly and, seemingly, obliviously, against my back for the third time, and tried to breathe normally. I felt sick, but I knew it wasn't the alcohol. On the stools nearest to me, a woman in a black leather miniskirt was running her fingers lasciviously up the pinstriped thigh of a shaven-headed man, who responded by leaning over and licking her neck, slowly and noisily. I shuddered, downed my whiskey and gestured to the barman for another. He nodded, busy with an order, and further down the bar another lone drinker winked at me. I looked at him for a moment – he was quite attractive in a louche, Bill Nighy type of way – then looked away, my fingers tapping an impatient rhythm on the countertop.

Shit. My head was beginning to pound, my stomach churning. I was still in shock, I thought. Had that really happened at Thea's? Had she really asked me those questions, made those accusations? How much did she really remember? I shivered, despite the heat of the bar. I'd been terrified this might happen, that her memories might start to return. The traumainduced amnesia, or whatever it was called, had been such a gift, but now …

'There you go, love. Add it to your tab?'

Another whiskey had appeared in front of me. I pushed the empty glass towards the barman, mumbling an appropriate reply to his question, and picked up the new one, trying to ignore the tremor in my hands. As I drank, the fiery liquid searing my throat, I thought of those early days, the days when Thea and I were both young and single, when we would sit side by side in bars like these, drinking together, and dreaming.

Until everything changed. I hated it when she had Nell, hated it more than Thea ever knew. I *hated* it. I despised this mewling being who had taken my best friend away from me, who had turned her into this alien mother creature. She tried to be the same, when we were together, but I could tell her heart wasn't in it anymore, not like it used to be, and it broke mine. Things improved a little when Nell got older, went to school, became less dependent on Thea, easier to leave at home. I even started to like the kid a bit, to find her entertaining and intelligent and quite sweet on occasion, which came as a massive shock to me. It made Thea happy though, and so for a while things were good.

And then the silly cow got pregnant again. Got pregnant by fucking Greg Garrington, and decided to keep the baby. Seriously? SERIOUSLY? Who does that, for Christ's sake, when they're married to someone else? But that was Thea, and there was no changing her mind.

I cried for days when she told me, although she never knew that. One kid had been bad enough, had stolen enough of her from me, but two? I kept her secret, though. Of course I did. I loved her, so I kept her secret, and kept my fingers and toes and legs and everything else crossable firmly crossed that this new baby wouldn't take us backwards again, that nothing would change.

But it did change, of course. It *really* changed, after Zander was born. It was never just the two of us anymore, or hardly ever, and I couldn't bear it. If we went for lunch, Zander was always there, in his pram, demanding attention, and then Nell needed picking up from school … if we went out at night, Thea'd always be running late because the baby needed to be fed or bathed, or she'd have to go home early because he'd be up in a few hours for his 1 a.m. feed, and blah and blah and BLAH.

It was insufferable, and it had been making me miserable. I'd tried to rationalize it, to tell myself I was getting too old anyway for the drinking and the partying, we both were. That I was being a selfish cow. That it was time I started thinking about settling down, too, about stopping the wild nights out and the one-night stands with men who had no interest in me other than a quick shag. That Thea and I were still friends, would always be friends, best friends, but just in a different way, a more … a more *adult* sort of way.

It wasn't as simple as that though, of course. Thea and I were far more than just friends. I don't mean we'd ever been sexually involved, nothing like that. But there was something intense between us, a deep connection, something entirely different to the connection I had with any of my other friends. I'd felt it that first time I met her, the evening when she spilled a drink all over me in that bar in London, and clumsily tried to wipe it off, her face all flushed. I felt it then, and I know she did too, and so many years on nothing had changed, not really. We just *got* each other, like nobody else did.

Except it *had* changed now, hadn't it? Now, suddenly, she didn't trust me anymore, had flung these horrible accusations, questions, whatever they were at me, and worst thing was, the most dreadful awful thing, the thing that made me sick to my stomach, was that she was right. I'd done something terrible, and I'd thought I was safe. But now Thea was remembering, and suddenly I wasn't safe anymore, and I had no idea how to handle it.

I swallowed the last of my drink, the alcohol starting to make my head swim, and looked for the barman. He was down at the far end of the bar, so I waved a hand, trying to get his attention.

'Jaz! Lady here needs a drink!'

The barman turned and nodded, and the Bill Nighy lookalike grinned at me.

'He won't be long,' he said. His voice was deep and mellifluous, and I held his gaze for a moment, then smiled a brief thank you and looked away. *Any other night, Bill,* I thought. *Not tonight though. I can't.*

'Same again?'

Jaz was standing in front of me, wiping his hands on his black apron.

'Make it a double,' I said.

I hadn't planned to drive the car home. I'd actually thought

Thea wouldn't really be drinking much that day, not with both the kids there. I thought she'd have one glass, maybe two maximum, which would have been fine over a couple of hours with a big lunch. But when we got there, to the pubby restaurant place out on the London Road, with the lovely sunny terrace and views over the fields, and ordered champagne, it was as if the old Thea suddenly re-emerged. Two, three glasses disappeared effortlessly, and then we were ordering another bottle. She didn't seem to notice that I was barely touching my drink, was drinking mainly water and just the odd mouthful of champagne.

I'm not even sure myself why I decided to do it ... it certainly hadn't been planned, hadn't been in my head at all when I'd got into the car with Thea earlier, heart sinking as I realized not just one but *both* of the bloody kids were coming too, *again*. I just suddenly thought, I suppose, that maybe I could somehow use this to change things a bit. That maybe if I kept a clear head, stayed relatively sober, but Thea got really pissed, out of her head drunk, when she was supposed to be in charge of the kids, that Rupert would ban her from taking them out again like this, and that I'd get her back to myself. That in future, she'd have to leave them at home. That I could have a quiet word with Rupert later, say how concerned I was that she'd drunk so much, that the kids had been distressed, that sort of thing. I knew how he'd react. Rupert was predictable like that.

This all sounded dreadful now, sounded as if I was trying to portray my friend as a terrible mother, but that wasn't what I intended, not at all, because she wasn't. I just wanted a little bit more of her for *me*, I suppose. I wanted her to come out and spend time with me, alone, and if Rupert told her she couldn't take the kids out when we were drinking, then I'd get what I wanted.

Selfish, or what? God, so, so bloody selfish. But at the time, it had seemed like a good idea. And so I sat there, the sun burning my skin, sipping my champagne and drinking my water, and I let her get drunk. Properly, steaming drunk, despite the steak and French fries we ordered along with the bubbly. Zander was kicking happily in his car seat, in the shade under our table, playing with some coloured plastic animal, and Nell was down there with him, staying out of the sun, engrossed in a game on Thea's iPad.

'Can't see it in the sunshine. And it's nice down here. Can you just pass me a drink now and again?' she'd asked, and every now and again a slender hand would emerge from under the table and Thea and I would laugh, and one of us would put apple juice with a straw carefully into it, and it would disappear for a minute then re-emerge, waving the empty bottle.

Shortly before three o'clock we decided it was time to go home. I'd noticed Thea's eyes looking bleary, dark shadows under them. She looked exhausted suddenly – she never got enough sleep anyway, but the heat and alcohol were clearly making her everyday weariness significantly worse that day. She was slurring her words by then, wobbly on her feet when she stood up, almost falling over when she reached down to grab Zander's car seat, dropping her car keys onto the hot stone of the patio. Good. I wanted her like this, worse than this ideally, when Rupert got home.

We could have some more wine back at the house, I thought, as I retrieved the keys, then gently took the baby seat from her, Zander sound asleep now, and carried it to the car myself, slotting it carefully into place. Nell, who'd still been tapping away on the iPad as she walked behind us, seemingly oblivious to the state her mother was in, clambered into her own seat, yawning and complaining about how hot the car was.

'We'll put the air con on, Nell. It'll cool down in a minute. Sssshh, you'll wake your brother,' I said, slipping into the driver's seat and turning the key in the ignition, then getting out again to deal with Thea.

'I'll drive,' I whispered to her, as she stood unsteadily by the bonnet of the car, blinking in the bright sunlight, the alcohol clearly really getting to her, and she nodded mutely. I opened the passenger door, helping her in, clipping her seat belt into place, then climbed back into the driver's seat. Behind me, Nell was leaning back in her seat, eyes closed, headphones on, hands limp on the iPad which was resting on her knee. Next to her, Zander was also still sleeping, head tilted to one side, long lashes resting on his creamy cheeks. To my left, Thea was slumped in her seat, chin on her chest. Was she asleep too, already?

I sat there for a moment, trying to calculate how much I'd actually had to drink. Was I really safe to drive us home? I felt sober enough, but it had probably been somewhere between two and three glasses of champagne in total. That should be OK, shouldn't it, with all the water and food?

And so I drove the car back to Montpellier Terrace, and amazingly there was a space right outside the house, and I manoeuvred the car into it and turned off the engine. As I did so, Thea and Nell opened their eyes simultaneously, Nell suddenly shrieking that she needed the loo, reaching for the door handle, and I leapt out too, realizing I was in desperate need of a wee myself, telling her I'd race her, and she laughed and scampered up the path to the front door. Thea was climbing out of the car herself at that point, so I left her to it. She'd get herself and Zander inside OK, I reckoned ... she was drunk, but not entirely incapable. And as I chased Nell into the coolness of the hallway, something in me hoped that maybe outside Thea would be making a bit of a mess of it. That she'd trip, or stumble, as she came up the path with the baby, that the neighbours would see, that somebody else as well as me would have a little word with Rupert about the state his wife was in, would add fuel to this fire I was building, this fire that would bring my friend back to me. The fire that, as it turned out, burned out of control instead, and nearly destroyed my friend. Nearly destroyed all of us. A fire which clearly, I now realized, was still smouldering, ready to flicker into life again ...

There were beads of sweat on my forehead now, and I wiped them away with the back of my hand, wondering vaguely how it was possible to be so cold and yet sweating at the same time. I took another gulp of whiskey, not even enjoying the taste anymore but needing it, needing the oblivion it was slowly bringing, the events of that sticky September afternoon still racing through my mind.

It was pretty well documented what happened next, of course. Or what the *police* thought happened next, anyway. When they questioned us, afterwards, I told them the last thing I remembered was falling asleep. And when they asked about the events leading up to that, and asked me why I had got into the car with Thea, knowing how drunk she was, I realized that she must have told them that it was her ... that *she* had driven us home. She'd obviously been so drunk she simply didn't remember ... she'd just assumed that she'd been behind the wheel. It was her car after all – I suppose it was a natural assumption.

And so I'd gone along with that. I could hardly say it had been me, not at that stage, could I? What would be the point? A drink-driving charge was the least of Thea's worries, and I relied on my licence so much for work. I wasn't even sure if I *had* been over the limit, not when I'd driven the car home, but we'd drunk more since then. If I was breath-tested, would they believe me if I said I'd been fine at the time? I didn't know how far the police would go to prove that someone was drink-driving, but what if they went to the pub we'd had lunch in, asked people, waiters, bar staff maybe, if they'd noticed how much we'd both drunk? I had no idea if they could do that or not, but what was the point in risking it?

So I just agreed, said Thea had driven. I lied and said I hadn't realized she was so drunk, that if I had I would never have let her drive, that I would never have left her alone to look after Zander, to bring him inside ...

I'd lied to them. I'd lied to everyone. All I'd wanted to do was teach Thea a lesson, shake things up a bit. But what I'd done that day, the consequences of it ... my stomach heaved, and I took a deep breath, willing it to settle. My glass was empty again. I stared into it, my vision blurring, then jumped as a hand gently touched my arm.

'Penny for them, Red?'

The Bill Nighy guy was standing next to me, looking at me quizzically. I straightened up, pushing my hair back off my hot forehead, and felt a sudden surge of recklessness, my eyes roaming from his full lips to his taut biceps, the flat stomach under his close-fitting black sweater.

'I'm Isla,' I said, and held out my hand.

31

THEA

'What time is Millie coming, Mum?'

I looked up from my laptop.

'Around one thirty, I think. So in about ten minutes?'

'Ace! I'll be up in my bedroom, OK?'

'OK, darling. I'll send her straight up when she gets here.'

Nell, grinning, nodded and raced from the room. She seemed absolutely fine this morning, bright and cheerful, with no mention of last night and her sudden appearance downstairs, shaking and screaming. I wondered if she even remembered it – she had seemed to be sleepwalking, and she hadn't said a coherent word as I'd comforted her and guided her back to bed, stroking her back gently until the sobs subsided and her eyes closed again. The incident had reinforced my concern about her state of mind, though, and I decided I had to talk to Rupert about taking her back to see Karen Ballerton. One session had clearly *not* been enough.

I picked up my phone, checking for new texts or emails for the umpteenth time today, but there was still nothing from Isla. I hadn't heard from her since she stormed out of here last night, even though once I'd calmed Nell down I'd called repeatedly, left a voice message and several texts, apologizing and asking her to please call me back. She was obviously way too pissed off to oblige, though, and I didn't blame her.

What had I been thinking of, suggesting that maybe she could have been lying to me about what happened? How could I have thought even for a second that my friend for so many years could have done anything to hurt me? It had seemed logical at the time, to ask everyone who was there that day, but I now realized I should have left Isla off my list. It was just ridiculous to think that *she*—

'BRRRRING. BRRRRING.'

I jumped as the doorbell rang, and leapt from my seat to answer it, foolishly hoping that I might see Isla standing on the doorstep. It was, of course, Millie, Greg standing behind her holding her overnight bag. The girls were spending the afternoon here with me, but Rupert was due to collect them at five, with plans for a theatre trip to Bath before a sleepover at his place. Mia wasn't part of tonight's plans, and for that I was grateful. Nell was in a fragile enough state at the moment without the stress of meeting Daddy's new girlfriend, and I was pleased that Rupert seemed to be aware of that, and was taking things slowly.

'Millie, welcome! Nell's upstairs, do you want to go on up?'

Millie beamed up at me, her golden bob sleek, freshly brushed. Annabelle always did turn her children out extremely well.

'Hi, Thea. Yes, please. Bye, Daddy!'

She turned, standing on tiptoes to peck her father on the cheek, and he bent down to meet her.

'Bye, baby. Have fun.'

Millie scooted past me and thundered up the stairs, and I watched her disappear then turned to Greg.

'Greg … I need a quick word. Have you got time for a coffee?'

He hesitated for a moment, then shrugged.

'Sure. Shall I just leave this here?'

He waved the overnight bag awkwardly at me, and I nodded.

'Yeah, just leave it in the hall. Come on through.'

223

He wiped his feet vigorously on the doormat and came in, dropping the bag and following me down the hallway to the kitchen. I flicked the kettle on then crossed the room again to close the kitchen door. *I don't want Nell or Millie to hear this,* I thought, a rush of nervousness making my stomach roll. I busied myself making the coffee, making idle chitchat over my shoulder about the weather and weekend plans, then, placing the two mugs on the table, took a deep breath.

'You might want to sit down,' I said.

'Ohhh-kaaaay.'

Greg, who'd been leaning against the kitchen counter, suddenly looked wary. He looked very handsome today, I thought, as he crossed the room to sit down opposite me. He was wearing a pale blue denim shirt which somehow made his eyes an even deeper grey, and his hair looked as if it had been recently cut, tightly cropped at the temples, a little longer on top. A memory flashed through my brain, an image of my hands gripping that head as he thrust into me, his cheek rough against mine, and I felt an unexpected little shiver of desire. I'd been drunk, very drunk, the night Greg and I had slept together, the night we conceived Zander. But I knew the sex had been good. Not something to think about now, though. *Bloody hell, Thea. Concentrate.*

'What's up?'

He looked nervous, fingers running around the rim of his coffee mug.

'I ... I just wanted to talk to you about ... about the day Zander died. You know I've had a sort of amnesia? That I haven't been able to remember much, well, anything really, about that day?'

He nodded.

'Yes. So I've heard.'

'Well, recently I've started having, I don't know, flashbacks, little bits of memory coming back. And it's confusing me, you know? Because what I'm remembering doesn't quite seem to fit with what everyone says happened that day. And the trial's only about a month away now, so I'm trying to get everything clear in my head. I thought it might help to talk it through with everyone who was around that day, here in the house I mean. Do you mind?'

I was trying to keep my voice calm, steady, but even I could hear the tremor of anxiety. Greg shifted in his chair.

'Flora mentioned something about this, after you had her round? And Annabelle too – she said she bumped into you, had a coffee. But I didn't really get it. I thought it was pretty obvious what happened, wasn't it? Thea, I know it was an accident, OK? I know you'd never hurt a child, your child. Not deliberately. I mean, everyone was shocked, horrified but … well, we've known you for years, and terrible things happen to good people, and we've tried not to judge …' He shifted again, looking uncomfortable. 'But … well, OK, if you need to go through it, if it will help. But I was out in the garden, with Rupert, when … I mean, I don't know what I can tell you, Thea.'

I was silent for a moment, looking at him. And then – and I had no idea why I said it, where it came from – I simply said quietly: 'You know, don't you, Greg? You know he was yours?'

He jerked backwards, as if I'd hit him. For a few seconds his mouth opened and closed, opened and closed, like a fish struggling to breathe on land. Then he said: 'I … I didn't know, not for definite. But I guessed, yes. He just looked so … so like me. So like my kids. But – are you sure, Thea? How can you be sure?'

His voice sounded tight, as if something was squeezing his throat. I stared into my coffee. I'd have to confess everything now, I supposed. But what did it matter, at this stage?

'I went through your pockets, when you left your coat in the hall one day. I found a comb with some hair in it. Had a DNA test done. He was yours all right. Well, 99.9999 per cent definitely anyway, they said, to be precise. Which is about as definite as you can get.'

225

His eyes widened, eyebrows raised.

'Wow, Thea. Little miss detective or what?'

'I suppose. Sorry. For sneaking around I mean. And for doing it without your permission. I should have told you. But you know, I was thinking of Rupert … and Annabelle, of course. Actually, I suppose I wasn't thinking straight really for a while there, if I'm honest. I was feeling depressed, struggling to cope, and I just didn't see the point in telling anyone. I thought it would just make everything worse, split up my marriage probably, and yours. And you never said anything, and Rupert never did. So … well, I just kept quiet,' I finished lamely.

Greg reached a hand across the table and rested it on mine for a moment, then withdrew it again.

'Thank you,' he whispered. 'Thank you for telling me, finally. And please, don't apologize. I'm the one who should be sorry. I am, you know? I'm so, so sorry. I did wonder, right from the beginning, when Millie came home and said Nell's mummy was having a new baby. I wondered then, if it could be mine, the timing seemed to fit, you know, after we … but then you never said anything, so I just let it go. But when I saw him, that first time … I knew, Thea. I just knew. He was … he was so beautiful.'

His voice cracked, and I realized he was crying, his eyes brimming with tears. He stood up, turning away from me, and I stood up too.

'Greg … Greg, please don't cry.'

I could feel myself starting to go too, my throat tightening, and I needed to try to keep emotion out of this, finish this conversation. I walked closer and gently took his arm, turning him back round to face me. He wiped his face with both hands, shaking his head.

'God, sorry. What a moron.'

'You're not a moron, it's fine. Here, let me get you a tissue.'

There was a box on the worktop and I pulled out a handful

226

and handed them to him. We both sat down again, and Greg took a deep breath.

'OK, so ... you said earlier, you're starting to remember things? What did you mean by that?'

I thought for a moment, wanting to choose my words carefully. I didn't want a repeat of last night with Isla.

'It's just the timeline. The order things happened in, I suppose. It's a bit hard to explain, but ... when you arrived with Millie that day, Greg, that was at around five thirty, right? Can you talk me through what happened, after you got here?'

I knew the timings by heart by now. He crinkled his brow, looking puzzled.

'OK, well ... yes, it was about five thirty, I suppose. Rupert opened the door to us, said hi and so on. Then Millie ran straight upstairs to see Nell, like she did today. Rupert asked me if I fancied a beer while I waited for her, and I said yes, so we came through here to the kitchen and he grabbed a couple out of the fridge. Then we headed out into the garden.' He gestured towards the back door behind me. 'It was cooler out there, nice and shady under the tree. It was hellish hot that day ...' His voice tailed off. 'Shit. Sorry.'

He covered his face with his hands and groaned.

'It's OK, honestly. I'm sorry, to ask you all this. But ... what happened then? Anything you can remember?'

He raised his head, looking at me in silence for a moment.

'We had a bit of a row,' he said.

'Who did?' I was taken aback. I didn't know anything about a row.

'Me and Rupert. Well, not a row exactly. But he started ... well, not *accusing* me, not exactly, but insinuating ...' He paused.

'Insinuating what?'

Another pause.

'Insinuating ... well, that I fancied you. I can't remember what he said, not the exact words. But he sort of implied that he

227

thought I fancied you, and to keep off. It was all jokey at first, but I suddenly got scared, Thea. I thought … does he know? Does he know what we did? Or at least suspect? I mean, Zander didn't look like either of you, not at all, did he? So I wouldn't have blamed Rupert, for being suspicious. I suddenly wondered if he suspected, was testing the water maybe, seeing how I'd react. And instead of just laughing it off, moron that I am, I got defensive. Asked him why on earth I'd want you when I had a beautiful wife like Annabelle …'

I snorted. '*Thanks.*'

'Oh shit, I didn't mean it. You know I fancied you, Thea. It would never have happened if I hadn't. I'd always thought you were gorgeous, every time I saw you, right from the beginning at that first school gathering we went to when the girls were small. I was just trying to protect myself, and you I suppose …'

'OK, OK, I was only joking. So how long did it go on, this row? What happened next?'

'Well, as I said, it wasn't really a row. But the next thing, it was about six fifteen, I think, well, we heard the screaming. Flora, screaming. And we dropped the beers and came running in, and—'

He stopped talking abruptly. I nodded, swallowing hard. I knew the rest.

'So … from the time you arrived, you and Rupert were together the whole time?' I asked.

He frowned.

'Errrm … yes, I think so. He went back in to get another couple of beers at one point but that was just into the kitchen. Only took a few seconds. Why?'

I shrugged. This had been a waste of time. All of it was just a waste of time, wasn't it? I'd destroyed my friendship with Isla, was probably going to destroy what was left of my relationship with Rupert next. And for what? A desperate attempt to convince myself that I didn't kill my child. That somebody else was responsible.

What the hell was wrong with me? I needed to let Greg go, leave it, stop digging. He was a victim in this too, if you thought about it, wasn't he? He'd lost a child, just as I had.

'Nothing. Just trying to get everything clear. I'm so sorry, Greg. Sorry to make you relive it again. I know it's not easy, for any of us. But especially you, especially now you know for definite. I'm so sorry, Greg. For your loss. Sorry for both of us.'

'So am I. And for Zander. I know you had your problems, Thea, but what happened to Zander … it was terrible. I can't … and now I know, that he really was my son …'

Oh God. I felt the tears welling again and swallowed them back. Greg was clearly trying to control his emotions too, his fists balled on the table in front of him, eyes fixed on the smooth wood, his breathing laboured. We both sat there for a few moments, then I exhaled and stood up.

'I need to get back to work. Thank you for that. I … I'm so sorry, Greg. For everything.'

He stood too, shaking his head.

'So am I,' he whispered.

32

GREG

I drove home in a daze, my hands gripping the steering wheel so hard my knuckles were white. Zander was *my* baby. My son. My fourth child. My *dead* child. Deep down, I'd known it from the start, known it from that very first time I'd seen him lying there in his pram, but I hadn't dared admit it even to myself, not really. I'd looked, and known, and then cast the thought out again, refusing to allow it to stay, terrified of what it meant.

I'd tried to avoid looking at him after that, sick with fear, with guilt. Wishing he would just go away. Wishing he wasn't there, that he didn't exist. And then, the day he actually did stop existing, my initial reaction to his death horrified me. Appalled me, then and now, every time I thought about it, every time I let my mind go there. Because my first feeling, the first emotion that hit me when I saw that tiny body in Flora's arms, wasn't one of grief, or loss, or sadness. My first reaction was a second, just a brief moment, of overwhelming relief. He was gone. I'd wanted him gone, and it had happened.

And then, almost as soon as that terrible, sick thought entered my head, it rushed out again, and the guilt roared back, sweeping over me like a tidal wave, making it almost impossible to think, to breathe. The hideous, never-ending sense of shame, that I could feel, even for a second, relief about the death of a child. A baby. *My* baby.

Annabelle mistook it for shock and sadness, of course. Night after night, my wife cradled me in her arms, stroked my hair, tried to soothe away the pain.

'Just such a terrible thing for you to witness, my darling. I'm so, so sorry, that you had to see that. That poor little mite, I can't bear it. That woman is a monster. To leave your own baby in a car, to *forget* about him ...'

And that, of course, made it all so much worse. I knew Thea wasn't a monster. She wasn't perfect – who was? – but she was a good woman, a good mother.

But why had I slept with her? Why? That should never have happened, didn't need to happen. It was one thing fancying the pretty mother of your daughter's best friend – and hell, yes, I always thought Thea was incredibly attractive, that lithe body, those cheekbones. But it was quite another to get pissed out of your head and shag her in a hotel room on a wild night out, shag her and not use any fucking protection.

I'd had flings before, now and again, but not for ages, years, and I'd never slept with any of them. It had never gone further than a snog before, a quick fumble. I loved Annabelle, and I had no intention of leaving her, of abandoning my marriage. It was just that sometimes ... well, she was always so busy, so stressed, so tied up with the children, the business. No excuse, I knew that. Pathetic, really. *My wife's too tired, so I'm looking elsewhere.*

I'd even tried it on with Flora, a little. She was so pretty, so nice, and I'd seen the way she'd looked at me too, sometimes. But I'd stopped myself – what was I thinking, right there in the house, under Annabelle's nose? Again, pathetic. But I'd wondered, too, if she might know about Zander. She and Thea had been close, and it had crossed my mind once or twice that she might know something, and that frightened me. If I could get closer to her, maybe I could find out if she knew, and if so, make her promise to keep it to herself. Because if she told Annabelle ...

But why did I have to try it on with her? Why not just *talk* to her, for fuck's sake? Midlife crisis or what? I sometimes thought Annabelle knew – not about Thea, but about some of the others – or suspected anyway, but she never said. Didn't want to know, I supposed. Didn't want to admit it to herself, a bit like me with Zander, because then what?

I slowed for a red light, my heart thudding dully in my chest, aware that I could feel the pulse in my throat. The bigger question now was *now what*? I hadn't asked Thea if she'd told anyone else, I suddenly realized. *Did* anyone else know that I was Zander's father? And what was she starting to remember, about the day he died? I hadn't asked her that either. She'd been the one asking all the questions. What had she said? That she didn't think things had happened like everyone said they did that day? A shiver ran through me, my body suddenly deathly cold despite the heat pumping out through the car's vents. *What did she remember?*

I sat rigid in my seat, my limbs leaden. The court case, the trial, was just weeks away now. It was something I'd started to worry desperately about in the past few weeks, something I'd tried to blame on work stress when Annabelle asked me why I was so tense, so distracted. It had suddenly occurred to me that if my suspicions were true, if I really was Zander's biological father, that it might come out at the trial, and the thought horrified me.

Now that I knew for definite about Zander, the fear was suddenly becoming paralyzing. Would everyone find out that I was Zander's father? Rupert had left Thea anyway now, so what did it matter if it all came out at her trial? Their marriage was over. A bit of infidelity thrown into the mix wouldn't change anything, not at this stage, would it? Would she do that to me, to him?

I swallowed hard, then jumped as a loud honk came from the

car behind. Shit. The lights had changed, and I waved a hand in apology, moving the car off, suddenly unsure if I was actually fit to drive. My legs had started shaking, my foot jerky on the accelerator pedal. During those long, dark nights in the weeks after Zander died, I'd begged the universe, begged a god I didn't believe in for forgiveness, vowing that my life was going to change, vowing never to cheat on Annabelle again, promising that if my dreadful secret could remain a secret I'd make a new start, become a new, better person. But I realized now that, somehow, in the past hour, my life had started to fall apart. That's what lying did to you, in the end, didn't it? Your lies always find you out. Do terrible things, and terrible things happened to you. Karma, they called it.

The road ahead was clear now, and I put my foot down, Annabelle's face suddenly floating into my mind. The pain, the grief in her eyes, if she were to find out about Zander, about what I'd done, from somebody else. From Thea. From the police. A sense of panic gripped me. I needed to go home. I needed to talk to my wife. I needed to confess.

33

ANNABELLE

'Heart-shaped invitations, heart-shaped biscuits, heart-shaped balloons, pink champagne in heart-shaped glasses, heart-shaped pizzas … *heart-shaped pizzas*? Seriously? Ugh. Tacky or what?'

I giggled at the undisguised disgust in Flora's voice. She really was *not* the hearts and flowers type.

'Well, it *is* a Valentine's Day party. People like hearts on Valentine's Day, Flora, what can I say? We give the client what the client wants. She can have heart-shaped flipping loo roll in the bathroom if she wants it.'

Flora's eyes widened.

'Someone makes heart-shaped loo roll? How does that work then? How does it fit on the … oh, very funny.'

Still laughing, I moved to one side as Flora threw her pen at me.

'Ouch, don't! Sorry, it was just your face as you read the list of heart-shaped stuff … you don't realize how funny you can be, Flora.'

'Hmmph.' She snorted in an exaggerated fashion, but there was a little smile playing on her lips now.

'Well, I'm glad I amuse you. Shall I pour the tea?'

'You do. And yes, please. I'm just going to move Olaf into the living room. Every time I stand up I worry I'm going to trample him, poor love.'

I bent down and gently picked the kitten up, stroking his soft head as I carried him into the front room and gently deposited him on the hearth rug, where he immediately curled into a sleepy ball. Remarkably, the very next day after the Hamish tragedy, Greg had seen an advert in the local paper offering Persian kittens for immediate rehoming. To Sienna's intense joy, the adorable ball of white fluff now known as Olaf had joined us that very evening, and after just a couple of days already felt like part of the family.

Smiling – he really was the sweetest little thing – I returned to the kitchen, where my tea was waiting for me. Flora and I had just settled down at the kitchen table for a quick debrief on last night, and a look ahead to Wednesday, when we'd be throwing the Valentine's party for Lara Foster, the Cheltenham Town footballer's wife. The pyjama party had been a resounding success – Octavia had been thrilled, hugging us both as we left and pressing an extremely generous cash tip into my hand. When we'd arrived home just after midnight, I'd handed most of the money to Flora.

'For all your hard work recently,' I said. 'You deserve it.'

She'd gaped at the notes and then, to my surprise, flung her arms around me. When she released me a few moments later, she had tears in her eyes.

'Oh Flora, sweetie, don't cry! It's only money. I'll take it back if it upsets you!' I laughed.

She laughed too, stuffing the cash into her jeans pocket.

'No way! Thank you so much, Annabelle. I'm sorry, I'm an idiot. It's just that … well, you're so kind to me. I feel … I don't know, sort of *valued* here. And sort of part of the family too. You've made me so welcome, and I love my job. I appreciate it so much, and I'm sorry if … well, I'm sorry if I don't often show it. I'm not that good, with emotion …'

She wiped her cheeks with the backs of her hands, and I felt a sudden wave of affection. She was so young, really, and I remembered how insecure I'd been at twenty-five and suddenly wondered if I should be doing more to show how much I appreciated her. She worked so hard, and was so great with the kids. I really couldn't imagine life without her now.

'Oh my goodness, don't apologize,' I said, and reached for her hands, squeezing them. 'You are absolutely part of the family, and highly valued, and I should tell you that more often too. Treat yourself to something nice with that money, please. You've more than earned it.'

We'd headed for bed after that, and I'd fallen asleep with a warm glow, remembering the smile on Flora's face as we'd parted on the landing. I was glad she was finishing the day on a high note. Earlier, as we'd eaten breakfast together, I'd mentioned Thea, and what she'd said to me when we'd bumped into each other in Cheltenham. I hadn't mentioned seeing her former employer to Flora when we met up again to drive home after our shopping, not wanting to sour the mood, so why on earth had I mentioned it now?

I knew instantly by Flora's face that I'd made a mistake, and mentally kicked myself. What Thea had said to me, about remembering things about the day Zander died, about the fact that she thought someone else had been responsible, had haunted me the evening after I'd seen her, but I'd been vague when I'd mentioned it to Greg, just saying that Thea's memories were returning and she was feeling confused. He'd been there that day after all, and the more I thought about it, the more ludicrous Thea's claims sounded. She had looked wretched, broken – was that why she had temporarily convinced me that there might be some truth in what was she was saying? Was it just sympathy for a woman whose life was crumbling that had made me believe her? Probably. So why had I brought it up now, with Flora? What was wrong with me, always going on about the Ashfields, when I knew she couldn't bear to talk about them, when I knew she was still traumatized by what had happened there?

'Oh, gosh, I'm so sorry, Flora. There I go again. Forget I said anything.'

I stopped buttering my toast and turned to look at her. Her eyes were fixed on her plate, her hands still working her knife and fork, cutting up a sausage, but her body looked stiff, her movements suddenly jerky. She shrugged, not looking at me.

'It's OK. It's the same sort of stuff she said to me, that time she asked me to go round to see her. I think she's crazy, Annabelle, honestly, and I hate saying that. But I think she's lost it a bit. I don't blame her – I can't even imagine what she's going through; it must be horrendous; it was bad enough for me, for the rest of us, seeing … well seeing Zander like that. But she was his *mother*, and I'm almost not surprised that her brain is finding it impossible to accept what she did; it must be unbearable. Even so … what she's saying, that she doesn't think she did it … I mean, it's bonkers, right?'

I sat still for a moment, thinking, then nodded slowly.

'Yes. It probably is. And it's just the saddest thing in the world, isn't it?'

Flora's eyes met mine, and she nodded too.

'It's the worst thing I've ever had to witness,' she said quietly, then dipped her head again, spearing a piece of sausage with her fork.

We ate in silence after that, and the more I thought about it, the more I knew Flora had to be right, just like Greg was.

I was thinking about it again now, as we sat at the kitchen table sorting out the final details of the Valentine's party, my mind constantly drifting away from pink confetti and heart-shaped everything to Thea. She had been so convincing, when she had told me what she'd told me, but now that I could look back on our meeting with a level of objectivity, it seemed insane to think that anyone other than her could have been responsible for the baby's death. Who on earth would do something like that?

CRASH.

Flora and I both jumped as, down the hallway, the front door banged open, flung inwards so hard it bounced back against the wall. I pushed the notes on the Valentine's do aside and stood up, alarmed.

'Greg? Is that you?'

It was. My husband was staggering down the corridor, his face deathly white.

'Annabelle.'

His voice was a hoarse gasp, and my alarm grew as he flung himself into an empty chair. His eyes were red-rimmed, his hair wild, as if he'd been running his hands through it repeatedly.

'Greg! What's wrong? Has something happened? Have you … have you been *crying*? Oh no, no no no … please don't tell me it's one of the kids? Greg, talk to me!'

I was standing over him, practically screaming, panic gripping me. My husband sank his head into his hands, and I turned to look at Flora, who looked as horrified as I felt.

'Greg … Mr Garrington? What is it? Please, you're scaring us,' she said, her voice shaky.

Greg raised his head and looked at me.

'The kids are fine. Well, *our* kids are anyway.'

Relief flooded through me, to be instantly replaced by more fear.

'What do you mean, *our* …?'

He was looking at Flora now, ignoring me.

'I've just been talking to Thea,' he said. 'She told me something. Confirmed something, Something I've suspected for a long time. Something I'm wondering if you already knew, Flora.'

Flora frowned, and then her eyes widened.

'Oh.'

Her voice was a whisper. Simultaneously, they both turned to look at me, and the expression in their eyes sent a chill down my spine.

'*What?* For God's sake, what is going on?'

'Annabelle.'

There were tears in my husband's eyes now, and I had a sudden terrible sense of foreboding, a sudden absolute knowledge that whatever this was, whatever he was about to say, was going to change everything, was going to destroy life as I knew it.

'Greg. Don't, please …' I whimpered the words, but he wasn't listening.

'Annabelle. I have something to tell you.'

look at me and the expression in their eyes sent a chill down my spine.

'Thea, for God's sake, what is going on?'

'Aunt Jie...'

There were tears in my husband's eyes now, and I felt a sudden terrible sense of foreboding, a sudden absolute knowledge that whatever this was, whoever he was about to say, was going to change everything, was going to end the life as I knew it.

'Greg, Don't, please...' I whispered the words, but he wasn't listening.

'Annabelle, I have something to tell you...'

34

THEA

I looked at my watch for the fifth time in about three minutes. Ten to five. Rupert could be here any time now, I thought, and I resumed the nervous pacing, up and down the dining room, that I'd been doing periodically ever since Greg left so abruptly a few hours earlier. He hadn't even called up the stairs to say goodbye to Millie, barely looking at me as he departed, his voice sounding hoarse as he muttered that Rupert had arranged to drop Millie off at home tomorrow morning after the sleepover so I didn't need to worry.

Our encounter had left me unsettled, jittery, unable to get down to work or even watch television. The girls were playing happily up in Nell's bedroom, emerging just once to ask for a drink and some biscuits before running back upstairs again, and that at least gave me some peace of mind.

An afternoon and evening with her best friend would be good for Nell – for Millie too, probably, as I feared that things might not be particularly good at the Garrington home this evening. Greg had seemed so shaken, so terribly upset, even though he said he'd suspected all along that he might be my son's father. The confirmation that he'd been correct had seemed over-whelming to him, though, and the dreadful guilt I was now feeling

240

about not telling him sooner was slowly becoming mixed with fear. What if he went straight home and told Annabelle? Would he?

I'd stopped my pacing as this thought struck me, suddenly frozen. Shit. The possible repercussions terrified me. If Annabelle knew I'd slept with her husband, had his child, what would that mean for Millie and Nell? She'd never let her daughter through my door again, and that would be devastating for Nell. I'd thought about this before, of course – tortured myself for months, after that night with Greg, after I found out I was pregnant. But as time went on, and Zander was born, and nobody said anything, I foolishly let myself believe that it would never happen. If Greg never asked if the baby was his, and Rupert never confronted me, we could all just go on as we were, and Annabelle would never find out the truth. Nobody would.

But now ... I shivered, and slumped down on the nearest chair, feeling a little queasy. He wouldn't tell Annabelle, would he? Of course he wouldn't. I was just being paranoid. What would he have to gain? It would probably destroy his marriage, and for what? A baby son who was no longer around to be a problem for him? I took a deep breath, trying to calm myself. No, it would be OK. He'd get over it, in time.

I needed to put Greg out of my head now anyway, because Rupert would be here soon. Rupert, the only other person in the house that day. The only person who really had both time *and* motive. The person who, of everyone there, had the biggest reason to want to hurt me, to punish me. But could I really confront him? As I ran through the words I wanted to say to him in my mind, I began to feel woozy, as if my brain was floating outside my body. Was I actually about to do this? Was I really about to accuse my husband of killing our baby? Well, of killing *my* baby?

He hated me enough already, his whole family did. My parents, dead so long before it had happened, had been spared the terrible shame, hadn't had to go through this ordeal. But Rupert's parents

241

… they'd come to the funeral, that dark day which I could barely remember now, the pain so great it robbed me of all speech, of all coherent thought. They'd come, and they'd looked at me with so much hate, so much contempt, that I was left reeling. They expressed their disgust that I'd even been allowed to attend, and then they'd left, and I'd never heard from them again. And now, would Rupert leave too, forever, after what I was planning to say to him today?

The futility of what I was doing suddenly struck me. Was there really any point? After all, what had I gained by talking to Flora, to Isla, to Greg? All I'd done was upset them all, offended them deeply. Made them think I was crazy, if they didn't already.

Should I even do this? Things between Rupert and me were tense enough already, and with Nell so fragile … I closed my eyes briefly, and it ran through my head again, like a scene from a movie. My arms, reaching into the back of the car. Zander, head heavy on my shoulder, sound asleep. My feet on the path, slightly unsteady with alcohol. My lips brushing his skin as I laid him in his pram. How then? HOW? How could he still be in the car hours later? How, when I *remembered*? My heart rate had speeded up, the dizzy feeling worse now, and I rubbed frantically at my face, then dropped my head down between my knees, willing myself not to faint, trying to breathe normally. No, it was no good. I had to do this. I had to see his reaction. I had to ask Rupert the questions that had gone round and round in my head for weeks, the questions I so desperately needed the answers to.

BRRRRR.

The doorbell rang. I stayed motionless, trying to get back in control of my body, knowing that Nell would probably answer it anyway, hearing her pounding feet on the stairs and her shriek of 'Daddy!' a moment later. By the time the dining room door opened and she and Rupert walked in, I was on my feet, making a show of tidying some papers on the table.

'Rupert. How are you? Nell, go and make sure you have

242

everything in your bag, will you? And maybe check Millie's, too. If she's forgotten anything we can lend her something of yours to bring. I just need a quick word with Daddy, OK?'

'OK!' Nell grinned at me, then turned and ran out of the room, thundering up the stairs as she shouted: 'Mills! We have to check our bags and then we can go!'

I waited until I heard her bedroom door close, then turned to Rupert, who had a puzzled look on his face.

'What's up? I don't have a lot of time, I promised the girls a burger before the play and we have to drive to Bath first ...'

'This won't take long. I just need to ask you something. I'm putting together my thoughts for the trial,' I gestured at the piles of paperwork on the table, 'and, well, my mind is clearer now, Rupert. The amnesia seems to be easing, and things are coming back to me. And these things ... well, some of them don't make sense.'

He was frowning now, staring at the papers on the table.

'What doesn't make sense?'

I said nothing for a few moments, then took a breath, the words coming quickly, practised so many times in my head.

'Rupert, everyone said I left Zander in the car. Even *I* thought I left Zander in the car. But in the past few weeks, I've started to think that's not how it happened. I remember, you see – the memories, they've started to come back. And now, I remember bringing him in and putting him in his pram, before I sat down with Isla to have another drink, and then fell asleep. And yet, a few hours later, Flora found him in the car. And the only way that could have happened, if I didn't leave him there, is that somebody took him back out and put him there. And I have no idea why anybody would do something so horrendous, so sick, but Rupert, I—' I stopped speaking, suddenly aware that my husband was staring at me openmouthed, his face flushing a dark, angry red.

'You ... hang on, let me get this right. You think *somebody put*

243

him back out there? What the *fuck*, Thea? Are you fucking mental? Has all the drinking rotted your fucking *brain cells*? Tell me you're not serious, please!'

He took a step towards me, a wild look in his eyes, his fists clenched in front of him, and a little ripple of fear ran through me. Was he … was he going to *hit* me?

'It's what I remember, Rupert. I can't help it.'

My voice was small, feeble, even to my own ears. He took another step forward, his eyes narrowed, his breathing heavy, and I backed away, fear like an icy bubble running up my spine.

'Rupert, please …'

And then, quite suddenly, he turned away from me, walked to the window, and began to laugh. I was so shocked, so relieved, that I sat down heavily on the nearest chair again, watching him. It wasn't his usual laugh – Rupert had an infectious, almost girlish giggle normally, the kind of giggle that set everyone else off too, even if they weren't quite sure what the joke was. But today his laugh had a hysterical quality, and I suddenly realized that he was crying and laughing at the same time, tears running down his cheeks. I sat, perfectly still, not knowing what to do, desperate for him to stop, to talk to me. To say something. To say *anything*.

'Rupert? Are you OK?' I said eventually.

I expected him to ignore me but he stopped laughing, crying, whatever it was, quite abruptly, and turned to look at me.

'OK? You're asking me if *I'm* OK? Christ, Thea. You're the one who's not OK. You think *somebody else* put Zander back into the car? And who is this somebody else, then? Can I assume that as it's me you're telling about this, that you think it was me? You think I … what? Sneaked in when nobody was looking, stole him out of the pram and put him back into a hot car to die? Are you fucking *serious*? I mean, I know you're trying to stay out of prison, but surely even you can't be that desperate?' His voice was rising, his face reddening again, the anger back.

'Rupert, please. I'm not accusing you. I'm not accusing anyone.

244

I just remember what I remember, and it doesn't make sense. So I'm trying to work out how ...'

I stopped, my throat suddenly tight, my own eyes filling with tears now. I shouldn't have done this, I shouldn't, I *shouldn't*. What was it going to achieve, except make Rupert hate me even more than he did already? All I'd done was alienate everyone, at a time when I needed them more than I'd ever done. When I was going to court, and most likely, I realized now, to prison too; for what jury would believe me when I said I remembered taking my child to safety, when I'd already taken responsibility for his death months ago? I'd ruined it, ruined it all, and for what?

My head was spinning, and I gripped onto the seat of the chair for support, aware that Rupert was talking again.

'What are you trying to work out, Thea?' His voice was quieter now, calmer, but with a hint of menace. 'Are you, by any chance, trying to work out how to tell me that Zander wasn't actually my son?'

I gasped, as if he'd thrown a bucket of cold water on me. Had Greg ... had Greg called Rupert, as soon as he'd left here earlier? Surely not ...

Rupert was still talking, moving closer to me again.

'Because he wasn't, was he, Thea? Whose son was he? WHOSE SON WAS HE?'

He screamed the final words, banging a fist on the table, his face so close to mine a fine mist of spittle sprayed my face as he spat the words out, and I shrank back in my chair, the tears streaming again. I had no choice now, did I?

'He was ... he was Greg's. Greg Garrington's. But it was only one night, I swear ...'

'FUCK! FUCK FUCK FUCK!'

He spun on his heels and stomped across the room, hands clawing at his scalp, and an anguished wail escaped him, the sound of a wounded animal in pain. And then suddenly there was another noise, another wailing sound, but this time more

245

high-pitched, more frightened, and I turned to see Nell standing in the doorway, a look of terror on her face, her whole body visibly shaking.

'STOP IT!! STOP IT!' she screamed.

35

RUPERT

'You two OK there for a bit? We'll leave for Bath in about half an hour, OK?'

Nell, calm again now, although her eyes were still red, nodded.

'OK, Daddy.'

She and Millie were in front of the TV in the small lounge of my rented flat, watching some old sitcom. It was *Friends*, actually, I realized as I left them to it and headed to the kitchen. I hadn't known it was still running. I closed the door behind me and sat down at the narrow breakfast bar, exhaling heavily. What an afternoon. What a shitty, shitty afternoon. First Thea and her revelations, and then my daughter, who was clearly still not right, not right at all, despite her visit to that bloody counsellor woman. Waste of money that was, then. When she'd appeared in such a state, Thea and I had both tried to comfort her, but she'd been inconsolable, her little face red and wet with tears.

'I want to just go, *now*,' she said, over and over again, pushing us both away, begging us to stop arguing. In the end, Thea, in tears by then herself, told me to take the girls and go, and that Nell would eventually calm down, and she was right. With a white-faced Millie, clearly traumatized by the whole thing, by her side in the back seat of my car, Nell's sobbing gradually lessened during the short drive to my flat on the edge of town, and now she seemed more or less fine again, which was more than I could say for myself.

The last, the very last thing I wanted to do this evening now was take two kids to eat burgers and sit in a theatre watching a dramatized version of some kids' TV programme – I'd rather sit here and drink myself into oblivion – but there was nothing I could do to get out of it.

I rubbed my eyes hard with the heels of my hands, then stopped rubbing and just sat there, resting my head in my hands, brain racing.

Greg Garrington. **GREG FUCKING GARRINGTON.** I'd suspected it, of course I had, for so long, but somehow I'd managed to convince myself it wasn't true, it couldn't be true, certainly at the beginning. Thea and I had had our issues, but she'd never be unfaithful, would she? It was one of the reasons why I hadn't fought her for sole custody of Nell, when I'd finally left her after that horrific day last September.

I couldn't live with her anymore, I knew that. The love that had been fading, shrivelling, had finally died when Zander died. But despite all that, despite the nightmarish days and weeks that followed, I still felt that Thea was basically a good person. So many people tried to change my mind about that – friends, colleagues, even strangers. *How can you ever trust her again?* they'd ask. *How can you leave your daughter with a monster like Thea?* But I'd known Thea for years, and I knew they were wrong. She'd always been a good person, a good wife, a good mother. Not a *perfect* wife, not a perfect mother, clearly. But then what mother, what parent, what marriage, was perfect?

She was a better mother than I was a father, that was beyond doubt. Work, to my shame, had always taken precedence for me, certainly during the early years of our marriage. And Nell adored her mother, and my little girl had suffered enough. To take her entirely away from her mum, her home, after what she'd gone

248

through? No. I needed to make sure my daughter was safe, and happy, and at the time it had seemed to me that the best way to ensure that was to let Thea share in her care, even if it was for less than half the week.

And even though I couldn't stay with my wife, couldn't bring myself to comfort her, could barely look at her in those early days, I couldn't cause Thea anymore pain either. She'd lost her baby – how could I take her only other child away too?

But now, for the first time, I was regretting that decision, the decision I'd made to spare her anymore suffering. More fucking fool me. *Greg Garrington.* My fists clenched under my forehead. OK, so we weren't the closest of mates, but we'd always got on, always had a laugh when we bumped into each other. He was the father of my daughter's best friend, a bloke I'd so often shared a beer with, talked footie with. Shared a fucking wife with too, it now seemed.

I banged my fists hard on the table, suddenly filled with a red-hot anger. How often had it happened? *When* had it happened? Was it still going on? Did Annabelle know? And who else knew that Zander wasn't mine? Isla must know, surely? Thea told her everything. But who else? Had they all been laughing at me behind my back, all this time? I stood up, pushing my stool back so violently it toppled over onto the floor.

'FUCK!' I shouted, then remembered the girls in the living room and groaned. I had to keep it together, for this evening at least. But tomorrow, when I dropped Millie off at home as agreed … I clenched my fists again, wanting nothing so badly right at that moment than to slam them into that bastard's smug face. How fucking *dare* he drink my beer, sit chatting with me in my own back garden, knowing all the time that he'd been shagging my wife? Getting my wife *pregnant*, for fuck's sake? And as for her …

I walked to the kitchen window and looked out onto the tiny paved courtyard that now served as my back garden. I'd loved

Cheltenham so much when we'd first arrived here, this classy town with its Regency terraces and ornamental parks, and we'd been so happy for a while in our Montpellier home, me and Thea and Nell. My rental was bleak, featureless, unloved, but I'd seen it as a stepping stone: somewhere to rest my head and put myself back together before I could move on again. But how easy was that going to be, really, after this?

I bent to pick up the fallen stool, breathing heavily. The doubts had started from when Zander was born, and he looked so different to what I'd expected. Somehow, though, I'd buried the feelings, refusing to acknowledge what my gut was telling me. OK, so the kid didn't look like me, didn't look anything like Thea or Nell either, with all that white-blond hair and blue eyes. But these things happened, right? Nature, genetics, were quirky things. We've all seen the stories in the newspapers about the black parents producing white offspring, some throwback to a mixed-race ancestor, right?

So I ignored how he looked, tried as hard as I could to bond with my son, tried to keep my relationship with Thea on track, even though somewhere deep inside the suspicions were growing, the questions bubbling to the surface. *Was* he mine? But if not, whose? Yes, Greg Garrington crossed my mind again from time to time, but apart from the hair and eye colour, well ... I couldn't see it, him and Thea. He was just one of Nell's friends' dads – fair enough, the one we saw the most of, but even so. Just a dad, someone we met at drop-offs and pickups at the school gates and the occasional social thing. I hadn't even noticed Thea talking to him much, ever, even now as I thought about it hard, running some of the parties or events of the past couple of years through my mind. So how the *fuck* ...?

So Greg remained on the periphery of my mind, and somehow I carried on behaving completely normally around him. Christ, I even confided in him about Mia, back in the summer, when we got pissed at some festival thing across the road in the park. I never told him about Flora, though, hadn't told anyone about that.

I still didn't really know why I did it, and did it so many times, with her. Yes, of course, she was attractive – fit body, cute smile, always there in the house, always a temptation. But when I looked back, I think being with Flora was a way of silently punishing Thea, punishing her for the doubts in my mind about Zander, for the problems in our marriage, for her tooregular nights out with bloody Isla. I was shagging Mia at work at the same time, for the same reasons, and when one day Flora suddenly told me it was over between us, it was almost a relief. My life was too complicated anyway, and for a while I thought maybe I could pull things back together, stop seeing Mia, too, concentrate on rebuilding my marriage, pretend all was well.

I managed it until just before Zander died. A few weeks before my son – *his* son – breathed his last. It was as if it hit me all of a sudden – the truth that had been staring me hard in the eyes for so long, the truth I'd tried to ignore. Greg had come round to pick Millie up, passing the time of day with me and Thea in the lounge while the kid gathered her belongings, and he'd wandered over to look at Zander, asleep in his pram. I'd walked over to join him, and suddenly it was there, right in front of me. I looked at Zander, looked at Greg, looked at Zander again, and it was as if somebody had rammed a fist into my throat, making me gasp. They weren't just a bit alike, they were … they were *identical*. The hair, the eyes, the shape of the fucking jawline, for fuck's sake.

I left the room, fast, saying I'd remembered an urgent work call I had to make, my heart beating so fast I thought I might keel over. And even then, I never confronted her. Never confronted either of them. I still hadn't known for definite, of course, and my suspicions, strong as they were, could have been wrong.

But inside me, the anger was growing. And although if what I feared was true, it was Greg I wanted to hurt – wanted to *kill*

251

– the main force of my anger was directed at Thea. At my wife, my cheating whore of a wife. So while I maintained an amicable relationship with her, most of the time, and mainly for the sake of the kids – it wasn't Zander's fault, after all, and certainly not Nell's – I started sleeping with Mia again, and this time I was deliberately careless. I would very obviously leave the room to take Mia's calls, leave dinner and hotel receipts in my pockets, even on my bedside table once, hoping that Thea might get suspicious. Hoping to hurt her. To cause her pain, like the pain I now believed she'd inflicted on me. But, well – she didn't even notice. She was too wrapped up in the kids, in *Just Enfant*, in Isla, as usual. And so I got angrier and angrier, and I knew I had to do something, something drastic. Something to confirm everything I was thinking, something to bring all this to a head, once and for all.

And so came that last day. That's how I thought of it now, the last day … the day life as my family knew it ended for ever. The day I finally found the guts to confront Greg Garrington in the garden, to ask him if there was anything, ever had been anything, between him and Thea. The day Zander died. A shudder ran through me, as the image of his face, his limp body, flashed through my mind. He didn't deserve that. No child deserved that. But then I thought of Thea. Of Thea, who had slept with another man, brought his child into the world and tried to pass it off as mine. My wife, who had betrayed me in the worst possible way. I thought of Thea, and *her* face when she saw her dead child in Flora's arms. Her screams of anguish. Her screams of *guilt*, finally. And I smiled.

36

THEA

It was all over. I sat, slumped on the end of the sofa, in complete despair. The room was warm, the central heating on, but I felt cold, chilled to the bone, my fingers numb, my skin covered in goose-bumps. Why hadn't I kept my mouth shut? Even Nell was gone from me now, my beautiful daughter, the child I'd hurt so much, damaged so much. I remembered her face, twisted in grief as she begged Rupert to take her away from here, away from me, and I felt a physical pain, a spasm that shook my body. Why had I let these delusions of mine take hold, make me confront people who might have supported me, make me throw such ridiculous, terrible accusations at my friends, my family? What was wrong with me?

I was responsible for Zander's death, nobody else. I had to be. Why couldn't I just accept that? Well, I had now. Rupert's reaction had finally opened my eyes. It was over. I'd had hope, these past few weeks – tiny tendrils of hope, frail but still there, still strong enough to hold me together. Now that hope was gone, and I could feel myself starting to fall apart. In a few weeks' time I'd be heading to prison, and my whole life – my family, my home, my business – would be gone. Done. Changed for ever. There was no way out of this now, nobody else to talk to, nobody who could help me. I was alone.

I cried then. Cried for everything I'd lost, and everything I was about to lose.

And then I reached for the gin bottle.

37

NELL

'Millie. Millie, I need to tell you something.'

We were sitting on the sofa, me and Millie, and *Friends* was on. I loved *Friends*, but today I couldn't concentrate. It felt as if butterflies ... no, something worse than butterflies, something with flappy wings, but heavier – what was heavier than a butterfly though? Birds? – were fluttering around in my tummy.

Out in the kitchen, Dad was banging around, and I was pretty sure I'd heard a bad word too. He was angry, and Mum was upset, and everything was horrible. So, so horrible. Things had been horrible for a long time now, and I knew that it couldn't go on like this any longer. I needed to tell somebody something, something really, really important. Something really, really bad.

I knew I should have told somebody ages ago, but I'd been told not to, because it was a big secret, the biggest secret ever, and I was just ... well, I was just really scared. At first, the scaredness (was scaredness a real word?) was that something really terrible would happen to me if I broke my promise not to tell, because bad things can happen if you tell a secret, can't they?

And then I got less scared of that, but more scared of how angry Mum and Dad would be with me, for not saying anything for so long. And so I didn't know who to tell. I'd tried to tell

Millie once, a long time ago, but she hadn't really believed me, and then I'd thought I shouldn't have told her after all, so I pretended I'd been joking. And then I'd thought about telling that nice counsellor woman, Karen, but I started and then got scared and changed my mind again, and only *sort of* told her, but she didn't really get it, and she was really kind and told me none of it was my fault, and that made me feel better for a while, because I thought about it really hard and I thought she was right, and it wasn't my fault at all.

But then my head got all confused again, and I kept having really bad dreams, and now I just didn't think I could keep it in anymore. I needed to tell somebody, and I thought that Dad might be the right person, and then he could tell Mum, or maybe we could go home and I could tell them both at the same time, and then … well, I didn't know what would happen then. It might be an awful mistake, doing this. But I suddenly knew that I had to do it. And I had to do it now.

'Millie?'

She turned away from the telly, where somebody – Joey? – was running around with a turkey stuck on his head, her face a big smile.

'This is SO funny! What, Nell?'

'Millie, I …' The words seemed to be stuck in my throat. I did a little cough and tried again.

'I need to go and tell Dad something. And Mum too. About the day Zan … Zander … you know, that day?'

She crumpled up her forehead.

'What about it?'

'Something. Something bad.'

I felt as if I was going to cry all of a sudden, and Millie must have noticed I looked a bit strange because she picked up my hand and held it.

'What's wrong, Nell? Shall I go and get your dad?'

I shook my head.

'No, let's go into the kitchen. I think I want him to take me back to Mum's.'

'But what about the theatre?'

I shook my head again, and now there was a big lump in my throat and I couldn't say anything. I pulled my hand away from Millie's and stood up, and she stood up too, her face all frowning.

'OK, come on, let's find your dad. You look awful, Nell, do you feel sick?'

I was already walking out of the room, down the little short hall and into the kitchen, and Millie followed me. Dad was sitting on one of the high stools, like the kind you see in a pub, and he was just staring at the breakfast bar, not doing anything. He looked up when we came in, and smiled, but it wasn't a proper smile, it was just his lips moving upwards.

'What's up, girls? We don't need to go for a few minutes yet.'

I took a step forward, and swallowed hard so the lump in my throat went down a bit.

'Dad. I need to tell you … I need to tell you something. And Mummy. Can we go back, so I can tell you both at the same time?'

'Huh?' He looked really surprised all of a sudden, as if somebody had just put a big box in front of him and he'd opened it and it was full of lizards or something.

'Don't be silly, Nell. We're off to Bath, remember? And you begged me to take you *away* from Mummy's. You were in a terrible state. And now you want to go back? Don't be ridiculous. Tell me whatever it is now, and tell Mum when you go home. It can't be that important.'

'It is. It's really, really important.' My voice sounded all squeaky, and my chest felt all funny, as if somebody was sitting on it. I looked sideways at Millie, and she looked at me, and then at Dad.

'Nell told me it was something about Zander, Mr Ashfield,' she said, and Dad stared at her for a few seconds and then looked back at me.

'About Zander? Oh love, come here. It's all going to be OK, you know? If Mummy does have to go to jail, I'll look after you, everything will be fine ...'

He got off his stool and started walking across the room, and I backed away, banging into Millie who was standing just behind me, and she moved backwards too, and I suddenly felt scared again, so scared that I started to feel dizzy, and then the words just started to bubble up inside me, like they were coming from my tummy and up through my chest and then into my mouth and I knew that I was going to say them, and then they all came out in a shout, the loudest shout I'd done for ages and ages, and I shouted:

'MUMMY DIDN'T LEAVE ZANDER IN THE CAR IT WAS ME I PUT HIM BACK OUT THERE WHEN SHE WAS ASLEEP!'

And then all three of us were standing totally still, still like the stone statues in the park, and Daddy was staring at me with his mouth open, and a little gasp came out of Millie's mouth, and then I spoke again, and this time all the shouting was gone and it was just a teeny little whisper.

'But it wasn't my idea. Somebody made me do it,' I said.

258

38

THEA

I tipped the glass sideways, pouring the remains of my gin down the kitchen sink, then rinsed the glass out and sat it upside down on the draining board. I'd only drunk a few mouthfuls when Rupert had rung, sounding frantic, terrifying me. Had something happened to Nell, an accident? He told me everyone was fine, but something had happened and they were on their way back, and he'd explain everything when they got here, and then despite my barrage of questions and demands for him to tell me what was wrong *now*, he'd cut the call.

What the hell was going on? I could smell my own sweat, the acrid smell of perspiration and fear, and knew I should take a shower, but I couldn't make myself go upstairs. Instead, I wandered through the downstairs rooms, straightening cushions, tidying papers, walking to the dining room window every minute to see if his car was outside. When the doorbell finally rang I almost tripped over the coffee table in my rush to open it.

'Rupert! Nell, are you all right? What's wrong?'

I ushered them in, the three of them, and realized they all looked pale, shaken.

'Come in here, into the lounge, sit down. What happened?

259

Did you see an accident or something? Nell, darling, baby, come here. You look like you're in shock.'

Rupert was still standing in the doorway, shaking his head.

'No, nothing like that. Nell just needs to tell you something, Thea.'

I dragged my eyes from Nell, who was perched on the edge of the sofa next to Millie, both of them looking white and scared, and looked at my husband. He had a strange expression in his eyes, one I couldn't work out.

'What? Tell me what? Why didn't you just phone? What's going on, Rupert?'

In reply, he stepped further into the room and waved an arm at Nell.

'This couldn't be done over the phone. Nell, come here. Come here, and say it again. Tell Mummy what you just told me.'

Nell sat very still for a moment, then stood up slowly, and walked a few steps nearer to me. She looked up at Rupert with frightened eyes, and he smiled a tight smile, obviously trying to reassure her.

'It's OK, Nell. You're not going to be in trouble, all right? But you need to tell Mummy. This is very, very serious. Tell her exactly what you just told me. Go on.'

What the hell? I looked at Rupert and then at Nell, waiting, my mind racing. What 'very, very serious' thing could my eight-year-old daughter possibly have to tell me?

'Nell, darling ... whatever it is, I promise I won't be angry, OK? Come on, spill.'

I tried to keep my tone light, but the fear in her eyes was still there, and then she opened her mouth, took a little, gasping breath, and said something so bizarre, so unexpected, that I almost laughed.

'I put Zander back in the car, Mummy. That day, when he died. You took him out, then you went to sleep, and I put him back in.'

260

Her voice was so quiet, so steady, and when she'd said the words she stood completely still for a few seconds, looking at me, then turned away and walked slowly back to the sofa, where she sat down again next to Millie.

'What?' There was a tremor in my voice, halfway between a giggle and a sob.

'What did you say? Rupert, what's …?'

He was looking at Nell, that weird look still in his eyes, and then he turned to me.

'That's what she said to me too. At the flat. Thea, I just don't know. I don't know why she's saying it, or if it's true, and if it *is* true, why on earth … but she said something else too. She said she did it, but that somebody *made* her do it.'

A chill ran down my back. Somebody … somebody *what*? I turned to Nell again.

'Nell … why? Who? What are you saying? You would never do that, not to Zander. Why would you say something like that?'

She was staring at the floor now, motionless as if in a trance, ignoring me, but Millie's eyes were darting between me and Rupert.

'Mrs Ashfield – I think she's telling the truth. She said something to me once, about doing it, about someone making her do it, but then she said she was joking; but I was worried, so I told somebody about what she'd said, and they said it wasn't true, and that I should forget about it … but now, I think maybe it *was* true …'

'JESUS!'

Rupert crossed the room suddenly, standing next to me, the two of us shoulder to shoulder now, the girls perched on the sofa in front of us.

'JESUS,' he said again. 'Jesus Christ, Millie! Who, for fuck's sake? Who made her do it? And who did you tell, and why didn't they tell *us*? Who the fuck are these people you're talking about?'

'Rupert.' I began to admonish him for swearing and then

wondered why on earth it mattered right now. This couldn't be real, after all. Could it? Could this possibly be happening? Was this conversation actually taking place, or was this some sort of dream?

Millie had started to cry, a fat tear running down her pale face.

'I don't know who made her do it. I—'

'AAARGH.' Rupert made an angry, strangled kind of noise, and I put a hand on his arm.

'Let me,' I said quietly.

'Thea, I just …' He started to speak then shook his head.

'It's OK.' Why did I feel so calm, suddenly? I walked to the sofa and crouched down, putting my right hand on Millie's knee and my left on Nell's. Nell jumped slightly, as if she'd just woken up, and her eyes were wet now, too, and I leaned forward and spoke very softly, looking from one tearful face to another.

'OK, I think we all know how serious this is now, don't we? So what's going to happen, girls, is that you're going to tell us everything. You're going to tell us the truth about what happened, you both are. And you're going to start now. Go.'

262

39

ANNABELLE

I wasn't quite sure why I wasn't crying. Instead, a sort of numbness had crept over me, seeming to freeze any emotion that might be trying to surface. I felt, in fact, very relaxed – unnaturally so, for someone who was always as anxious as I was. It was weird, very weird, and I didn't really know how to deal with it. I knew, in my head, that I should be reacting in some intense way right now – screaming, sobbing, howling, shouting – but I just wasn't, and I didn't know why. Maybe I was in shock? I mean, actual, medical shock? After all, my husband had just told me that he'd fathered a child with another woman. Was that sort of bad news enough, though, to send a human body into actual shock?

I turned to look at my husband – my cheating, scumbag of a husband, I thought now, calmly – who was slumped at the kitchen table, head in his hands, then returned my gaze to the garden, where Flora, wanting to give us some alone time, had just returned from a run and was leaning against a wall, balancing on one leg and using a small stick to poke the mud off the sole of the trainer on the opposite foot. Flora, who had probably known about this all this time, and who had never told me. I would talk to her about it later, but I began to wonder, casually tossing the thoughts

263

around my brain, about how I was going to tell the children that I was highly likely to be sacking my assistant, and that their parents' marriage was over, that their dad had come home from dropping Millie off at Nell's this afternoon and blown our world apart.

Because our marriage *was* over, wasn't it, now? Or did women actually stay married to men who did things like this? Did they? Did they forgive husbands who slept with the mothers of their daughters' friends, and impregnated them? Impregnated. What a strange word that was—

'AAAAGH! NO, NO, NO!'

I jumped violently at the anguished, terrified scream.

'Sienna?' It was coming from the lounge, and before I could think I was running, aware that Greg was on his feet too and following me.

'STOP IT! OLIVER, STOP IT!'

Sienna was still screaming, and as I reached the door to the lounge and shoved it open, gripped by a sudden dreadful fear, I heard Oliver bellowing back at his sister.

'SHUT UP! SHUT UP, YOU STUPID LITTLE BITCH.'

'Oliver!'

'What the f ...?'

Greg and I spoke at the same time, and the fear intensified as I tried to take in the scene in my living room. Oliver was standing on the sofa, Sienna clawing at his legs, sobbing hysterically. In my son's left hand was Olaf, the little kitten, wriggling and mewling, the fur around its neck streaked with red. And in Oliver's right hand, a kitchen knife, the bloodstreaked blade angled towards the animal's throat.

'OLIVER!' There was a roar from Greg as he flung himself at our son, twisting his arm violently behind his back, making Oliver scream with pain, the knife falling onto the sofa cushion and then, as if in slow motion, sliding to the floor, leaving smudges of blood where it had been, and then Olaf was on the floor too, mewing piteously.

I ran to Sienna, pulling her into my arms, dragging her onto the other end of the sofa, then reached for the kitten too, scooping him up, fingers probing the wound at his throat. It was bleeding, but not a lot, and I snuggled him into the crook of my arm, stroking his trembling body gently, muttering soothing nonsense. I'd have to get him to the vet, but he'd live. But what on earth?

'Oliver!' Even I could hear the fear in my voice as I turned to look at my son. Across the room, a puce-faced Greg was standing over Oliver, who was crouched on the floor now, rubbing his shoulder and rocking backwards and forwards, words spilling from him in a low, shaky monotone.

'I'm sorry, I'm sorry, I'm so sorry … I didn't mean to do it, she just makes me so angry … I'm so sorry, I know that wasn't right, I don't even remember getting the knife, is he OK, Olaf, is he dead, Mum?'

'He's not dead. He'll be OK. Maybe a few stitches. But Oliver … however irritating you may find your little sister, there's no excuse … I mean I just can't believe …'

Still cradling the kitten and clutching a sobbing Sienna to me, I stared at my son, suddenly remembering Hamish again, knowing without any doubt now that my worst fears had been realized.

'Olly … you killed Hamish, didn't you?'

The memory of the cat's mutilated body flashed into my mind, and I suddenly felt sick. Greg, who'd been staring at me, a horrified look on his face, turned back to our son.

'Holy shit, Olly. Did you? Oh CHRIST.'

Oliver was nodding, tears streaking his cheeks now.

'I'm sorry. I'm so sorry—'

BRRRRING.

In his pocket, Greg's mobile phone had started ringing. Cursing, he pulled it out, not looking at the screen, and put it to his ear.

'Thea? No, this isn't a good time … what?'

I rolled my eyes. Great timing, Greg's baby mama, I thought, with a flash of anger. On the floor, Oliver was still muttering, still apologizing.

'I'm so sorry, so, so sorry. It wasn't my idea, it wasn't …'

Still feeling sick and shaky, I moved Olaf gently to my lap and pulled Sienna closer, trying to listen to both Greg and Oliver at the same time.

'Thea, you're not making sense. Nell said *what*? She did what?'

'I would never have done it, I would never have thought of doing it, Mum; it was supposed to make me feel better; she said it would …'

'She said *who* made her do it? What the fuck, Thea, are you serious?'

'I like cats. I liked Hamish, I like Olaf, but it's just when I get mad and I don't know how to deal with it, she said it would help …'

What? What did he say? I released Sienna suddenly, handed Olaf to her, then stood up and walked to where Oliver was huddled on the floor, still rocking.

'Oliver, what are you talking about? Who said it would help?'

'Gosh. What's happened here?'

Flora, her voice cheerful, face still flushed from her run, trainers dangling from her right hand by their laces, was standing in the lounge doorway, looking from one of us to another, her smile fading as she took in the scene.

'Is … is everything OK?'

Her tone was hesitant now, a puzzled frown creasing her brow, and she dropped her trainers on the floor, her left hand moving to her right wrist, her fingers rubbing at the flesh.

'Hang on, Flora,' I said. 'Oliver—'

'Annabelle. That was Thea. I need to talk to you, urgently …'

Greg interrupted, stepping towards me, looking from me to Flora. He had a panicked, frightened expression on his face that

266

I couldn't understand, and I looked at him for a moment, perplexed, then decided he could wait.

'In a minute,' I said fiercely, then turned back to Oliver.

'Olly – are you saying that hurting Olaf … killing Hamish too, was somebody else's idea? Whose, for goodness' sake?'

My son raised his head, his eyes pink and puffy. And then he lifted a shaky hand and pointed. Pointed straight at Flora.

PART THREE

PART THREE

40

FLORA

Three months later

I didn't realize I was probably a psychopath until I went to university. I'd always known I was a little bit different to other kids I knew, never really had close friends growing up. But I didn't realize I was *that* different until I started at Northampton Uni, doing my English and Psychology degree, and there it suddenly was one day, on the big screen in front of me in a crowded lecture theatre – a checklist of psychopathic personality traits. A checklist of *my* personality traits.

Superficial charm
Need for stimulation/proneness to boredom
Pathological lying
Cunning/manipulative
Lack of remorse or guilt
Lack of empathy
Failure to accept responsibility for own actions

The list went on, but by then I was no longer listening to the lecturer, that weedy little man with the oversized glasses and bad breath who had just opened my eyes to what I was. I had all of those traits, to some degree or other, and while this realization might have horrified some people, it didn't really bother me at all. It was a relief, more than anything, an explanation of why I was the way I was, why I'd done the things I'd done. My reaction was more like: 'Ohhhhhhhh!' – another sign of my psychopathy, maybe.

After that lecture I went online, read more about it. Apparently, about one per cent of the population has psychopathic tendencies, but not all become criminals, murderers, social outcasts – far from it, many control and channel their personality traits, using them in careers where having a lack of morality and little empathy could be a bonus for those wanting to get ahead in tough businesses like finance, the military, or politics. All psychopaths are different, after all, just like 'normal' people. It isn't one size fits all.

I started thinking back, then, trying to analyse my childhood, to pinpoint when it had first started to show itself. As a child ... and I can say this now, after the therapy I've been having over the past months, the counselling sessions, the healing conversations ... as a child, I was abused. I can't think too deeply about it, not yet, maybe not ever. But I'd opened up about some of it. Told them about the times when as a seven- or eight-year-old my father, on one of the rare times he was actually home, would handcuff me to a bed, and then bring his friends in.

They would hurt me, those men, as they took their turns, as they huffed and humped on top of me, causing me such unimaginable pain that I could still feel it sometimes, even now, when I woke in the dark in the early hours, sweating and aching. I tried, so hard, to stop them, always fought back, despite their size and strength; and the scar on my right wrist was testimony to that, my badge of honour, my reminder that I never gave up, the handcuffs digging in as I struggled against them, the cold metal cutting into my skin.

My therapist asked me why my mother didn't know what was going on, why I didn't tell her. But the fact was that I think my mother *did* know. She just chose to ignore what was happening to me, her career and life outside our home far more important to her. She didn't care, my mother. Didn't love me. Neither of them did. Maybe they were psychopaths too, who knows?

And so I didn't love them either, and as soon as I could I made my escape. After I left for Northampton, I simply never went home again. I used to tell people I made an annual trip home, to catch up with 'the olds', but it wasn't true. I never saw them again. I never asked them for money either, from the day I left, working my way through university with bar jobs and waitressing, leaving my childhood behind me.

I thought about going back, once or twice. Thought about punishing them, for what they'd done to me. But by then I'd moved on, mentally as well as physically. Started to heal, maybe. What good would it have done, going back, raking up the past? And I'd caused enough damage already, over the years, because of them.

I'd coped, you see, with the abuse, the lack of love, in what I later realized was an extremely psychopathic way. I started to hurt people, like my father had hurt me. Not sexually, I don't mean that. I'd never do that, not to anyone. Even psychopaths have standards.

But because my abusers were too strong for me to control, I began to control what I could. Smaller, weaker things. Insects at first – what a cliché of a psychopath I was, I now realized, pulling the wings off butterflies! Crouching in the back garden, toying with my prey, loving the sense of power it gave me. Then a hamster, given to me by a well-meaning neighbour who always saw me playing alone and was worried I was lonely. It lasted a week, before being crushed under the wheel of my mother's car as she left for work one morning – a double whammy, that one, a carefully crafted 'escaped' pet, its life beautifully snuffed out, and the horror on my mother's face as she heard my screams and was forced to scrape the furry mess from her rear wheel, the spatters of it from her bumper, creasing her perfectly tailored black suit and smearing her powdered cheek with blood.

I even enjoyed the planning, the thought and care that went into hurting, into killing these animals. The knowledge that I'd planned so well that nobody would ever know I was behind it. Another psychopathic trait, I later discovered, and why I was a psychopath and not a sociopath – they were messier creatures, emotionally unstable, impulsive, lacking in patience. Psychopaths make fewer mistakes. I looked down on sociopaths, and even as I realized this I was amused by it. It was a bit like an alcoholic looking down on a drug addict, wasn't it?

The sexual abuse stopped when I got to sixteen. I was stronger then, fitter, less easy to control, and, of course, by then I was legal too, wasn't I, so where was the fun in that for them? But the damage was done.

I managed to suppress the memories, the fear, for months at a time, as I finished secondary school and moved on to uni, but then something would happen, a scene in a film, a throwaway comment from a friend, and I would be back there, shivering on that bed, kicking and squirming, rubbing my wrists raw as the next one forced his way into me.

And so, somebody, something would have to get hurt. An anorexic found her power by controlling everything she put into her body; a self-harmer did it by cutting. For me, it was about controlling – not myself, but others.

After the hamster, though, things changed. As I watched my mother trying to pick the remains of the squashed, dead animal from her pristine paintwork, I realized that this was what gave me the *real* sense of power. Who cared about a hamster's life, after all? What I'd done that day was to make my *mother* into a killer. It was she who had driven over it, after all, not me.

After that day, whenever I felt the panic, the compulsion, the need to hurt, I simply got somebody else to do it for me. At seventeen, babysitting for a neighbour, I got the nine-year-old son to break his younger sister's legs. She had these angel wings, left over from a school nativity play, and he persuaded her they were magic – that if she put them on, and jumped out of her bedroom window, she'd be able to fly. I was good with kids – that old psychopath charm, I suppose, they always adored me – and it was so easy to tell him what to do, and then to act horrified when he did it perfectly, and she jumped.

I still remember the delicious snap of bone, the rush of power it gave me, the panic on his face as he tried to explain what he'd done to his parents, the fear as he looked at me, remembering how I'd threatened to kill him if he ever told the truth. I was good at that too, the threats. They never told, not ever. Well, not until now.

I wondered for a moment what had gone wrong. I'd changed tactics in recent years, stopped the threats, used charm instead. Made them love me so much they'd do anything to protect me. But had I gone too far, with Nell and Oliver? I pondered that for a moment, then shrugged. What did it matter now, anyway? I'd had more than enough successes, inflicted more than enough pain for one lifetime, hadn't I?

It had gone on and on. At uni, I persuaded a desperately unhappy fellow student to commit suicide, an almost comically easy one to pull off, for everyone knew he was on the edge. Why would they suspect pretty, distraught little Flora of – metaphorically, of course, he died of an overdose – pushing him off it? Pathological liar – big tick on the psychopath list.

By the time I left Northampton, though, and started working, I was pretty much in control. A couple of years and I began to wonder if my past could actually be left behind me. I was happy, probably for the first time ever – work that kept me busy and interested, money in my pocket, casual boyfriends, a social life when I wanted it.

When I got the job with Thea I was in a good place, and I stayed there for nearly two years. Thea was good to me, and good *for* me. I was, for the first time in my life, part of a family. Valued, respected. Loved, even. Even a psychopath can love. Well, I could – a form of love, anyway. Children, especially, were so easy to love, and so loving in return, and Nell and I became … buddies, friends. She trusted me, trusted me implicitly, and her love for me was so sweet and pure that it stirred something inside me. I loved her back, in my way, and even though I ended up using her, using her horribly, that love never went away. So yes, Nell, Thea, even Isla, eventually. I was *part* of something.

It was the same later on, at Annabelle's. More love, more friendships. I'd never thought it would happen, that someone like me could have a life like that, have those feelings, and it made me feel almost normal. Made me feel *happy*. I even had Rupert, for a while, although now that I looked back, I realized he'd probably only started sleeping with me to hurt Thea. He didn't love me, did he? He used me too, just like all the other men, the ones I'd tried to forget. The ones I *had* forgotten, to an extent. Strange, how it was only older men who turned me on, though, when it was older men who had damaged me so badly, wasn't it? I still hadn't got to the bottom of that one.

But in general, back then, I was content. Things were good. And then they all turned bad again.

One morning, when Zander was about eight months old, a letter from my father arrived. A letter, to tell me that my mother had died, cancer taking hold and killing her in the space of six months. Immediately, everything flooded back, the old pain searing through my veins. I had cut off all contact with my family when I'd decided to cut them out of my life, and I had no idea how he had tracked me down to Cheltenham. I destroyed the letter, of course, didn't attend the funeral, never replied to my father's plaintive appeal to put the past behind us, and I thought I could carry on as before, carry on being happy, carry on with my new life, where I was good and useful and valued.

I couldn't, of course. And so, yes, I did what I did. I did what

276

I needed to do, to heal my pain, to regain control. I needed to hurt somebody, and Zander was the obvious choice, the easiest target. It sounds sick, to others, I know that. I couldn't help that though – others would always react how they would react. That wasn't my problem. It was just something I had to do, the only way to get back on track.

So I planned it, and it worked, so beautifully. I waited until the next time Thea was drunk, and then I made Nell put Zander back out in the car, and then I went running out to find him, to bring him in, and pathologically lied my little socks off about the whole thing.

But this was the thing, the thing that made me feel like I was maybe not such a bad psychopath as I had been before. The thing that made me think my time at Thea's had somehow healed me a little, if that was even possible. We're not supposed to show remorse, you see, or guilt, us psychopaths. Or to have empathy. We're not supposed to *care*. But after I found Zander, after I carried that tiny corpse inside … it *killed* me.

When I saw him, when I picked up his little dead body, and felt its heat, and knew that he was gone, I would have done anything, *anything*, to bring him back, to turn the clock back just a few hours. Anything to take the grief and agony away from Thea, from Nell. It was like a physical pain, a pain that no pain-killer could touch. And it had carried on, that pain. It was still there even now. And that was remorse, wasn't it? Or guilt? Or *something*?

'Miss Applegate.'

A nurse had slid unnoticed into my room, wheeling her little trolley with its dishes of coloured pills.

'Claire. How are you?'

I smiled at her, and she smiled back, and as she checked her list, scribbling something on it with her silver pen, I turned to look out of the big bay window to the left of my chair. It was nearly five o'clock, the weather warm for May, the sunshine still

277

streaming in. Outside, a couple of residents were playing boules on the lawn, and their laughter drifted in through the open window.

'You should join them, sometime, Flora love. Weather's been glorious today,' Claire said, as she held out a little paper cup of water along with my bowl. 'Do you good. Perk you up. These happy pills will help, definitely. But your depression needs other things to help it too. Fresh air, sunshine. Nature's medicine. You should go outside. Promise me you'll think about it?'

I nodded, but there was a hollow sensation in my chest now, my body sore and stiff, my scar throbbing. I was tired, so very, very tired, but Claire was smiling at me, and I suddenly didn't want to let her down, wanted to give her the answer she needed to hear. Wanted to please her.

'Maybe tomorrow, Claire. Maybe tomorrow,' I said.

41

THEA

'Daddy will be here in a few minutes, Nell. Run and get your things, darling.'

Nell looked up from her iPad, on which she was playing some sort of fashion, dressing up game, and grinned.

'OK. What are you going to do tonight?'

'Annabelle's coming round. I'm going to cook, and then we're going to talk about the show.'

'OK. Sounds nice.'

She put the tablet carefully to one side, jumped up and ran from the room, high-fiving me as she passed, making me laugh. I was doing a lot more laughing recently. Loads of it actually. Everything seemed brighter these days, colours more vivid, music sweeter, the sunshine warmer. It was as though I'd been trapped in a long, dark tunnel for so many months, with no prospect of anything but more darkness ahead, and now suddenly I was out in the world again, and it was a joyous place, full of promise.

Nell was a different child these days, the burden of guilt finally taken from her slender shoulders, her angry, tearful outbursts a thing of the past, for good I hoped. After that dreadful day – dreadful, and wonderful in equal measure, I often thought now, because it was the day everything finally made sense, the day the truth was finally exposed – she'd gone into a residential mental health care unit for six weeks, a wonderful, transformative centre near Oxford where she stayed Monday to Friday, going to school classes and undergoing treatment and activities, and coming home to me at weekends.

Rupert and I had been terrified at first that she'd be prosecuted, forever labelled a child murderer like the killers of James Bulger, but after the police had carried out their investigation, they'd decided that she hadn't been in charge of her actions that day – that she had been coerced, forced to do something terrible, but that it hadn't been her fault. She was so young, and so vulnerable, a victim too, just as much as Zander had been. The revelations had been enough, though, for the charges against me to be dropped, and for the newspapers and social media to go crazy yet again, my status changing overnight from the worst mother in Britain to the victim of a psychopathic monster.

That's what they dubbed Flora, now. Annabelle had described in great detail to me, to the police too, what had happened on that last day– how Oliver had turned to Flora, pointing at her, just as I was telling Greg on the phone what Nell had said. And how Flora had literally crumpled, slowly collapsed onto the floor, 'like a teddy bear that's been dropped', Annabelle said, and had lain there silently for a full minute, and then had begun to scream.

She'd carried on screaming, on and on, even as the police and ambulance had arrived, and taken her away. And then, when she'd finally stopped, she had apparently admitted everything, said that what Oliver and Nell had accused her of was absolutely true.

She'd been assessed then, and judged too ill to face trial, and instead had been sent under the Mental Health Act to Croft Park, a high-security psychiatric hospital in Wales. But the police were able to tell me they believed now that Zander's death was entirely down to Flora, and Nell had been only her unwitting, innocent accomplice.

'She told your daughter that the two of them were going to play a little joke on Mummy, while you were asleep,' Detective Chief Inspector Alan Brook, the senior investigating officer, had told me, when he'd visited a week or so after Flora had been taken into custody. It had been raining before he'd arrived, but when I'd opened the door to let him in the sky had suddenly been lit by the most beautiful rainbow, the bands of colour mesmerizing.

'She said that Nell had often told her she was upset by your drinking, Mrs Ashfield, and that she told Nell that if you got a fright, and thought you'd left the baby in the car, that might stop you using alcohol.'

I'd swallowed hard and stared at the carpet, shame washing over me, but he'd kindly told me to 'please, don't torture yourself about that now', and carried on.

'Miss Applegate said she would keep watch, and that Nell should sneak in and take the baby from his pram, then run out and put him back into his car seat outside. Miss Applegate said that she would then make some noise in the house a couple of minutes later and wake you up, whereupon you would notice your child was missing and panic, and he would then quickly be found in the car. Nell thought this sounded reasonable, and went along with it.'

'So this was ... about three thirty, four o'clock?' My brain was racing, trying to work it out.

DCI Brook nodded.

'Around then, yes. It seems Nell went straight upstairs after carrying the baby out, wanting to sort some things out to show her friend who was coming round later, and simply trusted that Miss Applegate was going to do what she had promised and wake you up shortly afterwards. She didn't, of course.'

I shook my head.

'I still can't believe ... I mean, I'm just struggling to reconcile the image I had of her, Flora I mean, with what she did. I know all this stuff's come out about her being abused as a child and everything but …'

I shook my head again, more violently this time.

'Everyone's really struggling with it. Annabelle … the things Flora made poor Oliver do too, this weird control thing, making other people do terrible things to make herself feel better. Apparently she started working on Oliver, making him hurt flies and kill that cat, to make her feel better about what she did to Zander. I've never heard of anything like it. Is she really a psychopath? I thought they didn't do guilt? And if she was, she certainly hid it well.'

'They generally do,' said DCI Brook.

He'd finished explaining then, telling me that Flora had been concerned that when Rupert came home, at around five o'clock, he might glance into the car parked out front and see Zander inside, and the same when Greg and Millie arrived a little later on.

'Sadly, none of them did,' he said. 'And so it wasn't until the passers-by saw the child shortly after six that the ruckus started, and Miss Applegate was able to pretend she had been alerted by them and *discovered* what had happened, and—'

I raised a hand then, not wanting to hear anymore. We all knew what had happened after that.

'I still don't really get why Nell didn't just tell me, tell you, tell *anybody*, what had really happened though. And how she could still be so fond of Flora afterwards, when she realized what the result of her little *joke* was,' I said.

I'd forgiven Nell, of course I had, but I was still finding the whole thing difficult to understand.

The detective sighed.

'She was very much in thrall to Miss Applegate, it seems. It was almost like brainwashing, in a way. Miss Applegate had grown very close to Nell in the months leading up to the incident … Nell had used her as a confidante when she was anxious about

282

your drinking, your marital ...' He coughed, 'marital disagree-ments.'

The shame washed over me again.

'It meant that when the baby was found, and everyone, you included, thought *you* had been responsible, all it took was a quiet word from Miss Applegate, and Nell kept shtum. Miss Applegate told her that it had to be a huge secret, that the two of them would get into terrible trouble if she told, and that it was an accident, the baby was never meant to die, accidents happened, and that if you got the blame it might be a good thing, might help you to change. She said, apparently, that Nell would "have a better mummy" at the end of all this.'

Tears pricked my eyes then, and I looked at DCI Brook and nodded slowly.

'Do you know what? She was right. I'm going to be.'

And it was true. Three months on, I had kicked the booze habit, taken on a new assistant now I was no longer a pariah, cut down on my working hours. Nell was getting more of my time, and she was happy. I knew she was, and it warmed my heart, filled it to bursting. I *was* a better mummy now, and I knew this was a change that would stay, for ever. There would be no looking back, and no going back. I'd promised Nell that, and she knew I meant it.

There had been, DCI Brook had also told me, one incident which could have blown it for Flora much earlier.

'The one time where Miss Applegate thought everything might come crashing down around her was when you sent Nell to a counsellor, a therapist?'

I nodded.

'Karen Ballerton. She practises up in Reading.'

'Indeed. Well, Miss Applegate was fairly horrified when she heard about that – she thought Nell might have spilled the beans to this woman. She didn't, of course. It seems she told the ther-apist simply that she felt terrible guilt about not checking that the baby had been taken inside from the car. True, of course, but the woman must have assumed she was talking about earlier, when you all arrived home. And so she did the counsellor thing, and told her that it wasn't her fault, that the baby was your, its mother's, responsibility. And that made Nell feel a little better, for a few days at least.'

I sighed, remembering.

'Yes, she did seem better for a few days. It all went downhill again after that. My poor baby.'

'Indeed. Strangely, Miss Applegate also said she was glad that Nell felt better. It seems as though she did have some genuine affection for her, and had been worried that what she'd made Nell do would damage her permanently. She claimed, in fact, to have had great affection for you too, and for Mrs Garrington's family, although clearly that still didn't prevent her actions. Not the behaviour of your archetypal psychopath, maybe, though.'

He'd left then, promising that it was unlikely Flora would be released from hospital for many years, if ever, leaving me to my thoughts, my jumbled mess of shame and guilt, grief and rage.

Now, in the glorious May sunshine, the mess was smaller, the pain less acute. It was still there, of course it was – it always would be – but as each day passed, I was learning to live with it, cope with it, a little bit more. Learning to look to the future, to live with hope, to find the good in every day, to be thankful, so thankful, for everything I still had. My daughter, whole and healthy again. And my husband, soon to be officially my *ex*-husband, but now a friend again. Rupert would never forgive me for sleeping with Greg, for fathering a child with another man, not entirely. And I would never forgive him for sleeping with Mia during our marriage, not just after we split, as I had later learned – and for sleeping with Flora too.

He'd confessed it all, eventually, but by then, I thought, what did it matter? So much had happened, so many bad things, that a couple more made no real difference. It was time to move on, and we were both trying to look to the future now, a future where we could be friends. We would always share so much, and watching Nell grow, learning to be a person, happy again, was all that really mattered, after all.

It had struck me, shortly after the day we found out the truth, that almost everyone *had* been lying about something, not just Flora and Nell. Not lying about what had happened to Zander – only Flora and Nell had known that – but lying about *something*.

Me, hiding such a big, dirty secret from Rupert. Him, living a lie too, pretending he believed Zander was his, sleeping with Mia and Flora behind my back. Greg, hiding what he'd done from Annabelle. And Isla, keeping my secret from Rupert, and lying about me driving the car home. She admitted that, eventually. Said she couldn't hide it anymore, didn't want me to think I was going mad.

'You're mad enough already, Ashfield,' she said, and then burst into tears.

I'd gone to court on that charge only, in the end. I told Isla I deserved some sort of punishment for what I'd done to Nell, and to Rupert. She cried again then, told me over and over again how sorry she was, how she would get help, how she would go to the police and tell them it had been her behind the wheel, but I wouldn't let her.

I was banned from the road for twelve months, but I was OK with that. There were trains, taxis. I could manage. And I had plenty of offers to drive me around these days, when I needed it – guilt, maybe, on the part of Isla, Rupert, Greg, Annabelle, Rupert's parents, my wider circle of friends again now too, everyone who thought I'd killed my child and now knew the truth.

But I could have done it, that was the thing. It could easily have been me who left him in the car. I knew that, even if they didn't. And so I was grateful, so very, very grateful, for what I had now, for what I still had, when a few short months ago I thought I had nothing.

BRRRRRRR.

The doorbell rang, and I went to open it, Rupert leaning in to peck me on the cheek with a smile as he said hello. He'd started doing that again recently, and I liked it. I liked Mia, too, rather to my surprise. More importantly, Nell liked her. I turned to the stairs for a moment to yell: 'Nell! Daddy's here!', then gestured at Rupert.

'Come in. She'll be down in a minute.'

He stepped inside, smiling again and meeting my eye as our daughter's happy shriek echoed down the hallway.

42

ANNABELLE

I scribbled 'advertise for second assistant/part-time' on the end of my evergrowing to-do list, put my pen down, leaned back in my chair and stretched my arms above my head, trying to ease the tension in my shoulders. Good tension though, I thought. The sort that came from hard work, not stress or anxiety.

Along with Verity, the girl I'd taken on six weeks or so after Flora – well, after Flora *went* – I'd spent yesterday trying different chair layouts at the Pittville Pump Room, the beautiful Grade I listed former spa building in Cheltenham which would be the venue for Thea's first major fashion show. We'd picked the main hall for the catwalk, deciding its crystal chandeliers and striking domed ceiling would be perfect to impress the hundreds of buyers, fashion photographers and magazine journalists on the guest list, and I was confident we were going to pull off a fabulous event next week. It *had* to be fabulous, because it was for Thea.

I snorted softly, as I often did when I paused for a moment to contemplate our friendship. I was heading to Cheltenham this evening, to chat through final arrangements for the show, to eat dinner with Thea, and although this was now a regular thing, the unexpectedness of it all still tickled me sometimes.

We'd first got together just days after Flora had been sectioned, oddly both writing emails to each other within the same hour and saying almost exactly the same thing, expressing a desire to talk through everything this girl had done to us. When we met, for coffee in town, we ended up chatting for two hours, finding common ground and shared ambitions that we had somehow managed to go through years of acquaintance without discovering. We talked too, of course, about the elephant – or, the great big hairy mammoth, elephant somehow seeming too small a creature – in the room: the fact that my husband and Thea had slept together, and produced a child.

Very, very strangely, though, that no longer seemed important to me. Greg and I had talked it out, through two long, tearful days and nights, and I'd somehow, for reasons unclear even to me, decided to forgive him. I finally understood now the real reason he'd been so distracted in the run-up to Thea's trial date, his anxiety about what might be revealed gripping him, and that had almost been a relief. He'd gone through so much pain, and I loved him, and I knew that he loved me, and was truly, desperately sorry.

I knew, too, that I'd neglected my marriage, too caught up for years in work and my children. That was still no reason for him to sleep with another woman on a drunken night out, and I knew many of my friends would call me a fool, if they knew. But they didn't, nobody did except our little circle, the Garringtons and the Ashfields, and Isla Laird, and we'd all agreed to keep the secret. Flora knew too, of course, but she didn't matter anymore.

And if I could forgive Greg, then I could forgive Thea too. She sobbed when I told her that, gripping my hand across the table, promising that it had meant nothing, and I believed her. Fool again, maybe, but I didn't think so. It was time to move on, and so we did. Even Greg and Rupert were OK now, all of us agreeing to leave the past where it belonged. Now, Thea and I were real friends ... *proper* friends, 'like me and Nell', as Millie had pronounced with great delight.

The kitchen door opened slightly and Oliver's head appeared in the gap.

'Mum, me, Millie and Sienna are going to walk down the fields to the village shop to get our mags. Need anything?'

I felt a little surge of love.

'No, thanks, darling. Walk carefully.'

He snorted. 'How do you walk *un*-carefully? See you later.'

Then he winked at me and vanished, his big trainers squeaking on the tiled floor of the hall, his still-boyish, high-pitched voice raised as he called for his sisters to hurry up. He was nearly twelve now, my son, my first born, and I wondered how long it would be before his voice broke, before my baby turned into a man.

He was well again, happy again now, my Oliver. It had only dawned on us afterwards that the changes in his behaviour had only begun after Flora arrived. It was almost as if he'd been brainwashed by her – something Thea had said too, about what she'd done to Nell.

The police officer in charge of the case had come to see me, not long after Flora had been taken away, screaming and shaking, leaving us chilled and frightened, stunned by what we had just seen and heard. DCI Alan Brook had told us, calmly and matter-of-factly, that 'Miss Applegate' had started to use Olly to try to regain her own sense of control, when the guilt she felt over what she'd done to Zander threatened to overwhelm her.

'Guilt? I thought the whole point of being a psychopath was that they never felt remorse or guilt?' Greg had said angrily, and the police officer had shrugged.

'There's a spectrum, maybe,' he said. 'She has certainly expressed some level of remorse, and of depression, as a result of her actions.'

So our son had become a victim too, like Nell, like Zander. She had started gradually, using his frustration with his little sister, telling him he would feel better if he released his feelings by taking control, by having power over weaker lives. I still shuddered every time I thought about the wingless, helpless flies, Hamish's limp, damaged body lying in the mud, the blood streaking through Olaf's fur. But it was the potential consequences for Sienna that still woke both Greg and I up in the early morning hours. We knew that if Flora had stayed much longer, if Nell hadn't finally spoken out, it might have been Sienna who was Flora's next victim: that she might, if Oliver had been as taken in, as brainwashed by her to the degree we believed he had been, have made our son murder our daughter.

Oliver knew that too, now, and like Nell, he had spent some time in residential treatment, emerging a calmer, quieter, more thoughtful child. I had watched him closely for weeks after he returned, panic shivering through me every time I realized he and Sienna were in a room alone together, but now I knew it was over. He had made his peace with what he had done, accepted that it had not been his fault, forgiven himself, and even apologized to Sienna; although she, just turned four, had simply looked puzzled and told him he was a 'big silly'.

So we had made peace with it too; Greg and I exchanging contented looks these days when Sienna would run eagerly to her big brother when he got in from school, waving her latest drawing, and he would dump his schoolbag on the floor, scoop her into his arms and inspect her work carefully, dropping a kiss onto her forehead before depositing her again.

Millie was OK again now too. Distraught for weeks after Flora had been taken away, she had told us how Nell had confessed to her, months ago, that she had put Zander back into the car, and that somebody had made her do it. She'd quickly withdrawn the claim, telling Millie it had been a joke, but Millie had worried about it, eventually going to Flora and asking her what she should do. Flora, of course, had told her that it simply wasn't true, that Nell was confused, that losing a loved one could play tricks on your mind and to just forget about it, and so, of course, poor, trusting, loyal Millie had never breathed a word. We'd talked to her at length, Greg and I, reassuring her, telling her nothing was her fault, and she too seemed happy now, everything right with her world again, the darkness lifted.

I heard voices outside the kitchen window and stood up to look, watching as my three children headed down the garden to the gate in the fence at the bottom, from where they would trek across the fields, their shortcut to the village. Oliver and Millie were jostling each other, Millie giggling as he tried to grab her little denim handbag from her shoulder, Sienna skipping ahead of them. My children, My family. My life. My heart swelled with love, and I stood there, watching, until they were just three little bobbing dots in the distance.

EPILOGUE

CROFT PARK HOSPITAL

One month later

'Where is Fran?'

Staff nurse Claire Browning, who was reading through some patient notes, looked up to see who was asking. Ward manager Gemma Evans was leaning on the counter of the nurses' station, frowning.

'Errm … I'm not sure, actually, Gemma. I haven't seen her for a while.'

'Hmmm. I hope she hasn't gone off for a sneaky nap again. I did warn her …'

Claire shook her head vehemently.

'No, no, I'm sure she hasn't. She was mortified about that, and really upset that she'd had a verbal warning. She wouldn't. Not again.'

'Where is she then?' Gemma looked left and right, but the long corridor was empty. It was just coming up to four a.m., and the high-security hospital was quiet, most of its residents soundly sleeping.

'I really don't know.' Claire was frowning now too. 'I mean, I saw her probably about half an hour ago. One of the patients

292

buzzed, so she went down to see what was wrong; it was her turn. And then Margo in room two wet the bed, so I went to deal with that, and just got back here five minutes ago, and Claire still wasn't back. It can't have been anything serious, though, or she'd have rung for back-up …'

'Which patient? Which patient buzzed?'

The alarm in Gemma's voice sent a nervous current through Claire.

'Errm … room eight, down the other end. Applegate. Why?'

'Shit. Come with me, quick.'

Gemma turned and began to run down the corridor, and Claire, suddenly feeling panicky, leapt from her chair and followed. The door to room eight was ajar, the light off.

'Fran? Fran are you there?' Gemma pushed the door open and flicked the light switch. 'Oh my … GOD! Shit. SHIT!'

'Gemma … what … what's happened?' Claire clamped her hands to her mouth, eyes bulging as she gaped at what was lying on the floor of room eight. Fran – at least she thought it must be Fran, although it was rather hard to tell, because her face was covered in so much blood, but it was certainly Fran's long red hair – was lying on her side, wearing only bra and knickers, one arm twisted unnaturally behind her. Her nose looked broken, and there was a small pool of blood under her head, the metallic tang of it sharp in the air. Gemma was on her knees, groping for a pulse, repeating the word 'shit' over and over again.

'Got it. She's alive. Only just though. Get help, Claire, quick, for fuck's sake.'

'Sorry. I'm on it.'

Claire dragged her eyes from her friend's slumped body, ran to the phone which sat on the bedside table, and hit the emergency button.

'They're on their way.'

'Good girl.'

Gemma was rubbing Fran's hand gently, murmuring reassuringly.

Claire took a deep, shaky breath and moved a step closer, then stopped as something struck her. *Why* was Fran half naked? Where were her clothes, her belt with all the keys and security passes, her shoes? She looked around the room, but it was neat and organized, no clothes anywhere. A horrible suspicion suddenly flashed into her mind. Could the *patient* ...?

'Gemma. *Gemma,*' she said. 'Where is Flora Applegate?'

NEWSFLASH

A woman who killed a baby and framed his mother for the crime has escaped from a high-security psychiatric hospital. Flora Applegate was detained under the Mental Health Act in February, after admitting the manslaughter of eight-month-old Zander Ashfield. On Saturday morning her bloodstained clothing was found on a bridge two miles from the secure Croft Park Hospital in south Wales.

Miss Applegate, who staff described as 'disturbed and depressed' in the days leading up to her disappearance, attacked a nurse before making her escape, leaving the thirty-year-old woman with serious injuries.

South Wales Police say she is potentially extremely dangerous, and should not be approached …

ACKNOWLEDGEMENTS

Am I Guilty? was inspired by an American true crime podcast I listened to during my commute between Gloucestershire and London for work. Season two of *Breakdown*, a podcast by legal affairs writer Bill Rankin of the *Atlanta Journal-Constitution*, was called *Death in a Hot Car: Mistake or Murder?* and featured the case of Justin Ross Harris, who was convicted of killing his 22-month-old son Cooper by leaving him in his car while he went to work on a hot day in Atlanta in June 2014. Harris was charged with murder and sentenced to life in prison in 2016. As I write these acknowledgements, in autumn 2018, twenty-nine people have died in a similar manner in the USA so far this year. The podcast made me think: what would happen if something like that happened here, in the UK, where such incidents are incredibly rare? And hence Thea's story began to take shape. *Breakdown* is a brilliant podcast – thank you so much for keeping me company on my long, dark drives to work and for the inspiration.

With such upsetting subject matter, it was very important to me to get the details correct, and I'd also like to thank Adam Grinsell from RoSPA (The Royal Society for the Prevention of Accidents), for information and statistics on deaths in hot cars.

I am also grateful to Ian Evans from CAPT (the Child Accident Prevention Trust), and Maryellen Clare from the NSPCC (the National Society for the Prevention of Cruelty to Children) for their help and advice.

A big thank you once again to former senior police detective Stuart Gibbon, for his always valuable advice on police and CPS practice and procedure.

I've never thanked a cat in my book acknowledgements before. Here we go – thanks to Hamish, next door's beautiful ginger cat, who is thankfully very much alive and well at the time of writing, for letting me use his name and description; and to my other neighbour, David Wares, for the use of his name too.

Huge thanks and much love to my husband, family, friends and work colleagues for their unwavering support and enthusiastic promotion of my novels to anyone who will listen, and to all the wonderful members of the book blogging and reviewing community, who never cease to amaze me with their passion, generosity and kindness. Your support means so much.

And finally, an enormous thank you to my fabulous agent, Clare Hulton, and to everybody at HarperCollins and Killer Reads, especially my brilliant editor Kathryn Cheshire, fantastic copy editor Janette Currie, marketing whiz Claire Fenby and Micaela Alcaino who designed the book's gorgeous cover. Thank you all for helping me make *Am I Guilty?* the very best it could be.

KILLER
READS

DISCOVER THE BEST
IN CRIME AND THRILLER

**Follow us on social media to
get to know the team behind
the books, enter exclusive
giveaways, learn about the
latest competitions, hear from
our authors, and lots more:**

/KillerReads **/KillerReads**